ROU
JUSTICE

True Story

By

Robert Steele

Grosvenor House
Publishing Limited

The right of Robert Steele to be identified as the author of this
work has been asserted by him in accordance with Section 78
of the Copyright, Designs and Patents Act 1988

The book cover picture is copyright to Oleksandr Marynchenko

This book is published by
Grosvenor House Publishing Ltd
28-30 High Street, Guildford, Surrey, GU1 3EL.
www.grosvenorhousepublishing.co.uk

A CIP record for this book
is available from the British Library

ISBN 978-1-78148-811-9

LEADING TO
MY FIFTEEN YEAR
BATTLE FOR JUSTICE

A TRUE STORY

By

Robert Steele

R Steele

29-5-2013

CHAPTER ONE

On the 8th June, 1992 I took up employment with St Helen's Council as a Temporary Security Officer.

When I first started with the Council there were two static duties in Sherdley Park; one on the greenhouse and one on Pets Corner. Mick Gornall, Head of Security told me I had to check both compounds because there were no men for Pets Corner. I was out checking Pets Corner in the dark when Jimmy Johnson (Security Officer and Shop Steward for T& GWU) turned up and ask me what was I doing. Jimmy went mad and told me Mick had no right telling me to check Pets Corner, as it was not safe to do so.

I had only been in the job a couple of weeks and I went into work and Alan Duckworth, another Security Officer, said I have seen your job application form, then Mick came out of his office and said, "I have had your job application form out again".

I found this bad man management; showing other Security Officers my application form. I was not happy about it but said nothing as I had just started in the job and looked at it as an incompetent manager.

In 1994 I was made permanent and a couple of weeks later all the Security Officers signed a vote of no confidence against Mick Gornall, Head of Security.

As I got on with Mick very well I refused to sign the vote of no confidence. I was the only permanent member of staff not to sign it. He had one temporary member of staff who told the lads he would have signed it if he had been in permanent employment.

I did not realise how much the Security Officers hated Mick Gornall. Within weeks, after the Security Officers signed a vote of

1

no confidence, they put up in the Rest Room abusive words about Mick and also cartoon pictures of him over a weekend. Alec Grant and Keith Jones were the supervisors for security that weekend and the lads were advised to take them down,but ignored their advice. I think it was Keith Jones who took them down in the end and I now have one of the cartoon pictures and one of the lads cut out Hitler's head and put it on the cartoon of Mick. I did find the cartoon characters funny as they looked so like Mick and showed him as a scruff.

Since I started in June 1992 all the Security Officers accused Mick Gornall of underpaying their wages. Atmy interview Mick Gornall told me that they had a restructure in 1991 and all Security Officers were on Manual Scale 3, plus allowances and they were all calculated together. They were put on staff rates of pay and Mick said it came to Scale 3 of A.P.T. & Conditions of service.

Around 1994/95 Mick took over the contract for fitting alarms inside empty council houses. An outside company was originally doing the job. Mick was asking Derek Anders, supervisor for security what was Paul Molyneux like as a person as Derek knew Paul. Alan Duckworth (already with the Security Department) wanted the job to get off shifts and Mick never advertised it and brought Paul Molyneux into our department as the Housing Officer.

Again, around 1994/95 the council wanted Security Officers to collect fines for overdue library books from peoples houses. Security Officers refused to do it so Brendan Farrell, St Helens Council Personnel Manager put Phil Ward into Security to do the job. Phil was Brendan's favourite – the job finished within six months and Phil had no job in Security but Mick kept paying him wages instead of redeploying him or making him redundant.

Sometime between 1994 and 1995 Mick reckoned he had too many men in Security and myself and Jebby Robinson, another security office were taken to see Peter Mavers in the Assistant Directors office. Because of a 'last in first out' basis we were told by Peter, 'Mick doesn't want to lose us as we were his best two officers' and we were told we had to go to the building department or be made redundant.

Fortunately, two other Security Officers went over to building. Before I went to Peter's office I made a complaint that Paul Molyneux the Housing Officer for Security was the last person in the job and he should have been one of the two to be made redundant or moved to the building contracts department. Peter told me he carried five years service over from another company. If they were to make him redundant they would have to paid him five years redundancy, I am not sure this is the truth. I believe Mick wished to keep Paul as he was a close friend.

When Paul Molyneux allegedly carried his five years service over Phil Ward never had a job in Security and when Mick decided to make two men redundant from Security he gave Phil my job as security officer as I only had two years service and Phil Ward had a longer service with the Council. This did not give Mick the right to give him my job as I was in permanent employment for that particular job and at the end of the day it was Phil's job that was redundant and when he became a Patrolling Officer he only lasted a few weeks and he would not do the job because he refused to work nights. Again Mick kept him in Security with no job. In my opinion this was because Brendan Farell was Personnel Manager and Phil Ward was a close friend. Once again my job was put at risk when it should have been safe.

Sometime in 1995 there was a bomb scare in the depot over the weekend. John Swift, Supervisor of Security, was on 8 till 8 days and when his shift finished at 20.00 hrs he went home. Keith Jones, Supervisor of Security, booked four hours off his shift and came in at midnight. It was in Mick's contract to cover for the supervisors.

Over the weekend the safe in security was robbed and I am certain it was robbed on the night shift, as that was the only time one person was left on their own. Due to staff shortages there were only two men on nights when there should have been three men. Had this been the case there would have been two men in the Control Room.

On the Monday I turned up for work at 1400 till 2200. When I got in Kenny Watterson, a Security Officer told me the safe had been robbed. I thought he was messing until John Swift (Supervisor for Security) came out of his office and confirmed it. John sent Kenny and I out on the cash run and Kenny finished at 1600.

Eric Clarke a Supervisor for Security had replaced John and told me to bring Kenny back to base as he finished at 1600. Eric sent Brian Wright a Security Officer out with me to finish the cash run. When we were leaving the depot Brian started telling me what premises the bags were stolen from and how much was in each bag, to the last penny. I don't know how Brian knew this as only so many bags were stolen and so many bags left behind. I thought to myself 'f****n hell' Brian how do you know this. It made me think he had robbed the safe.

On my next 1600 till 2400 shift I was in the rest room and Ged Philbin a Security Officer was sat next to me and I was telling the lads that Brian Wright told me which premises the bags were stolen from and how much was in each bag to the last penny. Ged said, "how does Bri Wright know this?" I said, "I don't know".

One of the lads reported what I told them to Alec Grant (Supervisor for Security) and when I came in on my next shift Alec asked me had Brian Wright told me where the bags were stolen from and how much was in them? I said "yes he told me he has informed Mick Gornall but Mick never took it any further.

John Swift, Keith Jones, Keith Hackett and Brian Wright, Supervisors and Security Officers were suspended. Derek Anders (Supervisor for Security) told me he had told Mick not to put the safe in the Control Room and to put it in Mick's office and he ignored him. This comment was made by Derek well before the safe was robbed.

If anyone should have been suspended it should have been Mick – John never forgave Mick for what he had done to him and left the Council altogether.

Mick Gornall suspended John for leaving the supervisor's door open where the keys were kept and a couple of weeks later Mick left his safe keys in the safe with the doors wide open and left the Council building.

A complaint was made to the Yard Manager, Brian Williams and he came in and locked the safe and removed the keys. Mick came back and said "silly me". Nothing happened to him.

Eric Clarke ex Supervisor told me today (11/2/2011) that he should have been on shift from 2000 till 0800 the night of the bomb scare and that he had booked holidays and Mick told him he had to come in for four hours 2000 till midnight as there was no cover. Eric insisted he was booking the whole shift off and Mick had to honour his request as Supervisors did annualised hours. Keith Jones had to cover Eric's shift but could only cover from midnight till 0800 leaving 2000 – 2400 hours with no cover. As already stated it was in Mick's contract to cover for Supervisors and Mick decided not to.

Mick then had a 'brainwave' and decided to get rid of Alec Grant (Supervisor for Security) – he was set up. Alec's own words are:

"REF EARLY RETIREMENT: in my mind I was forced out of my job by Mr Gornall and Farrell the now Acting Assistant Director. They accumulated three incidents over a period of time they thought serious enough for disciplinary action. I feel they should have dealt with these incidents as they arose. Mr Gornall did say at the time he would note it but take no further action. What should have taken place was;

5

I received a verbal, a written and a final written warning before being dismissed if found negligent.'

Alec was told to take early retirement or if he made one more mistake, they would sack him. He was bullied into early retirement. I found this a total disgrace and in 2009 Mick Gornall used exactly the same tactics to finish Mick Rimmer a Security Officer on early retirement. They also got Mick into the office and told him if he makes one more mistake they will sack him and advised him to take early retirement. Mick was put under pressure and took early retirement.

Again I found this a total disgrace. What annoyed me most is when Paul Molyneux became Deputy Head of Security I was getting regular feedback that he was constantly making mistakes and some believe because he was Mick Gornall;s best mate they were 'brushed under the carpet'. He made more mistakes than Alec Grant and Mick Rimmer put together.

Not long after, I was in Mick's office and I heard him telling Paul Molyneux he can persuade another supervisor to finish on ill health and he also finished five security officers on ill health. I am sure they were all capable of staying on in their jobs. All six finished within weeks of one another. Before Gary Wainwright, Office Helper, was finished he kept coming to me for advice as Mick was trying to finish him on ill health. I had to keep telling Gary that I would like to help him, but Eric Clarke was his Shop Steward. Gary was concerned about losing his job. In the end he came to me and said he was going to take their offer and go on ill health. I felt sorry for the lad and wanted to help him but my hands were tied as I was not his Shop Steward.

In October 1999 Clive Portman, District Auditor, wrotea report on ill Health.

Your concerns regarding ill-Health retirement. Abuse of ill-health retirement process of 6 men to finish on ill health grounds.

Council's response: employee's files contain appropriate medical certificate signed by Doctor. There are appropriate termination letters on file and the employees concerned did not appeal against the decision.

District Audit follow-up work and confirmed factual accuracy of the Council's response.

I wrote to Clive - 19/10/99.

"Ref ill-health

I have sent you copied statements of some of the six people who finished on ill-health."

Keith Hackett,Security Officer; statement is as follows:-

I was off sick with anxiety and depression for about six weeks because of the shifts and the hours. The Council Doctor that I was sent to recommended I finish on ill health. M Gornall said that as there were no other jobs in the Council I would have to finish.

K Hackett

Peter Waine, Security Officer; statement is as follows:-

"My employment was terminated with St Helens Council on the grounds of ill health (depression). It was recommended by Mr M Gornall (Head of Security) and Mrs P Gray (Personnel Officer).

Yours faithfully,
Mr P Waine

Jimmy Johnson, Security Officer; statement is as follows:-

"When I wanted to take voluntary redundancy I was advised by B Farrell to take ill health as the Council would probably not give me redundancy – so I had an appointment with the Council doctor and finished on ill health – this was recommended by B Farrell".

J Johnson

I find it strange after John Swift leaving and getting rid of Alec Grant when Mick did his re-structure in 1996. Security were over manned by six men and six men finished on ill health. There is something seriously wrong and I am concerned the Councilis abusing the ill health system.

Clive Portman responded to my letter dated 15 December 1999.

"Ref Ill Health

You say you have included copied statements of some of the six people who finished on ill health. What relevance do these statements have and what is being alleged?

Is it being suggested that the Council incurred more costs as a result of ill health retirements, which were contrived? Are you suggesting that the Council's doctor certified people as being unfit to work when they were fit to work?"

Yes, in my opinion I believe these six people were not ill and I am saying the six officers were finished by the works Doctor, when they were fit to work.

Keith Jones (Supervisor for Security) came into work to start his shift and Mick Gornall took him to Brendan's office and was finished on the grounds of ill health and went home for good the same morning.

In my opinion the situation on ill-health was covered up by Clive Portman to protect the Council.

When Mick did the restructure in 1996 he had two day shift men on days and only one job – they were Paul Molyneux (Mick's friend) and Phil Ward (Brendan's friend) Brendan who is now Acting Assistant Director. Mick decided to create a job for Paul so Phil could have his job and brought back the Client Liaison Officers job that was disbanded long before I started in 1992 because it was not cost effective. Terry Cunliffe, who had been with Security for a number of years and had also done the Client Liaison Officers' job in the past, put in for the job but Paul got it with no experience in Security – he only knew about fitting alarms to council houses and had no experience with the schools whatever. It's not how good you are at your job it's if your one of Mick's boys!

In October 1999 Clive Portman did a report on un authorized post.

> Your concerns that further management favouritism led to the creation of a Liaison Officer post for a specific officer and that this post was not included in the structure presented to the Committee in 1996 (Personnel sub 20/9/96).

Council's response –

> *The 1996 review did not allocate specific tasks related job titles to Security Officers. JCC Minutes of the 8/10/1996 meeting indicated that one of the 22 new Security Operatives posts would be a Client Liaison Officer and that this post would be open to application from all members of the Security section.*

> *The post was advertised and two officers applied. District Audit follow up work included review of the Liaison Officer was discussed and that the post was to be advertised. We*

have seen the advert for the post and are satisfied that two people applied for the position."

Firstly, I will comment that the Liaison Officer was not one of the 22 officers in Security as we had 17 Patrol Men, 4 Market Officers and 1 Housing Officer. This adds up to 22 Security Officers.

It was discussed with Brendan in a JCC meeting on the 8/10/96 but the Sub Committee had already passed the proposals for Security and Liaison Officer was not part of it.

When Paul Molyneux got the job some of the security officers believed all he did was sit in Mick's office with Derek Anders and talk rugby and attend meetings with Mick, which did not concern him or his position as Liaison Officer.

I attended an alarm activation with Andy State a Security Officer at a school over the Christmas period. We went into the school and could not find the zone so we re-set the alarm and went outside and it went off again. I isolated the zone and re-set the alarm when we got outside.

I could hear running water. It was in the building next door – another part of the school that was not on the map, so I drew a map and put the zone on it. This should have been done a long time ago by Paul Molyneux as he was the Liaison Officer for the schools. Had he been doing the job he was paid to do, this would have been sorted months earlier.

Had I not heard the running water, Andy State and I would have been disciplined because the building had a burst pipe and was flooded.

Before I became Shop Steward there was a lot of overtime going at Stanley Bank Farm. John Swift (Supervisor) rang me up at home and asked me if I wanted to do any overtime. I said, "I have done more overtime than the other lads, ask them and if you cannot get anyone then I will do it". John rang me back and said Keith Hackett is doing it. When I went into work Mick called me in to his office and asked why did I let Keith Hackett do the overtime? I told him I had done more than the others – he said, "so what, they would not have done that for you". I got the feeling he did not like Keith and he definitely did not want him to do the overtime.

In 1996 the GMB Shop Steward left Security. As the Security Officers continued to complain they had been robbed of their wages, I told them I would put in for Shop Steward and investigate the wages.

Around June 1996 I was elected the Shop Steward for the GMB.

As I had never met Brendan Farrell (Acting Assistant Director) I went down to Personnel and told Pam Gray I wanted to meet Brendan Farrell. She told me I had to make an appointment to see him. I went back to the Security Office and Brendan phoned me and told me "I've got five minutes", so I went down to his office.

I told Brendan that Mick keeps telling the lads that if they don't do what he tells them his job's safe. I did tell Brendan this is off the record.

Brendan told me no one likes Mick, I told him I got on with him very well. At the end of the meeting I told Brendan, if he sticks to the management rules and I stick to the Union rules we will get on fine.
　　Brendan responded with a verbal threat –"if you cause me any problems I will ring the Town Hall and have you closed over night". I was in Brendan's office for one hour, five minutes.

When I became Shop Steward I told Les Guilford (Convener for the GMB) I wanted to investigate Roy Simm a Security Officer's disciplinary as I knew it was wrong what Mick (and either Brendan or Peter Mavers) has done to him. Les gave me access to his file.

On my enquiry Derek Anders told me he had warned the Head Teacher and the Caretaker about the alarm panel. Firstly you could not see the information on the alarm panel nor did it have a countdown buzzer – there was no way whatsoever you knew whether it was set or not.

Roy re-set the alarm and later the school was broken into as the alarm panel did not re-set. Not long after Roy was sent back to that school and he made the Caretaker re-set the alarm. Again, it was broken into and the alarm did not re-set.

The school got the alarm repaired. You could now see the alarm had re-set and they also had the countdown buzzer fitted that also tells you the alarm is re-set.

The school was fully responsible and Roy should have never received a final written warning – he had no case to answer.

Roy came to me and asked me to make sure they had removed his final written warning. I wrote to Brendan on 1/7/96 reference Union matters.

1) **R Simm**
   I am informing you that Mr R Simms final written warning was given on the 15 June 1995."The twelve months are now up would you please inform me, in writing, that the warning has now been removed from his records."
   R Steele (Union Representative)

I again requested this in two other meetings with Brendan and he ignored my requests.

In one of the meetings Brendan told me that if Roy applies for another job he will have to tell them about his disciplinary. I believe this to be an out and out lie – once it is removed from your record it's gone for good with all the evidence provided. Roy should not have been disciplined and had no case to answer. Roy had been made a 'scapegoat' for the school's negligence.

Mick wanted to replace the Supervisors with six coordinators. Mick got me in the office and said no one has put in for coordinator. I told him we have all agreed not to put in for it, He told me, if he does not get six coordinators he will sack six men and take six people off the dole.

Brian Wright, now Acting Supervisor, came to me and told me himself and Phil Deighton have to take coordinators jobs so I put up a memo Ref. Contract Changes 7 July 1996.

I was informed by one of my members that Mick took it down and said 'more ammunition for me' and took it to Brendan's office.

I prepared my agenda for my first JCC meeting with management. I had seven issues concerning Union matters.

Heath & Safety

1. We are concerned that a member of staff who had medical problems is occasionally left by himself in the radio room for a considerable amount of time. This puts the workforce in a dangerous position. Mr Wainwright suffers from Epilepsy.

    We feel that the radio room should have full cover at all times, Mr Wainwright could have a medical problem at a vulnerable time i.e. when the crew are carrying cash and need immediate assistance.

    The radios that are currently in use are considered to be inadequate we understand that many different systems have been used without any success.

    One of the problems that could be solved and improve the communications is to have a base station working off a mast with a higher electric output than the present system.

Annualised Hours

2. The union membership at Security Services has expressed their concerns over annualised hours being introduced in the near future.

Bank Holidays

3. The Union membership feel that the implementation of the bank holiday rota has been unfairly introduced and would like to revert back to the old method, or have discussions on this matter.

Staff Rota and Shortages

4. The present rota system is clearly showing a staff shortage. This is an immediate problem that should be addressed now rather than later, as this affects everyone.

   The Union Membership know that corners are being cut which also affects the customer.

Uniforms

5. The standard of clothing is poor; we are being issued summer clothing through the winter months.

   The Head of Security has made it clear that the savings on clothing is being put towards the purchase of a computer – we find this statement and the fact that we are being denied the correct clothing unacceptable.

Mr P Partington, Security Officer

6. It is a regular practice that Mr P Partington has not been involved with the rota system. This is causing other members of staff to rotate around him.

Because of this unfair treatment it is the opinion of the Union Membership that he is moved to another department and replaced with someone who can work as part of the team.

Holidays

7. The booking of holidays for certain weeks in the year is being denied to the workforce. This is a direct result of the way the work rota has been produced and the fact we are short of manpower.

I attended my first JCC meeting on the 10 July 1996.

Brendan stated a keen Shop Steward; I like a good scrap with the Union.

A few minutes into the meeting I started to put the seven issues across to management. I got to issue six and Brendan Farrell stepped in and told me "it's not the time or the place, all you are doing is discriminating against Mick".

Brendan did not deal with any of the seven issues on the agenda.

I was told at a later date it was the time and the place to discuss the issues in a JCC meeting.

At the end of the meeting Brendan produced the copy of the notice I put up for the lads to read.

Reference Contract Changes 7th July, 1996.

To all Security Officers with regards to the current tension regarding the proposed changes in contracts I would like to draw to your attention the current employment law relating to contractual agreement.

WRITTEN CONTRACTS

Once an employer has offered a job and the offer is accepted there is a legal contract between employer and employee, even if there is nothing in writing. If an offer has been made and accepted and then the employer withdraws it, it may be possible to sue for breach of contract.

CONTRACT CHANGES

Once the employment contract has been accepted by the employee, then the employer should not make changes without agreement. Contracts may change if the parties agree to the change.

R Steele (Shop Steward)

Brendan then said that he could add a lot more to it.

Les Gilford (Convener for the GMB) said he hadn't seen it. Brendan then passed it over to Les and he read it and said nothing. I got the Union Rule Book out from my folder and dropped it on Les's legs and told him to tell Mike Titherington (Regional Manager for GMB) that his union Rule Book is wrong.

After the meeting I went back into Brendan's office to explain why I put the contract changes up.

I told Brendan that Mick Gornall had told me and the Union Members that if no one puts in for the Coordinators jobs he would sack six officers and take six people off the dole. Brendan then stated, "I will sack six men and take six people off the dole". I then complained to Brendan that there are too many men on days and not enough men to cover our shifts.

Brendan then phoned Mick and asked what does Paul Molyneux do, then he asked what Phil Ward does. Brendan put the phone down and said they need that many men on days or they would lose their contract.

I then said, "well what about our contracts".

Brendan said "what about your contracts?"

I said, "Education, Chief Executive and Ranger Service".

Brendan said, "you tell me about Ranger Service".

I told Brendan because we don"t have the staff level the static at pet's corner does not get a static put on it on a regular basis.

Brendan picked up the phone and asked Mick about the static at pet's corner. Brendan smiled and put the phone down and said, "Mick's not aware of this".

I again said it does not get covered on a regular basis. Brendan said then you tell me the last time it did not get covered.

I said Monday – I was on nights and we both went out on route.

Brendan picked up the phone and asked Mick what I had said. Brendan then put the phone down, he then put his hands over his face. I sat waiting for him to say something, then he moved his hands and stared at the wall – this went on well over a minute, then he said, "I think you had better go. I'll see you tomorrow at 4 o'clock with Mick".

I went back to the Control Room. Mick said to me, "you've got the Department in trouble – why didn't you keep your big mouth...", he then went quiet.

Mick and Jebby Robinson now Acting Supervisor, were sorting something out. They had the R.L.S log sheet out for that day.

I went to Brendan's office the next day with Mick. Mick said the reason Pet's Corner did not receive a static was that the shift supervisor did not distribute his men properly.

Brendan then asked me if I was happy and that it was an isolated incident and it won't happen again.

It was not an isolated incident. The reason for no static was staff shortages and it continued to happen on a regular basis.

Between the 11th and 16th July, 1996 I had a union meeting. I had been to Wages and got a copy of the figures for the restructure in 1991.

In the meeting I told the lads that I now have the figures and will investigate the wages. I also told them that if I find anything that will get Mick into trouble, or sacked, I would not take it any further.

Dave Anders a Security Officer stood up and said,"what are you protecting that "b*****d" for? If it was the other way around, he would sack you".

Jimmy Goodier a Security Officer then stood up and said,'why are you protecting that "b*****d"?'

After the meeting I went up to the Control Room and messing about with Derek Anders (Supervisor for Security), I said to him,"if I get you 01, will you give me 02?".

Derek grabbed my arm and said,"you want to watch who you say that to, they might take it the wrong way".

On the 17th July 1996 I was on night turn. At approx 10.10 am my phone rang – it was Keith Jones (Supervisor for Security). He said,"Mick has told me to phone you and Brendan wants to see you at 4 o'clock".

I said,"I'm on nights".

Keith said,"I'm only passing the message on".

At approx. 12.35 pm there was a knock at my front door. I went down and opened the door. It was Phil Deighton, Housing

Officer for Security. He had a letter from Brendan confirming the meeting at 16.00 hours in his office and that Les Gilford had been informed.

I rang Derek Anders at home and asked him if he knew what was going on.

He replied, "I haven't got a clue".

I said, "it must be serious for them to ring me and send me a letter and that Les Gilford has been informed."

Derek told me, "if there is a problem he would give me a character reference if I needed one."

Derek stitched me up to improve his chance of becoming Deputy Head of Security.

I got to Reception and met Les. He asked me what was going on; I told him I didn't know.

Kevan Nelson (Unison Convener) turned up. Les asked Kevan what was going on, Kevan said, "I don't know".

We then went into Brendan's office. I was asked, "did I say I had enough evidence to get Mick sacked?"

I said no but I did say that if I did find any evidence that would get Mick into trouble or sacked I would not take it any further.

I was then asked by Brendan, "did you say anything to Derek Anders?"

I said yes, after the meeting I did say to Derek, "if I get you 01 you give me 02".

Brendan said that disciplinary proceedings and dismissal could be brought against me.

Mick behaved like a 'big girl' and said, "you have really hurt my feelings".

Brendan then said to me he will put his answer in writing to me. A couple of days later I received his reply – he did not believe what I had said.

He replied 19 July 1996.

Re: Allegations against Mr M Gornall

I refer to our meeting on Wednesday 17 July 1996, which I convened following certain information that had come to my attention.

The information in question evolved from a Union meeting at which you claimed to have enough information to 'get Mike Gornall sacked' and a later conversation with Derek Anders during which you repeated the allegations.

The allegations in question I did not make in my Union meeting nor to Derek Anders.

He then went on – "during our meeting you denied making any comments at the Union meeting but you did admit to making the comments to Derek Anders which leads me to believe that the earlier comments were also true".

I did make a comment to Derek jokingly but not the one Brendan is accusing me of.

He then went on "as a recognised Shop Steward in this department you have certain responsibilities and I would advise you to refrain from making such scurrilous remarks about any employee of the Council. Not only are such remarks potentially slanderous but could also involve disciplinary proceedings being initiated against you. I would hope you heed my advice".

How can I heed his advice when I did nothing wrong?

I went to Mick's office and he said to me we will pretend it never happened and we will start again.

This made me not want to continue with the Shop Stewards job and what they planned worked – they shut me up.

A couple of months later Ged Philbin came to me and said, "you were like Les Gilford – a roaring bull, they shut him up, now they have shut you up" and he was right. I continued to do my job properly as a Shop Steward.

Mick got me into his office and told me he and Brendan were concerned about me being Shop Steward as you tell people things.

I went into the Health & Safety Officer's office in July 1996, as I wanted him to come out on patrol with me. Dave Sharrock the Health& Safety Officer said, "I'm not doing it as I live in Preston – ask her", meaning June Bracken a Health & Safety Officer. I asked June and she also said no.

In conversation with Dave I told him about an incident on an alarm activation where one of the Security Officers was threatened with a knife and he wanted to know why he was on his own.

I told him only one officer goes in hours of daylight.

He then stated to me, "there has to be two officers at all times".

I went to Mick's office and told him what Dave Sharrock said. Mick replied, "we've always sent one person" and totally ignored the request of the Health & Safety Officer.

It is now 2011 and he is still sending one officer to alarms in daylight hours, after ignoring the instruction of the Health & Safety Officer.

Because of the threat of sacking six men I told the lads to apply for the Coordinator jobs. In a meeting I told Brendan and Mick that the Coordinators jobs are for permanent staff only after Brendan put a memo out saying temps could apply. The next thing three temps were made permanent after three months, so that Peter Woodcock a Temporary Security Officer could have one of the jobs. This was not the Council policy – you have to be a temp for two years. The three men in question were Peter Woodcock, John Clayton and Bernard Day.

I wrote to Mick on 6 February 1997

Temps
Can you please clarify the position of the two temps who have been with the department for four months? Are they going to be made permanent and if so, could you please advise us when, given that the last three people who were temps were made permanent after three months.

I received a reply back from Mick 13 02 1997.

Temps
It is down to management discretion to decide when and if temps are made permanent. We will consider all possible future changes within the department before coming to a decision.

This was not what I understood to be policy.

The two men in question were Mick Rimmer and Andy State.

Minutes of JCC Meeting 18.11.98

Temporary Contracts

Kevan Nelson enquired about the status of temporary contracts. M Gornall responded that two officers have reached two years service (Mick Rimmer and Andy State). The issue was still on going with regard to the markets and nothing has been confirmed. The Security Officers working there are still employed by the Council.

G Philbin said the Officers need to feel secure in the job they are doing, we need to make a more secure workforce.

P Mavers (Assistant Director) responded that there are temps in most of the divisions in the department and a two years service period applies to them all.

This confirms that what Mick and Brendan did with Peter Woodcock, John Clayton and Bernard Day was wrong.

In 1996 Phil Houghey (Shop Steward for the TGWU, also a Security Officer) rang me at home and said "Mick wants you to do a 2 – 10 shift instead of my 4 – 12, as he wants to speak to us reference a new rota.

I got to the office around 2 pm and Phil met me at the door and told me he had picked Rota A for his lads. We both went to Mick's office and I had two rotas put in front of me A and B. I looked at both of them and Mick said, "which rota are you having?"

Phil said to me "your not happy with either are you?"

I said "no". I told Mick I will take both rotas and ask my members.

Mick said to me "what's up Rob haven't you got the balls to decide?" I replied "I don't make decisions for my members – they decide not me".

Around September 1996 I applied for a Coordinator job.

I received a reply 19.11.96
Re: Security Coordinator

I refer to your recent interview for the post of Security Coordinator and confirm the information given to you verbally. That is you were unsuccessful.

May I thank you for your interest and apologise for the delay in writing to you.

On the 19.10.95 I was given a reference from Mick.

TO WHOM IT MAY CONCERN

Re: Mr Robert Steele
'*Since 8 June 1992, when he commenced work as a Security Officer with St Helens Metropolitan Borough Council's Security Services, during his time with us Robert has shown exceptional ability and his work record is exemplary. He is honest, trustworthy, and totally reliable and can be relied upon to carry out any task using his own initiative. He has a pleasant courteous personality and his attendance record is excellent. I would be sorry to lose his service but have no desire to stand in the way of his personal ambitions.*'

I could not believe I did not get the Coordinators job after receiving a glowing reference on the 19 October 1995 from Mick Gornall. I put this down to conflict with Mr Gornall and Mr Farrell and for my honesty as Shop Steward.

Eric Clarke told me he was putting in for Deputy Head of Security. I told him not to bother as Derek was going to get it.

Eric said, "I've as much chance as anyone else." I know how Mick Gornall works and I knew that job was for Derek, even though Eric had more experience.

I made a complaint to Mick about Phil Partington (Security Officer) regarding two incidents with him. The first one was when he was on the radio; the three route men were radioing into base and Phil Partington, threw the mike across the work top and said 'F**k Em'.

I lost my temper with him and told him if anyone of them officers gets hurt I would hold him responsible.

The other incident concerned myself: I was checking a school and there was a van on the premises and when they saw me they shot off so I got into my van and chased them. I got on the radio and gave Phil Partington the vehicle registration over the radio. He kept saying "I can't hear you".

When I got back to base Mick Hutton (Security Officer) told me he could hear everything that was said.

Six months later Eric Clarke left as Coordinator and Phil Partington got his job, without the job being advertised.

I went in to Mick and complained, he said, "my boss told me to give him the job" (meaning Brendan). I warned Mick it will be on their heads if anything happens to any of the Patrol Officers because of Phil Partington's attitude.

This is now the second time Mick and Brendan have broke Council procedures and Union agreements. After Alec Grant was pushed out of his job Mick decided to restructure Security.

On the 12 November 1996 I went to my Convener, Les Gilford, as I wanted to know what was going on.

He told me to go and see Brendan, so I went to Brendan's office and said, "I want to know what's going on". He made a verbal attack on me and said, "it's been passed by the Town Hall and it's coming in whether you like it or not". This was without any consultation with the Unions.

Brendan told me if I go on strike I would get to the gate and turn around and I would be on my own. Brendan and Mick both knew they could do what they wanted with Security and the workforce would let them, as the Security Officers were 's**t' scared of losing their jobs.

I came to work to start my 4 o'clock shift and Brian Wright (Acting Supervisor) told me to get my stuff – I'm up at the Crematorium. He said, "it's a new job". I went mad and he told me to calm down.

I got to the Crematorium and I saw the Manager Dominic and I kicked off again.

Brian showed me the job and left. We had to do an extra two weekends every 17 weeks for no extra pay. This should have been discussed as they were 12 and seven hour shifts at weekends with no extra pay.

Les Gilford asked me to take Mike Titherington (Regional Manager for the GMB) and Charlie Lenard (Full Time Officer) around the Nursing Homes as they were trying to recruit members.

I took advantage of this and I was telling Mike everything that was going on in security with Mick.

Mike stated, "he sounds a right 'F******g W****r'. He told me when to call a status quo and how to go about it. He told me then to leave it to the 'big guns', meaning himself and Charlie.

On the 18th November 1996 I phoned Brendan over the new proposed rotas and wages. Brendan told me to get Mick and go to his office.

Mick and I attended Brendan's office. We discussed the new rota. I said the members don't want 12 – 12 shifts. Brendan asked Mick "is there anything we can do about this problem".

Mick said, "yes we will only change the floating shifts if both the 12 – 12 man and the 17.00 -00.00 man are both off.

Mick broke his promise, as usual and changed the 8 – 8 floater to 12 – 12 on a regular basis and he even changed the 8 – 8 floater when both 17 – 24 and 12 – 12 shifts were covered – which was not what he had previously stated.

I then said my wages are wrong, I showed them a breakdown of the wages. I was told by Brendan I am not on manual grade 3 but on APT & C scale 3.

Brendan told me he could get a private security firm in to do my job cheaper and I replied, "and I can get someone from the private sector to do your job for half the price". This statement shut Brendan up.

I then arranged for a meeting with Les Gilford for the next day, Tuesday 19th November at 16.00 hrs.

On the 19th November 1996 both Les and myself attended the meeting with Brendan and Mick. I again said my wages are wrong.

Brendan told Les I tried to tell Rob he is on APT & C Scale 3 not on manual grade 3. Les then asked Brendan "if Rob was on manual wage would his wages be right".

Brendan said "yes".

I then asked them to show me my bank holiday payments. I was told it's all built into the system by Mick.

I then brought up six Security Officers who had been given an upgrade to run the Control Room. I told them that members of the Union had been told that they had to help out in the Control Room whenever required. I said if that's the case then lets talk money.

Brendan stated Mick would like you in the Control Room. I'm saying it's not your job and you don't go in the Control Room.

Wednesday 20th November I had a rota put with the signing on sheet saying the new rota starts Monday.

Thursday morning I called into Les's office and told him to call a status quo. Les said, "I would have to ask for permission from Brendan".

I told Les you don't have to ask for permission as I have spoken to Mike Titherington the Regional Officer of the GMB. He told me I instruct you to call a status quo.

Les told me he had spoken to Mick about the rota and he gave me another two weeks – what's he playing at?

Les then faxed a memo to management stopping the rota coming in. Unfortunately I don't have a copy of it.

Later that day my phone rang and it was Derek Anders. He told me that the Conveners have been in a meeting all afternoon and Brendan wants to see you tomorrow. A few minutes later the phone rang – it was Derek again. The meeting has now been put forward to 09.00. The phone rang again – it was Phil Houghey asking me what's going on and saying Derek had rang him twice. I told Phil I've called a status quo.

I then phoned Les up that evening and asked him what the meeting was about. He knew nothing about it. Les was not invited as Brendan, Mick and Tommy Twist (Convener to T&GWU) were all involved in the 1991 figures and it seemed to me that the three of them were trying to 'worm their way' out of the problem with the wages.

Les sent Brendan a letter 21/11/96 which to this day I have not seen.

Brendan arranged for Phil Houghey to go to his office. Ged Philbin and the rest of his members told him to keep his mouth shut and I believe that Phil went down and 'squealed like a pig'.

I came in to work on my next shift and all his members asked me for membership forms to join my Union.

Phil later came to me and said, "I don't have any members – I may as well join your Union".

On the 21/11/96 Brendan replied.

RE Security Officers Pay Structure

> *I refer to your letter of 21/11/96 and I must admit to being perplexed by its contents. I would remind you that the revised shift rotas were chosen by the workforce and as far as I am aware present no problems. Indeed I have met the T&GWU Steward who again agrees there is no problem.*

> *In terms of the repeated requests you have made for information as to the pay structure, the only suggestion I can make is for you to sit down with Mike Gornall and work out what Security Officers were earning before the new arrangements of an all inclusive grade were implemented in 1991.*

> *Irrespective of this, your argument is irrelevant given that Security Officers have been employed under APT & C conditions since that time. I would hope that this clarified the matter and will arrange a meeting for Friday 22 November 1996 am.*

Les and I went to Tommy Cranston for help with the wages as he was the ex Convener of the GMB at the time of the restructure.

Tommy Cranston wrote as follows:

Les, Rob

1) *Check contract of employment to make sure APTC payment and conditions of employment come under the purple book!*

2) *If so, confirm with Horace Taylor that there have been no amendments to pages 49 – 50 section 3 paragraph 38.*

  • *Rotating shifts CIV*
  • *General and public holiday working*
  • *Extra statutory holiday working*

When confirmed, arrange a meeting with Security management asking them to confirm contract of employment, then explain that contract.

Re above – it does not conform with the purple book and would they make the appropriate adjustments from when contract started, also making the adjustments to contract of employment?

When Tommy wrote this information down he knew it was wrong what they did with the wages, as he was one of the Conveners who dealt with it in 1991 and he gave us the relevant information to rectify our wages.

I called into Les's office and he told me I have opened a can of worms that should have been left alone.

On Friday we attended the meeting with Brendan, Mick and also present was Tommy Twist, Convener for the T&GWU. I again brought up the subject of my wages, which were wrong. I said I'm on £3.96 per hour.

Brendan then rang wages. He then told me Cleaners are on £3.85 per hour, he then worked out on his calculator and replied, "you are on £4.13 per hour. The only way I could have been on this wage is to have been on manual Grade 3.

I kept going on that my wages were wrong. Brendan then stated, "why did you take the job". This statement was repeated to me several times by Brendan. Tommy put his arm around me and said, "I assure you the wages were correct".

He, Mick and Brendan checked the figures in a meeting yesterday.

Brendan said he is bringing the rota in on Monday 25th November. Phil shrugged his shoulders and I looked at Les for support and got nothing.

The rota came in after I had called a status quo to stop the rota coming in until we received a pay deal for all the extra weekend working and to put us on the correct wage and that would have been the same pay as the Park Rangers and the Hall Keepers – that was APT&C Scale 4 plus allowances that they should have received in 1991.

Because of Les's apparent lack of knowledge I went for help from Charlie Lenard a full time GMB Officer and he told me to go and see Les – which is what he gets paid for, this was the last straw.

I was going home in December 1996 after my shift and not being able to get to sleep as I was thinking how the hell are they getting away with all of this and I was trying to find a way to put it right and put a stop to what Mick and Brendan were doing.

Because of the lack of support I received from the GMB in January 1997, I made an appointment with Unison and I had a meeting with Eddie Tickle (Branch Secretary of UNISON) and Kevan Nelson (Convener of Unison).

I took my file and showed them what was going on. Eddie kept saying "they can't do that; we will sort that after the meeting".

I was impressed with the response I got so I wrote to my Members on the 11th January 1997.

To All Union Members

'I have taken the decision to resign as your Staff Representative.

The reason for my resignation is that I feel that I am no longer receiving the support of the present Union Area Representative, which is required during negotiations.

I joined Unison and the lads asked me to get them membership forms and they wanted me to continue as their Shop Steward'

This was my biggest mistake joining Unison myself and my members were 100 times worse off.

Les Gilford phoned Security and asked to speak to me. I told the Security Officer to tell him I will go to his office and see him face-to-face.

I went to Les's office and he blamed me for him losing his members. I told him it had nothing to do with me and it was his and Charlie Lenard's fault. I resigned himself for lack of knowledge as a Convener and Charlie Lenard for sending me away when I requested help.

As agreed with Unison a meeting was arranged for 23 April 1997 with Paul Hounch (Regional Officer of Unison). After the meeting Paul wrote to Mike Fitzsimmons (Head of Local Government of Unison 10/09/97).

'Dear Mike,

Re Security Service Staff at St Helen's

Later last year the branch recruited these 30 or so members who were formally with the GMB.

Their Steward, Rob Steele, had discovered that the deal agreed between the GMB and the Authority disadvantaged financially the bulk of his members. Indeed he had investigated at length in great details the agreement struck prior to his employment.

I have looked at the case and find it difficult in industrial terms to find a channel for effective recourse as essentially the staff was badly represented by the GMB. However, there maybe a legal avenue but this expires on the 1st October, 1997 when the case would become statute barred. I think it might be advisable to seek Thompsons' advice just in case we have picked up a liability when we recruited the members.

Perhaps you could let the Branch know directly if they can arrange the meeting forthwith, especially as they think it is worth pursuing in terms of our PR vis-à-vis the GMB. This perhaps is a case worth more in the long run than it is in the immediate future.

Rob Steele has worked very hard on this case but the employer is refusing to deal with him because of his tenacity in pressing his member's case which is exposing the Authority as a 'con merchant'.'

Paul Haunch (Regional Officer). Shortly after sending this letter he was moved on. At a much later date I met Paul in the Unison Office and I asked him why he went, he told me he did not want to go and he was 'moved aside'.

Paul said to me, "You look terrible" and told me to go home and rest, he told me he was a male nurse before he joined Unison and that I should take his advice.

This was towards the end of 1999, when my health started deteriorating rapidly with severe depression. Paul had seen for himself how ill the management had made me. It is my opinion that they had to move Paul to one side as you had two honest men working side by side and Unison knew he could not be bought.

Between February and April 1997 I attended a JCC meeting with several of my members.

I raised an issue concerning Dave Anders and Roy Simm. I told Brendan and Mick, Dave had approached me as whilst on patrol he stood on a nail and ruined a new pair of boots that cost £70 and that he wants to recover the cost from the Council and that it is in the accident book.

Mick replied 'no it's not in the accident book'.

I replied that I was told by Dave it was put in the accident book. Mick replied it's not. Then I said Roy slipped walking around the school and broke his glasses and he would like to recover the cost of his new pair.

Brendan told me to arrange to see June Brachen (Health & Safety Officer) and she would sort it out for both of them.

I sent both of them to June and she told them they could not claim.

After the meeting Kevan Nelson told me to stop my members coming to JCC meetings as they are causing problems – both he and I would deal with the issues. What I did not know at the time was he was getting rid of my witnesses.

I then went to the Control Room and 'railroaded' Dave for telling me his accident was recorded in the accident book. Dave went and got the accident book and it was there in black and white.

It stated:

Date: 16/2/97
Time; 16.55

In what room or place did the accident happen?
Outside Ex Carr Mill Community Centre.

How did the accident happen?
Whilst walking around premises slipped. Stood on board, nail went through boot and into my left foot.

Tetanus injection refused – already covered.

I apologized to Dave and he told me he wanted to make a complaint about Mick.

I told him to put it in writing and I would take it up.

It reads as follows:

> *'I David Anders approached my Shop Steward reference my boots being ruined whilst on duty hoping to be reimbursed for the cost of my boots. Mr Steele brought my request up at the next JCC and I was told afterwards by my Shop Steward that Mr Gornall was not aware of the incident because it had not been entered in the accident book.*
>
> *I assured my Shop Steward that the incident had been entered into the book by Mr B Wright. I am disappointed that I have not received any payment for my boots being ruined and that I have been made to look a liar by Mr Gornall.*
>
> *I, therefore wish for my Shop Steward to put in a Grievance on my behalf.'*

I took this letter to Kevan Nelson and he read it and to my disbelief, he said, "I'm not taking it any further".

I attended the JCC meeting on 24/4/97 with Kevan. In the meeting the minutes of the last meeting were discussed.

Ever since I became Shop Steward every issue I had brought up was not put in the minutes of all the JCC meetings I attended.

The management then went on to discuss the three points on their agenda.

Kevan then said he had to leave to go to a meeting and left the office.

I then put three points across on the Union agenda to the management. As usual I received feeble answers to the issues I put forward.

I then pointed out to the management that officers were still not receiving meal breaks. One officer went 16 hours without a break.

I told the management this is down to the new system and the system does not work. Brendan Farrell started laughing when I said the old system was a better system. He told the person writing the minutes to write down, "*Rob says the old system with six supervisors is better*".

I replied."hold on who mentioned Supervisors – I said our old system was better".

I then said I received a complaint that 94 premises were outstanding – again I said this is down to the system not working.

Mick Gornall replied, "Some Officers are making it not work, for instance one officer was seen doing 20 mph from one premises to another".

I then said, "some schools are getting three or four visits in one day to catch up on visits". The agreement for the schools is one visit Monday to Friday and two visits Saturday and Sunday.

Brendan replied that some schools would rather have seven visits in one night. I don't believe that is the case.

I replied, "that is not the agreement we have with the schools" and I produced the agreement with the schools.

Mick then asked me "where do you keep getting all this information from?"

I replied "no comment".

Brendan said this is out of date. The Manager has changed and the supervisors have gone.

I replied, "but the school contracts haven't changed or gone, that is still the agreement.

I then produced a list of premises, a total of 96, which needed follow-up calls.

Brendan then asked who gave me them. I said it's unfair to give you that information.

Brendan then asked Mick "do you know who it is?"

Mick replied, "I have an idea but Rob's not going to tell us".

I can now tell you it was the temp they made Coordinator, Peter Woodcock. They can't do anything to him because he left many years ago.

Brendan then said that this is confidential information and if it got into the wrong hands it would be damaging.

Brendan then stated the Chief Executive would sack him.

I replied, "no, he won't".

Mick then commented about it getting into the wrong hands. I said it's staying in my file.

Brendan then replied, "I'm going to give the schools their money back and get rid of 10 men – I'm not getting sacked".

I replied, "your threatening me now Brendan".

Brendan then picked up the list of premises and said "and you're threatening me". I replied "they are facts, not threats".

Brendan then asked Mick to find out why the premises were not checked on time. I replied part of it was down to alarm activations and lack of manpower on this system, I also said that I was stuck at a school for three and a half hours waiting for SMC to attend and one Officer waited over four hours. This problem is caused by never having an alarm response man on shift that the customer is paying for due to constant staff shortages.

Brendan then told me I'm not having any more men and then told me to see Mick at 15.00 hrs on the 27/4/97 and he will see me and Mick in his office next week. I replied I'm on a course next week. Brendan then said make it the week after.

I told Brendan that one of my members was being disciplined because his vehicle was broken into and his bag was stolen, along with the gate keys to the schools.

I told him this had been decided before an investigation had taken place and I thought there was a procedure for this.

Brendan replied, "yes, there is a procedure for this and I don't want to hear any more as you will be coming to me for an appeal".

Mick replied there was an investigation –I believe to be another lie. I was on nights when Mick walked in that morning and was told Tony Marsh a Security Officer's gate keys have gone missing and Mick turned around and said to me, "you are going to be doing another disciplinary".

That statement was made on the spot before he could have made any investigation, as I stated, I believe this is not true.

I was on the night shift when Tony came in and said his gate keys and his bag had gone missing. I got another vehicle key and opened his driver's door with it.

On my next shift Derek said to me, "between you, me and these four walls, Mick and Andrea Duff the Personnel Officer asked me to lie and say the key did not open the van when he tried it. The first thing I did was inform Kevan what Derek said to me and I also told Tony.

I defended Tony on his disciplinary and the case was dropped, as there was no case to answer. A couple of weeks later the same thing happened to Terry Cunliffe a Security Officer and I went on his disciplinary with the same defence as Tony Marsh and he was given a warning and Terry told Mick he is very disappointed. Terry should have got the same as Tony Marsh NO CASE TO ANSWER. Bernard Day had a radio stolen out of his vehicle.

All three incidents happened within a few weeks of each other. I told Mick if stuff keeps being removed from the vehicles I am going to the Police as I believed this was an 'inside job'. After making this comment they suddenly stopped.

The management had spare keys for all the vehicles and the three vehicles in question were not broken into.

At the end of the meeting I said to Brendan, "I believe in fairness".

He replied "so do I" – again I do not believe this is correct.

Something happened between Brian Wright and Phil Ward and Brian was removed from Security leaving his position as Coordinator vacant.

Derek Anders, now Deputy Head of Security, called me into his and Mick's office. He nodded his head towards his desk I said "what". He did it again. I looked down and there were a pair of Security Coordinator epaulets on his desk. He then said to me "there yours".

I replied, with disgust, "Oh no Derek I was not good enough first time – I'm not good enough now". I looked at Mick; he had gone red in the face and put his head down. Once again they were giving a job without advertising it.

After what went on between Brian Wright and Phil Ward, Phil would not continue to do his job as Housing Officer. Mick and Paul Molyneux used to go to Housing Meetings, which did not concern Paul or had anything to do with his job.

They got friendly with Peter Lawton who had nothing to do with the Council. Phil's job as Housing Officer became available and it was not advertised internally and I don't believe to this day that it was advertised externally.

Peter Lawton got the job and I was told it had been advertised in the Job Centre so I asked all six Coordinators if anyone came for the job interview and only one said, "yes, Peter Lawton". Bernard Day told Mick he wanted the job and Mick told him, "I did not think you wanted the job".

The job should have been advertised internally first and had Mick done that, he would have known Bernard wanted the job. He again gave a job to someone outside the Council. He has got no excuse as every week there is a list for internal jobs in the Council.

Mick Rimmer was doing a routine patrol when he arrived at Rainhill High School. The police were there and Mick told them he would assist them. He drove around the back of the school and got 'bogged down in the grass'. Mick gave him a written warning for 12 months and I went on his appeal with Brendan.

Brendan reduced his warning to six months. On both occasions I defended Mick and both times I told Mick Gornall and Brendan he had no case to answer.

Later in 1997 Paul Fahay a Security Officer got 'bogged down in the grass' at the same school on a routine patrol and he should have walked around the school. He was not disciplined and he did have a case to answer.

Jimmy Goodier and Terry Cunliffe were off sick. Terry had hurt his leg climbing Snowdon and I was talking to Derek about staff shortages.

Derek said "blame your colleagues" meaning Jimmy and Terry. He said if it was down to him he'd sack the 'b******s'. Derek also made this same statement about me at a later date.

I came into work for my 4 o'clock shift and Damian Finnan had been on days as the Coordinator in the Control Room. I walked into the Control Room and Damian was furious – he said "that 'b******d' has been in Mick's office all day talking rugby and done no work", meaning Paul Molyneux, "get it f*****g sorted". I understood where Damian was coming from as Mick, Derek and Paul had left him to do all the work.

1) I attended an alarm activation in Birley Street, Newton-le-Willows at the school. I went into the building and checked it out and went out to my vehicle. Alec Grant got on the radio and told me to phone him on the school's phone, so I did. He told me Mick Gornall had rang him and told him to get that 'bag of s**t' inside – meaning myself. I told Alec to ring Mick back and tell him if he ever calls me a 'bag of s**t' again, I will 'stick one on him'.

Mick Gornall lived a few doors down from the school and was watching me. He never had the balls to come and say it to my face. What Mick was complaining about was that the back of my shirt was sticking out of my trousers as I was constantly getting in and out of the vehicles and it pulled the back of my shirt out of the trousers.

In my opinion there is only one 'bag of s**t' in Security and that was Mick Gornall. He looked like a tramp in uniform. The cartoon character the lads had put up of him fits him to a tea – it shows what a 'scruffy git' he really is.

2) I was sent to premises 106 St Aeldrids, Birley Street, Newton-le- Willows to an alarm activation around 6 o'clock in the morning. I was half way round checking the building when Eric Clark got on the radio and told me to leave the premises and go to the special school down the road to let the Police in as I had the gate key. So I left. When I got there, there were about six Police Officers and two of them had climbed over the fence and had arrested Jamie Spencer – the same person who pulled a knife on Mick Fairclough a Security Officer at Penkford Special School. It was also Jamie Spencer that Mick Hutton pulled out of a cupboard at premises 64 in That to Heath a few weeks after he had pulled a knife on Mick Fairclough.

When I had finished with the Police Eric called me back to the Control Room. When I got back Eric said the Caretaker had rang him and said a window had been forced open and I had missed it. Had there been enough men on nights then there would have been two of us at the alarm activation and we were key holders for that school and should have gone in and checked the zone that had gone off and we would have found the window had been forced also one of us could have stayed at the school and checked the whole school whilst the other officer could have gone to the other school around the corner and assisted the police.

Again it was Jamie Spencer who had forced the window and set the alarm off and then went down the road to the other school and was caught by the Police breaking in.

Once again this problem arises from staff shortages and once again, I could have been on my own and faced the person who threatened Mick Fairclough with a knife months earlier.

Mick Gornall does not care about the health and safety of his Officers or he would have took the instruction of his Health & Safety Officer (Dave Sharrock) and made sure two men attend all alarm activations at all times. I believe he would rather cut costs than cover the safety of his Officers.

3) Mick Gornall called me into his office and complained to me that Tony Marsh was 30 minutes in front of himself on the route.

When Mick Gornall was out in his car and he sees a patrol he writes down the time and place he sees them and the next day he checks the time on the R.L.S sheet. He did it to me in a park in Haydock. I had only radioed out 10 seconds earlier so he had nothing on me.

If Mick had a problem with Tony Marsh being 30 minutes in front on his times then he should have got him in the office and told him instead of being 'gutless' and complaining to me about it.

4) Mick Gornall took a static on at Stanley Bank Farm on overtime he covered as many shifts as he could off shift.

After many months Mick got me in the office and said *"I'm getting rid of Stanley Bank Farm – I'm not having Security Officers on more money than me"*.

I did quite a bit of overtime on the Farm so he was also getting at me. When he decided he was getting rid of the overtime he did contact the department in the Council responsible for the Farm and he got them to put a private security firm on the Farm to prevent us earning more money than him.

What he did not understand was we had to work hundreds of hours overtime to earn the same money as him – I believe this just shows what a selfish 'b*****d' he is.

Ref. arranged meeting with Mick 27/4/97

I went into Mick's office about 15.25 hrs. The first thing that was discussed was why the 96 premises were behind on visits.

I again repeated it's still down to the system not working. I also replied I told you and Brendan that this system would not work well before you implemented it.

Mick again put the blame on my members and said, "if it carries on I will change the rota". I told him if he tries I will call a status quo.

Mick replied the management decides what goes on here, not the Unions. The Unions have tried to stop rotas coming in before and failed.

I replied, "it was me who instructed Les Gilford to call the last status quo in November 96". The reason the system has never worked in Security is because he has never got the manpower to carry out the duties the client is paying for – I believe it is embezzlement. This problem has been going on since Mick took over as the Head of Security in 1991.

It is now 2011 and if I went into Security and got the duty sheet and the rota out I could prove he is still cutting corners with his clients i.e. cannot provide the service they are paying for because of staff shortages.

I then said, "Brendan took the 'p**s' out of me at the JCC meeting".

Mick replied "have you told Brendan this". I said "not yet, but I will".

Mick then said, "I knew what you were on about but Brendan did not".

I also said to Mick, you and Brendan treated me like a total idiot and don't underestimate me. Mick then said the old system had gone and will never come back. Mick then said I have six dedicated Officers.

I replied, "that made £1,000 of mistakes over Christmas.

Mick denied this and said it was £167 and on your old system the Officers made £900 of mistakes in one month. They sent a plumber to a dripping tap and to a toilet that wouldn't flush. The Coordinators were called in to Mick's office over the Christmas period for the mistakes they made and Mick told them it was £1,000 of mistakes.

The statement Mick made 'I have 6 dedicated Officers' - if that was the case why did Derek Anders (Deputy Head of Security) have a meeting with four of the Coordinators and tell them they had a weak link in the team?

Eric Clarke came to me and asked why Ian Adams handwriting was all over Peter Woodcock's paperwork. I told Eric it was not Peter's fault he got the job and the lads were willing to train him up.

I then asked Mick why he gave a new member of staff the job as Coordinator when he had two ex Coordinators on the highest wage in Security and they never got a 'sniff in'?

I told Mick that Peter Woodcock told me and other Officers he did not know what Citizen's Charter was.

Mick replied he answered all six questions and answered them well.

I replied, "you only gave him the job to get at the other members who put in for it".

I then said he would not have got the job if Pat Wright a Temporary Security Officer would have stayed. I took Pat out on route and she told me that you had discussed a Coordinators job with her on her interview for Security Officer. I told her I was going to see you about it and she asked me not to say anything to you. This is why you made the temps permanent after three months so he could have the job.

Mick replied, "well you will know".

I replied, "yes I do know – I know how you work".

I then said to Mick I would challenge him and Brendan in a meeting at the Town Hall with Dave Watts (MP for St Helen's), Carole Hudson (Chief Executive for the Council) and Russ Damson (a Manager in the Town Hall).

Mick stated Brendan wouldn't let it go that far. Mick then told me the Officers are to stay out till 2 am patrolling. I replied first it's 12.30 am, then 1 am, then you move the goalposts to 1.30 am and now you want 2 am.

I then told Mick the agreement time for checking premises is 12.00 am and we wind down for 12.30 am.

Mick replied, "I'm not having Officers doing nothing all night".

I replied, "there not, we go on standby at 12.00 am for alarm activations that is what the night turn is for".

Mick said nothing had been agreed.

I replied, "the Union and the management will have to negotiate then."

In fact the agreement was made with the schools in 1991 and the patrols were to be finished for midnight. I then left the room slamming the door behind me.

I went on my Steward's induction course 30 April – 2 May 1997 at the Vetex Training and Conference Centre, Little Carr Lane, Chorley. I took my file of grievances, which I had been dealing with since becoming Shop Steward in June 1996. I had three Tutors over the three days – they were Stephanie Thomas, Bill Campbell and Angela Washington. Most of the course sessions were with Bill. Every lesson we had over the three days I had already been in conflict with management and in every lesson I got my paperwork out to show the Tutors.

All three Tutors asked me what the outcome was and when I told them they could not believe the outcome of the grievances. It did not look good for the Tutors who were trying to teach the other Shop Stewards how to deal with the issues I had already dealt with – all of which had ended up with a negative outcome.

In my last lesson with Bill, he said to me "don't tell me you have dealt with this as well".

I said "yes".

He said "I don't want to see it and told me there is something seriously wrong and I must go and see Kevan as soon as I get back.

I went to the Union office and told Kevan what Bill had said and to my dismay Kevan told me I must remember they are in the same Union as you.

After my course Mick told me I had to book three days holiday for doing my course.

I told him that, "Brian Chadwick from Cleansing was on the same course and he did not have to book holidays to go on the course so I'm not."

Mick said he was going to see Pam Grey (Personnel Manager) about it. I told him to go ahead and see her. I am still not booking holidays when Brian did not.

Mick backed down.

Mick Rimmer rang me at home and told me his mother had passed away. I told him I would ring work and let them know he wouldn't be in.

Mick told me he was down to work Monday, Tuesday and Wednesday 16.00 24.00. Mick rang me again on the following Monday and said he's on 21 – 8 nights and he wants to have a drink after the funeral so I told him I would sort it out for him.

I rang work and told them he won't be in for two shifts. I then found out that Mick Gornall told him he had to book the two 11 hour shifts as holidays. I was furious.

I wrote to Mick on the 6th February.
Bereavement Leave

> *A member of Security has recently been granted bereavement leave for one week by you. However his working week consisted of fifty-four hours and you have only credited him with 39 hours – can you please clarify this?*

Mick replied 13 February 1997

> *As mentioned in our meeting on 4 February 1997 this was a personal matter that should have been dealt with between the individual concerned, yourself and management. It should not have been discussed during a general meeting you convened on 30 January.*
>
> *Chief Officers are allowed to give 39 hours with pay and 39 hours without pay bereavement leave.*
>
> *Also in your letter you stated that his working week was 54 hours. In fact the leave was spread over 14 days and not one week.*

It was not Mick's fault the funeral was the following week. The problem was to do with the backlog of funerals over the Christmas period. I have the rota and Mick was down to work Monday 16.00 24.00 and Saturday 09.30 21.30 Sunday 9.30 21.30 and the following Tuesday 21.00 24.00 into Wednesday 00.00 08.00, 21.00 24.00, Thursday 00.00 08.00, 21.00 00.00 Friday 00.00 08.00.

He was down to work a total of 7 days over 2 weeks – a total of 54 hours.

I found out that Mick went back to work Saturday and Sunday and I was disgusted to find out that he was put on the Crematorium patrolling the Cemetery.

Over a seven day period and not 14 days like Mick stated in his letter. Mick had a total of three days off leading to a total of 30 hours and not 39 and 22 of the hours he had to book off as holidays.

In total Mick Rimmer got eight hours bereavement leave. In my opinion this just shows what a nasty piece of work Gornall is. John Sexton, Tony Marsh, Keith Jones and Derek Anders all had a week off, with full pay, when one of their parents died and John Swift had a month off and got full pay.

When Derek came back off bereavement leave and told me that Mick said to him he should have had more time off and said when my parents die I will be off months.

Mick Fairclough had a day off to go to a family funeral and was given the day off by Mick. I went to a family funeral and I had to book a day's holiday.

I was on 8 – 8 days with Keith Hackett and Kenny Watterson. The three of us were in the Control Room. Eric Clarke was the Supervisor and went out. Kenny had gone to the Rest Room for his dinner. Eric later came back and looked at the alarm monitor. Keith had missed a house alarm and Eric told Keith to send a patrol to go and check it out.

Alan Bolger went and on arrival the Fire Brigade was there. He got on the radio and said three houses had burnt to the ground.

Eric turned around and said "someone's head is going to roll".

As I was Keith's Shop Steward I went to his defence. I phoned the Fire Station up and asked them what time they received the call and I asked them how long it would take to get there. They replied a few minutes. I checked the times of the alarm and the time of the phone call and the time it took to get there. The alarm was activated after the Fire Brigade got there and it was one of the Firemen who activated the alarm. Whether Keith would have sent someone right away or not – it would not have changed the outcome of the damage to the Council houses. No one was disciplined.

Mick Hutton a Security Officer did not like Mick Gornall and swapped his day turns for nights so he did not have to work with him. Mick had been doing this for quite a considerable amount of time.

Around May 1997 I was feeling the strain from the behaviour of the Management. To avoid conflict with them I started swapping my days for nights. I came in on an afternoon shift and Derek came into the Control Room and told me I am not allowed to swap any more day shifts for nights. He made a statement that I did not want to work with himself or Mick.

They stopped me doing mutual swaps and let Mick Hutton and others continue to do so. There is no question about it, In my opinion this was victimization.

Jimmy Goodier was on Gerards Bridge depot and injured himself patrolling around the depot. Mick later made a statement to me that Jimmy had injured himself at home and said he was putting in a claim against the Council. Not long after, I was on nights with Ged Philbin and he injured his ankle on a rocking flag stone in the Depot.

Derek Anders came to me and said Ged had come to work with his injury and is trying to put a claim in. As I had always looked at Derek as a good friend, I told Derek that I was on nights with Ged when he injured himself going to the Rest Room. I told him not to get involved as Mick is going to get himself into trouble.

This brings back an incident concerning myself. I was out on route and a car ran into the back of me when I was stationary. I was at Penkford Special School in Newton-le-Willow. Keith Jones came out to me and said I had to go to the hospital – as he was my Supervisor he took me. I was told I had whiplash and they put my neck in a collar. I went back to the Control Room and Keith told me to go home. I told him I was OK and I that I would help out in the Control Room.

Colin Pinder a Security Officer was on alarm response and an alarm went off at the school. Colin had come back to the depot and I had got the keys and the information for the school out. When he came into the depot I went out and handed him the keys and the information.

He said "look at the state of your hand".

I looked at my left hand and it was swollen like a balloon. As he was my Shop Steward he told me to go back to the hospital. I went back to the hospital and they took X-Rays and put my arm in a sling.

I called into work as I had to pick up the insurance from the garage to show it to the Police. I called into Mick's office – he saw my hand was badly swollen and said I had smashed my hand with a hammer to get an insurance claim. I was later told by one of my work colleagues that Colin had had words with Mick about the comments he made about the hammer. I find Mick to be a very dangerous person.

I attended a meeting called by management on Tuesday 24/6/97 in Brendan Farrell's office where Brendan, Mick Gornall and Derek Anders and I were present.

Brendan asked who had called the meeting. I told him management had and I also had points to bring up.

The first discussion covered uniforms i.e. peoples appearances and hygiene. Brendan told me that no one will be employed in Security who had tattoos on their hand and face, nor anyone wearing earrings. I could not understand him saying this as he, being an ex Personnel Manager, should have know this was sex discrimination.

Furthermore, to my disbelief, he said that John Sexton and Phil Partington both Security Officers 'stink' and were making the Radio Operator's chair 'stink'.

I could not believe what I was hearing. It had nothing whatsoever to do with me as a Union Representative and should have definitely not been discussed with me. If they did have a problem with their hygiene they should have had a private word with them.

Mick Gornall and Derek Anders put this information about John and Phil into Brendan's mind, as Brendan only knows what's going on in Security by the information passed on by Mick and Derek.

We then went onto holidays. It was to do with Ged Philbin booking off four hours on his 12 – 12 shift. I told them I would mention it to him, which I did.

I then brought up that the Patrolling Officers are being 's**t' on and that we wanted to be treated like the rest of the Department.

Brendan then tried to blackmail me and said "go on annualised hours and you can".

I said "the Coordinators are on annualised hours and are being paid overtime to cover Brian Wright's shifts. Yet when we covered Phil Partington's shifts, who is now a Co-ordinator for three and a half months, we had to do it off shift and the money saved should have been divided between the 16 men who covered his shifts.

Brendan replied you covered it off shift and did not need overtime.

I said "yes we did cover it off shift but we all did extra work to cover it and we should have been paid for the extra work".

Brendan again said "how can I justify paying you when you covered it off shift?"

Again, corners were cut, and a man was down on shift, adequate cover was not there to cover the duties required for which the customer was paying for.

The rota, the duty sheet and the RLS sheet will prove what I have been saying all along is 100% right.

I then said that if we went on a work-to-rule it would prove the job would not get done.

Brendan replied, "I'm not having you on a work-to-rule, it's bad enough with the bin men working on a work-to-rule and the Union has to ballot for industrial action.

I replied "I do know how to ballot and that you receive the result of the ballot".

Brendan replied "go ahead and work-to-rule".

He then threatened me and said I will give the schools back the money and we would lose work. The department would close and I would see that Mick and Derek were redeployed, as they had not caused the problem.

I said we will be redeployed too.

Brendan then said "I will make you all redundant ".

I then said "if I lose my job the 's**t will hit the fan' and I will write to the Minister of Office of Public Services and get something done.

Brendan replied, "that's threatening".

I said "no Brendan it's not a threat I don't make threats I'm telling you I will do it".

I then told Brendan "I have written to Solicitors telling them they are 'b******s' and that they have the brain of an amoeba. I have also written to 10 Downing Street calling the Solicitor a 'b*****d' and he has the brain of an amoeba.

I have copies of the letters if you want to see them, so you can see I don't make threats I go ahead and do it".

I then said "threatening is what you do Brendan. You said in the last JCC Meeting when I showed you the 96 outstanding premises and you said you would get rid of 10 men and pay the schools back the money – that's threatening Brendan".

Brendan replied, "I don't recall saying that". I then reminded him of the first time I met him and I told him that if he sticks to the management rules and I stick to the Union rules we would get on fine and you replied, "if you cause me any problems you would ring the Town Hall and close you down overnight. That's threatening Brendan".

Brendan again stated, "I don't recall saying that and if I did then I would have only said that if you were threatening me".

I said "you did Brendan and I have already told you I don't make threats".

I then said Market Officers and the Coordinators are on annualized hours to cover their own duties and the 17 Officers on our rota should only cover our duties.

Mick said "you've always covered the markets".

I then said "I will investigate into this matter further.

Again, taking men off one rota to cover other jobs elsewhere is leaving a shortage of men to cover the daily duties the client was paying for.'
I then asked for Police 'Bomber' jackets.

Brendan then said we would look like 'Bouncers'.

I said the Police wear them.

Brendan then said "it's fine by me but it's up to them", meaning Mick and Derek.

Derek then said "I will do a deal with you, you wear your hats and we will give you the jackets".

I said "I'm not wearing a hat - when I was in the Army I got pains in my forehead and the top of my nose.

Brendan then said that some people could not wear hats and that he has tried four or five hats playing golf and couldn't wear one.

Mick then said that all our uniforms have to have a logo on them for tax reasons. I totally disagreed with this. The reason he wanted to do this was because he spoke to me about odd members of Security using their shirts and trousers when not at work.

I went on to them about how the job had changed since Mick and Derek were Patrolling Officers. I went on and told them how difficult the job has become with Youths drinking on the premises and the problem with drugs. It was alright for Mick and Derek when they went out on patrol, they went out in twos, the pair of them would not have the 'balls' to do it on their own – Mick especially would 'have diarrhoea running down his legs'. It was Mick who introduced one man patrols in his restructure in 1991 when he became Head of Security.

I challenged Brendan to come out on route with me to see how difficult the job was and to show how vulnerable the Security Officers were at some of the schools on their own. Brendan, being an ex Time and Study man and ex Personnel Manager, would have seen the risk factor – he declined to do so.

I then commented not even the Health and Safety Officers want to take me up on the same offer.

Brendan then said "are you telling me the Health and Safety Officers refused to check on a health and safety problem?"

I replied, "no, I gave them the same challenge I put forward to you and they also declined".

I then told Brendan "our wages are wrong".

Brendan said "I couldn't agree more".

I replied "you're not getting the point – our wages had been wrong since 1991".

Brendan replied "you agreed the wages were right in 1991. When I checked Mick's figures they did add up". I have since added them all together and they don't correspond with the APT&C scale.

Mick said "I hope you haven't told the lads this because the wages are right and they will take it out on you."

"I told them that I have been in a meeting with Paul Haunch for three and a half hours and he told me to tell my Members there is a wage discrepancy and he is doing a full investigation".

Brendan said "he has not said anything to me".

I said "that's because he hasn't finished his enquiries yet".

Mick again said "I hope you haven't told the lads this".

I again said "yes, I have – Paul Haunch told me to tell the Members there is a discrepancy and that he is doing a full investigation".

Mick then said "well if I've got it wrong then so have other qualified people".

When we discussed the wages in the meeting 27/4/97 Brendan made a statement that it's Kevan Nelson's fault you are on Scale 3 all-inclusive as he said that was good enough for Security Officers. We then finished the meeting.

I went to see Kevan about this and he denied it in this meeting and said Brendan is a liar. Mick, in the next meeting made the same statement that Brendan had said in the last meeting so I went back to Kevan's office and said both Brendan and Mick have stated it's you who put us on Scale 3 all inclusive. With aggression in Kevan's voice he alleged they are 'f*****g liars'.

Mick Gornall rang me up at home and asked me to attend a meeting in Brendan's office that afternoon and that Eddie Tickle would be attending so I rang Eddie to find out what the meeting was about. Eddie told me, "it's nothing to do with you; you don't need to be there".

I rang Mick back and told him what Eddie had said. Mick said he wanted me to go to the meeting.

I attended Brendan Farrell's office on 3/7/97 at 4 o'clock. Present were Pam Gray (Personnel Manager), Brendan Farrell, Mick Gornall, Derek Anders and Eddie Tickle.

Brendan started off by launching a verbal attack against me. He started off by telling me I was militant, a troublemaker and that I am causing all the problems in our department. He then said, "you've caused more trouble than all the Shop Stewards put together".

He then told Eddie Tickle he wanted another Shop Steward.

At the end of the day it's not up to Brendan who he wants as Shop Steward – it's up to my Members who elected me as their Steward.

I told Brendan I am not militant. I then got into a dispute over manning levels as they wanted to take an officer off shift to cover the Courier from the Town Hall.

I then challenged Mick to go and get the Coordinators and Market Officers rotas and I will prove we are under manned. I challenged him three times on this in this meeting that we do not have the staffing levels to cover the contracts with the client and they are paying for this and not getting the service they are paying for.

I then got the Security Officers rota out of my file. I had coloured all the duties in that we need to cover our contracts and built into the rota is two floating shifts per day to cover for sickness and holidays but there was only one floating shift Monday to Friday and none Saturday and Sunday. So if more than one person was off Monday to Friday the department could not provide the service to the client that they were paying us to do and if one or more were off on the Saturday and Sunday, this affected the client even more than on a Monday to Friday.

I then passed it to Brendan and asked him to show me how two men can be off when we don't have any spare floaters. Brendan said "sort it out between the three of you" (meaning myself, Mick and Derek).

Mick said the two 8 – 8 men can do a route and a half each. I said the 8 – 8 man has never done it like that and we never have done. If you look at the rota, even if the 8 – 8 men would have done a route and a half this would have made no affect to covering the client's contracts.

It got so heated between myself and Mick and Brendan, Eddie Tickle stepped in and told me to go outside. He came out with me and told me to calm down. I told Eddie that Kevan told me I'm not to go into any more meetings with management on my own as they had already 'stitched me up' meaning the issue with Ged Philbin.

Eddie said "you should have told me".

We went back into the office and a heated argument started again. Mick told Eddie that, "Rob won't listen". Unfortunately I don't listen to lies.

Brendan then said "we will continue this tomorrow".

I said "I won't be here I'm going to Cheltenham".

When I got back to the Control Room I pulled Mick up and told him "I'm not militant".

Mick replied, "I didn't know what Brendan was going to say". It was Mick and Derek who had planted the seeds in his head for Brendan to launch the verbal attack on me.

On the 31 July 1997 Eddie Tickle rang me to inform me that Brendan Farrell and Mick Gornall had stormed into the Union office demanding to see him about me. He told them he was not going to see them unless I was present.

I told Eddie that I am in about 4 o'clock. I will no doubt find out what it's about.

I went into the Control Room at 4 o'clock and Mick came out of his office and told me not to go anywhere as I am going to Brendan's office.

I said "is Eddie or Kevan going to be there".
He said "no".
So I said "I'm not going".

Mick then said "are you refusing to go to Brendan's office". I said "if you are putting it like that then yes".

Mick and Derek stormed off to Brendan's office and they came back and Mick asked me could he have a word with me and I went into his office. He looked at the clock and it was five to five – Mick said "from 5 o'clock tonight you don't speak to myself or Derek about Union matters.

I was in the Union Office around September, October talking to Steph and in conversation She thought I was talking about something else and she said Eddie wasn't happy about the letter either. I asked her about the letter and Brendan had written to Eddie about myself and Eddie and Kevan kept it from me.

Kevan came in and I told him I want a copy of the letter. Kevan was reluctant to give me a copy but I insisted. I got it; Kevan gave me a copy and told me not to put it in circulation.

The letter read as follows:
31 July 1997

Re: Rob Steele – Unison Shop Steward - Security

I refer to the above and becoming increasingly concerned in respect of Mr Steele's behaviour and conduct within the section.

He is disrupting a critical service with apparently no concept of the issues and procedures of Employee Relations. He had now informed Mike Gornall today 31/7/97 that he will not speak to management on pay issues, except in your presence.

This stance has no bearing on the operation of the section and I now fail to see why I should afford him any facilities in respect of his trade union duties.

Accordingly I have advised Mike Gornall and Derek Anders in respect of any dealings with Mr Steele as I have no confidence that management or service delivery issues are capable of being addressed in this climate.

I await an early meeting to resolve this issue.
Yours sincerely,

Brendan Farrell
Acting Assistant Director

ccM Gornall
D Anders
Mr E Tickle, Unison, 91 Corporation Street, St Helen's

What happened to the statement Brendan made in my first JCC meeting 10 July 1996 when he stated a he liked a keen Shop Steward, I like a good scrap with the Unions.

Not only was I a keen Shop Steward but also an honest one. I don't like liars, bullies and thieves. I believe that Mick had bullied, lied and thieved from his workforce and clients. In my opinion Brendan has also bullied and lied and was made well aware of the thieving and did nothing – he was also heavily involved in the wage structure in 1991.

Approximately six weeks before I went off sick in August, I serviced Derek's car. I went into work and Mick asked me to service his car. He said he would keep it discreet as the lads would not be happy me doing his car. He said "you don't have to do it if you don't want".

I said I would do it for him. He came to my home in the afternoon when he should have been at work and I serviced his car. I gave it a major service, which took two hours.

Mick asked me how much did he owe me and I said, "give me the £25 I paid for the parts". He turned around and said I want to give you £30. I thought to myself, 'big deal'.

Then Paul Molyneux brought his car to be serviced.

Mick bringing his car to me in works time reminds me when Derek was Supervisor. He brought his car to my house on a Saturday when he was on shift and he got a Security Officer to follow him and take him back to work.

I lived 15 miles away in Liverpool.

When I had changed the front wheel bearing, he got another officer to bring him back to collect his car. The two officers he brought to my house were Dave Watterson and Brian Wright both Security Officers. If it would have been a Security Officer that had done that, they would have been sacked.

I attended a JCC meeting 14/8/97. Present: Brendan Farrell, Mick Gornall, Derek Anders, Paul Molyneux, Kevan Nelson, Ann Jones, Dave Sharrock and myself.

I asked Dave Sharrock did he know what a bong was, he replied "no". So I told him it's a drugs machine. The reason I brought this up was I attended an alarm response in the hours of darkness.

When I got there all the lights were on in the building. I contacted control to let them know all the lights were on and Derek got on the radio and said "the Police have just left – go in and check it out". When I got upstairs there was a gang of youths there and when they saw me they ran out of the building. There were two ways down. I was blocking one way and they ran the other way.

On one of the tables was a bong, they were taking drugs. Derek put my life in danger. One he should not have sent me into that building on my own, especially in the hours of darkness. I took the bong back to the Council and put it in one of the cupboards in the Rest Room to produce at the JCC meeting but forgot to take it with me.

I then reminded Dave of the challenge I put to him of coming out on route with me and he and June Brachan both declined. I said I made the same challenge to Brendan and he also declined my offer.

Mick then stated that the Coordinator's annualised hours are not working.

I replied, "I told you they don't work. They did not work with the Supervisors and they don't work with the Coordinators.

Mick said he wants to pair up the Coordinators to cover each others shifts. I again said this will not work, this is a stupid idea. It would have been a bigger disaster than he already had.

Mick then discussed the depot merger. He wants the night shift to do constant patrolling of the depot when not on alarms.

I then asked Mick why did he make four men redundant from Gerards Bridge who were patrolling the depot.

He replied, "because we had cameras put in".

I said "the depot has six cameras and you are putting another four in and you want us to do constant patrol of the depot. If you want constant patrolling of the depot you better take the four men back and let them do it".

Brendan replied, "it will cost us £60,000".

I replied, "So what, I'm not doing it".

Brendan then asked, "does the depot get checked now". Derek said "sort of".

I said "if someone wants a bit of fresh air they will say book me on the depot".

Brendan then said, "that will do".

I replied, "he will only do what he wants and we will end up constantly patrolling the depot". Once I had gone off sick, he did just that.

I then blamed Brendan for making us check door handles in the dark when it was made clear, when one-man patrols were introduced in 1991 that you are to walk a safe distance from the building.

Brendan said it wasn't me. Again this was Mick's demands and again putting Patrol Officers' health and safety at risk. Kevan told me to bring up the issue concerning Ged Philbin.

I got into an argument with Mick and he started explaining to Brendan how I agreed to the night shift having to book off the whole shift and not part of it. I said "no I never it was to do with Ged Philbin booking off four hours on his 12 – 12 shift".

Mick replied, "yes you did". I lost my temper and said, "you're not making me look like a liar". As I got up I grabbed the table and lifted it off the ground. I grabbed my file and stormed out of the meeting. Why he was explaining this matter to Brendan God only knows, as in Mick;s letter to me Brendan witnessed it.

Here is Mick's letter
St Helen's Metropolitan Borough Council

To: R Steele, Unison Shop Steward
Our Ref. MG/DP
Extension HBD 2145 (M Gornall)
Date: 14 July 1997

Re Holidays

Following our meeting on Tuesday 24 June 1997 in which B Farrell and D Anders were also present, it was agreed by you to adopt the following.

If leave is required on the following shifts, one on Saturday and Sunday, the full shift and not part of it must be requested.

12.00 – 24.0,019.00- 07.00 and 21.00 – 08.00

Reason for this was:

1) *Difficulty to cover four hours due to floating shifts being 12 hours.*
2) *Could be refused leave for a full shift because Officers already on four hours holiday etc.*
3) *Could create conflict between Officers if someone has their 08.00 – 20.00 shift altered to 12.00 – 24.00 just to cover someone on holiday 20.00 – 24.00.*

M Gornall
Head of Security Services

Here is my reply to Mick's letter

2nd July 1997
Mr M Gornall
Head of Security
Contract Services
HARDSHAW BROOK DEPOT

Dear Mr Gornall,

Re: HOLIDAYS
I refer to your memorandum of 14th July 1997 in which you confirm a purported agreement reached at our meeting of 24th June 1997.

Whilst I recall an agreement in relation to a specific individual (Ged Philbin) there was no discussion about general guidelines. Therefore, I will regard your memorandum as a proposed restriction, which I will discuss with Security Officers as soon as possible and report back to the next Joint Consultative Committee.

Yours sincerely

Rob Steele Unison Steward

As I stated in a previous meeting with Mick and Phil Houghey present, it's my members that decide what goes on. I am not having people telling lies that I have agreed to something I haven't agreed to. I never once made a decision for my members, everything I did went through my members and I got them to sign signatures on certain issues.

I went to work that evening and Derek met me at a school in Garswood Premises no.5 and he said to me I had frightened Anne Jones the Secretary the way I left the meeting. I finished my shift on the morning of the 15/8/97 and had to go off sick with stress.

I consider that the behaviour of the management had gone far beyond acceptable standards of behaviour and the negotiations in the workplace context all amounted to a culture of bullying.

I had been off work a couple of weeks when I went to Brian Wright's house when Mick Gornall turned up at Paul Molyneux's house as Paul and Brian were next door neighbours. Mick said to me *"are you all right Rob?"*

I said *"no I'm not you and Brendan have made me ill"*.

Mick replied *"how's that then?"*

I said *"you've 'f****d' my head up that's how"* – I then walked off.

CHAPTER TWO

These are all the grievances I was dealing with during my time as Shop Steward for the GMB and Unison – they are in no particular order.

PROBLEMS IN SECURITY

INDEX

WAGES

1. SECURITY OFFICERS

In 1991 Mick Gornall had a restructure in Security and wanted to put the Security Officers on APT & C conditions of service i.e. staff rather than being manual workers. Security Officers were paid manual grade 3 which consisted of basic pay, shift allowance, weekend allowance and bank holidays paid at double time and a day in lieu.

This is the diagram of the wages in 1991:-

Manual Grade 3 pay 1991

Manual Grade 3

= £3.7482 per hour = £146.18 per week = £7,601.36 per annum

Basic Pay	£146.18
16% shift allowance	£ 23.39
26.93% weekend allowance	£ 39.36
TOTAL	**£208.93**= £5.36 p.h.

Each Officer was down to work 28 hrs. p.a. on bank holidays = £300.16 pa

Each Officer was entitled to a lieu day for being off on a rest day for each bank holiday. The rest days are as follows:-

Mon	Tue	Wed	Thurs.	Fri	Sat	Sun
12	9	13	13	10	9	9 = *Total of 75 days.*

Over a week ÷ 75 days by 7 days which gives you an average of 10.71 days x by 8 bank holidays = 85.68 days x by 8 hours = 685.44÷ by 28 men = 24.48 x £5.36 = *£131.21*

Basic Pay p.a.	£10,864.36
Bank Holiday Payment	£ 300.16
Lieu Time	£ 131.21
TOTAL	**£11,295. 73**

This is the wage Security Officers were earning before they went on to APT & C conditions of service i.e. Staff Pay.

LIEU TIME should have been given to each Officer who worked a bank holiday. Therefore, £147.01 is to be added to the pay grade in 1991. This works out as follows:-

12 men per bank holiday x 8 bank holidays = 96 men x 8 hours = 768 x £5.36 = £4,116.48 ÷ 28 = £147.01.

£11,295.73
£   147.01 this is equivalent to point 21 scale 4
£11,442.74

Brendan Farrell sent a letter to all security officers on the 31 October 1991 "I assure you that no one will lose money on the proposals and if you see Mick Gornall he will demonstrate this to you".

This statement includes new starters as he made it quite clear no one would lose money.

This is how Mick Gornall worked out the APT & C Staff Grade.

SECURITY OFFICERS PAY ALLOWANCES FOR NEW ROTA

Shift Allowance - 16%
Weekend Allowance - 26.48%

Manual Grade 3 pay will be:-
$$\begin{array}{r} £140.28 \\ +£\ 22.44 \\ +£\ \underline{37.14} \\ =£\underline{199.86} \\ \text{Hr. Rate} =£\quad 5.12 \end{array}$$

BANK HOLIDAY PAYMENTS STAFF LEVELS

0000 – 0800	3 men = 24 hrs x 8 = 192	
0800 – 1600	3 men = 24 hrs x 8 = 192	
1600 – 2400	4 men = 32 hrs x 8 = 256	

6 hrs.on 417 Sherdley Park 6 hrs x 8 = 48
- = 688 hrs 1 year
- ÷ number of men (26)
- = 26.46 hrs. per Officer x £5.12
- = £135.48
- = £2.60 per week extra for each Officer

Weekly Pay   =   £202.20   Annual   £10,514.40
Monthly Pay   = ...   New   £ 9,963.00

ALLOWANCES FOR ROTA

Shift allowance–16% = £22.45
Weekend Allowance 195 hr Sat & Sun every 28 wk
- = £292.5 every 28 wk.
- = £10.446 every week
- = 543.19 hrs / annum

X 100 x no of hrs/ann   = 543.19
=X x 2028   = 543.19
   100

= 26.78% = £37.57

39 hours at Grade 3 (1991)
↗

BASIC PAY £140.29 + Allowances
= 200.30 – 39
= £5.13 per hour

PAYMENT FOR BANK HOLIDAYS
WORKING 12 SHIFTS PER BANK HOLIDAY

= 12 x 8 x 8
= 768-8 x 8 (no. that any new starters could work)
= 704 hours –(1)

T FOR WORKING WOULD BE SAME AS (1) – 704 ÷ (2)
T FOR REST DAYS 10 OFFICERS 1 B HOL
= 80 X 8
= 640 – 8 X 8 (no taking new starters)

PAYMENT
(1) + (2) + (3)
=   1984 hrs. between 25 men
=   79.36 hrs each
=   79.36 x £5.13
=   £407.11
=   £33.93 / month

TOTAL MONTHLY PAY WOULD BE:-
    200.30 x 52 ÷ 12 = £33.93
    = £901.90
PROTECTION WOULD BE £71.65 / month

EXAMPLES OF GRADES AND THEIR SPINAL COLUMN POINT NUMBERS

Security Officers manual wage should have been equivalent to spinal point 21 scale 4 of APT & C – that is, £11,232.

Mick's own figures £10,822.80 put them on spinal point 19 Scale 4 of APT & C and decided to put them on Spinal Point 16, that is £9,963.00 *reducing Security wages by £1,479.74 p.a.*

Mick's own figures show he reduced their wages by *£859.80*. The reason my figures are different to Mick's figures is because he did not calculate the pay rise in November 1991 nor has he calculated lieu time for Security Officers working bank holidays. He only calculated lieu time for Officers on Rest Days.

Again, in my opinion he robbed his Officers of their wages.

Here is a statement made by Brendan Farrell (Personnel Officer) dated 31.10.91 to the Security Officers.

Again what happened to Brendan's statement *"I assure you that no one will lose money on the proposals".*

Security Officers lost £619.94 per annum and new starters, like myself, lost £1,479.74 per annum.

Security Officers were given a protection of £859.80. I believe this was introduced illegally. This will be discussed in detail when I get to Peter Maver's letters.

In 1990 Brian Cook was Head of Security and made a 'sort of' reasonable deal with Security personnel. Here is his letter:-

2 February, 1990

Dear Mr Twist,(Convenor for T & GWU)

Application for re-grading Security Personnel

With reference to our meeting on Friday 2 February 1990 it is proposed to implement the following with effect from Monday 19 February 1990, subject to your acceptance of the conditions outlined:-

Proposals

1) *Deputy Officers to be re-graded to APT & C Scale 4 (plus relevant shift and weekend allowances).*
2) *Mobile Security Officers (permanent staff only) to be re-graded to APT & C Scale 1 – 2 commencing at SPC 8 (plus relevant shift and weekend allowances).*

Conditions
As a condition of this re-grading, management would expect the following:-

1) *Total flexibility between the Duty Officers and Security Officers.*

    a) *Duty Officers to carry out the coordinators duties between 0001 and 0800 hours and to carry out Security Officers duties, if necessary.*
    b) *Security Officers to carry out the Duty Officers operational control room and coordinators duties, when necessary.*

2) *Control room duties to be carried out by means of computer equipment, following on site training.*

3) *Security Officers to continue to work a 39-hour week.*

4) *ALL APT & C staff to be paid monthly.*

5) a) *Any overtime to be paid at basic rate only without time and a half or double time enhancement.*
   OR
   b) *Use of selected temporary personnel to provide cover for absence through sickness, holidays etc.*

Brian Cook
Head of Security Services

2. GERRARDS BRIDGE OFFICERS PAY 1991

Basic Pay   = £146.18 p.w. = £7,601.36 p.a.
Shift Allowance   = 16% = £ 23.39 p.w. = £1,216.28 p.a.
Weekend Allowance = Sat £1.88 x 24 hrs =
                           £ 45.12 x 52 weeks =   £2,346.28 p.a.

Sun   = £   3.75 x 24 = 90 x 52 weeks = £4,680
£2,346.28
£4,680.00
£7,026.28 ÷ 4 = £1,756.57 ÷ 52 weeks = £33.78 p.w.

Basic Pay   =   £146.18
Shift Allowance 16%   =   £ 23.39
Weekend Allowance   =   £ 33.78
Total: £203.35   =   £5.22 p.h.

Bank holidays = 8 bank holidays x 24 hrs = 192 hrs x £10.44
= £2004.48 ÷ 4 = £501.12

Lieu Days = Mon to Fri 1 x 8 = 8 x 5 = 40 x £5.22 = £208.80
Lieu Days = Sat and Sun = 2 x 12 = 24 x 2 = 48 x £5.22 =
£250.56
88 ÷ 7 days = 12.5714 x 8 = 100.57 x £5.22 = £524.97 ÷ 4 =
£131.24 for time off for rest days.

Basic Pay	=	£10,574.20
Bank Holiday Payment	=	£ 501.12
Lieu Time	=	£ 131.24
Total:		**£11,206.56**

Because you have two officers working 12 hr shifts they are entitled to lieu time. This has to be added to the figures above 8 bank holidays at 24 hrs = 192 hrs ÷ 4 = 48 x £5.22 = £250.56, making a total of **£11,457.12 APT & C Scale 4 point 21.**

Mick Gornall also put them on scale 3 point 16 £9,963 p.a., which gave them a pay cut of £1,494.12 p.a.

Let's go back to Brendan Farrell's statement 31/10/91 "I assure you that no one will lose money on the proposals" – in my opinion this is yet another lie.

3. SECURITY SUPERVISOR'S PAY 1991

Supervisors were paid APT & C Scale 3 plus allowances – breakdown as follows:-

Basic Pay	=	£10, 215 p.a.
Shift Allowance = 20%	=	£ 2,043
Weekend Allowance = 20%	=	£ 2,043
Total:		**£14,301** = £7.63 p.h.

Bank Holidays = 8 x 24 hrs = 192 hrs ÷ 5 men = 38.4 x £7.63 = £292.99 hrs per man = £292.99 x 2 = £585.98

Lieu Days = Monday to Friday = 3 men x 8 hrs = 24 hrs. = 24 hrs x 5 days = 120 hrs
Saturday & Sunday 2 men x 12 hrs = 24 hrs x 2 men = 48 hrs = 168 hrs 168 ÷ 724 24 x 8 = 192 ÷ 5 = 38.4 x 7.63 = 292.99

Lieu days for rest days = Monday to Friday = 2 men x 8 hrs = 16 hrs x 5 = 80 hrs Saturday to Sunday = 3 men x 8 hrs = 24 hrs = 48 hrs = 128 hrs = 128 ÷ 5 = 25.6 x 7.63 = **£195.33**

£14,301.00	£15,375.30
£ 585.98	£14,484.00
£ 292.99	£ **891.30**
£ 195.33	
£15,375.30	

This again shows a deduction in Supervisor's wages of **£891.30**.

They should have started at point 30 SO 1 and not scale 6 point 28.

Again let's go back to Brendan's statement "I assure you that NO ONE will lose money on the proposals" – I believe this is just a lie after lie after lie.

4. MARKET SECURITY OFFICER'S PAY 1991

Basic Pay	=	£146.18
Weekend Allowance	=	………..

312 hrs for Saturday x £3.75 = £585 time and a half
156 hrs for Sunday x £3.75 = £585 double time
Total   £1,170 ÷ 39 = £30

£146.18
£ 30.00
£176.18 = £4.52 p.h.

Lieu Time 1 man x 8 hrs = 8 hrs x 8 bank holidays = 64 hrs x £4.52 = £289.28 p.a. ÷ 2 = £144.64 ÷ 52 = £278.16

£176.18
£ 2.78
£178.96 = £9,305.92 p.a.

£9,963.00
-£9,305.92
£ 657.08

Market Officers were **£657.08** better off and when the pay rise came in, in April 1992 Market Officers got another rise of £681.

Security Officers got a pay rise of £681 like the Market Officers, then they got a reduction in their protected earnings of £244.20, giving them a pay rise of £436.80 compared to the Market Officers £681.

I have made a mistake in a letter to Peter Mavers on the figures and I will hold my hands up and say so but all these figures above are 100% correct.

Now I am going to show you Mick's figures for 1991, which do not add up.

Allowances for Market Security Officers

Shift Allowance	=	Nil
Weekend Allowance	=	12 hrs every other Saturday
		6 hrs every other Sunday

	=	156 hrs / annum for Saturday
	=	156 hrs / annum for Sunday
	=	312 hrs / annum

$$\frac{X}{100 \times hr / ann} = \frac{312}{100} \times 2028 = 312$$

= 15.38%

Basic Pay	= £140.29 + Allowances
	= £161.87
	= £ 4.15 per hour

Bank Holidays
8 Bank holidays / annum
Rest days will be 2 Officers off every bank holiday
8 x 8 hrs x 2 Officers = 128 / annum
= 32 hours each (128 ÷ 4 x 4.15 = £132.80 / annum = £2.55)

Total Pay £161.87 + £2.55 = £164.42   (£191.59 p.w.)

Equates to less than currently paid.

Pay remains the same and would go to APT & C Scale 3 Pt 16.

Mick's own figures show he gave the Market Officers a pay rise of £1,413.16.

I have here a copy of a letter from Mr P Partington requesting a breakdown of wages:-

11th May, 1994
Wages Department
Hardshaw Brook Depot
Parr Street,
St Helen's
EMPLOYEE NUMBER

Ref: BREAKDOWN OF EARNINGS

Dear Sir/Madam,

I am writing to you in connection with the above. Again, as this is my second request in the last week, could you therefore, give me the following details:-

a) Basic Pay (weekly)
b) Unsociable hours (weekly)

c) *Shift allowances (weekly)*
d) *Bank holiday enhancement (weekly)*
e) *No lieu time i.e. bank holidays when staff already on rest days?*

I thank you for your time.

Yours sincerely,

Mr P Partington

The next thing Phil gets told to stay away from wages or he will be disciplined. I know what they were trying to hide, I will demonstrate it to you next:-

A full breakdown of wages for 1996 / 97.

It is an all inclusive grade APT & C Scale 3 £11,646 p.a.£5.74 ph. Bank holidays to be deducted.

Each Officer works 28 hrs p.a.28 hrs x 2 = £321.44

Lieu Days on Rest Day

Mon	Tues	Wed	Thurs	Fri	Sat	Sun	
9	6	8	9	5	6	6	= **Total 49 days**

49÷7=7=49+7=56 days an average for 8 bank holidays.

56 x 8 hrs = 488 hrs 488 x £5.74 = £2,571.52
£2,571.52 ÷ 17 = £151.26

£321.44	£11,646.00
£151.26	£ 472.70
£472.70	**£11,173.30**

48 men x 8 hrs = 384 hrs x £5.74 = £2,204.16 = £129.66

£11,173.30	Basic Pay = £ 7,482.58 p.a.
-£ 129.66	Weekend Allowance 381 hrs = £ 2,064.55
£11,043.64	Shift Allowance 20% = £ 1,496.51
	£11,043.64

Basic Pay £3.689 ph = £143.895 pw = £7,482.58 p.a.

This is how it is broken down into basic pay. You will read later "it's impossible to break the wages down", I've done it!

In late 1996 I attended a JCC meeting and in the minutes of the meeting it states "R Steele asked for clarification on the terms and conditions of employment covering Security Operatives".

Pam Gray, Personnel Manager, confirmed that all security operatives are under APT & C conditions of service. APT & C conditions of service do not have all-inclusive grades. This reverts back to the notes Tommy Cranston made below.

Les, Rob

1) *Check contract of employment to make sure APTC payment and conditions of employment come under the purple book!*

2) *If so, confirm with Horace Taylor that there have been no amendments to pages 49 – 50 section 3 paragraph 38.*
   - *Rotating shifts CIV*
   - *General and public holiday working*
   - *Extra statutory holiday working*

When confirmed, arrange a meeting with Security management asking them to confirm contract of employment, then explain that contract.

Re above – it does not confirm with the purple book and would they make the appropriate adjustments from when contract started, also making the adjustments to contract of employment.

When Tommy wrote this information down he knew it was wrong what they did with the wages as he was one of the Conveners who dealt with it in 1991 and he gave us the relevant information to rectify our wages.

Minutes from JCC meeting 10/7/1996
Page 5 it states:

"B Farrell responded that in 1991 rates of pay were calculated to incorporate bank holidays etc. To ensure they were paid the correct rate Security Operatives representatives were involved in the calculation process. "

How come I never received any payments for bank holidays or for extra weekend working or shift allowance?

At my request Paul Haunch wrote to Mick Gornall for a full breakdown of Security Officers' wages.

22 July 1997
Dear Mr Gornall,

Security Officers – All Inclusive Grades

Further to your discussions with local Unison representatives at the Security Division Joint Consultative Committee, I request detailed breakdown of the basis of calculation of the all-inclusive grade for Security Officers, in particular with reference to bank holidays shift and weekend working allowances.

Yours sincerely,

Paul Haunch
Regional Officer

I called into the Union office around November 1997. I was off sick at the time. I was not told that Kevan Nelson, Jim Keegan of Unison were having a meeting with Ged Philbin and Jimmy Goodier upstairs in the Union Office.

It was Ged who told me they knew I was in the office and did not invite me into the meeting. They were doing it behind my back but they were using my figures, which they didn't understand.

Kevan then wrote to Mick Gornall on the 19 November 1997. I do not have a copy of this letter but here is Mick's reply:-

10 December 1997

M Gornall
Dear Mr Nelson,

Re: Security Officers All Inclusive Grade

In reply to your letter dated 19 November 1997, the following is a breakdown of the all-inclusive grade in 1991.

1) **Basic Pay**
   Basic rate of pay was manual grade 3 – £140.29 per week.

2) **Shift Allowance**
   Security rota covered 24 hrs 7 days a week as per manual workers handbook. This was classed as rotating shifts and given an allowance of
   16% which equals £22.44 per week (16% of £140.29).

3) **Weekend Allowance**
   Security rota covered a 28-week cycle and each Officer would work 195 hours on both Saturday and Sunday. As per Manual Workers' Handbook allowance for weekend working was time and a half for Saturday and double time for Sunday.

As single time was already incorporated into the basic pay, the allowances for Saturday was 97.5 hrs (half of 195) and 195 hours for Sunday.

TOTAL HOURS 292.5. Thus giving £10.44 hours per Officer per week (292.5 divided by 28).

Therefore, the percentage was 26.7% giving £37.57 per week (26.78% of £140.29).

4) ***Bank Holidays***

For payment in respect of bank holidays an hourly rate of £5.13 would be used. This figure is the combination of all the above totals as per Manual Workers' Handbook.

Allowances for bank holidays are:
If normal shift worked received an additional eight hours pay and also credited with eight hours lieu time.
If a rest day falls on a bank holiday Officer is credited with eight hours lieu time.

Therefore, payment would need to be made in respect of:-
 i)   working normal shifts
 ii) lieu time for working normal shifts
 iii) lieu time for lost rest day

The amount for (i) and (ii) would be the same calculation for each allowance.

There are eight bank holidays a year and a maximum of twelve Officers were required to work each bank holiday totalling 96 shifts per annum.

a) ***Normal Shift***

Allowance for working a normal shift was based on twenty-five of the twenty-eight Officers. To ensure fairness it was worked on an average that one of the three other Officers would work a shift each bank holiday (the precise figure was 1.29).

Therefore, the remaining eighty-eight shifts (704 hours) had to be covered by the twenty-five Officers.

Equalled 28.16 hours per Officer (704 divided by 25).

b) **Lieu Time for Working Normal Shift**
As lieu time is given like for like when working your normal shift, the figure is the same a (a) 28.16 hours per Officer.

c) **Lieu Time for Rest Days**
As per rota, rest days fell as follows:
Ten Officers on rest day every Monday and Wednesday
Eleven Officers on rest day every Tuesday and Thursday
Nine Officers on rest day every Friday
Seven Officers on rest day every Saturday and Sunday

To ensure fairness it was worked on an average of ten rest days per bank holiday and also as in (a) it was based that one of the three other staff would be on a rest day every bank holiday (precise figure was 1.02).

Therefore, the remaining seventy-two rest days (576 hours) had to be credited to the twenty-five Officers.

Equalled 23.04 hours per Officer (576 divided by 25).

Total allowance for bank holiday was 79.36 hours per Officer or £407.11 per annum.

Total Pay	*Weekly*	*Annually*
Basic Pay	£140.29	£7,295.08
Shift Allowance	£ 22.44	£1,166.88

Weekend Allowance	£ 37.57	£1,953.64
Bank Holiday	N.A.	£ 407.11
Total:		£10,822.71

The above annual figure was rounded up to £10,822.80 to give a monthly pay of £901.90.

Yours sincerely,

M Gornall
Head of Security

cc B Farrell

My comments on the above figures:-
Firstly, the basic pay of £140.29 is incorrect. I found a letter where it stated that the pay award for 1991 was only added in November that year. I also rang wages to confirm the basic pay awards for 1991 and they stated £146.18 p.w. Mick had made out a rota for these figures but they do not add up to the rota Security Officers were working.

Several months later the weekend working was 196 hours and not 195 hours - total hours 294 thus giving 10.50 hours per Officer. The percentage giving 37.57 was in fact 37.77 and the bank holiday rate was £5.14 and not £5.13.

There were 12 men off Monday and 13 men off Wednesday, not 10 as stated. There were also 9 men off Tuesday and 13 men off Thursday and not 11, as stated – also 10 men off Friday and not 9 and Saturday and Sunday there were 9 men off and not 7 as stated.

Mick's own figures using the correct rota would have been a total of £10,839.66 and not £10,822.71. Also Mick Gornall did not add lieu time for working normal shifts and had he done so his figures would be £10,965.53 not £10,822.71.

Kevan Nelson of UNISON replied as follows

9 February, 1998

Dear Mr Gornall,

Re: Security Officers All Inclusive Grade

Thank you for your letter dated 10 December 1997 which I received on 15 January, 1998.

I am now able to confirm that Unison wishes to challenge the calculations on the following basis:-

1) *By your own calculations the all-inclusive pay equates to Scale 4 rather than Scale 3.*

2) *It is evident that the individual protection arrangements are inadequate (a shortfall in the region of £300 per annum).*

I look forward to an early meeting at which, I will be accompanied by Jim
Keegan, Regional Office, to discuss this matter.

Yours sincerely,

Kevan Nelson
Convenor

I don't know how Kevan Nelson came to the conclusion that Security Officers protection was a shortfall in the region of £300. Point 19 is £10,824 and Mick's figures were £10,822.71, which he increased to £10,822.80 – that left a shortfall of £1.20.

Had Kevan, Jim Keegan and Ged Philbin not gone behind my back and included me in the meetings, they would have had someone who knew what they were talking about. Ged was trying to get all the glory for all my hard work when none of them knew what they were doing. Jim Keegan and Ged Philbin were told where to get off on the wages in a later meeting with Peter Moffat, Assistant Director.

Here is a full breakdown of wages for Security Officers, Market Officers and Coordinators

Full breakdown of wages for 1999 – 2000 for Security Officers all-inclusive wage APT & C Scale 3 = £12,663 = £6.58 p.h.

Bank Holidays
28 hours per Officer=28 hours x 2=**£368.48**

Lieu Days for Rest Days

Mon	Tues	Wed	Thurs	Fri	Sat	Sun	
9	6	8	9	5	6	6	Total: 49

49 ÷ 7 = 7 7 x 8 bank holidays = 56 days
56 days x 8 hrs. = 488 hrs x £6.58 = £2,947.84
2947.84 ÷ 17 = £173.40

Lieu Time for Working Bank Holidays
6 men working bank holidays x 8 bank holidays = 48 men=384 hours x 6.58 = £2,526.72 ÷ 17 = £148.63

> £12,663.00
> -£ 690.51
> **£11,972.49**

£11,972.49 – weekend allowance

17 weeks = 114 hours 114 hrs ÷ 17 men = 6.705 hrs per week
6.705 hrs x 52 = 348 hrs per annum
348 x £4.22 = £1,471.817 Sunday 735.908 Saturday
= £2,207.72

Basic Pay	=	£8,137.31 = £4.22 p.h.
Shift Allowance	=	£1,627.4620%
Weekend Allowance	=	£2,207.72 £4.22936
Bank Holiday	=	£ 690.51
Total:		**£12,663.00**

Full breakdown of Market Officer pay 1999 – 2000
£12,663 = £658 ph

Lieu Time 1 man x 8 bank holidays = 8 hours x 4 bank holidays
= 32 hours x £6.58 = £210.56

        £12,663.00
        -£ 210.56
        £12,452.44

Weekend allowance=364 hours
Saturday 156 hours
Sunday 208 hours TOTAL £1,980.16

Basic Pay	=	£10,472.28£5.44 p.h.
Weekend Allowance	=	£ 1,980.16
Bank Holiday Allowance	=	£ 210.56
Total:		**£12,663.00**

**FULL BREAKDOWN OF WAGES APT & C SCALE 4
COORDINATORS PAY 1999 – 2000**
£14,391 = £7.4797

Bank Holidays
32 hours per Coordinator = 32 hours x 2 = £478.70

Lieu Days on Rest Days

Mon	Tues	Wed	Thurs	Fri	Sat	Sun	
2	2	2	2	2	2	2	TOTAL 14

14 ÷ 7=2 2 x 8 = 16 days 16 x 8 = 128 hours 128 x 7.4797 =
£957.40 £957.40 ÷ 6 = £159.56

Lieu Time for Working Bank Holidays
4 men x 8 bank holidays = 32 days 32 x 8 hrs = 256 hrs 256 x
7.4797 = £1,914.80 ÷ 6 = £319.13

£14,391.00
- £   957.39
£13,433.61

Weekend Allowance
6 weeks = 31 hours 31 ÷ 6 men=5.166 hrs per week
5.166 x 52 = 268 hrs per annum
268 x 4.95 = £1,326.60 x 1.5=£1,989.90

Basic Pay	=	£ 9,536.43£	4.95 p.h.
Shift Allowance 20%	=	£ 1,907.28 £13,433.61	
Weekend Allowance	=	£ 1,989.90 £ 957.39	
Total:		**£13,433.61 £14,391.00**	

WAGE STRUCTURE FOR SECURITY FOR 1999 – 2000
Showing Hourly Rates of Pay in the Department
Showing Basic Pay

Head of Security = S02 = £21,549 = 36 hours per week £11.51 p.h
over 36 hours.

Deputy Head of Security = S0 1 = £19,770
£10.56 p.h over 36 hours

Supervisor Over Town Patrols
= APT & C Scale 5 = £16,194 = £8.65 p.h. over 36 hours

Liaison Officer = APT & C Scale 3 = £12,663 = £6.76 p.h. over
36 hours

Courier = APT & C Scale 3 = £12,663 = £6.58 p.h. over 37 hours

Housing Officer = APT & C Scale 2 = £11,622 = £6.04 p.h. over
37 hour week

Town Patrol = APT & C Scale 2   = £11,622 = £6.04 p.h. over 37 hours

Market Officers = APT & C Scale 3 = £10,472.28 = £5.44 p.h. over 37 hours

Coordinators = APT & C Scale 4 = £9,536.43 = £4.95 p.h. over 37 hours

Patrol Officers = APT & C Scale 3 = £8,137.31 = £4.22 p.h. over 37 hours

The lowest paid in Security should have been Town Patrols and Housing Officers and figures show quite clear they were on more than Security Officers by £3,424.72 p.a.– on basic pay they were better off by £2,097.16 p.a. than Coordinators and £1,149.72 p.a. better off than the Market Officers.

I had a meeting with the Council Leader, Mike Doyle and Peter Mavers, Assistant Director, on the 27/10/98. I asked Mike to get me a breakdown of wages, then I told him they will tell you there isn't one.

Mike replied, "I am not accepting that Peter, there has to be a breakdown of wages and I want it".

I then wrote to Peter 28/10/98

> *Further to our meeting yesterday 27/10/98 with Councillor Doyle present, can you please send me a copy of the Union Agreement for APT & C Scale 3 all inclusive salary for 1991.*
>
> *I also require a full breakdown of wages for 1998 – 1999. Like Councillor Doyle stated, there has to be a breakdown of wages and he will not accept there is not one i.e. an all-inclusive grade of £6.96 p.h.*

I received a reply 16 November 1998 from Peter

Peter did not mention the Union Agreement nor did he send me a copy of it. However, he did reply to the breakdown of wages as follows:-

"It is impossible to break down an all-inclusive grade into an amount of cash relating to each of the constituent parts. However the elements included are basic pay, weekend working allowance, shift allowance and bank holiday payment".

This is exactly what I told Mike Doyle they were going to say.

I went to my MP, Peter Kilfoyle, Walton, Liverpool even though the Wages had been confirmed to me over the phone that the basic pay for 1991 after the pay rise was £146.18. I wanted it in black and white as evidence.

Peter sent a letter to the Council as follows:-

13 January, 2003

Dear Mrs Finney,

Re: Mr Robert Steele, Avon Close, Liverpool L4 1XL
Hourly rate of pay for Manual Grade 3 Security Officers

Further to my letter to you of the 6 January, 2003 (copy enclosed) I would like to amend my enquiries to read:-

1) *What was the hourly rate of pay for Manual Grad 3 Security Officers before the 1991 pay rise?*

2) *What was the hourly rate of pay for Manual Grade 3 Security Officers after the 1991 pay rise?*

I apologise for any inconvenience caused and look forward to hearing from you in the near future.

Yours sincerely,

Peter Kilfoyle MP

The Council did respond to this letter but did not answer the questions as it would have shown that the pay rise was not calculated into the figures in 1991.

This is the Council's response:

20 January, 2003

Dear Mr Watts,

Re: Security Officers' Salary Rates (Mr Robert Steele)

Thank you for your letters dated 6 and 13 January, 2003. I have now received a reply from the Personnel Manager concerned and can respond as follows:-

You will recall that there has been a plethora of correspondence on this issue between yourself, Mr Steele and the Council and District Audit. I do not propose to reiterate the Council's position on the matter but would confirm it remains as stated in the Chief Executive's letter to you of 7 August, 2002,

I would comment that Mr Steele was not employed by the Council when the review of Security Officers took place in November 1991 nor has he been employed by the Council since November 1999.

The key Officer involved in this complaint is Pam Gary, Personnel Manager.

I hope this information is of assistance to you in responding to your Constituent.

Yours sincerely,

Peter Blackburn
Assistant Chief Executive

I wrote at the top of this letter *IT'S NOT MR WATTS, IT'S MR KILFOYLE* and at the bottom of the letter I wrote, *THIS LETTER IS A LOAD OF S**T – YOU DID NOT ANSWER THE QUESTIONS IN THE LETTER DATED 13/1/2003 COPYSENT. I WONDER WHY, BECAUSE YOU KNOW I'M RIGHT* and I sent it back to the Council.

On the 17/6/2003 I wrote to Mr Cunliffe, Solicitor for Jackson & Canter asking him to write to St Helen's Council for a full breakdown of wages for the Patrol Officers, Coordinators and Market Officers including basic pay, shift allowance, weekend allowance and bank holiday payments for 2003 – 2004.
MrCunliffe, Solicitor wrote as follows:

17 November, 2003

Dear Mrs Hudson,

Re: Our Client Robert Steele.

We refer to your letter of 27 October 2003 in which you indicated that Mr Farrell, Head of Human Resources, is dealing with this matter. We are unsure whether Mr Farrell should actually be dealing with this matter, as he was a party to the original wage transfers in 1991. You will appreciate these are the cause of our concerns.

We are further concerned to note that our client's MP Mr Kilfoyle did in fact write for those figures in January of this year, copy letter enclosed and neither of these letters have been responded to.

We are furthermore looking into the issue of single status as in discussions with Mr Steele that when single status adjustments applied in 1997 these were not afforded to Security staff who you will appreciate are also the Council's employees.

We also require full breakdown of wages for Patrol Officers including basic pay, bank holidays, shift/weekend working allowances and lieu time for bank holidays for 2003/2004 for Patrol Officers. This will give details of the basic wage and we can then track back to see if these Officers were afforded appropriate increases when single status was achieved.

Please also provide a full breakdown of wages for Coordinators including basic pay, bank holidays, shift and weekend working allowances – again for 2003/2004. Please also do the same for Market Officers in 2003 and 2004. We believe this will again show underpayments for all these staff.

We trust this information will be provided in this matter, which has now long been complained of and can be resolved.

We should like these issues resolved efficiently and quickly. From the evidence we have seen and been produced by Mr Steele there are clearly discrepancies in the pay of all these Officers, including Mr Steele himself at the relevant time all of which were, or appear to have been, brushed under the carpet by the Council and the Unions. Our independent accountants Mitchell Charlesworth believe there are issues to be addressed from looking at the Council's own figures.

We await details of the single status pay in the hope that these matters can be resolved.

Yours sincerely,

Mr G Cunliffe
Jackson & Canter

The Council's Principal Solicitor, Angela Boyle, replied as follows:-

28 November, 2003

Dear Sirs,

Your Client Robert Steele.

Thank you for your letter dated 17 November addressed to the Chief Executive.

The Chief Executive has complete confidence in the integrity of Mr Farrell to deal with matters in an impartial and professional manner.

In relation to Messrs Cliffe, Simm, Watterson, Fairclough and Anders, all of whom are current employees of the Council, a request has previously been made for you to supply their written authority for you to act on their behalf. We cannot trace receipt of this and look forward to you providing this in due course. A response to your queries as is relevant to these individuals will then be provided.

In relation to the queries raised on behalf of Mr Steele, I would comment as follows:-

Mr Steele accepted a job offer made by the Council on the then existing terms and conditions in 1992 initially this was on a temporary contract which was made permanent when he accepted a permanent position in 1994. His employment was terminated 1999.

He made application to the employment tribunal, an application, which he subsequently withdrew. The Council was prepared to defend its position in the employment tribunal. A bundle of documents had been prepared and provided to Mr Steele. This bundle included inter alia correspondence passing between Mr Steele and Mr Peter Mavers, Assistant Director in which Mr Mavers answered complaints made by Mr Steele regarding grading issues. Mr Steele has access to this documentation and I do not propose to repeat its contents.

The Council takes the view that having accepted a job in 1992 Mr Steele has no reason to question terms and conditions, which existed prior to his employment. Similarly, he has no reason to question the employment situation, which has appertained since his dismissal. The opportunity existed for him to challenge issues, which were relevant to his employment at the employment tribunal. His application was dismissed on his withdrawal.

Efforts have been made by the Council to deal with the issues Mr Steele has raised but our responses have never been acceptable to your client. Not unreasonably the Council has reached the view that there is unlikely ever to be consensus between us and sees no value in prolonging that correspondence any further. I trust the Council's position to Mr Steele's complaints is clear to you.

Finally, you indicate your concerns that two letters sent by Mr Peter Kilfoyle MP to the Council in January 2003 have not been responded to. I enclose a copy of the Council's response to those letters. Whilst I appreciate that Mr Steele will not have been satisfied with the response it is clear that a copy was provided to him. The handwritten notes on the copy letter are his.

Yours faithfully,

Angela Boyle
Principal Solicitor

Comments on the letter above

How can the Chief Executive have complete confidence in the integrity of Mr Farrell to deal with matters in an impartial and professional manner as he was involved in the restructure in 1991 and stated on the 31/10/91, "I assure you that no one will lose money on the proposals" and figures show that all Security Officers and Supervisors did in fact lose hundreds of pounds per annum.

I never withdrew my employment tribunal. My father wrote to them and informed the tribunal that I was too ill to attend, I never heard from the tribunal again. At the end of the day I was not well enough to attend a tribunal until August 2009.

Re Correspondence between Mr Steele and Mr Mavers

These will be set out later in this book. This again will show what I consider to be more lies by Officers of the Council.

Re The Council takes the view that having accepted a job in 1992 Mr Steele has no reason to question terms and conditions, which existed prior to his employment.

Mick Gornall accepted Head of Security on a lower wage in 1991 and his Supervisor, Eric Clarke, said that it's not the Council's rate of pay for the job and he got the correct rate of pay and received all his back pay, so I do have reason to question terms and conditions.

Re Efforts have been made by the Council to deal with the issues Mr Steele has raised

Show me one effort. I did receive replies to my letters but I was 'fobbed off' with the truth. A letter 10 February 1998 to me from Mike Doyle states,*"Further to our recent discussions you have provided quite a lot of information and raised concern about a number of issues that require detailed examination".* I have never seen this detailed examination.

I also asked Mike Doyle for a panel of six Councillors to get them face to face Brendan Farrell and Mick Gornall so I could get to the truth. I selected six Councillors and I can remember four of them, from Labour it was Tommy Hargreaves, from the Conservatives it was Betty Lowe and from Liberals it was Susanne Night and John Beirne – there was another person from Labour and Conservative.

Mike asked me why I selected two from each party.

I said "you don't think I am going to select all Labour and get 'fobbed off'".

He then said I can have the panel if I change John Beirne – he is not having him in the panel. In order to get the panel I agreed to get someone else from Liberal. I went to my MP Peter Kilfoyle and told him about the panel and he wrote to Mike as follows:-

6 July 1998

Dear Mike,

Re: Robert Steele.

However, Mr Steele tells me that it was agreed with you to give him an opportunity to debate with Messrs Gornall and Farrell before a panel of independently minded Councillors to hear his allegations of Spanish practices within the Security workforce and managements' rebuttals of them. If that is the case can you please let Mr Steele and myself know of arrangements for such an informal Panel hearing?

Yours sincerely,

Peter Kilfoyle MP
Liverpool Walton

Mike Doyle replied as follows:

9 July 1998

Dear Peter,

Robert Steele

Thank you for your letter dated 6 July regarding Robert Steele.

I have spoken to Robert on a number of occasions regarding his circumstances, as you will be aware. I have in fact advised him that I am unwilling to convene the informal Panel he requested in the light of his appeal next week. Following the outcome of that appeal I will speak again to him to discuss what, if anything could be gained from such a meeting. I will however keep you fully informed.

I trust this will be of some assistance.

Yours sincerely,

Councillor Michael J Doyle JP
Leader of the Council

I won my appeal and nothing was ever arranged by Mike Doyle and his statement, "*what, if anything, could be gained from such a meeting*" – what could have been gained was all my grievances would have been put on the table and I could have returned to work to a healthy environment and all my grievances would have been sorted!

I went to my MP's office in 2005 – my MP is now Shaun Woodward and I spoke to Seb Dance and asked him, "can I select a Panel of six Councillors and put Farrell, Gornall and Peter Mavers in front of them".

He said "I don't see why not". I again selected two from each party.

From Labour Pat Robinson and Bessie Griffin; from the Liberals John Beirne and Susanne Night; from the Conservatives Wally Ashcroft and Tony Brown.

I wrote to Seb as follows:-

27/4/2005

Dear Seb,

When I met you a few weeks ago, I asked you could I select six Councillors of my choice and get Farrell and Gornall in and confront them and you said I don't see why not. You then said, "see what the District Audit do first".

What I am asking is for me to select the Councillors and invite Judith Tench of the District Audit along then what she cannot deal with, the Councillors can deal with it – it will "kill two birds with one stone".

I would also like you to attend so you can see for yourself what has been going on. If you agree to this I will contact you with the six Councillors and you can give them a month's notice to attend and I will contact my Solicitor to attend and you can send the District Audit the date to attend.

If you get me, Farrell and Gornall together the truth will come out. If you speak to me and then speak to them nothing gets done and this is why the District Audit has not done their job properly.

I hope to hear from you soon asking the names of the six Councillors.

Yours faithfully,
Mr R Steele

I then wrote to Seb as follows:

4/5/2005

Dear Seb,
I have not heard from you with my letter dated 27/4/2005.
I have picked the six Councillors; they are Bessie Griffin
Labour, Pat Robinson Labour, Susanne Night Liberal, John
Birne Liberal, Tony Brown Tory and Wally Ashcroft Tory.

Can you arrange a date for us all to meet at the Town Hall,
give them a few weeks notice and contact Judith Tench,
District Audit to be there and if you give me enough notice,
I will contact my Solicitor. I will leave it to you to contact
Brendan Farrell and Mick Gornall. I would also like Peter
Mavers there as I believe he has covered up for them.

This is why the truth will come out once and for all and I can
try and let go and get on with my life. I hope to hear from
you as soon as possible with arrangements for us to meet.

Yours faithfully,

Mr R Steele

I then went to the library and got the six Councillors phone numbers and I rang them and explained what was happening and would they sit on the Panel. All six said they would.

I went to see Seb and he told me he will have to contact the six Councillors to see if they are willing to sit on the Panel.

I said *"I have already rang them and all six said they would"*.

I again went back to see Seb to arrange the Panel and he said I can not have the Panel as it's illegal. So again I never got to put my grievances across and I don't know why it was illegal as the Councillors have a right to know what misdemeanours are going on in their Council.

In the purple book National Joint Council for Local Authorities Administrative Professional Technical and Clerical Services.

SCHEME OF CONDITIONS OF SERVICE

SHIFT WORKING

It states:-

Rotating Shifts
Three shifts on a rota basis including a night shift over 7 days a week 20% of salary.

When they were put on APT&C they were entitled to this 20% of salary – it also states allowances, weekend working.

For work on a Saturday or Sunday as part of the normal working week, payment shall be at time and a half for all hours worked.

The authority made an agreement with the Trade Unions that they would pay double time for Sunday.

Security Officers and Supervisors did not receive any of these payments until 2008 when the Coordinators took the place of the Supervisors. In 1996 – they also did not receive their entitlements.

In February 2008 the management admitted their wages were wrong and put the Security Officers on Scale 2 plus all allowances and did not back pay them. The Coordinators got Scale 3 plus allowances and also did not get paid any back pay. In fact the Security Officers should have been paid Scale 4, the same as Park Rangers and Hall Keepers. At the end of the day they are all some form of Security.

In 2009/2010 the Hall Keepers had to take a pay cut to Scale 3 and they appealed three times and on the third time they were put back on Scale 4 and got all the back pay.

The Coordinators are working supervisors, as they are also responsible for the shift. They should have got the Supervisors' rate of pay Scale 5 plus all allowances.

I am surprised that Eric Clarke did not put in for Scale 5 plus allowances when he got Mick Gornall the manager's wage in 1991 as all the Supervisors in the Council received Scale 5. When Mick Gornall made his best mate Paul Molyneux Supervisor in 1999 he paid him Scale 5 for permanent days Monday to Friday.

Tommy Hawks started with Security as a Security Officer and was put on point 17 Scale 3 straight away and all other temps had to start at point 14 and work their way up to point 17 over a two-year period. This is because he knew Brendan Farrell and Peter Mavers.

Two other temps complained to Mick Gornall and he told them it's because he was on a high wage at Pilkington's Glass. These two Officers went to the Union and they got put on point 17 and received all the back pay but all other new starters since had to start at point 14. Mick set a precedence and everyone should have been put on point 17 when starting in Security.

5. Bank Holidays

In a JCC meeting in 1996 with Brendan Farrell and Mick Gornall I told them that all Security Officers who started after 1991 do not get paid for working Bank Holidays. Brendan said we can have a lieu day for each bank holiday until February 2008. This was never granted.

The agreement in the Purple Book reads:

For work on a general or public holiday in addition to the normal pay for that days payment shall be plain time for all time worked within an Officer's normal working hours. At a later date time off with pay shall be allowed as follows:

When time worked is less than four hours half a day off.
When the time worked is four hours or more full day off.

However, the agreement with the Local Authority and the Unions was payment for bank holiday was double time and a day in lieu.

Mick Gornall's own figures for bank holidays show double time and a statement in writing from Peter Jennings, Assistant Director, states as follows:-

Bank holidays payment is included within aproposed grade and a day in lieu of working a bank holiday will be given.

Not one Security Officer since 1991 until February 2008 received this lieu day. Mick had deliberately deprived his workforce of thousands of pounds a year and over the 17 years it runs into hundreds of thousands of pounds.

6. Market Officers have never worked Bank Holidays since it started in 1991.

Around 1999 Mick Gornall put the Market Officers working Bank Holidays and never paid them.

Kenny Watterson went into Mick's office and asked to be paid for the Bank Holidays.

Mick told him, *"it's all inclusive in your wage"*. This statement is not true and they should have been paid double time and a day in lieu.

If you refer to number 4 pages 53, 54 and 55, Market Security Officers pay 1991 it shows quite clear that no payment for working Bank Holiday was calculated – I believe yet another lie.

7. In 1994 Peter Mavers told the Patrol Officers in a JCC meeting that they have to patrol premises on Bank Holidays. Till this day

in 1994 Security Officers did alarm response only. The reason for this is Mick Gornall had charged the customer for the service since 1991 and also failed to give them the service they had paid for.

This was brought to light when the Head Teacher at Willow Tree Primary School complained she never had her school checked.

Mick did tell her, *"we don't do patrols on bank holidays,"* but she insisted she had paid for it and she wanted it checked. She got it at the expense of the Patrol Officers – again this is not giving the client what they are paying for and at the end of the day it was wrong.

On the 28/11/94 in a JCC meeting Peter Mavers (Assistant Director) made a statement as follows:

P Mavers accepted it was not possible to visit all premises with a reduced staff level and felt it was sensible to visit the high profile sites and vandal areas.

What about the clients who are paying for the service and not getting it. Again this statement is deceiving the customer who should be refunded for no visits on Bank Holidays – but never were.

In 1996 Mick Gornall had the Coordinators doing 32 hours Bank Holidays for no extra pay and when he reduced his Coordinators from six to four. They increased their Bank Holiday working to 48 hours for no extra pay. Yet everyone else in the Council was getting paid double time and a day in lieu.

On investigating the bank holiday with people from other departments of the Council they confirmed they were paid double time and a day in lieu.

9. On the 23/12/94 the Chief Executive gave all the Officers in the Council an extra day off and in a JCC meeting 28/11/94 C Pinder

requested time off in lieu for 23 December in line with other Officers of the Council.

P Mavers responded that the Security Service were a specified service and therefore, excluded from the arrangements outlined on the recent memo from the Chief Executive. At the end of the day Security is part of the Council and should not have been treated any different.

I am led to believe that Mick Gornall got the day off.

10. PROTECTED EARNINGS

Kenny Watterson and Mick Fairclough were on protected earnings for life when they went over to the Market Officer from Patrol Officer.

Mick Gornall took the protected earnings off them.

In a JCC meeting in 1996 I told Brendan Farrell that Kenny and Mick had their protected earnings taken off them and they were in the same department and on the same scale of pay. **How can you justify this?**

Brendan said he would give Kenny and Mick their protected earnings back and said to Mick Gornall, "*I will tell you later Mick*".

I went and told Kenny and Mick Fairclough they were getting their protected earnings back. They still never received their protected earnings back from 1996 until the markets finished also they never received their back pay.

When the Markets finished, around 2005 this protection was for life and in this timescale I believe Mick Gornall had withheld in the region of £12,500 from the two Officers plus their back pay. Again it was not a mistake and was done deliberately. This means he has deprived them of their wages.

11. John Sexton, Alan Bolger and Peter Waine were Coordinators and had nothing to do with Security. The management decided to put the three of them into Security in 1991 and make them Security Officers and gave them protected earnings. As this was the correct procedure for protected earnings, as they were earning more money coordinating than the Security Officers were being paid and this protection was for life.

John, Alan and Peter all complained that their protected earnings had been cut dramatically. I told them to put it in writing and I would deal with it for them.

I was off sick at the time but still officially their Shop Steward. The three of them put it in writing as follows:-

21/11/98

A Bolger
In 1991, when Scale 3 was introduced to Security Officers, inclusive of shift and weekend entitlements.

I never signed any document agreeing this.

A threat was forced upon us at the period of time, an outside firm Burns Security, would be brought in if not agreed.

I have, in writing, guaranteeing that when my Coordinating job ceased and merged with Security Force, my earnings would not decrease. Bank holiday payments would be double time and lieu days. Each time Security received a pay rise my protected earnings diminished.

A Bolger

21/11/98

P Waine

I would like to state that I, P Waine, at no time attended any meeting or signed any contract concerning Working Practices or Pay Structures. The only time I was aware of the above was by an internal memo by Mr Farrell. Please note my protected earnings were reduced.

Yours faithfully

Mr P Waine

25/11/98

J Sexton

When Scale 3 was offered in 1991 I never signed any form accepting this. I was also told that my wage from Coordinator would be protected i.e. bank holiday payments would be paid at x2 plus lieu days. This is not the case.

J Sexton

Here are three extracts from Alan Bolger's wage slips proving they reduced their protected earnings dramatically over the first five months:-

31/12/91	Protected earnings	£218.24
31/1/92	Protected earnings	£137.77
31/5/92	Protected earnings	£116.77

Within 5 months Alan lost £101.47 a month on his protected earnings, which were for life, again this has been done deliberately and it again was contrary to the agreement.

12. In 1991 there were 28 Patrol Officers and four Security Officers at Gerrards Bridge Depot – a total of 32 Security Officers.

Twelve of the Officers were temps and 25 Officers received protected earnings and five of them were temps and the other seven did not get protected earnings.

Mick Rimmer, Gaynor Kay, Jeff Unsworth, Brian Wight, Denis Ashton, Phil Deighton and Les Barker were the seven to fall foul to Brendan and Mick's restructure in 1991.

At the end of the day none of the 22 Officers were entitled to protected earnings, as they were not removed from a different job title at a higher wage. That is how protected earnings work – the way the Coordinators got their protected earnings in 1991.

The Security Officers always believed their protected earnings were for going onto one-man patrols from two men.

When I investigated the wages I informed them protected earnings were given to them for bank holidays and weekend working.

I brought this issue up in a JCC meeting with Brendan and Mick. Mick Gornall found it highly amusing, explaining to Brendan the Security Officers' thought their protected earnings were for one-man patrols and not for Bank Holidays and weekend working.

The way that the twenty-two Security Officers received their protected earnings was in my opinion illegal and this is not the way they agreed to implement protected earnings in the agreement reached between the Local Authority and the Trade Unions.

I contacted the District Audit and one of the issues was protected earnings.

This is Clive Portman's reply:-

Protected earnings – your concern is that following the 1991 restructure four temporary employees were given protected earnings.

Council's Response

Five rather than four employees fell into this category.

The Council indicated that the 1991 restructure was a radical proposal that met with strong Trade Union opposition.

Agreement was reached with employees in post at the time of the restructure that they would not suffer any financial detriment – hence a protected allowance was paid to five Officers concerned.

It was viewed that there would have been little or no chance of any agreement had existing Officers, whether temporary or not, suffered any form of financial detriment.

District Audit follows up work included – review of the report which went to the Personnel Sub Committee on 7/10/1991. This report states that –*at the point of entry to the new staff grade there would be no detriment to existing levels of pay. We have also viewed copies of the letters that went out to the five Officers following the assimilation to the post of Security Officer. The letters state that the staff are to receive a protected allowance.*

In our view the Council's actions are justifiable in the circumstances.

I replied to Clive on the 19/10/99:

Re: Protected Earnings

At the time of the restructure there were 12 temporary staff and only five got protected earnings. Phil Deighton, Les Barker, Gaynor Kay, Jeff Unsworth, Dennis Ashton, Mick Rimmer and Brian Wright were not given protected earnings.

You state agreement was reached with employees. I have sent you 18 statements, 17 did not agree and one was forced to sign with his job and four others have also told me they did not sign. They have all suffered financial loss and if you meet up with me I will show you this.

Yours faithfully,

Mr R Steele

Clive replied to my letter 15 December, 1999

Ref: Protected Earnings

You say that at the time of the restructure there were 12 staff and only five got protected earnings – what point is being made by this statement? Are you suggesting that all 12 staff should have received protected earnings or that none of them should have received protected earnings?

These seem to me to be contractual issues between the Council and it's employees and I do not, on the basis of the information provided, see what relevance they have to my audit of the Council's accounts.

Clive Portman
District Auditor

I cannot understand why Clive did an audit in October and give me his reply and when I challenge him on his findings that he has accepted the Council's response in favour of the Council. He then tries to get out of it by stating 'I do not, on the basis of the information provided, see what relevance they have to my Audit of the Council's accounts'. If this is the case, why did he investigate protected earnings in the first place? I believe Mick Gornall was trying to cover up for the Council.

13. When the Security Officers received their pay rise in February 2008, the remaining Security Officers from the 25 Officers who received their protected earnings, had them taken off them by Mick Gornall.

This again is unacceptable as when they were given the protected earnings in 1991 they were for life – as long as they stayed a Security Officer. In that job they could not take the protected earnings off them, no matter how many pay rises they received. Again I believe that this was not a mistake and has financially penalised his staff.

14. OVERTIME PAYMENTS

Brian Wright was removed from Security over an issue concerning Phil Ward. The Coordinators were granted overtime to cover Brian Wright's shifts. Then Mick Gornall and Brendan Farrell wanted the Coordinators to do afternoon shifts and nights Monday to Friday and cover the weekend days, afternoons and nights, so Phil Ward could do the Coordinator's job Monday to Friday on permanent days as he would not work shifts. The Coordinators refused to do this so Brendan and Mick stopped their overtime payments.

An internal memo was put out as follows:

Internal Memo

To: Coordinators   *Date: 3.7.97 Time: 10.00*

From: D Anders (02)   *Ref: B Wright*

I have been instructed to cease overtime payment in respect of cover for B Wright.

All future shifts worked will be deducted from annualised hours total.

D Anders (02)

This was done for spite as the Coordinators refused Brendan's and Mick's demands. This in my opinion was because Phil Ward was Brendan's friend and had no job in Security.

15. Phil Partington was removed from the Patrol Officers rota and put on the Coordinator's rota. The Patrol Officers had to cover for Phil's shifts over a three month period. Cover for Phil should have been paid at overtime as it was the same reason the Coordinators were paid overtime because the Security Officers did not get paid like the Coordinators did for exactly the same reason.

I brought it up in the J.C.C. Meeting 24/6/97. I told Brendan the Coordinators are on annualised hours to cover each others shifts and are being paid overtime to cover Brian Wright's shifts. Yet when we had to cover Phil Partington's shifts for 3½ months we had to do it off-shift and the money that was saved should have been divided between the 16 men who covered his shifts.

Brendan replied, *"you covered it off-shift and did not need overtime"*.

I said *"yes we did cover it off shift but we all did extra work to cover it and we should be paid for the extra work"*.

Brendan again said, *"how can I justify paying you when you covered it off shift?"*

The Coordinators could have covered Brian Wright's shifts off-shift but were granted overtime. Covering Phil's duties left a man down and corners were cut to cover his shift for a three month period, at the expense of the client once again. Not giving them the service they were paying for. Phil's shifts should have been covered on overtime to provide full cover for his shifts.

16. There was overtime at the weekends on the Patrol Officers rota. Brian Case who was the Courier for security and Peter Lawton who was the Housing Officer got the bulk of the Patrol Officers' overtime, who had nothing to do with their shifts. This overtime should have only been given to the Officers who work that rota and know the job.

Again I made a complaint to Clive Portman, the District Auditor. It read as follows:-

Overtime– Your concerns that management showed favouritism by giving the bulk of any overtime to day men rather than Patrol Officers. Also you had concerns that this practice was uneconomic as the day men were employed at higher rates than Patrol Officers.

Council response:

Overtime was allocated on a fair and equitable basis. High level of Union recognition in security. If there was favouritism it would have been highlighted by now. Day men not paid higher rates than shift Patrol Officers.

District Audit follow-up includes review of overtime paid between April 1998 and April 1999.

No evidence found to indicate favouritism towards Day men. Also we noted that the hourly rates for Day men are less than for Patrol Officers.

I wrote to Clive Portman 19/10/99

Ref: Overtime.

If you look between September and December 1997 you will see that Peter Lawton and Brian Case got all the overtime on the Patrol Officers rota at weekends (Golf Shop, Crematorium).

15 December 1999

Clive's reply is as follows:-

Ref. Overtime

You say that between September to December 1997 Peter Lawton and Brian Case got all the overtime on the Patrol Officers' rota at weekends. Again what is being suggested by this statement? What relevance does it have to my current audit of the Council's accounts? Is the suggestion that overtime is being paid when it is either unnecessary or when it has not been worked? Is the suggestion that other staff should have received some of the overtime instead of Peter*

Lawton and Brian Case and if so, what relevance does that have on my role as the Council's external Auditor?

Again Clive has accepted the Council's response as being correct. Again I told him he had looked at the wrong times and told him to look between September and December 1997. Again, why did he investigate the overtime payments and when I told him to look at the correct dates he asks *"what relevance does that have to my role as the Council's External Auditor?"* Again, in my opinion he seems to be trying to cover up for the Council.

Several Patrol Officers complained to me about Peter and Brian getting their overtime and if you refer to below you will see Housing Officer basic pay was £6.04 ph in 1999 – the Couriers pay was £6.58 and the Patrol Officers basic pay was £4.22 so how can Clive Portman say this?

Also we noted that the hourly rates for day men were less than for Patrol Officers. He also states there was a high level of Union recognition in security. What you have read so far – do you think there would be the vast amount of problems unsolved if there had been a high level of Union recognition in security?

WAGE STRUCTURE FOR SECURITY FOR 1999 – 2000
Showing Hourly Rates of Pay in the Department
Showing Basic Pay

Head of Security = SO 2 = £21,549 = 36 hours per week £11.51 p.h over 36 hours.

Deputy Head of Security = S 01 = £19,770 £10.56 p.h over 36 hours

Supervisor Over Town Patrols = APT & C Scale 5 = £16,194 = £8.65 p.h. over 36 hours

Liaison Officer = APT & C Scale 3 = £12,663 = £6.76 p.h. over 36 hours

Courier = APT & C Scale 3 = £12,663 = £6.58 p.h. over 37 hours

Housing Officer = APT&C Scale 2 = £11,622 = £6.04 p.h. over 37 hour week

Town Patrol = APT&C Scale 2 = £11,622 = £6.04 p.h. over 37 hours

Market Officers= APT&C Scale 3 = £10,472.28 = £5.44 p.h. over 37 hour week

Coordinators = APT& C Scale 4 = £9,536.43 = £4.95 p.h. over 37 hour week

Patrol Officers = APT&C Scale 3 = £8,137.31 = £4.22 p.h. over 37 hour week

The lowest paid in Security should have been Town Patrols and Housing Officers and figures show quite clearly they were on more than Security Officers by £3,424.72 p.a.– on basic pay they were better off by £2,097.16 p.a. than Coordinators and £1,149.72 p.a. better off than the Market Officers.

17. CLIENT LIAISON OFFICER
The job as Client Liaison Officer was cost effective in the 1980's and was made obsolete. Mick Gornall had two people with only one job available. So in 1996 Mick brought back the Liaison Officers job for Paul Molyneux. Mick waited until after the restructure of 1996 was passed by the Sub-Committee before he created the job, which was given to his close friend Paul.

If they did need to bring back the Client Liaison Officers' job it should have been put back on the shift rota in the minutes of the J.C.C. Meeting on 8/10/96. M Gornall explained in more detail what would be expected from the Client Liaison Officer. The post holder would be expected to meet with and advise clients. The hours would be regular days, not shifts.

On a memorandum dated 14/10/1996 from Brendan it states:

Security Officer – Client Liaison Officer – Grade Spinal Column Point
14 – 17 (£10,884 – £11,646)
Job Description
Client Liaison Officer
Grade Scale 3 (inclusive of shift allowance and weekend working allowances).
Hours of work 36 on shift patrol agreed with Head of Security.

Paul worked regular days Monday to Friday and was given a rate of pay for shift and weekend allowances. He was also put on a 36-hour week when Security Officers had to work a 39-hour week. When Mick did the restructure in 1991 all Security Officers should have been automatically put on a 36-hour week when they went on APT & C conditions of service.

When Paul was promoted to Deputy Head of Security in 1999, the Liaison Officers job was re-advertised and Terry Cunliffe was given the job – second time lucky. The hours of working were increased to 37-hours a week and if single status had not been introduced in April 1999 Terry would have had to work a 39-hour week. Also on the Grade APT&C Scale 3 point 14 to 17, one of the officers had written on the job description sheet '*Wot no shift allowance*' – he was having a dig at Mick for removing the shift and weekend allowance, which was paid when his friend, Paul Molyneux was the Liaison Officer. You can also see below the other comments made on the Liaison Officer's job.

When Mick did the restructure in 1996 he had two men on days and only one job – they were Paul Molyneux and Phil Ward. Mick decided to create a job for Paul so Phil could have his job and brought back the Client Liaison Officers job that was disbanded long before I started in 1992 because it was not cost effective. Terry Cunliffe, who had been with Security for a number of years and also done the Client Liaison Officers' job in the past, put in for the job and Paul got it with no experience in Security – he only knew about fitting alarms to Council houses and had no experience with the schools whatever. It seems to me that it's not how good you are at your job it's if your one of Mick's boys!.

In October 1999 Clive Portman did a report on unauthorized post. "Your concerns are that further management favouritism led to the creation of a Liaison Officer post for a specific officer and that this post was not included in the structure presented to the Committee in 1996 (Personnel sub 20/9/96)."

Council's response –

The 1996 review did not allocate specific task related job titles to Security Officers. JCC Minutes of the 8/10/1996 meeting indicated that one of the 22 new Security Operatives posts would be a Client Liaison Officer and that this post would be open to application from all members of the Security section.

The post was advertised and two officers applied. District Audit follow up work included a review of the Liaison Officer, it was discussed and decided that the post was to be advertised. We have seen the advert for the post and are satisfied that two people applied for the position."

Firstly, I will comment that the Liaison Officer was not one of the 22 officers in Security as we had 17 Patrol Men, four Market Officers and one Housing Officer. This adds up to 22 Security Officers.

It was discussed with Brendan in a JCC meeting on the 8/10/96 but the Sub Committee had already passed the proposals for Security and Liaison Officer was not part of it.

When Paul Molyneux got the job all he appeared to do was sit in Mick's office with Derek Anders and talk rugby and attend meetings with Mick, which did not concern him or his position as Liaison Officer.

I attended an alarm activation with Andy State at a school over the Christmas period. We went into the school and could not find the zone so we re-set the alarm and went outside and it went off again. I isolated the zone and re-set the alarm when we got outside.

I could hear running water. It was in the building next door – another part of the school that was not on the map, so I drew a map and put the zone on it. This should have been done a long time ago by Paul Molyneux as he was the Liaison Officer for the schools. Had he been doing the job he was paid to do, this would have been sorted months earlier.

Had I not heard the running water, Andy State and I would have been disciplined because the building had a burst pipe and was flooded.

18. HEALTH & SAFETY

I was on nights with Ian Adams and Ian asked me if he have to go into a building to re-set the alarm panel where there was asbestos. I knew nothing about this so I told him he is not to go into that building whatsoever. I did my investigation through the night into this matter. I found out that John Sexton had been sent to Windle Pilkington School to re-set the alarm and there was an asbestos warning sign inside the building and he refused to go in and re-set the alarm.

I found out that Mick had got his Coordinator (Brian Wright) to write an internal memo out and it reads as follows:-

Internal Memo

To: Coordinators   *Date: 22/4/97 Time: 10.15*

From: 01/02 (Mick Gornall & Derek Anders)Ref 329

Ref: Asbestos Warning Signs Inside of Premises

Leave to Patrol's discretion on whether or not they want to enter for re-setting alarm. If not – leave word for day turn to inform key holder.

When I read this memo I went 'up the wall'. I then checked the daily summary sheets and I found on Wednesday 23/4/97 a Patrol attended at 02.10 and re-set the alarm at 02.33 and the building was all clear at 02.36.

A Patrol also attended Tuesday 6/5/97 at 16.50. *Patrol attended and re-set at 16.54 and the building was all clear at 16.57.*

That morning the Yard Manager, Brian Williams, came in and as he had done a Health and Safety course, I spoke to him about the asbestos. I came into work that night and Brian Williams had tipped Mick off about the asbestos and Mick had removed the Internal Memo. It was too late, as I had photocopied all the relevant information.

I then went to the Tech College as the building belonged to them. I spoke to Patricia Brearton, the Health and Safety Officer. She informed me it was blue asbestos that they use in pipes as lagging and it's the most dangerous of the lot. She saidto me,"*I cannot reassure you that asbestos particles are not in the air.*"

Again it appeared that Mick might has put his Security Officers lives at risk. I did speak to Mick about this and he said he did not know Brian Wright had written the memo. I asked Brian about the memo and he claimed was told to write it by Mick.

An internal memo was put out by Derek Anders as follows:-

To: All Security Officers   *Date: 09/05/97*

From: D Anders (02)   *Ref: 329 (Asbestos)*

I spoke to Lesley Bretherton (Safety Officer, St Helen's Tech College).
She has assured me that the above site is now cleared of asbestos and the site is now clear for us to enter. We are in the process of getting a clearance certificate. The building is due to be demolished this month.

D Anders (02)

Had I been sent to the above premises, I would have gone in and re-set the alarm as I was not informed of the situation and nor were a number of other Officers. It was going on for over two weeks before I found out.

Once again, employees health had been put in danger.

18. PATROLS UP UNTIL MIDNIGHT

Since 1991 the agreement with the schools had been till midnight to patrol the schools. Due to the constant shortage of staff Mick tried to get the Officers to patrol through the night until the patrols were finished. The times to patrol were Monday to Sunday 16.00 – 24.00 and 08.00 – 16.00 Saturday and Sunday. These were the times from 1991.

In 1996 they changed to 19.00 – 24.00 Monday to Sunday and 08.00 – 16.00 Saturday and Sunday.

Mick's own paperwork that was laid out in 1996.

Ref. Client Specifications
Routine patrols – 3 Routes
Each establishment to receive nine visits per week with times varied each shift unless otherwise stated as follows:

One per evening between 18.00 – 24.00 could even be 19.00 – 24.00,
One during the day Saturday and Sunday.

A letter was put out by Peter Moffat (Assistant Director) 11/6/92.

19. Patrolling

When patrolling do not walk too close to the buildings. Keep about six to eight feet away from the building line, especially when approaching doorways, recesses or corners. This will give you an even chance if someone is lying in wait.

Method of Patrolling

When one-man patrols are operating during daylight, they will be required to carry out physical checks of buildings.

When one-man patrols are operating between hours of darkness, they will carry out visual checks only from a safe distance of the whole premises.

Then Mick put out a memorandum.

Memorandum

To: All Mobile Security Officers

From: Mick Gornall   *20 March, 1998*

Ref: Security Patrols

There appears to be a misunderstanding in respect of Security patrols after midnight.

This has been discussed at various J.C.C.'s (see attached memo sent to all staff at the time). Therefore, in order to clarify the situation, the following will apply:-

If there are premises still to be checked after midnight then one-man patrols will continue until routes are completed.

The above would also apply when checking both depots and any ad hoc patrols requested after midnight.

M Gornall
Head of Security Services
cc Security Co-ordinators *6

In 1996 in Mick's own handwriting, he states:

Weekend 3 patrols afternoon 4 – 12 x 3 Mon to Fri 16.00 – 00.00 patrols x 3.

Then he puts:

Nights
Mon to Fri Night Shift Cover 3 Men Parks, Depot, Alarm Response and Pets Corner.

There was no mention of night shift patrolling after midnight because this was not the agreement with the schools or the Security Officers.

I was on nights with Ian Adams and Phil Deighton was the Coordinator and the night turn was already a man down. Phil wrote a list of premises for me and a list for Ian to go and check after midnight. There were about 20 premises each.

I told him it's not my job to patrol after midnight and I'm not doing it. Phil said to Ian go and do these premises and Ian said *'Rob's just told you we don't check premises after midnight'*. Two hours later Phil said to Ian, *'are you going to check these premises?'* and Ian said *'no'*.

When I came in on my next afternoon shift I was expecting to be called into the office but nothing was said to me. A while later I had a Union meeting and Eddie Tickle and Kevan Nelson attended. I was telling my members it's not our job to patrol after midnight and Dave Anders did not go out patrolling after midnight.

I was called into the office and Mick told me he had given Dave a warning that he will be disciplined next time and I'm going to get my members disciplined for not patrolling after midnight. Mick complained to Brendan about us not patrolling after midnight.

Brendan put a memo out on 18 July 1996:-

To: All Security Personnel
(this is an extract from that memo)

There are no exceptions to these arrangements including patrols after midnight.

Mick put a memorandum out:-

To: Security Officers

From: Mick Gornall

Date: April 13 2000

Subject: Patrolling After Midnight
There are no alterations to the procedure for one-man patrols after midnight.

The original arrangement is to continue without exception.

Any Officer refusing this procedure will be disciplined accordingly.

Mr Mick Gornall
Head of Security Services

If I had still been in Security he would not have got away with that. It's not the night shift job to patrol after midnight. He is bullying people to go out after midnight when the contract should have been completed by midnight. It's not the night shift's fault he has never got the manpower to complete his contractual duties and it was not in the original agreement to patrol after midnight. The agreement was made in 1991, patrols will finish at midnight.

Going back to the meeting with Mick Gornall Friday 24/4/97, Mick then told me the Officers are to stay out until 2 am patrolling. I replied first it's 12.30 am then 1 am then you move the goal posts to 1.30 am and now you want 2 am. The agreement for checking premises is 12.00 am and we wind down for 12.30 am.

Mick replied, *"I'm not having Officers doing nothing all night"*.

I replied *"they are not – we go on standby at 12 am for alarm activations that is what the night turn is for"*.

Mick said nothing had been agreed. This statement is in my opinion also an out and out lie, an agreement had been made with the client in 1991 and has never been changed. At the end of the day he is just bullying his officers to get his own way once again.

Mick Gornall making the statement, *"I am not having Officers doing nothing all night"* is a big joke. When Colin Pinder left security they had a 'whip round' and everyone signed a card and Mick Gornall put a photo of himself fast asleep on the canteen tables whilst on night turn. He wrote on the card "remember the good old days". One rule for Mick Gornall and another rule for the rest of the security officers – that is really hypocritical.

20.C.I. T. RUN

St Helens Council were not insured to carry cash in transit, nor were the vehicles equipped to carry cash i.e. armoured –they were just basic Vauxhall Nova vans and Vauxhall Astra vans and the Security Officers carrying the cash were not given any protected clothing or helmets. This again, put the Security Officers health at risk.

21. Sometime in 1996 I was on the cash run with Dave Anders and we were booked into the wrong premises by Gary Wainwright. Dave said to me he wants to make a complaint as he felt his life had been put in danger because of this error.

In the J.C.C. meeting 10/7/96 I raised the issue Ref Health & Safety – it states as follows:-

R Steele raised a point concerning CIT operations. CIT (cash in transit) needs an Operative on the radio at all times. R Steele said that calls occasionally do not get answered or answered incorrectly. R Steele then referred to an incident (as above).

M Gornall said that the incident raised was caused by a clerical error and was not a matter of Health and Safety. Had the vehicle been attacked and the emergency button had been pressed, then the Police would have been sent to the wrong premises so, in fact, it was a Health and Safety issue and Mick was prepared, once again, to put Security Officers lives at risk.

22. After I raised the issue in the J.C.C. meeting 10/7/96 that calls occasionally do not get answered, Jimmy Goodier was out on the cash run and was constantly not getting answered, so he pressed his emergency button and still never got an answer.

I went into work for my 4 o'clock shift and Mick got me into his office and said Jimmy Goodier had pressed his emergency button because he could not get through and had we sent the Police we would have looked stupid.

Firstly, Mick was out of order as once that emergency button was pressed, contact should have been made with the Officers involved immediately and the Police should have been informed immediately, whether it was a false alarm or not.

He then said that pressing the emergency button, you still have to wait in a queue to be answered. This statement was another lie,

I worked on the radio and when an emergency button is pressed the screen on the monitor goes red and the call automatically went to the top of the queue.

The real reason the call was not answered was that there was no one sitting at the radio when the call came in. As I stated in the JCC meeting 10/7/96, there needs to be an Operative on the radio at all times and again this was, ignored leading to Jimmy pressing his emergency button in frustration.

Again this is a situation putting Security Officers' lives at risk.

23. Because of the above issue it raised concerning Jimmy Goodier, I wrote to Mick as follows:-

Health & Safety   *6 February, 1997*

Dear Mick,

During a recent incident on a CIT run a Patrol Officer was unable to communicate with base so he then pressed his emergency button again and could not receive communication as channel one was still busy. We find this unacceptable and request that this system is reviewed as a matter of urgency.

Mick replied as follows:-

13/2/97

Dear Mr Steele,

Following our meeting on Tuesday 4 February, 1997 and your subsequent letter dated 6 February, 1997.

In your letter you make reference to an incident on a CIT run. I am unaware of any incident on a CIT run. It was explained by yourself that because the Officers were unable to contact base immediately on arrival at a location, they decided to use the emergency button thus jeopardizing the queue. They still had to wait and then complained to you about it.

As mentioned previously, the emergency button should only be used for real emergency situations and if in this instance we had phoned the Police, it would have been rather embarrassing explaining to the Police.

Ref Mick Gornall stating he is unaware of any incident on the C.I. T. run on the 13 February 1997 again I believe this is not true. Firstly, Mick got me into his office and complained to me about Jimmy Goodier pressing the emergency button and secondly, I raised two issues in the J.C.C. meeting 10/7/96 ref Gary Wainwright and the other Jimmy Goodier – it just shows how, in my opinion, Mick Gornall keeps lying his way out of trouble. I would also like to point out that Mick Gornall did know about the incident on the CIT run as what he previously stated above proved he was aware of the CIT incident, I believe this is more lies from Mick Gornall.

24. I wrote to the Security Industry Authority about Mick Gornall's letter, as follows:-

21/2/07

Dear Sirs,

I am writing to inform you that St Helen's Council have their own Security force and make their own rules as they go along. Mick Gornall, Head of Security, has made it quite clear to one of his Coordinators that he is not going to apply for SIA licenses.

In February 2007 I have been informed that, if a company does not comply they will be fined heavily and each person can be fined up to £5,000.

The department does a cash run twice a week and I have been informed to carry cash they need an SIA license. Gornall will tell you he did not know anything about it. In my opinion he is telling lies. He has discussed this with his Coordinator. Here is an address to contact them, its Mick Gornall, Head of Security, Hardshaw Brook Depot, Parr Street, St Helen's WA9 1JR.

Can you let me know the outcome of this letter and if you make them apply for SIA licenses.

Yours faithfully,
Mr R Steele

PS If you do take action against them and you want me to give evidence, I will.

I received a reply from SIA as follows:-

Security Industry Authority
Date:07 March 2007

Dear Mr Steele,

Thank you for your recent letter dated 21 February, 2007 the information that you have provided has been recorded.

Any information supplied to us on unlicensed activity or breaches of license conditions is treated seriously and in confidence. SIA investigations are conducted following full analysis of information or intelligence gathered from the Police, other enforcement partners or from the public.

However, I am sure you will understand that to avoid compromising investigations we and our enforcement partners are unable to report back on individual cases.

If you work in a licensed security role or employ or supply unlicensed security staff without an SIA license the penalties are as follows:-

Summary conviction at a Magistrates Court, a maximum penalty of six months imprisonment and/or a fine of up to £5,000 or trial on indictment at the Crown Court an unlimited fine and/or up to five years imprisonment.

I hope that the content of this letter addresses the points that you have made.

Please don't hesitate to contact us if you require further information.

Yours sincerely,
SIA Contact Centre

Within a couple of months of my letter St Helen's Council Security no longer did cash runs.

At the end of the day Mick stated on the 13/2/97, '*I am unaware of any incidents on a CIT run*'. Again I believe this is not true a she had discussed the two incidents with me before he made this statement.

25. BREAK-INS

Mick Fairclough was sent to an alarm activation at premises 117 Penkford Special School in 1995. He went around the back of the school and he found a window broken. He found the intruder still inside the premises. As he approached him he pulled a knife on him and threatened him – the intruder got away; the person was known to the police and was picked up.

A few weeks later Mick Hutton attended an alarm at premises 64 That to Heath, this was about four miles away from the last break in. Mick Hutton pulled the same person who threatened Mick Fairclough with a knife out of a cupboard.

I personally attended four alarm activations. One at Carmell College where I chased two youths across the golf course and this incident would have been logged on the summary sheet. I also attended Newton Tech College and the intruders were still on the premises and they dropped two boxes of crisps and ran off. I recovered the crisps and Eric Clarke came out and left a note for the Head Teacher.

I was also sent to the Crematorium to meet Tony Marsh at an alarm activation whilst Tony and I were waiting outside Dominic turned up and as we went to meet him the gates rattled and Tony said *'what's that?'*

I said *"the intruder has just jumped the gates and got away"*.

I also attended Carr Mill Community Centre. This is the incident with the bong where I was sent into the building full of youths.

I wrote to Mick Gornall on the 6 February 1997:-

Health & Safety

Due to the constant break-ins in the Newton area over the last couple of months, Unison feels that one-man patrols in this area are no longer safe and requests that two-man patrols are used until the culprits are caught or the break-ins decline rapidly.

Mick replied 13 February 1997:-

Health & Safety
I accept there has been a spate of break-ins in the Newton area, not constant break-ins.

The majority of break-ins have been at schools that are not part of our regular patrolling service e.g. Newton Primary, Newton High, St Aeldreds (patrol weekends only), St Mary's Infants and St Mary's juniors. The latter two now have a patrol as a temporary measure.

On speaking to the Police they have a good idea who is responsible for the break-ins but like everything else, they need evidence.

In all the break-ins the alarm has activated and when our Officers arrived the intruders have fled.(Try asking Mick Fairclough, Mick Hutton and myself this, again he was prepared to put Officers at risk and I don't believe he is telling the truth). All six incidents where the intruder was still on the premises, would have been logged on the summary sheet. Mick Gornall would have known of the incidents where the intruder was still on the premises.

Our manning levels and rota only allows for one-man patrols on shift it would be operationally impracticable to have a two-man patrol in the Newton area at all times.

I suggest a possible solution is available to the Officer if they feel strongly about it they could volunteer to work Monday to Sunday, one officer 19.00 – 24.00 on a rest day and then any time accrued can be taken off from the floating shift further along in the rota.

Firstly, if an alarm goes off at the above schools mentioned, the Patrol Officer is sent to the school automatically if the alarm goes off at any one of those premises and he could just be around the corner and it was quite possible the intruder could have still been on the premises.

Mick knew damn well no one will come in for a five hour shift, especially when they don't work annualised hours. He always took a man off shift to cover the Markets, the Town Hall Courier and any other jobs he took on but he could not afford an extra man on one route for five hours reference a health and safety issue. It was also operationally impracticable to remove men to cover the markets and Town Hall courier and all the jobs he took on but he did – in my opinion he is just one dangerous liar.

26. ANNUALISED HOURS

In 1991 Mick Gornall wanted Security Officers to do annualised hours on their new shift rota. The Security Officers totally voted against them and they were never introduced to the rota.

On the 8 May 1992 Mick Gornall sent a memorandum out:-

With reference to the meeting on 8 May 1992 between T Twist, J Johnson, T Cranston, C Pinder, B Farrell, P Moffat and myself, it is proposed that the attached rota would be implemented on a four-week trial as from 00.01 on 1 June, 1992.

The following conditions would apply:-

1) Floating Shifts

> *a) These would be entered on the rota as a set shift i.e. floaters Monday – Friday would be 16.00 – 24.00; floaters Saturday & Sunday would be 08.00 – 16.00 & 16.00 – 24.00. Security Officers would work that shift if not told to the contrary. Management reserve the right to either change the floating shift to any other that is required to cover holidays/sickness etc during that particular day or to cancel the floating shift altogether if not required to meet the emergencies of the service and the time owed would be set aside to be used if necessary elsewhere in the rota.*

b) *As much notice as is reasonable practical would be given to either change or cancel floating shifts.*

c) *Under normal circumstances Officers requested to work when not rota'd for a floating shift would not be penalised if eg they refused to work because they had made previous arrangements. Management would, however, expect that if ample notice was given then the Officers would work.*

If an Officer persistently refuses to work when time is owed, then this would have to be viewed on it's merit and the necessary action taken. Officers would be asked to work on rest days in turn to ensure any inconveniences are evenly distributed within the workforce.

d) *Floating shifts would be up to 8 hours long unless Officers are willing to work more. Working 12 hours instead of 8 hours on floating days would result in either additional days off or if absolutely necessary, overtime payments.*

Again Mick tried to introduce annualised hours and again it was rejected by the Security Officers.

I started Security 8/6/92 and in my contract it states an annualised hours system is in operation – again I don't believe this to be true.

When I was in Brendan's office 12/11/96 he asked me to go on annualised hours and I said no. He asked me if he could put a letter out to the lads for them to read. I said yes, but they won't accept annualised hours.

Brendan put a letter out to the lads 13/11/96 asking Patrol Officers to work annualised hours.

Dear Mr Steele,

Re: Annualised Hours Floating Shift.

I refer to our discussions yesterday in respect of the above and as agreed, I am writing to you in an attempt to clarify any misunderstandings and outline position.

The subject of annualised hours seems to strike terror in the minds of some Security Officers who feel that if they accept our annualised working system they will be hauled into work on every rest day. Can I assure you that this is not the intention? In fact the converse is true in that my objective is for Security Officers to enjoy more days off than they may enjoy at present.

This situation would be possible if employees only attended work for floating shifts if they were needed. The credit hours could then be accumulated and as far as I am concerned, if there was not further need to work those credit hours then those hours would be gained by Security Officers. Of course in emergency situations employees with credit hours may be asked to work on occasions but Mick Gornall believes these situations will be few and far between.

I understand the scepticism and it is entirely up to you and your colleagues to take up the offer. I will not be forcing the issue. Can I suggest that a three or six month trial period is set up with the provision that I give you my assurance that at any time you wish to abandon the trial period this will be done immediately.

As far as I see it you have nothing to lose as you can revert to the current situation anytime you chose. I repeat; you have my word on that in the long term however, you may see the benefits of such a system.

Can you please let me know as soon as possible?

Yours sincerely,
Brendan Farrell
Acting Assistant Director

c.c. Les Gilford
Mr R Steele
GMB Shop Steward
Security

Brendan making the above statement as you can see it is in my opinion untrue when you read how Damian was treated below for working annualised hours.

Damian Finnan was on his day off and because Damian worked annualised hours, Mick wanted Damian to go into work with no notice whatsoever, to cover a shift. Mick got Phil Partington to ring Damian's house every hour and also send a Patrol to his house every hour till they got hold of Damian. Mrs Finnan was very annoyed and when Damian came home he was furious.

The Security Officers totally rejected this offer. At the end of the day several Officers would have got away with working many hours and the rest would have to work all the hours extra. It is an unfair and unjust system – that is why we all rejected the offer. We had seen the situation with the Supervisors and Market Officers who worked annualised hours – how it didn't work and how unjust they are.

27. In May 1997 John Clayton and Alan Bolger came to me and said Mick Gornall has put them on annualised hours. I told them to put it in writing and I would sort it out.

Internal Memo

To: Rob Steele   *Date: 19/5/97 Time: 16.00*
From: John Clayton   *Ref: Ann Hours*

Ref: My Alteration to the Floating Shifts.

From 24 to 28 July I noticed that it has run into my rest day. This is annualised hours, which I have not agreed to.

J Clayton

Internal Memo

To: Rob Steele   Date: 19/5/97 Time: 16.00
From: Alan Bolger   Ref: Ann Hours

Regarding the alteration to week 7 on rota. I was not informed regarding being changed Wed 30th Floating Shift 16.00 – 24.00 off to working Mon 28th Rest Day 14.00 – 22.00 this to me is working annualised hours which I have not agreed to.

A Bolger

Mick also put Bernard Day down to work a rest day week ending 01 Dec 96 Wednesday 08.00 – 20.00 when in fact the floating shift in the week is only 8 hours.

He also did it to Roy Simm when he was on a rest day week ending 27 July 97, 14.00 – 22.00 on the Monday.

He also did it to John Sexton week ending 03 Aug 97 when he was on a rest day he put him on 14.00 – 22.00 on the Monday.

I was in Brendan's office and Mick complained to Brendan about John Clayton and Alan Bolger not doing annualised hours and Brendan said, "wait till they want something."

28. I went to see Dave Watts (MP) in July 2002 with Alan Bolger. Dave wrote to the Council and an extract from the Council's reply is as follows:-

6 August 2002

Dear Mr Watts,

Thank you for your letter dated 16 July 2002. I have now received a reply from the Head of Human Resources and can respond as follows.

Firstly Brendan Farrell is the Head of Human Resources and he states as follows:-

In 1991 a review of the Security services took place which involved transferring the employees from manual to APT&C conditions of service on an all-inclusive grade and on annualised hours working pattern.

This is in my opinion again another lie from Brendan Farrell. As above, as already stated, in 1991 the security officers refused to work annualised hours. This was also rejected in 1992. Brendan personally wrote to me on the 13 November 1996 asking patrol officer to work annualised hours again the third request was rejected. So to state to Dave Watts MP that security officers were on annualised hour working patterns was yet again not true.

29. A rota 7/5/03 was given to me as Mick Gornall put at the bottom of the rota

'Officer to stay until 00.30 when only two on nights'.

He wanted an Officer to work an extra 30 minutes per night Monday to Sunday above their 37-hour week. Good job I was not there, I would have told him where to get off. He was in my opinion, bullying them to work more hours than their 37-hour week. This is not even annualised hours he is just an out and out bully.

30. **MEAL BREAKS**

Set times have always been set for meal breaks 8 – 8 shift 12 o'clock; 4 o'clock; 4 – 12 shift 8 pm; 5-12 shift 8.30 pm. Mick Gornall decided to make their meal breaks staggered so you would have your meal break on your own.

This was to stop the Security Officers talking about him.

Ged Philbin was on 8 – 8 days and Mick put his meal break at 11.30 to 12.10 and 16.30 to 17.00. The 8 – 8 men should have their meal breaks at 12 and 4 o'clock. I would have refused to have my dinner at 11.30.

Internal Memo

To: Coordinators   *Date: 30/7/97*
From: Mick Gornall   *Ref. Meal Breaks*

Please ensure that all Security Officers have their meal breaks at the times stipulated on the duty sheets. Obviously if an officer is dealing with an incident then the meal break will have to be altered.

M Gornall

Mick was paranoid that all the Officers did was talk about him in the Rest Room so he split them up.

31. Coordinators working 4 – 12 shift should have a 40 minute sit down meal break at 8 pm and they don't get one and the 00.00 – 08.00 does not get a meal break at any time because they are on their own all night. Both the 4 – 12 and the 00.00 – 08.00 men are entitled to a 40 minute sit down meal break away from the desk by law.

Ref: JCC Meeting 14/8/97 Kevan Nelson raised the following issue:-

Coordinators Breaks

K Nelson reported that it appears that the Coordinators are not getting proper meal breaks. M Gornall responded that it was originally set up at times the meal break will need to be taken in the office at the desk. Problems have occurred because the Security Officers refused to cover whilst the Coordinators have a break. At times Coordinators cannot leave the office or go for a meal but they can eat at the desk.

Mick's statement *'at times the meal break will need to be taken in the office at the desk'* as it was original set up this isn't the case – the 16.00 – 24.00 00.00 – 08.00 man has never had any cover to go for a break since he brought this system in in 1996. The Coordinators could not even go to the toilet – one Coordinator p****d in a cup and threw it out of the window on his shifts as the Control Room had to be manned 24-hours a day. The same Coordinator had to go to the toilet because he had diarrhoea and left the Control Room unattended. This would have never happened with the old system.

Going back to Mick's statement about having their meal breaks at the desk. When I was the Radio Operator John Swift was Supervisor and let me go to the 'chippy' as I was on nights. I came back to the Control Room and Derek came in at midnight to take over from John Swift and he told me to get out of the Control Room with my tea as there is a Rest Room to eat it in. I threw it in the bin in disgust, as many a night turns I was on with Derek he brought his tea into the Control Room and ate his tea at the desk and his office was a few steps away in the same porta cabin.

A rule for one and not for others.

Going back to 19/11/96 Brendan Farrell stated 'Mick would like you in the Control Room'. I'm saying it's not your job and you don't go in the Control Room. This statement was made when I made a statement that members of the Union had to help out in the Control Room whenever required and I said if that's the case let's talk money and that's when Brendan made the statement above.

Also going back to the JCC meeting 24/4/97, when I complained a Coordinator went 16 hours without a meal break and I told the management that this is down to the new system and it does not work. That's when Brendan started laughing, when I said the old system was better.

At the end of the day the old system had three men in the Control Room that gave everyone a meal break away from the office as they were all on the same pay and covered for one another.

Also going back to the meeting with Mick Gornall 27/4/97 – I again repeated it's still down to the system not working. I also said I told you and Brendan that the system would not work well before you implemented it. Mick then said the old system has gone and will never come back.

32. BREAK PERIODS NIGHT SHIFT

Internal Memo

To: All Security Officers   *Date: 23/1/97*
From: D Anders (02)   *Ref: 19000700 Shift*

When you work the above night shift you know you are going to be on patrol, which will start at 1900 hrs. and should finish around 0030. Baring no incident your break will commence at 0100 and not before. Do not try to apply pressure to any of the Coordinators otherwise it may just result in a rota change to incorporate the routes i.e. 17.30 – 00.30.

Thanks

D Anders (02)

This is just bullying and 17.30 00.30 would have been better all around, especially for the client as there would have been three route men at all times. They would not have carried out this threat as they would have had to employ another three men to do it. Ever since the system came in, in 1991 the night shift got two 30-minute meal breaks, one at 0000 and 0400. I would not have stayed out until 0100.

Ref. J.C.C. meeting 20/1/98

G Philbin said that during night shift Security Operatives are quite often unable to have a break.

P Moffat responded that he could not agree with this statement from the information he had received so far, which indicated they do get breaks which are paid breaks at least equal to minimum entitlements.

G Philbin said employees are sometimes working a 13-hour shift when they try to get a break they are called to do a job.

T Marsh said that the Security Patrols think that it is the Coordinators sending them out on patrols but it is not. The Coordinators are following instructions from management.

P Moffatt agreed that there may be occasional nights where the Security Operatives are very busy but the standard night does not appear to prevent employees having a break.

(This is not true, if you are very busy and there is only two men on nights you do not get a break).

K Nelson asked if a set break time could be established.

P Moffat responded this is not possible – if an alarm goes off the section must respond. We can programme a standard target break time into the night but if the bell rings we must answer and take a break later, if possible.

There was already a standard target break time 0000 and 0400 – this was always the case since 1991 and Derek tried to change it in 1997.

T Marsh said that the Coordinators, when on 8 – 8 shift are unable to leave the office to have a break because there is no cover.

K Nelson said the facilities make the problem worse. The toilets are not easily accessible.(Like I stated earlier, one Coordinator was p*****g in a cup and throwing it through the window and also left the Control Room unmanned when he went to the toilet with diarrhoea).

P Moffatt said reasonableness was expected from the Security Officers in terms of this situation. A Security Officer could sit in the Coordinators chair while the Coordinator took a natural or refreshment break. If a supervisory decision was requested the Coordinator was still on site to be contacted.

At the end of the day, Mick took the job off the Security Officers and made it quite clear he has six dedicated Officers and gave them a pay rise so the Coordinators job does not concern the Security Officer whatsoever. Also, going back to the statement Brendan Farrell made on the 19/11/96, *Mick would like you in the Control Room I'm saying it's not your job and you don't go in the Control Room.*

Again, I warned Mick and Brendan this system would not work. As Mick said, *'the old system had gone and it's gone for good.* It's his negligence bringing in the new system after being warned by myself it won't work which has caused all the problems.

33. Market Officers have always had a paid meal break since the Market Security started in 1991. When single status came in, in April 1999 the working week went from 39-hours to 37-hours and Mick had to cut the Market Officer hours by two hours per week.

Mick kept their hours the same and took their paid meal break off them to lose the two hours the Market Officers had gained. This was well out of order. Several years later Mick amalgamated the markets with the security rota and gave them the paid meal break back.

The more you read about Mick Gornall the more you will see why I consider him to be a despicable person he really is.

34. ALARM RESPONSE

Since the restructure of 1991 there has been an alarm response man built into the system to cover 24 hours a day, seven days a week. However, nine times out of 10 there is never alarm response man on between 1600– 0000 due to staff shortages and the Client is paying to have this cover 24-hours a day and again is not receiving what they are paying for. This also causes a problem with the routes as, if an alarm goes off, they send a man off another route to go and meet up with the Officer whose route the alarm has gone off, preventing the patrols finishing their patrols off by midnight.

Alarm Activations

A memorandum was sent to all Security Officers

30 January 1992   *From: M Gornall*

If you have to send someone on their own to an alarm activation during hours of darkness then ensure they do not check the property unless it appears safe to do so, i.e. staff on premises etc.

The Officer is to wait until another Security Officer key holder, or the Police, attend.

In 1995 I was on nights with Ged Philbin and the Supervisor was not on shift and the night shift was also a man down. Once again

Mick Gornall should have come in and covered the shift but left me and Ged to do the night shift on our own.

I was sent to an alarm at premises 117 Penkford Special School and Ged phoned the Police to meet me. I waited over one hour for the Police and I wanted to go home, so I went into the building and re-set the alarm. If anything had happened to me, he would have put the blame on me when in fact it would have been his fault as once again we didn't have the manpower to cover our duties. On numerous occasions we have been short staffed and have phoned the Police for assistance and they have told us they are too busy and cannot assist us, leaving Council buildings vulnerable to burglary because of staff shortages.

36. STAFFING LEVELS

Since I have been employed as a Security Officer in June 1992 I have known of staff shortages in Security and when people leave Mick either takes months to replace them or does not replace them at all.

In April 2003 Security were three men down on their rota. Mick Rimmer was finished the end of 2009 and Graham Davis was finished in 2010 and he has not replaced them. It is now February 2011 and he is two men down on his rota. This again has a knock on effect to the customer as once again corners are being cut constantly since the end of 2009 when Mick Rimmer left and things would have got worse when Graham Davies left in 2010.

JCC Meeting 7 July 1994
Manpower Levels
J Johnson stated there is a manpower problem – a man has recently left and not been replaced.

JCC Meeting 10 July 1996
Staff Rotas / Shortages

T Cunliffe asked Mick Gornall what was going wrong?

M Gornall responded that problems had arisen because they were waiting for the outcome of the review.

R Steele said that 19 people were manning a 24 operative rota.

M Gornall said he knew of the problems and was looking to recruit. This statement is inacurate, as he had just got rid of six men on ill health and within a couple of months he reduced the rota to 17 men.

T Cunliffe referred to a situation when there was not enough cover.

M Gornall responded that this incident was because someone had gone sick. Again this statement inacurate as the rota has two floating shifts per day to cover for sickness and holidays. The reason was due to staff shortages.

15 August 1996

Sickness

B Farrell asked M Gornall if current sickness levels were causing any problems.

M Gornall responded that there were problems, especially because of a lot of holidays at the moment need to provide cover. Temporary employees were an option but would cost more money. Once again Mick sat back and did nothing about the situation again leaving the Clients without the service they were paying for.

B Farrell said it is essential that services are covered.

JCC Meeting 24/4/97
Recruitment

R Steele said he felt that the timescale for filling a recent vacancy was *too long.*

M Gornall explained the recruitment process and said there were exceptional circumstances.

B Farrell said there is now a full quota of employees in the division but problems arise when employees go off sick. Had there been a full quota of employees then there would not have been a problem when employees go off sick, as there are two floating shifts to cover for sickness.

R Steele said that the old system of working was better. Than the current method, when employees were sick, other employees could cover. The new system has caused problems and some premises are not being visited. R Steele referred to a recent weekend when premises were missed.

(These notes have been altered drastically to what was said, compared to my notes dated 24/4/97 – mine were 100% accurate) below.

B Farrell responded that he has received no complaints about premises not being visited. M Gornall to investigate R Steele's report that premises were missed.

B Farrell said there is enough manpower in the division to do the job.

R Steele said that there is no manpower at weekends for alarm response.

M Gornall disagreed – there are resources built into the alarm response rota to include weekends.

(There is a man built into the rota but he never has the full quota of staff to cover the job.)

Brendan Farrell started laughing when I said the old system was a better system. He told the person writing the minutes to write down, *"Rob says the old system with six supervisors is better"*. I replied hold on *"who mentioned Supervisors – I said our old system was better"*.

I then said I received a complaint that 94 premises were outstanding – again I said this is down to the system not working.

Mick Gornall replied, "Some Officers are making it not work, for instance one officer was seen doing 20 mph from one premises to another".

I then said, "some schools are getting three or four visits in one day to catch up on visits". The agreement for the schools is one visit Monday to Friday and two visits Saturday and Sunday.

Brendan replied that some schools would rather have seven visits in one night. This statement is not true.

I replied, "that is not the agreement we have with the schools" and I produced the agreement for the schools.

Mick then asked me, "where do you keep getting all this information from?" I replied "no comment".

Brendan said this is out of date. The Manager has changed and the supervisors have gone. I replied, "but the school contracts haven't changed or gone, that is still the agreement.

I then produced a list of premises, a total of 96, which needed follow-up calls.

Brendan then asked who gave me them. I said it's unfair to give you that information.

Brendan then asked Mick, "do you know who it is?" Mick replied, "I have an idea but Rob's not going to tell us".

I can now tell you it was the temp they made Coordinator, Peter Woodcock. They can't do anything to him because he left many years ago.

Brendan then said that this is confidential information and if it got into the wrong hands it would be damaging.

Brendan then stated the Chief Executive would sack him.

I replied, "no he won't". Mick then commented about it getting into the wrong hands. I said it's staying in my file. Brendan then replied, "I'm going to give the schools their money back and get rid of 10 men – I'm not getting sacked".

I replied "your threatening me now Brendan". Brendan then picked up the list of premises and said "and you're threatening me". I replied "they are facts, not threats".

Brendan then asked Mick to find out why the premises were not checked on time. I replied part of it was down to alarm activations and lack of manpower on this system, I also said that I was stuck at a school for 3½ hours waiting for SMC to attend and one Officer waited over four hours. This problem is caused by never having an alarm response man on shift that the customer is paying for due to constant staff shortages.

Brendan then told me I'm not having any more men and then told me to see Mick at 15.00 hrs on the 27/4/97 and he will see me and Mick in his office next week. I replied I'm on a course next week. Brendan then said make it the week after.

St Helen's MBC Security
Daily Duty Sheet

Saturday   *Date: 16 Aug 1997*

John Clayton on holiday – no cover for Pets Corner 2100 – 0800 on nights.

No man to do route two 1700 – 2400

No man to cover the market 0630 – 1830 Saturday 16 August 1997 the job was a total of 3 men down for their duties.

Internal Memo

To: Derek   *Date: 20/8/97*

From: Tony

Could you please sort out the staff for Thurs. No one available for 417 (Pets Corner) 21.00. No alarm response man neither.

This had already been stated on the 10 July 96 in the J.C.C. meeting.

The present rota system is clearly showing a staff shortage. This is an immediate problem that should be addressed now rather than later as this affects everyone. The Union Membership knows that corners are being cut which also affects the customer.

Monday 21/7/97 St Helen's Crematorium from 16.30 to 20.30 due to lack of manning levels Officer arrived 1740 – no alarm response man.

Monday 28/7/97 no alarm response man.

Tuesday 29/7/97 Only two Officers on nights – should be three officers. No parks locked.

Wednesday 30/7/97 No alarm response man. No parks locked.

21/8/97 No. 417 (Pets Corner Static) 21.00 – 00.30 No alarm response man.

Because I was receiving all of this information Mick Gornall told Tony Marsh to tell me I'm not welcome here any more – I was stopped from going into the Depot.

37. DISCIPLINARY'S

Mick Rimmer, Tony Marsh, Terry Cunliffe, Roy Simms' disciplinary's have already been dealt with.

Damian Finnan and Jebby Robinson were disciplined because the monitor on the cameras was not on rotating the cameras and it was not recording and allegedly a lawn mower was stolen off the depot and both Damian and Jebby were punished when only one of them was responsible for monitoring the cameras. At the end of the day none of them should have been disciplined.

Phil Deighton was also disciplined because intruders went on to the depot and he missed them. When the Coordinator is doing three men's jobs on his own then he will miss things.

Mick Gornall and Paul Molyneux were monitoring the cameras on days when Mick's motorbike was stolen from under their noses. It does not matter whose bike it was, it was still stolen from the Depot and neither Mick nor Paul were disciplined – what a joke.

38. ILL HEALTH

This matter concerning the six members of staff i.e. Keith Jones, Alan Proctor, Gary Wainwright, Peter Waine, Keith Hackett and Jimmy Johnson have been discussed earlier.

39. HOLIDAYS

Security Officers are entitled to 22 and 27 days holiday a year. Mick Gornall gave the Security Officers their holidays in hours, 176 and 216 hours instead of days.

Around half the rota are 12-hour shifts – this is why Mick put the holidays in hours so you have to book a day and a half for one shift. If you book the four night turns off you have used 6 days holiday instead of 5 days.

This worked to Mick's advantage. If you booked half your holidays at 8 hours and the other half at 12 hours, an Officer with 22 days holiday would only end up with 18 days holiday a year and an Officer with 27 days holiday would get 22.5 days a year. The rest of the Council get 22 and 27 days a year.

While I was off sick the Security Officers had a meeting with Jim Keegan (Full Time Officer for Unison). They told him that they had to book 12 hours off for a days holiday and he said it's wrong and they should be booking a day for a day and he would sort it out.

13 years later they are still booking 12 hours off for a days holiday.

On my contract it stated 20 + 2 days holiday not 176 hours, which is what Mick was giving us.

40. In 1999 when single status came out, Mick reduced the hours by 19 hours giving Security Officers another 2½ days less off a year, yet they still had to book 12 + 8 hour shifts off as holidays. Mick Gornall and the rest of the Security Officers on days got 22 + 27 days holiday in full. At the end of the day I consider that Mick is just a 'con man' who rips his staff off.

Here are the minutes from a J.C.C. meeting around September 1995:-

J Johnson raised the issue of booking holiday entitlement in hours. He felt this disadvantaged some people.

P Mavers instructed M Gornall to look into this but felt it would be very difficult to arrive at an alternative arrangement that would be acceptable to all. Perhaps an average number of hours per week could be used as a basis for calculation of holidays will be reported back at the next meeting.

Extract from JCC Meeting 10 July 96

The booking of holidays for certain weeks of the year is being denied to the workforce. This is a direct result of the way the work rota has been produced and the fact that we are short of manpower.

Ref J.C.C. Meeting 10/7/96

Holidays

R Steele stated that operatives were being denied holidays on certain weeks in the year due to the rota and staff shortages.

M Gornall responded that it is the need of the service, not necessarily a shortage of men and hopefully, this situation will be resolved when the new rota is produced.

B Farrell stated that within reason no one should be denied their holidays.

R Steele said that 21 operatives are needed to cover rota – they are down to 17 operatives.

M Gornall replied to R Steele that if he could produce a better rota then he should have a go and let him see it.

B Farrell said if the stewards could produce a rota covering the level of work, holidays, sickness etc., then he would be very interested.

Dave Anders came to me and said Mick had denied him holidays so I went into the office and reminded Mick that Brendan had stated that within reason, no one should be denied their holidays and Mick backed down and give Dave his holiday.

Security Services Holiday Application Form
Name: Damian Finnan

Days and Dates Sat 21/9/9620.00 00.00
Sun 22/9/9600.00 -08.00

Date Resuming Work: Sun 22/10/9600.00-08.00

Total number of days leave to be taken 12 hours.

Date: 11/9/96

Damian received a reply from Derek Anders:

Sorry unable to grant your holidays due to no floating shifts available.
D Anders (04)

Security Services Holiday Application Form

Name: R Steele   **Date: 22/6/97**

Day	Date	Shift	Hrs
Wed	2/7/97	08.00	8
Thurs	3/7/97	16.00	8
Fri	4/7/96	15.00	9
Sat	2/8/97	17.00	7
Sun	3/8/97	17.00	7
		Total Hours	**39**

Leave was granted for 2nd, 3rd, 4th July 97 and was rejected for 2nd and 3rd August 97.

Sorry Rob 2 Officers already off these days

D Anders

Daily duty sheets clearly showed that three men were off on certain days – a rule for one and not for the other.

Memorandum

To: Mr R Steele GMB Shop Steward
Mr P Houghey T & G Shop Steward

From: Mick Gornall   *Date: 26 July 1996*

Holidays

It was agreed that a better method of booking a weeks leave would be explored.

Possible options could be:

Class a weeks leave e.g. Saturday – Sunday as 40 hours and if your rostered shifts total more than 40 hours then the time would be worked elsewhere in the rota.

Class a day as 8 hours leave and again any hours over 8 would be worked elsewhere in the rota.

Obviously if rostered shifts are less than 40 hours or 8 hours / day then that number of hours could be booked as normal.

(The only way Security Officers should have booked their holidays is as to the contract agreement. A day for a day it's not the Security Officer's fault they have to work long hours at certain parts of the rota to cover client needs – it is the fairest and only way they should book holidays).

M Gornall
Head of Security

John Sexton booked holidays and booked his flight to, I think it was Bulgaria, and Mick Gornall told him he had to come back to work to cover one shift and told him if he could not get cover for the shift he could not go on holiday – in my opinion it shows what a 'p***k' Gornall really is.

Damian Finnan booked holidays to Wales and Mick told him he had to come back from Wales to cover a shift. Damian came to me and told me so I went to Kevan Nelson and he put a stop to Mick doing this. In some opinions Gornall is just one total nasty piece of work – no wonder he was unpopular.

I did produce a better rota with 19 men on it instead of 17 men. This would have given the Client what they were paying for and also covered for sickness and holidays and still gave full demands to the Client. It also gave the lads a one-on one-off weekend working instead of working three-on one-off at the weekend. I showed this to my members and they all agreed to my rota. I took it to Mick and he said it would not work and brought a 17-man rota in that definitely did not work, again leaving the Client's demands short.

The only reason he never brought my rota in was because there were 19 men on my rota and he would not employ extra staff and that he never thought of it himself.

41. FAILING TO RECOGNISE THE UNION

I have already mentioned the letter I sent to Brendan Farrell regarding Roy Simms disciplinary and the request at two meetings to confirm Roy's disciplinary had been moved from his record and Brendan totally ignored my requests.

42.8th July 1997
Mr B Farrell
Acting Assistant Director

Dear Mr Farrell,

Re: Library Courier

Further to our recent meeting regarding the above, I would be grateful if you could confirm in writing that when the library courier service is being covered by Security the rota will be fully staffed i.e. there is no sickness or holiday, therefore there would be no detriment to the existing service.

Yours sincerely,
E Tickle
Branch Secretary

As above, Eddie Tickle wrote to Brendan Farrell and told him not to use Security Officers to cover library courier when not fully staffed. Mick continued to do this after the letter 8 July 97 – he did it on 9, 10, 11 July;26,27,28,29 August;2, 3, 4, 12 September 97 and is still doing it to this day in February 2011.

Because Mick Keeps leaving our shifts short by doing other jobs i.e. library courier. I got my members to sign an agreement as follows:

26 January 1997

To comply with Union Unity, I will not attend work at short notice nor will I volunteer for Courier.

I did this so our shifts would not be short of manpower and certain officers liked doing the Library Courier as it was day shifts for them. At the end of the day it was leaving us short to cover our contracts.

Derek Anders put the following people on Courier:-

B Day	Wed 9 July 97
J Goodier	Thurs 10 July 97
J Sexton	Fri 11 July 97
P Houghey	26 & 27 August
A State	28 & 29 August
J Goodier	4 September
A Bolger	12 September

If Derek had put me down for it he would have been told where to get off.

43. THREATS BY MANAGEMENT

In 1991 Security had a restructure and the management told the Security Officers that, if they didn't accept what is on offer Burns Security would take over at 5.00 pm that day.

The management could not do this as CCT did not come in till 1994. In 1997 I had a meeting with Sheila Samuels (Head of Human Resources) and Russ Damson from the Town Hall. I told them that if security did not take what's on offer Burns Security would take over at 5.00 pm. Sheila Samuels told me in the next meeting with her that the management will tell you anything they want to get you to accept what's on offer.

It just shows you what a bunch of 's**thouses' St Helen's Council really is. All the Council workers got the correct rates of pay, apart from a percentage of security staff and nobody else has been threatened with their job.

44. Mick Gornall used to tell the lads that, if you don't do the extra work he wanted them to do, his job was safe – meaning, if they shut security down they will find him another job and the rest of the Security Officers would go on the dole. I heard him say this myself on a couple of occasions.

45. As already read, Mick Gornall threatening to sack six men if they didn't put in for Coordinators jobs and then getting the same threat by Brendan Farrell that he would sack six men and take six men off the dole. I got no support from the Union on this matter so I advised my members to apply for the jobs rather than to lose six jobs.

46. As already read ref. my first meeting with Brendan Farrell where I said –*"if you keep to management rules and I keep to*

Union rules we would get on fine".

He replied – *"if you cause me any trouble I will ring the Town Hall and have you shut down over night".*

47. You have already read about the 96 premises not getting checked over the weekend and making the statement – *"I'm going to give the schools their money back and get rid of ten men – I'm not getting sacked".*

Here is the list of premises that visits were missed. The number is the number of the premises and x whatever is how many visits they missed over the weekend. All the premises should have had four visits.

Internal Memo

	Route 1
To: Coordinators	*Date: 01/04/97*
From: D Anders(02)	*Ref: Unchecked Prems.*

Prems listed below require extra visits as per their contracts.

136 x 1	75 x 2
113 x 1	1 x 1
211 x 1	76 x 2
117 x 1	98 x 1
212 x 2	402 x 1
106 x 1	18 x 2
408 x 1	411 x 1
313 x 1	300 x 2
428 x 1	400 x 2

Internal Memo

	Route 2
To: Coordinators	*Date:01/04/97*
From: D Anders (02)	*Ref: Unchecked Prems*

Prems listed below require the stated amount of visits as per their contract:

318 x 2	43 x 2	86 x 1
426 x 1	416 x 3	427 x 2
404 x 2	11 x 3	414 x 2
433 x 2	225 x 3	68/69 x 2
130 x 3	114 x 2	418 x 1
133 x 3	508 x 2	419 x 2
115 x 3	415 x 3	
330 x 2	100 x 1	

Internal Memo

	Route 3
To: Coordinators	Date: 01/04/97
From: D Anders (02)	Ref: Unchecked Prems

Prems listed below require the stated amount of visits as per their contract.

81/82 x 1	61 x 1	447 x 1
85 x 1	27/28 x 1	94 x 2
34 x 1	41 x 1	36/37 x 2
38 x 1	421 x 1	
56 x 1	97 x 1	
101 x 1	64 x 2	
30 x 1	83/84 x 2	
468 x 1	488 x 2	

These are all the premises that were outstanding when I showed them to Brendan 24/4/97 and Brendan stated that 'this is confidential information and if it got into the wrong hands it would be damaging'. He stated the Chief Executive would sack him and this is when he made the statement he would give the schools their money back and get rid of 10 men.

I did report this issue to John Vis (District Auditor) and he replied 'coverage for schools not being in accordance with service level agreements (SLA's) i.e. not all premises visited, schools not visited within time ranges requested and patrols finishing after midnight N.B (completion of patrols prior to midnight is not specified in SLA but considered preferable by the security force management.'

Detailed review of radio log sheet over one week period showed that:-

99.3% of programmed visits were made.
87% of visits were made within the requested time ranges.
85.7% patrols finished prior to midnight.

I can tell you John Vis picked the best week for the above figures. Had he gone back three months like he did with the locking of the parks, the percentage would have been around 40%. In my opinion he to was protecting the Council. I believe if he had he done his job properly the statistics would have been totally different.

48. BULLYING BY MANAGEMENT

Damian Finnan reported Mick Gornall to the Union about bullying. They had a meeting with Peter Mavers (Assistant Director). Damian said to Mick *"are you calling me a liar"* and Mick said *"no"*, so Damian said *"well I'm calling you a liar"*. Like every other issue, it was brushed under the carpet and nothing happened to Mick. Mick said to Damian after the meeting' "we will pretend it never happened". This is the same statement he said to me when I was taken to Brendan's office 17 July 96 – not long after Damian left security.

49. When Mick made Peter Woodcock Co-ordinator and Brendan and Mick wanted Phil Ward to do permanent days Monday to Friday as Coordinator and the rest of the Coordinators were

asked to cover all the other shifts. All five Coordinators would not do what Mick wanted so Mick got Peter and told him "what right have you got to decide?" and told him to just leave the Council. Not long after Mick made this statement Peter left the Council.

50. Cath, Co-ordinator, rang the Chief Executive for help when the emergency plan was activated. Mick Gornall and Paul Molyneux must have had a 'bollocking' because Paul came out of the office and threw a file into Cath's chest and swore at her because she did not know what to do when the emergency plan was activated. Because of what had happened she went off long term sick.

At the end of the day Paul Molyneux should have been disciplined and removed from security because Paul was Mick's best mate, once again it was brushed under the carpet and Cath had to leave Security and move to another department.

51. Paul Molyneux's girlfriend was a cleaner and cleaned in the security office. Bernard Day asked her could he ask her a question and she said "yes". He said, "have you had a 'boob' job and she reported Bernard. Bernard was removed from security and away from the offices and became a Park Keeper.

What Paul did to Cath was a lot more serious and Paul stayed in security and Bernard was removed. There is no justice in Security or the Council.

52. Damian Finnan was on his day off and because Damian worked annualised hours, Mick wanted Damian to go into work with no notice whatsoever, to cover a shift. Mick got Phil Partington to ring Damian's house every hour and also sent a Patrol to his house every hour till they got hold of Damian. Mrs Finnan was very annoyed and when Damian came home he was furious.

53. Mick Gornall rang John Clayton at home when he was off sick with the flu and told him I've got the flu and I'm in work. John returned to work because of Mick's bullying – it was alright

for Mick he did not have the flu and even if he did, he is in a heated office all day and can have plenty of hot drinks throughout the day. John had to go out in adverse weather conditions.

54. Derek Anders phoned Mick Hutton while he was on the sick the same time as John Clayton. Mrs Hutton answered the phone and Derek told her he wants to speak to Mick. Mrs Hutton told him he is in bed with the flu and Derek told her to get him out of bed to answer the phone. I know Mrs Hutton well and she told me she was very upset the way Derek had spoken to her and that she was disgusted with his attitude.

55. This reminds me of when I went into hospital when I first started in Security and Derek rang the hospital to see when I was returning to work. I told him I had to have skin grafts on both my knees – I was in hospital for 15 days and the day I got out of hospital I was issued a sick note for three weeks.

Mick rang me up and asked me to go back to work so I went back and a week later Mick asked me to get a note from the hospital saying I am fit to work, so when I had my check up with the Consultant, Dr Green, I asked him for a return to work note and he said he thought it was a bit early to return to work as my skin graphs may not take.

He let me go back to work and I took the return to work note in. A few days later Mick came to me and said I had to get another note from the day I returned to work so I saw Dr Green and told him. I got a 'right bollocking' and he told me not taking advice could have set me back another couple of months. This was all down to Mick getting me to go back to work too early against the advice of the hospital. I felt intimidated.

56. NIGHT SHIFT

You need three Security Officers and a Coordinator to cover the night shift.

If the emergency plan is activated you need two men to go to the Town Hall and one man to pick up the DO 1 or DO 2 if requested. On occasions the third man was needed to pick up either the DO 1 or DO 2. You need two men to cover alarm response and a man to cover Pets Corner between 5 am and 6 am and then he goes off and opens the Parks for one hour – that takes him up to 7 am. The depot also needs opening at 5.30 am which takes around 20 minutes.

There is no way you can cover the Client's specifications without three men.

J.C.C. Meeting March 98
Staffing Levels

K Nelson raised this issue. Three persons are needed on shift during the night period. Kevan stated that recently there have been instances where there has been two or even one person on shift at night. The rota indicates that three Security Operatives should be on shift. Overtime or a casual supply list should be considered.

P Moffat responded that there are three persons on shift. One Coordinator and two Security Operatives – this is not the case.

G Philbin said that the requirements were three Security Operatives plus the Coordinator. There have been instances where three persons have been needed.

P Moffat did not agree with this and referred to item 4.3 of the previous minutes. Security Operatives do have time to have breaks and there does not appear to be a need to have an additional person on shift. The Division is meeting contractual commitments and customers are satisfied.

Again I do not believe this to be true – you cannot cover contractual commitments with only two officers on nights.

M Gornall said the reason the rota indicates three Security Operatives is to accommodate holiday sickness etc.

This again is not the case. For this to be true one of the night shifts would have been a floating shift and his rota states 19.00–24.00 to 00.07 on week one 21.00–24.00 to 00.08 on week 4 and 19.00–24.00 to 00.07 week 14. This again was leaving one man on his own for the last hour when you would need two men to cover alarm response.

Here is an extract from a letter from Mick Gornall 28/11/91.

Included in the rota are floating shifts which are used to cover for holidays / sickness etc"

The floating shifts for Monday to Friday were 16.00–24.00 except the floating shift to cover black bags.

Saturday and Sunday 08.00 – 16.00 none of the rotas have ever mentioned floating shifts on night turns but around 2008/2009 Mick decided to make one of the night turns a floating shift so most night turns have only two officers on shift.

None of the night shift duties have changed and it has been demonstrated quite clearly you have to have three men on nights to meet the contractual commitments to the customer and with two men you cannot do this.

There have been times when the Coordinator has had to take the man off Pets Corner and away from opening the Parks to give cover for the alarm response and there have been times when the Coordinator has left the office to go and open the Depot, leaving the Control Room empty when it should be manned 24 hours a day. Leaving the Control Room also leaves the officers at alarm activations vulnerable.

57. I went to the District Auditor, John Vis, in St Helen's Council in 1998.

Issues Raised

Inadequate staff cover in respect of initiating the Council's emergency plan.

Findings of work Undertaken

This area is not subject to formal agreement between the Security force and the Council. However, when incidents have occurred the security force has provided two officers. One officer at the Town Hall entrance and one to set up the incident room.

Staff cover can be stretched over the shift period from midnight to 8 am when only three officers are on duty, particularly if one officer calls in sick just prior to the start of the shift. However, the fact that the Head and Deputy Head of service are on call 24 hours a day provides, in my view, adequate cover. (Again this is not true).

Firstly I will state that on Mick's Client specification for 1996:-

In addition to the above also carry out the following on a weekly basis and the last specification is standby for major emergency plan.

At the end of the day it was subject to formal agreement.

I was taken to the Town Hall on two occasions to make sure I knew exactly what to do and where to go, along with all the other Security Officers because if there were any problems, the 's**t would hit the fan' like it did when Cath rang the Chief Executive up.

As for the Head and Deputy Head being on call 24 hours a day, I have known that on many occasions several of the Coordinators have rang Mick and Derek for help and neither of them have answered their house phone and their mobiles have been turned off. This is not giving adequate backup. John Vis seems to have covered up for the Council.

58. CONTRACTS

All Security Officers who started security before November 1991 did not have contracts for the restructure, which took place in 1991.

All Security Officers who started after the 1991 restructure were given contracts that were not correct. Firstly, in my contract it states an annualised hour's system is in operation – which in fact was not the case. It also stated:

Holiday Entitlements

A) Annual Leave

Your current holiday entitlement is 20 + 2 days per annum and after five years it increased to 25 + 2 days per annum.

Mick made us book our holidays in hours and not days, so we ended up with less days off per annum.

59. As already stated earlier in 1996 Mick Gornall and Brendan Farrell wanted to change our contracts and I ended up calling a status quo to stop them doing this. Brendan changed our contracts and brought the new rota in on the 25/11/96 without my consent, the members consent or the Union's consent. I believe he is another bully like Mick Gornall.

60. BEREAVEMENT LEAVE

This has already been discussed ref. Mick Rimmer and the treatment he received from Mick Gornall, showing in my opinion he is a despicable person who bullies people.

61. COUNCIL POLICY

These two issues have already been discussed. –one being the three temps being made permanent after three months when the Council

Policy is two years. The other issue was Tommy Hawks being put on to the top of Scale 3 when everyone else had to work their way up over a two-year period. This was also Council Policy.

62. PETS CORNER & PARKS

Ref: Pets Corner where I stated to Brendan Farrell – Pets Corner was not getting manned on a regular basis. After I went off sick I went to the Council leader Mike Doyle and in front of my Father, I told Mike Doyle that Pets Corner never gets a static put on it and Mick Gornall is charging his Clients for the static.

Mike Doyle turned around to my Father and said, *"do you know Mr Steele, someone your son does not know has told me that there is never a Security Officer on Pets Corner"*.

I also reported this issue to John Vis (District Auditor) who decided to 'brush it under the carpet. See para 64 below.

I then made a complaint to the Audit Commission and stated that John Vis' report was a disgrace and it was passed on to David Goodman, Regional Director, based in Widnes. I made an appointment to go and see him – I took my Father with me.

David said to me he is not happy that I said his District Auditor's report was a disgrace (meaning John Vis) and I said, "well it is a disgrace".

Clive Portman was with him, the same person who was with John Vis in the Town Hall. When I complained to John Vis about all my grievances David told me that Clive is going to be doing the Audit, so the first thing out of my mouth was Pets Corner never getting manned. Again Clive never investigated the matter.

So far I have reported Pets Corner to Clive Portman, David Goodman, Mike Doyle, John Vis, Brendan Farrell, Sheila Samuels and Russ Damson – a total of seven people and they all brushed this serious matter under the carpet as not one of them did anything about it.

The Ranger Service put a static on Pets Corner in 1991 from 22.00 to 06.00 am seven days a week and around 1996 they could no longer afford the costs and reduced the hours to 21.00 –00.30 and 05.00–06.00 am.

With only having two men on nights there will definitely be times when they are not going to have an Officer available to cover Pets Corner, especially if an alarm goes off between 05.00 – 06.00 as the two Officers will have to attend the alarm activation and it is now February 2011 and it still goes on.

63. I also reported to the District Auditor that the parks are not getting locked on a regular basis, when the Ranger Service are paying to have them locked.

On 23 March 1998 John Vis did a report as follows:-

Issue 3
The charging of security force clients for work not done and work not being done to standards set out in service level agreements.

Issues Raised
Charges being made to the parks and open spaces section for closing parks even though parks were not shut some evenings.

Findings of Work Undertaken
Review over three month period showed that on some occasions parks were not closed mainly due to an incident/ incidents occurring elsewhere during the evening. However, on each occasion that the parks were not closed, no charge was made to the parks and open spaces section.

Ref. incident/incidents occurring elsewhere should have no effect to the parks getting locked and each Security Officer has their own tasks to do and only if there is a shortage of staff would there be a problem which, on a regular basis, was the problem and as to *'no charge was made'*. I find this unlikely.

I went to speak to Eric Ashcroft (Head of the Rangers) and I asked him did he ever receive a refund. He said he recently stopped doing the costings but all the time he was doing the bills for Ranger Service he never got refunded for no static at Pets Corner, nor for the parks not being locked. I don't believe Mick Gornall has ever refunded anyone.

64. Over the Christmas period the Ranger Service asked for a Security Officer to cover the Café in Sherdley Park and Mick charged them for this. Once again he used the Officer on Pets Corner to cover the café instead of putting another man on Pets Corner to cover the café on overtime.

The officer on Pets Corner was called away to do alarm activations and the café was broken into. I reported this to John Vis and John Vis replied as follows:

Static security at Pets Corner, Sherdley Park not being maintained leading to a break in to the café between Christmas and New Year 1997. Security not to the standard requested by the Client.

The break in occurred during a lapse in cover during a shift change. This lapse in cover was accepted by the Client given that the request for cover was made at short notice over the Christmas / New Year period i.e. when staffing resources would be more stretched than usual.

The only days that the security is stretched are Bank Holidays and it did not happen on a Bank Holiday. Also there is supposed to be a static at Pets Corner every Bank Holiday – it's not true to say there was a lapse in cover during a shift change. The static at Pets Corner goes on at 21.00 hours and shift change over happens at 19.00 hours and 20.00 hrs. The reason this happened was the man was taken off Pets Corner to attend alarm activations. Had he put another man on Pets Corner the two of them could have done regular patrols of the café. He would have definitely got someone to do it on overtime; again this issue has arisen from having staff shortages once again.

The only reason the Client accepted their excuse was that they don't know how the system works and when they are being lied to. I know the system like the back of my hand and I definitely know when lies are being told.

John Vis, like the other six, did not investigate Pets Corner not being manned and not one of them looked into this issue. This was serious, as I believe many thousands of pounds was involved. I reported this to seven people who had the authority to solve the problem, which was ignored.

65. HOUSING OFFICER
I have already discussed this earlier about Peter Lawton getting the job as Housing Officer. I did go to John Vis, District Auditor, in February 1998 and he replied:-

Issues Raised
Temporary Security Officer / Alarm Installer appointed in Summer 1997 without the post being advertised internally or externally.

Findings of Work Undertaken
The post was advertised at the local Job Centre and recruitment processes used for selection of the successful candidate followed established Council policies and guidance.

The post was not advertised internally in accordance with established procedures on filling posts at the Security Officer / Alarm Installer level in short time scales.

This statement is absolute 'bulls**t',Phil Partington was moved to Coordinator from Security Officer the same day and Tony Marsh was made Coordinator within two weeks. The only reason he was not made Coordinator the same day was because he had booked holidays on the Security Officers rota or he would have gone to Coordinator the same day.

I brought it up in a J.C.C. Meeting 14/4/97 that it took three months to replace Phil Partington on our rota. Mick Gornall stated that's how long it takes to apply to the Job Centre and interview and select the correct candidate for the job. Yet the District Auditor states it's quicker to advertise the job through the Job Centre because of short time scales.

As you can see quite clearly it takes one day internally and three months through the Job Centre so once again another lie by the Council and the District Auditor.

I did not believe that the job had been advertised in the Job Centre so I asked all six Coordinators had anyone come for an interview for Housing Officer? Only one of them said 'yes' – Peter Lawton.

So I went to the Job Centre and asked had the job of Housing Officer been advertised between May and August 1997? She went away for ten minutes and came back and said *"I have to see my Manager"*. The Manager came to me and said she cannot giveme the information I require.

I believe it was because the job was not advertised. She would not have gone away for ten minutes and looked on the computer. She would have told me straight away they could not give me that information.

So I went to my MP Peter Kilfoyle and he wrote to the Manager on 20 April 1998 as follows:-

Dear Mrs Holden,

Vacancy for Temporary Housing Officer in Security, St Helen's MBC

I am writing to ascertain whether in fact the above vacancy was advertised in the Job Centre between May – August 1997.

I look forward to your response.

Yours sincerely,
Peter Kilfoyle MP.
Liverpool Walton

Gaynor Holden wrote back as follows:-

24 April, 1998

Dear Mr Kilfoyle,

I am writing in response to your request for information about a vacancy with St Helen's M.B.C.

I have checked Employment Service instructions on disclosure and confirmed with Employment Service Secretariat that I cannot disclose to you the information you request.

The reasons are because your enquiry is not about a constituent and employer and vacancy information is confidential to the employer or to candidates who were submitted to them.

If you would like further information about this policy you can contact Heather Gore, Employment Service Secretariat, Caxton House, Tathill Street, London.

Yours sincerely,
Gaynor Holden
Mrs Gaynor Holden
Business Manager

Peter Kilfoyle wrote back as follows:-

5 May 1998

Dear Mrs Holden,

**Re: Vacancy for Temporary Housing Officer in Security,
St Helen's MBC**

*Please find enclosed copy of your letter to me of 24th April
1998 for ease of reference.*

*In that letter you claim that you could not disclose the
information that I sought because your enquiry is not about
a constituent. In fact the enquiry does concern a constituent
of mine and I would be grateful, therefore, if you could now
provide that information.*

I look forward to hearing from you shortly.

Yours sincerely,
Peter Kilfoyle MP
Liverpool Walton

Gaynor Holden replied as follows:-

7 May 1998

Dear Mr Kilfoyle,

**In response to your latest letter about a vacancy at
St Helen's M.B.C.**

*I apologise for the explanation in my first letter, which had
led you to believe that I cannot disclose the information you
request because you are acting for your constituent.*

I was aware that your constituent had engaged your support and I have seen and spoken to him myself. In this case I shouldn't have used this as an example of a reason for not giving you the information.

The reason for non-disclosure in this case is because the information is about an Employer and their vacancy information is confidential to them.

You may be able to obtain the information from the Employer yourself.

If you would like further information about Employment Service disclosure policy and our position as a third party in your enquiry I recommend that you contact Heather Gore at the Employment Service Secretariat, Caxton House, Tathill Street, London.

Yours sincerely,
Gaynor Holden
Mrs Gaynor Holden
Business Manager

David Goodman from the District Audit replied to our meeting we had in Widnes as follows:-

April 1999

Failure to meet client specifications.

I have already referred to this in the context of Health and Safety.

Mr Vis letter 23 March 1998

We also discussed your dissatisfaction with the response you received from Mr Vis in respect of the concerns you raised

175

this time last year. Your main concerns were whether it was true that the alarm installer appointment in Summer 1997 was advertised in the Job Centre, as claimed and the adequacy of the sample of logs reviewed at Audit to assess whether the SLA had been complied with.

I said that I would check the position as to the advertisement of the Alarm Installer job. I have done so. The Job Centre has confirmed that it did advertise the job in accordance with its normal arrangements as to the adequacy of the sample audited. I should say that this involved a review of 700 logged items. I share Mr Vis' view that that was a reasonable sample to have taken.

Next Step

As I explained to you the appointed District Auditor for St Helen's is Mr Clive Portman who is based here in Chorley. I have copied this letter to him and he will deal with matters as set out above. He will let you know the outcome of his enquiries.

Finally, thank you again for coming to explain your concerns.

Yours sincerely,
David Goodman
Regional Director

I do not believe that Mr Goodman has seen any proof of the job being advertised and why would the Job Centre not tell myself, or my MP Mr Peter Kilfoyle. Had the job been advertised there would have been no problem and again the Job Centre would not have taken my paperwork and gone looking for the relevant information – they would have told me straight away. They cannot give me the relevant information. The fact is the job was not advertised in the Job Centre and John Vis would have stated x-amount of people applied for the job and x-amount of people were interviewed for the job and he didn't. That's because only one person was interviewed for the job.

Also, the Coordinators would have known how many people came for an interview as everyone has to report to Security and only one person came for the job interview as the six Coordinators manned the office 24 hours a day. They might be able to fob any one else off but they can't 'bulls**t' me. At the end of the day I don't believe that job was advertised in the Job Centre.

66. HARASSMENT

It has already been stated about Damian Finnan being harassed to go into work on his day off because he worked annualised hours and annualised hours don't work. They have to give so much notice to come into work, not a couple of hours and also ringing his house and getting Phil Partington to send a Patrol knocking on his door every hour is harassment.

67. It has already been stated about John Clayton receiving a phone call to go back to work when he was ill. This is also harassment and Derek Anders ringing Mrs Hutton up and telling her to get her son out of bed to answer the phone. Mrs Hutton was disgusted with the way she was spoken to by Derek – this was also harassment.

68. NO JOBS

Brendan Farrell put Phil Ward into Security to do the collection of debts and recover library books from people's houses. The job only lasted six months and because he was a friend of Brendan'she was retained in Security for six months on full pay when in fact he should have been redeployed or made redundant, but Mick Gornall found a solution by creating the job as Liaison Officer for his friend, so Phil Ward could have Paul Molyneux's job.

69. A Government scheme came up in Security to give people on the dole short time work and the Security Officers were told by

Mick Gornall they cannot apply for the jobs as they were only temporary jobs for people on the dole. There was a position for a temporary Supervisor.

Mick Gornall took his best mate out of a full time job and paid him Supervisors rates of pay. Within a few months the job finished and again Mick Gornall paid Paul Molyneux Scale 5 Supervisors rate of pay in Security for eight months with no job in the department. Again he should have been redeployed or made redundant, as these two people were an adverse strain on security finances.

70. PATROLLING THE DEPOT

In J.C.C. meeting 14/8/97, when Mick wanted constant patrolling of the depot and I told them if they want constant patrolling of the depot, they had better take the four men back and let them patrol the depot. Brendan said it will cost £60,000. I made it quite clear I'm not checking the depot nor were my members.

Since I went off sick Mick Gornall has had them constantly patrolling the depot. This was not part of the Security Officers duties. For night shift they had set procedures to carry out and patrolling the depot was not one of them.

In my opinion Mick Gornall is just a bully who bullies people into getting his own way. It's on Mick's contract to cover for Supervisors / Coordinators and I know for a fact, on occasions, there has been no Supervisor on shift and Mick has failed to cover their shifts when he should have done so.

71. ONE MAN PATROLS

The agreement for checking schools was physically checking buildings during daylight hours. Operating hours of darkness to carry out visual checks only – not checking windows and doors. Mick Gornall and Brendan Farrell enforced checking windows and doors in hours of darkness without the consent of the Union or the consent of the workforce, this issue is putting the Officers health and safety at risk.

Around 1994 C Pinder voiced concern regarding the instruction to Patrols to check doors (some debate ensued). M Gornall clarified that the instruction was to check doors only where there was no risk to personal safety. P Mavers underlined the importance of adhering to withdraw from checking any doors would be detrimental to the uptake / continuance of service level agreement.

Around 1996
Extract from Minutes of J.C.C. Meeting

Patrolling of Premises

M Gornall referred to an item in a previous J.C.C. regarding checking of doors. M Gornall said it had been brought to his attention that Operatives were still not checking doors.

T Cunliffe responded that it was never agreed they would check doors.

M Gornall said, if operatives are passing doors it is not unreasonable to check doors.

T Cunliffe stated that in a meeting two years ago Brendan Farrell said that they did not have to check doors as Caretakers are paid to check doors.

B Farrell said he did not recall saying this and said if it is safe to check doors, they should do so.

C Pinder said he did recall B Farrell saying they did not have to check doors.

Extract from Minutes of J.C.C. Meeting 10 July 1996

Patrolling of Premises

B Farrell replied that the Client expects windows and doors to be checked. It is expected and it is not unreasonable and should be done in accordance with the guidance cards.

Extract from Memorandum 18 July 1996 from Brendan Farrell

Checking of doors, windows etc. during evenings.

Again the service level agreement is based on the checking of doors, windows etc. I fail to understand how any Security Officer can believe that such a fundamental job is not part of their duties.

We do respect, however, that in these safety conscious times, there may be occasions when it is unsafe to carry out these activities. This scenario is clearly outlined in the Health & Safety Guidance card entitled Patrols Night Time Card No. 50 which states 'when you are patrolling premises / locations (during the hours of darkness) you must only carry out physical checks where there is good access, otherwise visual checks must be carried out from a safe distance.

It was Mick Gornall who wrote this card no. 50.

Extract from Minutes of J.C.C. Meeting 14/8/97.

Lone Working

R Steele said the problem in relation to lone working was specifically the checking of alcoves and dark areas during darkness.

M Gornall responded that no one should put themselves at risk. If the Officer feels that an area is a risk then it should be checked from a safe distance. If there is good lighting and good visibility then physical checks must be done.

Extract from Minutes of J.C.C. Meeting 18 November 1997

Lone Working (Trade Union Items on Agenda)

K Nelson said there are concerns, which have been raised before about the checking of doors in poorly lit areas at night. The advice card puts the onus on the Security Officer to determine if the area is a safe site. Specific specifications are required for premises that are patrolled.

Specific specifications were put out to one-man patrols.

28 November 1988

To: All Security Staff

Method of Patrolling
Any one-man patrols out between 20.00 and 08.00 will carry out visual checks only.
J Sanders
Acting Head of Security Services

Extract from letter from Peter Moffatt (Assistant Director) 11 June 1992

When one-man patrols are operational between hours of darkness they will carry out visual checks only from a safe distance of the whole building.

It was Peter Mavers, Brendan Farrell and Mick Gornall who tried to enforce the checking of windows, doors etc. when two-men patrols were out. Before 1991 they did have to check doors and windows in the dark. A safety procedure was put out twice for one-man patrols. Peter Brendan and Mick all decided to ignore the correct procedure and put the officer at risk. As stated a visual check only from a safe distance of the whole building.

As stated it was Mick Gornall who wrote Guidance Card No. 50 putting the onus on the Security Officers. At the end of the day they don't check windows and doors in the hours of darkness. Management have broken the procedure set out for one man patrols and Brendan Farrell never had the 'balls' to come out on patrol with me to see how difficult and how vulnerable the job was for security officers.

72. GRIEVANCES

This grievance has already been discussed ref Dave Anders' boots and Roy Simm's glasses where the Council did not reimburse either of them for their damage to their goods after Brendan Farrell stated they will receive their money back.

73. This grievance has already been discussed where I came into work and was told I was up the crematorium and I went mad as Mick Gornall brought the job in without any consultation with the Union and expecting Security Officers to do extra weekend working for no extra pay. The 1996 restructure made more weekend working hours than any other rota we had before and we had to do them for no extra pay.

74. The Patrol Officers had a static duty at Newton Cemetery and were stopped from using the Rest Room next to the Chapel.

Mick Gornall told the Security Officers to take their meal breaks in the van. This was a joke as; on numerous occasions there was not enough vans to send one up to the Cemetery so where were the Security Officers supposed to take their break? When there was a vehicle spare they were told to park their vehicle outside the Lodge. Terry Cunliffe did so and the people who lived there told him to move his vehicle as it was parked on private property.

The Security Officer was also instructed by Mick Gornall that they had to radio the Coordinator for permission to use the toilet. This was humiliating to ask a grown man to ask permission to use the toilet. Facilities were available until Mick Gornall stated someone heard a noise coming from the Rest Room – a TV or a radio. It was 99% certain it was voices coming from the radio handset that this person heard and not a TV or radio like Mick Gornall tried to suggest.

Mick Gornall put out a memorandum:-

To: All Security Officers
From: Mick Gornall   *01 May 1997*
Re: Newton Cemetery – Use of Cabin

1) *Due to a complaint received concerning use of TV/ Radio in the cabin at the side of Chapel of Rest – NO ONE will be allowed to use the room except for:-*

   i) *Use of toilet*
   ii) *Use of Washing Facilities*

Any refreshments will have to be taken in the vehicle. When the use of toilet/washing facilities is required then you must inform the Coordinator when entering/leaving, who will log the times down.

2) *Vehicle must not be parked up to the Chapel of Rest. The vehicle can be parked at side of the Lodge as you drive through the main gates on the right – see attached sketch of location to park the vehicle.*

Failure to follow the above may result in disciplinary action being taken.

Obviously it goes without saying that TV/Radios are forbidden on any static duty.

M Gornall
Head of Security Services

I was on duty on a weekend when one Officer said he needed to warm his food up and had no facilities as they were not allowed to use the Cabin. I told him to leave the Cemetery and come back to base and have his meal break. He told me had had no vehicle at the cemetery so I went up there and covered for him and he took my vehicle back to base and had his dinner.

Mick Gornall and I had heated words about this issue as he told me it's not to happen again I told Mick it will happen every time I'm on shift. If I, or any of the Officers, had been disciplined for this then I would have refused for any of us to cover the Crematorium, or the Cemetery, ever again.

75. RADIO HAND SETS

14/8/97 in a J.C.C. Meeting

I requested that the handsets be put on channel 2 for Health and Safety reasons. Mick Gornall stated that what I was requesting was already the procedure – that statement was not true.

Only one month earlier Derek Anders put a memo out as follows:-

Internal Memo

To: *All Security Officers*   Date: *04/7/97*

From: *D Anders (02)*   Ref: *Handset Radios*

If on the odd chance you have to use the talk through facility for any reason, please ensure that once the incident/problem has ended, please put your handset back into the silent mode operation.

Handsets are not to remain in the talk through mode.

D Anders (02)

The J.C.C. Minutes read as follows:-

R Steele asked if it was possible for vehicle radios to be on channel one and handsets on channel two.

M Gornall responded that this is the procedure now. M Gornall to check that all Officers are following this procedure.

Derek's memo was not a mistake and we were instructed to put our radios on channel one – the silent mode and not the talk through mode on channel two.

This was the reason I brought this matter up in the JCC meeting 14/8/97 as it was a Health & Safety issue and as you can see Mick Gornall's statement was not the procedure we were instructed to do. More lies and it's not as if it was a mistake as Mick and Derek shared the same office and it was only around 12 foot by 14 foot and it is Mick who instructs Derek to put the internal memos out. He was just covering his back on a Health and Safety issue.

76. SECURITY OFFICERS REQUEST FOR SCALE 4 APT & C

P Houghy requested for Security Officers to be on Scale 4 like the Coordinators to cover their shifts when needed. This request was refused by B Farrell.

In a meeting 19/11/96 B Farrell stated, *"Mick would like you to help out in the Control Room".*

I'm saying, *"it's not your job and you don't go in the Control Room"*

Ref minutes from JCC meeting 8-10-96 as follows:

P Houghy suggested that all security operatives should be paid scale 4 as instances may arise, where scale 3, security operatives would need to cover for the scale 4 security coordinators.

B Farrell responded that re-grades needed to be justified. Employees cannot be paid more if their duties and responsibilities have not been increased. Anyone who covered for the security coordinators would be paid in accordance with APT & C conditions.

This statement is not correct as security officers and coordinators were not paid in accordance with APT & C conditions. At the end of the day they should have been as they are Council employees. The Coordinator had the same responsibilities as rest of the supervisors in the Council if not more and the supervisors were paid scale 5 plus allowances. Security officers had more responsibilities than the Hall Keepers and Ranger Service who were paid scale 4 plus allowances.

Why has a percentage of security been denied the Councils correct rates of pay? Security Officers should have been on scale 4 plus allowances and Coordinators should have been on scale 5 plus allowances and not scale 3 and 4 all inclusive and they would have all been paid in accordance with APT & C conditions like Brendan Farrell stated.

77. COORDINATORS

When there is a problem in Security the Coordinators have been told they are Supervisors and are told to give supervisory decisions at times when needed, yet when they ask for supervisors pay they are told they are not Supervisors.

This was a similar issue the Security Officers had. There were times when it suited management. Security Officers were told one minute they were staff and the next minute, they were manual workers.

So I put a stop to that when in a JCC meeting I asked Pam Gray to confirm whether we are APT & C staff or whether we are manual workers and Pam Gray confirmed we were under APT & C conditions of service which meant we were entitled to our allowances which we never received.

186

Extract from minutes of JCC meeting 20-01-98

P Moffat (Assistant Director) said reasonableness was expected from the Security Officers in terms of this situation. A Security Officer could sit in the Coordinators chair while the Coordinator took a natural or refreshment break, if a supervisory decision was required the Coordinator was still available on site to be contacted.

This statement confirms the Coordinators are Supervisors and were paid from 1996-2008 scale 4 inclusive and should have been paid the Supervisors rate of pay scale 5 plus allowances and in February 2008 the Coordinators pay went from scale 4 all inclusive to scale 3 plus all allowances. As already stated, they should now be on scale 5 plus all allowances.

With reference to security officers sitting in the coordinators chair its a non starter, as Brendan Farrell made it quite clear that Mick would like you to work in the control room, I'm saying it's not your job and you don't go in the control room. Brendan made this statement when I told him that members of the union had to help out in the control room when ever required and I said if that's the case lets talk money. Brendan made the above statement quite clear on the 19th November 1996.

78. JOB VACANCIES IN SECURITY

It is Mick Gornall who decides who gets the jobs in security and it is not how good you are at your job in security. Mick gives the jobs to his "favourites", it does not matter whether you can do the job or not or how rubbish at the job you are, you will get the job as myself, Alan Duckworth, Bernard Day, Phil Deighton, Terry Cunliffe and Eric Clarke all found out as they were all more experienced in security at their jobs and Mick's favourites got the job.

79. I wrote to the Audit and Councillors of St. Helen's Council on the 16/3/99.

To Audit and Councillors.

Security section has new posts on the new deal scheme for patrolling the town. Security Officers have been told they cannot apply for the posts as they are for out of work people aged 18-25.

They also have a post for a Supervisor on scale 5. APT & C, this post should also be given to someone on the new deal. I will state now the job will go to Paul Molyneux, best friend of the Head of Security and his position of Liaison Officer will no longer exist. I have always stated this position was never needed.

I was informed on the 28/3/99 that Paul Molyneux was interviewed on the 19/3/99 for the Supervisor's job and filled the position on the 23/24-3-99 and to my surprise; Mick Gornall gave Terry Cunliffe the job as Liaison Officer.

At the end of the day the Supervisors job should have gone to someone off the dole and not to Paul Molyneux as it was a temporary job to take people off the dole. It just shows how devious Mick Gornall is.

80. The Deputy Head of Security has not yet been proposed, when the job does become available Phil Deighton will get the job as Derek Anders Deputy Head of Security has already made this statement to some of the security officers.

Paul Molyneux's job came to an end after several months and he had no job in security for eight months. The Deputy Head's job finally became available and Paul Molyneux got the job.

What no one saw was Mick Gornall giving Paul Molyneux some experience as a Supervisor so he could give his best mate the Deputy Heads job. At the end of the day Phil Deighton had done all the jobs in Security and was more qualified than Mick's best mate Paul Molyneux. His mate always came first before experience.

Once again Alex Grant and Mick Rimmer were called into the office and told to take early retirement or be sacked if they make one more mistake and Paul Molyneux made more mistakes than Alex and Mick Rimmer all together as Deputy Head of Security and they were brushed under the carpet, as he was Mick Gornall's best mate.

81. The Yard Manager's job again has not been proposed. When the job does become available the Deputy Head of Security, Derek Anders, will get the job. Derek and another person put in for it and the other person used to cover for Brian Williams, Yard Manager when he was off, and guess what Derek Anders, with no experience, got the job leaving his position as Deputy Head open for Mick's best mate to fill it as he had no job in Security for eight months and should have been re-deployed or made redundant.

I got two of the three jobs right and if I had known Paul Molyneux was going to have no job in Security for eight months I would have stated he would definitely have got the Deputy Head's job.

82 PATROLLING TIMES

On the 11-6-92 Peter Moffat sent out a letter – the following is an extract from it:

> *"It remains critical however that security patrols be carried out in a thorough and diligent manner so we can demonstrate best value for money from our 10, 15, and 20 minute patrols".*

The small premises that get patrolled are a 10 minute check and since I started in 1992 I know for a fact that most Security Officers only stay for two to three minutes, I used to give them 5-6 minutes as you would not have been able to finish your route in time.

At the end of the day the client is paying for 10-15 and 20 minute patrols for the time stated and that is the time the officer should stay at the premises and to check the premises to agreement.

Premises 101 Rain hill High School: to check it properly in daylight hours it takes 30 minutes. If the RLS duty sheets would have been checked, you would find the 10 minute visits get between 2/3 minutes, 15 minutes checks got between 6-8 minutes and 20 minute checks got around 10-13 minute checks, if that, which once again is cutting corners with the clients, while the cost to the client are not reduced.

At the end of the day, if they do not give the customer what they are paying for then they should not have the contract. Mick Gornall has cut corners from the day he took over as Head of Security in 1991 and is still cutting corners now in 2011 at the client's expense.

83. SECURITY SERVICES DRESS CODE.

The Security services dress code went far beyond peoples human rights and were also discriminating for certain people.

They were based higher than military standards; this issue should have been addressed at the time as the people in question were Council employees and not in the armed forces. Here is the dress code Derek Anders put out after being a Sergeant Major in the Territorial Army.

St. Helen's Metropolitan Borough Council Security Services Dress Code.

Objectives:

1. *To portray a professional IMAGE FOR S. Helen's MBC*
2. *To promote the image of St. Helen's MBC*
3. *To be clean smart and correctly dressed.*
4. *To take care of any uniforms issued*
5. *To always wear uniforms whilst on duty.*

Standards:

1. *Appropriately groomed and short length hair*
2. *Clean shaven for every shift or beards to be kept trimmed and short*

3. *Personal hygiene to be maintained to a high standard.*
4. *No visible tattoos allowed on hands or face.*
5. *No types of pierced jewellery to worn eg earrings etc.*
6. *No loose jewellery to be worn around the neck or wrist.*
7. *Only wedding rings plus one other type of ring to be worn.*

Uniform issue must be worn whilst on duty as follows:

- *Shirt with epaulette shoulders with long or short sleeve options.*
- *Black trousers.*
- *Black sweater – Dependent on weather.*
- *Black Anorak – Dependent on weather.*
- *Black over trousers – Dependent on weather.*
- *Black clip on tie – At management discretion between 1st June and 31st August, otherwise must be worn at all times: when the tie does not have to be worn only the top button of the shirt may be undone.*
- *Epaulettes – Worn when in shirt-sleeve order.*
- *Epaulette flashes – To be worn over outer garment epaulette*
- *Peak cap – Optional if issued.*
- *Footwear – Not issued but must be either black or dark brown shoes or boots.*
- *Safety footwear – If a specific duty requires the wearing of safety footwear then these will be issued and must be worn for that particular task only.*

D. Anders
Deputy Head of Security.

Two of the Officers deliberately grew beards to get at Derek, they were Alan Bolger and Jimmy Goodier and Derek could not do anything about their beards, as they were grown in protest to Derek's dress code.

John Sexton and a few others never wore a tie all year round since 1991 Derek gets made deputy head of security and starts his bulling tactics.

A friend of mine went for an interview for Security and I put a good word into Mick Gornall for him and because he went for the interview on a motorbike and had earrings in both ears Mick came out of his office when I was on shift and told Dave Anders that I got this lad to come for an interview and called him rotten and 'slagged him off' for coming for an interview on his motorbike and wearing an earring in both ears.

Bernard would have done the job properly and would have made a better Security Officer than most of the officers he already had.

A few years later Mick started to come to work on a motorbike – what a hypocrite he is.

Phil Houghy, when I first started in Security in 1992, wore an earring with a cross hanging from it, for a good couple of years, and in 1993/94 Andy Tie had an earring in when he swapped jobs with Alan Duckworth. On one shift he had a big bust up with Derek Anders when Derek told him to take his earring out and Andy refused and continued to wear it till he left Security – once again Derek could do nothing about it.

The dress code Derek and Mick Gornall brought in has gone far beyond discrimination and human rights.

You have now read 83 grievances and not one of them was dealt with and all of them were a genuine reason for concern and needed addressing with a possible outcome and not bushed under the carpet by the Council and District Auditors.

CHAPTER THREE

I am now demonstrating my summary of facts and chronology of events a total of my 57 grievances St. Helen's Council, the Unions and the Police – all covering up for St. Helens Council.

1. June 1996 Mick Gornall threatened me he was going to sack six men because he could not get his own way as on a last man in first out basis I was one of the six men to be sacked, this is now the first time I was threatened with the sack.

2. June 1996 – In my first meeting with Brendan Farrell I told him if he sticks to the management rules and I stick to the union rules we will get on fine and Brendan threatened me – if I cause him any problems he will ring the Town Hall and have us closed down over night.

Brendan threatened us all with our jobs if he does not get his own way. In less than a month of being Shop Steward I have now been threatened with my job **twice** as I was not prepared to let Mick and Brendan bully me and let them get their own way like they did with all the other Shop Stewards.

3. In my first JCC meeting 10th July 1996 Brendan Farrell told me I was misleading my members and he could add a lot more to it – that statement was not true, what I wrote about the contract changes were written from the Union Rule Book word for word – it was as follows:-

Reference Contract Changes 7th July, 1996.

To all Security Officers with regards to the current tension regarding the proposed changes in contracts I would like to draw to your attention the current employment law relating to contractual agreement.

WRITTEN CONTRACTS

Once an employer has offered a job and the offer is accepted there is a legal contract between employer and employee, even if there is nothing in writing. If an offer has been made and accepted and then the employer withdraws it, it may be possible to sue for breach of contract.

CONTRACT CHANGES

Once the employment contract has been accepted by the employee, then the employer should not make changes without agreement. Contracts may change if the parties agree to the change.

R Steele (Shop Steward)

If any person with legal experience reads the above they will know 100% that I was not misleading my members and that the information I wrote was 100% correct and they will also know that statement made by Brendan Farrell stating he can add a lot more to it is wrong – like the statement he made that I was misleading my members was also untrue.

After the JCC meeting I went back into Brendan's office to explain why I put the contract changes up as Mick Gornall threatened to sack six men if he did not get six Coordinators and he told Brian Wright that himself and Phil Deighton would be sacked if they didn't put in for Coordinator.

Brendan turned around and said, *"If I don't get six Coordinators I will sack six men and take six men off the dole".* As on a last in first out basis I was one of the six to be sacked this is now the **third** time I have been threatened with the sack in less than six weeks of becoming Shop Steward.

4. 17th July 1996 Brendan Farrell threatened me with a disciplinary and dismissal.

Between the 11th and 16th July, 1996 I had a union meeting. I had been to wages and got a copy of the figures for the restructure in 1991.

In the meeting I told the lads that I now have the figures and will investigate the wages. I also told them that if I find anything that will get Mick into trouble, or sacked, I would not take it any further.

Dave Anders stood up and said,*"what are you protecting that 'b*****d' for? If it was the other way around, he would sack you"*.

Jimmy Goodier then stood up and said,*"why are you protecting that 'b*****d'.*

Dave Anders made a statement ref union meeting July 1996, last year Rob Steele stated he was going to look into the wages but if he found anything wrong in his file discriminating M. Gornall he would not take it any further. I then raised the question why? Because if it was the other way round we would be sacked. Another union member agreed with me on this matter,

D. Anders

Dave never stated how it was exactly said. My version above is 100% accurate.

After the meeting I went up to the Control Room and messing about with Derek Anders (Supervisor for Security), I said to him,*"if I get you 01, you give me 02"*.

Derek grabbed my arm and said,*"you want to watch who you say that to, they might take it the wrong way"*.

On the 17th July 1996 I was on night turn. At approx 10.10 am my phone rang – it was Keith Jones (Supervisor for Security). He said, *"Mick has told me to phone you and Brendan wants to see you at 4 o'clock"*.

I said, *"I'm on nights"*.

Keith said, *"I'm only passing the message on"*.

At approx. 12.35 pm there was a knock at my front door. I went down and opened the door. It was Phil Deighton. He had a letter from Brendan confirming the meeting at 16.00 hours in his office and that Les Gilford had been informed.

I rang Derek Anders at home and asked him did he know what was going on. He replied, *"I haven't got a clue"*. I said *"it must be serious for them to ring me and send me a letter and that Les Gilford has been informed"*.

Derek told me if there wasa problem he would give me a character reference if I needed one.

Derek stitched me up to improve his chance of becoming Deputy Head of Security.

I got to Reception and met Les. He asked me what was going on; I told him I don't know.

Kevan Nelson (Unison Convener) turned up. Les asked Kevan what was going on, Kevan said, *"I don't know"*.

We then went into Brendan's office. I was asked, did I say I had enough evidence to get Mick sacked. I said no but I did say that if I did find any evidence that would get Mick into trouble or sacked I would not take it any further.

I was then asked by Brendan, *"did you say anything to Derek Anders?"*

I said yes, after the meeting I did say to Derek, *"if I get you 01 you give me 02"*.

Brendan said that disciplinary proceedings and dismissal could be brought against me.

Mick behaved like a 'big girl' and said *"you have really hurt my feelings"*.

Brendan then said to me he will put his answer in writing to me. A couple of days later I received his reply – he did not believe what I had said.

He replied 19 July 1996.

Re: Allegations against Mr M Gornall

I refer to our meeting on Wednesday 17 July 1996, which I convened following certain information that had come to my attention.

The information in question evolved from a Union meeting at which you claimed to have enough information to 'get Mike Gornall sacked' and a later conversation with Derek Anders during which you repeated the allegations.

The allegations in question I did not make in my Union meeting nor to Derek Anders.

He then went on – 'during our meeting you denied making any comments at the Union meeting but you did admit to making the comments to Derek Anders which leads me to believe that the earlier comments were also true'.

I did make a comment to Derek jokingly but not the one Brendan is accusing me of.

He then went on, "as a recognised Shop Steward in this department you have certain responsibilities and I would advise you to refrain from making such scurrilous remarks about any employee of the Council. Not only are such remarks potentially slanderous but could also involve disciplinary proceedings being initiated against you. I would hope you heed my advice".

How can I heed his advice when I did nothing wrong?

This is now the **fourth** time I've been threatened with the sack.

5. I applied for the job of Security Coordinator sometime around September 1996. I received a letter from Mick Gornall 19th November 1996 telling me I was unsuccessful, after receiving a glowing reference on 19th October 1995. I put this down to conflict with Mr Gornall and Mr Farrell for my honesty as Shop Steward.

I received a reply 19.11.96

Re: Security Coordinator

I refer to your recent interview for the post of Security Coordinator and confirm the information given to you verbally that is you were unsuccessful.

May I thank you for your interest and apologise for the delay in writing to you.

On the 19.10.95 I was given a reference from Mick.

TO WHOM IT MAY CONCERN

Re: Mr Robert Steele

'Since 8 June 1992, when he commenced work as a Security Officer with St Helen's Metropolitan Borough Council's Security Services, during his time with us Robert has shown exceptional ability and his work record is exemplary. He is

honest, trustworthy, and totally reliable and can be relied upon to carry out any task using his own initiative. He has a pleasant courteous personality and his attendance record is excellent. I would be sorry to lose his service but have no desire to stand in the way of his personal ambitions.'

I could not believe I did not get the Coordinators job after receiving a glowing reference on the 19 October 1995 from Mick Gornall. I put this down to conflict with Mr Gornall and Mr Farrell for my honesty as Shop Steward.

6. On the 24th April 1997 Brendan Farrell threatened to sack 10 men on a last in first out basis I was one of the 10 men. This is now the **fifth** time I have been threatened with the sack.

Extract from JCC Meeting 24/4/97

Brendan replied,*"I'm going to give the schools their money back and get rid of ten men. I'm not getting sacked"*. This was after I had complained that 96 premises were not checked over the weekend.

Here is the extract from the minutes of the meeting:-

B Farrell stated there will be no increase in staff. If the division cannot provide the required service then we will have to tell the schools this, then there would be no need for a security service and the establishment would be reduced accordingly.

These minutes were not what was said. My notes from the extract from the JCC meeting above are 100% true and accurate.

The trouble with Mick Gornall and Brendan Farrell is they haven't got the 'balls' to repeat what they have said because they would be in serious trouble, whereas I don't care – I will repeat what I have said or anyone else – word for word.

7. Sometime at the beginning of 1997 Paul Molyneux showed me a large tray in the boot of his car, which Mick Gornall gave him. Paul told me Mick had six of these trays in his office so I went into Mick's office and asked Mick for one for my garage so I could put my nuts and bolts in. He said, *"No, it's not fair on the other lads as he has not got enough for everyone"*. No one else wanted one, yet his best mate was given one when he asked for one. Once again, I was singled out by Mick Gornall.

8. Sometime around May 1997 Derek Anders came out of his office into the Control Room and told me I was not allowed to swap any more shifts as I did not want to work with himself nor Mick Gornall. Yet Mick Hutton had been swapping his shifts for years to avoid Mick Gornall and he and the rest of the security officers were allowed to continue to swap their shifts. In fact Derek Anders put out an internal memo a few months later but it excluded me. It read as follows:

Internal Memo

To: All Security Officers   *Date: 7/7/97*
From: D Anders (02)   *Ref: Mutual Swaps*

Please ensure when you do a swap with someone that you enter on the R/H/S of the signing on sheet who you have swapped with. Failure to do this may result in swaps not being allowed.

Thanks
D Anders (02)

9. **Below is an Extract from meeting with Management Tuesday 24/6/97**

I said that if we went on a work to rule it would prove the job would not get done.

Brendan replied, *"I am not having you on a work to rule. It's bad enough with the bin men and the union have to ballot for industrial action."*

I replied, *"I do know how to ballot."*

Brendan replied, *"Go ahead and work to rule. I will give the schools the money back and we would lose work and the department would close. I would see that Mick and Derek were redeployed as it's not them who have caused the problem"*.

I said, *"we would be redeployed too"*.

Brendan said, *"I will make you all redundant"*. This is the **sixth** time I have been threatened with the sack in 12 months.

10. On the 3rd July 1997 I received a phone call from Mick Gornall telling me to attend a meeting at 4 o'clock with Eddie Tickle. I rang Eddie up to see what the meeting was about and he told me it does not concern me and I don't need to be there.

So I rang Mick back and told him that Eddie told me I don't need to be there. Mick asked me to attend the meeting at 4 o'clock, so I turned up and met up with Eddie and he asked me what I was doing there. I told him Mick wanted me to be there and we went into Brendan's office.

Pam Gray (Personnel Manager) was there with an A4 notepad. Brendan started off with a verbal attack on me by saying I was Militant and a troublemaker and you are causing all the problems in our department and you have caused more trouble than all the Shop Stewards have put together. Then he told Eddie he wants another Shop Steward.

Firstly, Pam Gray was there for one reason and one reason only – Mick Gornall and Brendan Farrell brought me in on a disciplinary and never informed me of it. When Eddie got me to leave the meeting to calm down, I told Eddie they have brought me in for a disciplinary.

Both Mick and Brendan broke the rules for a disciplinary by not informing me of it and they cannot deny it as they brought the

Personnel Manager in Pam Gray and she was asking me questions and not one question was written down on Pam Gray's A4 notepad. I got the better of the three of them Mick, Brendan and Pam Gray.

Secondly, I am not a trouble maker or Militant nor did I cause all the problems in security. When my members come to me with a grievance then I take it up as any good Shop Steward should do.

Thirdly, it is not up to Brendan Farrell whether he wants another Shop Steward it's up to the Union members who they elect as their Shop Steward, not Brendan Farrell.

What happened to Brendan's statement in the JCC meeting 10th July 1996 – *"A keen Shop Steward, I like a good scrap with the unions"*. Mick and Brendan did not like a good scrap with me, they could not handle me and could not stop me pursuing my members grievances – I was a thorn in their side.

11. On the 31st July 1997 I received a phone call from Eddie Tickle telling me Brendan Farrell and Mick Gornall stormed into the Union office demanding to see Eddie about myself. Eddie told them he's not seeing them without me present. I told Eddie that I will find out what it's about as I am in work for 4 o'clock.

I got to work for 4 o'clock shift and Mick Gornall told me not to go anywhere as I'm going down to Brendan Farrell's office. I asked Mick *"is Eddie or Kevan going to be there?"* He said *"no"*, so I said *"I'm not going"*.

Mick Gornall then asked, *"are you refusing to go to Brendan's office?"*

I said, *"If you are putting it like that, then yes"*.

Mick Gornall and Derek Anders stormed off to Brendan's office. They came back and Mick asked me to go into his office.

He looked at the clock and it was 5 to 5. Mick then said from 5 o'clock tonight you don't talk to me or Derek about Union issues. The management no longer recognised me as a shop steward for doing my job properly.

12. On the 6th August 1997 I attended a Branch Committee Meeting in the Unison office and in the minutes of the meeting Eddie Tickle brought up *security problems in Security re. victimisation of the Steward – full-time official to look into this.* The full-time official was Jim Keegan and he never looked into this matter – it just never happened.

13. On the 14th August 1997 in the JCC meeting Kevan Nelson told me to bring up an earlier issue with Mick Gornall ref. Ged Philbin. Mick called me a liar – I could not take any more and I stormed out of the meeting. I went to work that evening and that was my last shift with St Helen's Council.

14. Sometime between August and September I called into work with my sick note in the evening and Derek Anders was there.

We got into an argument over the job and I reminded Derek when he was a Patrol Officer, how he used to sit in the Rest Room all night playing cards and booking in and out of premises when in fact they were sat in the Rest Room.

Derek replied aggressively that the job got done. I said the job got done on paper but not physically like it should have been. Derek then threatened me – he is going to send me to the work's doctor. I stayed very calm and said, *"if that's what you want to do then do it".*

At the beginning of September I was sent to the Works Doctor. 10/11/98 I wrote to Peter Mavers (Assistant Director) as follows:

A member of staff was off sick a week before I went off. I was sent to the Works Doctor after three weeks and he was off for five weeks and not sent (WHY).

Peter Mavers replied on the 24/11/98.

I understand that when you brought your sick note in to the Security Office you invited the Supervisor to send you to the Council's Doctor. All medical appointments are made on an individual basis subject to the individual employee's circumstances.

Firstly, it was the Deputy Head of Security who sent me to the work's doctor and not a Supervisor and secondly, I was sent to the work's doctor because I got the better of Derek when I told him the job only got done on paper when he was Patrol Officer and not physically done and Derek 'spat his dummy out' and sent me to the work's doctor – again I have been singled out.

15. On the 10th September 1997 Paul Haunch (Regional Officer of Unison) wrote to Mick Fitzsimmons, Head of Local Government North West Region), stating that, *their Steward, Rob Steele, had discovered that the deal agreed between the GMB and the Authority, disadvantaged the bulk of his members. Indeed he has investigated at length in great detail the agreement struck prior to his employment. Rob Steele has worked very hard on this case, which is exposing the Authority as a con merchant.*

16. Sometime in September 1997 I called into the Council Depot to have a cup of tea and a chat with the lads, when Tony Marsh came out of the office and told me Mick Gornall told him to tell me,*"I'm not welcome here anymore"*. I found this remark rather strange as I was still employed with the Council. This made me feel they were trying to get rid of me out of Security and out of the Council.

I wrote to Peter Mavers 10/11/98 – here is an extract from my letter:

Mick Gornall told the Coordinators that I am not welcome in the depot anymore. This was well before any termination of employment took place.

Peter Mavers replied 24/11/98 – here is an extract from his letter:

The decision that you should not be allowed into the depot was taken by Mr Moffat who felt that as you were suffering work based stress, coming into work would only exacerbate your situation.

This statement is not true, the decision was made by Mick Gornall and only Mick Gornall. The instruction came from Mick Gornall that I was not welcome there any more and not Peter Moffat. If it would have come from Peter Moffat then Tony Marsh would have stated it was him and not Mick Gornall. Also Peter Moffatt would have put it in writing to me. They are all just trying to cover up for each other and all they are doing is 'banging more nails in their coffins'.

17. Sometime in October 1997 I was on the Market and met up with Kenny Watterson and Mick Rimmer. They invited me into their security office and I had a cup of tea with them. As I was leaving, Paul Molyneux and Bernard Day turned up. Paul Molyneux went back to the office and told Mick Gornall that I had grabbed Bernard around the throat. Mick Gornall later asked Bernard and Bernard said it didn't happen.

A few weeks later I was sat in the Rest Room next to Ged Philbin and Bernard came in and we were talking about Paul Molyneux saying I had grabbed Bernard around the throat. Bernard turned around and stated that Mick Gornall got him in the office and told him if you would have said Rob Steele grabbed you around the throat I could have got rid of him straight away. He wanted Bernard to tell lies to get rid of me (i.e. sack me). This is now the **seventh** time they have threatened me with the sack.

I wrote to Peter Mavers on the 10/11/98 – here is an extract:

Gornall's mate Molyneux told Gornall that I grabbed Bernard Day around the throat. Gornall got Bernard in to the office and told him he would get it sorted.

Peter Mavers replied 24/11/98 – here is an extract from his letter:

The Head of Security did indeed interview Mr B Day regarding an incident involving yourself at the Market. Other issues were alleged by Mr Day but to date these have not been taken any further.

What these other issues were I have not got a clue and I have not said anything to Bernard that would raise any issues – more lies.

18. Just before I went off sick I serviced Mick Gornall's car and Derek Anders and Paul Molyneux's cars. Mick asked me if I would service his car and said if you think you will get grief from the lads you don't have to do it. I told Mick I would service his car and he said to me he will keep it discreet to prevent any tension from the other Security Officers. This was in July 1997 and sometime in October 1997 Mick Gornall told the lads, *"I don't know why Rob hates me so much – he serviced my car just before he went off sick"*. He made this statement to them as they hate him and he wanted them to fall out with me as it was the lads who were giving me all the ammunition to fire at him and he wanted to cause trouble between them and myself.

At the end of the day it failed as Tony Marsh, Phil Houghy and Dave Anders were giving me all the information and paperwork I required up until 2008 when they got their pay rise. I was just being used to get them what they wanted and when they got what they wanted they would not give me any more information so I could get my justice.

19. In October 1997 I called into the Union office and I was talking to Steph – in conversation she thought I was on about something completely different and she said that Eddie Tickle was also disgusted with the letter Brendan Farrell had sent Eddie so I quizzed Steph about the letter and I found out it was about myself. Kevan Nelson came into the office and I told him I wanted

a copy of it – he was reluctant to give me a copy, butI insisted he gave me a copy and told me it's not to be put in circulation.

The letter read as follows:

31 July 1997

Re: Rob Steele – Unison Shop Steward – Security.

I refer to the above and becoming increasingly concerned in respect of Mr Steele's behaviour and conduct within the section.

He is disrupting a critical service with apparently no concept of the issues and procedures of Employee Relations. He had now informed Mike Gornall today 31/7/97 that he will not speak to management on pay issues, except in your presence.

This stance has no bearing on the operation of the section and I now fail to see why I should afford him any facilities in respect of his trade union duties.

Accordingly I have advised Mike Gornall and Derek Anders in respect of any dealings with Mr Steele as I have no confidence that management or service delivery issues are capable of being addressed in this climate.

I await an early meeting to resolve this issue.

Yours sincerely,

Brendan Farrell
Acting Assistant Director

cc M Gornall
D Anders
Mr E Tickle, Unison, 91 Corporation Street, St Helen's

The statement Brendan has made he had now informed Mike Gornall today 31/7/97 that he will not speak to management on pay issues except in your presence is also untrue as I did not discuss any such thing that day 31/7/97.

The first thing I did with this letter was to take it to my MP Peter Kilfoyle.

20. Between my first and second visit to the Work's doctor someone contacted me from the Council. I'm not quite sure but I'm convinced it was Pam Gray, Personnel Manager and whoever it was told me what the Work's doctor had said about me. I don't remember what was said but I was not very happy about it. When I went on my second visit to Dr Fiona Page I repeated what the Council had said to me and I swore at her for setting me up in the last meeting with her. I told her *"you are all p*****g in the same pot"*.

Dr Page then stated,*"I have been used"*.

Also in my consultation with Dr Page she told me to hand my file over to the Union and I told her no way am I handing my files over to the Union as I don't trust them. The files are staying in my possession.

After our consultation, because of what happened with the Council, myself and her, she read out exactly what she was going to write to the Council so there was not a repeat of her being used to get at me again.

On the 21st October 1997 Occupational Health Physician Dr Fiona Page wrote to the Council:

Mr Steele is very poorly. I have suggested further treatment via his GP. It would be prudent for the Council to limit contact with him as far as possible. Contact will only serve to exacerbate his condition.

21. On the 28th October 1997 I called into the Union office. Thelma told me that Brendan Farrell had contacted her on the phone and told Thelma that he wanted to see me in his office on Tuesday.

I went mad in the union office and I told Thelma and Steph that the Work's doctor told them not to have any contact with me as I am very poorly and contact will only exacerbate my condition. Steph told me to calm down and forget it; I was really annoyed as this was after receiving advice from Dr Page to stay away from me.

22. My Doctor asked me to see a Psychiatrist and on the 3rd November 1997 Dr Dutta, Psychiatrist, visited my home. I talked to him in great detail about what was going on in the Council. I talked to him for two hours. As Dr Dutta got up to leave he stated, *"they have used a psychological approach to wear you down"*.

23. I went to Peter Kilfoyle the first Friday in November as his surgeries are every first and third Friday in the month. I told Peter Kilfoyle MP the problems I was having with the management and I was in dispute with them. I also told Peter about Brendan ringing Thelma in the Union office trying to get me in to work after the work's doctor had told them to stay away from me. Peter asked me if I had a sick note in and I told him it was for three months. Peter wrote to the following people, as follows:

11 November 1997

Dear Mr Farrell
Dear Mr Gornall
Dear Mr Nelson and Mr Tickle,

Re Robert Steele, Security

Mr Steele, as you are aware, has been in some dispute with management. I have dealt with Mr Steele before on a different issue and understand that the stress under which he was placed by the problems he faced at that time.

I am given to understand that his general practitioner has signed him off work for three months due to the very great stress he is now undergoing. However, Mr Steele tells me that he is being heavily pressed to go into work, despite his medical certification.

Will you please tell me how you see this matter? Is he in fact being pressed to come into work? If so, what are the circumstances, which merit him attending work despite his doctor's advice to say home?

Yours sincerely,
Peter Kilfoyle MP
Liverpool Walton

Brendan Farrell wrote back as follows:

18 November 1997

Dear Mr Kilfoyle,

Re Mr Robert Steele, Security Officer St Helen's Metropolitan Borough Council.

I refer to the above and have respectfully taken liberty of replying on behalf of myself and Mr Mike Gornall (Head of Security) who has received a similar letter from yourself.

I can confirm that Mr Steele is employed within the Security section and that he holds the position of a representative with the local branch of Unison. However, I would take odds with Mr Steele's assertion that he is in dispute with management and I am sure that this can be confirmed by the Unison Branch Secretary at St Helen's MBC.

There are obvious routine issues that require resolution but these will be addressed via the Local Consultation procedures. I do feel though that perhaps these issues may have had an effect on Mr Steele and have contributed to the stress he is now suffering.

In terms of his being pressed into returning to work. I can categorically assure you that this is not the case. Mr Steele has been absent since 21 August 1997 and in accordance with Council procedures has been referred to the Council's Occupational Health Advisor. In support of this contact was made with Mr Steele via his trade union (due to the sensitive circumstances) to arrange a welfare visit to him. Unfortunately Mr Steele has misinterpreted the motives of this welfare visit and become even more distressed.

Mr Steele will continue to be monitored in accordance with the Council procedures and hopefully, he will resume his duties in the future.

If I can be of any further assistance then please do not hesitate to contact me.

Yours sincerely,
Brendan Farrell
Personnel Manager

I would firstly like to comment on Brendan stating, *"however, I would take odds with Mr Steele's assertion that he is in dispute with management and I am sure that this can be confirmed by the Unison Branch Secretary at St Helen's MBC"*. If the 83 grievances and the 23 personal grievances you have already read are not a dispute with management then what is he – I believe he is just a liar.

Secondly, *"there are obvious routine issues that require resolution but these will be addressed via the local consultation procedures"*.

These issues have already been dealt with in previous JCC meetings that were brushed under the carpet and they were not addressed via the Local Consultation procedures. They went far beyond routine issues. Again more lies.

Also, if the Branch Secretary would have confirmed that I was not in dispute with management then he would have also been lying as on the 6th August 1997 the Branch Secretary stated, *problems within security re victimisation of the Steward – full time officer to look into this.*

Thirdly, contact was made with Mr Steele via his Trade Union (*due to the sensitive circumstances*) to arrange a welfare visit. This statement was is not true as it was Mick Gornall who rang me at home and told me that personnel are visiting me on the 6th October 1997.

I told Kevan Nelson they were coming and he said he is going to cancel it as they have already 'stitched you up'. I was not complaining to Peter Kilfoyle about the welfare visit on the 6th October 1997 but the statement Brendan Farrell made to Thelma on the 28th October 1997 where he told her he wants to see me in his office on Tuesday.

I know for a fact if I would have gone to his office I would have received another verbal attack and even been threatened with the sack. Brendan Farrell never had the 'balls' to admit he had rung Thelma and arranged this meeting – he just tried to lie his way out of it.

Eddie Tickle wrote to Peter Kilfoyle as follows:

13 November 1997

Dear Mr Kilfoyle,
Re: Rob Steele
I refer to your letter of 11th November 1997.

I am able to confirm that Rob is an accredited Unison Steward for the Security Division of St Helen's MBC by whom he is employed as a Security Officer.

As you are aware Rob is currently absent on sick leave. During his absence he has maintained contact with his office and in the near future, he will be attending a Unison Convalescence Centre. On the 26th November 1997 he will be visited at home by Kevan Nelson, Branch Convenor and Jim Keegan, Regional Officer.

I can assure you that to our knowledge Rob is not being pressed to go into work although it was recently agreed that Personnel and a Unison Branch Officer visit him on a strictly welfare basis.

I am satisfied that the trade union is providing the appropriate support to our member.

Yours sincerely,
E Tickle
Branch Secretary

To say that *'to our knowledge Rob is not being pressed to go into work'* when Thelma and Steph both knew about the phone call from Brendan Farrell telling them he wants me in his office on Tuesday and both of them being secretaries in the Unison office would have had to inform either Eddie Tickle or Kevan Nelson to cancel the meeting on the Tuesday – so Unison did have knowledge. I was being pressed to go into work and also when Mick Gornall rang me to arrange a meeting on a welfare visit on the 6th October no Unison Branch Officer was going to visit – now I believe Eddie is telling lies.

24. Sometime in November my phone rang at 21.25. It was Alan Bolger, he told me to be careful playing snooker as Derek Anders has told a couple of the lads if I catch Rob Steele playing snooker I will sack the b*****d.

I put the phone down and rang Kevan Nelson at 21.30 and told him what Alan had said. Kevan informed Jim Keegan and a couple of days later Jim phoned me and told me he would arrange for me to see Thompsons Solicitors.

From November 24th to January I had left numerous phone messages to find out about going to Thompsons and eventually Jim rang me in January and said I would be seeing Thompsons Solicitors Feb 8th 1998. On two separate occasions I rang Stephen Pinder of Thompsons and Jim had still not made me an appointment. It was a couple of months later. Jim Keegan finally made me an appointment with Thompsons. This is now the **eighth** time I have been threatened with the sack in a 16 month period.

I wrote to Peter Mavers on the 10/11/98 regarding Derek Anders. I took up snooker and Derek Anders said to the lads, *"if I catch Rob Steele playing snooker I'll sack the b*****d"*.

Peter replied 24 November 1998:

> *Derek Anders has no recollection of the allegation you make but in any case would have no power to carry out the nature of the threat made in your allegation. As a trade union representative I would have thought you would understand the Council's disciplinary procedure.*

In the same letter I also brought up Derek Anders saying to a member of staff, *"blame your colleagues off sick I'll sack the b*****s"* – meaning myself and Jimmy Goodier.

I got the same comments as above from Peter Mavers. I know for a fact Derek made these statements as he made the same statement to me when we were discussing staff shortages and Derek said to me, *"blame your colleagues off sick – I'll sack the b*****ds"*. That remark was to Jimmy Goodier and Terry Cunliffe. This comment was Derek's favourite saying so I know dam well he said it, especially when he made the statement to myself.

25 On the 24th November 1997 Kevan Nelson, Unison Convener and Jim Keegan, Regional Officer for Unison, came to my house. The first thing Kevan said to me was, *"under the circumstances you should leave the Council altogether"*.

I said, *"yes, I would go now – let's talk tribunal"*.

Kevan said *"what for?"*

I said, *"discrimination of a Shop Steward, ill-health, loss of earnings, intimidation, harassment and anything else you can throw at them"*.

Kevan did a complete U turn and said I should get back to work as soon as possible.

I then said to Jim Keegan, *"if Kevan 'f****d up' you would cover his arse"*.

Jim replied, *"yes I would"* and Jim Keegan did just that when I reported Kevan to the General Secretary of Unison.

I wrote to the General Secretary on the 4/3/98:

Dear Mr Bickerstaffe,

I wrote to you on the 20/2/98. I received your reply dated 25 February 1998 on behalf of David Picking.

I have twice rang Brian Devine and he has not returned my request to speak to him.

I have reported several things to Kevan Nelson. He has told me I must remember they are Unison members too. I told him that Brendan Farrell and Mick Gornall have twice accused him for us being on a low wage.

Kevan Nelson and Jim Keegan both came to my home on Monday 24th November. Kevan said under the circumstances we feel you should leave the Council altogether. I said "yes I would go now, let's talk tribunal".

Kevan said, "what for?"

I said, "ill-health, loss of earnings, discrimination of a Shop Steward, harassment, intimidation".

Kevan did a complete U TURN and said, "we will get you back to work as soon as possible". I said to Jim Keegan, "if Kevan fucked up you would cover his arse". He said, "yes I would".

There is a lot more I can tell you. I spoke to Jerry Birmingham, MP for St Helen's about our wages on Saturday 28th Feb 98. He told me it's a case for a tribunal. This is twice Jim Keegan had denied our department a tribunal.

I am seeing Peter Kilfoyle MP on Friday 6/3/98 and I'm telling him what's going on. I have kept photocopies of my letters. I will expose your Union to the papers.

Yours faithfully,
Mr R Steele

Mike Fitzsimons, Head of Local Government for Unison wrote back as follows:

19 March 1998

Dear Mr Steele,

I refer to the Regional Secretary's letter to you of 4 March. I would advise you that I have received copies of your correspondence and I am now investigating your complaint.

I shall be back in touch with you as soon as my investigations are complete.

Yours sincerely,
Mike Fitzsimmons
Head of Local Government

Mike Fitzsimmons then replied 29th April 1998:

Dear Mr Steele,

Complaint to General Secretary.

I have been asked by the Regional Secretary to respond to the terms of your 4 March 1998 written complaint to the General Secretary.

Your letter was received at Unison headquarters on 10 March 1998 and as you will recall acknowledged by Mr Pickering on 13 March 1998. I am sorry for not replying sooner but it has been necessary to consider the terms of your complaint in detail.

Your case raises a number of point,s which merit a response as follows.

Firstly, there is clearly a misunderstanding regarding the 24th November 1997 visit to your home as Kevan Nelson and Jim Keegan have a different recollection of what was said. I know from my Regional Officer that his principal concern throughout has been for your health on the one hand and securing your employment with the Council on the other.

I consider this to be a load of b******s. I believe the Regional Officer had done nothing whatsoever. Jim did tell me I had an appointment with Thompsons Solicitors on the 8th Feb 98 after I had put pressure on him to get me to the Solicitors and when

I rang Stephen Pinder at Thompsons he knew nothing about the appointment. My MP Peter Kilfoyle had to write to Jim Keegan three times to get him to do his job and help me.

> *My understanding is that the consistent advice given you by Unison is that your interests are best served by securing your return to your substantive post as Security Officer with the Council. This of course is on the basis such a return accords with the advice of your GP etc and is in line with your own wishes. Unison would assist you in achieving this.*

I would like to know what this consistent advice given by Unison was – they never approached me with any.

> *If this is not practicable for whatever reason, then our advice would be for you to secure redeployment to another suitable position with the Council on agreed terms and conditions of service. Again, Unison would provide all necessary advice and assistance with this option.*

> *Only if your medical advice was strongly to the effect that you should end your employment with the Council and this accorded with your own wishes, would we consider advising on this option. Again Unison would lend any necessary advice, assistance in this process.*

> *As none of the above processes have yet been exhausted Unison cannot accept that you have been denied access to or support for industrial tribunal proceedings. On the contrary, our advice has been to try to resolve your position without the need for tribunal proceedings arising.*

The only advice I received was from Kevan Nelson telling me to leave the Council altogether, which would have been a reason for tribunal proceedings arising.

> *As regards your payment position, both the Branch Officials and my Regional Officer agree that the earlier consolidation/*

assimilation exercise should have resulted in a Scale 4 grading instead of the Scale 3, which currently prevails. However, this agreement was entered into by another Trade Union and I understand predates your employment with the Council. Given this providing the Council are paying you in accordance with your contract i.e. Scale 3, then there is no right to refer to a tribunal under the provisions of the Employment Rights Act 1996.

As earlier advised by the Regional Officer those employees in the post at the time of the agreement who received protection of salary, would have the right to go to tribunal if the protected level of salary was not being paid to them. We are not aware this is the case for any of those employees.

Paul Haunch informed Mike Fitzsimmons by letter 10th September 1997 so he was aware. Here is an equal pay claim for 400 cooks. Dinner ladies want the same deal as men. A group of more than 400 school cooks could open the floodgates for multi-million pound payouts if they win their case for equal pay.

The workers, all women, employed by St Helen's Council believe they are entitled to the same pay and conditions as Council workers in manual jobs such as road sweepers and bin men who are mostly men.

Manual workers boost their pay by up to two-thirds with performance bonuses but these are not available to catering employees on the same grade. An employment tribunal preliminary hearing in Liverpool on 13/1/2003 heard that the Council thought they were liable and settled the equal pay claims in December 1999 in a £1.25 M settlement. The tribunal was told that they had also agreed with the Unions to introduce a fair pay structure but problems with the scheme caused delays. More than three years on the structure is still not in place, which is why the union Unison is taking the Council to an employment tribunal.

The Union is pressing for the Council to pay out more than £4M.

Unison wants the same agreement that was given to a breakaway group of 39 St Helen's workers who took their case to an earlier tribunal and won. Mr Keegan added the value of these claims ran into millions of pounds and could have seen the collapse of the school dinner service in St Helen's. We understood the authority would get on and conduct reviews and this would yield equal pay but as the Council has not done this, then they are vulnerable to claims.

Brendan Farrell, Head of Human Resources for St Helen's Council, said the agreement was that if their jobs were kept in-house then the equal pay claim would be withdrawn. The spirit of the agreement was here is some cash now and we will address the gradings in the future with everyone else. They did not deal with security until five years later 2008 and put them on a scale 2 instead of scale 4 to be in line with the Hall Keepers and Park Rangers.

Landmark fair pay award for 36 dinner ladies St Helen's Council may have to pay massive legal costs to a group of dinner ladies after a lengthy legal battle over equal pay.

They lost their case in the House of Lords last Wednesday (April 25) when they ruled unanimously that 36 women had been victimised by Town Hall bosses. Now the Council Chiefs will have to pick up the pieces which will include compensation costs, the legal costs of the court cases and making sure that pay is equal across the board.

GMB Secretary, Brian Strutton, who has backed the women from the outset said this is a landmark ruling and just shows how far these dinner ladies had to go to prove they had been badly treated.

If the Council had admitted their wrong doings in the first place, St Helen's taxpayers would not be out of pocket. Now they will have to foot the huge bill.

The Law Lords condemned the Council saying this is a clea- cut case of the victims being victimised in their ruling.

The Court heard how in 1998 510 dinner ladies claimed equal pay with male Road Sweepers. These men were getting paid more than they were, but on the same pay scale.

After many negotiations the majority accepted the terms of a Council settlement but the remainder (the 36 dinner ladies) took their case to the Employment Tribunal and won.

Just two months before these claims were heard a senior Council official sent letters saying that, if they did not back down then there could be redundancies and the price of school dinners across the Borough would go up to cover the extra legal costs.

Mr Strutton said the women who decided to continue fighting the Council were told in no uncertain terms, that their decision to continue with the case would have a detrimental effect on those in the schools.

Michelle Cronin, the women's Solicitor at Thompsons, said this judgement should make it clear once and for all to employers what their response to equal claims should be. They can negotiate with the Trade Unions and their Solicitors by all means to avoid litigation for all parties but they cannot intimidate the individuals and expect to get away with it.

A Council spokeswoman said the Council stands by it's defence that it sent the letters as an honest and reasonable employer attempting to settle equal pay claims whilst ensuring that the claimants were aware of the financial consequences of not doing.

I have experienced first hand that St Helen's Councilare not an honest and reasonable employer and everything you read will confirm my statement.

What you have read above – there is no right to a tribunal under the provisions of the Employment Act 1996 has been blown right out the window. Tommy Twist T & GWU, Les Gilford GMB, Charlie Lennard GMB, Kevan Nelson Unison, Eddie Tickle Unison, Jim Keegan Unison, Mike Fitzsimmons Unison – all had the opportunity to put our wages right and failed to do so.

On the general position of grading, the Branch are continuing via the security JCC to press the case for Scale 4 grading to apply as soon as possible. The whole question of grading and allowances will have to be reviewed as and when single status negotiations get underway within the Council.

This was stated April 1998 and Security did not get single status until February 2008 – 10 years later and they did not get Scale 4 like Mike Fitzsimmons stated they got Scale 2 when in fact it should have been Scale 4 to be on the same pay as the Hall Keepers and Ranger Service.

Finally, on the question of harassment by Messrs Farrell and Gornall and the affect you say this has had on your health. I was happy for your case to be referred to Thompsons for assessment in the first instance and I believe Jim Keegan communicated this to you. Since then, however, you have stated in your correspondence and at meetings with Unison that you feel your position arises in part because of Unison's failure to properly support you in your role as Steward.

Because of the implications this has for both yourself and Unison, then on advice from the legal department it is felt best if you now seek independence advice on this matter.

Jim Keegan did tell me I had an appointment with Thompsons on the 8th February 98 and when I contacted Stephen Pinder he knew nothing about it. I did not trust the Union since 24th November 1997 when Jim and Kevan came to my house and told me under the circumstances you should leave the Council altogether. The above letter from Mike Fitzsimmons confirmed I should not trust the Union.

I replied to Mike's letter as follows:

5/5/98

Dear Mike,

1) *I have received your letter 29th April 1998. Firstly, there is NO misunderstanding regarding the visit to my home. I know what they said and I will swear on the Bible – on my Mother and Father's lives – they said that.*

2) *When I first went off Kevan told me he wanted me back at work within a month on the 24th of November. Kevan told me it's in the best interest that I leave the Council altogether. When I said I will go and asked for a tribunal. Ref. their interests have been to get me back into work – this is incorrect.*

3) *I saw Personnel in the Town Hall the last week of March. I was told I am not going back to Security. I also saw them on the 1st May 98 and I have been told they are going to finish me. Jim, Kevan and Eddie all knew about these meetings.*

4) *This should never have happened. I should have had assistance when these problems started. Kevan and Eddie both knew what was going on. Branch Committee Meeting 6/8/97 Section 8 Security – problems within Security re victimization of the Steward. Full-time official to look into this? What has been done – it's now May 98.*

5) *I requested a tribunal on the 24/11/97 when I was told Derek Anders said, "if I catch Rob Steele playing*

snooker I will sack the b*****d". I rang Kevan at 21.30 and told him I received a phone call a couple of days later and Jim told me he would arrange for me to see Thompsons Solicitors. I had to leave numerous messages then Jim contacted me in January 98 and said I would be seeing the Solicitor February 8th 98. Unison have denied me access and no support whatsoever.

6)   When I went on the interview for the job as Security Officer I was told by Mick Gornall that in 1991 they were on manual grade 3 plus allowances and they added them all together and it came to APT & C Scale 3. This is incorrect; it came to P.T. 19 Scale 4. Talking about my contract it states I will receive a rest day for each Bank Holiday I work. I also should have received a rest day for each bank holiday that falls on a rest day. I have never received any in the six years. This is not a mistake it's been brought up in previous JCC meetings that was never minuted.

7)   I have spoken to the leader of the Council. I have selected six Councillors from St Helen's Council and I will be going through the wages with them. I have done the figures and I'm the only person who understands them. Unison have kept me in the dark ref single status. I have sent you a copy – these figures are for 97 – 98. You can see how much the Patrol Officers are being robbed.

8)   Jim rang Thompsons to make arrangements for me to see them. I rang Thompsons twice to see if Jim had made me that appointment. Both times I was told NO. I then complained to the General Secretary. No effort was made by Jim and I would have been at Thompsons, week commencing 8th Feb 98.

The Cabinet Office Minister believes me (Peter Kilfoyle).
Jerry Birmingham MP of St Helen's believes me.
Now the leader of the Council (Mike Doyle) believes me.

Things I have stated that have been denied have come to light. You cannot escape the truth, it comes out in the end. It may have cost me my job. I am going to continue to get the Patrol Officers what they are entitled to because no one else is.

Yours faithfully,
R Steele

I first got suspicious about the Union when Eddie Tickle told Peter Kilfoyle MP, *"to our knowledge Rob is not being pressed into work"* and when Kevan told me, *"under the circumstances you should leave the Council all together"* confirmed my suspicions and I did not approach my Union until I wanted to take the Council to court for personal injury in February 1998 and I still continued to deal with my personal matters with the Council as I did not trust Kevan, Eddie and Jim Keegan.

I visited Dr Dutta, Psychiatrist, on a domiciliary visit on the 20 February 1998 and he wrote to Dr Page, Occupational Health Physician. In February he told me that he has been victimised and is going for a tribunal. He talked at length as to what the management and the Union representatives were doing. He said they are all in a clique together. He also said that he believed there has been a cover up between his managers and the Union bosses.

Mike Fitzsimmons did not have the decency to reply to my letter 5/5/98. I wonder why. I did not trust the Union. Two Security Officers saw Brendan Farrell and Kevan Nelson going into a pub together in the evening. I confronted Kevan about this and he said, *"I will drink with who I like"*. Brendan and Kevan were best of friends and that's why I consider I received no support from the Union.

Had I got the support and the truth came out Brendan and Mick Gornall would have been sacked. They rather got rid of me, an honest Shop Steward than what I believe to be a corrupt management.

I had a couple of meetings with Sheila Samuels and Russ Damson in the Town Hall about all the problems I had with management and I told them both. *"I do not trust the Union"* and I continued to take my campaign all the way on my own as I stood a better chance not being stabbed in the back by my union representatives.

Because I got no where with Sheila Samuels, Head of Human Resources and Russ Damson, Manager in the Town Hall, I went to Mike Doyle, Council Leader and I went to his place of work and I told him everything that was going on in Security and he told me they are very serious allegations I was making. I said, *"they are not allegations, they are facts"*.

26. On the 10th February 1998 Leader of the Council, Mike Doyle wrote to me:

Dear Mr Steele,

Further to our recent discussions you have provided quite a lot of information and raised concerns about a number of issues that require detailed examination.

This was never dealt with I had a couple more meetings with Mike and my father came along to witness the lack of support I was getting. Mike Doyle told my father that someone who does not know your son has told me it's a waste of time having Security on Pets Corner as there is never a Security Officer up there and Mike Doyle, being leader of the Council, should have done something about it, along with all my other grievances.

27. *March 1998 ref JCC meeting. Peter Moffat referred to a recent investigation of Security by District Audit. The complaints made are unfounded and Peter was certain that Audit would confirm this.*

Peter had looked into the allegations personally and found them to be spurious. Audit were always welcome in sections under Peter's management but these allegations appeared mischievous.

Peter was disturbed that it appeared that someone within the Security Services was passing information to a member of the service who was currently off sick. This type of behaviour was corrosive to team spirit. Any issues should be raised via the normal chain of command.

If people were reluctant to raise issues with their Supervisors they could be raised directly with Peter or via the Union. It was a waste of time having a JCC meeting if issues were not raised in this forum.

I have raised 83 grievances in total and in the region of 80 were discussed in previous JCC meetings and most of them were not minuted and not one issue was put to bed.

In my opinion Peter Moffat is talking 'out of his a**e'. Also Peter claims he had looked into my grievances when in fact he had not seen them and found them to be spurious. I believe that two District Auditors covered up a total of 10 of the grievances and did not look at the other 73 – I had and it was a majority of the security officers passing me the information, not one individual as they looked at me to solve their problems.

Kevan Nelson said the actions were not supported by Unison. No one in Security Services had colluded with this member of staff. Ged Philbin is the Steward and issues should be raised with him accordingly.

I pulled Ged up about him being Shop Steward and he told me you're the Shop Steward, I'm just standing in for you until you come back. Kevan Nelson no longer recognised me as the Shop Steward and Ged Philbin was not elected Shop Steward until after I was finished in September 1999. Once again in my opinion the Union was stabbing me in the back.

28. The first week in March 1998 I went to my MP Peter Kilfoyle and told him what was going on. Peter told me he is not having

this as the Council were ganging up on me and he said he is going to write to Mike Doyle Council leader to stop them ganging up on me.

29. On the 10th of March 1998 Peter Kilfoyle wrote to Mike Doyle as follows.

Dear Mike.

Ref: Robert Steele Security Officer St. Helen's MBC.

I understand you have spoken with Mr Robert Steele as indeed has Gerry Birmingham MP.

I did assist Mr Steele through a very protracted and complicated Building Society problem some years ago and understand well the stress he endured at that time.

However he seems to be even more stressed by his work situation, he feels that he is subjected to what his GP described as psychological warfare. His most concern has been the halving of his wages whilst he is on sick leave.

It would be in the interest of both the Council as employers and Mr Steele as an employee, for Mr Steele's situation to be resolved as quickly as possible. Would it help for you and me to meet and try to find a way forward?

Best Wishes
Peter Kilfoyle MP.
Liverpool Walton
Cc Mr R Steele
G. Birmingham MP. St. Helens
D. Watts MP. St. Helens

I did tell Peter it was my Psychiatrist Dr Dutta who made the statement not my GP and I also told him they have used a psychological approach to wear me down and not psychological warfare – it means more or less the same thing but I want it right.

Mike Doyle replied 16 March 1998.

Dear Peter.

Robert Steele Security Officer St. Helen's MBC.

Thank you for your letter dated the 10th March 1998 concerning one of your constituents Mr Steele an employee of St. Helen's MBC.

Mr Steele has had a number of meetings with both myself and senior officers from the personnel department, but continues to remain in a very stressed state. We have encouraged him to take the advice of his medical staff in an attempt to aid his recovery, but unfortunately this advice is not taken.

I feel it would be beneficial if we could meet to discuss the precise details of Mr Steele's case and would ask you to please ring my office to check diaries.

Yours Sincerely
Mike
Councillor Michael J Doyle J.P.
Leader of the Council

Firstly it is obvious, in my opinion that senior management from personnel are going to cover up for Brendan Farrell as he was the ex personnel manager. When he finished as Acting Assistant Director, he ended up as the senior person in personnel (Head of Human Resources)

In an attempt to aid my recovery they could have given me my panel of six Councillors and I could of confronted Brendan Farrell and Mick Gornall face to face and rectified the grievances and

I could have returned to work in a healthy environment with immediate effect.

Peter Kilfoyle MP wrote back to me on 7 April 1998:

Dear Mr Steele

Your message left at my office when you called has been passed to me by my staff and I have noted your comments.

However I will be meeting with Councillor Doyle leader of St. Helen's Council after the Easter holidays and will then decide how best to proceed with your case.

Yours Sincerely

Peter Kilfoyle MP
Liverpool Walton

At the end of the day I do not believe that a meeting ever did take place between Peter Kilfoyle MP and Mike Doyle leader of St. Helen's Council.

Once again I was let down by the system.

30. On the 1 May 1998 Russ Danson, Personnel Manager, Control and Monitoring, the man I complained to also along with Sheila Samuels in 1997 wrote to Peter Moffat:

Re: Robert Steele, Security Officer.

I have met with Mr Steele today in order to assess his future employment prospects.

Mr Steele was examined by the Council's Occupational Health physician on 28 April 1998, the Physician's opinion being that Mr Steele is unfit for work for the foreseeable future. Mr Steele's view on re-deployment is that his substantive post is Security Officer and he does not wish to return to any other employment in the Council.

Given this situation and the length of time Mr Steele has been on sick leave, I believe that the appropriate recommendation to you is that you consider terminating Mr Steele's employment on the grounds of ill-health.

Should you decide on this course of action, Mr Farrell, your Departmental Personnel Officer will advise on the correct procedure to be used.

RJ Danson
Personnel Manager, Control and Monitoring

Russ Danson, being the person I had three previous meetings with regarding my grievances with Mr Gornall and Mr Farrell in the Town Hall,in my opinion failed to do anything about my grievances and make my workplace habitable for me to return to a healthy environment, failed in his duty to do so as he was Brendan's boss. He decided to cover up for him and then got Brendan involved with my termination, what a joke.

I had a meeting with Peter Moffat, Assistant Director, on the 20th May 1998. Peter asked me to bring my father to the meeting but I decided to go on my own.

Eddie Tickle and Kevan Nelson were informed of the meeting and made no effort to offer me any support so I attended it on my own. Peter also mentioned to me being re-deployed to another job but no job was offered.

I told Peter,'I am going back to Security to sort Gornall out'.

Peter replied, 'What do you mean sort Gornall out'.

I said, 'To stop him bullying and to put the department right'.

Peter then turned round and said, 'Mr Farrell is in a position and staying in a position, Mr Gornall is in a position and staying in a position, therefore I'm terminating your employment'.

I have not only been threatened with my job eight times, I have now been sacked because nothing is going to get done about all the misdemeanours I consider Brendan Farrell and Mick Gornall have done and for me being the honest Union Representative, once again the Council would rather terminate my employment rather than sort out the grievances that made me ill in the first place and give me a healthy environment to return to with immediate effect.

Peter Moffat wrote to me as follows:

22 May 1998

Dear Mr Steele

Re: Termination of Employment

I write to confirm my decision on 20 May 1998 when I met with you to discuss your employment position and medical status. Mrs Gray, (Personnel) attended the meeting and you had been offered but declined the opportunity to be accompanied/represented.

During your nine months of absence, you have been medically examined by the Council's Occupational Health Advisor on several occasions. Her final report indicates that you are still unfit for your duties as a Security Officer and will not be fit for the foreseeable future. You agreed with the opinion and described the symptoms that prevented you from work. You informed me that you are receiving treatment under the care of a specialist which will continue at least until your next appointment in September 1998. I explored with you the possibility of a return to a different post but you were not in favour of pursuing this.

Taking all these circumstances into account my decision was to terminate your employment on the grounds of your incapacity to fulfil your contractual duties. You are entitled to a period of notice totalling six weeks and I will arrange for a payment to be made in lieu of this notice via payroll. When your employment ceases, you will also receive payment for any outstanding leave that you may have.

You have the right to appeal against my decision under the Council's internal procedure and/or to the relevant statutory bodies, e.g. Industrial Tribunal. Should you wish to exercise your right of appeal under the Council's procedures, please advise me in writing within 10 working days of delivery of this letter. As you were not represented at our meeting you may wish to take appropriate advice as to your statutory rights. If you do not wish to appeal, please contact myself on the above number or Pam Gray (456704) to enable the arrangements for payment in lieu of notice to be implemented.

I have, as you requested, addressed this letter to Avon Close from where you confirmed you do receive mail.

Finally, I would like to thank you for your service to the Security Section over the last six years and wish you a full recovery in time and best wishes for the future.

Yours sincerely

P Moffat
Assistant Director

I find Peter Moffat to be a total hypocrite as in March 1998 Peter stated he had looked into my allegations personally and found them to be spurious. The only allegations he could have looked into were the six selected by the District Auditor and there were a total of 83 and the six allegations if he did look into them then he would have seen they were not spurious but were true. To make the statement, 'my decision was to terminate your employment on the grounds of your incapacity to fulfil your contractual duties,' is in my opinion not correct.

In our meeting on 20 May 1998 he never mentioned terminating my employment on the grounds of ill-health but stated, 'Farrell is in a position and staying in a position, Gornall is in a position and staying in a position, therefore I am terminating your employment'. My employment was terminated because the Council had no intentions of investigating Brendan Farrell and Mick Gornall so they had to get rid of me.

I replied to Peter's letter on 4/6/98

Dear Mr Moffat

I am replying to your letter dated 22 May 1998.

I have taken Solicitors advice and I am appealing against your decision to terminate my employment. I am a bit concerned with a couple of things you have put in your letter.

Firstly, you had been offered but declined the opportunity to be accompanied/represented. I recall being asked to bring my father along and that's all. I had no offer from the union or anyone else.

Secondly, I explored with you the possibility of a return to a different post but you were not in favour of pursuing this. I will agree with you, you did mention re-deployment, at no time was I offered a different post. I also told you at this moment in time I am not fit enough to work anywhere and I told you I want to return to Security when I am, to sort Gornall out. I recall you asking me, 'what do you mean, sort Gornall out'. I replied, 'stop him bullying and put the Department right'.

I asked you had you worked Single Status out for the Security Department and you replied, 'I've had a dabble'. I then told you I worked it out at over £16,000 for last year. You replied, 'It's for the management and the union to negotiate. You're wrong Peter, Single Status is Single Status, it's not negotiable. It's the management and the unions negotiating in 1991 that has cost me my job. Farrell and Gornall have both told me the money was there for Scale 4 and Kevan Nelson said Scale 3 was ok. I have told Kevan this both times it was said to me. I know for a fact that in 1991 the union asked for Scale 4 and Farrell said no.

I look forward to my appeal.
Yours faithfully

Mr R Steele

31. I went to the Town Hall for my appeal on the 4 September 1998 after a letter from Peter Kilfoyle to Jim Keegan asked him whether or not he is representing me at my appeal. Jim Keegan came with me.

In the meeting Peter Moffat gave evidence against me so I told the Chairperson, Councillor Fletcher that I want to ask Peter Moffat a question. He said we don't do it in normal circumstances and he asked the panel of Councillors if they agree to it and none of them objected to it so I said to Peter, 'Did you say to me Farrell is in a position and staying in a position, Gornall is in a position and staying in a position, therefore I'm terminating your employment'.

Peter replied, 'I recall saying that Mr Farrell is in a position and staying in a position, Mr Gornall's in a position and staying in a position therefore I'm terminating your employment'. He made this statement after telling the Councillors that he finished me on the grounds of ill-health. The Councillors, hearing this statement had no alternative but to reinstate my employment, as had it gone to tribunal, the Council would have lost.

As we left the building Russ Danson came over to me and Jim and said, 'I don't know why you give him support, he did nothing but call you rotten'. As Russ walked off I told Jim I did tell Sheila Samuels and Russ Danson that I did not trust the Union because of the way I had been treated by the Union meaning Jim, Eddie Tickle, Kevan Nelson and Mike Fitzsimmons. I also reminded Jim about him covering up for Kevan Nelson when they visited my house on the 24 November 1997 and Jim said I don't remember. Jim replied I understand you're not well.

Kevan saying what I told Jim about Kevan telling me under the circumstances you should leave the Council altogether. Jim lied to me as he was looking across at Kevan when he said it to me. Also on that day I told Jim if Kevan f****d up you would cover his a**e and Jim replied, 'Yes I would' and I believe Jim did just that. Russ Danson being the man I complained to about Farrell and Gornall in September 1997, the same man who covered up for them with their misdemeanours instead of investigating my 83 grievances plus my 30 or so personal grievances.

32. I had just been reinstated with the Council when I received my P45 in the post. I went to Mike Doyle and complained to him about me receiving my P45. Mike sent Peter Mavers a memo and sent the same memo to Sheila Samuels on the 2 October 1998.

Subject: Mr R Steele, Avon Close, Walton.

Could you give a full account as to why the error occurred with regard to Mr Steele receiving his P45 from your section.

At a time when Mr Steele is convinced that we have some kind of vendetta against him, how am I to convince him otherwise.

I shall await your comments.

Mike Doyle
Councillor Michael J Doyle JP
Leader of the Council

A letter was sent to Sheila Samuels on the 12 October 1998

Mr B Farrell is dealing with this matter.

Dear Sheila

I refer to Councillor Doyle's letter in respect of the above and outline the explanation for Mr Steele's receipt of his P45 after the date of his reinstatement.

There are no excuses as you will deduce but I assure you that all Personnel, Wages and Security Management are aware of the issues surrounding Mr Steele and are acutely conscious of the sensitivity in dealing with this matter.

You will be aware that Mr Steele received his termination letter on 12 June 1998 with an effective date of termination of 24 July 1998. Normal procedures requested the input of a leaver to generate the P45 and this would be done irrespective of an appeal. However, due to the sensitive nature of this matter and pending the outcome of the appeal, which took place on 14, 29 July and 4 September 1998, we took a decision not to input the leaver until the matter was resolved. Had we done what we agreed to do, this problem would not have arisen.

Mr Steele was reinstated on 4 September 1998 and even before written confirmation arrived (11 and 16 September 1998), Pam Gray spoke to Anne Mason on 7 September 1998 and told her that Mr Steele had been reinstated and to check the financial position in terms of his sick pay entitlement.

Then for some unexplainable reason, Anne input a leaver for him around the 14 September 1998 which was contrary to what we had originally agreed to do and despite Pam's telephone call.

I have spoken to Anne three times about this matter and she is understandably very upset and distressed. She acknowledges her mistake and has apologised.

I have seen cover-ups before when I believe Mick Gornall got Jebby Robinson to take the wrap for Mick Gornall not having enough men to cover the shifts and getting Brendan to tell me Jebby had not distributed his men properly. I'd been in security too long to accept that feeble excuse and once again Brendan Farrell has used this Anne Mason as a scapegoat. If someone tells someone not to do something then they don't go and do the opposite. How come Brendan Farrell, the man I have been complaining about for all his misdemeanours is involved with all issues concerning myself? I know Brendan is also trying to cover up the issue with the P45!

33. On 12 October 1998, Sheila Samuels wrote to Jim Keegan as follows:

Dear Mr Keegan

I am writing in response to your letter dated 6 October 1998 addressed to Mr Leach in my office. Given our previous discussions on matters relating to Mr Steele and my concerns regarding a number of issues surrounding the whole sequence of events involving Mr Steele, yourselves and management within the Council, I have decided to respond personally to your letter.

Firstly, as you are aware the Authority's decision is that Mr Steele is reinstated as a Security Officer with the Authority. This being the case and as he is still unfit to undertake the duties of his post, he remains subject to the Authority's procedures in respect of long term sickness.

On the matter of the P45, I was made aware that the Department had made this error and I immediately instructed them to write to Robert explaining the position and offering an apology. A copy of that letter is attached which is self-explanatory.

With regard to the way forward, there are a number of issues, which concern me and I do not feel that it is sufficient in this case to deal with Robert's sickness absence in isolation without having regard to the many wider issues which have and continue to be raised by him in relation to his employment with the Authority.

It is my view that unless there is a frank and open debate with yourselves and management regarding these issues and all the issues put on the table, which has not been the case to date, it is likely that they will continue to fester in Robert's mind and may prejudice not only his return to full health but the ability to re-build links with the Council and facilitate a return to work. There are also issues around how best he is working towards recovery and the role in which you as his representative and the Council can play to assisting this.

As you know, Officers on many occasions have tried to ascertain the extent of his grievance against his Managers and the little information provided to the Council has been looked at by ourselves and the District Auditor. Whilst reference has been made to a dossier, full details have not been produced to the Council. Notwithstanding this, you informed me some time ago that the two officers about whom Robert has continually made assertions have approached you as members for advice expressing their concerns about the allegations. As you rightly pointed out to me, the Council has an obligation towards those two employees also.

In summary, my overriding concern is to put the necessary framework in place, which will:

1) *Ensure that Robert continues to be treated appropriately by the Department in terms of the application of the Authority sickness procedures.*

2) *Ensure that any allegations of Robert's which the Council should be addressing regarding other employees are clearly laid out so that in conjunction with yourselves, they can be dealt with appropriately.*

3) *Establish the parameters and way forward in respect of Robert's health and framework for achieving a return to work in the future, which will no doubt necessitate re-building links and relationships in the Authority.*

In order to move forward, I wish to hold a meeting with Managers and you as Robert's representative and specifically request that either Kevan Nelson or Eddie Tickle are also in attendance. I will also be seeking input either by written advice or attendance of our Occupational Health Unit.

I suggest 2pm on Wednesday 21 October as a suitable date and time to meet in my office. I think that it is an important issue to address and therefore hope that diaries can be adjusted to accommodate this. Please could you confirm whether or not you are able to meet at the suggested date and time.

Yours sincerely

Sheila Samuels
Head of Human Resources

Comments on Sheila Samuels' letter:

Firstly, Sheila stated unless there is a frank and open debate and that all issues are put on the table, I was not made aware of this meeting till after August 2009 when I put my case together and found the letter amongst my paperwork. As for a frank and open debate, there never was one. They did have the meeting on the

21 October 1998, issue one was discussed but issues two and three were not discussed. None of my allegations were clearly laid out and they were not dealt with appropriately and no building links and relationships in the Authority ever took place, in my opinion these points were not discussed.

Sheila Samuels stated to Jim Keegan as you rightly pointed out to me, the Council has an obligation towards those two employees, also meaning Brendan Farrell and Mick Gornall. The Council also had an obligation towards me along with the Union but they both decided to protect Brendan Farrell and Mick Gornall knowing of all their alleged wrongdoings and myself who only wanted justice, was sent down the river.

Sheila Samuels wrote to Jim Keegan on 10 November 1998 as follows:

Dear Mr Keegan

Mr R Steele, Housing Environmental & Contract Services Department.

I am writing in connection with the above employee with particular reference to the meeting between Unison, Peter Mavers and myself on 21 October 1998.

It was agreed inter alia at that meeting that in due course, arrangements would be made for a further appointment with our Occupational Health Unit as part of the long-term sickness monitoring procedures. We were all concerned to ensure that further information was available regarding Mr Steele's health status and progress towards recovery.

In accordance with this, I can confirm that an appointment has been made for Mr Steele to attend at the Occupational Health Unit on 20 November 1998 at 2:00pm. A separate letter is being written to Mr Steele by the Department.

In relation to the other issues we discussed at our meeting, you had agreed to make two points to Mr Steele and confirm this to us:

a)   That Unison is dealing with the issue of the pay rates for security force and

b)   That it was not in his or others interests for him to make assertions and/or threats regarding other staff members.

Perhaps you could confirm whether the above points have been made by Unison. I am aware that issue (a) is still being pursued by Mr Steele in the form of detailed correspondence to the Assistant Director.

Regarding issue (b), I confirm that to date the position remains as at the date of our meeting with no specific allegations having been made.

This letter was from Sheila Samuels, Head of Human Resources

Jim Keegan did not discuss or inform me of the above nor did I know of any letters on the 12 October 1998 or 10 November 1998 and that a meeting had taken place on Wednesday 21 October 1998. The first I knew of any of this was when I started sorting out my file in August 2009. I also had every right to make my assertions on my 83 grievances and as for making any threats to other members of staff it is total bullsh*t. I never made any threats towards Mick Gornall and Brendan Farrell whatsoever.

34. When I was out patrolling at Peter Street Community Centre, a gang of youths saw me and dropped three crates of Fanta and jumped over a fence and ran off. I picked up the cans of pop and put them in my vehicle and Eric Clarke, my supervisor informed the Police.

The Police came and the youths were stood on the corner and they caught one of them and the Police took the three crates of pop with them. I went round to Eric Clarke's house on 10 November 1998 and he asked me did I remember the incident at Peter Street Community Centre.

I told Eric, 'I do remember all of it'. He asked me did I know what happened to the 72 cans of pop.

I said 'the Police had it and it went back to the owner'.

Eric then said,'what if I told you I found the chitty in my pocket and went to the Police station and recovered the 72 cans of pop'.

Eric said he took the cans of pop into Mick Gornall's office and said they belong to Rob Steele. I replied,'I don't know anything about that'.

The same day, 10 November 1998, I wrote to Peter Mavers about the pop, here is the extract form that letter:

Dear Peter

Today I was asked if I remember an incident at Peter Street Community Centre. I did recall all of it and I was asked what happened to the 72 cans of pop. I said the Police took it away. He (Eric Clarke) then said the pop was collected from the Police station and ended up in Gornall's office.

I would like to know the whereabouts of the pop as it was not Council property and legally belonged to me. I did not know it had been recovered. You being a Magistrate will know it belonged to me and this is theft, and that is a sackable offence. I want to know where my pop went.

Peter Mavers responded on the 24 November 1998:

You wrote with regard to the cans of pop which were recovered from the Police. It is not correct to say you are entitled to their return as you discovered them in your capacity as a Security Officer. In my view the property therefore belongs to the Authority and to suggest they have been stolen from you is inaccurate.

I don't know how Peter could state the cans of pop belong to the Authority as Peter Waine received the set of ladders he found and later sold for £150 and Mick Fairclough found a mountain bike and he was given that and Terry Cunliffe found a knife and he kept that after it being released from the Police, yet once again I was singled out as Mick Gornall took my goods at the end of the day. In my opinion Mick Gornall stole my goods and Peter Mavers covered up for him.

I again went to Eric Clarke's house and Eric told me that Mick Gornall had rung him and asked him what had hed one with the cans of pop. Eric replied, 'I haven't got a clue'. Mick then said to Eric 'I must have shared them out with the lads'. Eric replied, 'I don't think so'.

I was speaking to one of the Security Officers about the pop and he told me that Mick Gornall was in his office and shouted to Paul Molyneux, 'Do you know what I did with the pop?'

Paul shouted back, 'You gave me a crate for the rugby team'. I believe it would have gone to Paul Molyneux's house as he has two kids and Mick Gornall had the other two crates for his two kids. At the end of the day Mick Gornall stole my cans of pop and kept it from me that they had been recovered. I only found out two to three years later from Eric Clarke or I would have been none the wiser.

I also went to ASDA and told the head of security what had happened and he was really annoyed and said that if anyone should have had the pop it should have been me.

I also wrote to the Chief of Police on the 10 December 1998 and explained the above and I told him it was PC Mike Hudson that dealt with the matter. I received a reply from the Mersey side Police on 16 December 1998.

Dear Sir

Thank you for your recent correspondence regarding the above.

Your letter has been passed to the incident management unit based in St Helen's who have responsibility for researching and analyzing complaints of this nature, and who will contact you in due course.

If you have any further problems or need to speak to the Officer dealing with your complaint, please contact Sergeant Wright at the Incident Management Unit.

Yours faithfully

Richard Williams
Area Commander

PC Mike Hudson rang me and said the Police should not have released the pop in the first place as it was evidence. He also told me that there was not enough evidence to bring charges against Mick Gornall for taking the pop as it was theft, yet there was enough evidence against two of the youths that took the pop in the first place.

At the end of the day I consider that Mick Gornall stole the pop knowing the pop was mine as Eric Clarke made it quite clear to Mick when he took the pop into his office and told him, "that's Rob Steele's pop".

The police brushed it under the carpet. At the end of the day Mick Gornall should have been sacked by the Council for theft and charged by the Police for theft. Both the Council and the Police decided otherwise. Had that have been any other member of Security that did it, they would have been sacked and charged.

35. I rang work on the 27 March 1999 to let them know I was returning to work on the Tuesday as I was going to my doctor on the Monday to get a return to work note.

Peter Mavers wrote to me on Monday 29 March 1999 and sent the letter to my home address and my parents' address by courier that day.

Dear Mr Steele

I have been informed by the Security Section that you telephoned on Saturday 27 March 1999 and indicated that you would be returning to work on 30 March 1999.

You will recall in previous discussions that you should direct all issues surrounding your employment position via myself. In respect of your statement on Saturday, I am informing you that I am not in a position at this time to allow you to return to work.

If you have anything you wish to discuss with me, please contact me at the above address.

Yours sincerely

P R Mavers
Assistant Director

I found Peter's statement rather strange and I knew they did not want me back. Also I was not aware in previous discussions that I had to direct all issues surrounding my employment position via Peter. The correct procedure is to contact your department by phone, which I did. I used the correct procedure for sickness. Like I said, at the end of the day they just wanted rid of me at all costs.

36. Once again Brendan Farrell got involved with my second termination.

He wrote to Dr Page as follows:

6 April 1999

Dear Dr Page

I am writing following discussions with Jan Ahmed in respect of the above. I understand that Mr Steele has failed to attend current medical examinations whereby I understand you are to make a final decision on his current medical condition and fitness for employment.

You will be unaware that Mr Steele has contacted his Manager stating he is about to return to work. He has also again begun to repeat spurious allegations against his colleagues and Managers. In addition Mr Steele has made it public knowledge, both verbally and in writing, that he has a psychiatric report which renders him permanently unfit to carry out his duties.

As I told Mrs Ahmed, I cannot compel Mr Steele to attend his medical without certain sanctions such as a breach of contract issues. I am also of the opinion that he too knows this and will deliberately fail to attend. In these circumstances I do feel the decision needs to be taken on his future and I would be grateful for your opinion, albeit based on the evidence you currently have.

Could you please provide me with your opinion in order that the Council can take the appropriate Management decision?

Yours sincerely
Brendan Farrell
Personnel Manager

Again Brendan Farrell is now involved for the second time with my dismissal. The same man who threatened me five times with dismissal during my time of being shop steward over a 14-month period, has now stuck the knife in to get me finished.

He is only the person I reported for all his wrong doings with Mick Gornall and the Council gave him the power to terminate my employment for the second time. I knew from the first few weeks I was off sick when Mick Gornall told Tony Marsh to tell me, "I'm not welcome here anymore", they were trying to get rid of me and I knew this for definite when Kevan Nelson, my convenor, came round to my house on the 24 November 1997 and told me under the circumstances you should leave the Council altogether.

As for me missing my medical, I did not deliberately fail to attend for the reason Brendan Farrell stated. When I went off sick in August 1997 I turned to drink and I had a drink problem. I was in the pub from opening to closing, drinking 10 pints plus a day, seven days a week. I ended up with a serious drink problem caused by the way St Helen's Council treated me and I went to the work's Doctor p****d and she said, "Why have you done this to me?"

At that time I went to the pub and got p****d instead of going to the work's Doctor because of what St Helen's Council did to me. Drink was my life till I became seriously ill with depression around September 1999 when the Council terminated my employment for the second time.

37. On the 11 May 1999 Dr Page visited my home and in front of my father told me to finish work on ill-health and told me to think about it. I said, "I am going back to work" and she stated my health has greatly improved but she was not prepared to let me to return to that environment as it will make me ill again.

I believe that Dr Page made this statement because she had been influenced by Brendan Farrell's letter to her on the 6 April 1999,

Brendan Farrell making the statement, "he has also again begun to repeat spurious allegations against his colleagues and Managers". Firstly I did not make any allegations against my colleagues and secondly they were not spurious allegations I made against Brendan Farrell and Mick Gornall, in my opinion they were facts.

Dr Page sent a medical report to the Council after her visit to my parents' home, it reads as follows:

I reviewed this Mobile Security Officer at home in the presence of his father and Jan Ahmed from Occupational Health. Medically there is no doubt he has improved since I last saw him in November but he still has residual symptoms and remains under close specialist supervision.

As you know, I have on file a specialist report and I have considered this together with my own observation today and I feel that Mr Steele is permanently unfit to work in his previous post as a Mobile Security Officer. I did explain this to him during the course of our consultation and it is clear that he is of the mindset that he wishes to return to work.

Notwithstanding that, I am clear in my opinion that he is permanently unfit to undertake this role.

In my opinion Dr Page knew I was well enough to return to work. She said, my health had greatly improved but she was not allowing me to return to that environment as it will make me ill again. I also believe Brendan Farell had made written statements to Dr Page, in which he made spurious statements about his coleagues and managers, which put the spanner in the works for me.

I also believe Dr Page knew if she let me return to work it would make me ill again In my opinion I was fit to undertake this role and could have gone back at anytime between August 1997 to September 1999 had St Helen's Council sorted my grievances out.

In March 1999 I was ready to take St Helen's Council on again and sort out all the grievances. I was also prepared to put up a bigger battle than before. I believe that Dr Page knew this was the case and she terminated my employment rather that see me ill again Also my opinion is Peter Mavers would not let me return to work on 30th March, 1999 because St Helen's Council did not want me back. I would also like to comment how the security department had six staff too many, according to the restructure of 1996, and six staff were finished on the basis of ill-health, within weeks. But I am not allowed to state this because of libel laws.

38. I believe I was wrongfully sectioned under the Mental Health Act and my Community Psychiatric Nurse, Brian Langshaw went to the Police and informed them I had been sectioned in April 2001.

About 10 weeks later I was allowed home for weekends and Mick Gornall found out I was out and phoned the Police and told them I had threatened to harm him. When I got back to the ward, Andy, the Ward Manager, called me in to his office and said the Police have been on to him and said I have threatened to harm Mick Gornall. I told him, 'I don't have a clue what you are on about; and I was stopped from going home at weekends.

A few weeks later Andy said I can go home Saturday and had to go back that evening and could go home again Sunday for the day. This was another ploy to discriminate my character for when I went to Court. At no time at all did I threaten Mick Gornall other than to take him to Court, apart from when I bumped into to him at Safeway and I wrote to him that if he ever stares me out again I will not be held responsible for any actions I may take against him.

Dave Anders told me when I visited him that the lads have been winding Mick Gornall up again. Dave only ever told me one of the things they were saying and that was what Jebby Robinson had told Mick and that was I was a crack shot with a rifle in the Army and that Mick replied, 'I'm a crack shot with an air rifle'.

Dave also told me that the lads have got Mick Gornall frightened to death of me. I found it amusing when Dave told me Mick had security locks on the Security portacabin and a panic alarm fitted because the lads have got him paranoid. Where Mick went wrong was he was saying all the threats I was making were against himself. If I had made these alleged threats, then they would have also been aimed at Brendan Farrell, as I hated them both as much as each other.

39. I was discharged from hospital in August 2001. A few days later there was a knock at my door, it was Detective Sergeant Steve Lowe who I met at the hospital and he came with a Detective Constable. They came into the house and Steve Lowe said I had rung Mick Gornall up and threatened to kill him.

I said "no I haven"t' and the DC said, 'we have got your voice on tape'.

I said, "you haven't got my voice on tape because it wasn't me'.

Steve Lowe said, 'you have told someone you are going to kill him slowly'. I told Steve to get that person to say it to my face as I have not said it. I then told Steve, 'he is provoking me to go and get him' and Steve said 'that was the last thing we want to do'.

Steve then threatened me he would have me put away indefinitely and take my driving licence away from me. Steve then asked me for the house phone number.

When Steve and the DC were leaving, the DC turned around and told me to pack it in. How can I pack it in when I have done nothing to pack in?

Between me being discharged from hospital and my visit from the Police, I called at Dave Anders house and he asked me, 'Had I rung Mick Gornall up and threatened to kill him?'

I said, 'No why?'

He said it was someone who knew the system as they knew how to contact Mick. Dave told me that Cath answered the phone and Mick came out of his office and asked her who was that on the phone and she said Guss. Mick Gornall then rang the Police and told them it was me on the phone. Again Mick Gornall was trying to have me put away. Dave Anders saying to me it was someone who knew the system did not sink in for a number of years but when I thought about it years later, it could have only been someone from Security who made that phone call.

I am suspicious Mick Gornall masterminded it as he knew it was not my voice on the phone yet he told the Police it was and why would he go in the control room and ask Cath who was it on the phone if he knew it was me? The phone call did take place because Cath answered the phone; that was obviously part of the plan to have a witness. It was definitely someone from Security who made that phone call and definitely someone well in with Mick Gornall. I'm not stupid,in my opinion Mick Gornall was involved in the plot as he was trying to set me up.

40. I have now decided to write to Carole Hudson, Chief Executive of St Helen's Council as follows:

15 March 2003

Dear Mrs Hudson

Your letter dated 7 August 2002 to Peter Kilfoyle, MP you say extensive correspondence took place between 1998 and 1999, this is not true, it has been going on since 1996.

You also denied a miscalculation took place, so what you are saying is the wages were cut deliberately. How many other departments in the Council have took a pay cut ever – NONE.

I know what Farrell and Gornall did with the wages in 1991. It's funny over the years I have been fighting the wages.

I have been given different reasons why the wages are like they are. My MP wrote to Susan Finney asking for hourly manual workers rate of pay before and after the 1991 pay rise. The question was never answered. Why? Because I am right. I have sent you a copy with this letter.

I tried to speak to you in 1997 about the problems in Security. I ended up with Sheila Samuels and Russ Danson who covered everything up. I have a file over four inches thick with evidence against Farrell and Gornall. I had over 45 Grievances as a Shop Steward. To this day Security Officers are coming to me with their problems. The Council have a policy on bullying, Cath. Dave Anders and a couple of others in Security have been bullied, they have reported it and it has been covered up. They have three years to take it to Court and I'm going to advise them every step of the way.

I have been informed that you are going to get an anonymous letter from a member of Security telling you exactly what is going on in the Department. He is sending me a copy for my file. People are not telling you the truth about what has gone on. The reason I have got nowhere is because you are all p*****g in the same pot, the Council, Union and Auditors.

I am going to expose the Council, the Unions and the Auditors to the St Helen's Star, St Helen's Reporter and the Liverpool Echo newspapers. When the time is right I can expose you all what I have got on file.

I will get you all into Court and have my day. WATCH THIS SPACE.

Mr R Steele

P.S Your Legal Department may tell you I have only three years to put my case into Court and that has passed, WRONG, see you in Court.

I then wrote again to Carole Hudson as follows:

8 April 2003

Dear Mrs Hudson

I acknowledge your letter dated 24 March 2003 and you say my letter 15 March 2003 is receiving attention. I don't know what attention it can be receiving because I have not told you anything.

I don't trust you but I will give you the benefit of the doubt. I am going to give you three grievances they have now, not when I was Shop Steward:

1) *The Market Officers since 1991 have been paid overtime for their Christmas hours. Two years ago Gornall told them they have to do the Christmas hours as annualised hours. He cannot do this, what I want you to do is get them their back pay and stop him from doing this. I know they work annualised hours but this has never included Christmas overtime.*

2) *You have had a Mr Hawks startin Security a few months ago because he knows Farrell and a couple of others high up in the Council. He started at the top of Scale 3 and people who started before him are working their way up the scale. One lad went into Gornall and asked why he was on £100 less than him a month when he's been in the job longer than him. Gornall told him it's because he was on a high wage at Pilkington Glass. You cannot take the money off him now, by law, you will now have to put theother peoples wages to the top of Scale 3 as you cannot give one and not the other and all new starters will have to start at the top of Scale 3. This is Gornall's fault.*

3)   *Ste Cliffe was on alarm response and was sent out to check schools. This is not the alarm response man's duty. He is there to attend alarms. He finished at 12pm and came in at 11:45 hours to finish his shift. He was told to wash the number plates and windscreen on his vehicle. This also is not the job of the alarm response man. Ever since I have joined Security in 1992 we have never washed the vans and it is not their duty to do so. They have a car wash on the depot that Gornall won't pay to use it.*

Ste Cliffe was given an oral warning for coming into the depot without asking to return to the depot and not washing his vehicle. He has three charges against him and he had no case to answer.

If I were Shop Steward I would get my members to work to rule and the job would not get done until his warning was removed from his record. How many people have been told to wash their vehicles – NONE. How many people have just come into the depot – ALL OF US. How many people have been disciplined for it – NONE, so why has Gornall picked on Ste Cliffe? These issues are all to do with Gornall, he is responsible for them.

I will come into a meeting with you, Gornall and myself and have it out face to face. He will fill you full of s**t as that is the type of person he is.

I believe that Gornall and Farrell are thieves and the biggest pair of lying bastards going and I can prove it. If you sort out the three grievances and I am satisfied you have been honest, I will give you the other problems they have. I would like you to put it in writing to me what you have done.

The best way to deal with this is for yourself, myself and Gornall to thrash it out. It's the only way you will get the truth. I look forward to hearing from you with a date to meet.

I still have near 50 other grievances from my time as Shop Steward, most of them to do with Farrell and all of them to do with Gornall. Do you not find it funny that I won't go away? If I was Chief Executive I would want to know what is going on and I would want the truth,

Yours sincerely

Mr R Steele

The reason Mick Gornall picked on Ste Cliffe was because he came to my Solicitor with me, also Dave Anders, Roy Simm, Kenny Watterson and Mick Fairclough came with us. Mick Gornall did get Ste Cliffe into his office and told him that he is fraternising with the enemy and said to Ste, 'You might win the battle but you won't win the war'. Mick Gornall also told Roy Simm that, 'if you make me ill again I will make you all suffer'.

Carole Hudson replied to my two letters on 24 April 2003:

Dear Mr Steele

RE Your letters dated 15 March and 8 April 2003

Thank you for your recent correspondence which my Personal Assistant has acknowledged on my behalf.

As I indicated to Peter Kilfoyle, MP in my letter dated 7 August 2002, the issues you have previously raised have been considered and it is unlikely that there will ever be agreement between us in relation to them. It was unsurprising to me therefore, that in your letter dated 15 March 2003 you disagreed with the comments in my letter.

For the reasons previously given, I see little point in our continuing correspondence on matters which took place several years ago, in addition, I do not intend to meet with you to discuss them.

I understand that your previous dealings with the Council have resulted in it being made clear to you that you are not to attend the Town Hall or Hardshaw Brook Depot and that if you do so, the Police will be called immediately. That position remains the same. The Council has already been obliged to involve the Police due to your actions in the past and will have no hesitation about doing so in the future. I hope the Council's position is now clear to you.

Yours Sincerely

Carole Hudson
Chief Executive

In my opinion the Chief Executive has ganged up on me. I have never been told whatsoever I am not to attend the Town Hall or Hardshaw Brook Depot and the Council has not been obliged to involve the Police due to my actions in the past. I don't believe the Chief Executive is telling the truth.

I replied to the letter above on the 6 May 2003 as follows:

Hudson

I am disgusted with your spurious allegations you have made against me. If you are going to believe liars then they are going to get you into trouble.

In my letter 15 March 2003 I wrote 'you are all p*****g in the same pot', your actions have proved I am right. In my letter 8 April 2003 I told you 'I don't trust you but I give you the benefit of the doubt'. I was right not to trust you. I gave *you three simple grievances and you did nothing about them, some leader you are.*

I am going to the Police station and making a complaint against you and Gornall. I am also going to contact Peter Edwards, a Solicitor, about your allegations against me. I am going to the papers in the next few weeks and exposing the Council as thieves and corrupt.

Don't bother replying to this letter, as I don't want anything else to do with you.

SEE YOU IN COURT.
Mr R Steele

I've seen Inspector Vaudrey on the 6 May 2003 at St Helen's Police station. I took the above letter with me and I showed it to Inspector Vaudrey and he said the Council couldn't stop me going into the Town Hall and Hardshaw Brook Depot as they are public buildings and the Police have not put any order on me telling me otherwise. He said if the Council do phone the Police to remove me from a Council building they will not attend.

I then told him about a Detective Sergeant coming to my house from CID. I described him as having short red hair and a beard and slim, as I did not know his name at the time and Inspector Vaudrey said he did not know who it was. I told Inspector Vaudrey how he set me up in 2001. I later found out his name when I asked my Community Psychiatric Nurse Brian Langshaw and he told me it was Detective Sergeant Steve Lowe who is now Detective Inspector Steve Lowe. I decided to go and see him on the 26 June 2003.

I again went to the Police Station on 26 June 2003 and spoke to Inspector Steve Lowe. I took my file of grievances with me. I told him that Mick Gornall is provoking me and I want him to see Mick and stop him saying things about me.

Firstly, Gornall told Kenny Watterson that if Rob Steele comes on the market you are to remove him immediately. Secondly, Mick told Bernard Day that he has an injunction on me to keep me away from him. Thirdly, Dave Anders told me that Mick Gornall told him that he is not frightened of Rob Steele.

Steve Lowe then said if I see him I will have to tell him who it was that told me and they will get into trouble. 'You don't want that do you?'

I said no.

Steve Lowe never told me who said I was going to kill Mick Gornall slowly. Steve was protecting Mick Gornall as he did not have to tell him who said it. I then told Steve about Mick charging Pets Corner for a Security Officer on a static duty and never putting a man up there. I then got my file out and showed him five of my grievances and Steve replied theirs lies, bullying and alleged embezzlement. The second he mentioned alleged embezzlement he should have investigated it and once again like the Council he brushed it under the carpet.

I wrote again to Carole Hudson on the 1 July 2003 as follows:

Mrs Hudson,

I have been to the Police Station again on Thursday 26 June 2003 and I spoke to a Detective Inspector Steve Lowe. He is the officer Gornall spoke to when he was Detective Sergeant.

I have shown him your letter and he has stuck up for you by saying you Have been misled by your officers. The allegations you have made against me are untrue and if I want to visit the Town Hall or Hardshaw Brook Depot, the Police cannot stop me as it's a public place and I have not been told to stay away by the Police or anybody else.

I have shown Steve Lowe, Farrell saying one thing then denying it later. I also showed him Gornall saying one thing and then denying it later, (i.e. telling lies). Gornall will tell you I have got nothing on him. If you ring Steve Lowe up and ask him he will tell you otherwise as he has seen some of the 76 grievances I have against him. Steve has told me there is bullying and alleged embezzlement in what I have shown him, as well as the lies. I have also forgotten to show him the theft from Gornall.

Steve Lowe has told me to let the Solicitor, Barrister and the Courts deal with it and to keep my file safe. I did warn you about Farrell and Gornall and you took their side and now they have blackened your name.

If you don't believe me, phone Merseyside Police on 0151 7096010 and ask for St Helen's Control Room, then ask for Detective Inspector Steve Lowe and ask him.

I have also written to the T&GWU and the GMB about them allegedly agreeing to the wages in 1991. I also spoke to them on Thursday 26 June 2003 and the T&GWU aregoing to write to you and want to see proof. The GMB have a meeting with Farrell next week and if it's found to be untrue, the GMB are going to take the Council to Court for slander.

I am the Council's biggest nightmare and I'm going to get justice for myself and the lads I represented as Shop Steward.

I am going to get them their wages and sort out their grievances. I have not yet been to the papers as my Solicitor has told me the time is not right.

Yours

Mr R Steele

The T&GWU and the GMB told me what they were going to do when I told them that they agreed to the wages in 1991 and they were gutless and did nothing. They both lied to me when I spoke to them on the phone.

41. On 7 July 2003 I bumped into Mick Gornall in Safeway. When Mick saw me he stared me out. I lost my temper and shouted, 'you f*****g fat thieving b*****d' and he walked off. I was with my mate's wife and when she found out it was Gornall she encouraged me to leave the supermarket. I was so wound up with him staring me out I wrote to him on 15 July 2003 as follows:

Gornall

If you ever try and stare me out again like you did in Safeway on Monday 7 July 2003, I won't be held responsible for what actions may be towards you. Don't you ever try and stare me out again.

I have been informed by the lads that have had a member of staff in your office and told him to have nothing to do with me or you will make their jobs very difficult for them. You also told him 'you might win the battle but you won't win the war'.

You have frightened the lads in the past with your threats; it's not going to work this time as they know it's only a matter of time before Security closes. They all want what you have stolen from them and I'm going to get it for them.

Mr R Steele

42. I received a phone call from Detective Inspector Steve Lowe on 14 August 2003.

He said I had threatened Security Officers for money.

I said 'no I haven't'. I have asked the lads who I know for £20 to pay for an Accountant's report on the wages and I have asked Dave Anders, Phil Haughey and Tony Marsh to see if any of the new starters want to pay it and for them to collect it. Phil and Dave did collect the money from some of the new starters.

DI Lowe replied 'we will leave it at that then'.

I won't leave it at that, Mick Gornall accused me of threatening members of Security for money to Detective Inspector Steve Lowe to get me into trouble. Once again I believe he is telling more lies.

DI Lowe then said about the threatening letter I sent to Gornall. I told him Gornall deliberately stared me out and he said it's a threat but not a direct threat. DI Lowethen said I have sent abusive letters to the Council and I asked him had he seen any abusive words in the letters they have sent him? He said no. DI Lowe then moaned at me for writing to the Chief Executive and telling her what he had said in our meeting 26 June 2003 and said I behaved like a big kid going ner ner ne ner ner. In my opinion DI Lowe behaved like a big kid for coming out with that statement. He spat his dummy out because I told the Chief Executive what he said in our meeting. He then alleged he has been told by the Chief Executive of the Council to send me a harassment order and wants me locking up. DI Lowe told her he's not going to lock me up.

I received a letter on the 14 August 2003 as follows:

Merseyside Police, copy for Council

Inspector Steve Lowe
St Helens Police Station
College Street
St Helen's
0151 777 6878

14 August 2003

Mr Robert Steele

Dear Sir

This letter and the attached warning Notice under the 1997 Harassment Act is to explain and confirm the details that were told to you by myself on the telephone at 13:00hrs today.

Any legitimate business that you may have with the local authority must be addressed to the head of the correct department and not personal employees. The content must not contain any threats or implied threats and not contain derogatory remarks or references to individuals. I strongly advise you correspond via a third party such as your legal advisor by letter or telephone.

The letters you have sent have caused harassment, alarm and distress to the receivers and having read and retained them myself I can confirm this.

Any other act by yourself from the time of this warning will render you liable to be arrested and charged with harassment. In view of the period of two years history and consultation since you were last seen by the Police and the fact that you have been into hospital during that time, I have not ordered you to be arrested on this occasion (there is sufficient already to put before the Court).

If you have genuine cause or grievance against the Council, then you must follow correct channels. By sending threats in the letters it will weaken any case that you may have. They will not be dealt with but filed as evidence for harassment.

Inspector 8403 Steve Lowe

I don't know how my letters have cause harassment, alarm and distress as I only told the truth in them and my letters were sent to the head of the correct departments. I never sent letters to personal employees and myself telling DI Lowe about Pets Corner and my concerns about possible embezzlement should have raised the alarm for himself to do something. In my opinion all DI Lowe was interested in doing was to shut me up and in doing so I consider he ganged up on me and set me up.

Merseyside Police
OFFICIAL WARNING

PROTECTION FROM HARASSMENT ACT 1997

A complaint has been received from ST HELEN'S COUNCIL EMPLOYEES (Human Resources, Security and Chief Executive) IN RESPECT OF YOUR CONDUCT, NAMELY confrontation, threats, letters containing abusive and threatening words, phone calls.

At 13:00 hrs on Thursday 14 August 2003 an OFFICIAL WARNING UNDER THE PROTECTION OF HARASSMENT ACT 1997 HAS BEEN ADMINISTERED TO YOU BY DETECTIVE INSPECTOR LOWE by telephone.

2nd Posted direct.

SHOULD YOUR FUTURE CONDUCT CAUSE THE COMPLAINANT ANY FORM OF HARASSMENT, ALARM OR DISTRESS, THAT ACTION MAY RENDER YOU LIABLE TO ARREST.

Detective Inspector 8403 Lowe
St Helen's Police Station

Signed Steve Lowe (Officer Administering)

Posted to Clockface Road after verbal acceptance and explanation by telephone.

Print name   Signed/Refused
(Person receiving)

*Delete as appropriate

Now DI Lowe has added confrontation and phone calls to his harassment order, both these issues were not mentioned on the phone or in his letter dated 14 August 2003. He also mentioned letters containing abusive and threatening words. DI Lowe told me on the phone he had not seen any abusive words in the letters the Council sent him and only one letter had sort of a threat in it. DI Lowe even stated on the phone it was not a direct threat. In my opinion DI Lowe has ganged up on me and also set me up to try shut me up.

I then wrote to the Police Complaints Authority on 26 October 2003 making a complaint against Steve Lowe as follows:

Dear Sirs

I am writing with a complaint against the Police.

In August 2001 I came out of hospital and a few days later two Police Officers from CID came to the house, one I had met in hospital. I let them in and Detective Sergeant Steve Lowe alleged I rang Gornall and told him I was going to kill him. I never rang him so I denied it. The other Police Officer said we have got your voice on tape. I then told him 'you have not got my voice on tape because it was not me'. DI Lowe then said I had told someone that I was going to kill Gornall slowly. Again I denied this and told him whoever said it to say it to my face.

I don't think DI Lowe believed me and I think he suggested he was going to have me sectioned indefinitely and made other threats towards me. I went to see the Psychiatrist and told him what he had said and he told me that he cannot do this.

Several months ago I went to the Police Station with a complaint about St Helen's Council and made a complaint against DI Lowe. I spoke to an Inspector Vaudrey. I showed him a letter from the Council and told him I have never been told to stay away from anywhere and the Police have never been called out to me. He told me they cannot stop me going to public places and if they do call the police they will not attend.

I then told him about the two Police Officers that came to the house. I told him they were from CID and one was called Steve. I described him to him as tall, short hair and a beard and his name is Steve from CID. He told me he did not know who I was on about.

I told my CPN and he told me his name was Steve Lowe and he has been promoted to Detective Inspector. I rang him up and told him I wanted to see him about Gornall.

I went to see him and told him that three of the lads had told me what he had been saying about me. I asked DI Lowe to go and see him and stop him saying things about me. He told me he would only pick on the lads who have told me what he had been saying.

I then got my folder out with 76 grievances against Gornall. I showed him some of them and I believe he told me there are lies, bullying and embezzlement and did nothing about it.

In August I bumped into Gornall in Safeway and he deliberately stared me out. I wrote him a letter telling him 'don't dare stare me out again'.

I then received a phone call from DILowe. He said the Police had issued a harassment order to me after the threats against

Gornall and for being abusive in two letters. The two letters the Councilsent to DI Lowe in my opinion I was not abusive in any of them. I then received the harassment order from DI Lowe. He alleged confrontation and threats that I do not believe I made and letters containing abusive and threatening words. The threatening words I did do but abuse was not in any of the two letters sent to DI Lowe. He also included phone calls. I don't know anything about phone calls unless these are the phone calls I was supposed to have madea couple of years earlier. The only thing I have done is threaten Gornall and DI Lowe said it was not a direct threat. In my opinion what I have done does not warrant a harassment order.

I would like to meet you and DI Lowe face to face, this way is better than seeing me and then seeing him. Get us both together and then there are no cover-ups.

Hope to hear from you soon with a date to meet.

Yours faithfully

Mr R Steele

I first sent this letter to the Police Complaints Authority who told me to send it to the Chief Constable of Greater Manchester Police.

They wrote back on 17 December 2003 as follows:

Dear Mr Steele

Re. Letter received 10 December 2003

I am writing to acknowledge receipt of your letter dated 7 December 2003.

Unfortunately when you wrote to the Police Complaints Authority they informed you incorrectly. Your complaint should have been sent to the Chief Constable of Merseyside Police, Mr Norman Bettison. Their address is as follows:

Merseyside Police
PO Box 59
Liverpool
L69 1 JD

To assist you in this matter I have forwarded your documentation to the above address, therefore you need not send it again. I have also contacted the Police Complaints Authority and informed them of the error in order for them to update their systems. May I apologise for the inconvenience this may have caused you.

Yours sincerely

Janine Sykes
Administration Assistant

Norman Bettison never even had the decency to reply to my letter. Again in my opinion the Police were covering up DI Lowe's wrong doings.

43. On the 25 March 1999 Mick Foy (Director of Housing Environmental and Contract Services) sent a letter out to all members of Security about the Single Status Agreement and at the top of his letter he states Mr B Farrell is dealing with this matter. After Brendan's dealings with Security in 1991 he was not in my opinion capable of dealing with this matter as I believe he had already stitched Security up in 1991. What confirms this statement was Security never received Single Status until February 2008 and were once again underpaid and never received any back pay.

I went to my MP's surgery at the beginning of November 2003 as I was concerned that Brendan Farrell was dealing with the wages.

Peter Kilfoyle then wrote to Carole Hudson on the 10 November 2003 as follows:

Dear Mrs Hudson

Re. Robert Steele, Avon Close, Liverpool

Thank you for your letter of the 3 November last and regarding my constituent above.

I note that the answer to Mr Steele's Solicitor on the same matter came from Brendan Farrell as Head of Human Resources.

He said he would give a substantive reply as soon as reasonably practicable. Given that Mr Farrell figures highly as one of the staff in the first place, is he the best person to give, after all this time, a substantive reply?

Yours sincerely

Peter Kilfoyle MP

c.c. R Steele

The Chief Executive, Carole Hudson got the Council's Solicitor to reply on 28 November 2003:

Dear Mr Kilfoyle

Re. Robert Steele, Avon Close, Liverpool

Thank you for your letter dated 10 November addressed to the Chief Executive.

The Chief Executive has complete confidence in the integrity of Mr Farrell to deal with any issues raised in a professional and impartial manner.

The Council has received correspondence from Solicitors who indicate that they act on behalf of existing Council employees. The Council's Legal Services section will deal with that correspondence and a reply is currently being prepared.

In relation to Mr Steele's complaints about his employment, these have been considered over a period of several years. The Council's position was set out in a letter to you dated 7 August 2002 (copy enclosed). That remains the Council's position.

Mr Steele was employed in 1992 (initially on a temporary contract until 1994) when he accepted the terms and conditions on offer. His employment was terminated in 1999. In my view, he has no right to challenge matters on terms and conditions of employment, which arose prior to the commencement of his employment or subsequent to its termination. He also has no apparent locus in relation to any complaints, which may be made by existing employees of the Council.

Mr Steele has had the opportunity to raise complaints about his own employment not least via the Employment Tribunal. From a review of previous extensive correspondence on the issues, which Mr Steele has raised, I am satisfied that the Council has made more than reasonable efforts to explain its position in the past. There is no requirement to continue to do so and it is not proposed to correspond on this matter further.

Yours sincerely

Angela Boyle
Principal Solicitor

Firstly, I don't understand how can the Chief Executive have complete confidence in the integrity of Mr Farrell to deal with any issues raised in a professional and impartial manner when he was involved with many of the issues that raised concerns in the first place? The Chief Executive gave Brendan Farrell the green light to cover his tracks and to prevent him being investigated.

Secondly, 'in relation to Mr Steele's complaints about his employment', these have been considered over a period of several years. I don't know how as they would not sit down with me and discuss the issues with me and the Council have not seen most of my grievances to date because they constantly refused to discuss them with me.

Thirdly, 'In my view he has no right to challenge matters on terms and conditions of employment that arose prior to the commencement of his employment or subsequent to its termination'. As set out in the current union rule book, No. 7 states pay and conditions of my role as Shop Steward, I had every right to challenge matters on terms and conditions of employment that arose prior to my commencement of my employment and I have every right to pay and conditions after leaving the Council, as I have the right to work out my loss of earnings for Court.

Fourthly, 'Mr Steele has had the opportunity to raise complaints about his own employment, not least via the Employment Tribunal'. How can this be the case when my father had to write to the Tribunal and tell them I was too ill to attend? In my opinion my illness was caused by the wrong doings in the Security Department by Brendan Farrell and Mick Gornall, so I was not given the opportunity to raise my complaints to a Tribunal as the Council have wrongly stated.

44. I wrote to the Council leader, Brian Spencer on 13 February 2010.

Here is an extract from the letter:

Hi Spencer

Yes it's me Rob Steele, the Council's biggest nightmare. As you well know,I have been fighting the Council for the last 12 years.

Mr Murray sent me a letter 26 January 2010 where it states this Authority is under a duty to protect public funds. We all know this statement is a load of s**t. The Council had a number of chances to deal with this problem and decided to protect Farrell and Gornall. Had you dealt with this matter at the time,I believe Farrell and Gornall would have been sacked and I could have returned to work with immediate effect. It would not have cost the Council a penny.

The Council covered up for Farrell and Gornall. Now I am seeking one million pounds plus in the European Court of Human Rights, so Mr Murray's statement 'this Authority is under a duty to protect public funds' is a load of nonsense. If this statement was true, Farrell and Gornall would have been sacked a long time ago. I would have returned to work to a healthy environment and this would not have cost the Council a penny. Justice would have been done.

I took the letter to the Town Hall in person and I wrote on the envelope, 'My Best Mate Brian Spencer' from 'Your Best Mate Rob Steele', hand delivered.

I then received a letter from Peter Blackburn, Assistant Chief Executive on 18 February 2010.

Dear Mr Steele

The executive leader has asked me to respond to your letter of 13 February 2010.

The matter to which you refer appear to claims, which you have raised previously with the Council. For the avoidance of doubt, I have asked Mr Murray to confirm the position in that respect.

May I also remind you that the order restraining you from the Town Hall is still in force.

Yours sincerely

Peter Blackburn
Assistant Chief Executive
(Legal and Administrative Services)

Now I consider Peter Blackburn has ganged up on me and has stated that the Order restraining me from entering the Town Hall is still in force. I don't believe this to be true as there has never been a restraining order on me.

After I had dropped my letter off to Brian Spencer, I received a phone call on Wednesday 24 February 2010 from a Police Constable telling me if I go near the Town Hall I will be arrested. I asked him did he know DI Lowe and he said he had spoken to him about this matter. I told him that I believed DI Steve Lowe is already in serious trouble and I will go to the Town Hall when I like. The Police Officer again said I would be arrested. I told him where to get off and put the phone down on him.

I wrote back to Peter on 26 February 2010:

Dear Peter Blackburn

Hudson and Spencer are too gutless to contact me. They have used you to once again bully me. This has now been going on for 12 years. Your name has now gone on my list of 22 February 2010 people who I believe have set me up (copy sent with this letter). There is also another name to add to this list, O'Brien, Consultant Psychiatrist.

This case is so close to going to Court and you might think a judge is not going to believe one person over 28 people, watch this space.

But we've got a psychiatric report that states I'm a paranoid schizophrenic. I don't need someone like that who has never met me or known me to write reports like that about me. I know what it is exactly that's wrong with me, it's stress, depression, frustration and anxiety, all brought on by St Helen's Council for not telling the whole truth about the corruption that in my opinion was going on in Security.

In my opinion embezzlement was going on and every person who was informed covered it up and most of their names are on that list. I'm telling you now, I will go to Hardshaw Brook depot, St Helen's markets and the Town Hall whenever I like. I will be bringing this letter into the Town Hall on Monday. No one but no one is going to stop me. You can get Hudson to get Steve Lowe to contact me or even arrest me like he told me on the phone on Wednesday.

Lowe also has not got the guts to do it himself. All three of these gutless people are in serious trouble. I have done a massive assault on a number of senior people in the country and have fired the bullets on all those names on that list I have sent you on 22 February 2010. I will also tell you now I have done a massive assault on the Courts and they have finally taken the hint. I am not going away and they have given me vital information I required on two issues and I am still attacking them for the last piece of the jigsaw. I will get it and it's all hands on deck to get my Court Hearing I have waited 12 years for.

It does not matter what your Solicitors or Barristers tell you, you're going to Court. It's only a matter of time before the atom bomb explodes on you. When you set me up and ruined my life for not telling the whole truth, you did it to the wrong person. That's all you need to know at this moment in time. Watch this space.

Yours

Mr R Steele

Because of DI Steve Lowe's assistant phoning me and telling me I will be arrested if I go to the Town Hall, I took the letter to Peter Blackburn personally on the 1 March 2010.

45. After our discussion in the Town Hall I wrote to Peter Blackburn on the 17 March 2010 reminding him to send me a copy of the restraining order as of today's date, 14 April 2011. They still have not sent it as there never has been one.

The letter I sent is as follows:

Dear Peter Blackburn

Reference our discussion in the Town Hall

Monday 1 March you told me you were going to send me a copy of the order restraining me from the Town Hall. I have still not received this. WHY? I have not got a problem with you but don't think they are going to use you to get information out of me. You will only be told what I want you all to know.

I have made it quite clear to everyone I do have a grudge against St Helen's MBC and I don't have a problem putting it in writing for everyone to see. That list with all the names on I sent you, I will expose them all. I know your name's on it but that's a minor incident at this moment of time as you may turn out like the rest of them.

I am sorry Peter, I don't take s**t from anyone, the Courts or Government or the Police. When I do something wrong then I will accept my punishment and I will never deny anything I have said or done. I have put one of my claims into Court today and I am ringing your insurers tomorrow and if they don't make me an offer to pay in full my second claim, then I will be putting it into Court tomorrow. If I don't get justice on my claims in the County Court,then it *will be put into the Court of Appeal and again if I don't get the justice there, then I will take these matters to the Supreme Court and then to the European Court of Human Rights.*

I don't care how much it costs me, I will win my case and recover all monies owing, plus all costs.

The biggest mistake St Helen's MBC did was doing what they did to me. I have said it before and I will say it again, they s**t on the wrong person because he won't go away till justice has been done.

I have sent you a copy of the letter I have sent to Gordon Brown, 26 February 2010 and even his government will go to the ECHR if they don't pay me £500 for the loss of my TV. I can tell you this matter is being dealt with at this moment of time by the Department for Culture, Media and Sport and if they don't pay up when they contact me, they will be put into Court with immediate effect.

My first claim with you is for £1026.33 and when in Court I will be pointing out to the judge ruling on CPR 16.2 of the law and will be claiming for £1100 interest on my loan. If you do decide to settle this claim out of Court, it will be a total of £2126.33 full and final settlement.

The ball is now in your court.

Yours faithfully

Mr R Steele

Peter Blackburn wrote back to me on the 18 March 2010:

Dear Mr Steele

Thank you for you letter which is dated 17 March and which I have received today.

I have been trying to trace a copy of the Order, which I mentioned when we spoke on your visit to the Town Hall on 1 March. I believe that it took the form of warning under the Protection from Harassment Act 1997 and was issued by Inspector Steven Lowe of Merseyside Police in August 2003. I understand that you were advised that you cannot enter the Town Hall or Hardshaw Brook depot and must not telephone individual employees. I am unclear as to whether that was the extent of the prohibition.

As I indicated when we spoke, I will send you a copy of the document once I have been able to locate it.

Yours sincerely

Peter Blackburn
Assistant Chief Executive
(Legal and Administrative Services)

For Peter Blackburn to say I believe that it took a form of a warning under the Protection from Harassment Act 1997 and was issued by Inspector Steven Lowe of Merseyside Police in August 2003,I don't believe this to be true. When I went to school I was taught that April comes before August but at the school Carole Hudson was educated they taught her that August comes before April, as on the 24 April 2003 Carole Hudson wrote to me,'I understand that your previous dealings with the Council have resulted in it being made clear to you that you are not to attend the Town Hall or Hardshaw Brook depot' and according to this statement, it's made quite clear this order was already in force before 24 April 2003, when in fact I don't believe there has never been any such order against me.

Peter then goes on to say, 'I understand that you were advised that you cannot enter the Town Hall or Hardshaw Brook depot and must not telephone individual employees'. Again, these comments in my opinion are not true. Going back to DI Lowe's harassment order it states, 'In respect of your conduct, namely confrontation, threats, letters containing abusive and threatening words and phone calls', it does not state I cannot enter the Town Hall or Hardshaw Brook depot and also does not mention I must not telephone individual employees as Peter has wrongfully stated. What DI Lowe did state was 'any legitimate business that you may have with the local authority must be addressed to the head of the correct department and not to personal employees'. Why DI Lowe made this statement I have not got a clue as all of my letters I sent were to the head of the correct departments and not one letter was sent to personal employees.

Peter then went on to say, 'As I indicated when we spoke, I will send you a copy of the document once I have been able to locate it'. This statement was made on the 18 March 2010 it is now 24 April 2011 and I still have not received any such document as there has never been one. In my opinion it's just lie after lie after lie.

I replied to Peter Blackburn's letter on 23 March 2010 as follows:

Peter, Peter, Peter, who's filling you full of bulls**t mate? I have not got a problem with you, you seemed decent enough when I met you but someone is filling your head full of s**t. Your letter 18 March 2010 has just dug a bigger hole for St Helen's Council. Whoever is giving you this information is putting more nails in the Council's coffin. There are more and more lies being directed at me from whoever is giving you this incorrect information about me.

Gornall told the lads, that's more ammunition for him when he took my letter Exchange of Contracts down and took it to Farrell. This was not more ammunition for him, just another nail in the coffin. Yourself and John Murray have given me new ammunition to fire at you with new evidence of lies from three letters you have sent me recently. I can tell you that I believe I have written proof that Gornall has lied, Farrell has lied, Hudson has lied, Mavers has lied and your good friend Lowe has lied in black and white. Yes, they have all set me up. I can tell you I have photographic memory. I can remember 80% plus of my case without looking at my paperwork. My paperwork at this moment of time is with a Solicitor. The date you have put in your letter of August 2003 is niggling at me for some reason.

I believe this was the date Hudson sent me a letter stating what you have stated in your letter 18 March 2010. Apart from phone calls, I did receive a harassment order from DI Lowe. Again I believe this was at a later date. I am not 100% sure about this, I am convinced this is correct. If it is, then this is how good my memory is. When my barrister had my file, I told him over the phone,times, dates, places and he found what he was looking for from my memory. When I finally receive my paperwork back, I will be able to confirm this 100% true or whether I have got it wrong and that's not very often. I will hold my hands up and be the first to admit it, as that's the straightforward person I am. I can tell you none of you know the law.

I listen and absorb the law and use it to my advantage. I bet you I do a better job than any Barrister or Solicitor you throw at me. My main case will go to Court, possibly in the European Court of Human Rights unless the Courts in this country pull their finger out.

You do know I have two small claims in Court against you at the moment and when I get my paperwork back off my Solicitor, a third claim will be in the small claims Court. This will show you just how good I am at winning my cases. For the big one of up to three million, see you in Court.

Hudson's letter could have been 2002 and Lowe's could have been August 2003, I will not know till I receive my paperwork back.

Yours faithfully

Mr R Steele

The letter I sent to Peter Blackburn 23 March 2010, I did get a bit confused with the dates as the letter I was thinking of that Carole Hudson sent was to Peter Kilfoyle on the 7 August 2002. I totally forgot about the date of the letter Carole Hudson sent to myself 24 April 2003 but I did remember the contents of it further into my letter to Peter Blackburn. I remembered Lowe sent me a letter August 2003 with his harassment order.

46. I called round Dave Anders house and Dave told me that Mick Gornall told him that he believed I had slashed his tyres. Dave told me that it was a member of staff from another department that did it as Mick had gone spying on him and took photographs of him and got him sacked, so he slashed his tyres.

47. I was once again round Dave Anders house and Dave told me that Mick Gornall alleged that I kept ringing him at 4 o'clock in the morning. Dave told me that Mick had gone to Reception and checked on the phone monitors and knew it had been done from Security and that Mick knew it was John Sexton but Mick tried putting the blame on me once again.

48. Damian Finnan and Tony Marsh both asked me did I ring Mick Gornall's wife up and call her a slag as Mick Gornall told them I had rung his wife up and called her a slag.

49. Sheila Samuels sent me a letter dated 12 February 1998. I was so annoyed with the contents of the letter I rang my Community Psychiatric nurse, Hillary Bedson up and told her to ring Sheila Samuels up to explain my illness to her. Hillary rang Sheila up and spoke to her. Hillary then rang me and told me to go straight to my parent's house and she would meet me there within one hour. Whatever Sheila said to Hillary made her frightened of me and she rang my dad up and asked him to be in when she got to their house. On the strength of Sheila's comments on the telephone I believed she convinced Hillary to have me sectioned.

Dr Dutta, psychiatrist, came out to the house about 6pm with the house master and asked me a few questions and told me I don't need sectioning. After what happened, I got rid of Hillary Bedson, my Community Psychiatric nurse and refused to have another psychiatric nurse for a good 18 months.

50. In February 2005 I contacted a Councillor, Wally Ashcroft, about my grievances and he came out to the house and I got my file out and he told me it's a massive and complex case and is too big for him to handle. He then wrote the District Auditor on the 8 March 2005.

51.30 April, 2 May 1997, I attended a Shop Steward Induction course with Unison over the three day period. I had three tutors, Bill Cambell, Angela Washington and Stephanie Thomas. Every subject we did I had already dealt with. Bill told me there is something seriously wrong and when I get back I must see Kevan Nelson. I told Kevan and he said to me "I must remember they are in the same union as you", meaning Brendan Farrell and Mick Gornall. Kevan knew what was going on and in my opinion decided to cover up for them as Brendon and himself were good drinking buddys.

52. I was constantly on at Unison to get me to their solicitors. After several months of requesting I got to Thompsons solicitors around 1998. Jim Keegan rang me and told me he had made an appointment with the solicitors for February 1998. I rang them up and Stephen Pinder, solicitor, told me that Jim Keegan had not contacted them. I had to continue to request that I go to the solicitors before Jim Keegan made the effort to make that appointment.

53. On the 30 April 1998 I called at Millbrook Care Home to see Ann as she was a fellow shop steward. She said to me in the past that if she ever needed backing up she would come to me for help. I called at Millbrook to let her know how I was being treated by the Union and for help with the problems. Eddie Tickle found out I had called on Ann and asked to speak to me in his office and told me not to discuss my case with other shop stewards and he sent me a letter dated 6 May 1998 confirming this. What was the Union trying to hide?

54. Peter Kilfoyle, MP, wrote to Jim Keegan on three separate occasions trying to get him to support me. Peter wrote letters on the 9 June 1998, 5 October 1998 and 21 December 1998. This proves that Unison was stalling on helping me. They did not want to take this case to court.

55. Sometime in 1999 I went to the Union office and Steph, secretary for Unison told me I was no longer allowed in there and she got the instruction from Eddie Tickle, Branch Secretary. I found this strange as I was still a Unison member and still officially the shop steward for my department and still employed by St Helen's Council. When I finished with the Council in November 1999, Unison took the subs out of my last pay packet. I also did not automatically become an honourable member of Unison and all the other members that finished with the Council did. I believe I was singled out once again.

56. On the 9 November 1999 Peter Mavers wrote to Jim Keegan that he was not aware of any complaints of bullying and harassment by Mr Steele and on page two of his letter, Peter states Mr Gornall informed me at a meeting on 14 April 1998 that you personally advised him to complain to the Police about the threats made by Mr Steele. At no time at all have I threatened Mr Gornall or Mr Farrell. It proves the union were stabbing me in the back with Jim Keegan's remarks and these are all spurious allegations to ruin my reputation.

57. On the 6 March 2001 a letter from Jim Keegan to myself registration of itself does not imply further Unison support for your case. You should be aware that your local branch considers that your claim has little prospect of success and on this basis should not be supported. I was also told by Jim that I would have to defend myself at the tribunal as Unison were not going to give me any representation.

CHAPTER FOUR

From going off sick in August 1997 the following events took place:

1. Sometime between August and September I called into work with my sick note in the evening and Derek Anders was there.

We got into an argument over the job and I reminded Derek when he as a Patrol Officer, how he used to sit in the Rest Room all night playing cards and booking in and out of premises when in fact they were sat in the Rest Room.

Derek replied aggressively that the job got done. I said the job got done on paper but not physically like it should have been. Derek then threatened me– he is going to send me to the work's doctor. I stayed very calm and said, *"if that's what you want to do then do it"*.

Derek went ahead and sent me to the work's doctor at the beginning of September 1997.

2. Sometime in September 1997 I called into the Council Depot to have a cup of tea and a chat with the lads, when Tony Marsh came out of the office and told me Mick Gornall told him to tell me, *"I'm not welcome here anymore"*. I found this remark rather strange as I was still employed with the Council. This made me feel they were trying to get rid of me out of Security and out of the Council.

With all the evidence to date confirms that the Council just wanted rid of me.

3. Sometime in October 1997 I was on the Market and met up with Kenny Watterson and Mick Rimmer. They invited me into

their security office and I had a cup of tea with them. As I was leaving, Paul Molyneux and Bernard Day turned up. Paul Molyneux went back to the office and told Mick Gornall that I had grabbed Bernard around the throat. Mick Gornall later asked Bernard and Bernard said it didn't happen.

A few weeks later I was sat in the Rest Room next to Ged Philbin and Bernard came in and we were talking about Paul Molyneux saying I had grabbed Bernard around the throat. Bernard turned around and stated that Mick Gornall got him in the office and told him if you would have said Rob Steele grabbed you around the throat I could have got rid of him straight away. He wanted Bernard to tell lies to get rid of me (i.e. sack me). This is now the **seventh** time they have threatened me with the sack.

All Mick Gornall was trying to do was in my opinion find a good enough excuse to get rid of me, i.e. get me sacked!

4. In October 1997 I called into the Union office and I was talking to Steph – in conversation she thought I was on about something completely different and she said that Eddie Tickle was also disgusted with the letter Brendan Farrell had sent Eddie so I quizzed Steph about the letter and I found out it was about myself. Kevan Nelson came into the office and I told him I wanted a copy of it – he was reluctant to give me a copy so I insisted he gave me a copy and told me it's not to be put in circulation.

The first thing I did with the letter was I took it to my MP Peter Kilfoyle on the first Friday in November 1997.

5. Between my first and second visit to the Work's doctor someone contacted me from the Council. I'm not quite sure but I'm convinced it was Pam Grey, Personnel Manager and whoever it was told me what the Work's doctor had said about me. I don't remember what was said but I was not very happy about it. When I went on my second visit to Dr Fiona Page I repeated what the Council had said to me and I swore at her for setting me up in the

last meeting with her. I told her that in my opinion, *"you are all p*****g in the same pot"*.

Dr Page then stated, *"I have been used"*.

Also in my consultation with Dr Page she told me to hand my file over to the Union and I told her no way am I handing my files over to the Union as I don't trust them. The files are staying in my possession.

After our consultation, because of what happened with the Council, myself and her, she read out exactly what she was going to write to the Council so there was not a repeat of her being used to get at me again.

6. On the 28th October 1997 I called into the Union office. Thelma told me that Brendan Farrell had contacted her on the phone and told Thelma that he wanted to see me in his office on Tuesday.

I went mad in the union office and I told Thelma and Steph that the Work's doctor told them not to have any contact with me as I am very poorly and contact will only exacerbate my condition. Steph told me to calm down and forget it; I was really annoyed as this was after receiving advice from Dr Page to stay away from me.

7. My Doctor asked me to see a Psychiatrist and on the 3rd November 1997 Dr Dutta, Psychiatrist, visited my home. I talked to him in great detail about what was going on in the Council. I talked to him for two hours. As Dr Dutta got up to leave he stated, *"they have used a psychological approach to wear you down"*.

8. I went to Peter Kilfoyle the first Friday in November as his surgeries are every first and third Friday in the month. I told Peter Kilfoyle MP the problems I was having with the management and I was in dispute with them. I also told Peter about Brendan ringing

Thelma in the Union office trying to get me in to work after the work's doctor had told them to stay away from me. Peter asked me if I had a sick note in and I told him it was for three months. Peter wrote to the following people:

11 November 1997

> *Dear Mr Farrell*
> *Dear Mr Gornall*
> *Dear Mr Nelson and Mr Tickle*

This issue has already been stated on page 209 no. 23.

9. Sometime in November my phone rang at 21.25. It was Alan Boger, he told me to be careful playing snooker as Derek Anders has told a couple of the lads if I catch Rob Steele playing snooker I will sack the bastard.

I put the phone down and rang Kevan Nelson at 21.30 and told him what lan had said. Kevan informed Jim Keegan and a couple of days later Jim phoned me and told me he would arrange for me to see Thompsons Solicitors.

From November 24th to January 1st had left numerous phone messages to find out about going to Thompsons and eventually Jim rang me in January and said I would be seeing Thompsons Solicitors Feb 8th 1998. On two separate occasions I rang Stephen Pinder of Thompsons and Jim had still not made me an appointment. It was a couple of months later. Jim Keegan finally made me an appointment with Thompsons.

10. On the 24th November 1997 Kevan Nelson, Unison Convener and Jim Keegan, Regional Officer for Unison came to my house. The first thing Kevan said to me was,*"under the circumstances you should leave the Council altogether"*.

I said *"yes, I would go now – let's talk tribunal"*.

Kevan said, *"what for?"*

I said *"discrimination of a Shop Steward, ill-health, loss of earnings, intimidation, harassment and anything else you can throw at them"*.

Kevan did a complete U turn and said I should get back to work as soon as possible.

I then said to Jim Keegan, *"if Kevan 'fucked up' you would cover his arse"*.

Jim replied, *"yes I would"* and Jim Keegan did just that when I reported Kevan to the General Secretary of Unison.

11. I went to the Town Hall in January 1998 as I wanted to speak to the Chief Executive to tell her what's going on. Sheila Samuels, Head of Human Resources came out and said I have to see her. I went into an office and I spoke to her about the wages and some of my grievances.

12. A few days later I called into the union office and Eddie Tickle asked me 'have I been to the Town Hall again?'

I said 'no'.

He then said 'have you spoken to Sheila Samuels?'

I said 'yes I have'.

He said that I have frightened her and to stay away from the Town Hall.

13. After being told by Eddie Tickle to stay away from Sheila Samuels in January 1998 I contacted Mike Doyle, Council Leader and I met him at his workplace. I discussed some of my grievances in great detail and I produced reports and evidence to confirm my

allegations. When we left his place of work I continued to tell Mike what else was going on and Mike stated they are serious allegations. I said to Mike they are facts.

14. I went back to the Town Hall again as I wanted to speak to the Chief Executive. Sheila Samuels came out to see me. After what Eddie Tickle had said about what Sheila was supposed to have said about me, I said to her 'I am not speaking to you, I want to speak to the Chief Executive'.

Sheila told me I had to see her so I told her 'I am going to see Mike Doyle, Council Leader'. I went to Mike Doyle's workplace and he was not there so they sent me to the technical college where I bumped into him on the stairs and I told him I want to speak to the Chief Executive. He said he would tell her.

15. I again went back to the Town Hall to speak to the Chief Executive and I ended up speaking to Sheila on the phone in the Town Hall. She told me she would discuss the problems with me and could she bring a member of Audit with her. I said 'yes, I want Audit there and also the Chief Executive'. I went to the arranged meeting with her and she brought Russ Danson with her. I asked her was he from Audit, she said 'no, I may have misled you'. I told her I did not trust her and told Sheila that Eddie Tickle had told me I frightened her last time I saw her and Sheila denied that she had spoken to Eddie.

I showed Sheila a letter that I received from the Building Society in 1994 and told her I won that case and I meant business. Again we discussed the wages and other problems in the department. I told Sheila I am taking the Council to a tribunal and would not discuss anything that would affect my claim.

16. I received a phone call the same night as the meeting. It was about 6pm. It was Sheila Samuels and she told me it looks as if I am right about the wages and she gave me another time and date to meet her in the Town Hall.

17. I again went to the Town Hall and Sheila came out and we sat in the Reception area of the Town Hall. I told Sheila that in 1991 security officers were told that if they did not take what was on offer, Burns Security were going to take over at 5pm that night. I also told her that none of the security officers have signed their contracts. Sheila told me that if the wages are wrong, the Town Hall would hold their hands up and pay up. I then said they owe me £8,000 back pay and I then left the Town Hall.

18. Another meeting was arranged and it was with Sheila and Russ Danson. Again Sheila told me they could not fault my figures. Sheila then stated that the Town Hall had decided that the job was only worth Scale 3 all-inclusive. I replied Mick Gornall did the re-structure in 1991 and it was him that decided the wages were only worth Scale 3 all-inclusive. Sheila stated 'yes he did'. Sheila then said to me that the management are allowed to make threats on people's jobs to get them to accept what's on offer.

I then told Sheila and Russ that Mick Gornall had created a job for Paul Molyneux. The job was Client Liaison Officer and that this job was disbanded in 1988 because it was not cost effective and that this post was not on the re-structure presented to the Town Hall in 1996. I also told them Mick had two men on days and only one job so he created the Client Liaison Officer's job for Paul Molyneux. Sheila photocopied the paperwork on the Liaison Officer's job and the next thing I'm told Paul Molyneux is doing his job for the first time in 14 months. Sheila also told me to hand over my file to the union and she got the same answer as the work's doctor, no way am I handing my file over to anyone, it's staying with me.

19. Because of the Council's negative response, I went to my MP, Peter Kilfoyle to let him know what was going on. Peter told me to contact the District Audit as they are an independent body from the Council. I contacted them and they arranged a meeting for the 18 February 1998.

20. I attended Mike Doyle's office at the beginning of February and I spoke to Mike about single status and I showed him a breakdown of wages. Mike told me it's costing 1 million pounds for single status and if that's what our wages come to, then that's what you're entitled to. I also told Mike that we were on less than £4 per hour. Again I showed him this. I also told Mike that Brendan Farrell and Mick Gornall said there is no breakdown of wages and Mike stated there has to be a breakdown of wages. Mike Doyle replied as follows:

21.10 February 1998

Mr Robert Steele Avon Close Liverpool L4 1XL

Dear Mr Steele

Further to our recent discussions. You have provided quite a lot of information and raised concern about a number of issues that require detailed examination.

The District Auditor, as you are aware, has now taken an interest and is in the process of carrying out an investigation. The District Auditor is, of course, a person totally independent of the authority, and I consider we should allow him to carry out his investigation, and await his findings.

I have conveyed the position to Mr Bermingham MP and Mr Kilfoyle, and will contact you again once those findings are known.

Yours sincerely
COUNCILLOR MICHAEL J DOYLE JP
Leader of the Council

22. Sheila Samuels wrote to me on the 12 February 1998 as follows:

Dear Robert

I am writing to you following the issues you raised with me concerning the Security Service and to clarify with you the action being taken by the Council. I am also aware that you have met with Councillor Doyle and he has sent an interim response to you.

In the light of the information you presented, we have been looking into the matter thoroughly and will be producing a report for the Chief Executive and Leader. The District Auditor has also approached me following your approach to him and I will be liaising with him also. You can be assured, therefore that every step is being made to look into the issue.

I am conscious that you also made reference to other general issues which you had concern over relating to the workforce as a whole – gathered from when you were performing your role as Steward for UNISON, although you were not willing to pass over supporting documentation. I understand that you have asked to meet the District Auditor and no doubt he will take any issues up with the Authority that he feels able to do.

In addition to the above I have been in contact with Kevan Nelson as the appointed UNISON Convenor who is actively dealing with the wages issue from the Union side and will I believe take up any issues on behalf of the workforce should he consider it necessary. I would strongly suggest therefore that, given you current absence on sick leave, you should refrain from continuing to perform your role as Steward in representing issues on behalf of the workforce and should direct any issues of general concern via Mr Nelson.

It has been a matter of concern to me that, during your absence on sick leave you have continued to seek meetings with numerous individuals regarding matters which stem from your role as staff representative. Given the nature of your illness I do not feel that this is wholly conducive to your recovery. I understood from you that this also accords with advice you have received from, your psychiatrist.

In view of the above, and in an endeavour to assist your recovery, given that you have now drawn the matters of concern to the appropriate authorities I strongly recommend you to refrain from making contact with work over these matters and concentrate on assisting your recovery with the advice and medical assistance being provided.

I understand that you are to see the Occupational Health Physician next week and I have asked her to indicate to me your progress and of any further steps, which we can take to assist in dealing with your current illness. I or another member of the Personnel staff will contact you on this specific issue on receipt of the medical advice.

Yours sincerely

Sheila Samuels
Head of Human Resources.

What the above letter is telling me is to back off . Ref paragraph 5 – 'given the nature of your illness, I do not feel that this is wholly conductive to your recovery'. I disagree. The nature of my illness was because they would not listen or act on my grievances. The day I received the above letter I phoned my Community Psychiatric nurse up and I told her about the letter and would she ring Sheila up and explain my illness to her. Ten minutes later Hillary Bedson rang me back and she asked me to go to my parent's house straight away and she would meet me there within one hour. I went and she arrived four hours later.

Hillary told me I need to go into hospital and that the Psychiatrist, Dr Dutta is coming to see me. Hillary also told me to give my file to the union. My father came home and sat down. I said 'she wants me to hand my file over to the union'.

He said, 'you're not to do it'.

I then said 'she wants me to go into hospital'.

My dad then said, 'you're not going into hospital, no judge would listen to you'.

Hillary then said, 'I agree with you Mr Steele'.

23. Around 18.30 the Psychiatrist arrived with the house master from the hospital. Dr Dutta took one look at me said I don't need sectioning. He then asked me 'did I feel violent?'

I said 'no'. Then he had a chat with my father and then left the house. I refused to see Hillary again as I don't know what Sheila had said to her but she nearly had me sectioned under the Mental Health Act.

24. 18 February 1998 I attended a meeting in the Town Hall with John Vis and Clive Portman. I was with them for nearly three hours showing them evidence from my file to back up my allegations. The first thing I complained about was what I thought was embezzlement going on at Pets Corner. John Vis decided to look at six issues excluding the most important issue – embezzlement.

25. March 1998 ref JCC meeting. Peter Moffat referred to a recent investigation of Security by District Audit. The complaints made are unfounded and Peter was certain that Audit would confirm this.

Peter had looked into the allegations personally and found them to be spurious. Audit was always welcome in sections under Peter's management but these allegations appeared mischievous.

Peter was disturbed that it appeared that someone within the Security Services was passing information to a member of the service who was currently off sick. This type of behaviour was corrosive to team spirit. Any issues should be raised via the normal chain of command.

If people were reluctant to raise issues with their Supervisors they could be raised directly with Peter or via the Union. It was a waste of time having a JCC meeting if issues were not raised in this forum.

26. The first week in March 1998 I went to my MP Peter Kilfoyle and told him what was going on. Peter told me he is not having this as the Council were ganging up on me and he said he is going to write to Mike Doyle Council leader to stop them ganging up on me.

27. **On the 10th of March 1998 Peter Kilfoyle wrote to Mike Doyle as follows:**

Dear Mike

Ref: Robert Steele Security Officer St. Helen's MBC

I understand you have spoken with Mr Robert Steele as indeed has Gerry Birmingham MP.

I did assist Mr Steele through a very protracted and complicated building society problem some years ago and understand well the stress he endured at that time.

However he seems to be even more stressed by his work situation, he feels that he is subjected to what his G.P. described as psychological warfare. His most concern has been the halving of his wages whilst he is on sick leave.

It would be in the interest of both the Council as employers and Mr Steele as an employee, for Mr Steele's situation to be resolved as quickly as possible. Would it help for you and me to meet and try to find a way forward?

Best Wishes
Peter Kilfoyle MP
Liverpool Walton
Cc Mr R Steele
G. Birmingham MP. St. Helens
D. Watts MP. St. Helens

I did tell Peter it was my Psychiatrist Dr Dutta who made the statement not my G.P. and I also told him they have used a psychological approach to wear me down and not psychological warfare – it means more or less the same thing but I want it right.

Mike Doyle replied 16 March 1998:

Dear Peter

Robert Steele Security Officer St. Helen's M.B.C.

Thank you for your letter dated the 10th March 1998 concerning one of your constituents Mr Steele an employee of St. Helen's M.B.C.

Mr Steele has had a number of meetings with both myself and senior officers from the personnel department, but continues to remain in a very stressed state. We have encouraged him to take the advice of his medical staff in an attempt to aid his recovery, but unfortunately this advice is not taken.

I feel it would be beneficial if we could meet to discuss the precise details of Mr Steele's case and would ask you to please ring my office to check diaries.

Yours Sincerely
Mike
Councillor Michael J Doyle J.P.
Leader of the Council

Firstly in my opinion it is obvious senior management from personnel are going to cover up for Brendan Farrell as he was the ex personnel manager. When he finished as Acting Assistant Director, he ended up as the senior person in personnel (Head of Human Resources).

In an attempt to aid my recovery they could have given me my panel of six Councillors and I could of confronted Brendan Farrell and Mick Gornall face to face and rectified the grievances and I could have returned to work in a healthy environment with immediate effect.

Peter Kilfoyle MP wrote back to me on 7 April 1998:

Dear Mr Steele

Your message left at my office when you called has been passed to me by my staff and I have noted your comments.

However I will be meeting with Councillor Doyle leader of St. Helen's Council after the Easter holidays and will then decide how best to proceed with your case.

Yours Sincerely

Peter Kilfoyle MP
Liverpool Walton

At the end of the day no meeting ever did take place between Peter Kilfoyle MP and Mike Doyle leader of St. Helen's Council.

28. John Vis sent me his response from our meeting 18 February 1998:

Mr R Steele Avon Close Walton Liverpool L4 1XL

Dear Mr Steele

St Helen's MBC – Security Force

Further to our meeting on 18 February 1998 and to our phone conversations on 9 February 1998 and 10 March 1998, I write to respond to the issues you raised on those occasions.

My understanding is that your concerns related to three areas:

- *Issue 1 – pay grading of Security Force operatives following are view of the Security Service in 1991.*
- *Issue 2 – improper recruitment practices.*
- *Issue 3 – the charging of Security Force clients for work not done and work not being done to standards set out in Service Level Agreements*

I have looked at these three areas and outlined our findings and conclusions below.

Issue 1 – Pay grading of Security Force Operatives following the review of Security Services in 1991

Issue 1 – Findings

As the Council's external auditors we do not have a role to intervene in employer/employee disputes. However, we note that:

- *discussions are still on-going between Unison and the Council in respect of the 1991 calculation of the all-inclusion grade for the Security Force operatives.*

- *the Housing, Environmental and Contract Services Department has given a commitment to rectify any proven miscalculation if any is found.*

Issue 1 – Conclusion

The on-going discussions should resolve this issue in due course.

Issue 2 –Improper recruitment practices

Issue 2 – Findings

The issues you raised related to two items, I have detailed these in the following table along with the findings of the work undertaken to review these issues.

Issues Raised	Findings of Work Undertaken
Temporary Security Officer/Alarm Installer appointed in Summer 1997 without the post being advertised internally or externally	The post was advertised at local job centre and recruitment processes used for selection of the successful candidate followed established Council policies and guidance. The post was not advertised internally in accordance with established procedures on filling posts at the Security Officer/Alarm Installer level in short timescales.
Improper practices followed in the appointment of staff to 6 Security Coordinator posts in Autumn 1996.	No records exist to verify the basis of selection of the successful candidates. Current Council Guidance Notes For Managers on Recruitment and Selection require that records are retained for a minimum of six months. In the absence of the records the issue of whether improper recruitment practices were used is difficult establish. However there is no evidence that individuals raised objections to the selection process at the time.

Issue 2 – Conclusion

Where evidence is available it confirms that Council procedures were followed. A more detailed review in respect of the appointment of Security Coordinators would have been possible if concerns had been raised at or nearer the time of the selection exercise. Given that nearly eighteen months have elapsed since the selection exercise, the absence of detailed records does not indicate that proper practices were not followed.

Issue 3 – The charging of Security Force clients for work not done and work not being done to standards set out in Service Level Agreements

Issue 3 – Findings

The issues you raised related to various items, I have detailed these in the table below along with the findings of work undertaken to review the issues.

Issues Raised	Findings of Work Undertaken
Charges being made to the Parks and Open Spaces Section for closing Parks even though Parks were not shut on some evenings.	Review over a 3 month period showed that on some occasions parks were not closed, mainly due an incident /incidents occurring elsewhere during the evening. However, on each occasion that parks were not closed no charge was made to the Parks and Open spaces section.

Issues Raised	Findings of Work Undertaken
Static security at Pets Corner Sherdley Park not being maintained leading to a break in to the Cafe between Christmas and New Year 1997	The Security Force provision over the Christmas period 1997 accorded with that requested by the client. The break in occurred during a lapse in cover during a shift change. This lapse in cover was accepted by the client given that the request for cover was made at short notice over the Christmas/ New Year period i.e. when staffing resources would be more stretched that usual.
Inadequate staff cover in respect of initiating the Council's Emergency Plan	This area is not subject to a formal agreement between the Security Force and the Council. However, when incidents have occurred, the Security Force has provided two officers. One officer at the Town Hall entrance and one to set up the incident room. Staff cover can be stretched over the shift period from midnight to 8am when only 3 officers are on duty particularly if one officer calls in sick just prior to the start of the shift. However, the fact that the Head and Deputy Head of Service are on-call 24 hours a day provides, in my view, adequate back-up.

Issues Raised	Findings of Work Undertaken
Coverage for schools not being in accordance with Service Level Agreements (SLAs), i.e. not all premises visited, schools not visited within time ranges requested and patrols finishing after midnight. N.B. *(Completion of patrols prior to midnight is not specified in SLAs but considered preferable by the Security Force management)*	Detailed review of radio log sheets over a one week period showed that: • 99.3% of programmed visits were made • 87% of visits were made within the requested time ranges • 85.7% patrols finished prior to midnight

Issue 3 – Conclusions

The audit investigations do not support your concerns that there are significant problems in respect of charging of Security Force clients for work not done or of work not being done in accordance with SLAs. As may be expected minor operational problems have occurred in respect of Security Force service provision during the period under review. On balance, I do not consider that the issues arising have significantly limited service provision to the clients of the Security Service.

I thank you for the information that you have provided which we have been able to use during the course of our audit.

If you have any queries please do not hesitate to contact me.

Yours sincerely

John Vis Audit Manager

Letter copied to:
Carole Hudson - Chief Executive St Helen's MBC
Mike Foy - Director of Housing, Environmental and Contract
Services St Helen's MBC

Ref issue one conclusion:
The on-going discussions should resolve this issue in due course. The Council did resolve this issue 10 years later and only paid the security officers half of what they were entitled to and never back paid them any moneys owing.

Ref issue two conclusion:
Council procedures were not followed as John Vis has stated as temporary employees could not apply for full-time posts. I personally raised concerns near the time of selection when I informed Brendan Farrell in a meeting between August and November 1996 when I told Brendan that the job for Security Co-ordinator is for full-time employees only and that's when Brendan made the temps permanent because Mick Gornall had already decided Peter Woodcock was having one of the Co-ordinator's posts.

Ref issue 3 conclusion:
The audit investigations did not support my claim because if John Vis would have listened in the meeting, he would have seen that there was never a man on Pets Corner and that there was never an alarm response man for weekend and days 0800 to 2000 and afternoons 1600 to 0000 hours Monday to Friday, yet the customer was paying for these services all year round.

Once again, why did John Vis go back three months with opening and closing of the parks and only went back one week with the schools. Had he gone back three months his findings would have gone from 99.3% to around 40%. John Vis in my opinion covered up for St Helen's Council.

29. Because of what was going on in St Helen's Council, I decided to write to Tony Blair, Prime Minister as follows:

26 March 1998

Avon Close, Walton, Liverpool L4 1XL

Dear Mr Blair

Your Government keeps going on about getting people back to work and off benefits and one of your own Labour council's is doing totally the opposite.

I am a shop steward in St Helen's Council and have been for nearly two years. I rang the Assistant Director, Brendan Farrell to meet him when I took over as shop steward. I had never met him before. We had a chat and I said to him off the record, Mick Gornall, the manager of the department, he's telling his staff,'if you don't do what I want, my job's safe'. I also told Farrell that if he sticks to the management rules and I stick to the Union rules we would get on fine. He replied if you cause me any problems I will close the department over night.

I attended my first JCC meeting on the 10 July 1996. At the end of that meeting Farrell produced a Reference of Contract changes dated 7 July 1996. I put this up for my members as one of my members told me he had to take one of the jobs as Co-ordinator or they would finish him. Gornall told me if he does not get six Co-ordinators he would sack six staff and take six off the dole.

Ref the contract changes, Farrell told me I was misleading my members and not to put things up like this again. After the JCC had finished, I went back to Farrell's office to explain why I put it up, he then said I will sack six officers and take six off the dole. I also told him that there were too many staff on days and we didn't have the staff to carry out our duties. I made notes of this meeting the same day and wrote a full report on the 12 July 1996.

On the 17 July 1996 I was on night turn when I received a phone call at 10.10 hours. It was work. I was told that Farrell wanted to see me at 4 o'clock. At 12.35 there was a knock at my front door, it was a letter from Farrell telling me I had agreed to attend at 4 o'clock. I was told to be there. I was accused of getting Gornall sacked. I again made notes and wrote a full report on 25 July 1996.

On the 18 November 1996 I had a meeting with Farrell and Gornall. I told them the wages were wrong. I again saw the management the next day with Les Guilford. Again we discussed the wages. On 20 November 1996 Farrell called a meeting. I was told by Tommy Twist that he, Farrell, and Gornall had been in a meeting and the wages are right. I again made notes on the 18, 19 and 20 November and wrote a full report on the 23 November 1996. I again did a full report on the JCC meeting on 24 April 1997. I wrote this on 27 April 1997.

Farrell told me I'm not getting sacked for you, I'm giving the schools back their money and I'm getting rid of ten men. This was because I produced evidence the job was not getting done and we needed more men.

I had a meeting with Gornall on 27 April 1997. I had a disagreement on several items. I challenged him and Farrell at the Town Hall. Gornall replied Brendan won't let it go that far. I again wrote a full report on 28 April 1997. I had a meeting with management on 24 June 1997. Again I had a run-in with Farrell. He told me the department would close and he would re-deploy Gornall and Anders and the rest of us would be made redundant. I again wrote a full report on the 25 June 1997. I received a phone call from Gornall wanting me to attend Farrell's office at 4 o'clock. I went and Farrell told me I was militant, a trouble-maker and it's me causing the problems in our department. He also told me I've caused more trouble than all the shop stewards together. I left and made notes the same day – 3 July 1997.

On 14 August 1997 I attended a meeting for a JCC. Again I got into a disagreement with management. At the end Gornall made me look a liar. I got up and I was going to hit him. I managed to grab my paperwork and walked out.

I have been off work for eight months with stress caused by Farrell and Gornall.

In 1996 Gornall drove John Swift out. He also got rid of Alec Grant. Alec was told if he does not take early retirement if he makes one more mistake they would sack him and he would lose his pension. Alec was forced into early retirement. Then came the big one. Keith Jones, Peter Waine, Gary Wainwright, Keith Hackett, Jimmy Johnson, Alan Proctor all finished within three months on ill-health. Then Gornall forced Eric Clarke out of the department. Last month they finished Brian Wright off on ill-health. I have now been told they are trying to finish Jimmy Goodier off with blood pressure. They sent him to the work's doctor.

In December 1996 I started having sleeping problems. I also felt my body becoming drained. On 23 April 1997 I had a meeting with Paul Haunch, the full time union officer. I have sent you a copy of his letter dated 10 September 1997. On 30 April I went on a steward's course. Everything we covered over three days I had been involved in. All three tutors told me there is something seriously wrong and I must see the full time official. On 31 July 1997 Farrell and Gornall stormed into the union office demanding to speak to the conveners. Eddy Tickle rang me at home and told me he was not going to speak to them without me present. I said I am not speaking to them without you. I went into work at 4 o'clock and Gornall told me not to go anywhere as I had to go to Brendan's office. I told him 'I am not going without Eddy or Kevan present'. He said 'are you refusing to go to Brendan's office?' I said 'if you're putting it like that, yes'. Gornall went to Farrell's office and came back about five to five. He said 'have you got a minute?' I said 'yes' and went into his office. He looked at his clock, it was 16.55. He said 5 o'clock you don't discuss any union business with myself or Derek. They didn't recognise me as a shop steward. Farrell wrote a letter dated 31 July 1997. I have also sent you a copy with this letter. I took this letter to my MP, Mr Peter Kilfoyle. My MP wrote to Farrell and Gornall on 11 November 1997. Farrell replied on 18 November 1997. Both copies will be with this letter.

On 29 September Gornall saw me at B Wright's. He asked me how I was. I told him 'you and Brendan have made me ill'. He said how's that then?' I replied 'you've f****d my head up, that's how'.3 October 1997 Gornall rang me at home and asked me to see Personnel. He wanted me out and I knew it. 6 October 1997 K Nelson stopped me going to Personnel. He said 'they've already stitched you up'. A couple of weeks later I called into the union office and Thelma told me that Brendan has rung and wants to see me on Tuesday. I went mad. Their own doctor wrote to them and told them to stay away as I was very poorly. He only wanted to finish me.

On 24 November 1997 K Nelson and Jim Keegan came to my home. Kevan said to me 'under the circumstances we feel you should leave the council altogether'. I said I would go. Now let's talk Tribunal. Kevan said 'what for?' I said 'ill-health, loss of earnings, harassment, intimidation and discrimination of a shop steward'. Kevan replied I think we better get you back to work as soon as possible. Later that *day Alan Bolger rang me and said Dereck said 'if he catches Rob Steele playing snooker I'll sack the b*****d'. I rang K Nelson at 21.30 and told him.*

I went to the Town Hall in January to sort out the wages. I have since had problems with Sheila Samuels, Head of Personnel. She told me they wouldn't contact Hardshaw Brook on their enquiry. When I rang her to tell her I had a breakdown of the wages she already had them, she did contact them. She also told me if the Town Hall had got the wages wrong they would hold their hands up. Next time I saw her she told me the Town Hall decided the job was only worth Scale 3. I said Gornall did the re-structure and decided the wages. She said yes he did. I also told her that the management told the work-force that if they didn't take what's on offer, Burns Security will take over at 5pm. In the next meeting I had with her she told me that the management are allowed to make threats to people's jobs to get them to accept what's on offer.

I received a letter from Samuels on 12 February 1998. She started off being nice then came the threats for me to back off. I phoned my Community nurse up and asked her to explain my illness to Samuels. Ten minutes later the Community nurse phoned me back and asked me to go straight to my father's house. She will be there within an hour. She turned up four hours later and said I need to go into hospital. She said Doctor Dutta is coming to see you (the Psychiatrist). He turned up about 18.30 with the house master and he took one look at me and said I don't need sectioning. Whatever Samuels had said to the Community nurse failed. If I had been sectioned how many judges would have listened to me. They have all closed ranks and covering for one another including the union conveners. They are all scared of Farrell.

What needs to happen is a full enquiry with myself, Peter Kilfoyle MP, Gerry Birmingham MP, Dave Watts MP and the

Chief Executive and any legal people required. District Audit are involved and last Wednesday or a week last Wednesday Gornall told a Co-ordinator that he's sick of Rob Steele and his bloody audit. Gornall and Andrea Duff asked the Assistant Manager to tell lies on a disciplinary. I did seven disciplinaries within weeks. The Assistant Manager did the first two and was asked to be on the second one. He was not involved in the other five. I was called into the Town Hall on 26 March 1998. I have to go back on 1 May 1998. I believe they are going to finish me on ill health.

When you reply to this letter can you tell me when the Tories brought in CCT for council work. All the employees in one department need to be interviewed and also all of them who have finished on ill health.

Yours faithfully

Mr R Steele

Ps I have full respect for Peter Kilfoyle and I will not lie or mislead him in any way.

30. I never received a reply from Tony Blair so I wrote to him again as follows on 28 November 1998:

28 November 1998

Avon Close, Walton, Liverpool L4 1XL

Dear Mr Blair
I wrote to you on 26 March 1998. I received a note from Downing Street telling me the complaint had been passed to the relevant department and they will contact me. This did not happen. I have, with this letter sent you the five page copy.

Once again I am telling you there are serious problems in St Helen's MBC, i.e. corruption. I am asking you for a public enquiry. I would also like outside district auditors in to work with me.

The local district auditor has been in and given a report dated 23 March 1998 and in my opinion his findings are a disgrace. Both myself and Peter Kilfoyle, MP have challenged the auditors report. Peter wrote to the relevant people on 24 April 1998 and was denied the information requested. He again wrote on the 7 May 1998, again he was denied. He then wrote to Gerry Birmingham MP on 20 July 1998 and has again written to him on 23 November 1998 as he did not reply to his last letter.

I would like to go through with the public enquiry or district auditors or both, JCC meeting 10 July 1996 (2), allegations against Gornall (3), meetings on 18, 19, 20 November 1996 (4), JCC meeting 24 April 1997 (5), meeting with Gornall on 27 April 1997 (6), meeting with management on 24 June 1997 (7), problems with Head of Personnel (Samuels) 8 April 1998 (8), meeting with Farrell on 3 July 1997 (9), termination of employment on 22 May 1998 (10), letter to Gornall on 6 February 1997, reply from Gornall dated 13 February 1997 (11), District Auditors report dated 23 March 1998 (12), my letter to Peter Mavers dated 28 October 1998, his reply dated 16 November 1998 (13), my letter to Peter Mavers dated 10 November 1998, the reply when I receive it (14), my letter to Peter Mavers dated 23 November 1998 and my reply when I receive it (15), the next letter to Peter Mavers and his reply.

I have seen the works doctor on 20 November 1998 and she asked me to go into hospital and I said 'no'. She asked me can I honestly see myself going back to the Council? I said 'yes'. We asked the doctor and the psychiatrist back in August to return to work, this was not granted. I am again

309

asking to go back in December to sort this out. The doctor told me she cannot see me returning to the Council. I have told Peter Kilfoyle this and he has written to my solicitor asking him to contact Dr Page.

All this has led to me having financial difficulties. I have never been in debt in my life. I have always worked for a living and lived comfortably. I owned two cars and my home. Earlier this year I had to sell one car to pay debts off. I now have to sell my other car to pay off debts once again. I can also see me having to sell the house next year. I have had to pay two lots of £20 costs and one of £25 summons. I have also had to cancel my private pension, all this thanks to St Helen's MBC.

A few weeks ago Tony Marsh told me that Gornall said I had rung him for a week at 4am. Tony asked me did I do it. I said 'no'. I have been asked again by Damian Finnan about this the other night, this is slanderous.

I had a cup of tea with the market officers. Paul Molyneux turned up with Bernard Day. Molyneux went into Gornall and told him I grabbed Bernard around the throat and threatened him. Two weeks later he got Bernard in the office and asked him, Bernard said no. About four months later Gornall told Bernard if you would have said he threatened you, I could have got rid of him four months ago.

Since I have been off, Damian Finnan has been harassed. He has been down the office and said to Gornall,'are you calling me a liar?' and he said no, so he replied, 'well I'm telling you you're a liar'. This was in front of the union and Farrell. Later Gornall told Damian we will pretend it never happened and we will start again. I told Damian he said that 28 months ago. He will go out to get you. A few weeks ago Gornall rang Damian at home. His wife told him he was not in. Gornall got Phil Partington to ring his house every hour and if you don't get an answer, knock on his window. This is harassment and this is what I tried stopping Gornall and Farrell doing when I took over a shop steward.

Going back to bottom of page 1, top of two, I would like to add (16) minutes of JCC in March 1998 and (17) letter from Peter Kilfoyle MP to Farrell and his reply dated 18 November 1997.

I am also sending you copies of letters to Peter Mavers dated 28 October 1998, 10 November 1998 and 23 November 1998. You will see the complaint about the pop. I have been advised to speak to my solicitor, this I am doing Monday.

All this has led to me having a serious drink problem. If you look at my hospital records, you will see I was lucky to drink four pints a month. Now I can drink that by dinnertime and I will drink in the afternoon and nights. I'm out seven days a week. My best mate has got me to go with him on occasions to keep me out of the pub. I know he's only trying to help, I know that is something I do need.

I want to finish off with comments by my three tutors on the stewards induction course 30 April to 2 May 1997. Over the three days I had Stephanie Thomas, Bill Combell and Angela Washington. I took my file with me and everything we covered I had dealt with. All three tutors told me there is something seriously wrong and to see the union when I got back.

I also went to the Council leader, Mike Doyle when I first went off in August 1997 and he told me that what I have said are serious allegations. I don't consider them to be allegations, I believe they are facts. If they are serious then why has nothing been done. I require all members who have worked in Security since 1991 to be interviewed including the ex

Police Officer who lasted two weeks and said Gornall is more bent than the canteen forks.

What to be treated like this? This is one of your labour run councils. What are you going to do about it? These were your words. Enough is enough. Now let's see some action.

Can you make this a matter of urgency as I am very frustrated. I want full involvement in the enquiry.

Yours faithfully
Mr R Steele

31. Department Environment Transport Regions replied to my letter on 10 December 1998 as follows:

Mr R Steele, Avon Close, Walton, Liverpool L4 1XL

Dear Mr Steele

Thank you for your letter of 28 November 1998, addressed to the Prime Minister, which has been passed to this Division as we have policy responsibility for local government matters. In this correspondence, you express grave concern about alleged corruption in St. Helen's Metropolitan Council.

I am writing to let you know about the channels open to you for taking your complaint further.

Legislation provides a framework in which local authorities must operate. They are independent of central government although they are, of course, responsible for their actions and decisions to their electorate, their Auditor and to the courts. It follows that in the absence of specific statutory provisions to the contrary; the Government has no powers to intervene in the day-to-day affairs of a local authority.

The Commission for Local Administration (the Local Government Ombudsman) is unable to consider complaints against parish or town councils, the reason being that every local government elector for such councils has the right to raise any matter affecting parish/town business at the annual parish/town meeting. In this sense democracy is more direct than in the case of county and district councils and gives electors the means themselves to raise any concerns which they may have affecting the business of the conduct of the parish or town council. Nevertheless, parish or town councils, like other local authorities, must act within the law and are subject to challenge in the courts if they do not. And, as I have said, the town meeting provides a very direct way for local electors to air concerns about the conduct of the town council.

You will be interested to know that the Government have recently published proposals for a new ethical framework for local government. It is proposed that each local authority will be required to introduce a code of conduct based on a national model. In addition, councillors will be under an obligation to observe their own Council's Code. There will be arrangements for the prompt investigation and determination of all allegations of malpractice, which in all but the most trivial cases will be undertaken by a new independent body – a Standards Board. There are also proposals in respect of council employees, who will be required as part of their normal conditions of service to observe their council's code of conduct for employees. I enclose a copy of this green paper, which has recently been followed by a broader White Paper covering all of the Government's proposals for modernising local government, which is available from HMSO, price £12.50.

Yours sincerely

PHILIP PERRY

As for the statement made in the above letter, they are of course responsible for their actions and decisions to their electorate, their Auditor and to the Courts is in my opinion a load of bullsh*t. Firstly I contacted the Police late 2011 and I was told they cannot do anything, yet I am part of the electorate. Secondly, the District Auditor on two occasions has in my opinion covered up for the Council as previously explained in this book. Thirdly, I have done everything possible to challenge the Council in the courts and become a victim of a miscarriage of justice. There has been one massive cover up by everyone concerned.

32. I again wrote to Tony Blair on 16 April 1999 and I got nowhere with my last two letters to him as follows:

Avon Close, Walton, Liverpool L4 1XL

Dear Mr Blair

I have written to you twice before and have got nowhere. I still have problems with my employer St Helen's MBC. I am a shop steward for Unison and have been put under great pressure from the management. This has led to me being off work since August 1997.

The union is well aware of the problem but for some unknown reason they will not support my actions. As a shop steward I have a duty to carry out to my members that is all I have done, yet the union have failed to carry out their duty to support myself. I have been to two solicitors and have both told me the union has a duty to represent me and to use the union solicitor. I have also spoken to ACAS and they can't help. I have also informed the commissioner for the right of trade union members, they have told me they cannot make the union support me.

I have, with this letter, sent you a list of problems and have also documented them in more detail. I have a form for the local Government Ombudsman, however, matters relating to staffing issues are not appropriate.

I believe there is a Bill going through Parliament at the moment called Public Interest Disclosure Act 1998. This would have been of some use if it's passed but could be too late for me.

I have also sent you copies of letters – one from Paul Haunch, Regional Officer to Mike Fitzsimmons, Head of Local Government of Unison exposing the Authority as a con merchant. Also a letter from Peter Mavers, Assistant Director to myself.

As you are the Prime Minister and run this country, you tell me where do I go from here. All I want is the problems sorted and put right.

Yours faithfully
Mr R Steele

33. Once again the Department of Environment Transport Regions replied to my letter on the 21 May 1999 as follows:

Mr R Steele, Avon Close, Walton, Liverpool L4 1XL

Dear Mr Steele

LOCAL AUTHORITY PAY AND CONDITIONS OF SERVICE

1. *Thank you for your letter of 16 April to the Prime Minister about your employment with St Helen's Metropolitan Borough Council. I have been asked to reply as this Department has responsibility for monitoring local authority pay and conditions of service. I am sorry, but I have unable to find your previous letters to the Prime Minister, to which you refer.*

2. *Local authorities are independently elected, autonomous bodies and are largely independent of central government. Ministers have no power to intervene in their day-to-day affairs except where specific provision has been made in an Act of Parliament. Such specific provision is not made in relation to the detailed terms and conditions of local government employment, which are a matter for each individual authority to determine. Your concerns have been noted, but I cannot see a case for intervention here.*

3. *If local authority employees have any questions about their pay and conditions of employment, they should approach the local authority direct, or take their case to the relevant Trade Union. I am sorry that I cannot be of any further help.*

Yours sincerely

Mrs Nikki Hinde

Firstly, they say this department has responsibility for monitoring local authority pay and conditions of service yet in their next sentence they say I cannot see a case for intervention here, so all my findings on pay and conditions of service don't count. Also, to say they should approach the local authority direct is a joke as that is what I have done for the last three years and to say or take their case to the relevant trade union is also a joke as I also did that over a three-year period.

The Department of Environment Transport Regions gave me these two avenues to approach as a reason to fob me off knowing I had already done that over a three year period.

34. As I got nowhere with my last three letters to Tony Blair, I decided to write to him again on 21 June 2005 as follows:

Clockface Road, St Helens, Merseyside

Dear Mr Blair

I wrote to you on 26 March 1998, 28 November 1998 and 16 April 1999. I still have problems with St Helen's Council.

In 1998 I asked Mike Doyle, Council leader for a panel of six councillors to confront Farrell and Gornall of the wrong-doings they were doing and he said I could have it and, he never gave me the panel at the end of the day. I went to Marie Rimmer when she took over and she would not see me and she advised me to write to the Ombudsman and I did and he could not help me. She has just got a CBE for what she has done for the people of St Helen's. Why is it she would not see me

I went to St Helen's Police station and spoke to a Detective Inspector Steve Lowe on 26 June 2003 and I showed him some of the things St Helen's Council were doing and he told me there was lies, bullying and embezzlement. Again nothing has been done to the people responsible. I have been to the District Audit and they won't see me and have told me it's a matter for St Helen's Council to sort it out with me.

I have recently been to my MP's office, Shaun Woodward and I asked his case worker can I select six councillors of my choice and have a meeting with Farrell and Gornall and confront them on what they have done and let the councillors decide what action to take. He said I don't see why not so I selected the six councillors and arranged a date to the meeting and all six councillors agreed to it on the 6 July 2005 and I have been told today that my MP has no jurisdiction to get the councillors together. At the end of the day, I have the right to put my opinion across to the councillors.

In my opinion Gornall has been embezzling his clients since 1991 and is still doing it today and I can prove it. How can I get these councillors together with me, Farrell, Gornall and Mavers and confront them on what they are doing and have done.

I look forward to hearing from you soon with how to get a meeting with St Helen's Council.

Yours faithfully

Mr R Steele

Ps Officers of the Council must be responsible to someone for their wrong-doings, there must be a governing body they would have to answer to.

35. I received a reply on 29 June 2005 as follows:

From the Direct Communications Unit

Mr R Steele, Clockface Road, St Helen's, Merseyside

Dear Mr Steele

The Prime Minister has asked me to thank you for your recent letter.

Mr Blair would like to reply personally, but as you will appreciate he receives many thousands of letters each week and this is not possible.

The matter you raise is the responsibility of the Office of the Deputy Prime Minister, therefore he has asked that your letter be forwarded to that Department so that they are also aware of your views.

Yours sincerely

Mrs J A Guilfoyle

Now they are saying the matter you raise is the responsibility of the Office of the Deputy Prime Minister after receiving two letters from the Department Environment Transport Regions. I never received a reply from the Deputy Prime Minister's office so I decided to write to him on 10 July 2005 as follows:

Clockface Road, St Helen's, Merseyside

Dear Mr Prescott

I wrote a letter to the Prime Minister who has passed it on to you, copy sent with this letter.

I was shop steward and I was made very ill with what was going on with Farrell and Gornall. I have not been able to work for the last eight years and I am still not well enough to return to work. I had 76 grievances with St Helen's Council and some of them are still going on today.

All I want is for the truth to come out and for justice to be done. All I want to do is select six councillors of my choice and have a meeting with Farrelland Gornall and confront them face to face on what they have done. I have selected the six councillors, they are; Bessie Griffin, Labour; Pat Robinson,

Labour; John Birne, Liberal; Susanne Night, Liberal; Tony Brown, Tory and Wally Ashcroft, Tory. I would like these councillors to sit on a panel and put my grievances across to them and let Farrell and Gornall answer them. I would like a meeting as soon as possible with these councillors.

Hope you will arrange it soon. Give me enough time to contact my solicitor so he can be present.

Yours faithfully

Mr R Steele

36. I received a reply on 10 August 2005 as follows:

Office of the Deputy Prime Minister

Mr R Steele, Clockface Road, St Helen's, Merseyside,

Dear Mr Steele,

Thank you for your letter of 10 July to the Deputy Prime Minister about St Helen's Council. I have been asked to reply.

I must first explain that local authorities act independently of central government. Ministers have no remit to intervene in their day to day affairs except where specific provision has been made in an Act. Local authorities are however responsible for their actions to their electorate, their auditor and to the Courts.

It is also not for this Office to arrange meetings between councillors and the public, if you wish to bring any matter to the attention of a councillor, you should contact the councillor's office directly.

Yours sincerely

William Tandoh

Once again I was informed Local Authorities are however responsible for their actions to their electorate, their Auditor and to the Courts. As already stated, I contacted the Police as part of the the the electorate and they could not do anything and I contacted the Auditor who in my opinion covered up for the Council twice and I have been trying to get St Helen's Council into Court for the last fifteen years with no joy. I have just been fobbed off once again by the system.

37. The Monday before the 30 April 1998 I attended a meeting in the Town Hall with my father and Mike Doyle, Council Leader. I discussed the District Audit report John Vis had done on 23 March 1998. I made a list of comments on John Vis's audit report on the 9 April 1998 and Mike Doyle took a copy of my notes.

Mike made a comment to my father, 'do you know Mr Steele, someone who has no connections with Rob has told me that it's a waste of time having security in the park as there is never anyone up there on Pets Corner'.

The notes on John Vis are as follows:

Comments on District Auditor's report – John Vis 9/4/98

Reference findings from letter dated 23 March 1998, my comments are as follows:

Issue 1 – it was myself who did all the work on the wages and when I explained the figures to the union and on doing so I confused them. I am the only person who knows what's going on and I have been left out of any discussions. I find this a disgrace.

Issue 2 – Temporary Security Officer/Alarm installer – I don't believe and don't accept that this job could not have been advertised internally due to short timescales. Phil Partington was interviewed for Co-ordinator internally in the middle of December 1996 and was Co-ordinator the beginning of January 1997 two weeks later. It took 3½ months to replace him on the patrol officers side. I asked why does it take 3½months to replace a member of staff. This was asked in a JCC meeting on 24 April 1997. Gornall replied that's how long it takes to contact the Job Centre and then interview and select the right candidate for the job. Again in 1998 Tony Marsh was interviewed for Co-ordinator and was told he had the job within two weeks. He did start the job after three weeks because he had booked a week's holiday on our rota. Again this job was advertised internally. I went to the Job Centre in St Helen's and spoke to the supervisor. I took the District Auditor's report with me. I asked her to check if this job was advertised between May – August 1997. She took the Auditor's Report and was gone for approximately 10 minutes. She came back and said 'I'm going to have to speak to the Manager'. She came back and said 'I cannot give you any information'. I told this to Peter Kilfoyle, MP and he is writing to the Job Centre on my behalf. I am still waiting for the answer.

Issue 6 – Security Co-ordinators – Gornall made three temps permanent after three months so he could make one of them Co-ordinator. Council policy is to temp for two years. All other temps on Patrolling since the three made permanent are still temps. I wrote to Gornall on 6 February 1997 after a meeting with him on 4 February 1997. I told him he should make the two temps permanent as they had been there over three months. I was told it's down to management discretion. In my opinion this is not true. Two years you have to be a temp. When I was a temp Gornall told me I was his best officer and he wished he could make me permanent. I had to wait two years like the rest of the staff. I also had a run in with Gornall about the temp getting the Co-ordinator's job. This is in report 5 dated 28 April 1997. No objections were raised because we had no one to object to.

Issue 3 – changes being made to ranger service – incidents happening elsewhere should not affect the duties. The system has an alarm response man to deal with this. All this shows over the 18 months as Shop Steward I was right when I complained we were undermanned. Pet's Corner – I first reported this to Acting Assistance Director (Farrell) on 10 July 1997. I told him there was no static at Pet's Corner and this was a regular thing. Full details can be seen in report 1 dated 12 July 1996. I do not believe they received a refund for all those times nor for the parks. I asked Eric Ashcroft, Senior Ranger who was in charge of the finances at that time. I asked him since this report was done.

Reference emergency plan – if the Auditor would have checked he would have seen that only one man was on nights. I have done it myself. It's not just one night but two or more and if he would have asked the Co-ordinators, they would have told him there's time when they have rung Gornall and Anders and the mobiles were turned off and got no answer at home coverage for schools. I gave the Auditor a copy of 96 prems outstanding from report 4 dated 24 April 1997. He also took a copy of duties outstanding between 21 July to 21 August 1997. Again I find his findings were poor. I was with them for nearly three hours, I showed them evidence. I told them a lot more than this they didn't look into.

M Gornall leaving the keys in the safe after suspending a supervisor for leaving the door open where the keys are kept, on a bomb scare, Co-ordinators not getting meal breaks on some shifts, six Security Officers finishing on ill health within three months, Gornall creating a job as Liaison Officer as he had two men on days and only one vacancy. I told them mobile patrols of void council houses. This was put to Committee on 20 September 1996 and this has never been done since passed by the Committee. I did look for the review on the day but could not find it. Day men doing Patrol Officers over-time, Websters not being charged for admin.

38. Mike Doyle wrote to me on 30 April 1998 –

Dear Rob

Just a short noet to confirm that I am looking into the further points you raised at our meeting on Monday which require further comment and once I have received a response, I will contact you again.

Yours sincerely

Mike

Councillor Michael J Doyle, JP
Leader of the Council

39. By this time in April 1998, I started drinking heavily. I was drinking up to 12 pints a day and I did not have a care in the world and was driving home from the pub p****d. I had a serious drink problem. When I was well I could only drink four pints and I was p****d and the room would spin and I would be sick. When I became ill because of St Helen's Council, I was drinking up to 12 pints with no effect.

Around this time I turned up to a medical with Dr Fiona Page the work's doctor and I went in the afternoon p****d and I remember her saying to me 'why have you done this to me?'

40. I again attended the Town Hall and had another meeting with Mike Doyle. I asked Mike could I have a panel of six councillors and get Mick Gornall and Brendan Farrell in and thrash my grievances out and Mike said I could. I told Mike I will go away and select my six councillors and left the Town Hall.

41. I again attended the Town Hall and spoke to Mike Doyle. I took the six councillors names and when I told Mike who they were he asked me why had I picked them. I told him I'm not having six labour councillors and I have selected two from each party. Mike told me he was not having John Birne as one of the councillors and if I wanted the panel I had to pick someone else so I did.

42. Mike Doyle later rang me and told me he was not happy about this panel but he would let me have it.

43. I had a meeting with Russ Danson and Pam Gray from Personnel. I took my father with me so once again he could see how I was being treated by the council.

They basically told me they want to see me on 1 May 1998 and they will decide one way or the other whether they will finish me or re-deploy me. They will tell me one way or the other.

44. On 20 May 1998 I had a meeting with Peter Moffat, Assistant Director and Pam Gray, Personnel Manager. Peter wanted me to go into a different job and I told Peter, 'I am going back to Security to sort Gornall out'.

Peter said to me, 'what do you mean, sort Gornall out?'

I said, 'stop him from doing what he's doing'.

Peter then told me that 'Mr Farrell is in a position and staying in a position and Mr Gornall is in a position and staying in a position therefore I'm terminating your employment'. Now I have been sacked to protect Mr Farrell and Mr Gornall from their wrong doings.

I did tell Peter that I was not well enough to return to work as I wanted to return to Security and I was not prepared to go back to that environment till the problems had been sorted. Had they sorted the problems, I could have returned to work with immediate effect.

45. Dr Dutta, Consultant Psychiatrist wrote to my doctor on 3 November 1997. Here is an extract from the letter – 'he told me he has been victimized by his boss for the last 15 months as he is the shop steward and he is getting angry with people very quickly'.

46. Dr Schofield wrote to Jim Keegan of Unison on 3 August 1998. Here is an extract from the letter – 'He presented with a stress related illness with anxiety, agitation and symptoms of

depression. He has responded to treatment though I feel he is not fully recovered and a return to work now may lead to a setback in his condition though Mr Steele himself is keen to return to work as soon as he can.

I feel a full recovery is very possible in view of his improvement so far and eventual return to work beneficial to his condition perhaps as a gradual reintroduction'.

47. Dr Fiona Page employed by the Council wrote to Dr Dutta on 20 November 1998. Here is an extract from that letter – 'I have been asked to see him again by his employer to advise on his on-going fitness for work. However, he also stated that once he had successfully seen his campaign through to the end he intended to return to work for the local authority'.

48. Dr Page wrote to the Council on 20 November 1998. Here is an extract from that letter as follows:

'As you well know, Mr Steele's campaign continues and he intends to see this through to the bitter end. His health continues to suffer as a consequence. Whilst he has been given much consistent advice, it is the nature of his condition he is unable to comply with it'.

The Council knowing I will see it through to the bitter end decided to cover up for Farrell and Gornall knowing my health was suffering because of their wrong-doings and I would not get better till justice had been done.

49. Dr Dutta wrote to Dr Page on 8 December 1998. Here is an extract from that letter –'On the first occasion he told me that he has been victimized by his boss as he is the shop steward.

Since then I have seen him on a domiciliary visit on 20 February 1998 and on four occasions in my outpatient clinic. In February he told me that he has been victimized and he is going for a tribunal. He talked at length as to what the management and the union representatives were doing. He said they are all in a clique together. He also said that there has been a cover up between his managers and the union bosses'.

50. Dr Ben Johnson wrote to my doctor, Dr O'Donnell on 4 August 2000. Here is an extract from that letter as follows:

'He still believes that he was unfairly dismissed but there is no evidence of any aggression'.

51. I attended Dr Dutta's clinic on 6 April 2001 and I was seen by P Nkonde, Staff Grade Psychiatrist and she wrote to Dr O'Donnell on 9 April 2001. Here is an extract from that letter as follows:

'He told me that the sleeping during the day has improved since Depixol was stopped. He however lacks motivation to do things and spends most of the time at home doing nothing. He however reassured me that he is complying well with medication and he has not been hearing voices for some time'.

Firstly, my sleeping was most days up to 23 hours a day and this started September 1999 and went on until 2002. Since 2002 onwards, I sleep around 15 hours a day and still do now in December 2011. I can go several nights at a time without sleeping and many a time I haven't slept for up to 80 hours at a time and as for not hearing voices for some time is wrong. I have never told anyone ever I have heard voices because I have not once heard voices because I have never had schizophrenia in my life.

52. Brian Langshaw, my Community Psychiatric nurse visited me on 24 April 2001 and my mother was talking a load of nonsense to him about my dad and I lost my temper and ran across the room with my fists up at Brian Langshaw. For several weeks Brian was asking me to go into hospital as I needed a break and I kept saying 'no'. On this visit he again wanted me to go into hospital. He later left the house. Later that day, someone rang my dad and I heard him say it does not warrant that. About 6pm Dr Dutta and

another psychiatrist turned up at the house along with Brian Langshaw and a social worker and two Police officers. I was sectioned under Section 3 of the Mental Health Act.

When I got to hospital Brian Langshaw and the social worker came to my room and Brian told me he had to tell Mick Gornall and Brendan Farrell I had been sectioned. I have not got a clue why he had to tell them as in my opinion I was wrongfully sectioned because all I did was raise my fists to Brian and it had nothing whatsoever to do with Brendan Farrell and Mick Gornall.

I was seen by Dr Dutta on a weekly visit in the hospital and on week one Brian Langshaw said in the meeting that I wanted Farrell and Gornall dead. My first reaction was I told Brian I never said that and Brian knew I never said any such words and he shut up. If he had said anything I would have put him in his place as I had never even mentioned anything like that. I'm not having people putting words in my mouth that I have not said.

53. I have a Discharge summary from Whiston Hospital sent to Dr O'Donnell and it states reasons for admission (Signs and Symptoms) admitted on Section 3 – aggressive and unpredictable in community, paranoid thoughts about members of St Helen's Council and threatening to harm them. This statement is in my opinion a load of bullsh*t. At no time at all did I have paranoid thoughts about members of St Helen's Council and at no time at all did I threaten to harm them. Brian Langshaw made it up for a reason to have me sectioned and it worked. I will repeat once again the only thing I did was put my fists up to Brian Langshaw.

Also on the summary it states 'Management and Progress – slow progress. Long time till would open up to staff on ward'. In my opinion this statement is also a load of s**t as one of the staff came into my room, someone called Terry Jones who used to be a hospital porter before becoming a member of staff and I told him everything that had gone on and he said to me at the end of my discussions 'the b*******s'.

I did open up to staff right at the beginning of my time in hospital.

54. After DI Steve Lowe visited my home and in my opinion threatened to have me put away indefinitely. When I attended my next out-patients clinic with the psychiatrist, I told Dr Raja, Staff Grade Psychiatrist on the 14 September 2001 that DI Steve Lowe and another Police officer from CID came to my house in August 2001 and DI Steve Lowe said I had rung Gornall up and threatened to kill him and they have my voice on tape and I said you have not got my voice on tape as it was not me. DI Lowethen said I have told someone that I was going to kill Gornall slowly and I said, get that person to say it to my face as I never said anything and DI Steve Lowe said he will put me away indefinitely and take my driving licence off me. Dr Raja stated the Police cannot do that, it's only the psychiatrist who can do it and to ignore them.

Dr Raja then wrote to Dr O'Donnell on 17 September 2001. Here is an extract from the letter – 'he also informed me that he made a threatening phone call to the manager at the Council office. They were annoyed and told him he should be in hospital for good. He doesn't remember the threatening call to them'. At this stage I left it.

For Dr Raja to say I informed him I made a threatening phone call to the managers and then tell him I don't remember the threatening call to them makes me sound like a total p***k and that's one thing I'm not. What I said above is what I stated and not his version.

55. I attended Dr Dutta, Consultant Psychiatrist's clinic on 26 October 2001 and I told Dr Dutta word for word what I told Dr Raja about the visit from DI Steve Lowe in August 2001. Dr Dutta wrote to Dr O'Donnell on 8 November 2001. Here is an extract from the letter –'he complained of lack of motivation and lack of energy. He is still suspicious and threatens his ex bosses. The Police have warned him about this'. Once again, in my opinion another load of bullsh*t. They don't write down what you tell them and they totally get it wrong. Statements like this are getting

me a bad name and causing me a bad reputation. Like I have said, I am not having people putting words in my mouth when they are not true.

56.1 May 1998, Russ Danson, Personnel Manager, Control and Monitoring wrote to Peter Moffat. Here is an extract –'I believe that the appropriate recommendation to you is that you consider terminating Mr Steele's employment on the grounds of ill-health. Should you decide on this course of action, Mr Farrell, your Departmental Personnel Officer will advise on the correct procedure to be used'.

Brendan Farrell who has threatened to sack me on five occasions is now involved with my first termination.

57. On 16 September 1998, P Leach, Manager of Human Resources wrote to Brendan Farrell as follows:

St Helen's Metropolitan Borough Council
To: Mr B Farrell: Personnel Officer: Housing, Environmental and Contract Services Dept.

Our Ref: Pers/PL/R Steele Result Your Ref:

Extension: 6076   Date: 16 September 1998

Personnel Appeals Sub-Committee - 14 & 29 July& 4 September 1998 Appeal against Dismissal on Capability Grounds by Mr R Steele

Please find attached a copy of the memorandum received from Member's Services confirming that the Sub-Committee resolved that Mr Steele's appeal be upheld.

I would be pleased if you could undertake the necessary action to reinstate Mr Steele, including the adjustment of his pay as appropriate.

Advice is being sought from Legal Service's in respect of the reasoning behind the decision. When this is received I will offer advice on how it affects the management of Mr Steele's absence.

P Leach
Manager – Human Resources

On 12 October 1998 Brendan Farrell wrote to Sheila Samuels about the Council wrongfully sending me my P45 and tried to say it was a mistake. After all the grievances I had with Brendan Farrell he should not have been involved with any issues concerning myself.

58. On 6 May 1998 Eddie Tickle, Branch Secretary of Unison wrote to me as follows:

UNISON, St Helen's Metropolitan Branch

6th May 1998

Mr R Steele, Avon Close, Walton, Liverpool

Dear Rob,

Further to your meeting on Friday 1st May 1998 with Kevan and myself I am writing to confirm what was said in relation to your Unison activities. We asked that:-

If you require representation or advice at any time please ring the branch office and the staff will arrange an appointment for you to see whoever is appropriate. If it is just advice over the phone that you need somebody will talk to you if they are available. If not they will ring you back as soon as possible.

We also asked you not to contact any Unison Steward or member without contacting Kevan or myself in the first instance.

The guidelines were given following your visit to Millbrook on Thursday 30th April 1998. We feel it is in your best interests that you adhere to these guidelines.

Yours sincerely

E. TICKLE

Branch Secretary

The statement made by Eddie Tickle 'we will continue to give you advice and support and help with your on-going issues' is just one big joke. They never gave me any advice, support or help whatso-ever. In my opinion all they did was stab me in the back.

59. On 29 March 1999 I again wrote to Rodney Bickerstaff, General Secretary of Unison as follows:

Mr R B Steele, Clockface Road, St Helen's, Merseyside

Mr R Bickerstaff, Chairman UNISON

Dear Mr Bickerstaff

I find the situation quite ironic in that whilst UNISON is attempting to recruit new members, particularly from among the workforce who might be having trouble with their management, that I, a member, and shop steward of this Union, am still getting nowhere, at either local, or regional level, with my appeals for support in my own three year long problems with my own management.

Twice in the past I have written to you asking for your support, and you have referred my appeals back to regional level, where in my experience, the whole thing just grinds to a halt.

In exasperation I have attended a number of meetings, accompanied by my father, with such people as Mike Doyle, Leader of St Helen's Council: Gerry Bermingham, one of St Helen's two members of Parliament, and Mr J Goodman, District Audit or, and each of whom, having looked through my files, have all expressed their surprise and wonder at my union's apparent total lack of any support.

Moreover, my own MP, Mr Peter Kilfoyle has written twice since 21st December last, on my behalf to Mr Jim Keegan, and to date both of these letters have been ignored!

I have spoken to two separate solicitors, only to be told to consult my union solicitor, but this continues to be blocked by my local official's inertia.

I have a feeling that my problems with my management could be moved along if you could find some way of asking an official from outside this area to come and look into things with a fresh mind.

Of one thing we can all be certain; this thing is NOT going to go away. My local Lib Dem Councillors have 'taken a look' and are supporting me, and I have learned that Inland Revenue have taken an interest to the extent that they have informed the Audit Commission that 'something is amiss.'

Perhaps I could be forgiven for thinking that if my local UNISON people continue to sit on my problems, the whole affair is going to culminate in a blow-out which will reflect no credit on those I look to for support.

I remain, yours sincerely

R Steele

I did not get a reply from Rodney Bickerstaff so my father wrote to him on 18 April 1999 as follows:

Mr JP Steele, Clockface Road, St Helen's, Merseyside
Tel: 0174 ...

Mr R Bickerstaff, Secretary, UNISON

Dear Mr Bickerstaff

I am writing to you on behalf of my son, Rob Steele, who has heard nothing since he wrote to you on 29/3/99.

As a shop steward within the St Helen's, Merseyside, Council Security Service, he has worked hard to do his duty by his members, and this without a great deal of support from his local and area officials in resolving a long drawn out area of disagreement with his departmental managers.

It is now obvious that the resultant strain has cost him both his health and his job, and it is equally obvious that his Union (?) is not prepared to assist him with any back up in any legal action he may take, and I am personally alarmed to discover that he is taking steps to dispose of both his house and his car to part finance legal advice.

I understand that problems within his department still exist, with some new ones thrown in, and that his colleagues, out of fear for their jobs, are not prepared to complain.

My own view, which I have expressed to Rob, is that UNISON, certainly at this local level, coupled with a membership which, on the face of it, does not seem to have the courage to stand up for itself, has made Rob's efforts quite futile; my own opinion of course!

Rob is, I believe, enclosing some further details with this letter for your information.

Yours faithfully

JP Steele

Rodney Bickerstaff also totally ignored my father's letter to him. I wonder why?

60. I received a letter from Jim Keegan, Regional Officer of Unison on 6 March 2000. Here is an extract as follows – 'As advised on the telephone I have entered this application in order to preserve your rights. As far as timescales are concerned, Registration of itself does not imply further Unison support for your case, which will need to be determined following a full assessment of the merits which I intend to undertake. With this advice from Thompsons you should be aware that your local Branch considers that your claim has little prospect of success and on this basis should not be supported'. Eddie Tickle had already stopped me entering the Union office back in 1999. The Union did not want to support my case full stop. Unison had already decided to drop my case. However, on 7 March 2000 I received a letter from Steve Allen of Thompsons solicitors stating I will now be dealing with your case personally. I am the managing partner of the office. The reason for your papers being passed to me is that Mr Pinder has recently left the practice. Jim Keegan, Eddie Tickle and Kevan Nelson had already decided not to take my case any further.

61. Jim Keegan again wrote to me on 23 June 2000 as follows:

UNISON North West Region

Mr R Steele, Clockface Road, St. Helen's, Merseyside WA9 4LF

Dear Mr Steele

RE: SELF v ST. HELEN'S MBC ETC

Please find attached copy correspondence recently received from the Council, the terms of which are hopefully self-explanatory.

In line with my earlier letters and our recent telephone conversation, please note that I have now written to both the Council and the Employment Tribunals advising them UNISON is no longer able to act for you in your case. I have though left both your local appeal and your Employment Tribunal in place and asked that the Council and the Tribunals to now forward any correspondence directly to yourself.

As a consequence, it would now be my intention to close our file but in doing so, I send my best wishes for your future and especially hope that you will soon be able to enjoy good health.

Yours sincerely

James Keegan, Regional Officer

Now Unison is no longer supporting me on my appeal and Employment Tribunal and as to state.'I send my best wishes for your future and especially hope that you will soon be able to enjoy good health' is a joke. It is now January 2012 and I still suffer from a psychiatric illness in my opinion caused by St Helen's MBC for being an honest shop steward and doing my job properly.

62. Steven Pinder of Thompsons solicitors wrote to Jim Keegan on 22 July 1998. Here are some extracts from that letter –

'In the absence of medical evidence suggesting your members return within a reasonable period an industrial Tribunal application may fail. Even if it succeeds your member would be out of work and I can foresee that the Tribunal award would be one of moderate value. A positive statement about returning on any basis should be advanced and as we discussed your member's credibility would be improved by agreeing to renounce his trade union role upon his return, your member's prior attendance record and the written reference should also assist. This leads me on to the reason for your member's absence from work, namely his conflict with management in relation to his trade union role. Your member believes that his current illness has been caused by management and he wishes to claim damages for what are in essence, personal injury.

I could not hope to outline all of the matters raised, suffice to say that your member has encountered problems over several years, most of the problems have arisen since your member became a union representative in 1996.

There is a fine line sometimes between harassment and victimisation and robust industrial relations and it is clear that your member has stood up for his members and that he has pursued grievances for employees in the workplace.

On occasions management may have been pushing your member to the limit'.

63. Steven Pinder wrote to Peter Kilfoyle on 30 November 1998 as follows:

THOMPSONS

Mr P Kilfoyle MP, Liverpool Walton, House of Commons, London SW1A0AA

Dear Mr Kilfoyle
RE: ROBERT STEELE

Thank you for your letter dated 23 November 1998. The position in terms of my involvement in this case remains as set out in my letter dated 28 September 1998, and I have written to UNISON to ask whether they would like me to become more formally involved. I am sorry that I cannot offer any more positive information, but as you will appreciate I can only undertake work on a file if instructed to do so by the union.

Yours sincerely

STEPHEN J PINDER
For THOMPSONS

64. Steven Allen from Thompsons solicitors wrote to me on 7 March 2000 as follows:

THOMPSONS

Mr R Steele, 63 Clock Face Road, St Helen's, Merseyside

Dear Mr Steele

I will now be dealing with your case personally. I am the Managing Partner of the office. The reason for your papers being passed to me is that Mr Pinder has recently left the Practice.

I am presently awaiting your hospital records.

I would also like to see and consider your personnel records and occupational health records from work. Could you please sign and return to me the attached forms of authority.

As soon as I have all the records I will arrange to see you so that we can go through your case in detail.

Yours sincerely

Steve Allen
for THOMPSONS

Even though Steve Allen stated he will be dealing with my case personally, Jim Keegan had written to me the day before on the 6 March 2000 – 'itself does not imply further Unison support for your case. That your claim has little prospect of success and on this basis should not be supported'.

Unison had already decided not to support my case before Steve Allen had even looked at my case. Unison gave me no support from the day I became ill in August 1997 and since I became a Unison shop steward the only grievance they dealt with was the wages with Paul Hornch and Jim Keegan backed down on that issue.

65. I attended a meeting with Steve Allen and Jim Keegan at Thompsons solicitors on 18 April 2000. Here are Steve Allen's attendance notes:

ATTENDANCE NOTE   *SA/STEELE/S99V0058*

Attending Jim Keegan and Mr Steele on 18 April at 10am. Mr Steele was here a few minutes early and Jim Keegan was a few minutes late, held up in traffic. While we were waiting for Jim Keegan Mr Steele handed me a newspaper report from the Daily Mail for January. When Jim Keegan arrived I saw the two of them together. Jim Keegan explained that appeals had been entered against dismissal on two grounds namely against the medical assessment, namely that he is permanently incapable of doing his job and then against his dismissal to the elected members.

Jim showed me a letter from the GP of September 1999 which was not helpful. He said that in practice the appeal to the Independent Medical Assessor was unlikely to be successful. We had no medical evidence contrary to that put forward by the Council's doctor, Dr Fiona Page. Furthermore, if the medical appeal was not successful, the appeal to the elected members would not be successful, not least because this is the second time the client has been dismissed. His dismissal was withdrawn and he was reinstated in 1998, to give him more time to recover. A great deal of further time has now elapsed.

Mr Steel said he asked his own doctor to sign him back to work and it seemed his own doctor was prepared to do so in March 1999.

Jim Keegan pointed out that we have a letter from the GP in September 1999 which does not help. In response to a direct question Mr Steele told me that he did not know if he was fit enough to go back to work. He is on anti-depressants, still seeing the Psychiatrist Dr Dutta and seeing the Community Psychiatric Nurse who comes out and gives him an injection every three weeks to control his anger/violence.

I explained to Mr Steel that in my view his appeal would not be successful because there was no medical evidence to counter the employers and I told him also that his Employment Tribunal would not be successful. I explained to him that the background reason for his stress related illness was not relevant. I gave him the analogy of a workman who injured his hand in a machine so that he could no longer do his job. The employers might have been negligent, but they were still entitled to dismiss, provided they first checked whether the client could do the job with suitable modifications – the Disability Discrimination Act point – and provided they also checked whether there were any suitable vacancies for alternative work.

We then moved on to the stress related illness.

There was a significant background but the precipitating reason for coming off work in August 1997 was a row with the line manager Mr Gornall, which Mr Steele described as a big bust up. He also complains about Mr Farrell who was in the personnel department.

In response to a direct question he said that they did not know at work that he had seen a Psychiatrist back in 1995 for other reasons.

I told Mr Steele that it was clear that there had been a number of work related issues and disputes. However, it was not legally foreseeable that those would give rise to a psychiatric illness. I explained to him in detail the courts decision in the Walker case, and I quoted to him at length from the Rorrison case and indeed gave Jim Keegan a copy of the Judgment.

All that took a considerable length of time. Unfortunately, at the end of it and as the client was leaving he said that if the law did not help then he would take matters into his own hands and kill the two people concerned. Generally speaking throughout the interview Mr Steele had been polite and had not said a great deal.

After this I spoke to Jim Keegan who will make sure that the Branch gets to know what was said. The relevant managers are members of UNISON I believe. I also asked Jim to telephone the GP.

After further discussion it was agreed that I would do so. Due to other commitments I was not able to telephone until about 4pm and then spoke to Dr Schofield who felt that he was unable to do much. I tried Dr Dutta the Consultant at about 12 o'clock not long after the interview finished. I got no response from the hospital. I then tried again at 4.25pm and got a response from the hospital but no response from Dr Dutta's office.

I am not inclined to write to this client for the time being. Jim Keegan thought there would be a request from other solicitors now for the papers.

Engaged: 1 hour reading the papers prior to the interview.

1 hour 15 minutes with the client and Mr Keegan.

First, Steve states Jim showed him a letter from my GP of September 1999. I have never seen this letter and if Jim had showed Steve it then I would have seen it. Then on paragraph four Steve stated Jim pointed out we have a letter from the GP in September 1999. Steve Allen has contradicted himself. Secondly, to state 'however, it was not legally foreseeable that these would give rise to a psychiatric illness' is in my opinion a load of c**p. The evidence was available to Thompsons and they never bothered their a**e to look at it as Unison did not want them to.

For Steve Allen to say 'Unfortunately at the end of it and as the client was leaving he said that if the law did not help then he would take the matter into his own hands and kill the two people concerned', this is utter bullsh*t. I still remember what I said and it was not when I was leaving, I was in the middle of discussions with Steve Allen when he said to me because I had not gone back to work and gone off sick again there was nothing else he could do and I replied,'then I will take the law into my own hands'. At no time did I mention the word kill. In my opinion Jim Keegan stayed behind after the meeting and it was him who put those words 'kill' into Steve Allen's head because Mick Gornall had been telling Jim I was going to kill him.

At the end of the meeting Jim told Steve Allen that Mick Gornall is a bully and he was going to do something about it. Like everything else, Jim never did.

Damian Finnan, ex Security Officer and Co-ordinator told Milly Waine, Peter Waine's mum who was also an ex Security Officer, that some of the lads in Security have got Mick Gornall s**t scared of Robbie. This is where all the alleged threats of killing him are from, not me.

I believe that Thompsons solicitors should have advised me to return to work and had things not changed or been dealt with, go off sick again to safeguard a claim but from the start Unison did not want to support my claim. As for me not saying a great deal, it was because I was suffering from severe depression and had been doing so since September 1999 brought on by everyone concerned in this case.

66. Steve Allen wrote to me on the 13 June 2000 as follows:

Mr R Steele, 63 Clock Face Road, St Helen's, Merseyside

Dear Mr Steele

Many thanks for your letter and enclosure,s which I received on 8th June 2000.

I think I have seen all these documents before, and I certainly considered them in detail before we met on 18th April.

As we discussed, it is perfectly clear that there were a number of work related issues and disputes. However, as I tried to explain to you, I do not think that we could establish in your case that it was legally foreseeable that those problems would give rise to a psychiatric illness.

The leading case in this area of law is Walker -v- Northumberland County Council. In that case Mr Walker was subjected to extreme stress over a period of time. It was all minuted and recorded by the employers. He had a nervous breakdown. After a few months he recovered and he went back to work on the employers assurance that they would provide assistance etc. When he got back to work the employer's assurances were not honoured. As a result he was once again exposed to a great deal of stress, and suffered another nervous breakdown.

When the case came to Court the Judge found that although the employers knew all about the stress he was under before the first breakdown, nevertheless the first nervous breakdown was not legally foreseeable. Having suffered the first breakdown, however, the second breakdown <u>was</u> foreseeable and the employers were accordingly negligent in respect of the second breakdown.

Having considered your case in detail, I do not think that you would overcome the legal foreseeability hurdle.

As you know, we discussed all of this when we met. I do not feel there are any realistic prospects of proceeding successfully with a personal injury claim on your behalf.

I am very sorry that this is the case.

I should warn you however that normally any legal proceedings must be commenced within three years of the relevant event. In your case the three year period would run from the date in August 1997 when you came off work ill. If proceedings are not commenced within that time limit your claim would probably be out of time and statute barred.

I am extremely sorry it has not proved possible to pursue a claim successfully on your behalf.

If there are any further points you would like me to consider or if you think I have missed anything, please do not hesitate to let me know.

Yours sincerely

Steve Allen
for THOMPSONS

To say 'I do not think that we could establish in your case that it was legally foreseeable that those problems would give rise to a psychiatric illness', to think something is not a direct answer, Jim Keegan had already decided my case was not going to court and Steve Allen used this answer I think to get rid of me. The only way I would have found out whether I had a case or not was to put my case in front of a judge as a decision of the court of appeal in COTT VIBC Vehicles LTD (2006). The times 21 April where Lord Justice Sedley is reported to have stated that in an action founded on negligence the question is not whether the particular outcome was foreseeable but whether the kind of harm for which damages were sought was foreseeable and the decision in this case appears to have relevance to my claim.

To state 'In your case the three year period would run from the date in August 1997 when you came off work ill', Thompsons gave me a two month warning to get my case into court knowing that another solicitor would not touch the case with too little timescale to put my case forward. Thompsons should have dealt with this matter earlier and when I was well enough to take my case elsewhere and get justice.

67. I wrote to Mike Doyle on 19 July 1998 as follows:

Avon Close, Walton, Liverpool L4 1XL

Dear Mike

I have had several meetings with you and spoken to you on the phone on a number of occasions, I now feel it should be in writing.

I first came to you at your workplace about 10 months ago. I told you about the problems in Security and how I have been victimized by Farrell and Gornall. I produced reports and evidence to confirm my allegations.

When we left the building, I continued to tell you what's going on, and you said they are serious allegations.

Peter Kilfoyle, MP wrote to you on the 10 March 1998 and you replied on the 16 March. The next time I saw you, I told you your letter had Sheila Samuels' written all over it. I also spoke to you about single status and showed you a breakdown of wages. You yourself told me it's costing 1 million pounds for single status and if that's what our wages come to that's what we're entitled to. I also told you we were on less than £4 per hour, again I showed you this. I also told you that Farrell and Gornall said there is no breakdown on wages and you said there has to be.

I next saw you with my father. We went through the District Auditor's report dated 23 March 1998. You took a copy of my comments on District Auditor's report 9 April 1998. You told us that a member of the Council had made the same allegation on Pets Corner, I had. This was about three months ago, I asked you for a panel of Councillors, and I selected six, you later rang me and said you're not happy about this panel but you will let me have it. The end of May I had my employment terminated.

I have put an appeal in, however I don't stand a chance of getting my job back. I am concerned that Farrell and Samuels are involved with my appeal. I find this a disgrace. I saw Peter Kilfoyle again and you rang me at home and I told you Peter was writing to you as I asked him for Farrell and Gornall to be at the hearing, so we can have it out once and or all. You then told me I have to wait till after my appeal because of the law. But in your letter to Peter you have stated you're not willing for this appeal till after the outcome of the appeal.

Whether I win or lose, I want that hearing. In the minutes of the JCC (March 1998) meeting, Peter Moffatt has stated I am spurious.

In your last telephone call you told me all I want is justice. That's all I want, the truth out.

Yours faithfully

Mr R Steele

Ps Sent you copies of my debts caused by shortage of income.

68. I then received a reply from Mike Doyle on 23 July 1998 as follows:

St Helen's Metropolitan Borough Council

Mr Robert Steele, Avon Close, Walton, Liverpool L4 1XL

Dear Robert

Thank you for your letter dated 19 July 1998.

Whilst I sympathise with your obvious frustrations, until your Appeal is considered, I am unable to progress your request for a further meeting.

Yours sincerely

COUNCILLOR MICHAEL J DOYLE JP
Leader of the Council

69. I again wrote to Mike Doyle on 11 January 1999 as follows:

Avon Close, Walton, Liverpool L4 1XL

Dear Mike

I am writing to you, firstly to inform you that the specialist I am under, has written to Dr Page 'works doctor' and stated I am unfit for work as a Security Officer and can be regarded as permanently unfit for work.

I have trusted you, and allowed you to deal with this problem. I have had several meetings with you, I have phoned you on numerous occasions, and you have failed to return many of my calls. You also asked me not to go to the papers, on three occasions and I did not. You were made well aware of the problems, back in August 1997 and you stated these are serious allegations you are making. I feel you have failed to look into this matter, and have let myself and my members down.

It's a good job I did not know the TV was going to be at United Glass when you were interviewed, because I would have confronted you on this matter. If you do as much for the workers of United Glass, as you did for us, they may as well forget their jobs.

I partly blame you for my health problem, and losing my job, if you would have acted when I first came to you for help, then none of this may have happened.

I feel under the circumstances you should resign as Council Leader and let someone who will deal with these matters have the job.

I am now going to deal with the matter my way, and I will get to the truth and see justice. I and Milly Waine are seeing Councillor John Beirne tomorrow and will be informed of all the goings on in Security.

I have written to the Auditors Commission, asking them to investigate my facts, and not allegations. I have also got a meeting with the tax inspectors over the wages.

I don't care whose toes I tread on: the truth is going to come out. St Helen's Council is supposed to be run by Councillors <u>NOT</u> the Chief Executive, and its officers.

One disillusioned shop steward.

Yours faithfully
Mr R Steele

70. I then received a reply from Mike Doyle on 21 January 1999 as follows:

St Helen's Metropolitan Borough Council

Mr Robert Steele, Avon Close, Walton, Liverpool L4 1XL
Dear Robert

Thank you for your letter dated 11 January 1999. I am rather disappointed by your remarks that you feel I have failed to look into your complaints. As you are aware, I have discussed at some length the issues you raised both with yourself, your father, your MP and Senior Officers of the Council, in an attempt to find solutions.

I am sorry that you have been declared permanently unfit for work, however, I do not accept that my actions have attributed to this in anyway. You are, and always have been, free to contact whomever you care to and if the individuals named, or the newspapers can achieve your aims, I wish you nothing but success.

I have nothing else to say on the matter.

Yours sincerely

COUNCILLOR MICHAEL J DOYLE JP
Leader of the Council

Firstly, discussing at some length with myself, my father, my MP and senior officers of the Council is not a solution, giving me my panel of six Councillors would have been the solution or meeting my MP, which was agreed may also have led to a solution. I was also declared permanently unfit for work by a psychiatrist who from somewhere came up with the idea I have schizophrenia. I do not accept his diagnosis and do not believe I have not got or never have had schizophrenia like illness. This was in December 1998. If Mike Doyle had done his job then I could have returned to work with immediate effect, as the problems that were making me ill would have been sorted.

71. Mike Doyle, leader of the Council wrote to Peter Mavers, Assistant Director of the Council on Friday 2 October 1998 as follows:

MEMO

To: Peter Mavers, Assistant Director – HECS
Sheila Samuels, Manager – Human Resources & Employee Support

From: Councillor Michael Doyle, Leader of the Council
Date: Friday, October 2, 1998

Subject: Mr Robert Steele, Avon Close, Walton

Could you give a full account as to why the error occurred with regard to Mr Steele receiving his P45 from your section.

At a time when Mr Steele is convinced that we have some kind of vendetta against him, how am I to convince him otherwise.

I shall await your comments.

COUNCILLOR MICHAEL J DOYLE JP
Leader of the Council

72. Peter Mavers wrote to Jim Keegan, Regional Officer of Unison on 4 December 1998 as follows:

St Helen's Metropolitan Borough Council

Mr J Keegan, UNISON, Civic House, 131 Katherine Street, Ashton-under-Lyne OL6 7DE

Dear Mr Keegan

Re: Mr Robert Steele

I refer to the above and for your information enclose various items of recent correspondence from Mr Steele. I also enclose a copy of a letter from UNISON in respect of Mr Michael Gornall, Head of Security.

My purpose in writing to you as Mr Steele's representative is that I am concerned about the effect Mr Steele may be having on the Security Section. Mr Gornall is concerned on a personal basis for his family and via UNISON has requested that a dedicated telephone line linked to Security be installed at the Council's expense. This will enable his private line to be rendered ex-directory.

Also I have been made aware that Mr Steele has been into the Security Offices on Sunday 30 November 1998 between 11.00pm and midnight and on Monday 1 December 1998 at midnight. His continued comments about Mr Gornall are both unhelpful in terms of his medical condition and are exacerbating Mr Gornall's anxieties.

Due to the sensitivity I do not feel it prudent to contact Mr Steele directly at this time, but I do feel that a meeting between ourselves would be of assistance. Could you please contact me to arrange.

P MAVERS
Assistant Director

Encs

73. Peter Mavers again wrote to Jim Keegan on 9 November 1999 as follows:

St Helen's Metropolitan Borough Council

Mr J Keegan, UNISON, Civic House, 131 Katherine Street, Ashton-under-Lyne OL6 7DE

Dear Mr Keegan

Re: Mr Robert Steele

I refer to your letter of 27 October 1999 and am somewhat puzzled by the contents. For your information I am unaware of any complaints of bullying and harassment by Mr Steele. Accordingly I am not aware of any documents relating to the bullying and harassment of Mr Steele. Your requests are further puzzling in that the local UNISON branch have consistently informed the department that they have no issues with any complaints made by Mr Steele. The only indication of complaint that I can recall is a meeting between Mr Steele, myself and Cllr Doyle on 27 October 1998. At this meeting Mr Steele outlined a series of general complaints about the activities of the Security Section and I have enclosed copies of Mr Steele's complaints and my response, which was copied to Cllr Doyle.

The matter of Mr Steele's treatment is further confusing in that the UNISON Branch-Secretary and Convenor appear to take a different perspective than yourself. I outline this as follows:-

A letter to Mr P Kilfoyle MP from Kevan Nelson on 13 November 1997 indicated that there were no issues concerning Mr Steele's treatment by his managers.

UNISON via Kevan Nelson requested that Mr Mick Gornall receive a funded alternative phone line due to offensive telephone calls he was receiving.

On 3 August 1999, Kevan Nelson and Eddie Tickle requested a meeting with myself on behalf of Mick Gornall the Head of Security. At the meeting Messrs Tickle and Nelson requested assistance to combat the harassment and threats of violence and abuse that had been directed towards Mr Gornall by Mr Steele.

Mr Gornall has informed me that at a meeting on 14 April 1998, in the presence of Kevan Nelson that you personally advised him to complain to the Police about the threats made by Mr Steele.

Given the above I feel that you need to consult with the Local Officials, and if necessary I will request written statements from the Convenor and Branch Secretary to confirm my understanding of these issues.

On the matter of notice pay, it is the Council's practice to make payments in accordance with the Occupational Sick Pay Scheme during the notice period, pending the outcome of the appeals process. However, as Mr Steele's notice ended on 8 November 1999, he will be paid for the 7 weeks notice on the next pay date i.e. 22 November 1999. He will also receive payment for untaken annual leave accrued up until 8 November 1999. I have written to Mr Steele to confirm this, and enclose a copy for your information.

I would request that you provide Mr Steele's medical evidence that contradicts that of the Council's Medical Advisor and his nomination for the independent Medical Advisor within the next 28 days. If I do not receive these within this timescale, I will assume that you are not pursuing the medical appeal.

Yours sincerely

PR MAVERS
Assistant Director

Encs

For Peter to say 'I am unaware of any complaints of bullying and harassment by Mr Steele', Peter wrote to Jim on 4 December 1998 – 'Mr Gornall is concerned on a personal basis for his family and via Unison has requested that a dedicated line linked to Security be installed at the Council's expense'. Things had been said to Peter and he denied it in his letter dated 9 November 1998 and on page 2, 'Mr Gornall has informed me that at a meeting on 14 April 1998 in the presence of Kevan Nelson that you personally advised him to complain to the Police about the threats made by Mr Steele'. I never made any threats to Mr Gornall at any time. They are all in my opinion lies to discredit me, to cover up his wrong doings and to prevent me returning to work. Also if I had threatened Mick Gornall, the same threats would have also been aimed at Brendan Farrell as I hated them both the same.

74. Because I had been fobbed off by Mike Doyle, Council Leader, Sheila Samuels, Head of Human Resources, Russ Danson, Personnel Manager, Carole Hudson, Chief Executive and Eddie Tickle, Kevan Nelson and Jim Keegan, all of Unison, I decided to write to Peter Mavers, Assistant Director on the 28 October 1998 as follows:

Avon Close, Walton, Liverpool, L4 1XL

Dear Peter

Further to our meeting yesterday, 27 October 1998 with Councillor Mike Doyle present.

Can you please send me a copy of the Union agreement for APT & C Scale 3 all-inclusive salary for 1991.

I also require a full breakdown of wages for 1998/1999. Like Councillor Doyle stated, there has to be a breakdown of wages and he will not accept there is not one IE an all-inclusive grade = £6.06ph.

Here is my breakdown of the wages.

Basic Pay	*£6,982.59*
Shift Allowance 20%	*£1,396.51*
Weekend Allowance	*£3,417.84*
Bank Holiday Allowance	*£499.05*
A total of per annum	*£12,295.99*

This gives you a weekly wage of £134.28 and an hourly rate of £3.44, these figures are on a Patrol Officer's basic pay.

I would also like to know how you justify the Market Officer's wages going from £8,416.20 per annum to £9,963.00 in 1991, an increase of £1,546.80 and the Patrol Officer's wages going from £10,840.70 to £9,963.00, a loss of £877.71. The members were informed that they would receive a protected earnings of £71.65 a month for going on one-man patrols.

However, this was reduced to £50.65 and the officers were told they had made a mistake.

If you look at review of Security Services 31 October 1991, page two, paragraph 2. This does not mean any cuts in wages to employees, as you can see above, this is untrue.

If you look at Gornall's letter to Mr Nelson 10 December 1997. By his own calculations the wages equate to Scale 4 and not 3. You yourself stated it came to Point 19 of Scale 4.

I worked out the wages and informed the members that their protected earnings were their Bank holiday payments and not for going on one-man patrols. I confronted Gornall on this matter in a JCC meeting and he told Farrell that they are their Bank holiday payments and they think the money was for going on one-man patrols. I have spoken to members after leaving you and they have confirmed this to me.

I also would like in writing why the members were threatened that if they don't take what is on offer Burns Security will take over the department at 5 o'clock that evening. At this time compulsory tendering was not available.

I have also had confirmed that they did not sign their contracts as the shop steward at the time told them not to (Jimmy Johnson). He is no longer with the Council but will give evidence in a later meeting or a Court of law.

When I had my interview for the job in 1992, Gornall told me that in 1991 they had a review in security and the Bank holidays, weekend allowance, shift allowance and basic pay were all calculated together and came to Scale 3. We all know it now that it came to Point 19 of Scale 4. I have not been paid for my Bank holidays. I would also like to inform you that if security would have stayed on a manual grade they would now be on £13,445.24, they would be better off by £1,149.25 pa, the whole idea of going on APT & C was to be better off.

I look forward to your reply within 10 working days of you receiving this letter.

If an agreement has not been made then I will send copies of this letter, along with your reply to 10 Downing Street, Peter Kilfoyle MP and Mike Doyle.

Yours faithfully
Mr R Steele

75. Peter Mavers replied on 5 November 1998 as follows:

5 November 1998

Dear Rob

I refer to your letter dated 28 October 1998, which I only received yesterday (4 November 1998).

Following our meeting last week I promised to review your calculations and to attempt to clarify the signatories to the review of Security Service agreement in 1991.

Unfortunately, the Head of Security was on leave until Monday this week and I was only able to begin the research upon his return.

I will, however, respond to you in detail as soon as it is practicable to so do.

Yours sincerely

P R MAVERS
Assistant Director
Housing. Environmental and Contract Services

cc Councillor M Doyle

76. I then received another reply from Peter Mavers on 16 November 1998 as follows:

16 November 1998

Dear Robert

May I first offer my apologies for the length of time taken to respond to you following our meeting with Councillor Doyle on 27 October 1998. As I explained in my earlier note, I was unable to progress any investigative work immediately because the files were unavailable.

In responding I have found it helpful to refer to your letter dated 28 October 1998, which seems to summarise much of what was discussed the previous day.

One of the points you make most forcibly is that you believe there was no agreement to the proposals put forward to the

Security Service in 1991. In researching this matter I see from the files that the proposals were necessary because the Security Service was going through a difficult phase both commercially and in terms of its credibility with its customers. Indeed, there is a letter on file dated August 1991, from the joint trade unions involved, requesting that a survival plan be drawn up and presented to elected members as a matter of urgency. This request was met when a report was presented to the Trading Services Committee in October 1991. The report outlined the difficulties faced by the Security Service, the inflexibility and constraints associated with the existing structure and shift patterns, and the problems of demarcation and working practices.

The Committee report outlined proposals to resolve the difficulties, which included annualised hours, an all-inclusive grade and changes to the Staff Structure. The grade recommended for Security Officers was Scale 3 (point 16) and the grade was inclusive of shift and weekend allowances and Bank Holiday pay.

The report contained the mandatory section regarding the need for consultation with the relevant trade unions. Though the file does not contain any record of the meetings held between management and trade unions, it is clear from correspondence that agreement was reached with the senior trade union representatives of the day.

As part of my investigations I have interviewed two of the three trade union convenors involved in the agreement, the third regrettably in now deceased. Both convenors interviewed confirmed their involvement in and assent to the proposals on behalf of their respective members as outlined in the Committee report.

I have further seen copies of a large number of individual security officers, including two of the shop stewards at the time, agreeing in writing to the proposed conditions of service, grades and new working arrangements.

It seems fairly clear to me that the proposals were properly discussed, approved by committee and were accepted by the workforce at the time. There was protection offered to existing post holders but new personnel to the service, obviously including yourself, were recruited on the revised conditions.

Whilst interviewing the now UNISON convenor relating to the agreement, he advised me that UNISON have informed you that they are to take up the grading issue once again and it may therefore be a duplication of effort to be investigating the matter solely at your behest. In light of these comments I intend therefore to concentrate on the major issues you raised relating,to the calculations.

It is impossible to break down an all-inclusive grade into an amount of cash relating to each of the constituent parts, however, the elements included are basic pay, weekend working allowance, shift allowance and Bank Holiday payment.

Turning to my analysis of the figures you produced at our meeting on 27 October 1998, there are some elements in which I am unable to follow your reasoning. On page A of your document you begin by using a figure of 196 hours weekend allowance to be included in the calculation. The rota for the relevant period gives a figure of 195 hours and consequently the figure of £37.80 you have in your summary is incorrect.

Referring to the Bank Holiday payments, you show 28 hours at double time when in fact this should be single time because the officer would already have been paid single time in the basic pay line for the particular day on which the Bank Holiday falls and is therefore only entitled to a further single time payment plus 28 hours at lieu time as you have correctly shown.

The combination of rest days on Bank Holidays which you have shown do not coincide with any rota on file and certainly do not represent the situation in 1991.

Your figures on page A seem to more or less agree with those produced by the Head of Security for basic pay £140.28 pw and for shift allowance at £22.44 pw. However, your figure for weekend allowance of £37.80 on page A is replaced in your assertion of 'How management should have broken down the old grade' by a figure of £37.14, which I can see no basis for and is in fact less than the figure allowed in the Head of Security's calculation (i.e. £37.57).

I can see no basis for your figure of £8.28 for Bank Holiday allowance, there seems to be no substantiation or other refer-ence to the figure. Perhaps you would wish to explain your understanding in this respect.

No doubt you will be able to explain your thinking in relation to the original calculations and the figures used as a basis for the agreement to the UNISON officials as they take up the issue corporately.

In relation to the other points you raised, the pay of the market officers seemed an issue. You suggested in your letter that the market officers were paid £8416.20 per annum but as I under-stand the position there was no discrepancy between the rate of pay for the market officers and the remainder of the security officers. Prior to becoming responsible for market security, the four officers involved were part of the regular rota and paid on exactly the same basis as the other officers on the rota.

You state in your letter that protected earnings of £71.65 per week were indicated for converting to one-man patrols.

My understanding is that the protected earnings were paid for a commitment to increased weekend working and payment for Bank Holidays. There were no payments or protection offered for converting to one-man patrols. One-man patrols were essential to the survival of the Security Service.

You suggest in your letter that the protection element was reduced to £50.65. I am advised that this did happen at the time when the security officers received their annual increment. This is the way in which the Council administers a protection and guarantees that staff do not get a lower wage than at the point when the new structure began.

Referring to the Head of Security's letter to Mr K Nelson in December 1997, the figures were provided to indicate the element of protection to existing staff and nothing to do with the scale 3, which was agreed as the new grade for the future of the service.

You next refer to an allegation that security officers were threatened with the introduction of a private security company. I have interviewed the officers concerned and am informed that the security officers were informed that if they did not report for duty on 9 November 1991, supervisors and senior managers would provide the service. It is likely that during the course of the meetings reference was made to the inevitability of private companies taking over the service if the necessary cost reductions and amended working practices were not effected.

You suggested at our meeting and again in your letter that the security staff did not sign to confirm their agreement to the corporate agreement negotiated by their trade unions. I have seen letters of acceptance from quite a number of those concerned, including 2 of the 3 shop stewards involved in the negotiations. The fact is that all of the officers took up their new duties and no one felt strongly enough to use the Council's procedures to pursue any objections to the agreement.

In conclusion it seems to me that the proposals considered by the representatives for the Security Service were a last ditch attempt to rescue the service in the face of commercial disaster. Credibility of the service was low and costs were too high for customers to continue using the service.

I am satisfied that protection of existing employees' earnings was made and honoured in the way in which the Council usually undertook such matters. Grade 3 was agreed as the substantive all-inclusive grade and all new starters were offered and accepted this rate of pay.

The allegations you have made in our recent meeting seem to me to be unfounded on your evidence presented thus far. However, I am prepared to keep an open mind when the whole issue is raised corporately by UNISON.

You may have further queries arising from my response and I would be happy to consider any new information you may have, although this may be most appropriately directed through UNISON.

Yours sincerely

P R MAVERS
Assistant Director

Housing, Environmental and Contract Services

cc Councillor M Doyle

My calculations on my letter of 28 October 1998 were wrong, I calculated the weekend allowance by the hourly rate of an all inclusive wage of £6.06 per hour when it should have been calculated at £4.10 per hour so it should have shown as below:

Basic Pay	£ 7,903.79	*£4.10ph*
Shift Allowance 20%	£ 1,580.76	
Weekend Allowance	£ 2,312.40	*564 hours*
Bank Holiday Allowance	*£499.05*	
A total of per annum	*£12,296.00*	

Peter goes on to say on page A of your letter document, you begin by using a figure of 196 hours weekend allowance to be included in the calculation. The rota for the relevant period gives a figure of 195 hours and consequently the figure of £37.80 you have in your summary is incorrect. This statement is in my opinion untrue I took the rota to Mike Doyle and I got him to calculate the number of hours on the rota and he replied, '196 hours'.

Referring to the Bank holiday payments, you show 28 hours at double time when in fact this should be single time because the officer would already have been paid single time in the basic pay. This statement is also in my opinion an out and out lie as Bank holiday payments are paid at double time plus a day in lieu making it treble time, which the rest of the Council are paid.

Ref combination of rest days on Bank holidays which you have shown do not coincide with any rota on file and certainly do not represent the situation in 1991. I have the rota that security was working from in 1991 and it shows quite clearly that the combination of rest days does indeed coincide with the relevant rota. This rota was passed down to me by the ex shop steward, Colin Pinder.

For Peter to say prior to becoming responsible for market security the four officers involved were part of the regular rota and paid on exactly the same basis as the other officers on the rota, the four officers in question did not work as many hours, nor did they work shifts or Bank holidays, so why were they paid the same pay?

For Peter to say my understanding is that the protected earnings were paid for a commitment to increase weekend working and payment for Bank Holidays is also in my opinion untrue as protected earnings were paid when a job finished and the person was moved to another job that was less pay and not for increased weekend working and Bank Holidays.

For Peter to say 'you suggest in your letter that the protection element was reduced to £50.65. I am advised that this did happen at the time when security officers received their annual increment. This is the way in which the Council administers a protection and guarantees that staff do not get a lower wage than at the point when the new structure began'. This is again in my opinion untrue as this is NOT how the Council administers a protection and how come the security officers were worse off by £244.20 a year and the four market officers were once again better off by £244.20 a year plus the £657.08 a year thanks to Mick Gornall.

Peter saying 'Referring to the Head of Security's letter to Mr K Nelson in December 1997, the figures were provided to indicate the element of protection to existing staff and nothing to do with the scale 3. So why did Kevan Nelson write to Mick Gornall on the 9 February 1998 and state I am now able to confirm that Unison wishes to challenge the calculations on the following basis:

1. By your own calculations the all -nclusive pay equates to scale 4 rather than scale 3.

2. It is evident that the individual protection arrangements are inadequate (a shortfall in the region of £300 per annum).

Once again Peter has tried to cover up or Gornall and fobbed me off.

For Peter to state, 'I am satisfied that protection of existing employees earnings was made and honoured in the way in which the Council usually undertook such matters' is in my opinion all untrue. The protected earnings were not honoured as previously stated by myself. Alan Bolger's protected earnings were cut by over £100 a month and the rest of the security officers had theirs cut by £20 a month and it has never been the way the Council usually undertook such matters as security were the only department in the whole of the Borough Council to have been robbed of their wages up until this date – January 2012.

Peter stating, 'the allegations you have made in our recent meeting to me to be unfounded on your evidence presented thus far'. The evidence I have provided proves, in my opinion that Peter was covering up for Farrell and Gornall to protect them.

77. I again wrote to Peter Mavers on the 10 November 1998. I wrote this letter to Peter before I received my reply to my last letter dated 28 October 1998. It reads as follows:

Avon Close, Walton, Liverpool, L4 1XL

Dear Peter

Further to my letter I wrote to you on 28 October 1998, I have other queries I require answers to. Today I was asked do I remember an incident at Peter Street community centre? I did recall all of it and I was asked what happened to the 96 cans of pop. I said the Police took it away. He then told me the pop was collected from the Police station and ended up in Gornall's office. I would like to know the whereabouts of the pop, as it was not Council property and legally belonged to me. I did not know it had been recovered, you being a magistrate will know it belonged to me and this is theft and that is a sackable offence. I want to know where my pop went.

I am very concerned that you are dealing with the wages. Gornall wanted John Swift and Derek Anders to do a course on a rest day and they did not attend and you stopped them a day's pay. This was contravention of the Wages Act 1986 and you had to give them it back. This is what I meant when I said to you in the meeting on 27 October 1998 about you all pissing in the same pot.

Today is 11 November 1998. I have been to the Police station about the pop, they told me the pop would be returned to the owner and if not found would go to the finder. The finder was me and not St Helen's MBC. I am writing to the Head of the Police with all the information and see if I can bring charges against the person/persons responsible.

I have been to Alec Grant's today and asked him did he lose any money on his protected earnings? The answer was no, can you now tell me why John Sexton, Alan Bolger and Peter Waine lost money each year on their protected earnings as they were all in the same department? I have also seen a letter from Farrell to them telling them they won't lose money.

I'm now going back to that meeting I had with you on 27 October 1998. You said to me in your own words the client liaison officer no longer exists. I have sent you a copy of a memorandum dated 7 November 1998 and at the bottom it states client liaison officer, can you tell me why you thought this?

I confronted you over a member of staff carrying five year's service over from another employer and you told me that he was sub-contracted to IDS. This is incorrect, he was employed by IDS. Why were you of the opinion he was a Council employee? I look forward to your answer as this nearly cost me my job.

In discussion you told me the union had to be involved in the re-structure of the department before Council would pass it.

I told you that did not happen on the re-structure of 1996. I was the steward at that time and Farrell told me it's coming in whether I like it or not. I even called a status quo and he still brought it in. You're telling me St Helen's Council are not corrupt.

This is about the harassment I have received since being off sick.

1. *A member of staff was off sick a week before I went off. I was sent to the work's doctor after three weeks and he was off for five weeks and was not sent – WHY?*

2. *Gornall rang me at home and asked me to visit Personnel.*

3. *I told the works doctor that management were harassing me and she wrote and told them I'm very poorly and to stay away. A week later Farrell rang the union office and said he wanted to see me on Tuesday.*

4. *I took up snooker and Derek Anders said that if I catch Rob Steele paying snooker I'll sack the bastard.*

5. *Anders asking members of staff has Rob Steele been round your house, he's been round Alan's.*

6. *Samuels trying to have me sectioned.*

7. *Gornall's mate, Molyneux told Gornall that I grabbed Bernard Day around the throat. Gornall got Bernard in and told him he would get it sorted.*

8. *Gornall told the Co-ordinators that I am not welcome in the depot any more. This was well before any termination of employment.*

9. *Terminating my employment.*

10. *Sending my P45 after winning my appeal.*

11. *Anders saying to a member of staff, blame your colleagues off sick. I'll sack the bastards (i.e. myself and Jimmy Goodier).*

Both Russ Danson and Peter Moffat had the cheek to say I have been left alone to get better, what a joke.

Last weekend Gornall told a member of staff that they are underpaid and they are going to get a pay rise and not getting back pay. What's up as Gornall shouted s**t and you and Mike Doyle have jumped on the shovel. I have been to the Town Hall twice this week looking for Mike Doyle over this matter.

I am going to phone Derek Hatton on Radio 105 and discuss corruption in St Helen's Council. I would like you and Mike to be on the air and let's see what the public have to say.

I look forward to your reply.

Yours faithfully

Mr R Steele

78. Peter replied to my letter on 24 November 1998 as follows:

24 November 1998

Dear Robert

I write in response to your letter of 10 November 1998.

You wrote with regard to the cans of pop which were recovered from the Police. It is not correct to say you are entitled to their return, as you discovered them in your capacity of a Security Officer. In my view the property therefore belongs to the Authority and to suggest they have been stolen from you is inaccurate.

I am sorry that you are concerned that I will be involved in the issue you have raised regarding the grading and wages of the Security Section. However, I am currently responsible for that service and whilst so, will do my utmost to resolve any proven anomalies. It seems to me that a number of people have looked into the grading issue and have independently come to the same conclusion I have reached on the evidence presented thus far.

As I indicated in my earlier letter, all officers were treated in the same way regarding protection and Mr A Grant was no exception. No one has lost any money by comparison to the grade paid in 1991.

Your reference to Paul Molyneux and his substantive post was correct and my understanding in this instance was in error.

Your reference to service with another employer is hardly relevant because the fact is it did not cost you your job. Of course, if you had been redeployed as was the proposal then the issue would have become relevant. The fact is that because the employee concerned was acting as a contractor to the Council, then any transfer of the undertaking i.e. the alarm-setting task, enables the employee to be transferred to the new undertaker i.e. the Council and that his conditions and service have to be honoured.

You next refer to the need for Trade Unions to be involved in departmental restructuring and that you were the shop steward at the time. The fact that the Acting Assistant Director met you and discussed the changes surely means that you were involved in the process. In addition, you will recall that several meetings took place in respect of the restructuring, with the GMB Convenor, Mr L Gilford, and the UNISON Convenor, Mr K Nelson.

Referring to your numbered points:

1. *I understand that when you brought your sick note in to the Security office, you invited the supervisor to send you to the Council's doctor. All medical appointments are made on an individual basis subject to the individual employee's circumstances.*

2. *The Head of Security did contact you at home but this is not extraordinary, indeed managers are expected to monitor progress of staff who are subject to lengthy periods of sickness absence. Further to this, it is part of the Council's procedure to keep in contact with staff and to carry out welfare meetings, so that resource planning can be facilitated.*

3. *Following your medical on 21 October 1997, Dr Page advised the Council to limit contact with you as far as possible. However, as your employer, the Council does need to contact you from a welfare point of view. The meeting arranged to see you was probably the one arranged for 6 October 1997 but was cancelled at Kevan Nelson's request.*

4. *Derek Anders has no recollection of the allegation you make but in any case would have no power to carry out the nature of the threat made in your allegation. As a trade union representative I would have thought you would understand the Council's disciplinary procedures.*

5. *Derek Anders says he may have asked the questions you suggest but indicates that it would have been in general conversation and with no ulterior motive. I am unclear how these comments, if made, could be construed as harassment.*

6. *I am not aware of the detail involved in this allegation.*

7. *The Head of Security did indeed interview Mr B Day regarding an incident involving yourself at the Markets.*

Other issues were alleged by Mr Day but to date these have not been taken any further.

8. *The decision that you should not be allowed into the depot was taken by Mr Moffatt, who felt that, as you were suffering work-based stress, coming into work would only exacerbate your situation.*

9. *Termination of employment is permissible under the Council's procedures but in your case members were not satisfied that the dismissal was justifiable.*

10. *I have explained in an earlier letter that the incident with your P45 was a genuine mistake.*

11. *Same comments as number 4.*

12. *The Head of Security believes he may have been discussing the issue Single Status and the effects that a job evaluation exercise might have on various grades within the Council. Of course, as you will realise, any job evaluation exercise is likely to take quite some time to effect, even if the Council decides it is necessary. The issue was also discussed by Mr Keegan at a meeting with Mr Moffatt.*

13. *I understand from the Head of Security that there was a conversation regarding Single Status wherein there is the possibility of a job evaluation exercise. This comparison of grades for various types of work within the Council may or may not yield changes to a whole host of pay rates but the Head of Security will not be the determining officer.*

I have to say that your allegations of corruption within the Council are yet in my view to be substantiated. You seem to have convinced yourself that you have legitimate grievances but I can only take action in response to positive proof. I have yet to be so convinced.

I still have an open mind if you are able to substantiate any of the claims you make but I fail to see how the incidents you list in your letter, even if proof were available, could possibly be construed as harassment towards yourself. I know that you are still receiving treatment for your illness and under medication and in order to speed your recovery I suggest that you set these allegations to one side until your health improves. I fear that your constant involvement in matters relating to your work could impede your progress.

Yours sincerely

P R MAVERS
Assistant Director
Housing, Environmental and Contract Services

For Peter to say the cans of pop are in my view the property of the Authority and to suggest they have been stolen from you is inaccurate so why did Peter Waine get the ladders he found and Mick Fairclough get the mountain bike he found and Terry Cunliffe get the knife he found? Because Mick Gornall took the cans of pop that were rightfully mine and stole them from me. Peter Mavers a JP and a Christian lied to me and covered up for Gornall stealing my cans of pop.

79. Because of Peter's actions I wrote to the Chief of Police on the 10 December 1998 as follows:

Avon Close, Walton, Liverpool L4 1XL

Dear Sir

About four weeks ago my ex supervisor asked me did I recall an incident at Peter Street community centre. I said about the pop, I remember it very well. He said 'yes' and 'do you remember what happened to the pop?'. I said the Police came and took it away in their car.

He then asked me did I know where it went after that. I replied 'back to the owner I suppose'. He then said what would you say if told you about four months later I found the ticket you had in my pocket and I called into the Police station to see if it was still there and collected the pop. He then went on and told me he took it to the office and gave it to the manager and explained what had happened. I replied, 'I don't know anything about that'.

I wrote to the Assistant Director on the 10 November 1998 asking him what happened to the pop and if it was claimed, then I was the finder and it belonged to me.

The ex supervisor told me the manager had rung him at home and said he thinks he shared it out between the lads. He replied, 'I don't think so'.

I have been told by a member of staff that the manager shouted loud enough for him to hear, 'I don't know what I done with the pop Paul'.

'I do Mick, you gave me some for the rugby team'.

I have received a reply from the Assistant Director on 24 November 1998. You wrote with regard to the cans of pop, which were recovered from the Police. It is not correct to say you are entitled to their return as you discovered them in your capacity of a security officer. In my view, the property therefore belongs to the authority and to suggest they have been stolen from you is inaccurate.

The ex supervisor thinks the night in question was October 1993, I think it was January 1994. The Police officer was PC Mike Hudson and had just started with the Police from the

Air Force. I do know I gave a statement to him in March 1994 and two youths were charged with theft.

The officer also told me the pop belonged to ASDA so how the Assistant Director can say it belongs to the Authority I don't know.

I have spoken to ASDA today and if I can get dates and proof the pop belongs them they will take this matter further. I need to speak to pc Hudson. He can contact me on ...... (St Helen's). The head of security at ASDA also seems to think that I was the finder and I should have received the pop. Can you give me your opinion on this matter?

I would also like to stress that had the manager approached me and I would have taken the goods, then I would have been as bad as the youths that stole it as I knew who the owner was. Again, if he had come to me and asked about it I would have told him 'it's ASDA's'.

Being Head of Security department, I thought it obvious to enquire about it rather than just give it to your mate. I still say it was not his to give away and an offence had been committed.

When I wrote to the Assistant Director, I told him it was 96 cans to see what answer he would give. It was a total of 72 cans. He has still not answered the question what happened to the pop.

If I had stolen from the Council ten years ago and evidence came up last week, I would be disciplined accordingly.

If you wish to speak to me, leave a message on St Helen's ...... I can go to the Police station any time (College Street, St Helen's).

Yours faithfully

Mr R Steele

80. I received a reply from the Area Commander on 16 December 1998 as follows:

Merseyside Police
16 December 1998

Dear Sir,

Thank you for your recent correspondence regarding the above.

Your letter has been passed to the Incident Management Unit, based at St Helen's who have responsibility for researching and analysing complaints of this nature, and who will contact you in due course.

If you have any further problems or need to speak to the officer dealing with your complaint, please contact Sergeant WRIGHT, at the Incident Management Unit on 0151 777 6969.

Yours faithfully

Richard Williams
Area Commander

Mike Hudson did contact me about the pop and told me there is not enough evidence to charge Mick Gornall with theft, yet there was enough evidence to charge two of the youths with the same evidence. In my opinion the Police covered up for the Council and Mick Gornall.

Peter saying it seems to me that a number of people have looked into the grading issue and have come to the same conclusion I have reached on the evidence presented thus far, then all of them, as well as Peter have in my opinion lied and covered up for Farrell and Gornall.

Peter saying 'no one has lost any money by comparison to the grade paid in 1991' as you can see is in my opinion another out and out lie to protect Farrell and Gornall.

For Peter to state, 'the fact that the Acting Assistant Director met you and discussed the changes surely means that you were involved in the process'. The truth is I met with Brendan Farrell after the re-structure had been passed and I was told it's coming in whether I like it or not and I don't recall several meetings took place in the respect of the re-structuring with Mr L Gilford and Mr K Nelson. This statement is in my opinion an out and out lie as Mr K Nelson had no members in Security at that time as the two convenors that were involved were Les Gilford and Tommy Twist and the only meeting they had was with me and Phil Houghey on 22 November 1996 and the re-structure was passed in August 1996 without any meeting with any union reps whatsoever. More lies by Peter I believe.

Peter saying, 'you invited the supervisor to send you to the Council's doctor' is in my opinion untrue. I got into an argument with Derek Anders, Deputy Head of Security and he spat his dummy out and told me he's going to send me to the work's doctor.

Peter saying, 'the meeting arranged to see you was probably the one arranged for 6 October 1997' is in my opinion more lies. I made it quite clear to Peter it was to do with the meeting Farrell arranged with Thelma in the union office. Peter was just covering Brendan Farrell's back.

Peter stating other issues were alleged by Mr Day, but to date these have not been taken any further. I spoke to Mr Day in November 2011 and he told me he had not said anything and told me a number of things Mick Gornall and Paul Molyneux had done to him.

Peter saying, 'the decision that you should not be allowed into the depot was taken by Mr Moffat', is in my opinion also untrue.

Tony Marsh made it quite clear to me it was Mick Gornall who told him I am no longer allowed into work.

81. I again wrote to Peter Mavers on 23 November 1998 as follows:

Avon Close, Walton, Liverpool L4 1XL

Dear Peter

I have received your rely to my letter dated 16 November 1998 and I will challenge you on this with Mike Doyle in the Town Hall.

1. *Going back to our meeting on 27 October 1998 I asked you to tell me what other departments who are all on APT&C who work 39 hours and 36 hours doing the same job. Can you please let me know?*

2. *I also spoke to you about checking door handles in the dark and that it was you who made us do it and you replied the client were paying for the service. So what you are saying is Gornall has charged them for this service since 1991 and not provided it.*

3. *It was also you who started patrol officers checking premises on Bank Holidays. When I started with security we did alarm response only. Again you stated the client was paying for this service. So are you again saying Gornall charged for this service since 1991? I look forward to your answers.*

4. *Can you tell me why the four security officers, who were employed at Gerrards Bridge depot did not receive protected earnings on the APT&C scale 3, as they were employed by security at the time of the re-structure.*

5. *Can you also tell me why Kenny Watterson and Mick Fairclough lost their protected earnings when they moved to the Markets?*

6. *Can you confirm to me that the Council procedure for temporary employment is two year? It's a straightforward question, yes or no.*

7. *If an employee is disciplined for something and another employee does the same thing, they should be punished the same. Again, it's a straightforward yes or no. I look forward to your answers.*

Peter, the questions for the wages are to show what a shambles Gornall has made and people backing him will end up blushing when I've finished.

I have spoken to the ex Council Leader, Brian Green and hopefully be contacting him again, along with Derek Hatton.

I am going through my file with a fine tooth comb and you will be hearing from me again requiring more answers.

I will beat you all at the end of the day.

Yours faithfully

Mr R Steele

Ps I know about the phone call Gornall made about the pop.

82. *I again wrote to Peter Mavers on 1 December 1998 as follows:*

Avon Close, Walton, Liverpool L4 1XL

Dear Peter

I am starting off with your reply of 16 November 1998, page 2 paragraph 3. I have spoken to 20 of these members and 17 have given me signed statements and out of the 20 members, only one states he did sign and he was threatened with his job to do so. Because of the confusion, I have sent you a list of 28 names. Can you write yes or no? No means you have not and return it to me. I have sent you a copy of an employee's contract. I have removed his name and date of employment. You will see here is no signature.

I have written to 10 Downing Street requesting a public enquiry or outside Auditor to investigate St Helen's MBC. On this I will challenge you, on the rest of your letter dated 16 November 1998, along with everything else.

Looking back at the rotas, I see that M Rimmer, G Kay and J Unsworth were employed on the 29 man rota and the re-structure was for the 28 man rota. Can you tell me why they also did not receive protected earnings?

I have heard two different stories where the pop went. One, given out between the lads and two, given to the rugby team. No matter who he gave it to, it was not his to give away.

I can confirm that I now have outside help and have plenty of Council experience.

I had a few more questions to ask but I will now save them for the enquiry. I still have the Auditor's Commission to contact.

If you would have replied to my letters dated 10 and 23 November 1998, I would have sent you a copy of the five page letter I sent to Downing Street.

I went to war with the Bradford & Bingley, they used three lots of solicitors to destroy me. Every time they knocked me down I bounced back. I was right but the law was on their side and they were protected by red tape and had all loop holes covered, but I STILL BEAT THEM.

You have none of these, you've left yourselves wide open and I'm going to expose all.

At the end of the day I WILL WIN.

Please return the list of names completed asap.

Yours faithfully

R Steele

Please complete 'Yes' or 'No' to show you have signatures agreeing to the re-structure of 1991:-

	Name	Yes	No
1.	T Cunliffe		
2.	P Haughey		
3.	M Hutton		
4.	P Partington		
5.	I Adams		
6.	G Philbin		
7.	A Bolger		
8.	M Fairclough		
9.	A Proctor		
10.	C Pinder		
11.	A Duckworth		
12.	T Marsh		
13.	J Brown		
14.	D Robinson		

	Name	Yes	No
15.	K Hackett		
16.	K Watterson		
17.	J Goodier		
18.	J Sexton		
19.	J Johnson		
20.	D Anders		
21.	B Tracey		
22.	R Simm		
23.	D Finnan		
24.	P Waine		
25.	J Unsworth		
26.	M Rimmer		
27.	P Almond		
28.	G Kay		

J Johnson, Havelock Close, St Helens

In 1991 when Scale 3 was introduced for shift and weekend allowance I was shop steward for the TGWU representing some of the security officers at Hardshaw Brook Depot, St Helen's Council. I did not agree with any of the proposals and me and all the staff were intimidated at the time with our employment if we did not agree. I never signed any agreement accepting the new working practices.

J Goodier, Bowness Avenue, Clinkham Wood, St Helen's

I did not attend the meeting. I recall I was working that day. I know for a fact that I did not sign a contract because other members were in dispute. The shop steward told us not to sign anything.

Roy Simm, Fearnley Way, Newton-le-Willows

In 1991 I did not sign any agreement to Scale 3. They said private security would be forced in this job.

A Duckworth, Tickle Avenue, Parr, St Helen's

I remember the meeting in 1991 asked to go on the Grade 3 scale. I never signed any documents because I did not agree with the one -man patrols. I was told that our wages would go up every six months until we reached the top of the grade but was told after we were put on the Grade 3 that everything was put together and we were on the right grade. The Bank Holiday allowance was never in my mind mentioned. A private security firm was mentioned that if we did not agree we would be out and they would be brought in. I do not work on security any longer I am now a Caretaker.

P Partington, Morgan Street, St Helen's

I wish to point out that in 1991 I was present at a meeting to change the working practices of the services.
This involved Scale 3 all-inclusive to include Bank Holiday working etc. I remember being informed that if we didn't accept then it could go to a private security firm.
I am under the impression that I have never signed an agreement for the above mentioned scale even though worked it as per every other security officers.

K Hackett, Parbold Avenue, Blackbrook, St Helen's

I remember attending a meeting in 1991 regarding re-structuring. I did not sign any document because we did not agree to one-man patrols or anything else. We were told that if we did not agree we would lose our jobs and a private firm brought in. We were also told our wages would go up every six months till we reached the top of Grade 4.

M Hutton, Link Avenue, Blackbrook, St Helen's

I remember attending a meeting informing us of re-structuring. It was regarding one man patrolling. I did not sign any document because I asked where the Health and Safety point of view was.

We were forced into this stating we would lose our jobs and that a private security firm was on stand by to take over. We were also told our wages would go up every six months.

T Cunliffe St John Street, Newton-le-Willows

I attended the meeting in 1991. We were offered an al-inclusive grade which included a protection amount for what I understood would be for 1 man patrols and going on monthly pay. Bank Holiday payment was __not__ mentioned on that day. I don't recall signing an agreement. I do recall it being said that we had no choice as other plans were in place should we not agree and we could be replaced at the drop of a hat.

I recall it being a hostile meeting as I as others thought it both unsafe to work alone and unfair on the client as they would receive a lesser service. I don't recall any minutes being taken. I also understood that on APT&C we would be entitled to two increases per year until reaching an upper limit at the top of Scale 4.

M Fairclough, Mendip Grove, Parr, St Helen's

I did not sign an agreement in 1991 and I did not attend any meeting about the re-structure.

P Haughey, Brynn Street, St Helen's

I was not at the 1991 meeting. Also I did not sign any form to agreement of Scale 3 in 1991.

K Watterson, Holly Road, Haydock, St Helen's

I Kenneth Watterson attended a meeting in 1991 at Hardshaw Brook Depot where I was told to do one-man patrols under the threat we could lose our jobs and an outside security firm would take us over and I ca"t recall signing anything to agree to this meeting. I was given protected earning of £71 per month, which was reduced to £58 until I moved over to the markets and this £58 was taken away from my monthly pay. I was under the understanding that the protected earnings which I first received was for doing one-man patrols.

At this meeting we were on Grade 3 and promised to be upgraded.

A Proctor, Beechwood Close, Clockface, St Helen's

In 1991 I did not agree to sign for Scale 3 on the threat that if we would not sign that Burns Security would be coming in. Also the Unions did not agree to this. Also the Unions and the workers did not agree to work annualised hours and the annualised hour system never came into operation. I never signed any documents agreeing to Scale 3 or the annualised hour system when I was employed by the Security Services.

P Almond, Buckfast Avenue, Haydock, St Helen's

In the year 1991 I was employed by St Helen's Council as a permanent patrol person. I attended several meetings. I can remember being threatened with a private security firm coming in to take over our jobs. To the best of my knowledge I did not sign any documents ref. my patrolling on my own because I happen to be an insulin dependant diabetic.

This idea seemed stupid to me if I had any difficulties due to illness driving and patrolling alone was out and all the lads agreed with me. This still sticks in my mind. I am now retired due to bad health.

D Anders, Downway Lane, Parr, St Helen's

I recall back in 1991 we, the security personnel were forced into accepting one man patrols and if we did not accept this we would be replaced by Burns Security at 0:00 hours on a certain date.

I was also told if I did not sign for this I could be sacked on the spot at any time.

J Sexton, Firthland Way, Parr, St Helen's

When Scale 3 was offered in 1991 I never signed any form accepting this.

I was also told that my wage from Co-ordinating would be protected, i.e. Bank Holiday payments would be paid at x2 plus lieu days. This is not the case.

P Waine, Grace Street, Sutton, St Helen's

I would like to state that I, Mr P Waine at no time attended any meeting or signed any contract concerning working practices or pay structures. The only time I was aware of the above was by an internal memo by Mr Farrell. Please note my protected earnings were reduced.

A Bolger, Redruth Avenue, St Helen's

In 1991 when Scale 3 was introduced to Security Officers inclusive of shift and weekend enhancements I never signed any document accepting this.

A threat was forced upon us. At the period of time an outside firm, namely Burns Security would be brought in if not accepted.

I have in writing guaranteeing that when my Co-ordinating job ceased and merged with Security force, my earning would not decrease. Bank Holiday payments would be double time and lieu days. Each time security received a pay rise my protected earnings diminished.

D Finnan, Whalley Avenue, St Helen's

In 1991 when Scale 3 was offered to Security Officers inclusive of shift and weekend allowance I never signed any document accepting this proposal because I felt forced into the working agreement.

We were threatened into this working proposal or Security would be taken over by a private security firm (Burns).
Also, Bank Holiday working was not included in the proposals, none of the shop stewards at this time agreed to including Bank Holidays into Scale 3.

I was also advised not to sign any documents by my shop steward, at the time Mr James Johnson, I took his advice.

83. I received a reply to my letter on 14 December 1998 from Peter Mavers as follows:

14 December 1998

Dear Robert

I refer to your undated letter, which I received on 2 December 1998.

As I explained in an earlier letter the issue of grading is to be taken up byMr J Keegan of UNISON as I understand it and it may be counter productive for you to be pursuing the matter in parallel with that process. I will not be providing information from personnel files in terms of employees signatures.

In relation to the other document you sent with your letter, this is a Statement of Particulars and not a Contract of employment. The statement has no requirement to be signed by the employee.

The three employees referred to in your letter were temporary employees at the time the restructure took place and their contracts were not renewed at a later date. The three employees would therefore not have been entitled to the protected earnings.

Finally, I repeat the comment I made in earlier correspondence, that you should allow your trade union to take up the issue of the grading, for the benefit of your own recovery. I am not sure what it is you wish to 'win' at but your efforts cannot be helpful to your state of health. As I have said both verbally and in writing if there have been any errors in calculation they will be addressed by the trade union and rectified by the Management. As yet I have seen no evidence, which supports the suggestion.

In closing can I remind you that on more than one occasion you have been asked not to call at the depot. I am informed that in recent times you have visited the Security offices late at night in direct contradiction to the instructions. The request that you do not come in to the workplace is primarily to avoid your exacerbating your medical condition by being concerned with operational issues, but secondly my concern that you may compromise the Security of the Depot by distracting the duty staff.

P MAVERS
Assistant Director

When I challenged Peter and sent him signed statements proving he had not seen a large number of individual security officers agreeing in writing at the time and he did not see two of the shop stewards agreeing in writing as Jimmy Johnson has made a statement saying otherwise, and Colin Pinder the other shop steward told me he did not sign anything. That's why Peter wrote, 'I will not be providing information from personnel files in terms of employees signatures'. I caught Peter out because I went round the majority of the security officers and got it in writing, in my opinion Peter was lying once again.

Peter saying, 'The three employees referred to in your letter were temporary employees at the time the re-structure took place and their contracts were not renewed at a later date. The three employees would therefore not have been entitled to the protected earnings', what a load of bulls**t. Had Security not been reduced from 28 men to 24 men two years later then they would have been made permanent. Plus Mick Gornall would not have known this at the time also.

I wrote to Peter on 23 November 1998 asking him, 'can you tell me why the four security officers who were employed at Gerrards Bridge depot did not receive protected earnings on the APT&C scale 3 as they were employed by Security at the time of the re-structure and two of these people were made permanent?' That was Brian Wright and Phil Deighton but Peter declined to reply to my letter.

84. I wrote again to Peter on 3 January 1999 as follows:

Avon Close, Walton, Liverpool L4 1XL

Dear Peter

I see that you have failed to reply to my letter dated 23 November 1998.

Going to your letter dated 14 December 1998 last paragraph, 'In closing can I remind you that on more than one occasion *you have been asked not to call at the depot'. This is bullsh**t. I have been told once by Tony Marsh, his words were 'Gornall said you're not welcome here anymore, can you leave the depot?'.*

You have replied to three of my letters and I find your answers a total disgrace.

Since August 1997 I have made serious allegations against St Helen's MBC and nothing has been done (WHY?) I also feel you have perverted the course of justice and I am writing to the Lord Chief Justice asking for you to be suspended and if found guilty, struck off as a Magistrate.

Just before Christmas I spoke to a government official, he is arranging for me to meet two officers, he told me they won't just stop at Security.

I also know that 18 vehicles were broken into after security officers were instructed to turn the lights off at 7pm and then told, 'don't let anyone know they were turned off or we will be in trouble'.

I have informed Mike Foy, Neil Jervice, Joe White and Jeff Dancer I am also writing to Mike Doyle.

You will no doubt know I have been regarded as permanently unfit for work by the psychiatrist, don't party too early, I'm going nowhere. I might be finished with the Council but the fight still goes on.

Do you know you lot make me sick. In your letters you go on about my health and really you don't give a s***t. If you cared so much you would have solved the problems back in 1997 and stopped Gornall and Farrell using psychological warfare with my mind.

The only time I want to see you is when you are being interviewed by the auditors commission.

Yours faithfully

Mr R Steele

Ps You were wrong to say the pop belonged to the authority, I have spoken to the owner of the pop, even they said I should have received it, if anyone. Merseyside Police are dealing with this matter.

85. Peter replied on 15 January 1999 as follows:

15 January 1999

Dear Robert

I refer to your letter of 3 January 1999, which I received on 5 January 1999.

You referred in your letter to my failure to respond to your letter of 23 November 1998 but I am unable to find a letter of that date on my file. However, I suspect you refer to an undated letter, to which I responded on 14 December.

You still maintain that nothing has been done with regard to your 'serious allegations' against the Council yet as I have said in previous correspondence, I have been unable to find substantiation to your allegations on the evidence presented so far. I understand from the files that your allegations have been investigated by other officers of the Council and in addition the District Auditor, and they cannot agree with your claims either.

I am disgusted by your spurious allegations against me personally and have informed the Clerk to the Justices of your accusation.

Your comment regarding the vandalism to the Council vehicles shows no understanding of the operational difficulties and highlights the danger of misinformation in the wrong hands.

Yours sincerely

P MAVERS
Assistant Director

Peter stating, You still maintain that nothing has been done with regard to your "serious allegations, writing letters which in my opinion are covering up for Farrell and Gornall is not dealing with the situation.

Also Sheila Samuels stated on 12 October 1998 ,that it is my view that unless there is a frank and open debate with yourselves and management regarding these issues and all issues are put on the table which has not been the case to date, shows just how far Peter will in my opinion go to cover up the truth and lie for his colleagues. Some magistrate and Christian he is in my opinion.

Over the years I have asked for a panel of six councillors to confront them face to face and I also asked the District Audit to confront them face to face and they all declined to do so. So nothing has been done to date – January 2012. Also Peter did fail to respond to my letter dated 23 November 1998 as all my letters to him were sent undated was sent on the 1 December 1998 and not the 23 November 1998. All he is now doing is covering his own back. There was also no misinformation regarding the vandalism to the council vehicles, the only thing I was misinformed was 17 vehicles were vandalised and not 18 as stated and Mick Gornall did instruct his officers to turn the lights out on the depot at 7pm leading to the vandalism on 17 vehicles.

CHAPTER FIVE

1. I decided to write to the Audit Commission on 6 January 1999 as follows:

Avon Close, Walton, Liverpool L4 1XL

Dear Sir

I am writing to you because I have a serious problem and you can help.

I became shop steward for Security in June 1996, my problem first started on 10 July 1996 in my first JCC meeting. Over a 14-month period my life was made a living hell.

In August 1997 I went off sick with the pressure put on me by management.

I saw the Council leader Mike Doyle and told him what was going on, he told me they were serious allegations. I have had several meetings with him and he has failed to do anything.

My MP, Peter Kilfoyle has been involved for over 12 months. He advised me to contact the District Auditor, this I DID BACK IN March 1998. He has had to put pressure on the union in August and December 1997 to get them to represent me. I have spoken to Peter a few days before Christmas and he has stated I need to back up my allegations as this matter will end up in Court.

Going to the District Auditors report, firstly I find his findings a disgrace. A Mr John Vis did the audit and he is based in St Helen's, also Sheila Samuels, Head of Personnel worked with him. The same woman who tried to have me sectioned under the Mental Health Act a month earlier.

Assistant Director Peter Moffat said he had looked into the allegations and found them to be spurious. The same man who told my appeal committee when asked, he finished my employment on the grounds of ill- health and not of the problems. I then chatted to him and he then said that Farrell and Gornall are in employment and not going anywhere, therefore I'm terminating your employment, a complete U turn.

The Assistant Director Peter Mavers has stated to me in a letter dated 16 November 1998 that the officers did get a £21 a month reduction when they received their annual increment. The wages should have gone up not down.

I have written four letters to Peter Mavers dated 28.10.98, 11.11.98, 23.11.98 and 1.12.98, he has failed to reply to my letter dated 23.11.98, I wonder why? I have sent you a copy of the letter dated 23.11.98. His reply to my other letters were a joke.

Acting Assistant Director Farrell wrote to the union on 31 July 1997 about my behaviour. I took a copy of this letter to Peter Kilfoyle, MP. He wrote to Farrellon 11 November 1997. Farrell replied on 18 November 1997. In it he replied 'however I would take odds with Mr Steele's assertion that he is in dispute with management'.

What I would like from you is go through my file with me and let me work with you on interviewing all members of staff that have worked with Security since 1991 and all management concerned.

I have sent you a copy of a list of problems I wish to discuss with you, I have also sent you a copy of Farrell's letter he sent to the union.

Can you also bring along an accountant so we can go through the wages.

I hope to hear from you soon.

Yours faithfully

Mr R Steele

Ps I missed my union course I did in March – April 1997. When I was on the course every subject we covered I had dealt with.

I had three tutors over a three-day course and they all told me to see the union when I get back, there's something seriously wrong.

Also, half the information I gave the District Auditor was not dealt with.

2. I contacted Councillor J Beirne of the Liberal Democrats and he wrote to the Audit Commission on my behalf on 4 February 1999 as follows:

St Helen's MBC

Dear Sir/Madam,

I am writing to ask whether or not you have received a complaint against St. Helen's Council from Mr R Steele, Avon Close, Walton, Liverpool, L4 1XL.

Mr Steele has contacted me and expressed concern about a serious allegation he has made against St Helen's Council and I would be grateful for any information you could give me on the matter.

Yours faithfully
Councillor John Beirne, Marshalls Cross Ward Councillor

3. The Audit Commission wrote back to Councillor John Beirne on 31 March 1999 as follows:

Audit Commission

Dear Councillor Beirne

ST HELEN'S MBC

Thank you for your letter of 4 February 1999, acknowledged by us on 8 February 1999.

I can confirm that the Audit Commission has not, itself, received a complaint against St Helen's Council from Mr R Steele of Avon Close, Walton, Liverpool L4 1XL.

You will be aware that auditors appointed by the Audit Commission act independently of the Commission and it is possible that such a complaint has been made direct to the District Auditor. I have therefore forwarded a copy of your letter to the District Auditor and asked him to reply direct to you.

I am sorry that we have been unable to help on this occasion.

Yours sincerely

JC Golding
Associate Controller

For the Audit Commission to state, I can confirm the Audit Commission has not itself received a complaint against St Helen's Council from Mr R Steele is in my opinion a lie, now they are making me look a liar.

4. I then wrote to a Mr Bressington and a Mr David Goodman of the District Audit on 18 February 1999 as follows:

Avon Close, Walton, Liverpool L4 1XL

Dear Mr Bressington / Goodman

I see that the Audit Commission has passed my complaint to you. I would like a meeting with you as a matter or urgency to discuss this matter in full detai;, this will take more than a day as my file is over three inches thick.

I have also sent you copies of letters sent to Tony Blair dated 28.1198 and 26.3.98.

Also letter to Peter Mavers dated 28.10.98, 23.11.98, 10.11.98, 1.12.98 and 3.1.99. I am still waiting for a reply from 23.11.98 letter, all letters were sent recorded delivery.

Also letter to Mike Doyle, Council Leader 11.1.99.

I have also sent you a copy of a list of problems I wish to discuss with you.

Gornall is now telling members of staff that I am finished in the Council and are no longer on the books. I have not been informed of this verbally or in writing.

I look forward to speaking to you soon.

Yours faithfully

Mr R Steele

5. John Beirne wrote to Mr Goodman of the District Audit on 18 February 1999 as follows:

St Helen's MBC

Dear Mr Goodman

I am writing to you on the understanding that you have received a complaint against St Helen's Council (financial matter) from a Mr R Steele, Avon Close, Liverpool L4.

As an Elected Councillor to St Helen's Council, I would be grateful for any comments you may have on this matter, as I am sure you are aware of the serious nature of these allegations.

Yours sincerely

Councillor John Beirne
Marshalls Cross Ward Councillor

'Even John Beirne stating, 'I am sure you are aware of the serious nature of these allegations' knew how serious my allegations were.

6. I decided to write to the Audit Commission again on 16 September 2003 as follows:

Clockface Road, St Helen's, Merseyside

Dear Sirs

I have had a visit from the Ombudsman investigator today, Tuesday 16 September 2003 about St Helen's Council. I have over 76 grievances with them and he told me it's a matter for the District Audit and the Police fraud squad.

I have been to the District Audit twice before on 18 February 1998 and around April 1999 and both times they did not investigate what I had told them and what they did investigate they gave very poor answers.

I would like a meeting with you and not the District Audit to discuss my 76 grievances with you and then have a meeting with St Helen's Council with yourself, myself, the Police and my solicitor present.

The investigator told me to go to the papers but my solicitor wants me to wait till the time is right.

I have written to the Audit Commission before back on 6 January 1999 and you put me on to the District Audit. This time I want to deal with you. I hope to hear from you soon with a date to meet and discuss the problems.

Yours faithfully

Mr R Steele

7. I received a reply from a Rowland Little, Head of Complaints on 8 October 2003 as follows:

Audit Commission

Dear Mr Steele

Thank you for your letter dated 16 September.

The Commission itself has no powers to investigate grievances in a local authority. The Commission's appointed auditor has certain powers but I note from your letter that you have already been in touch with the District Auditor in 1998 and 1999 and that he examined your concerns where they fell within his remit before writing to you to explain his position and findings.

The Commission will not investigate your 76 grievances but it is able to consider a complaint that an auditor has failed to carry out his duties – see enclosed leaflet. However, we would be reluctant to investigate a complaint against the District Auditor relating to events which took place over four or five years ago.

I would ask that you carefully consider the leaflet and my comments above before deciding whether to refer your concerns against the District Auditor to me at this point in time.

Yours sincerely
Rowland Little
Head of Complaints

8. I again wrote to Rowland Little on 10 October 2003 as follows:

Clockface Road, St Helen's, Merseyside

Dear Mr Little

Thank you for your letter dated 8 October. I went to the District Audit in 1998 and I was with a Mr John Vis for over 2 hours telling him what was going on. He investigated 6 of about 60+ grievances I told him about. I found his findings a disgrace, he blatantly let them off with alleged embezzlement.

I again went to the District Audit in 1999. I went to Widnes to see a Mr David Goodman and a Mr Clive Portman. Again I was with them over 2 hours. I took my file with me and showed them written evidence. Again I told them 60+ grievances and they investigated 4 issues, let them off with alleged embezzlement was not dealt with.

You say you are reluctant to investigate the complaint because it took place four and five years ago, I will let you know I was ill for 3 years where I did not speak to anyone. This was down to the Council and the Audit failing in their duties. If I would not have been ill, it would have been dealt with a lot sooner.

I am going to see my MP Peter Kilfoyle next Friday to discuss this matter with him. No doubt you will hear from Mr Kilfoyle regarding this matter.

I am also going to the papers with this as I feel the Auditors have failed in their duties and have covered up several issues.

I would like to meet an external Audit and go face to face with the Council so we get to the bottom of this matter and get to the truth once and for all.

I will leave this for you to sort out and hope to hear from you very soon with a date to meet.

The two Auditors who dealt with me should be investigated for covering up for St Helen's MBC. I am seeing my solicitor to see if I have a claim against the Audit for failing to do their duties and contributing to my illness.

Yours faithfully

Mr R Steele

9. I again received a reply from Rowland Little on 16 October 2003 as follows:

Audit Commission

Dear Mr Steele

I am writing in connection with our recent exchange of correspondence and our telephone call earlier this week.

I confirm that I have requested the District Auditor's case file setting out the history of your concerns and the work carried out by the auditor. I will contact you again once I have received and considered the information therein.

Yours sincerely

Rowland Little
Head of Complaints

10. I again wrote to Rowland Little on 28 December 2003 as follows:

Clockface Road, St Helen's, Merseyside

Dear Mr Little

I am writing to you to see how you are getting on with your investigation as I have not heard from you since your phone call back in October.

Reference our phone conversation I told you about the embezzlement I reported to the two auditors on Pets Corner that was going on for over two years. I also reported this to Brendan Farrell in 1996, he was the Acting Assistant Director at that time and it still went on. Gornall was also charging for an alarm response man and there never was one. Gornall makes sure it gets done now, what he is doing now is taking a man off nights leaving a route not getting done. He should have three men on nights – two for routes and one for Pets Corner and still there is never alarm response man between 1600 – 2400 and he is charging for it. He has a 17 man rota, 4 market officers and he was 5 men down for months and at this moment of time he is 2 men down and his clients are paying for these people and he's not provided them. He has not had a full rota for nearly 1 year.

I would like to meet you, the two auditors who did the investigation and Farrell, Gornall, Mavers, Carole Hudson, my solicitor, the Police and 6 Councillors who I select, all in the Town Hall and thrash this out. I would like you to let me have your opinion on the meeting. This is the only way we are going to get it out in the open and get to the truth. If you give me a date and you arrange for the two auditors and the people from the Council who I have mentioned and I will arrange for my solicitor and the Police to be there.

Yours faithfully

Mr R Steele

Ps I have sent you a copy of a letter from Peter Kilfoyle MP to Clive Portman. I have also informed him of your investigation on the District Audit. I will be visiting Peter Kilfoyle again in the New Year to make him well aware of this letter. Again it is public money that Gornall is not using properly as his clients are paying for a service and not getting it.

Once I get the go ahead from my solicitor I will be going to the newspapers with all this information and what has gone on.

11. I again received a reply from Rowland on 13 January 2004 as follows:

Audit Commission

Dear Mr Steele

Further to my letter of 16 October 2003, I am writing to inform you that I have now had the opportunity of examining the District Auditor's case file relating to your concerns and complaint.

The file contains evidence of communications between yourself and District Audit since February 1998 and indicates that your concerns have been taken seriously and investigated. The files record the involvement of both the District Auditor and the Regional Director of District Audit. I am satisfied that District Audit has acted properly and appropriately in pursuing your concerns and that the matters raised by you are essentially for action and resolution by St Helen's MBC.

I note that you have made recent contact with the District Auditor in December 2003. I believe that the only matter for action on my part is to copy your most recent correspondence to the new District Auditor, Tim Watkinson, and ask that he considers whether there is any new information or issues therein which have not been considered previously by his predecessor.

In respect of your request for a meeting, this will be a matter for the District Auditor to consider and decide. The Commission itself has no powers or locus to become involved in a meeting of this nature.

In conclusion I am satisfied that the District Auditor has dealt with your representations in accordance with the Commission's Code of Audit Practice and I regret therefore that the Commission is unable to help you further in this matter.

Yours sincerely

Rowland Little
Head of Complaints
Audit Policy & Appointments

12. I replied to Rowland's letter dated 13 January 2004 on the 16 January 2004 as follows:

Clockface Road, St Helens, Merseyside

Dear Mr Little

Thank you for your letter 13 January 2004. How did I guess you were going to defend the two District Audit reports. I will start with John Vis' report. Issue 1 – the Housing Environmental and Contract Services Department has given a commitment to rectify any proven miscalculation if any found so why are the Council so hostile in rectifying this, this is a matter for the District Audit as this is public money, so you are satisfied it's nothing to do with the District Audit? Issue 2 – Temporary Security Officer, the post was not advertised internally because of the short timescales, tell me how Phil Partington and Tony Marsh advertised internally and got the job within two weeks? I can tell you a lot more on this matter. Again you are satisfied with the District Audit. Six Security Co-ordinators in a JCC meeting with Farrell, he told us the temps can apply for the job. I told him the jobs are for permanent staff only. The next thing the temps are made permanent so Peter Woodcock could have one of the posts. Council procedures were temp for two years. I can tell you a lot more on this matter. Again you are satisfied with the District Audit. Issue 3 – charges being made to open spaces. Parks were not closed mainly due to incidents, this is not an acceptable excuse, I bet you it's because he never had a full shift on duty because he was short staffed. No charge was made to parks and open spaces section. I can get a witness who will tell you he never received a refund. Gornall has never refunded anyone. Again you are satisfied with the District Audit. Static at Pets Corner leading to break in at the café, there was no static on Pets Corner, that is part of the normal duty and the Ranger service paid for a static to be put on the café because of the gypsies on the park. This would have had to be done on overtime. There should have been two statics on the park and there was none, again due to staff shortages. Again I can comment on the District Auditor's report, again you are satisfied with the District Audit.

Council's emergency plan – this area is not subject to a formal agreement between Security and the Council. This is in my opinion a lie, it is listed on client specifications, it also says they have provided two officers when incidents have occurred. They have provided three officers and not two. I can tell you a lot more on this matter. Again you are satisfied with the District Audit.

Schools not being visited within time ranges and finishing after midnight – the agreement with the schools is one visit between 0800 – 1600 Saturday and Sunday and one visit 1900 – 0000 seven days a week. This is not happening, again because of a shortage of staff and making staff go out after midnight. The Auditor went back one week and found 85.6% patrols finished prior to midnight. I bet you he picked the best week to make it look good. If he had gone back one month or even three months like he did with the parks it would have been a different story. Again you are satisfied with the District Audit.

Clive Portman's report:- 1 – Ill-health retirements – the re-structure on 1996 was six men too many and six men finished on ill-health – NOT a coincidence. I sent Clive written statements from some of the people who finished, I can tell you a lot more. Again you are satisfied with the District Audit. 2 – Overtime between September to December 97 was given to two day men at weekends. On the patrol officer's rota since this report, the Co-ordinators have got the overtime on the patrol officer's rota between October to December 03. Again I can tell you a lot more on this matter, again you are satisfied with the District Audit. 3 – Unauthorised post – management favouritism led to creation of Liaison Officer. Gornall had two mates on days and only one job for them, this job was disbanded in 1988 because it was cost effective. I can tell you more on this matter, again you are satisfied with the District Audit. 4 – Protected earnings – five officers got protected earnings and seven officers did not get them, they all should have got them. I can tell you more on this matter, again you are satisfied with the District Audit.

Have you seen the two letters dated 19.10.99 and 14.01.2000 that I sent Clive? I have a lot more grievances that may interest the District Audit. I am far from satisfied with the two District Audit reports, realistically, I find them a disgrace. If I don't get satisfaction from you, then I will get my Barrister to subpoena John Vis and Clive Portman to

Court when I go. As far as I am concerned, the District Audit and St Helen's Council are allies. It's only a matter of time before I get to the truth. I am willing to meet you, John Vis and Clive Portman and I will bring my evidence with me and we will thrash it out.

Yours faithfully

Mr R Steele

Ps I have NOT made recent contact with the District Audit in December 2003. I wrote to you personally, copy sent with this letter. My MP, Peter Kilfoyle has written to them in 2003, not me. You are also satisfied the District Audit did nothing about the embezzlement on Pets Corner, that was going on for over two years and also the parks not being locked.

13. I received a reply from Rowland on 22 January 2004 as follows:

Audit Commission

Dear Mr Steele

I am writing to confirm receipt of your letter dated 16 January 2004.

Yours sincerely
Rowland Little
Head of Complaints
Audit Policy & Appointments

Rowland never had the guts to reply to my comments above because he knew I was right in my allegation that the District Audit covered up for St Helen's Council.

14. Peter Kilfoyle MP wrote to Clive Portman on 22 December 2003 as follows:

Dear Mr Portman

Re: Robert Steele

You wrote to me on the 19/7/02, in response to my letter of the 8/7/02.

In that letter, you pointed out that, 'It is the Council who need to be persuaded that a miscalculation has taken place because they are the body to rectify the matter if it can be established that they have made an error'. Now, the Council's principal solicitor, Angela Boyle, has written to me saying that. 'it is not proposed to correspond on this matter further'.

Yet only last month, Mr Steele's solicitor – Graham Cunliffe, of Jackson & Canter – wrote to Carol Hudson – CEO of St. Helen's MBC – saying 'Our independent Accountants, Mitchell Charlesworth, believe there are issues to be addressed from looking at the Council's own figures.'

Thus, we are told by you that you have no locus, despite the fact that this is public money; we are told by the Council that they will no longer speak with us; and accountants say there is something amiss. Who, then, do I go to as a concerned Member of Parliament? Do I seek leave to speak on the matter in Parliament, disparaging almost by definition all parties to this dispute; or can you suggest a way beyond the present impasse?

Yours sincerely

Peter Kilfoyle MP

cc Mr R Steel
G. Cunliffe

15. A Tim Watkinson replied to Peter's letter on 8 January 2004 as follows:

Audit Commission

Dear Mr Kilfoyle

Robert Steele

I reply to your letter to Clive Portman dated 22 December 2003 as I have now taken over as the District Auditor to St Helen's MBC.

I wonder if you, Mr Steele or Mr Steele's solicitor could provide me with further information regarding the 'issues which need to be addressed', so that I can consider if there is any action that I ought to take as the District Auditor.

You may be aware that Mr Steele has raised some concerns about the issues he has previously raised, with the Audit Commission nationally. I wonder whether the points you are now raising with me are connected with these concerns. Consequently I am copying this letter, together with your letter to me, to Rowland Little, Head of Complaints for the Audit Commission, who is currently considering these matters.

Yours sincerely

Tim Watkinson
District Auditor

16. I decided to write to Tim Watkinson on 23 November 2004:

Clockface Road, St Helen's, Merseyside

Dear Mr Watkinson

I have rung you several times and not been able to get hold of you, so I am putting it in writing to you.

You sent a letter dated 8 January 2004 regarding the issues which need to be addressed. I want to meet up with you and go through the 73 grievances I have with St Helen's Council, 11 have been dealt with the Auditors that need looking at again as I have evidence the Auditors were wrong and the rest need looking at.

I am paying a Barrister to go through my file to prove I was right in what I was saying and take St Helen's Council to Court and the union.

I have seen my MP Shaun Woodward and his case worker has told me to contact you and go back to him with the outcome.

If I don't hear from you within the next 10 days I am sending a copy of this letter to Roland Little and going back to my MP. I do want to meet you and show you what I have got on file, all I want is the truth.

Yours faithfully

Mr R Steele

17. I received a reply on 30 November 2004:

Audit Commission

Dear Mr Steele

St Helen's MBC

Thank you for your letter dated 23 November 2004.

As far as I am aware, there are no outstanding matters which require my consideration or attention. All the material has been considered by Rowland Little who has concluded that the audit processes have been appropriately applied and that the matters you have raised are essentially for action and resolution by St Helen's MBC. Do you believe there are any 'new' issues that have not been properly considered by the District Auditor?

At this point in time, I don't think there is any merit in meeting, given my comments above. But I'd be pleased to consider this further when I hear back from you.

Please also note that I am no longer the District Auditor to St Helen's Council. Judith Tench has taken over this responsibility from me. However, it would be helpful if you could respond to me directly on this matter for now.

Yours sincerely

Tim Watkinson
District Auditor

18. I again wrote to Mr Watkinson on 2 December 2004:

Clockface Road, St Helen's, Merseyside

Dear Mr Watkinson

Thank you for your letter 30.11.04.

Firstly I must tell you Roland Little has seen very little that I have on file and there are a lot of outstanding matters that need to be looked at.

I wrote to Roland Little on 16.1.04 and he never replied to my letter, I will be writing to him and asking him why, copy sent with this letter.

I have spoken to my solicitor today and asked him to arrange a meeting with the Barrister to look through my file. I am going to take this matter as far as the European Court of

Human Rights. I have the money from my house sale to do so. This is not a matter of compensation, this is for justice and to get to the truth.

I also think you should look at the evidence I have, that the Auditors were wrong in their reports.

The District Audit has a commitment to look at these matters as it's tax payer's money that is being used.

Yours faithfully

Mr R Steele

19. Tim Watkinson replied to my letter on 10 December 2004:

Audit Commission

Dear Mr Steele

St Helen's MBC

Thank you for your letter dated 2 December 2004. I have passed this to Judith Tench, the current District Auditor for St Helen's MBC, who will respond as soon as possible.

Yours sincerely

Tim Watkinson
District Auditor

20. I also wrote to Rowland Little on 2 December 2004:

Clockface Road, St Helen's, Merseyside

Dear Mr Little

I have written two letters to Tim Watkinson, copies I have sent with this letter.

I wrote to you on 16.1.04 and you never gave me a reply, I have sent you a copy of this letter and hopefully you will reply to it.

As you are Head of Complaints, I would like you or the District Audit to look at my file and let me prove what I have been saying is right.

I have £90,000 to take this to Court and I will spend every penny, money does not mean anything to me, at the end of the day I want the truth and I'm going to get it with or without your help.

Yours faithfully

Mr R Steele

21. Rowland Little replied on 23 December 2004:

Audit Commission

Dear Mr Steele

Thank you for your letter dated 2 December with enclosures.

Please may I refer you to my comments in my letter to you of 13 January 2004. As I indicated therein, it is a matter for the District Auditor and not the Commission to decide how to deal with your submissions. I have noted that you are in correspondence with Mr Watkinson and note his request to you in his letter of 30 November.

I am sorry that the Commission is not able to help you further on this matter.

Yours sincerely

Rowland Little
Head of Complaints

Rowland Little once again stated it is a matter for the District Auditor and not the Commission to decide how to deal with your submissions. The District Auditor would not take this case any further because in my opinion it would have got John Vis and Clive Portman into serious trouble for covering up for St Helen's Council. Also Rowland Little did not respond to my comments I made about him being satisfied with John Vis and Clive Portman's reports in my letter 13 January 2004.

22. I decided to write to Judith Tench on 30 December 2004:

Clockface Road, St Helens, Merseyside

Dear Mrs Tench

I would like to meet with you as soon as possible to discuss the grievances I have with St Helen's Council. I know you won't be able to deal with all of them, we can go through them and sort out the ones you can deal with.

I have a letter dated 23.12.2004 from Roland Little saying it is a matter for the District Auditor and not the Audit Commission.

Tim Watkinson has passed you the letter dated 2.12.2004 for you to deal with, I would like to meet up with you before I see the Barrister, so can you get in touch with me as a matter of urgency as I am waiting to report back to my MP's office.

Hope to hear from you soon.

Mr R Steele

23. Judith Tench replied on 14 January 2005:

Audit Commission

Dear Mr Steele

Thank you for your letter of 30 December, which I received today along with copies of your recent correspond-ence with Mr Tim Watkinson and Mr Roland Little. Please accept my apologies for not being in a position to reply sooner.

Before I reply in any detail or meet with you I would like to familiarise myself with the remaining correspondence and reports to which you refer.

In the meantime please contact Louise Hartley in my office who will arrange a convenient time for us to meet at the beginning of February.

Yours sincerely

Mr Judith Tench
District Auditor

24. Louise Hartley, Admin Support Officer from the District Audit wrote to me on 31 January 2005:

Audit Commission

Dear Mr Steele

Following my telephone conversation with your father on Tuesday evening I'd like to confirm in writing your new appointment with Mrs Judith Tench, District Auditor.

Your new appointment is 11am Tuesday 15 February at The Heath Business & Technical Park.

Yours sincerely

Louise Hartley
Admin Support Officer

25. I received a letter from Judith Tench on 9 February 2005:

Dear Mr Steele

St Helen's MBC

Further to my letter of 14 January I have now personally reviewed the correspondence and other papers relating to your concerns regarding St Helen's and your complaint to the Audit Commission.

Having done that I have concluded that there is no reason for us to meet next week as originally planned. My colleagues, and St Helen's council, have invested significant amounts of time in reviewing and responding to your concerns in recent years and I can see no 'new' issues in your letter to me that have not already been properly considered.

Your concerns have been thoroughly investigated by my predecessors who have each concluded that there are no remaining matters where the auditor should or could take action. Furthermore their work has been reviewed by Roland Little, (the then Head of Complaints at the Audit Commission) who concluded that your concerns have been appropriately considered by the District Auditor and that the matters raised by you are essentially for action and resolution by St Helen's council.

I now consider this matter closed. Please note that our meeting next week is cancelled and that I will not be at the Runcorn office as previously arranged.

Finally, thank you for taking the time to write to me; I am sorry that I cannot be more helpful on this occasion.

Yours sincerely

Judith Tench
District Auditor

26. I wrote back to Judith Tench on 12 February 2005:

Clockface Road, St Helens, Merseyside

Dear Mrs Tench

You say in your letter 9 February 05 'My colleagues and St Helen's Council have invested significant amounts of time in reviewing and responding to your concerns', the only thing St Helen's Council has done in my opinion *is spend time covering up and as for your colleague Clive Portman, was given written evidence that his report was wrong and still continued to protect St Helen's Council and if we would have met, I would have shown you this.*

I have spoken to a Councillor from St Helen's Council who is going to go through my file with me and he has told me if he finds my allegations to be true, which he will, he is going to the Standards Board and they will make the District Audit act on the information I have given them.

Also in your letter you write, 'Furthermore their work has been reviewed by Roland Little. Letter dated 16.1.04 tells Roland Little what I think of his findings and he did not reply to it. You should have seen this. I feel the reason you won't see me is you have been got at.

416

Yours faithfully

Mr R Steele

27. Conservative Councillor Wallace Ashcroft wrote to Ms Tench on 8 March 2005:

St Helen's Council

Dear Ms Tench

Mr R Steele, Clockface Road, St Helen's

With reference to your letter to Mr Steele, dated 28 February 2005, I would confirm that I have met him at his home.

Having seen the vast amount of correspondence regarding his complaint I feel that it is too big and complex for me to handle personally.

I wonder if you could offer me some guidance as to the best course to take in order to progress his complaint. Would it be better for Mr Steele to book an appointment to see his MP Shaun Woodward or does your department have anyone who could look into it?

I look forward to an early reply

Yours

Councillor Wallace Ashcroft (St Helens MBC)

28. Judith Tench replied to Wallace Ashcroft on 10 March 2005:

Audit Commission

Dear Councillor Ashcroft

Mr R Steele

Thank you for your letter of 8 March, referring to your meeting with Mr Steele. You may be aware that Mr Steele has written to me recently and that I have properly considered whether he has raised any issues that I need to take account of in carrying out my statutory audit duties. I concluded that there were no matters where I should or could consider taking any action and I wrote to Mr Steele to explain this on 9 February this year (copy attached). In reaching my conclusion I reviewed both Mr Steele's recent letters to me as well as his correspondence with my predecessors and concluded that there were no new issues being raised that had not already been properly considered.

The matters raised by Mr Steel have been thoroughly investigated by my predecessors and it has already been established that there are no remaining matters where the auditor should take any action. This assessment has been reviewed in the past by the Audit Commission's then Head of Complaints, Rowland Little who concluded that Mr Steele's concerns had been appropriately considered by the District Auditor and that any remaining matters were for the Council to consider.

I have explained to Mr Steele that I now consider this matter to be closed as far as any audit involvement is concerned. If Mr Steele wishes to pursue the matters he has raised with the Council then I could only suggest that he should consider using the Council's complaints procedures or failing that then he should write to the Chief Executive to set out his concerns.

I am sorry not to be more helpful on this occasion – the issues raised have already been reviewed and I do not believe there is any further action for me to take. I am copying this letter to the Chief Executive.

Yours sincerely

Judith Tench
District Auditor

Cc Carole Hudson, Chief Executive, St Helen's Council
Mr R Steele, Clockface Road, St Helen's

Judith Tench in my opinion was just taking the p**s. I had already used the Council's complaints procedures and I had written to the Chief Executive (Carole Hudson) on numerous occasions. Just to in my opinion be lied to, this is one big cover up from all parties concerned.

29. I wrote again to Judith on 10 March 2005:

Clockface Road, St Helens, Merseyside

Dear Mrs Tench

The Councillor has written to you on 8 March 2005 and has found the case too big for him to take on.

May I suggest that we meet and go through my file and I will ring my MP's office tomorrow and see if his case worker will come with me to the meeting. As I know you won't be able to deal with all the grievances, the ones you cannot deal with we will let the case worker have them.

It will take several hours to go through it all, at the end of the day I want the truth and I will get it.

I look forward to hearing from you as soon as possible.

Yours faithfully

Mr R Steele

30. I received a reply from Judith on 14 March 2005:

Audit Commission

Dear Mr Steele
St Helen's MBC

Thank you for your letter of 10 March. I trust that you have now received a copy of my letter to Councillor Ashcroft.

My position remains as set out in my letter to you on 9 February. I do not believe that there is any further action that I need to take as the council's external auditor. The matters raised by you are essentially for action and resolution by the council and I have suggested that you use their complaints procedure to pursue your concerns. If you remain dissatisfied you may then wish to consider contacting the Local Government Ombudsman. Her contact details are:

Patricia Thomas
Local Government Ombudsman, Beverley House
17 Shipton Road York YO30 5FZ

Tel: 01904 380200 Fax: 01904 380269

Thank you for taking the time to write to me; I am sorry that I cannot be more helpful on this occasion.

Yours sincerely

Judith Tench
District Auditor

c.c Councillor Ashcroft, St Helens

31. I again wrote to Judith on 12 March 2005:

Clockface Road, St Helens, Merseyside

Dear Mrs Tench

I have received a copy of the letter to Councillor Ashcroft.

May I remind you your predecessors were, in my opinion *wrong with the answers they gave. I produced written evidence that his findings were wrong and he did nothing.*

As to Roland Little's investigation, I sent you a copy of a letter I sent him dated 16.1.04 that I never received a reply, I again reminded him on 2.12.04 and he has still not replied to that letter.

Since 1991, Gornall has in my opinion *had several £100,000 out of his clients that* in my opinion *he has stolen from them i.e. (embezzlement), that is still going on today and if you would have met me I would have shown you this.*

I will now contact my solicitor and get the Barrister to look at my file that I will pay for and will take the Council to Court and will subpoena John Vis and Clive Portman to Court.

I will go to the papers and expose you all for being allies and covering up corruption.

Yours faithfully

Mr R Steele

c.c. Councillor Ashcroft
MP's office
(Graham Cunliffe, Solicitor)

32. Judith replied to my letter on 11 May 2005:

Audit Commission

Dear Mr Steele

St Helens MBC

I am writing in response to your letter dated 12 March 2005, which appears to have 'crossed' in the post with my letter dated 14 March. I apologise for the delay in replying fully to your letter until now, this is an oversight on my part.

Since my last letter to you I have ensured that all the material held in our audit files that relates to your allegations about St Helen's Council has been reviewed. I am satisfied from this, and from my earlier review of the correspondence, that the allegations you have made to me, and my predecessors, against St Helen's Council have been thoroughly and properly investigated. The allegations you have made to date have been taken seriously and my predecessors, including the then Regional Director and the Audit Commission's then Head of Complaints have found there are no matters for the auditor to consider taking any formal audit action. As I have told you previously if any matters remain to be resolved then they are for you and the Council to resolve together.

With regard to the serious allegation you make in your letter of 12 March regarding 'Gornall'. If you can provide any evidence that substantiates your assertion about embezzlement then please provide me with that evidence in writing and I will consider it as part of my audit. If you are unable to provide evidence to support your allegation then I will consider this matter to be closed.

Yours sincerely

Judith Tench
District Auditor

As you can see, Judith Tench did not want to take matters any further in my opinion to protect her predecessors and as you can see, St Helen's Council have NOT been thoroughly and properly investigated and as for her stating, 'if any matters remain to be resolved, then they are for you and the Council to resolve together', what a joke. That's why I went to the District Audit in the first place as St Helen's Council would not speak to me. I also believe that I have provided enough evidence over the years about the embezzlement going on in Security to take someone's money for a service and not give it to them is stealing their money, that is embezzlement.

33. I once again wrote to Judith on 13 May 2005:

Clockface Road, St Helen's, Merseyside

Dear Mrs Tench

Thank you for your letter 11 May 2005.

I told both your predecessors about the alleged embezzlement and they never even looked at it. I told Steve Lowe, a Detective Inspector what I told your predecessors and he stated 'it's embezzlement'. WHY did they not look into it at that time? He is still charging his client's money and not providing them the service they are paying for. I have spoken to my MP's office and I have selected 6 Councillors of my choice to attend a panel with Gornall, Farrell and Mavers and confront them on what they have done and covered up. I have also asked my MP to contact you with the date and to make you attend as you have a duty as the Audit Commission to investigate these matters.

You say in your letter, 'my allegations have been thoroughly and properly investigated', how could they when you have not seen my evidence. I look forward to seeing you at the panel and proving you all wrong.

Yours faithfully
Mr R Steele

I never received a reply to my letter dated 13 May 2005 so I gave up writing to the District Audit and the Audit Commission as I believe they were all protecting one another, i.e. p*****g in the same pot as they all covered up for St Helen's Council and John Vis and Clive Portman of the District Audit.

34. My MP, now Shaun Woodward wrote to Judith Tench on 4 April 2005:

Re: Mr Steele, Clockface Road, St Helen's, Merseyside WA9 5LD

I have recently been visited by a constituent, Mr Steele, who has come to me with some concerns regarding the practices of particular employees of St Helen's Council. He has been in contact with your office and was, after consideration, refused the opportunity to have an appointment with you.

I would be very grateful if you could briefly outline the reasons for this refusal so that I may pass on your comments to my constituent.

In addition, Mr Steele has amassed a considerable amount of possible evidence, and he has assured me his barrister is committed to go through this evidence at some point in the near future. He would very much like to know if you would consider taking the opportunity to go through this evidence at some point with him.

Thank you for your assistance in this matter.

Yours sincerely

Shaun Woodward MP

I never did see a reply to this letter so it shows quite clearly that the District Audit did not want to investigate my grievances.

Nor would the District Audit outline the reason for this refusal and they also did not want to go through this evidence with me at some point because the truth would have had to come out and in my opinion a number of people in the Council and the District Audit would have been in serious trouble.

35. Because I got nowhere with Mike Doyle, Council Leader, I decided to contact Marie Rimmer Councillor for St Helen's MBC as she was the ex Council Leader to let her know what was going on in the Council.

36. Marie Rimmer wrote to me on 8 April 1999:

St Helen's MBC

Dear Mr Steele

Further to our telephone conversation and my subsequent enquiries, it is evident you have raised your concerns with a number of Councillors in an attempt to try to resolve your on-going grievance.

Unfortunately, despite the efforts of many, including the District Auditor, the unions and your own Member of Parliament Peter Kilfoyle, we are unable to bring this matter to any sort of conclusion that will satisfy you.

My advice therefore, as you still feel aggrieved, is to consider approaching the Local Government Ombudsmen, who have powers to investigate independently complaints relating to the Council. I enclose their information which I trust will be of some assistance.

Yours sincerely

Councillor Marie E Rimmer

I was not surprised by her actions as she was the Council Leader at the time of most of the problems. I also attended the Town Hall in 1999 when she was reinstated as Council Leader. I spoke to her on the phone and she told me she was not going to meet with me and discuss my grievances and that Mike Doyle should have never had meetings with me.

37. Because of the negative response I got from the Labour Councillors I decided to have a meeting with Brian Spencer, Leader of the Lib Dems and Suzanne Knight, Deputy Leader of the Lib Dems. We discussed the wages issue and I showed Brian Spencer the evidence and he sided with Peter Maver that the Security officers had already been paid time for Bank Holidays in their wages. Suzanne tried to stick up for me but Brian soon shut her up and Brian would not take the issue any further.

CHAPTER SIX

1. I visited Alan Bolger an ex workmate after being sectioned and I told him what had gone on and he told me his wife used to work for a mental health solicitor in Liverpool called Peter Edwards. He gave me his contact number so I rang him and he told me to contact Jackson and Canter in Liverpool, so I did and I had a solicitor called Graham Cunliffe dealing with my case. Alan Bolger and his wife took me to see Mr Cunliffe several times in 2002 and Mr Cunliffe kept repeating 'it's bizarre'. I took Kenny Watterson, Mick Fairclough, Dave Anders, Steve Cliffe and Roy Simm to see Mr Cunliffe, all from Security, for them to inform him of what was going on and once again he kept saying 'it's bizarre'. Mr Cunliffe wrote to Carole Hudson on 27 February 2003 as follows:

Jackson & Canter

Dear Madam

Re: OUR CLIENTS:
STEPHEN CLIFFE – MOBILE SECURITY OFFICER
ROY SIMM – MOBILE SECURITY OFFICER
KENNY WATTERSON – MARKET SECURITY OFFICER
MICK FAIRCLOUGH – MARKET SECURITY OFFICER
DAVE ANDERS – SECURITY CO-ORDINATOR

We have been consulted by the above named clients in relation to queries over wages, gradings, protected earnings and single status enquiries.

All our above named clients complaints relate to wages received over the course of their employment with the Council in the Security Force.

In particular, there are several areas which require explanation to which no satisfactory explanation has been given in relation to changes in their salary and wages over a 12-year period.

Patrol Officers
Both our above named clients who are Patrol Officers, Messrs Cliffe and Simm, have enquiries regarding payments received and grade changes over the last 12 years. The enquiry in relation to these two Officers in the first instance goes back to the pay rises in 1991 when they believe there is discrepancy between pre and post pay rise earnings. Please give details of the pay pre-1991 pay rise, and post-1991 pay rise. We believe these changes took place in about November 1991.

Pay Scale
We understand that in 1991 certainly Mr Simm, who was employed at the time, should have been a Scale 4 APT&C and yet was only paid on a Scale 3 basis. Please clarify the position and let us have the appropriate information. We understand this pay scale went from 1991 to 1999.

Please also provide details in Mr Simm and Mr Cliffe's case of the scale of pay and allowances since 1999, with particular reference to single status, as we believe after 1999 other Officers were on better basic pay conditions than Mr Simm and Mr Cliffe despite the fact that Mr Simm had been at the Council for 18 years, and had probably been on the wrong scale from 1991. In relation to the two above named clients please provide a breakdown of their wages from 1991, including shift allowance, weekend allowance, Bank holidays and lieu time together with a copy of their respective employment contracts to explain our clients genuine enquiries as to the apparent discrepancies in their pay.

Co-ordinators
In this aspect we are instructed by David Anders.

Please provide Co-ordinators details, from 1996 to 1999 pay scale details for Co-ordinators from 1996 to 1999. And pay scale details for Mr Anders from 1999 when he was appointed Co-ordinator in order that a proper comparison can take place. Please also provide information as to why the Co-ordinator position was paid less than a Supervisor position, which we understand, was Scale 6 and which was changed in 1996. We understand that a Co-ordinator was required to do extra work over and above that of a Supervisor yet was paid less money. Please clarify the position. Please give a breakdown of Mr Anders' pay and conditions, including shift allowance, weekend Allowance, Bank holidays and lieu time, if appropriate.

Market Officers
In relation to the above we are instructed by Kenny Watterson and Mick Fairclough, both had been working with the Council in excess of 13 years.

Both these gentlemen have, we understand, had protected earnings reinstated to them during a meeting some time in 1996 but these earnings were not paid to either Mr Watterson or Mr Fairclough. Please clarify this position.

Please also provide a complete breakdown of wages, including weekend allowance and lieu time for Market Officers in order that these can be appropriately compared with their earnings.

This information has been requested both by ourselves and in correspondence by Mr Cliffe. Surprisingly Mr Cliffe has been the subject of disciplinary proceedings as soon as his letter was received. The grounds of those proceedings are apparently grounds that have not existed before for disciplinary matters, and would seem to have been instituted within a few days of Mr Cliffe making a written enquiry for his wage details.

The implication of this is there for all to see.

We expect a reply to our reasonable enquiries within the next 21 days. We do not believe this information is anything other than that our clients are entitled to under the terms of their employment contracts, and is indeed reasonably requested. We would point out that we trust a response will be received in the time requested without the heed for further correspondence or application to the local County Court for this information by way of disclosure.

We await hearing from you.

Yours faithfully,

JACKSON & CANTER

2. I wrote to Graham Cunliffe on 17 June 2003 asking him for a full breakdown of wages for Patrol Officers, Co-ordinators and Market Officers from St Helen's Council as follows:

Clockface Road, St Helen's, Merseyside

Dear Mr Cunliffe

Ref our telephone conversation, can you write to St Helen's MBC and ask them for a full breakdown of wages for Patrol Officers including Bank Holidays, shift and weekend working allowances and lieu time for 2003-2004.

A full breakdown of wages for Co-ordinator including Bank Holiday, shift and weekend working allowances and lieu time for 2003-2004.

A full breakdown of wages for Market Officers including Bank Holidays, shift and weekend working allowances and lieu time for 2003-2004.

Getting this information will prove that they are underpaid and should have received single status in 1999.

Can you send me a copy of the letter for my file.

Yours sincerely

Mr R Steele

For Mitchell Charlesworth to set out the correct figures they require manual grade three, hourly rate of pay before and after the 1991 pay rise.

For single status Mitchell Charlesworth will require a full breakdown of wages for Patrol Officers including basic pay, Bank Holidays, shift, weekend working allowances and lieu time for Bank Holidays for 2003-2004 = £14,532.

A full breakdown of wages for Co-ordinator including basic pay, Bank Holidays, shift and weekend working allowances and lieu time for Bank Holidays for 2003-2004 = £16,515.

A full breakdown of wages for Market Officers including weekend working allowance and lieu time for Bank Holidays for 2003-2004 = £14,532.

3. Graham Cunliffe wrote again to Carole Hudson on 8 October 2003 as follows:

Jackson & Canter

Dear Ms Hudson

Re: OUR CLIENTS:
STEPHEN CLIFFE – MOBILE SECURITY OFFICER
ROY SIMM – MOBILE SECURITY OFFICER
KENNY WATTERSON – MARKET SECURITY OFFICER
MICK FAIRCLOUGH – MARKET SECURITY OFFICER
DAVE ANDERS – SECURITY CO-ORDINATOR

We write further to our recent enquiries concerning security officers.

We enclose copies of previous correspondence to which we have not had a substantive reply. We enclose a preliminary draft report of Mitchell Charlesworth Chartered Accountants in relation to the position as regards security officers being underpaid since 1991. This is very much a draft report and is based only on the Council's figures, and is not a completed report in relation to certain other outstanding issues. On the basis of the Council's own figures, it would appear to us that each individual security officer has been substantially underpaid over a period now of 13 years.

We think you should give urgent attention to this and look at it very carefully as we also consider that when single status was brought in in 1999, the security and patrol officers will have a further substantial loss.

No doubt you will have a substantive explanation for all these discrepancies, failing which we will have to consider what action the security officers will take in relation to these problems.

We trust you will write to us urgently.

We also enclose a copy of a letter from the District Auditors to Mr Steele in March 1998, which shows commitment to rectify any proven mis-calculation in earnings. We trust you will investigate this matter properly and rectify any mis-calculations, which has led to the underpayment of wages for all the security staff.

Yours sincerely
Mr G Cunliffe
JACKSON & CANTER

4. Brendon Farrell, the man I have constantly complained about was requested to respond to Mr Cunliffe's letter on 27 October 2003 as follows:

St Helen's MBC

Dear Sir

I refer to your letter of 8 October 2003 addressed to the Chief Executive, to which I have been requested to respond.

Given the time span of the information requested, it will take some time to research and I will endeavour to give a substantive reply as soon as reasonably practicable.

Yours sincerely
Brendan Farrell
Head of Human Resources

5. Graham Cunliffe wrote back to Carole Hudson on 17 November 2003 as follows:

Jackson & Canter

Dear Ms Hudson

Re: OUR CLIENT ROBERT STEELE

We refer to your letter of 27 October 2003, in which you indicated that Mr Farrell, Head of Human Resources, is dealing with this matter. We are unsure whether Mr Farrell should actually be dealing with this matter, as he was a party to the original wage transfers in 1991. You will appreciate these are the cause of our concerns.

We are further concerned to note that our client's MP, Mr Kilfoyle, did in fact write for these crucial figures in January of this year, copy letters enclosed, and neither of these letters have been responded to.

We are furthermore looking into the issue of single status, as in discussions with Mr Steele that when all the Council's low-paid employees achieved single status adjustments in 1999, these were not afforded to security staff who, you will appreciate, are also the Council's employees.

We also require full breakdown of wages for patrol officers, including basis pay, bank holidays, shift/weekend working allowances and lieu time for bank holidays for 2003/2004 for patrol officers. This will give details of the basic wage and we can then track back to see if these officers were afforded appropriate increases when single status was achieved.

Please also provide a full breakdown of wages for Co-ordinators, including basic pay, bank holidays, shift and weekend working allowances, again for 2003/2004. Please also do the same for market officers in 2003 and 2004. We believe this will again show underpayments for all these staff.

We trust this information will be provided in this matter, which has now long been complained of can be resolved.

We should like these issues resolved efficiently and quickly. From the evidence we have seen and been produced by Mr Steele, there are clearly discrepancies in the pay of all these officers including Mr Steele himself at the relevant time, all of which were or appear to have been brushed under the carpet by the Council and the Unions. Our independent Accountants, Mitchell Charlesworth, believe there are issues to be addressed from looking at the Council's own figures.

We await details of the single status pay in the hope that these matters can be resolved.

Yours sincerely

Mr G. Cunliffe

JACKSON & CANTER

6. The Chief Executive, Carole Hudson got Angela Boyle, Principal Solicitor to reply to Mr Cunliffe's letter on 28 November 2003 as follows:

St Helen's MBC

Dear Sirs

Your Client: Robert Steele

Thank you for your letter dated 17 November addressed to the Chief Executive.

The Chief Executive has complete confidence in the integrity of Mr Farrell to deal with matters in an impartial and professional manner.

In relation to Messrs Cliffe, Simm, Watterson, Fairclough and Anders all of whom are current employees of the Council, a request has previously been made for you to supply their written authority for you to act on their behalf. We cannot trace receipt of this and look forward to you providing this in due course. A response to your queries as is relevant to these individuals will then be provided.

In relation to the queries raised on behalf of Mr Steele, I would comment as follows.

Mr Steele accepted a job offer made by the Council on the then existing terms and conditions in 1992. Initially, this was on a temporary contract. which was made permanent when he accepted a permanent post in 1994. His employment was terminated 1999. He made application to the Employment Tribunal, an application which he subsequently withdrew. The Council was prepared to defend its position in the Employment Tribunal. A bundle of documents had been prepared and provided to Mr Steele. This bundle included, inter alia, correspondence passing between Mr Steele and Mr Mavers, Assistant Director, in which Mr Mavers answered complaints made by Mr Steele regarding grading issues. MrSteele has access to this documentation and I do not propose to repeat its contents.

The Council takes the view that, having accepted a job in 1992, Mr Steele has no reason to question terms and conditions which existed prior to his employment. Similarly, he has no reason to question the employment situation, which has appertained since his dismissal. The opportunity existed for him to challenge issues, which were relevant to his employment at the Employment Tribunal. His application was dismissed on his withdrawal.

Efforts have been made by the Council to deal with the issues Mr Steele has raised but our responses have never been acceptable to your client. Not unreasonably, the Council has reached the view that there is unlikely ever to be a consensus between us and sees no value in prolonging that correspondence any further. I trust the Council's position in relation to Mr Steele's complaints is clear to you.

Finally, you indicate your concern that two letters sent by Mr Kilfoyle, MP, to the Council in January 2003 have not been responded to. I enclose a copy of the Council's response to those letters. Whilst I appreciate that Mr Steele will not have been satisfied with the response, it is clear that a copy was provided to him. The handwritten notes on the copy letter are his.

Yours faithfully

Angela Boyle
Principal Solicitor

7. Angela Boyle again wrote to Mr Cunliffe on 16 December 2003 as follows:

St Helen's MBC

Dear Sirs

Your Clients – Messrs Cliffe, Simm, Watterson, Fairclough & Anders

Thank you for your letter dated 5 December enclosing the letters of authority from your clients.

I have discussed the issues, which you raised with the Council's Personnel Section and I shall set out the Council's comments firstly on a general basis before turning to the individual cases of your clients.

In October 1991, the Council's Trading Services Committee considered and approved a report, which reviewed the Security Services. The review was considered necessary for a number of reasons, as the service had come under criticism from client departments and Council Members for:-

1. *lack of accountability;*
2. *not being cost effective;*
3. *inadequate supervision;*
4. *lack of feedback to clients;*
5. *poor response to incidents;*
6. *indiscipline amongst members of the Section;*
7. *poor operational procedures;*
8. *excessive overtime;*
9. *high sickness levels;*
10. *inadequate specifications by clients;*
11. *certain restrictive practices prevailing.*

In order to demonstrate that the Security Service could be a viable, accountable service, a full review of the Section's activities, including revising operational procedures, organisation structures, remuneration packages and working practices was undertaken in conjunction with client departments providing definitive specifications.

The organisational structure at that time included various classes of Security Officers (Mobiles, Static, Depot and Temporary Officers), employed on differing terms and conditions of service and demarcations existed between them. To achieve a greater degree of flexibility across the operations, a generic Security Officer role was introduced, to receive common conditions of service and expected to carry out the entire range of functions and duties.

The review entailed introducing an annualised hours system and an all inclusive rate of pay. At the time of the review, Security Officers were paid on Manual Grade 3, plus weekend working and Shift Allowance. Contemporary rates of pay were £104.29 per week, plus 16% shift allowance and enhanced rates for weekend working. This equated to £10,822.71 per annum. The review transferred Security Officers onto APT & C Conditions of Service, to be paid at Scale 3 (£9,516 to £10,215 per annum, all inclusive).

The review assimilated Officers to spinal column point 16, £9,963 per annum. As this was less than annual earnings of existing Officers, it was agreed that permanent Security Officers would be paid an allowance of £71.65 per month (£859.80 per annum), which would maintain their level of annual income of £10,822.71 as it was immediately preceding the review. There was no loss of income to Security Officers employed at the time due to the review. When the Officers received their annual increment to spinal column point 17, in May 1992, giving them an annual salary of £10,215, the allowance reduced to £50.65 per month (£607.80 per annum), resulting in annual income of £10,822.80. This again maintained previous earning levels of permanent Security Officers. Officers in receipt of this allowance in 1991 continue to receive the allowance, which has been increased from £607.80 with pay awards over the years. Such Officers currently receive a salary of £14,532 plus £870.48 per annum.

The review was fully consulted and agreed with trade union representatives, and all employees received a letter explaining the reasons for the changes (copy enclosed dated 31 October 1991). Following that, individual letters of assimilation to the posts, on the above terms were issued, and I enclose a sample letter for your information.

It is not accepted that the 1991 review resulted in a loss of earnings to Security Officers employed at that time. One of the purposes of the review was to make the service more efficient and cost effective, and as new recruits to the service were employed they were offered and accepted employment on the new terms and conditions of employment. The review was necessary for sound business reasons.

I can also confirm that Security Officers deployed in St Helen's Markets are paid at APT & C Scale 3, on an all inclusive basis, similar to that of Officers employed on patrol duties.

The 1996 review was in response to changing client needs and to address the supervisory requirements following a reduction in numbers of Security Officers employed, due to a decline in the client base. At the time of the review, in addition to the Head of Security, there were 5 posts of Security Supervisors paid at APT & C Scale 6, spinal column points 26-28, and 28 Security Officers on Scale 3 as described earlier. Two of the supervisory posts were vacant. The demands for mobile patrols had diminished, and where they were required it was generally during evenings and weekends. When the structure had been established in 1991, it was on the basis of the two-tier structure being operational for a 24-hour period, 365 days per year. The decline in workload called into question the need for blanket supervisory cover at all times. In addition, the introduction of a revised radio communications system, closed circuit television and Citizens Charter initiatives focused attention on the activities carried out in the Security Base office.

To address these issues a dedicated team of six Officers was established whose primary responsibility would be to co-ordinate activities from the Security headquarters. These were designated as Security Co-ordinators, remunerated at APT & C Scale 4, spinal column points 18-21, on an all-inclusive basis. There was then and remains no supervisory responsibility attached to these posts. All Security Supervisor posts were deleted from the structure and a post of Deputy Head of Security was created. Recruitment to these posts were from internal Security Officers and Supervisors in accordance with the Council's ring fencing and assimilation arrangements.

Again, the review was consulted and agreed with the relevant trade union representatives. Applications were invited from employees in the Security Service for the newly created posts, and subsequent appointments offered and accepted.

The Single Status Agreement of 1999 did not result in any changes to the scale of the posts for either Security Officers or Co-ordinators. Rather, the Agreement maintained levels of wages whilst reducing the standard working week from 39 hours to 37 hours. In Security Services, this reduced their annual working hours from 2028 to 1924 per annum.

I am not able to provide a breakdown of earnings for Security Officers or Co-ordinators from 1991 to date as these posts are paid equal twelfths of a salary each month, which is an all inclusive rate for the posts, as agreed in 1991 and 1996 respectively.

Stephen Cliffe

Mr Cliffe commenced employment with the Council in February 1999 as a temporary Security Officer. The reviews referred to in 1991 and 1996 are not relevant to his employment. I enclose a copy of his written Statement of Particulars as requested.

Roy Simm

Mr Simm was appointed to the permanent position of Security Officer in March 1986. I enclose a copy of his written Statement of Particulars following his assimilation in the 1991 review, as requested.

Mr Simm has remained in the same post to date and continues to be paid on a protected salary in accordance with the details provided in my general comments.

David Anders

Mr Anders was appointed to the post of Security Officer in November 1989. He was assimilated to his post in 1991 and paid on a protected salary. In November 2000, Mr Anders applied for and was successful in obtaining the post of Security Co-ordinator on Scale 4. It was clearly Mr Anders' choice to apply for the post in question on the terms and conditions as stipulated.

Kenny Watterson

Mr Watterson had a number of temporary contracts as a Security Officer before being assimilated to the permanent post in November 1991.

In August 1996 Mr Watterson was appointed to the post of Markets Security Officer. Whilst similar in its terms and conditions, this is a different post and upon his appointment to it, Mr Watterson was no longer entitled to receive a protected salary. His protected earnings therefore ceased and he was paid in accordance with the grade i.e. Scale 3.

Mick Fairclough

Mr Fairclough was appointed to the post of Security Officer in 1986. He was assimilated in the 1991 review on a protected salary. In February 1996, he was appointed to the post of Markets Security Officer. This is also a Scale 3 post but, whilst it is similar in its terms and conditions to the Security Officer's post, it is a different post. Upon his appointment to it, Mr Fairclough was no longer entitled to receive a protected salary.

The Council has attempted to address the queries, which you have raised. I must leave it to you to determine how to convey this information to your five clients whilst respecting their individual right to confidentiality.

Yours faithfully

Angela Boyle
Principal Solicitor

Angela Boyle's figures are wrong. Had Security Officers been on £104.29 pw as she stated, they would have been on £8017.54 pa not £10,822.71 pa.

You will also see No. 3 inadequate supervision – yet she states there was then and remains no supervisory responsibility attached to these posts meaning Co-ordinators, yet Peter Moffatt stated in a JCC meeting on 20-1-98 a security officer could sit in the Co-ordinator's chair while the Co-ordinator took a natural or refreshment break if a supervisory decision was required. The Co-ordinator was still available on site to be contacted so the Co-ordinators are supervisors. Angela Boyle is wrong.

8. Graham Cunliffe again wrote to Angela Boyle on 23 December 2003 as follows:

Jackson & Canter

Dear Ms Boyle

Re: OUR CLIENTS
WATERSON, FAIRCLOUGH & ANDERS

Thank you for your letter of 16 December.

We have noted this with interest and have asked Mr Steele and the other people involved to comment on the contents.

With respect, we think you may have missed the point here.

What we are actually after is details of the change in salary structure in 1991. Our report, and all the evidence we have seen indicates that the security employees actually suffered a loss of earnings when they were transferred in 1991 to the new all-inclusive contract basis. They did not receive the pay that they were entitled to at the relevant time that they were earning pre-working on an all-inclusive basis.

You seem to be completely ignoring this point. We do understand the balance of your letter but you have simply missed our point. We are alleging that on the transfer of all the security employees in 1991 from an hourly based pay structure to an all-inclusive contract, the men actually lost pay; allowing the Council to artificially reduce all their wages. It is from that basis that we have calculated the losses through our Accountants, Mitchell Charlesworth.

You have not addressed any of the issues they have raised in their report nor that we have suggested in our letter. The crucial point here is that when all the men were transferred they should have gone to scale 4, given their pre-transfer levels of earnings, and not scale 3. Therefore the Council shifted the basis upon which they were paid irrespective of whether they were union negotiations at the time. It appears that the point is that the Council managed to achieve a substantial reduction in the men's earnings.

No one appears to have dealt with or analysed this situation correctly.

We cannot understand your comments that you are not able to give a breakdown of earnings for Security Officers from 1991 onwards. Does that imply that you can give a breakdown prior to 1991, or why can you not give a breakdown of how the initial pay structure was assessed in 1991 when it was transferred to an all inclusive basis? You will appreciate that the answer to this question will in actual fact prove our arguments that the Council has been underpaying its Security Force artificially for a number of years.

We are forwarding a copy of this letter to Peter Kilfoyle to keep him up-to-date, and we would really like to see the answer of these enquiries, which is what our clients and many of your current employees have been requesting now for several years and months.

We cannot see why you cannot answer this basic question. We again reiterate that you have not answered the enquiries of Peter Kilfoyle MP, in his letters of January 2003. This information must be available and will surely answer the simple enquiry that we have made.

We await hearing from you.

Yours faithfully

JACKSON & CANTER

9. Peter Kilfoyle, MP wrote to Graham Cunliffe on 5 January 2004 as follows:

House of Commons

Dear Mr Cunliffe

Thank you for your letter of the 23 December. As you will be aware, I am exploring every area, which I think might have some potential for stimulating St Helen's Borough Council into responding.

The apparent failure of the trade union concerned to do its job, allied with the council's hostility to outside interference, have made the task of eliciting any information, extremely difficult.

I must now await the outcome of my enquiries with the District Auditor, the National Audit Office and the Office of the Deputy Prime Minister.

Yours sincerely

Peter Kilfoyle MP

Things went quiet for some time when Mr Cunliffe sent me to a Barrister in Liverpool and he told me he worked for Thompsons Solicitors and that he agreed with them, so I told Mr Cunliffe I had found another Barrister and he said I was entitled to a second opinion.

10. My brother gave me a health and safety information document written by a public barrister, Robert Spicer. I contacted the company it was written for and they contacted Robert Spicer and he told them to give me his contact number and in September 2005 I contacted Robert Spicer and he arranged for me to go and see him in Bristol on 4 October 2005. When I met him he had a barrister friend called Candia and we discussed my case for two hours. Both Robert Spicer and Candia told me I would get a fair hearing in the European Court of Human Rights as I have not been given a fair hearing in Britain.

I arranged to get my file off my solicitor, Graham Cunliffe, and I took it to Robert Spicer on 1 November 2005. Robert Spicer invited another of his barrister friends to sit in and he told me there is a problem with the limitation period and that my case would be struck out of court and I told him what Robert Spicer and Candia told me about getting a fair hearing in the European Court of Human Rights. He too said I would get a fair hearing and I told both of them I was going to take my case all the way to the European Court of Human Rights. Robert Spicer told me he would take my case all the way to the European Court of Human Rights. When I was leaving Robert Spicer's barrister friend shook my hand and said 'I will see you in the European Court of Human Rights'.

In January 2006 Robert Spicer told me to sack Graham Cunliffe as he had done nothing for me and Robert told me it's not going to be easy but he will do my case on his own and that he does not need another solicitor.

11. Robert Spicer wrote to me on 20 June 2006 as follows:

Frederick Place Chambers, Bristol

Dear Mr Steele

Further to our telephone conversations, I now enclose a letter for you to sign and send by recorded delivery to Weightmans.

I also enclose a copy of a list of fees for starting a claim. These relate to the county court. If we start proceedings in the High Court, the fees may be different. The list will give you some indication of the expense you will incur. I would point out that these fees are payable to the court and not to me. One reason why I have advised you not to start proceedings before now is that these fees may be wasted if the other side admit liability.

I would also state that my own fees are generally based on an hourly rate of £80.00 plus 17.5%, which is approximately half the fee charged by a high street solicitor. I also charge £25.00 plus VAT for drafting a letter. I enclose a fee note for this amount. I would again point out that there is no guarantee of success in this matter and that you should give serious thought to the prospect of your incurring considerable expense once proceedings are started.

Yours sincerely

Robert Spicer

There was no reason to give serious thought of incurring considerable expense once proceedings are started, as agreed with Robert Spicer, we had agreed to take my case all the way to the European Court of Human Rights.

12. Around the end of July 2006, Robert Spicer told me he needs a solicitor on board and he has found a local firm of solicitors called Bevans in Bristol. He told me they are very good and I should listen to them. Bevans took my case on, it was a Nicole Fellows.

Nicole Fellows did a report on 21 September 2006 as follows:

Bevans Solicitors

Dear Mr Steele

Re: Claim against St Helen's Metropolitan Borough Council

I have now had the opportunity to fully review all papers forwarded to me by Robert Spicer on your behalf. There are several issues which I feel ought to be raised with you, namely the issue of limitation in relation to a claim for breach of contract or alternatively for Personal Injury, the prospect of succeeding in a claim for breach of contract or for personal injury, a potential negligence claim against Mr Robert Spicer, your public access barrister and finally the issue of costs.

It is clear that the issue of limitation is integral to the prospect of proceeding with your claim set out in your letter to the above named organisation on 26 January 2006 and so have dealt with this first.

Limitation issues

As no doubt you have discussed on previous occasions with Mr Spicer, the time frame in which a claim can be brought is subject to time limits as laid out in the Limitation Act 1980. With regard to limitations for the purposes of a Personal Injury Claim, you have only a period of three years in which to issue your claim at court. Contract claims have a longer shelf life of six years. There are of course exceptions to the time limits, which are explored further below, but it is worth noting at this point that these exceptions are not lightly applied. A further complication to the issue of limitation is deciding a starting point from which your claim began to accrue, i.e. effectively a start date (date of accrual) from which the limitation period will begin to run.

Date of accrual – breach of contract

In the circumstances of your case and for the purposes of a breach of contract claim, the operative date is that at which your employment was finally terminated, being the 8 November 1999. Therefore the limitation period would have expired on 8November 2005 being two months after you instructed Mr Robert Spicer to advise you in relation to a claim.

Date of accrual – personal injury

With regard to the potential personal injury claim, the date of accrual is less obvious though the Limitation Act does offer guidance to assist in establishing the operative date. Section 14A of the Act stipulates that the starting date for reckoning the three-year limitation period for personal injury is the earliest date upon which you first had the knowledge, which you might reasonably have been expected to acquire, necessary to bring a legal claim against the Council. You must therefore have known the material facts, have known that the damage caused by the Council's acts (or omissions) was serious enough to justify the issue of legal proceedings and must have known the identity of the potential parties to the action, before the three year period starts running. This effectively means that the three-year period did not start to run until you were aware that there was a problem and the parties involved which can in some cases be some time after the event

The difficulty with your claim in this respect is in establishing when you had all of the above knowledge. This could arguably have been at the point that you decided to leave work due to ill-health on the 14 August 1997, or on the 2 August 1999 when the Council's Occupational Health Physician stated that you had a disability and no potential adjustments would allow your continued employment. However the latest date at which you could argue that you had sufficient knowledge to warrant initiating a claim, would be the 24 April 2001 at which date you were admitted to Whiston Hospital as an inpatient under Section 3 of the Mental Health Act. This admission meant that you were unable to proceed with an Appeal against your prior dismissal on the 8 November 1998. For the purposes of personal injury, any potential claim has therefore exceeded the three-year limitation.

Possible exceptions to the Limitation Period

I am aware that Mr Spicer has explored the possibility of exceptions with you and therefore seek to both summarise the position regarding exceptions and apply this to your particular circumstances by way of clarification.

There are a number of exceptions to the general three and six year rules which can stop or delay time running for breach of contract and personal injury claims under the limitation period. In addition the court has a wide discretion, which it rarely exercises, to extend the limitation period. Reliance on the courts discretion is a high-risk strategy and if the limitation period has expired then the court will only allow the issue of legal proceedings in very exceptional cases. The main exceptions to the general rules include:-

- *The limitation period does not start to run for children and young adults until they reach the age of 18 years. This means that the period expires on the eve of the 21st birthday.*

- *People who suffer from mental incapacity may be able to issue proceedings at any time, as in severe cases; the three year period may never start to run. The limitation period may however start to run if mental capacity returns.*

Mr Spicer has suggested that there is some scope with regard to the second exception, indeed in 1999, as noted above, the Council's Occupational Health Physician did find that your psychiatric condition was of such severity that your were in fact disabled and unable to continue your employment. The question is however, whether you remain incapacitated for the purposes of the above exception, as the limitation period will begin to run if mental capacity returns.

In consideration of the medical evidence that has been supplied, your GP records certainly bear out the fact that you have been prescribed a significant amount of medication since August 1997 and that this is subject to regular reviews. The GP records and correspondence between Dr Dutta and Dr Schofield are indicative of the fact that you are managing to lead a comparatively normal life only as a result of your continued medication, which does occasionally require adjustment.

Despite these records, there does not appear to have been a further report concluding that your mental capacity remains impaired to the extent that you would have been unable to initiate proceedings during the limitation period. Your admission to Whiston Hospital between 24 April 2001 and 7 August 2001 is illustrative of your incapacity at that time but is of short duration. It would be impossible to argue that a stay of 14 weeks in an institution prohibited you from issuing a claim during a six-year limitation period. You forwarded a letter addressed to the Principal Solicitor of the Council dated 8 November 2005 in which you state 'My health has recently improved and I am now capable of managing my own affairs.' This could be detrimental in the sense that you were arguably in a position to issue your claim before this date, which you may note above is the date of the expiry of the limitation period for breach of contract claim.

The above position is mitigated by a letter from Dr Kurzeja of Four Acre Health Centre dated the 19 June 2006 in which she briefly states that you suffer from Schizophrenia and currently benefit from the care of your local mental health team. Further, the letter states that you are unable to live a normal lifestyle. Should you decide to proceed with this matter, it will be imperative to secure a further, much more comprehensive report in order to establish that your mental health issues have been of such severity that you have never had the mental capacity to initiate a claim. In this scenario the limitation periods would never begin to run. It should also be borne in mind that should the Council attempt to establish that your illness improved and at some point in the past six years you gained sufficient capacity to initiate a claim, the limitation periods would be deemed to run only from that point in time.

The issue of limitation remains a considerable hurdle to overcome. Should we issue a claim on your behalf, it is almost guaranteed that the Council will object on the grounds of limitation. With the current evidence available, it is not possible to guarantee being able to successfully deal with the limitation problem and I would ask you to bear that in mind when considering the costs involved in proceeding with litigation. There is an alternative approach based on a claim in professional negligence against Mr Spicer, which I will discuss in more detail below. In summary, Mr Spicer received your papers at some point in September 2005 and had sufficient time to assess your case in terms of potential litigation and deal with the pending expiry of the limitation period by issuing a protective claim form. Had Mr Spicer issued the claim, you would have been able to pursue compensation for breach of contract.

Prospects of success

Breach of contract claim

In the event that you are able to overcome the limitation period, a breach of contract claim could be pursued in the terms laid out in your letter of claim dated 26 January 2006. The actions of your employer (the Defendant) could arguably amount to a breach of an implied term (meaning it does not need to be expressly written into the contract to permit the employees reliance on it) of mutual trust and confidence on the grounds that the Defendant behaved in a way calculated or likely to destroy or damage the relationship of confidence and trust without reasonable and proper cause.

The onus is upon the employee to prove that the relationship broke down as a result of the deliberate and overt acts of the employer, which were sufficiently serious to amount to a breach of the implied term of trust and confidence. If this can be proven it would inevitably mean that there has been fundamental breach going necessarily to the root of the contract.

In relation to the circumstances of your case; the following examples could arguably be used to illustrate deliberate acts of your employer to undermine the relationship of trust and confidence;

- *July 1996 – being told that if six people did not apply for a new role of co-ordinator, that six men would be sacked and replaced*
- *November 1996 – unilateral changes to the terms of the contract of employment made without consultation.*
- *Being subjected to malicious and abusive language*
- *Being provided with insufficient staff to carry out your duties properly*
- *August 1997 – being accused of lying in front of a number of my colleagues*

– *November 1998 – a letter written to the Assistant Director set out your complaints and grievances and a response was received from the Assistant Director. In November 1999 however, he stated that he was unaware of any complaints by you of bullying or harassment.*

I note that the above list is by no means exhaustive. The cumulative effect of your employer's actions may be sufficient to satisfy the requirements of proving a breach in relation to mutual trust and confidence. However, it is worth noting that evidencing the same could prove very difficult. Cases of this kind have a particularly high failure rate and it would appear that only the most blatant and extreme cases are brought against employers with any degree of success.

There may be insufficient evidence to substantiate each of your complaints and for this reason, I am bound to advise that a claim of this sort could be very risky and it would be impossible to guarantee a successful income.

Personal Injury Claim

In the event that the claim is not struck out on the basis of expiry of the limitation period, a personal injury claim could be made instead of a breach of contract claim. You would need to establish that your illness was a direct result of the actions of the Defendant in other words, you would need to show that the acts of the Defendant during the course of your employment caused the illness from which you began to suffer. It could then also be claimed that the further omission of the Defendant to investigate your complaints or to take adequate measures to prevent the behaviour of it's staff was instrumental in perpetuating your illness to the point that you were unable to continue in your employment.

There is sufficient evidence to show that you were suffering from a mental illness at the time of the termination of your employment. The claim would be assisted by the fact that the Defendant terminated your employment on grounds of ill-health, the difficulty would be in establishing that it was the act and/or admission of the Defendant, which caused the illness and the onus of proving this lies with you. In order to show that the Defendant acted in breach of its statutory duty of care, you will need to prove not only that the Defendant was aware of your difficulties but took no steps to address them. This could be difficult in light of the lack of documentation prior to the 14 August 1997.

It is also worth mentioning at this point that after your dismissal and subsequent reinstatement in September 1998, there is evidence to show that the Defendant adopted procedures that were designed to facilitate your return to work and to health even though they were never utilised. Further to the above, there does not appear to be a contemporaneous psychiatric report prepared at the time of your dismissal (one may have been produced but not placed with the files – please confirm if in fact such a report does exist). Such a report would have been a vital piece of evidence, which may have assisted in forging a link between your illness and the termination of your employment. There is also an issue in relation to whether your subsequent illness was a reasonably foreseeable consequence of your previous employer's actions. It is arguable that the Council could not have anticipated that their alleged actions would have resulted in your current illness.

In the event that it is possible to overcome the evidential difficulties of this claim, the losses that you are likely to recover will reflect any loss of earnings incurred (subject to receipt of sick pay and other benefits) including future loss of earnings. Further compensation in the event of a successful claim is difficult to quantify as psychiatric harm deals with more intangible factors such as your ability to return to work and to lead a normal and fulfilling life. I am unable to advise more specifically regarding likely compensation as it there is insufficient detail in the files provided at the moment.

Professional Negligence claim

As mentioned above, the problem of the expiration of the limitation could have been avoided had a claim form been issued before 8 November 2005. In the event that the problem regarding limitation cannot be overcome, a professional negligence claim against Mr Spicer could provide an alternative route of compensation.

The basis of this claim would be professional negligence, i.e. if someone who possesses a special skill undertakes to apply that skill for the assistance of another person who relies upon that skill; a duty of care will arise. Robert Spicer was therefore under a duty to provide appropriate and professional advice in relation to the circumstances of your claim. One of the issues of which he ought to have been aware is the expiry of the limitation period. Robert Spicer would have been fully aware that there would be a six-year bar in relation to the breach of contract claim and should have taken appropriate action to protect your potential claim by issuing a protective Claim Form with the court. As a result of Robert Spicer's inaction you have essentially lost the opportunity to bring your claim.

The potential claim against Robert Spicer could only relate to the lost opportunity of bringing the breach of contract claim as this is the only limitation period that Robert Spicer missed. The limitation period regarding the personal injury claim expired some time before Robert Spicer was instructed by you.

The compensation available for such a claim would depend on the court's view of the likely damages you would have recovered if you had in fact been able to bring the breach of contract claim. The court can only speculate about the outcome of the original proceedings, which will involve a degree of consideration in relation to the probabilities of success and other contingencies.

There is of course a risk that the court may form the view that the prospect of success of the breach of contract claim is limited, bearing in mind my advice above that these particular claims are difficult to prove. In order to overcome the hurdle regarding whether or not the case would have been successful, we would need to show that you did in fact have a claim in law with some prospect of success at the very least. On the basis of the documentation I have to hand, we should be able to show that there was a meritorious claim, however, there will be a substantial element of risk involved given our ability to show that your employer's were at fault.

In conclusion

I perceive that there are two options available to you;

You can either issue proceedings for a breach of contract or a personal injury claim against your employer including our representations regarding limitation. It is to be anticipated that the Council will respond to the limitation issue quite strongly and potentially to apply to have the claim struck out on this basis. In the event that an argument regarding limitation is unsuccessful, you would still have the option of pursuing Mr Spicer in relation to a Professional Negligence claim. The further benefit of this course of action is that the court would conclusively decide whether the limitation period has begun to run or if in fact it has expired.

The costs issues in following this course of action could be prohibitive, you would incur substantial costs in relation to solicitors and barristers fees, court fees, preparation of experts reports and in the event that you are unsuccessful, the Council's legal costs as well. If unsuccessful, there is of course the opportunity to claim against Robert Spicer, however the costs again could be substantial and there is still a risk that you may not succeed.

Alternatively, you can issue a claim in the first instance against Mr Spicer for Professional Negligence. The benefit of this course of action is that you would not be incurring the cost of risky litigation against your previous employer, though you would still need to take into account that this claim alone could still be very costly in the event that it goes all the way to a hearing. It would be beneficial in either claim to reach an agreed conclusion before a full hearing became necessary. The compensation that you could potentially recover would depend to a certain degree on the prospect of the success of the claim for breach of contract had this not been barred by limitation.

As discussed above there are two factors to be borne in mind. Firstly, the claim would be quantified by the court with suitable deductions to take into account your prospect of success and the risk of litigation in general and Secondly, in order to be successful in your professional negligence claim, you will need to be able to show that not only was there an actionable claim for breach of contract against your employer but that there would have been some prospect of success. It is my opinion that it would potentially be an easier task to show that there was an actionable case with a prospect of success than to attempt to overcome the hurdle of the expired limitation period.

I am aware that there is a considerable amount of information contained above and that you may require some time to digest the same. I received the fax from Julie Waring that you authorised and confirm that I have sent her a copy of this fax in the event that this letter does not reach you in time for your meeting with her. I shall be in the office all day

tomorrow and would be happy, should you feel the need, to contact to discuss any of the points raised above.
In any event, I look forward to receiving your response to the above and hope that I am able to assist you further in the future.

Yours sincerely

Nicole Fellows

I told Nicole Fellows that I did not want to take Robert Spicer to court and I wanted to take St Helen's Council to court. I spoke to Robert Spicer on the phone and told him what Bevans had said about him being negligent and he replied 'oh dear' and asked me to send him the report straight away.

13. I received a letter from Robert Spicer on 4 October 2006 as follows:

Frederick Place Chambers, Bristol

Dear Mr Steele

Thank you for sending me the letter from Bevans dated August 17 2006. On August 14 2006, you paid me £400 plus £70 VAT in advance for future work on your case. I have done £50 worth of work, which was preparing and delivering the documentation to Bevans. I have been advised by the Bar Council that I should refund the balance to you and I therefore enclose a cheque for £411.25 as a full refund. As you are aware, all of the relevant documentation is with Bevans. I will return the remainder of the documentation to you under separate cover.

Yours sincerely

Robert Spicer

14. I was shocked by Mr Spicer's response. I contacted a Mental Health Advocate, Julie Waring to write to Robert Spicer and she wrote to him on 10 October 2006 as follows:

Mental Health Advocate

Dear Mr Spicer

ROBERT STEELE

I am supporting the above named with regard to his pursuance of a claim of Breach of Contract against St Helen's MBC. Mr Steele advises me that you have been very supportive towards him with regard to this matter until recently, when you advised that you could no longer continue with this case.

Mr Steele is now confused and disappointed with this decision and has asked me to establish and explain the reasons for this to him. He has stated that his only intention is to pursue St Helen's Council despite being given a number of options in a letter from Bevans Solicitors dated 17 August 2006, one of which was a professional negligence claim against yourself, which is clearly not an option for him.

I look forward to hearing from you shortly.
Many thanks.

Yours sincerely

JULIE WARING
Mental Health Advocate

15. Robert Spicer replied to Julie Waring on 11 October 2006 as follows:

Frederick Place Chambers, Bristol

To Mr Robert Steele

c.c Julie Waring, St Helens CDP

I have today received a letter from Julie Waring at St Helen's CDP asking me to explain to you the reasons why I cannot continue with your case. The reasons are as follows:

1) *Paragraph 603 of the Code of Conduct of the Bar of England and Wales states that 'a barrister must not accept any instructions if to do so would cause him to be professionally embarrassed'. Paragraph 603(d) states that 'this includes a matter where it will be difficult for the barrister to maintain professional independence'.*

2) *I have been advised by the Bar Council and by the Bar Mutual Indemnity Fund that this rule applies to me in relation to your case.*

3) *The fact that you have been advised that you have a potential professional negligence claim against me means that this rule applies. I have no alternative but to comply with this rule.*

4) *You are now instructing solicitors in this matter and this means that you are no longer instructing me.*

Yours sincerely

Robert Spicer

As for Robert Spicer to say 'you are now instructing solicitors in this matter and this means that you are no longer instructing me' is in my opinion just an excuse to drop my case. I never mentioned I am no longer instructing him.

16. I wrote to Nicole Fellows on 4 October 2006 as follows:

Clockface Road, St Helen's, Merseyside

Dear Nicole

461

Thank you for your letter dated 3 October 2006. Firstly I am shocked to find out I owe £1,211.43. When I spoke to you on the phone a few weeks ago I asked you how much more would it cost and you told me you are not going to charge me anymore than the £587.50 I sent you as you were learning experience from it. I have sent you a cheque with this letter for £1,211.43 and if you do recall our conversation you should not cash it.

I have read your report 21 September 2006 a couple of times and I have decided to go for a breach of contract against the Council. The Council have done a lot of damage to my health, they have left me physically and mentally disturbed by what I consider to be their lies, bullying, harassment and corruption and I want my day in Court and expose every one of them. They have destroyed my life and I will have my day in Court. I know you have told me it's going to cost me £80,000 so be it.

I am going to Cheltenham on 24 October and if you can pencil a day in on the 25 – 26 to come and see you, I think we're going to need two hours. I am going to need you to write three letters, one to Brian Langshaw, one to Mark, my ex CPN and one to my psychiatrist from 1999 when I was seriously ill and you could not have a conversation with me. I was sleeping up to 23 hours a day.

Can you let me know how much it will cost for two hours and three letters. I know how to get to Frederick Place, Clifton but I will need directions from there and parking. I will need the appointment between 12-2 or 2-4 to give me time to find you. I am convinced that my limitation period will be lifted till 2008 at the least.

Yours faithfully

Mr R Steele

As you can see, I decided to take St Helens's Council to court and not Robert Spicer for professional negligence.

17. I attended Bevans Solicitors on 25 October 2006 and had discussions about my claim with Nicole Fellows and William Ellerton and William told me to sue Robert Spicer rather than go after the Council. He told me that the maximum payout is £100,000 and I would get £20,000 to £30,000 out of court settlement. Firstly I did not want to sue Robert Spicer and secondly, twenty to thirty thousand pounds was not acceptable as I had lost in the region of a million pounds in loss of earnings.

18. Nicole Fellows wrote to me on 31 October 2006 as follows:

Bevans Solicitors

Dear Mr Steele

RE: St Helen's Metropolitan District Council

Thank you for attending our offices to give us the opportunity to meet you finally. I wanted to give you a brief re-cap of the meeting so that you can make a final decision as to whether to proceed against Mr Spicer.

Both William Ellerton and myself agree that your strongest claim is in fact against Mr Spicer, as opposed to that against St Helen's Metropolitan District Council. This advice is based on two main issues. Firstly, the limitation period has expired in relation to a claim against St Helen's and is a virtually impossible hurdle to overcome. Secondly, the current evidence relating to your mental disability appears to be insufficient to support a personal injury claim and also to substantiate a breach of contract claim.

You also raised the issue of previous solicitors, in particular the firm of Thompsons whom you instructed between 1998 and 2002. You noted that they did not take sufficient initiative to fully investigate your claim at the material time. It is worth noting that further evidence of your psychiatric well-being at this time would have been helpful. However, a claim brought against Thompsons for professional negligence based on the fact that they did not deal with your case effectively would be particularly difficult. In order to bring a claim against Thompsons for professional negligence, we would need to show that in the event that they had secured further evidence regarding your psychiatric health, your claim in personal injury would have been successful. Establishing that a successful claim would be a hurdle comparable to that of an expired limitation period.

The further points that you raised in relation to the treatment you received from St Helens are pertinent to a claim against Mr Spicer. We will need to show that there was a claim against St Helen's that had some prospect of success. However, it would be a disservice to suggest that a claim against St Helen's has the same chance of succeeding as a claim against Mr Spicer.

I await your further instruction in this matter. Should you wish to discuss any of the above, then please do not hesitate to contact me on the details provided on my card.

Yours sincerely

Nicole Fellows

19. After constant pressure from Nicole I gave in and agreed to sue Robert Spicer but I was not prepared to settle for an out of court settlement of twenty to thirty thousand pounds and I wrote to Nicole on 17 November 2006 as follows:

Clockface Road, St Helens, Merseyside

Dear Nicole

Thank you for your letter 31 October 2006. I feel I have two claims and they are both at Mr Spicer. Firstly we all agree he is responsible for the Breach of Contract.

I went and saw Keith Parks Solicitors in St Helen's and spoke to a solicitor called Adrian about Thompsons. He gave me several reasons why Thompsons were negligent and they would not take the case on because of the short time limit that ran out in July 2006, and who was going to pay the costs?

What I cannot understand is how a woman a few months ago got over £800,000 for stress at work and never accrued a mental illness from it. I have plenty of evidence of stress and depression. The first time the psychiatrist visited me at home he told me my employer had used a psychological approach to wear me down. I have since reminded him several times over the years in front of witnesses of this remark. William Ellerton said he could put a case together on things I told him what was going on, especially the wages.

I will remind you of some of the incidents.

1. *Gornall took the job of Head of Security on a pay cut and he accepted the job. His shop steward told him he is entitled to the Council rates of pay and the union got it him, Gornall – Head of Security. Molyneux has had four jobs in Security and has been on the Council's rate of pay in every job. He is Gornall's best mate and has got all the promotions in Security giving him the job of Deputy Head of Security. Ian Dillon is Courier for Security and is on days – Monday to Friday and gets Council's rate of pay. Terry Cunliffe is the Liaison Officer in Security and is on the Council rates of pay. The rest of the lads are on the same money and have to work weekends, shifts and Bank Holidays and lieu time for it and they have more responsibility.*

2. *I had only been off work a few weeks when Tony Marsh told me that Mick had told him to tell me I am not welcome any more at my place of work.*

3. *Peter Moffat told me in 1998 that Mr Farrell is in a position and staying in a position, Mr Gornall's in a position and staying in a position, therefore I'm terminating your employment.*

4. *The works Doctor told them I was very poorly and to stay away from me. A week later Farrell rang the union office and wanted to see me in his office.*

5. *Derek Anders told the lads that if I catch Rob Steele playing snooker I will sack the b*****d.*

6. *Derek Anders asked the lads, 'has Rob Steele been round your house, you can tell me he's been round Alans'.*

7. *When I wanted to return to work Peter Mavers told me to stay away and six months later finished me on ill health.*

8. *The Head of Human Resources wrote to the union and told them that if my grievances weren't put on the table it would fester in my mind and make it difficult for a return to work.*

Robert Spicer spoke to me on the phone and told me they wanted rid of me. I told him I already knew that from day one. The only way forward is to take Robert Spicer to Court and I can confront the Council as they will have to give evidence.

I am looking at starting my own business in July 2007 and William Ellerton reckoned I would get 30% of £100,000.

That would be very helpful to the business. I will have to think very seriously about it as I lost over £60,000 in having to sell my house.

Ref Thompsons, the solicitor told me a number of reasons they were at fault. I can remember three of them;

1)   *They never looked at my medical records, doctor's or psychiatrist;*
2)   *They never got an opinion from a barrister;*
3)   *They had my case up to a month before my time limit ran out and told me I never had a case and I was seriously ill at the time and could do nothing about it. If they would have told me earlier, I could have got another solicitor and got legal aid.*

I have just remembered number 9 – just before I went off sick I serviced Gornall's car for him. None of the lads liked Gornall so I never told them when I went off sick. Gornall told some of the lads, 'I don't know why Rob Steele hates me, he serviced my car'. The reason he told them was so they would not bother with me. I told them I did but it backfired in Gornall's face because they never fell out with me.

Let William Ellerton see this letter and see what he thinks and I will ring you on Tuesday.

Yours faithfully

Mr R Steele

Ps Number 10 – Robert Spicer asked me did they have a counselling service and asked me did they every offer me counselling. I said 'no'. He said this was very helpful to my case.

20. I again wrote to Nicole on 29 November 2006 as follows:

Clockface Road, St Helen's, Merseyside

Dear Nicole

I wish for you to proceed against Mr Spicer for negligence.

Ref my letter 17-11-06, I gave you ten reasons for breach of contract. I have remembered a couple more.

11) Jimmy Goodier was off sick two weeks before me and I was off sick three weeks and Jimmy had been off five weeks. I got sent to the works doctor and he never.

12) Single Status came into force in the Council in April 1999. I was still the shop steward even though I was off sick and I was the only person who knew what to do and what was going on. The Council paid 2 million pounds out bringing the lower paid up to the rest of the Council's pay. Most of the Security officers did not get a penny and they were also entitled to what their colleagues were getting but got nothing and most of Security got a pay cut in 1991 and were the only people in the Council to do so.

All this is down to Farrell and Gornall.

Yours faithfully

Mr R Steele

21. As I did not want to take Robert Spicer to court in the first place and as I trusted what Robert Spicer said to me about getting a fair hearing in the European Court of Human Rights, I rang the European Court of Human Rights on 12 January 2007. They confirmed what Robert and his two barrister friends told me was correct so I contacted Julie Waring my Mental Health Advocate

and asked her to contact Robert Spicer and see if he would continue with my case. Julie wrote on 22 January 2007 as follows:

Julie Waring,Mental Health Advocate

Dear Mr Spicer

RE: ROBERT STEELE, 63 CLOCK FACE ROAD, ST HELEN'S

Mr Steele has requested that I write to you to ascertain whether or not you would be willing to continue with his case against St Helen's Borough Council. He has contacted the European Court of Human Rights who have advised him to take this forward as they would be prepared to look at this despite it being out of the Limitation Period.

Perhaps you would be kind enough to advise either myself or Mr Steele direct at your earliest convenience. Many thanks.

Yours sincerely
JULIE WARING
Mental Health Advocate

22. Julie Waring wrote to me and told me Mr Spicer will take my case back on an 'advice only' so I wrote to Robert on 30 January 2007 as follows:

Clockface Road, St Helen's, Merseyside,

Dear Mr Spicer

I have spoken to Julie Waring today and she is going to contact you. She tells me you can only give me advice.

I spoke to the European Court of Human Rights on 12 January 2007 and they told me what you and your two barrister friends told me and I am awaiting a reply from their lawyers.

The problem I have got is I have to put my case into Court and have it struck out on the time limit. I have to take it to the highest Court in the country before I go to the European Court and if you cannot do this anymore, can you get your barrister friend to do this for me. I don't know his name but I met him at your office.

No matter what it takes, I am going to get St Helen's Council into Court. I blame Thompsons Solicitors and Jackson and Canter for my time limits running out. None of the solicitors I have instructed have been honest with me including Bevans.

I have received a copy of a psychiatric report done on behalf of Weightmans Solicitors and if I put my case into Court they are going to have it struck out on the grounds that it is statute barred. This will give me the opportunity to apply to the European Courts.

If you want a copy of my psychiatric report let me know.

I am going to need your help put my case into Court and issue proceedings against the Council.

I should hear from the European Court in the next week or two so I will be collecting my file from Bevans.

I have sent you a copy of the letter to the European Court.

Yours faithfully

Mr R Steele

23. I again wrote to Robert Spicer on 2 March 2007 as follows:

Clockface Road, St Helen's, Merseyside,

Dear Mr Spicer

I have sent you a cheque for £940 that puts me well in credit. I am putting a cheque in on Monday so I have put Wednesday's date on it to give my cheque chance to clear.

I have also sent Bevans a cheque on 1-3-07 so you should have the files by next week. When you get the file can you read their psychiatric report very carefully, especially (35) page 21. I became very ill towards the end of my termination where I was sleeping up to 23 hours a day and stopped talking. You could not get a sentence out of me. I did not bother with any of my friends for approximately three years; I lost contact with them all.

I have sent you some copies of statements from my friends that you might find helpful. I took them to Bevans and they would not even look at them. There is a good two years where they say I could have been incapacitated. If that's the case, my limitation does not run out till November 2007 we need to look at this as a matter or urgency.

Yours faithfully

Mr R Steele

24. Julie Waring wrote to Nicole Fellows on 13 February 2007 as follows:

Julie Waring, St Helen's CDP

Dear Ms Fellows

Robert Steele : Claim Against St Helen's MBC

You will recall I am supporting the above named who has requested that I write to you in connection with his claim as above. Mr Steele has been in touch directly with the European Court of Human Rights who have advised him that they will look at his case once it has been struck out of court. This is similar advice to what Mr Robert Spicer gave and it is therefore Mr Steele's intention to refer this matter back to Mr Spicer on an advice only basis.

I would be obliged therefore if you could send the file of papers directly to Mr Spicer without delay. Mr Steele has indicated that he feels there should be a refund of monies from yourselves as the information you gave him was misleading, particularly now as he has received confirmation from the European Court which confirms the original advice received by Robert Spicer. Perhaps you would be good enough to consider the above and reply direct to Mr Steele at your earliest convenience.

Yours sincerely

Julie Waring
Mental Health Advocate

25. I received a letter from Robert Spicer on 14 March 2007 as follows:

Frederick Place Chambers, Bristol

Dear Mr Steele

This is to confirm that I have now received the documentation from Bevans. They told me that the correspondence file will be returned to you. Could you please forward it to me when you receive it.

The next step, as you know, is for you to start proceedings. This involves filling in a claim form which you can get from your nearest county court. The form has to be accompanied by particulars of claim, which I am working on at the moment. The argument on limitation can also be included in the particulars.

The particulars of claim have to be accompanied by a Schedule of loss which sets out details of any past and future expenses and losses which you claim. This will involve a fair amount of work and in the meantime you could perhaps list every expens,e which your illness has incurred, details of loss of earnings etc.

The claim will not be an easy one. I have contacted two other lawyers who are willing to discuss your case. I will ensure that there is no repeat of the last eight months. Once again, I would ask you to consider seriously the prospect that you might incur significant expenditure for no satisfactory result.

So far, since you re-instructed me, I have spent 4 hours on your case. This means that you are 6 hours in credit. I will keep you fully informed of costs as we proceed.

Have you applied for exemption from the court fee?

I think that we will need a conference soon but I will deal with the particulars of claim first.

With best wishes.

Yours sincerely

Robert Spicer

26. I again wrote to Robert Spicer on 16 March 2007 as follows:

Clockface Road, St Helen's, Merseyside

Dear Mr Spicer

Up to date my legal costs to you are £5,076.25 and I have spent £2,391.13 with Bevans and my expenses up to date are £1,596, to date a total of £9,063.38.

Without the relevant information from the Council I cannot get an exact figure on my wages to date or for he future. What I do know is the weekend hours for Co-ordinator was 286.6666667 hours per annum from 1996 to 2003 and in 2003 it went down to 260 hours per annum. In 2005 or 2006 they went up to 312 hours and Bank Holidays were 32 hours per annum from 1996 to 2005 or 2006 and now they do 48 hours per annum for the same pay, a shift allowance of 20% on their basic pay.

I can tell you had I been on the correct pay in 2003 to 2004 my wages would have been £26,684.04 per annum. I do have the relevant paperwork to work it out to the exact amount for 2003 to April 2004.

I sold my house for £85,000 and they are now selling for £124,000 so I have lost £39,000 on the sale of my house. I also spent £30,000 doing it up and I left a couple of thousand pounds worth of tools and equipment in the garage.

I would say my loss of earnings would be around £700,000 plus and I would like compensation for the last 10 years for not being able to live a normal life and the possibility of never living a normal life again. You did say it's a massive claim.

Yours faithfully

Mr R Steele

I also spoke to Robert on the phone on 16 March 2007. I asked Robert when will my case be in court and he told me 'before I go away in May'. I again spoke to him on the phone on Monday 19 March 2007 and things were going ahead. Robert Spicer wrote to me on 22 March 2007 as follows:

Frederick Place Chambers, Bristol

Dear Mr Steele

Re: Your claim against St Helen's Metropolitan District Council

I have now had the opportunity to review your case in detail since you re-instructed me to provide advice only after you had terminated your instructions to Bevans. I have had an informal discussion with another personal injury specialist. My conclusion is that I would advise you, in the strongest terms, not to spend any more money on this matter. I realise that this may be very disappointing for you, but it is my professional duty to ensure that you are fully aware of, and understand, the financial implications of continuing with the claim and the potential complications of the Civil Procedure Rules. You have stated that you trust my judgment and I would ask you to seriously consider the points, which I make below. My reasons for this are as follows:

1. *It is possible to start proceedings, which means completing a claim form. This will cost £1700 court fee plus my own fees of an estimated 8 hours at £80 per hour.*

2. *The completion of the claim form involves drafting particulars of claim. This will be problematic, and will involve the preparation of a detailed schedule of past and future expenses and losses. It must also include a report from a medical practitioner. The other side have indicated that they will apply to have the claim struck*

out on the basis that the limitation period has expired and it will not be possible for me to deal with this unless a solicitor is instructed.

3. *If proceedings are started, you may be at risk as to the payment of the other side's costs. It is difficult to assess the chance of your liability for costs, but you must be aware that these could be substantial.*

4. *In my opinion, the complex nature of this matter and potential difficulties with procedural rules mean that I cannot carry out my public access instructions unless you instruct a solicitor. I have previously advised in similar terms. I do not have the administrative resources to deal with your case after the claim form has been issued. I do not feel able to advise on an appropriate solicitor, given the difficulties, which arose in August 2006.*

5. *You may wish to obtain a second opinion on these matters but I would advise you that this will involve significant further costs.*

6. *Your chances of success in this matter are not good because of the limitation issue and the question of causation.*

7. *In relation to your relationship with Bevans, this is essentially a matter between yourself and them. I would make the point that their advice to you was that you should make a claim against me for professional negligence. The basis of this was that I had failed to issue proceedings within the prescribed limitation period. I would point out that my client care letter, which is issued to all my clients including yourself, states very clearly that I am not able to conduct litigation, including the issuing of proceedings and the fulfilment of limitation obligations. Further, it is a criminal offence for me to issue proceedings because I am not an authorised litigator for the purposes of the Courts*

8. *You stated in your letter of March 16, 2007, that your legal costs to me have been £5076.25. This does not take into account the refund of £411.25, which I sent to you. I would point out that the fees, which I have charged you have been between one-third and one-half of the standard rate, which I charge. Since you re-instructed me, I have spent 10 hours on this matter at £80 per hour, amounting to £800 plus £140 VAT.*

In conclusion, I would remind you that I have advised you in writing, on a number of previous occasions, to carefully consider whether you should spend any more money on this matter. I can now restate this advice in the strongest terms. In my opinion, you should decide to draw a line under this matter.

I have written to your mental health advocate advising her, in general terms, of my advice.

I sincerely hope that your health continues to improve.

Yours sincerely

Robert Spicer

27. Sam Coles, his clerk wrote to Julie Waring on 23 March 2007 as follows:

Frederick Place Chambers, Bristol

Dear Ms Waring,

Re: Robert Steele

This is to let you know as a matter of courtesy that I have today informed Mr Steele that Robert Spicer has been advised by his doctor to suspend his practice for four weeks on medical grounds.

He has written to Mr Steele in detail.

Yours sincerely

Sam Coles
Clerk, Frederick Place Chambers

28. Because of the behaviour of Robert Spicer dropping my case, I wrote to him in March 2007 as follows:

Clockface Road, St Helen's, Merseyside

Dear Mr Spicer

I am shocked by your letters 22 and 23 March 2007. The first thing that came into my mind was you have been warned off. I have showed it my mate and he said he believes that you have been bought off, the only other reason is you screwed up big time. Another friend has said for you to be ill and drop my case, in his opinion *you have been threatened and I totally agree with her. It was only a week earlier you told me my case would be in Court 'before I go away in May'. I spoke to you on the Monday, 19 March 2007 and you were still fighting my case.*

I am writing to a multi-millionaire to sponsor my case and use his lawyers and barrister who will no doubt be a QC. This person knows what it's like to get justice and I feel there's a strong chance he will sponsor me.

You are right about the £411.25. I have paid you £4665 to date and I am seeing my advocate putting a letter to the Ombudsman for a full refund.

Yours faithfully

Mr R Steele

29. Julie Waring, Mental Health Advocate wrote to the Bar Standards Board to complain to them about Robert Spicer on my behalf on 22 October 2007 as follows:

Julie Waring, St Helen's CDP

Dear Ms Gunn

RE: Complaint by Robert Steele re: Robert Spicer

I am a Mental Health Advocate who has supported Mr Steele since September 2006. Mr Steele has asked me to reply to your letter dated 12 October 2007.

Mr Spicer initially took Mr Steele's case in 2005 and was aware that the Limitation period had expired but assured Mr Steele that this would not be a problem as he was a special case due to his mental health being affected by the way he was treated by his employers. Solicitors were required and Mr Spicer recommended Bevans. Bevans subsequently, after reviewing all case papers, decided that the best course of action would be a professional negligence claim against Mr Spicer (see Appendix 1).

Mr Steele, confused with this turnaround, advised Mr Spicer of Bevans findings (Mr Spicer had asked Mr Steele to be kept informed and sent copies of any correspondence from Bevans) but assured him that it was not his intention to follow this course of action. Mr Steele was adamant that he only wanted to pursue a breach of contract against his former employer (Appendix 2). Mr Spicer then wrote to Mr Steele on 04 October 2006, however he did not state clearly his intentions and when pressed for reasons why he could not continue (Appendix 2a), Mr Spicer replied to Mr Steele on 11 October 2006 (Appendix 3).

This effectively brought matters to a halt and an attempt by Mr Steele to secure Bevans services was also rejected due to him disclosing the contents of their original letter (Appendix 1) to Mr Spicer which they felt would now put Mr Spicer at an advantage, knowing details of their intended course of action. Now Mr Steele finds himself in a situation where he has no Barrister and no Solicitor and a considerable amount of money having changed hands. Mr Steele's mental health once again deteriorates as a result of this situation.

In January 2007 Mr Steele takes it upon himself to contact the European Court of Human Rights who advise him and he again contacts Mr Spicer on 22 January 2007 (Appendix 4). Mr Spicer subsequently telephoned my office on 26 January enquiring about Mr Steele's mental health. He stated that he had been in touch with the Bar Council who had agreed that he could take the case back in an 'advice only' capacity, which would mean that Mr Steele would need to instruct another firm of Solicitors and the same situation could occur again as with Bevans. Mr Spicer stated that he would need written assurance from Mr Steele that he would not take out a cause of professional negligence against him. Mr Spicer added that ideally he would like Bevans to send him a letter also, stating that it had all been a misunderstanding of public access rules. Mr Spicer said he realised this may not be possible but he was prepared however to re-start the case. He said he needed to be absolutely sure of this as it had very far-reaching implications for himself, and he had been very angry and upset by the actions of Bevans as it was he who had recommended them in the first place (see Appendix 5 and Appendix 6).

Mr Spicer wrote to Mr Steele on 14 March (see Appendix 7). To all intents and purposes the case is now back with Mr Spicer who sets out the next steps. Mr Spicer then wrote to

Mr Steele on 22 March 2007, only one week later (see Appendix 8) obviously having changed his mind regarding the pursuance of Mr Steele's claim. A further letter was received one day later (23 March 2007) from a clerk Sam Coles at Frederick Place Chambers (Appendix 9).

Again Mr Steele is faced with yet another disappointment and again his mental health deteriorates as a result of the situation. In June 2007 Mr Steele requested me to write to Mr Spicer with regard to returning some missing paperwork which I duly did and received a reply from Mr Spicer dated 18 June 2007 (Appendix 11).

Mr Steele now finds himself even further removed from the Limitation date, with very little prospect of his case being heard. He continues to search for representation to get his case struck out of court in order to take it to the European Court of Human Rights. Bevans Solicitors were adamant that the best course of action for Mr Steele to take was that of 'professional negligence' against Mr Spicer, so he is obviously not alone in now reaching this conclusion. After taking Mr Steele's case on a second time, Mr Spicer then within a matter of days, takes a complete reversal in his advice to Mr Steele. Surely this situation could have been avoided by Mr Spicer not taking this case on again a second time? Mr Steele has spent a considerable amount of time, effort and money in complying with legal representation and now feels let down by the whole process.

I hope this further clarifies the reasons why Mr Steele felt it necessary to take his complaint to yourselves and he looks forward to hearing from you in due course.

Yours sincerely

Julie Waring

Enclosures

I never did get a satisfactory response from the Bar Standards Board and Mr Spicer got away with it Scot free.

30. In 2006 Robert Spicer was writing letters for me to send to Andrew Cooper of Weightmans Solicitors, a firm of solicitors instructed by St Helen's MBC. Robert told me on the phone they are a massive firm of solicitors and he's not afraid to take on the big boys. Robert drafted a letter for me to sign and send to Andrew on 9 June 2006 as follows:

Clockface Road, St Helen's, Merseyside

Dear Mr Cooper

With reference to your letter of May 9 advising me that you were still in the process of investigating the claim, I have been advised to make the following points:

1. *While I appreciate that this is a complex claim and that some of the relevant facts occurred some time ago, I would point out that the three-month period for investigation, as prescribed by the pre-action protocol, expired some time ago. I have made every effort to comply with both the spirit and the letter of the protocol. My letter of claim was sent to the defendant on January 26 2006. Requests for documentation from Aon Claims Management and from Capita were promptly and fully dealt with.*

2. *You are no doubt aware that Rule 44.3(5)(a) of the Civil Procedure Rules provides, in general terms, that an unreasonable failure to comply with the protocol may have costs implications.*

3. *I would be most grateful if you could let me have a realistic assessment of the time within which you expect to be able to send a detailed letter of response.*

4.   *I do not understand why there has been such a long delay in supplying me with a copy of the insurance scheme documentation. This material may be crucial to my claim and I would be most grateful if this matter could be expedited.*

5.   *My letter of claim asked for my earnings detail,s which would enable me to calculate my financial loss. Again, I would be most grateful if this matter could be expedited.*

6.   **As** *you are aware, I am a disabled person suffering from a psychiatric illness. The continuing uncertainty about this matter seems to be adversely affecting my health.*

Yours sincerely

Robert Steele

31. I again wrote to Andrew Cooper on 23 June 2006 as follows:

Clockface Road, St Helen's, Merseyside

Dear Mr Cooper

Thank you for your letter dated 20 June 2006. I have spoken to my Barrister and we are issuing proceedings at the end of the month. If you do manage to strike my case out of court we will put it back into court and if you manage to strike it out again, then we are going to the European Court of Human Rights. I have been told been told by two barristers that I will get a fair hearing as I have not had one in Britain.

Aon requested medical evidence and documents referred to at page 9 of the letter of claim.

1.   *Occupational health records*
2.   *GP records*

3. *Psychiatric reports*
4. *Personnel files*
5. *Documents relating to employment tribunal*
6. *Documents relating in internal appeals*
7. *My contemporaneous handwritten notes and my grievances, district audit.*

You yourself requested 4 items you wanted to look at. You have received everything you have requested. I have requested the insurance scheme documentation that you have failed to send. The Council have failed to give me any information since 1996. Ref my earnings, I will require a copy of the rota for Security Officer and Co-ordinator. I also require the pay scales for local government workers for 2004-2005, 2005-2006 and 2006-2007. This can be obtained from the Unison office. I would also like a full breakdown of wages for 2006-2007 for both rotas. This includes basic pay, shift allowance, weekend allowance, Bank Holiday payments and lieu time. This has been requested on a number of occasions and never been given. Can you ensure I receive this information?

You will be getting a letter in a couple of days requesting the insurance scheme documentation. Again this is another failure on behalf of St Helen's Council.

Yours faithfully

Mr R Steele

32. I once again wrote to Andrew Cooper on 10 July 2006 as follows:

Clockface Road, St Helen's, Merseyside

Dear Mr Cooper

Thank you for your letter dated 5 July 2006. You have written you will be aware that you need to include any medical evidence with the proceedings. You have had all the medical evidence, not once but twice you were sent it from Capita and you yourself requested it. I have an up to date letter dated 19 June 2006 from my doctor and I will be getting an up to date psychiatrist report that you will be sent in due course. We are in the middle of negotiating with a solicitor to issue proceedings so it could take sometime before you hear anything.

Also in your letter you said together with a schedule of special damage in which you indicate your valuation of your claim. We cannot do this until you send me the relevant information from my letter dated 23-6-06. I should have had this by now as it takes a day for you to write to them and send it and it takes a day for them to get the information and send it back to you, then it will take a day to send it to me so I should have received this within three working days.

What I can tell you is I am claiming loss of earnings from 1992 until I retire, compensation for my illness, poisoning my body with drugs that I would not have to have taken, having to cancel my private pension, the loss in having to sell my house and if I win my case, I will be buying another house and I'm going to have to pay someone £50 a week to housekeep for me and I'm going to have to pay £50 a week to a gardener to keep the gardens done. I will be claiming for all of this.

Also, if I win my case I will be getting a garage and I'm going to have to pay someone £500 a week to do my job. I was capable of doing all of this and more till your clients made me ill.

Can you see I get the wages information and the insurance document asap.

Yours faithfully

Mr R Steele

33. Again I wrote to Andrew Cooper on 11 August 2006 as follows:

Clockface Road, St Helen's, Merseyside

Dear Mr Cooper

I wrote to you on 10 July 2006 and again you have failed to send me any information I have requested. I have requested for the sight of the insurance schemes on numerous occasions, again you have failed to disclose this information. I have also requested information of my letter 23-6-06 for disclosure of up to date rotas for Security Officers and Co-ordinators' pay scales for local government workers for 2004-2005, 2005-2006 and 2006-2007 and I also requested a full breakdown of wages for 2006 /2007 for both rotas. I will also need to now when the date the Co-ordinators started.

I have spoken to my Barrister and we are giving you 10 working days from the date of this letter to reply with all the relevant information requested then we are going to the Courts for disclosure of the material I need. You should be issued proceedings in the next few weeks.

Yours faithfully

Mr R Steele

34. Andrew Cooper replied to my previous letters on 1 September 2006 as follows:

Weightmans, Solicitors

Dear Mr Steele

Robert Steele v St Helen's MBC

Thank you for your letter dated 11 August, received during my annual vacation.

The Council is not obliged to send you copies of the insurance schemes between the Council and its personal accident Insurers for the following reasons:

1. *The scheme only covers accidents – you have not had an accident.*
2. *Your entitlement to any benefits would accrue under your Contract of Employment with the Council. The insurance scheme is therefore totally irrelevant. I assume that you have a copy of your Contract of Employment or, at least, have access to it. The Contract of Employment sets out the basis upon which an employee can seek benefits from his employer.*

I have asked the Council for details of any pay rises which you could reasonably have hoped to achieve had you remained in their employment. The answer is likely to come in the form of a percentage page rise. Your request for 'loss of earnings' documentation does not form part of standard disclosure. As a result, the Council will not be ordered to disclose such information before proceedings are issued. However, I will send you details of the percentage pay rises once I have them.

In any event, I am happy for you to issue proceedings without a fully detailed Schedule of Special Loss. You have indicated in previous letters that you believe your losses are significant. For now, this is sufficient information for the Council. Please do not refrain from issuing proceedings simply to await further pay rise details.

I will be touch as soon as I receive the pay rises.

Yours sincerely

Andrew Cooper

Partner

You will see quite clearly the statement made by Andrew – 'the scheme only covers accidents, you have not had an accident'. I already had a copy of the accident scheme. As you will see below, it states it does not pay out for any pre-existing mental or physical defect so my mental illness was not excluded as it was a new illness.

PERSONAL ACCIDENT - ALL DUTY INSURANCE SCHEME CONDITIONS

The scheme provides for:-

1. *Payment of lump sum benefits for employees who are killed or permanently disabled in the course of employment.*

2. *The benefits will apply to all employees of the St Helen's Metropolitan Borough Council other than persons over 70 years, of age.*

3. *All employees or their personal representatives shall be entitled to receive the payments set out in the schedule in respect of sustaining bodily injury by violent, accidental, external and visible means, as a result of which death or disablement occurs within 12 months of sustaining such Injury whilst engaged in the Council's business and on journeys connected therewith anywhere in the world, including travel between private residence and place of work.*

4. <u>*Exclusions*</u>

No payment shall be made in respect of death or disablement caused directly or indirectly by –

(a) *suicide or attempted suicide, insanity, intoxication, the illegal use of drugs, venereal disease', pregnancy or childbirth;*

(b) *any pre-existing mental or physical defect or infirmity of any person in respect of whom compensation would otherwise be payable but only if and to the extent to which such defect or infirmity prolongs the period of disablement or causes death or other permanent total disablement.*

(c) *racing of any kind or travelling in or on or entering or disembarking from any airborne craft.*

Travel as a passenger in duly licensed multi-engined conventional type passenger aircraft (other than helicopters) is not excluded.

5. *In the event of any accident or injury to an employee which results in the death or permanent disablement of that employee being brought about by or contributed to by the conduct of that employee, no benefit shall be payable as of right in accordance with the provisions of this scheme, but the Borough Council may in their absolute discretion pay all or any part of the benefit arising under this scheme.*

6. *Any employee who considers that he has become entitled to benefits in accordance with this scheme shall notify the Treasurer and state the extent of his injuries. Personal representatives of a deceased employee shall be required to supply the Treasurer with a death certificate, together with any further information, which may be required.*

7. *Any injured employee who considers that he has become entitled to benefits in accordance with the scheme shall make himself available for, and submit to, any medical examination which the Council may require, provided that the time and place of such examination shall be reasonable, and an employee who refuses to make himself available and submit to such examination shall not be entitled to payment of benefits under the scheme.*

8. *Payment of benefits shall be made as soon as possible after the degree of injury resulting from any accident has been ascertained, in accordance with the Schedule hereto, and no interest shall be paid to an employee in respect of any benefits.*

9. *Compensation in respect of any one person shall not be paid under more than one of the items in the Scale of Compensation in respect of the same period of time. Unless otherwise, agreed the Council shall not be liable in respect of any one person to make any further payment hereunder after a claim in respect of that person has been admitted in respect of permanent disablement of any kind.*

10. *Payments made under this scheme may, at the discretion of the Council, be reduced by the amount of damage or compensation recoverable in respect of particular injuries.*

12. *For the avoidance of doubt It is hereby declared as follows:-*

(a) *Loss of all sight in one eye together with the total loss of use of one limb occurring in the same incident shall be treated as loss of use of two or more limbs and the benefits payable under the scale of compensation shall apply.*

(b) *Loss of all sight in one eye or the total loss of use of one limb to an employee who has already lost the use of a single limb or all sight in one eye shall not be treated as the loss of use of two or more limbs or loss of sight in both eyes, within the scale of compensation.*

(c) *Compensation benefits shall not be payable under more than one of the sub-paragraphs referred to in the scale of compensation.*

(d) *Where employees undertake as part of their duties any precautionary action, whether searching premises or taking other precautionary action, in relation to or following a bomb warning, such activity is recognised as being within the scope of the Authority's employment and, in the event of death or injury sustained as a result of undertaking such action, the compensation provisions set out in the scale of compensation shall apply;provided that death is caused by violent external and visible means and results within 12 months of a bomb explosion or terrorist or other subversive activity.*

12. *Limit of Liability*

Capital sum – 5 times annual earnings

Compensation for each occurrence will be in accordance with the Scale of Compensation.

EMPLOYEES PERSONAL ACCIDENT INSURANCE
ALL DUTY
SCALE OF COMPENSATION

Item		Amount Payable The under mentioned percentage of the capital sum		
1.	Death, total and irrecoverable loss of all sight, in one or both eyes, total loss by physical severance or complete loss of use of one or both hands or feet at or above wrist or ankle, occurring within 12 months of sustaining injury within the meaning of this Schedule		100%	
2.	Permanent total and absolute disablement (other than as stated in Item 1), from engaging in or giving attention to any profession or occupation of any kind		100%	

Item		Amount Payable The under mentioned percentage of the capital sum		
3.	Permanent partial disablement (not otherwise provided for above) the percentage of the capital 'sum set against the' degree of disablement in the following table			
	(a) Total loss of hearing in both ears		40%	
	(b) Total loss of hearing in one ear		10%	
	(c) Complete loss of use of hip or knee or ankle		20%	
	(d) Removal of lower jaw by surgical operation		30%	
	(e) Fractured leg or foot with established non-unions		25%	
	(f) Fractured kneecap with established non-union		20%	
	(g) Shortening of a leg by at least 4 centimetres		25%	
	(h) Loss by amputation or complete loss of use of:	Right		Left
	(i) one thumb	20%		17½%
	(ii) one index finger	15%		12½%
	(iii) any other finger	10%		7½%
	(iv) one big toe	10%		!0%
	(v) any other toe	3%		3%
	(i) Complete loss of use of one shoulder or elbow	25%		20%
	(j) Complete loss of use of wrist	20%		15%

Memoranda

1. Benefits under (h),(i) and (j) shall be reversed in the case
    of a left handed person.

2. In the case of other permanent partial disablement not
    specified in item 3. The amount payable shall be such
    percentage of the capital sum as is commensurate with
    the degree of permanent disablement when compared
    with the degree of disablement specified in item 3.

Medical Referee

Any question relating to the degree of disability of this Scale
of Compensation shall be referred to a medical referee
nominated by the St Helen's Borough Council.

On 9 May 2006 Andrew Cooper wrote to me, 'I have requested
the insurance scheme documentation from St Helen's and will
forward the same to you as soon as it is received', I never received
this document.

35. On 14 August 2006 a Dr Stephen O'Brien a Consultant
Psychiatrist wrote a psychiatric report on me on behalf of Weightmans
Solicitors. I told my psychiatrist about this report and that he has
never met me and written about me. My psychiatrist told me it would
not stand up in court and it's only fit to wipe you're a**e on.

36. Weightmans Solicitors sent me a copy of the wages from 1/4/1999
to 1/4/2006. These figures are inaccurate to what Security should
have been paid. Here is the letter dated 4 October 2006 below:

Weightmans, Solicitors

Dear Sir

Robert Steele v St Helen's MBC

The Council can provide the following wages details. We understand that you were employed on SCP14 to 17 and were at the maximum of the scale at the end of your employment in November 1999. Below is the actual salary for this point, and percentage increases from the previous rate this represents. The salary from 1 April 1999 applied at the point of termination so is the starting point:

Date	Salary	% increase from previous rate
01.04.1999	£12,663	
01.04.2000	£13,044	3%
01.04.2001	£13,500	3.5%
01.04.2002 *	£13,905	3%
01.10.2002 *	£14,040	1%
01.04.2003	£14,532	3.5%
01.04.2004	£14,931	2.75%
01.04.2005	£15,372	2.95%
01.04.2006	£15,825	2.95%

* Annual pay award in two parts

We also enclose report from Dr O'Brien dealing with the question of limited and whether you had capacity to consult a Solicitor. You will see that Dr O'Brien believes that you did have capacity for the vast majority of the period since you left the Claimant's employment, although there may have been some small periods when you did not have capacity.

On the basis of Dr O'Brien's report, the Council intends to take the limitation defence should you proceed (in addition to defending the main action). We will ask for limitation to be dealt with as a preliminary issue and ask the Court to strike out your action on the grounds that it is statute barred. The Council denies liability. If you intend to proceed, please ensure that any proceedings are served directly on us.

Yours faithfully

Weightmans

37. Because Robert Spicer dropped my case for a second time, I contacted Matthew Wilkinson Solicitors in Middlesbrough. Matthew Wilkinson stated to me when I told him that William Ellerton, Head of the Litigation Department at Bevans Solicitors told me that the maximum payout for a claim against Robert Spicer was £100,000 and I would get an out of court settlement of 20 to 30 thousand pounds. Matthew told me there is not a maximum cap and 20 to 30 thousand pounds was not acceptable to me on a one million pound plus claim.

38. Matthew Wilkinson wrote to me on 30 April 2008 as follows:

Matthew Wilkinson, Solicitors

Dear Mr Steele

Re: Solicitors Negligence

Further to our last conversation I am sorry that it has taken a little longer than I expected to look through your boxes of papers.

As you know I agreed to look at a potential professional negligence claim as you had previously been advised that your 'direct access' Barrister Mr Spicer had been negligent in missing the limitation period for your claim against St Helen's Metropolitan Borough Council.

My advice is as follows:-

1. *You suffered a stress related illness in 1997 and it is well documented that you claimed this to be the result of your work including allegations of victimisation, bullying and harassment. You ceased to work in August 1997 and were subsequently declared permanently unfit to return to your employment. I note that you were sacked and then re-instated after an internal appeal procedure and you were then sacked once more on capability grounds (ill-health). I also note that you appealed this further dismissal and made a claim to the Employment Tribunal for unfair dismissal and also sought advice from the Union Solicitors with regard to a personal injury claim against your employers. As far as I can see the Union advised you in respect of the Employment Tribunal and Messrs Thompsons Solicitors in relation to the potential personal injury claim.*

The claim for unfair dismissal and any other employment claims ought to have been lodged at the Tribunal within three months of your second dismissal and I understand such an application was lodged. Unfortunately, the Union took the view that there were no realistic prospects of success with such an application because it was likely thatthe Tribunal would hold that after such a long-term incapacity and with the medical opinion as to your inability to return to work, it was reasonable for the employers to bring your employment to an end. Further, they took the view that the employers could not have taken any other reasonable steps to accommodate you due to your disability. I understand that as a result of the Union forming this view that they stopped supporting your Tribunal case sometime in mid-2000 for you to take it on yourself. It is not clear from the papers what became of it.

With regard to your claim for damages against the Council, Messrs Thompsons similarly formed the view that there were no real prospects of success because even if you could prove that your illness had been caused by your work it was unlikely that you would be able to prove that it was foreseeable for the employer that you would sustain injury. This was because they were not on notice until you ceased work that you had any mental health or psychological vulnerability or that stress at work was causing you health problems.

I note from your medical records that you are reported as having a significant previous mental health history (prior to 1997) but on your job application in 1992 you denied any previous mental health problems. I have not seen the pre-1992 medical records and therefore do not know whether this statement was accurate but in any event disclosure to your potential employer of past mental health problems is a double-edged sword. Whilst it may put the employer on notice of your psychological vulnerability in case of any future problems it is much less likely that the employer will employ you in the first place.

I have seen some criticism of Messrs Thompsons in that they did not obtain medical evidence to substantiate the causal connection between your work place and your psychiatric condition. The problem with this argument is that even if there was a causal connection you would still need to prove foreseeability and this would not depend upon an expert Psychiatrist's view as to whether you had suffered from a work related stress condition.

I know that you are probably very disappointed that your claim was not supported by the Union or the Union Solicitors and presumably did not agree with their advice as to the prospects of success of a claim against the Council for damages for the injury and consequential losses sustained by you. However, in assessing whether Messrs Thompsons were negligent we would have to show that in the work that they did and the advice they gave to you that this fell below the standards of a reasonably competent Solicitor dealing with this type of case. Unfortunately, there was very little in the documents that I saw which you could have used to argue that your employer was on notice or that it was otherwise reasonably foreseeable that you would suffer an injury from the stress that you were under. In fact the evidence I have seen suggests that you had a previous mental health history and were vulnerable to this type of injury but that this was probably not known to the employer. It is therefore understandable that a Solicitor dealing with the matter in June 2000 could advise you of the difficulties in the case and that it would not be supported by the Union and inform you of the relevant limitation date in case you wished to pursue the matter through other Solicitors. This is not to say that another Solicitor would not have done a better job or would necessarily have formed exactly the same view; only that the advice you were given could well fall within a range of advice which could be given to you by a reasonably competent Solicitor at the time.

2. *The original claim against the Council therefore had limited prospects of success. This does not mean that it had no prospects of success or that it was incapable of gaining sufficient evidence to improve its chances of success but only on the evidence available at the time it did not appear meritorious taking into account the risks and costs involved.*

3. *Your claim against the Council was always likely to be a personal injury claim. If you had tried to pursue the Council for breach of contract but did not claim that you had suffered an injury as a result of that breach of contract then it is difficult to see what significant losses you could have claimed. All your loss of earnings and future losses were caused by your inability to work, which was due to your injury/illness. If the injury/illness was not caused by your employer or more to the point*

was not claimed as being due to your employer, then none of those losses could have been claimed in a breach of contract claim. There would be no causation as the Council would say that your losses were caused by your illness and you were not claiming that your illness was caused by the employer. However, once you include your injury/illness into the claim it becomes a personal injury claim regardless of whether you are suing for breach of contract or for negligence or for some other breach of duty. In the circumstances the relevant limitation period was likely to be three years commencing on the date when you first knew that you had an injury/illness of any significance, which may be the result of your work. On your own admission in your Letter of Claim of January 2006 to the Council you had sufficient knowledge in August 1997. It is likely therefore that the three years began to run in August 1997 and unless interrupted by any mental incapacity time would run out by August 2000. This was confirmed to you by Messrs Thompsons Solicitors in June 2000. There is no evidence of mental incapacity preventing you from taking advice or pursuing your claims right up until June 2000. There are no copies of correspondence from the period of June/July 2000 through to July 2002 and it is possible that there was a period of incapacity as you were admitted as an inpatient in 2001 between April and August 2001. However, the three year period may well have expired prior to that period of incapacity (if any) and in any event there is little evidence after June 2002 of your inability to understand your position and your claims or to pursue them and give instructions. In the circumstances if the three-year period did not expire in August 2000 it was likely to have expired by August 2002. The Court does have a discretion in personal injury cases to allow claims to proceed outside of this time limit but it is unlikely that the Court would extend it by a number of years when you had been in a position to seek advice about the claim at an early stage. In the circumstances it does seem to me that by the time Mr Spicer took on your case that limitation had already expired.

4. *I know that Mr Spicer advised you that there was a possible way of proceeding for a breach of contract claim and relying on a six-year limitation period with periods of incapacity extending this so as to enable you to still proceed. I am afraid that I do not agree with this advice. It seems to have been adopted in part by Messrs Bevans but again they have misdirected themselves as to the relevant law. It is irrelevant whether the claim is made in contract or tort (eg. negligence) as to whether the three-year personal injury limit applies. What is relevant is whether you are claiming damages for personal injury. In the circumstances when Mr Spicer first took the case on from you, the only way he was likely to be able to proceed with the case would be if he could obtain evidence to demonstrate that you had been mentally incapable for a very long period of time and that therefore you were still in time or alternatively the Court within its discretion was likely to allow you to continue outside of the relevant time period under Section 33 of the Limitation Act 1980. Unfortunately, your medical records did not appear to support such an assessment and in any event your detailed correspondence over the years (apart from the gap referred to above) did not support an inability or incapacity to understand and pursue your claim.*

5. *It follows therefore that although Mr Spicer may have been negligent it is unlikely that he caused you the loss of your claim against the Council. There might be a case against Mr Spicer for wasted costs if he has continued to investigate and pursue a hopeless matter. In his defence he could say that he never said that you had a good*

claim. Perhaps he could be criticised for not obtaining or advising you to obtain a full up-dated Psychiatric Report, however, it is not clear whether had he done so whether you would have incurred any less sum in costs to the point that you could establish that you were not able to proceed. As you are probably aware the Defendant (the Council) did obtain through their Solicitors Messrs Weightmans, a Psychiatric Report from Doctor Stephen OBrien, which purports to be a comprehensive analysis and dismissal of your possible claims to mental incapacity so as to prevent time from running under the Limitation Act. Doctor O'Brien could not even bring himself to say that you had mental incapacity at the time that you were admitted to Hospital under the Mental Health Act in April 2001 but states that in any event this was only for a limited period and there was ample evidence during other periods when you were well able to understand and pursue your complaint. Doctor O'Brien is not the Judge but his evidence at the moment is persuasive and you would need strong psychiatric evidence in response to get anywhere near showing that your claim was not statute barred. Whilst an independent opinion might support you in this respect it is not looking likely at present having regard to all the evidence referred to by Doctor O'Brien.

6. *It is important to remember that the claim against the Council taken on by Mr Spicer was already probably statute barred and probably only had a small prospect of success once bolstered by further evidence. Further, even if we could prove that the Council were in breach of duty and this had caused you the illness and that this was reasonably foreseeable, your recoverable losses might not include the full value of compensation for the injury or illness as suffered by you or indeed your full consequential losses. I say this because you had a pre-existing history of mental health problems and you*

would be classed as vulnerable. The Defendant may well be able to obtain expert evidence to say that there were a number of things which could have set off further mental illness without there being any cause of action against the employer and if the employer had caused a reasonably foreseeable stress related illness that the Court would have to decide how much of this was down to the employers breach of duty and how much was down to any pre-existing or other causal/contributory factors. Further, Doctor O'Brien, the Consultant Psychiatrist employed by Messrs Weightmans, appears to have formed the view that you sustained an adjustment disorder (which is a psychiatric illness) as a result of your work related problems but that you then suffered a schizophrenic psychotic type illness, which was constitutional in nature. This means that instead of the condition being caused by some external factor such as an accident (or in your case stress at work) it is part of your constitution and make-up or would have occurred naturally without any outside causation. If the Court were to accept that a shorter period of psychiatric illness was caused by the stress at work from which you ought to recover and that you were then being prevented from working by a more serious schizophrenic psychotic disorder which was not caused by the stress at work then the larger part of your damages, including all consequential and future losses, would not be recoverable. This has a serious impact upon the value of any claim.

7. *In summary:-*

a. *Your claim against the Council is statute barred and was probably statute barred when Mr Spicer took it on.*

b. *Some of the advice given to you by Mr Spicer and by Messrs Bevans was incorrect. However, this did not cause you the loss of the claim against the Council. It might have caused some wasted costs but most of the costs might be justified if they were incurred and carried out on their assessments. Further,please note that being wrong as to the law is not necessarily negligent. If all lawyers took the same view on every case no cases would ever go to Court.*

c. *Although it could be said that there is still a potential case against Messrs Thompsons, I think it is unlikely that you will establish a breach of duty and/or a significant loss and that it is not worth taking the risks on proceeding with. Strictly speaking your six year limitation period in respect of Messrs Thompsons would have expired in August 2006 but you might still be able to proceed against them under the date of knowledge provisions in Section 14a of the Limitation Act 1980, which give you a further three years from your date of knowledge. This would be knowledge in respect of the case against Thompsons, not in respect of the case against the Council. I do not, however, recommend this course of action.*

One thing that is not clear is why you did not continue to pursue your claim (perhaps through other Solicitors) against the Council in June 2000 or if you were too ill then in and from June 2002. The delay between 2002 and 2005 obviously creates some very difficult problems on limitation. As you will appreciate,however, I am not only concerned about limitation but also about the prospects of the original case due to the problems on foreseeability of the injury and also the extent of the injury depending on what further psychiatric evidence is available.

I know that you will be disappointed with my assessment, however, I have tried to look at the papers in an objective and independent way and I am sorry that I cannot recommend a course of action which is likely to recover compensation for you.

Please let me know whether you require any further advice and what instructions you have with regard to the box of papers you left at my office.

Yours sincerely

Matthew Wilkinson

Mr Wilkinson stated, 'I note from your medical records that you are reported as having a significant previous mental health history (prior to 1997) but on your job application in 1992 you denied any previous mental health problems. I have not seen the pre 1992 medical records and therefore do not know whether this statement was accurate'. Then Mr Wilkinson states, 'in fact, the evidence I have seen suggests that you had a previous mental health history'.

I did not have a previous mental health illness as stated by Matthew Wilkinson, nor did I have a schizophrenic psychotic type illness like my psychiatrist stated. Dr Steven O'Brien's report was only fit to wipe you're a**e on.

39. Because of the letter Matthew sent me dated 30 April 2008, I wrote to him on 19 November 2008 as follows:

Clockface Road, St Helen's, Merseyside

Mr Wilkinson

When I first spoke to you on the phone I told you Bevans Solicitors took 10 hours reading my files and you told me for you to do that it will cost me £2400. Before I sent you the cheque I sent you copies of my letter of claim by Robert Spicer, Psychiatric Report by Dr O'Brien and a copy of a report written by Bevans Solicitors and asked you to let me now if I had a possible claim before sending you the £2400.

When I later phoned you, you told me I did not have a claim on the evidence you had seen and told me you need to see my file so I sent you the file along with a cheque for £2400. I again rang you a couple of weeks later to see if I had a claim and you told me you had not looked at any of my paperwork.

I received a report from you dated 30 April 2008 and in it it states, 'In fact the evidence I have seen suggests that you had a previous mental health history'. When I phoned you I told you I had no other mental illness. Also you stated, 'the delay between 2002 and 2005 obviously creates some very difficult problems on limitation'. Had you read all my files you would have seen letters from Jackson and Canter Solicitors for that period which I told you on the phone. You later confirmed this in your letter 19/05/08.

I also asked you had you seen the letter from Brendan Farrell to the Union. You said 'no', so I sent you a copy of it. I also asked you had you seen the letter from Thompsons to Peter Kilfoyle MP, you also said 'no'. I also asked you had you seen the letter from Peter Mavers to me, again you said 'no' and a letter to Jim Keegan from Sheila Samuels. You had not seen any of these and they were all in the file. I know for a fact you looked at a few pages from the Union and some of the Thompsons Solicitors letters and I know that you only looked at around 5% of my file that would have taken around 1 hour's reading.

I rang you up when I found out the Council had paid Security four and a half thousand pounds pay rise after me fighting for this for the last eleven years and you told me this does not alter my case. I have been informed it does alter my case as it's new evidence.

I also told you on the phone about the foreseeability on another matter where my employer saw I had a problem and you told me it changed everything, then you wrote to me and told me it had to do with work.

After all I have stated in this letter I request a full refund of £2400 and if I have not received this within 10 working days of this letter I will be taking further action.

Yours

Mr R Steele

40. Matthew wrote to me on 21 November 2008 as follows:

Matthew Wilkinson, Solicitors

Dear Mr Steele
Re: Solicitors Negligence

I thank you for your letter of the 19 November 2008.

I cannot confirm all the facts as stated by you but do accept that you contacted me in connection with a claim which other lawyers had tried to help you with and you had not been able to make any progress. I also confirm that you sent me a selection of papers initially and it was my view that they did not reveal a sustainable claim. Quite properly, however, I pointed out this was not a full assessment but if you wished me to carry out a full assessment I would have to charge for my services. I did not encourage you to ask me to carry out this assessment and as you readily admit I was clear in telling you that on the evidence I had seen you did not have a sustainable claim.

As you know you then sent me a considerable number of papers in two boxes together with a post-dated cheque for £2,400 being the agreed fee. You told me on the 13 March

2008 that the cheque would clear and it was presented on the 17 March 2008. At this point I was heavily involved in other commitments but completed the assessment of the papers between the 17 and 28 April 2008.

I confirm that my report referred to the papers (particularly the medical report) referring to previous mental health symptoms. This was not changed by the fact that you disputed that you had any such problems. In fact from my notes it was the medical report of Dr Stephen O'Brien that took account of previous mental health problems in coming to his opinion. I believe he was referring to two previous accidents with psychiatric evidence obtained at the time and also a dispute with a building society and surveyor, which had caused mental anxiety and other such symptoms.

With regard to limitation, the delay between 2002 and 2005 would still create a potential problem on limitation if you had not issued proceedings to stop time running. There is evidence of the involvement of Jackson & Canter but there was insufficient information and documents to show what they had been doing. I pointed out in my advice of the 30 April 2008 and again in my advice of the 19 May 2008 that it was not just a matter of finding someone to blame for not issuing the proceedings but also a matter of finding that the case against the Council was not hopeless as it would then have no real value.

With regard to your telephone conversation and the different items of correspondence which you have referred to, it would not be possible for me in a telephone conversation a week after my assessment was completed to remember specific letters from the two boxes of papers. If I asked you to send a copy letter to me it was because you were trying to persuade me to change my opinion and the most cost effective way of me considering the point would be to ask you to send the letter rather than me having to look through the files for it.

I do not think that I could have said that I had or had not seen a particular letter, which you quoted to me unless perhaps on my assessment I had considered it already to be so significant that it remained in my recent memory.

The allegations you make about the time I spent looking at the files is absolute nonsense.

With regard to foreseeability of a stress related illness, evidence as to the employer's knowledge would have changed the strength of the case against the Council but I quite properly pointed out to you that evidence of some stress related symptoms without any connection to your employment would not necessarily put the employer on notice that the work was causing stress.

With regard to the point about the pay rise, I do not agree that this can change your case on foreseeability or limitation. If you have received different advice you are of course free to proceed with a case based on that advice but I would not be prepared to take such a case on.

I am sorry to have to tell you that your dissatisfaction with my professional opinion is not a good ground for seeking repayment of the monies paid for my advice. I have carried out the work at the agreed price and have given you detailed advice and thereafter when you queried this I have given you further advice.

I am sorry that you had so many problems but these are not my responsibility. The assertions made in your letter are bordering on the insulting particularly bearing in mind that a large part of the time I spent reading through your files was during the evening in my own time. Nevertheless, I still wish you well for the future.

Yours sincerely

Matthew Wilkinson

Matthew states in his letter I had mental anxiety from two other accidents, this is not true. I did see a psychiatrist about the Building Society, it was Dr Dutta and he discharged me saying I don't have any mental health problems, all I was suffering from was stress.

41. I got Julie Waring, Mental Health Advocate to write to Matthew on 9 January 2009 as follows:

St Helen's CDP

Dear Mr Wilkinson

Re: Mr R Steele

I am a Mental Health Advocate and have been supporting Mr Steele since September 2006.

Mr Steele has requested that I write to you regarding your recent dealings with him. Mr Steele feels disappointed that he has paid you a considerable sum of money for reading his file of papers and he has stated that you do not appear to be aware of many of the points contained therein. Whilst acknowledging that you have perused some of the initial paperwork he sent you, Mr Steele considers that the majority was left unread. There are a number of points in your replies dated 30 April, 19 May and 21 November, 2008, which can be clarified in the file of papers Mr Steele forwarded to you. Therefore he feels that you did not complete the ten hours reading time that he was charged the sum of £2,400 for.

Mr Steele has requested that I ask you therefore for a full refund of all monies paid and to advise you that if you feel that this is not appropriate, he will have no choice but to take the matter further and raise this with the Law Society.

Yours sincerely

Julie Waring

42. Matthew wrote back to Julie on 12 January 2009 as follows:

Matthew Wilkinson, Solicitors

Dear Sirs

Re: Mr R Steele

We thank you for your letter of the 9 January 2009.

We believe that you must realise that the conclusion reached in the last sentence of the second paragraph of your letter is not necessarily a logical conclusion even though it may be a genuinely held belief of Mr Steele.

We have already answered this particular point in my letter of the 21 November 2008 and if you have seen my previous correspondence I am very surprised that you have written to me in these terms. However, there is no question of any refund in respect of monies paid for work done for an agreed price. We are enclosing with this letter a copy of our time ledger printout, which shows the actual time spent.

Please note this is a final response in relation to Mr Steele's complaints. If he still considers he has grounds to complain he should refer the matter to the Law Society.

Yours sincerely

Matthew Wilkinson

Enc

43. I wrote to the Law Society on 17 February 2009 as follows:

Clockface Road, St Helen's, Merseyside

Dear Sirs

I am writing to you to complain about Matthew Wilkinson Solicitors. I contacted him in January 2008 on the phone. I told him that Bevans Solicitors took 10 hours reading my files, he told me for him to do that it would cost £2400. Before I spent that amount of money I sent him copies of a letter of claim by Robert Spicer, Psychiatric report by Dr O'Brien and a report by Bevans Solicitors and asked him to see if I had a claim.

I rang him again and asked him did I have a claim? He said 'no', I need to see your file so I sent the file along with a cheque for £2400. I did not have enough money in the bank to cover the cheque so I dated it 31/03/08 when there would be enough money to cover the cheque.

I again phoned him and asked him did I have a claim? He told me he had not looked at any of my paperwork. I got suspicious and told my Mental Health Advocate he had not looked at my paperwork I first sent him. He did a report dated 30/04/08 and 99% of it was done on the paperwork I first sent him. He had looked at several pages from Thompsons Solicitors and a few pages from Unison. I contacted my Mental Health Advocate again and told her he had charged me £2400 and not looked at my files.

Too many things did not add up. For instance, in his letter 30/04/08 he states,'I note from your medical records that you are reported as having a significant previous mental health history prior to 1997'. My medical records do not show this at all and when I challenged him in my letter 19/11/08 he wrote back on 21/11/08. In fact, from my notes it was the medical report of Dr O'Brien that took account of previous mental health problems.

I will send you all the correspondence I have and you will find a number of issues that don't add up. I know for a fact he hardly read any of my files by what he has written. He had not seen any of the paperwork I challenged him on. Most of all, he wanted to charge me extra to see if I had a case against Jackson and Canter. He would have already known this had he looked at my files.

I would like a full refund and when you read the facts you will see why I am complaining about him. He misled me from the start and I hope you will do something about it. He cannot take advantage of sick people to line his own pockets. I would like to hear from you with your response as soon as possible as I need he money to pay a solicitor to do a proper job.

Yours faithfully

Mr R Steele

The legal complaints service made Matthew pay me back £650.00.

44. Matthew wrote to me on 30 April 2009 sending me my cheque for £650.00 as follows:

Matthew Wilkinson, Solicitors

Dear Mr Steele

Re: Complaint – Potential professional negligence claim

We enclose herewith our cheque in the sum of £650.00 being the amount agreed through the Legal Complaints Service as full and final settlement of the above matter.

We trust this concludes the matter and will now close our file.

Yours faithfully

Matthew Wilkinson Solicitors

45. In June 2009 I approached DAS Legal Expenses Insurance Company Limited to investigate a claim against Robert Spicer. They instructed a firm of solicitors, DWF in Manchester. A Bill Radcliffe took the case on. Mr Radcliffe wrote to Mr Spicer on 11 August 2009 as follows:

DWF LLP, Manchester

Dear Sir

Mr Robert Steele
Clockface Road, St Helen's, Merseyside, Letter of Claim
We act for Mr Steele, who intends to bring a professional negligence claim against you. This is the letter of claim in accordance with the professional negligence pre-action protocol.

Background

Mr Steele believes he developed psychiatric illness after he was subjected to bullying, harassment, threats and victimisation while working for St Helen's MBC ('the Council'). He left work on health grounds on 14 August 1997. The Council finally terminated his employment on the ground of incapacity on 8 November 1999.

You were first instructed by Mr Steele in relation to his dispute with the Council in September 2005.

On 4 October 2005, you wrote to Dr Dutta to say you had advised Mr Steele to seek his opinion on the cause of his psychiatric illness.

In your letter of 19 October you stated: '... It is difficult for me to assess the chances of success in your claim because of the present lack of evidence and the length of time which has elapsed since you left employment'.

You drafted a letter for Mr Steele to send to the Council dated 8 November. The letter ended: 'I am aware that there is a limitation issue in relation to these proceedings but I am advised that my disability is likely to be relevant to this point'.

On 9 November you wrote again saying:'... This matter has not yet progressed beyond the preliminary stage...'

You wrote to Mr Steele on 16 November to say you had 'looked at all the paperwork in detail'. You made the following points:

- *'It seems that in October 2004 Dr M Jasti of the Sherdley Unit, Whiston Hospital, stated in a letter to Dr Schofield that your health had greatly improved and that you were not expressing any psychotic phenomena. I think that this is important because we can perhaps argue that from 1998 until October 2004 you were unable to manage your own affairs and that the limitation period should start to run from October 2004. Is this correct? This would give us more time.'*

- *'I think that a new report from Dr Dutta is crucial... The key points for him to address are the cause of your illness and the period for which you were so disabled that you were unable to manage your own affairs.'*

In your letter of 25 November you said to Mr Steele: 'I am currently working on a possible claim for breach of contract, which may be a way forward'.

On 1 December you wrote to Mr Steele explaining the purpose of the letter of claim. Your advice on the claim itself was:

'At the moment, I think that the way forward is to claim, for example, breach of contract, and in particular that you were

subjected, for example, to bullying harassment and intimidation. Also, you would claim that your former employers failed to deal properly with your disability, and a number of other matters, for example the fact that you were sent a P45 after winning your appeal.'

You also warned that there was 'no guarantee of success' and that in 3 months' time, Mr Steele may have spent a good deal of money to no purpose.

You sent a draft letter of claim to Mr Steele on 25 January 2006. Although it is not absolutely clear from the letter of claim, it appears you included claims in respect of personal injury and financial loss (loss of earnings). The letter of claim also stated the following:

'Since 1997 I have been suffering from personal and psychological problems which have tended to inhibit me from raising court proceedings. I was not capable of properly instructing a legal adviser until September 2005. It has been stated that I lacked insight into the impact of my medical condition on the level of functioning and ability to carry out the demands of my job. I was therefore unable to fully understand the implications of legal advice, representation and proceedings.'

In your letter of 25 May you advised:

'In relation to the question of time limits, as I have previously advised you, I think that you are in some difficulty with any claim for personal injuries because the time limit is three years. We have concentrated on the breach of contract aspects of the matter where the time limit is six years. This makes it more realistic to deal with the time limitation matter'.

On 3 July you advised Mr Steele that the matter had reached the stage where there was;'no option but to issue proceedings'.

At this point you approached Bevans Solicitors to act for Mr Steele.

Bevans wrote to you on 11 July to say they would probably have to examine a potential professional negligence claim against you. You responded by letter of 17 July saying:

'I was unable to reach a view on this matter until I had examined all the documentation... It was not until December 2005 of thereabouts that I was able to take a coherent view'.

In their long letter of advice dated 21 September 2006, Bevans advised Mr Steele that he may have a claim for professional negligence against you. You then wrote to Mr Steele on 11 October to inform him you were unable to do any further work on his case because of the advice from Bevans.

In January 2007, you were approached by Mr Steele's Mental Health Advocate, Julie Waring, to take on Mr Steele's claim to the European Court of Human Rights. You agreed to act again for Mr Steele at the beginning of February.

In your letter to Mr Steele of 14 March, you said: 'The claim will not be an easy one'.

On 22 March you wrote a long letter of advice to Mr Steele. The opening paragraph of that letter said:

'I have now had the opportunity to review your case in detail since you re-instructed me to provide advice only after you had terminated your instructions to Bevans... My conclusion is that I would advise you, in the strongest terms, not to spend any more money on this matter. I realise that this may be very disappointing for you, but it is my professional duty to ensure you are fully aware of, and understand, the financial implications of continuing with the claim...'

Later in that letter you advised Mr Steele that his chances of success in this matter were not good because of the limitation issue and the question of causation.

The following day, on 23 March, you asked your clerk to write to Mr Steele informing him that you were suspending your practice for 4 weeks on grounds of ill-health. The letter pointed out that illness was a substantial reason for withdrawal from the case in accordance with Paragraph 609(d) of the Bar Code of Conduct.

Breach of Duty

It was an implied term of your retainer with Mr Steele that you would exercise reasonable care and skill in acting for and advising Mr Steele. Further or alternatively, you owed Mr Steele a similar duty of care in tort.

The limitation period for a claim for financial loss arising out of the Council's breach of contract probably expired on 7 November 2005. At this point, you had been instructed for nearly 2 months. You received the relevant documentation in October and early November 2005. On 16 November 2005 you told Mr Steele you had;'looked at all the paperwork in detail'.

It is reasonable to assume you had sufficient knowledge of the issues and the key dates to be able to advise Mr Steele of the need to issue proceedings for breach of contract by 7 November 2005.

Your failure to do so, or to advise Mr Steele to instruct solicitors to conduct the claim on his behalf, was negligent, notwithstanding that you did not have the authority to issue proceedings yourself.

At an early stage it is clear you formed the view that Mr Steele's mental condition may be relevant to the issue of limitation. In your letter of 16 November 2005, you said Dr Jasti's letter to Dr Schofield of 28 October 2004;'may be important' for indicating Mr Steele was unable to manage his own affairs between 1998 and 2004. You also told Mr Steele to obtain a report from Dr Dutta addressing the fact that he was unable to manage his own affairs.

You continued to advise Mr Steele in these terms, however, at no stage did you advise Mr Steele of the need to obtain an independent expert report to support this proposition. Independent expert evidence was essential for showing that Mr Steele lacked capacity during the period 1998 to 2004. Without this evidence, Mr Steele's case had no prospect of success. Letters from Mr Steele's treating physicians, including Dr Dutta, were unlikely to be persuasive one way or the other. You were, therefore, negligent for failing to take steps to obtain appropriate medical evidence.

When you were re-instructed by Mr Steele in 2007, you acted for little over 1 month and it seems very little, if any, progress was made during that time.

In summary, you did nothing to advance Mr Steele's case. You missed the limitation date for a claim for breach of contract and proceeded, within weeks, to carry out extensive work on a claim for breach of contract. You repeatedly encouraged Mr Steele that his mental condition may be relevant to the issue of limitation but you took no steps to obtain an independent expert report in support of this proposition.

As a result, you were pursuing a claim that was doomed to fail, and charging Mr Steele for work that was of no value to him. At the same time, your written advice to Mr Steele was always phrased in exactly the same way: 'there is no guarantee of success'. This was quite an understatement in the circumstances. It is striking that the first time you actively advised Mr Steele not to pursue the claim further was on 22 May 2007, the day before you stopped acting for Mr Steele.

Loss

In light of the above, it is Mr Steele's case that your work for him was of no value and there was a total failure of consideration.

Mr Steele paid fees of £4,665.00 between October 2005 and March 2007, the consideration for which totally failed.

In the alternative, Mr Steele has suffered loss of £4,665.00 as a result of your negligence and/or breach of contract.

Furthermore, Mr Steele has suffered additional stress and anxiety as well as considerable inconvenience as a result of your negligence and/or breach of contract. Mr Steele is particularly aggrieved by the fact that he had organised his various and substantial papers in an orderly way and requested you to maintain the papers in the same order as you received them. This did not happen and Mr Steele now has to re-organise the papers.

Mr Steele claims £500 for the additional stress, anxiety and inconvenience he has suffered.

Mr Steele claims:

1.£4,665.00
2.£500

3. Interest on the sum of £4,665.00 at 8% from 23 March 2007, amounting to £891.58 at 11 August 2009, and continuing to accrue at the daily rate of £1.02.

Settlement/ADR

In the event that you do not accept liability for the losses, which our client has sustained, our client would be prepared to consider appropriate means of dispute resolution as an alternative to litigation. Please indicate your position in relation to such alternatives as soon as possible. We consider that this case would be suitable for mediation.

Please confirm a copy of this letter has been sent to your professional indemnity insurers and acknowledge receipt within 21 days.

Yours faithfully

DWF LLP

I later had a telephone conversation with Bill Radcliffe telling me he had contacted DAS and told them my case had a 51% success. DAS did not want to support the case and pulled out with my case being over 50%. They should have taken my case to court. Once again I was let down badly by the system.

CHAPTER SEVEN

1. Because the Council were blaming the Unions for the wages being put on APT & C Scale 3 inclusive for Security Officers, I wrote to the relevant unions on 7 May 2003 as follows:

Clockface Road, St Helen's, Merseyside

Dear Mr Edmonds

In 1991 St Helen's Council had a re-structure in the Security Department. They changed the wages from manual Grade 3 to APT & C Scale 3, Point 16. The management's own figures show they should have gone on to APT & C Scale 4, Point 19.

The management also fiddled them out of the pay rise for that year and if they would have had their pay rise they would have been on APT & C Scale 4, Point 21. The Security Officers were underpaid. A solicitor is now dealing with the matter. The thing is, St Helen's MBC are blaming the GMB for the shortfall in wages and the solicitor is on about taking you to court. I can tell you it was not the union's fault.

Tommy Cranston was the convenor and Colin Pinder was shop steward. They both knew that the figures came to Scale 4, Point 19 and they asked Brendan Farrell, Personnel Officer for Scale 4, Point 19 and Farrell said 'no'. The Councilsaid the unions have agreed to it and cannot produce this in writing.

I am on your side on this matter. I want to see St Helen's Council done for fraud and not the union. I can tell you that Colin Pinder still works for St Helen's MBC and now works for the Ranger Service and is still a member of the GMB. You could get in touch with him and ask him what happened. You should write to Carole Hudson, Chief Executive, Town Hall, St Helen's, Merseyside WA10 1HP and ask her what she is doing blaming the unions for their problems. I can tell you this is the fourth reason I have been told the wages were cut.

I hope to hear from you soon and if you get any answers from the Chief Executive and you pass them on to me I will see the solicitor gets them.

Yours sincerely

Mr R Steele

I then received a reply from John Edmonds on 21 May 2003 as follows:

GMB

Dear Colleague

Thank you for your recent letter. I read its contents with considerable interest. I will consult our Liverpool Region to establish more of the background and determine how this matter might be taken forward.

All my best wishes.

Yours sincerely

John Edmonds
Retiring General Secretary

2. This matter was put into the hands of George Patterson in the St Helen's branch of the GMB. I spoke to George on the phone on 26 June 2003 and I told him that the Council were accusing the union of agreeing to the wages in 1991 and he told me he would

sue them for slander and that he was having a meeting with Brendon Farrell the following week and was going to discuss this issue with him.

He asked me to give him my file for a possible personal injury claim so I photocopied it and took it to his office and told him not to pass it on the Council.

3. I then received a reply from George on 13 October 2003:

GMB

Dear Mr Steele

ST HELEN'S MBC

As a result of your letter to John Edmonds, GMB General Secretary some months ago, I was asked by Paul McCarthy, Regional Secretary of the GMB Liverpool, North Wales & Irish Region, to investigate your complaint.

I thank you for providing me with the file and information with regards to the number of complaints identified within your letter and I have now had an opportunity to peruse this information and investigate the allegations.

Within the content of your letter it appears that you alleged that there could be misrepresentation from GMB 85 Branch Secretaries concerning changes to terms and conditions within contracts.

It appears that the majority of the changes had arisen when the Security Staff and yourself were members of the Unison Union. I am aware at this moment in time that there are a number of issues still on-going within the Council and the Security Guards and will suggest that any outstanding grievances be taken up with the Unison representatives.

Unfortunately, Tommy Cranston, who as you will be aware was the GMB 85 Branch Secretary, passed away some years ago. Les Gilford, who became the GMB Branch Secretary after Tommy, unfortunately as you will also be aware has had a stroke and we were unable to ascertain whether Les was party to any of the changes to terms and conditions.

I hope that this clarifies the situation and wish you every success in the future.

Yours sincerely

George Patterson

Organiser

cc Paul McCarthy Regional Secretary/Graham McDermott Senior Organiser Susan Lee GMB 85 Branch Secretary

For George Patterson to state 'it appears that the majority of the changes had arisen when the security staff and yourself were members of the Unison union' was incorrect. All apart from one person were GMB members when most of the changes had arisen and the other member was a member of Unison who was a Market Officer and these changes did not concern him for 1996 and the changes that happened in 1991, the majority of the union members were the T & GWU and the remainder were GMB members.

4. I then decided to phone Paul McCarthy in his Liverpool office and he replied by writing on 13 November 2003 as follows:

GMB

Dear Mr Steele

St Helen's MBC

I refer to your recent telephone messages left at my office and would advise you that unfortunately I have nothing further to add following my colleague; George Patterson's letter to you dated 13 October 2003. I am guided by George's experience in this matter and will, therefore, be unable to meet with you in this connection.

I would suggest that you may wish to take this matter up with Unison.

Yours sincerely
Paul McCarthy
Regional Secretary

Paul McCarthy saying I am guided by George's experience and that he has nothing further to add just shows makes me feel they are all covering up for one another. I also sent the GMB the letter Paul Haunch of Unison wrote to Mike Fitzsimmons on 10 September 1997 as follows:

Unison

Dear Mike

RE: SECURITY SERVICE STAFF – ST HELEN'S

Late last year the Branch recruited these 30 or so members who were formerly with the GMB.

Their Steward, Rob Steele had discovered that the deal agreed between the GMB and the Authority disadvantaged financially the bulk of his members. Indeed, he has investigated at length in great detail the agreement struck prior to his employment.

I have looked at the case and find it difficult in industrial relations terms to find a channel for effective recourse, as essentially the Staff were badly represented by the GMB.

However, there maybe a legal avenue but this expires on the 1st October 1997 when the case would become statute barred. I think it might be advisable to seek Thompson's advice just in case we have picked up a liability when we recruited the members.

Perhaps you could let the Branch know directly if they can arrange the meeting forthwith, especially as they think it is worth pursuing in terms of our P.R. vis-a-vis the GMB. This is perhaps a case worth more in the long run than it is in the immediate future.

Rob Steele has worked very hard on this case but the employer is refusing to deal with him because of his tenacity in pressing his members case, which is exposing the Authority as a 'con-merchant'.

Yours sincerely

PAUL HAUNCH

REGIONAL OFFICER.

CC: St Helen's Branch Secretary

In my opinion the GMB did not have the balls to challenge Unison on this letter and then tell me that it appears that the majority of the changes had arisen when the security staff and yourself were members of the Unison union, just cover up after cover up by the unions, they did not want to do the job we as members were paying for.

5. I once again wrote to John Edmonds on 22 November 2003 as follows:

Avon Close, Walton, Liverpool

Dear Mr Edmunds

I wrote to you on 7 May 2003, copy I have sent with this letter. You passed it on to Paul McCarthy who passed it on to George Patterson. I spoke to George on the phone and I told him the problems I had. He asked me to photocopy them and he would look at them and he would also look into a personal injury claim. I took the grievances to his office and his secretary told me he wants my personal file so he can put a personal injury claim in for me. I photocopied this and took it to his office and told them I do not want this getting into the Council's hands.

I was shop steward for the GMB back in 1996. I had a lot of problems with St Helen's Council and I was telling Mike Tithrington what was going on. He told me to call a status quo when we had a re-structure in 1996 and that they had to buy our contracts back off us. Les Gilford was the branch secretary and I asked him to call a status quo he said he would have to speak to Brendan Farrell and ask his permission. I told him 'you don't, I call the status quo'. We then had a meeting in Farrell's office and I told Farrell that he had to buy our contracts off us and in my opinion he told us a pack of lies why he did not have to.

I looked at Les for support and he shrugged his shoulders, he did not have a clue. I also found a discrepancy in our wages since 1991. I took this to Les and after a few meetings he told me I had opened a can of worms that should have been left alone. I was not happy with Les so I went to Charlie Leonard for his support and he told me to go and see Les, that's what he gets paid for. Because of the lack of support I received from the GMB I went and saw Unison and told them the problems I had. They said they would sort them out if we go into Unison. Both the GMB and Unison failed to do anything about the problems. I was going to get 20 odd members to go back into the GMB but with the attitude of Paul McCarthy and George Patterson, I'm not going to bother. I was on the GMB's side till now.

I would like you to get George Patterson to return all the information I have given him and if he has given any of this to the Council and it affects my personal injury claim my barrister will know by the Council's response and I will sue the GMB for thousands.

My solicitor has told me I have a claim against Unison. I am also going to find out if we have a claim against you. I was on your side and I'm disappointed with the attitude of your union members.

Yours faithfully

Mr R Steele

6. I again wrote to Mr Edmonds/Curran as I did not know which one of them was the General Secretary on 15 January 2004 as follows:

Avon Close, Walton, Liverpool

Dear Mr Edmonds / Curran

I wrote to you on 22 November 2003, copy I have sent with this letter. I have not heard from you so I have decided to write to you again. I must emphasise that I want the information that I have given George Patterson back as a matter of urgency, as that was confidential information I have given him and he was told not to give it to the Council.

If I do not receive this information within 10 working days I am going to the Police to come with me to get it back as if I go on my own I will lose my rag.

Yours faithfully

Mr R Steele

7. I received a reply from Kevin B Curran, General Secretary on 15 January 2004 as follows:

GMB

Dear Colleague

Thank you for your letter dated 15 Januar, which I have forwarded on to Paul McCarthy, Regional Secretary of our Liverpool Region as this is a matter for the Regional Office to take up. I am sure this is the best way of dealing with this matter.

Yours fraternally

Kevin B Curran

General Secretary

c.c. Paul McCarthy

I never heard anything else from the GMB union and I decided it was a total waste of time having anything else to do with them as I consider they were pissing in the same pot as the Council and Unison.

8. I also contacted Bill Morris, General Secretary of the T & GWU union on 7 May 2003. The same day I wrote to the GMB as follows:

Clockface Road, St Helen's, Merseyside

Dear Mr Morris

In 1991 St Helen's Council had a re-structure in the Security Department. They changed the wages from manual Grade 3 to APT & C Scale 3, Point 16. The management's own figures show they should have on to APT & C Scale 4, Point 19.

The management also fiddled them out of the pay rise for that year and if they would have had their pay rise they would have been on APT & C Scale 4, Point 21. The Security Officers were underpaid. A solicitor is now dealing with the matter. The thing is, St Helen's MBC are blaming your union for the shortfall in wages and the solicitor is on about taking you to court. I can tell you it was not the union's fault.

Tommy Twist was the convenor and Jimmy Johnson was the shop steward. Jimmy Johnson told me they put a load of figures in front of him and he did not have a clue. He came out of the meeting and told his members not to sign anything. The Council said the unions have agreed to it and they cannot produce this in writing.

I am on your side on this matter. I want to see St Helen's Council done for fraud and not the unions. I can tell you that Tommy Twist is now working for Helena Housing and still is a convener for the T & G in St Helen's. You could get in touch with him and ask him what happened.

You should write to Carole Hudson, Chief Executive, Town Hall, St Helens, Merseyside WA10 1HP and ask her what she is doing blaming the unions for their problems. I can tell you this is the fourth reason I have been told the wages were cut.

I hope to hear from you soon and if you get any answers from the Chief Executive and you pass them on to me, I will see the solicitor gets them.

Yours sincerely

Mr R Steele

9. Bill Morris replied on 12 May 2003 as follows:

T & G

Dear Mr Steele

I acknowledge, with thanks, receipt of your recent letter, from which I am sorry to learn of the difficulties you are experiencing.

I can advise that the Deputy General Secretary, Tony Woodley, has responsibility for membership liaison and I have therefore sent a copy of our exchange of correspondence, asking him to consider the issues raised and to respond to you direct. I have no doubt that he will be in touch with you shortly.

Yours sincerely

Bill Morris
General Secretary

10. I received a letter from Tony Woodley, Deputy General Secretary on 21 May 2003 as follows:

T & G

Dear Brother Steele

I am in receipt of your correspondence to the General Secretary and note with concern the comments you have made.

I would advise that I have forwarded your correspondence to our Regional Secretary, Brother Dave McCall, who is responsible for the North West area, asking him to look into the issues you raise and respond to you direct.

If I can be of any further assistance, please do not hesitate to contact me.
Yours sincerely

Tony Woodley
Deputy General Secretary

11. I then received a letter from Dave McCall on 4 June 2003 as follows:

T & G

Dear Mr Steele

I am in receipt of a copy of your letter addressed to the General Secretary, Bill Morris, received in this office on 22 May 2003, the contents of which have been noted.

I have passed this matter on to the Trade Group Secretary, Eddie Blackwell, who is based at our Wigan District Office, and, no doubt, you will be hearing from him direct in due course.

Yours sincerely

Dave McCall
Regional Secretary

COPY: Tony Woodley
Eddie Blackwell Wigan, for appropriate action

Dave did say I would hear from an Eddie Blackwell in the Wigan office but I never did hear anything from him. The T & GWU were also not interested in taking on the Council, along with the GMM and Unison, they all wanted your money each month but did not want to rock the boat and stick up for their members.

The experience I have had as a shop steward and a union member, means I would never join another union again as long as I live and I would advise anyone paying into a union to part company with them as all they want at the end of the day is your money to keep them in well paid jobs. I was sent down the river by the GMB and Unison and was also sent to Coventry by Unison for defending my member's rights and it's not as if it was minor issues, they were serious facts that needed addressing with immediate effect the day the issues were brought to light and the unions brushed them under the carpet.

CHAPTER EIGHT

1. Because I got nowhere with Tony Blair I decided to write to David Cameron, when he became leader of the opposition as I thought he might do something to gain brownie points for his chance of becoming Prime Minister, on 21 December 2006 as follows:

Clockface Road, St Helen's, Merseyside

Dear Mr Cameron MP

I was an employee for St Helen's Council for 7 years. I started in June 92 and finished in November 99 due to ill-health caused by my employer. In June 1996 I became shop steward for my department. I could not believe what my manager and Acting Assistant Director was doing. I had over 76 grievances in just over 12 months. I approached my convenor and branch secretary with my grievances and I was told I must remember they are in the same union as you. Things got so bad I had to go off sick in August 1997.

I went and saw the leader of the Council and told him what was going on. He told my father that someone who does not even know me had told him the same thing and he did nothing. In May 98 Peter Moffat, the Assistant Director terminated my employment. I appealed and was reinstated because of the reason he finished me. In March 99 I told work I was returning to work and they told me to stay away and in November 99 finished me on ill-health.

I wrote to Tony Blair several times and I never got a straightforward answer. Again nothing was done.

I went to the Police station and showed a Detective Inspector Steve Lowe six of my grievances and he told me there were lies, bullying and embezzlement and he did nothing about it. I have around two thousand pages of what was going on, along with the evidence to back it up. I have had three solicitors on the case and discussed it with a fourth and I have also had two barristers. They have all told me different things and between them have let the time limits run out for a personal injury claim and a breach of contract claim.

I don't know who's telling me the truth. At the end of the day all I wanted was to expose the corruption that was and is still going on today in St Helen's Council. All I wanted was my day in court and give evidence against them.

When I lived in Liverpool I went and saw Peter Kilfoyle MP and he tried to help me and he got a hostile response from the Council and the union. I am determined to take my case to the European Court of Human Rights and I would like you to help me as the legal departments have let me down. I would like to meet with you and discuss what has gone on. It will take a full day to go through it all. I have been to the House of Commons before when Peter Kilfoyle dealt with a different matter. I would like to have a public enquiry into the corruption in St Helen's Council and want to be part of it.

I hope you don't let me down and make arrangements to meet me. It is a big case and I will tell you everything that has gone on. I want to see you before I get on a plane to Strasbourg and speak to a barrister out there or go and see the European Court myself. I would like you to stand up in the House of Commons and tell Blair how a Labour council has destroyed my life.

Yours faithfully

Mr R Steele

2. Because I never received a letter from David Cameron I wrote to him again on 14 January 2007 as follows:

Clockface Road, St Helens, Merseyside

Dear Mr Cameron MP

I wrote to you on 21 December 2006 and I have not had a reply. I have sent you a copy of that letter in case you did not receive it.

I spoke to the European Court of Human Rights on Friday 12 January 2007 and they have told me to write to them. I have sent you a copy of the letter.

Can you reply to this letter as soon as possible as I may need your help put my case into the British court, to be struck out so I can go to the European Court of Human Rights.

Yours faithfully

Mr R Steele

3. I received a reply from Ian Philips, Office of the Leader of the Opposition on 15 January 2007 as follows:

Rt Hon David Cameron MP, House of Commons

Dear Mr Steele

Thank you so much for writing to David Cameron – he's asked me to thank you and to say that he appreciated your taking the time to let him know of your concern.

I should advise you that there is a strict convention in the House of Commons that stops an MP from acting on behalf of another MP's constituent. As David Cameron is not your local Member of Parliament, I am afraid he is unable to intervene personally in this instance.

I am sorry to send what I realise will be a disappointing reply.

With best wishes

Yours sincerely

Ian Philps

Office of the Leader of the Opposition

4. When David Cameron became Prime Minister I wrote to him again on 27 June 1010 as follows:

Clockface Road, St Helen's, Merseyside

Dear Mr Cameron

I wrote to you when you became Leader of the Opposition. At this moment in time I don't have it as it is with a solicitor. I wrote to Blair and Brown when they were Prime Minister and they ignored my pleas for help. Now you are Prime Minister I hope you are going to do something about my problems.

I was employed as a Security Officer with St Helen's Council. I became shop steward and in just over 12 months I had 76 grievances with my employer and not one was dealt with. I went to the Police and spoke to a Detective Inspector Steve Lowe. I only showed him 6 grievances and he told me there's lies, bullying and embezzlement and did nothing about it. The reason for this letter is a want to meet you and Nick Clegg and I also want a meeting with Works and Pensions Minister Mr Grayling.

As I was made very ill in 1997 and not been well since, I have spent 13 years campaigning for justice and have continuously been denied. Not one person has sat down with me and listened to what I have got to say. I voted Conservative in the election, now it's time for you to listen to me. I have sent with this letter, a copy of Particulars of Claim. I hope you and the other two, Nick Clegg and Mr Grayling take it home and read it. This is just the tip of the iceberg.

I will bring my file to 10 Downing Street and I will discuss this matter with the three of you. If you don't give me the opportunity to come to 10 Downing Street, I will just turn up and won't leave until we've discussed this matter.

I hope to hear from you with a date to come to 10 Downing Street soon.

Yours faithfully
Mr R Steele

5. David Cameron did not reply to my letter so I wrote to him again on 8 August 2010 as follows:

Clockface Road, St Helen's, Merseyside

Dear Mr Cameron

I wrote to you on 27 June 2010 and I've still not had a reply. Will you please respond to this letter, copy sent?

I am now writing for your Government to change the law on people who borrow money that they have to pay every penny back. Since I became ill with depression, I have lent people money and I cannot get my money back. I have taken two of them to court. The court ordered they pay the money back and I have not got the power to recover the money.

I have recently taken David Smith to court, he was working for 6 months and he signed an agreement that he would pay £100 a month till the debt was paid and while on the dole he would pay £20 a fortnight out of his money. The courts should get the power to take £10 a week out of their money till the debt is paid. I would like this matter dealt with as a matter or urgency so I can go back to the courts and recover my money. He can afford to smoke and drive a car but he won't pay me £10 a week.

In the six ties if you borrowed money you had to pay every penny back. At the end of the day I want my money back. The way things stand the law is an ass. I will be patient and give you and the courts time to change the law then I will take the law into my own hands. This person has owed me money since October 2006. I have been patient for the last four years, now my patience is running out. If people owe money, then they should be made to pay every penny back and the courts should be given the power to do this.

I hope to hear from you soon telling me to go back to the courts to take £10 a week out of his job seekers allowance. I have lent 7 people money, 5 of them are not paying me any money back at this moment in time and between them they owe me £19,590. I have got a mental illness and suffer from deep depression. It's only since my illness started I lent money out. I hope you have the decency to reply to both my letters and give me positive answers.

Yours faithfully

Mr R Steele

6. I again wrote to David Cameron on 18 September 2010 as he failed to reply to my last three letters, as follows:

Clockface Road, St Helen's, Merseyside

Dear Mr Cameron

Would you please have the decency to reply to my letters dated 27.6.10, 8.8.10 and 18.8.10 along with this letter.

I have suffered from a severe depression for the last 13 years and it's time someone listened to my grievances and gave me some support in getting justice. Everyone is blaming myself for my illness. I am an honest person and I will stand up when people are committing alleged embezzlement, bullying and telling lies and also robbing us of our wages.

I enjoyed my job and I did it well but I did not like what I saw was going on and I had every right to open my mouth. That's why I was a shop steward. I have sent you photos of my house that I lost and all the work done to it I did myself. I worked all the overtime possible to pay for it and I lost everything, including my health. I could do with someone from the Government to sit down and listen to me.

Hope to hear from you soon and hopefully put me on the right road for justice.

Yours faithfully

Mr R Steele

7. I once again wrote to David Cameron on 21 April 2011 as follows:

Clockface Road, St Helen's, Merseyside

Dear Mr Cameron

I had a good job that I enjoyed doing for St Helen's Council and I bought a house and spent £30,000 doing it up to my standards. When in 1996 I became shop steward for my department, the workforce constantly complained they were robbed of their wages so I decided to investigate this issue. That ended up with me dealing with a total of 83 grievances and 58 personal grievances.

I have started a book on a true story that is half-way through. I have sent you a CD disc with the 83 grievances and 29 of my personal grievances on it. I still have to get the other 29 grievances typed up for me. I have paid over £500 to get this typed up so far as I am going to get the book published. My aim is to sell one million copies and make £10 profit from each copy and I'm donating hopefully 10 million pounds to charities. They are as follows: (RSPCA) Royal Society for the Protection of Cruelty to Animals; (NSPCC) National Society for the Prevention of Cruelty to Children; Cancer Research (Clatterbridge Hospital, Merseyside); Help for Heroes (for the Armed Forces) and the Children's Alder Hey Hospital in Liverpool. I am hoping for all five charities to receive 2 million pounds each.

What I was put through at St Helen's Council left me with stress, anxiety and a severe depression for the last 14 years. I have not been in any fit state to work. I have a case in the European Court of Human Rights as the British legal system let me down badly. I am claiming loss of earnings of around one million pounds, damage to my health and care for the rest of my life as the depression has totally shut my body down. I lost the job I really enjoyed doing and I also lost my home as I could no longer afford to keep it or look after it. I have sent you some pictures of what I have done to the house and you can see I lost a lovely home that was my pride and joy.

Do one thing for me and print off my story from the CD and read it at your leisure and you will see for yourself exactly what I was put through that made me so ill. If I got awarded

100 million pounds from the ECHR it would not make me better. The way I have felt over the last 14 years I would not wish it on my worst enemy. One good thing that could come out of my illness is five charities could all receive 2 million pounds each.

You should look into St Helen's Council and the problems on my CD and remove the relevant people from the Council for their part in corruption and alleged embezzlement. If I went in there with you, I could show you it's still going on today.

Yours faithfully

Mr R Steele

8. I forgot to send the photos of my house to David Cameron when I sent the CD for him to read so I wrote to him again on 25 April 2011 as follows:

Clockface Road, St Helen's, Merseyside

Dear Mr Cameron

I wrote to you on 21 April 2011. I forgot to put the photos of my house in with the CD so I have sent this with this letter. I have also sent you a copy of a leaflet that David Lawrenson has put through my friend's door as he is standing for a Councillor and this will prove that what I have said in my book is true, as he himself has raised concerns about St Helen's Council and both of us have received harassment charges to shut us up, that were false.

David Lawrenson has told me if he gets elected as Councillor he is going to get Carole Hudson out of the council (Chief Executive). You need to bring in an MP to regulate problems like I and David have raised as the councils do not have to answer to anybody, they are a law to themselves and you need to bring in a governing body who they have to answer to.

Please read my book, as you will find it interesting knowing what local authorities are up to.

Yours faithfully

Mr R Steele

9. Here is a copy of David Lawrenson's leaflet. He put out to the ward he was a candidate in the local elections 2011 as follows:

Please Vote for me, David Lawrenson, the Independent Candidate for Moss Bank.

Just like you, my family, my friends and I have to deal with St Helen's Council on a regular basis. Most council staff work hard and honestly but some council staff are incompetent, deliberately obstructive and sometimes dishonest.

I have brought clear, simple evidence before the senior executives of the council and they have covered up libel, perjury and extortion.

I have shown all three Moss Bank Councillors some of my evidence and all agreed with me but are afraid to act. I have written to every councillor in the town and none has dared even reply. I announced that I was going to stand for the council to speak up on these issues. On 29th March I was arrested by the police and locked up on a false charge of harassment. They have ordered me not to contact any member of St Helen's Council, under pain or arrest and imprisonment. I was arrested on the words of Carol Hudson and Angela Sanderson, Chief and Deputy Chief Executives of St Helen's Council, for persistently insisting that the complaints of my family and friends be heard fairly. This is not Libya, Saudi Arabia or Communist China but St Helen's.

If you want an independent voice to stand up for you, please vote for me, unless you think you might be arrested for daring to do so.

I do not promise to bring down the government, get more money for the town, or turn straw into gold. I do promise that if you are mistreated by St. Helen's Council Staff, I will not be frightened to challenge the senior staff and executives of your behalf. I stand by all honest council staff. If I am elected, I will speak out on the matters that affect you and your family, even if it means getting arrested again on bogus charges.

If you do not want a coward to represent you, vote for David Lawrenson.

Who is David Lawrenson? I am an ordinary, sane 61-year-old man wanting to enjoy a quiet life. I have no criminal convictions and no wish to be a martyr. Iam luckily married to Gill and we have three amazing grown up children and six wonderful grandchildren. Both my sons have recently fought in Afghanistan. I have lived in the ward for over 50 years, initially in council houses in Windermere and Ullswater Avenues and for nearly 30 years in Crossdale Way. I go to St Patrick's church.

I have worked in brick and glass factories and also for the Council as a labourer in the Parks Department and as an ordinary teacher at Holy Cross, St. Alban's, De La Salle and the Tech College. I have also been a taxi driver, an amateur builder and been in the dole queue. I am as ordinary as you and claim no special gifts, though I consider myself to be the most fortunate man on earth.

My political views are these. Labour let a mad Scotsman drag us from prosperity to ruin, but won't admit it. The Tories are too frightened of the bankers and Europe to sort out the mess and the Lib Dems will say anything to appear to be important. The lunatics are in charge of the asylum.

In St Helen's, our local politicians are chickens, not in control of the executive officers and are too impotent to impose that control. All council staff, and that includes chief executives, work for us, are paid by us and must be answerable to us. They are not employed to cover up malpractice. Deceit and dishonesty must be dealt with. No one else should ever be imprisoned for speaking out against corruption

If you vote for me, you will have at least one voice on your side.

Carole Kavanagh is a harmless; well meaning lady and Dave Kent is a nice, quiet man. I bear them no ill will for turning their backs on me, my family and integrity. Jeff Fletcher heard my story, agreed with every word I said and promised to get back to me. Now he won't even acknowledge that he has spoken to me.

If you have the courage to vote for me, I pledge to speak and vote, not as I am ordered by a party leader but for you and according to my own conscience. Thank you for reading my appeal.

Best wishes whichever way you vote.

David Lawrenson

As you can see, he too has concerns about members of St Helen's Council. He was arrested on a false charge of harassment and I was threatened with arrest for harassment. This is somebody who I had never heard of till my friend showed me this leaflet and we have both had and received similar issues and hostility from the Council and the Police.

10. Alan Bolger wrote to David Cameron on my behalf on 10 May 2011 as follows:

Redruth Avenue, Laffak, St Helen's, Merseyside

Dear Mr Cameron

I am writing to you on behalf of my good friend, Robert Steele. You have been made well aware of the problems Robbie has endured. He first wrote to you on 21 December 2006 when you became leader of the Conservative Party. He last wrote to you on 21 April 2011 when he sent you a CD with half of his book on it to show you just how bad things have been for him.

Just as Robbie thought things could not get any worse for him, the European Court of Human Rights threw his case out for the following reason. The court found that domestic remedies had not been exhausted as required by Article 35-1 of the Convention.

I was in the court of appeal with Robbie when the judge told Robbie that he could take his case no further in Britain. Robbie told the judge he was taking his case to the European Court of Human Rights and he had received a letter from them. The judge asked to see it and read it.

When Robbie arrived home he rang the Supreme Court and asked to have his case heard in the Supreme Court and again he was told he could not take it any further in Britain so Robbie rightfully went to the European Court of Human Rights.

No matter how you put it, either the British court has lied to Robbie or the European Court have got it totally wrong.

Will you please have the decency to read Robbie's book and you will see just how badly Robbie has been treated.

All his family and friends would like you to use your power of being Prime Minister to resolve this matter with the British courts or the European Court of Human Rights for the sake of Robbie's health as this has knocked Robbie's recovery over the last nine years for six. Robbie's health has deteriorated dramatically since receiving the letter from Clare Ovey, it's just like when he appeared at my home in 2002 after disappearing for three years.

I am finding it very difficult to have a conversation with him again. It's like they have knocked back his recovery by nine years.

This problem needs resolving now rather than later for Robbie's state of mind. All Robbie ever wanted was the wrongdoings in St Helen's Borough Council put right, iie. justice for his members. The thing everyone being involved in has denied him his justice.

Yours sincerely

Alan Bolger

Alan did not, like myself on several occasions, receive a response to his letter.

11. I received a reply from 10 Downing Street on 8 June 2011 as follows:

10 Downing Street, London

Dear Mr Steele

I am writing on behalf of the Prime Minister to thank you for your recent letter and the enclosed CD.

Mr Cameron is most grateful for the time and trouble you have taken to get in touch.

I have been asked to forward your letter to the Department for Communities and Local Government, so that they too are aware of your views.

Thanks you, once again, for writing.

Yours sincerely

Correspondence Officer

12. On 29 July 2011, I eventually received a reply from the Communities and Local Government as follows:

Communities & Local Government

Dear Mr Steele

Council Complaint

Thank you for your letter of 21 April to the Prime Minister in which you raise various concerns regarding St Helen's Council and your concerns over corruption at the Council, and their treatment of you whilst you were employed there. As you will appreciate the Prime Minister receives a significant amount of correspondence on a daily basis and it is not possible for him to reply to each letter individually. In these cases, the correspondence is forwarded to the most appropriate Department for a reply. Your letter has been forwarded to this Department in view of our responsibilities for local government matters and I have been asked to reply. I am sorry for the delay in replying.

Whilst I am sorry to hear of your concerns, I should begin by explaining the relationship between central government and local government. Local authorities act independently of central government, and Ministers have no remit to intervene in the day-to-day affairs of local authorities, except where specific provision has been made in an Act of Parliament. Local authorities are accountable for their actions to their electorate and must act within their statutory powers.

Starting with your concerns over your employment, the Department has no locus to intervene here. I would recommend that you speak to the Employment Tribunal service, or to a legal adviser.

If you have any evidence or criminal wrongdoing or corruption at the Council, then this is a matter for the police, and you should contact them directly.

Yours faithfully

Mark Coram

For Mark Coram to state, 'Local Authorities are accountable for their actions to their electorate and must act within their statutory powers', is just one big joke and also stating, 'if you have any evidence or criminal wrongdoing or corruption at the Council then this is a matter for the Police and you should contact them directly', this I did to Detective Inspector Steve Lowe and all he did was threaten to have me arrested on harassment charges.

13. I wrote again to David Cameron on 2 August 2011 as follows:

Clockface Road, St Helen's, Merseyside

Dear Mr Cameron

I wrote to you on 21 April 2011 and 25 April 2011. The reason I am writing to you is your Correspondence Officer has sent the correspondence I sent you to the Department for

Communities and Local Government. I have waited since 8 June 2011 for them to contact me with a way forward to investigate St Helen's Council. I also take it you never had the decency to read my book that I sent you on a CD. If you had read my book, you would have known how serious this is. I have also had my case dropped in the European Court of Human Rights as I was misled and lied to by the British courts when I approached them for help and advice.

I am already suffering from stress, anxiety and depression because of the lack of getting justice against St Helen's Council. The lack of support from the courts has led to a further deterioration in my health. The British courts need to be made well aware of the facts and put my case back into court as my case is 100% a mis-character of justice.

I await yours and the Department for Communities and local government's response.

Yours faithfully

Mr R Steele

14. I did not hear from David Cameron so I wrote to Mark Coram of the Department of Communities and Local Government in reply to his letter dated 29 July 2011 on 29 August 2011 as follows:

Clockface Road, St Helen's, Merseyside

Dear Mark Coram

Thank you for your letter of 29 July 2011. You stated in your letter 'Local Authorities are accountable for their actions to their electorate' and that includes myself. The council's solicitor wrote to my MP, Peter Kilfoyle on 28 November 2003.

In my view, he has no rights to challenge matters on terms and conditions of employment, which arose prior to the commencement of his employment or subsequent to its termination so does this not include me as an electorate?

I also went to the Police station in 2003 and spoke to a Detective Inspector Steve Lowe and I showed him 6 of the 83 grievances I had and he said there's lies, bullying and embezzlement and did nothing about it. I made a complaint to the Police Complaints Authority and I had it sent to the Chief Constable of Merseyside Police, Mr Norman Bettison who totally ignored my letter and my complaint.

You also said the council must act within their statutory powers, I have sent you another copy of my book on CD and if you read it all, you will see the council have not acted within their statutory powers. So where do we go from here? I am also going back to the Police station in St Helen's and demanding to speak to the Senior Officer in the Police station and I look forward to hearing from you with what you are going to do about the council not complying with their statutory powers.

Yours faithfully

Mr R Steele

15. I received a reply from Mark Coram on 9 September 2011 as follows:

Communities & Local Government

Dear Mr Steele

Council Issues

Thank you for your letter of 29 August. I have nothing further to add to my letter of 29 July. As I indicated in that letter the Department cannot interfere in the day-to-day running of local authorities. I have provided advice as to the avenues open to you and I refer you back to my initial letter.

I am returning your CD.

Yours faithfully

Mark Coram

Mark Coram just fobbed me off in this letter and he did not read the book on the CD with around the first 200 pages on it and neither did David Cameron have the decency to read my book, who also received it on CD.

CHAPTER NINE

1. After getting nowhere with Tony Blair when he was Prime Minister I decided to write to Gordon Brown when he took over as Prime Minister as he stated he would listen to the people. I wrote on 27 June 2007 as follows:

Clockface Road, St Helen's, Merseyside

Dear Mr Brown

I have written to Tony Blair several times and got nowhere, now you are leader, I hope you are going to help me.

I have sent with this letter, copies of four letters sent to Tony Blair. In just over 14 months as being shop steward, I had 76 grievances with management and they have never had to answer to anyone. I need a lawyer to do my case on a no win, no fee and that's impossible to find. My case has to be put into court and it will be struck out on limitation and once it has been struck out of the highest court I can go to the European Court of Human Rights who have told me they will give my case a hearing.

I need a wealthy businessperson to sponsor my case. I personally think the government should pay my legal costs, as it's one of their council's that has caused my problems. I have been ill for the last 10 years and I am still not well enough to take a job and after what has happened, I may never trust another employer. Through the wrongdoings I lost my job, my health and my home. I had never been out of work before this happened. I have worked from the age of 16.

I would like you to conduct a public enquiry into St Helen's Council and for me to be part of it as I would like to confront the people responsible for the corruption that has gone on over the last 10 years. Thinking about it, it was going on in 1992 when I started and realised when I took over shop steward in 1996. The lads remember it months after Gornall took over as Head of Security.

If you don't do anything about this then I am contacting the EU to finance my case to get it to the European Court of Human Rights. If you wish to see me and discuss the corruption, I will come to 10 Downing Street or you can come to St Helen's. I have around 2000 pages of documentation. I am determined to get to court one way or another. I would like you to personally reply to this letter.

Yours faithfully

Mr R Steele

2. As I did not receive a reply from Gordon Brown I wrote to him again on 15 July 2007 as follows:

Clockface Road, St Helen's, Merseyside

Dear Mr Brown

I wrote to you on 27 June 2007 and I have not heard from you. I know you are very busy. I do need to know where I stand. I do want to meet you and discuss everything that has happened and I will tell you as it is no lies and nor will I exaggerate the truth.

When I saw the council leader in 1997 he told me they were serious allegations I was making and he did nothing. For me to go into great detail I need to sit down with you and I can produce evidence to back up my allegations and I can get ex supervisors to give evidence.

I went to the Police and spoke to a Detective Inspector Steve Lowe. I showed him 6 of my grievances and he told me there were lies, bullying and embezzlement and again nothing was done.

I hope you will meet me as soon as possible and I can tell you everything. Hope to hear from you soon.

Yours faithfully

Mr R Steele

3. I received a reply from 10 Downing Street on 12 July 2007 as follows:

10 Downing Street, London

Dear Mr Steele

The Prime Minister has asked me to thank you for your recent letter and enclosure.

He hopes you will understand that, as the matter you raise is the responsibility of the Department of Communities and Local Government, he has asked that your letter be forwarded to that Department so that they may reply to you on his behalf.

Yours sincerely

S Caine

4. Because I never heard from the Department of Communities and Local Government, I wrote to Gordon Brown again on 5 August 2007 as follows:

Clockface Road, St Helen's, Merseyside

Dear Mr Brown

I have written to you on 27 June 2007 and 15 July 2007. I did receive one reply on the 15 July 2007 and it was dated 12 July 2007. It says the matters you raise are the responsibility of the Department of Communities and Local Government. I have not heard from them again. I want to meet with them and tell them everything and show them the evidence.

I am going to the national papers to ask them to put an ad in for a wealthy businessperson to sponsor my case to the European Court of Human Rights. Can S Caine contact the relevant department and speed things up as I am waiting to hear from them?

Yours faithfully

Mr R Steele

5. I again received a reply from 10 Downing Street on 14 August 2007 as follows:

10 Downing Street, London

Dear Mr Steele

The Prime Minister has asked me to thank you for your recent letter and enclosure. I am sorry you have received no response to your original enquiry.

As your letter was referred to the Department for Communities and Local Government I have passed this further letter to them and asked them to ensure a reply is sent to you as soon as possible. Meanwhile, if you wish to contact the department direct you should write to the following address: Department for Communities and Local Government, Customer Liaison Group, Eland House, Zone 3/B5, Bressenden Place, SW1E 5DU.

Yours sincerely

G Edwards

6. I decided to write to the Department for Communities and Local Government Customer Liaison Group on 19 august 2007 as follows:

Clockface Road, St Helen's Merseyside

Dear Sirs

I have written to Downing Street three times and they have now sent me your address.

As you may already know, I was shop steward for security section of St Helen's Council and in just over 14 months I had 76 grievances with management. I showed just 6 of my grievances to Detective Inspector Steve Lowe and he told me there's lies, bullying and embezzlement.

I have two boxes of files with a lot of evidence that I want to bring to you and go through my case. It will take several hours to discuss it and provide evidence. A lot of people have covered up for one another and once I get to the European Courts, they will be exposed and hopefully punished.

I hope to meet with you soon.

Yours faithfully

Mr R Steele

7. Because I never received a letter from the Department for Communities and Local Government, I again wrote to Gordon Brown on 3 September 2007 as follows:

Clockface Road, St Helen's, Merseyside

Dear Mr Brown

This is my fourth letter I have sent you. I wrote to you on 27 June 2007, 15 July 2007 and the 5 August 2007. I have received two replies from Downing Street on the 12 July 2007. My letters had been passed on to the Department of Communities and Local Government. I then received a reply on 14 August 2007, G Edwards had passed on my further letter and asked them to ensure a reply is sent as soon as possible. He also sent me their address to write to them direct, this I did on 19 August 2007. To this date, I have not heard from them.

I have been waiting for a reply since 12 July 2007. Will you make them reply as a matter of urgency as I am seeking help putting a letter to the European Court for help as this country has failed to help me with my case.

Yours faithfully

Mr R Steele

8. I once again wrote to Gordon Brown on 27 February 2008 as follows:

Clockface Road, St Helen's, Merseyside

Mr Brown

This if the fifth time I have written to you and I am beginning lose my patience as I don't like being ignored. I again will send you copies of the letters I have sent you and two copies of your replies, along with a copy of a letter sent to your Department of Communities and Local Government.

I want someone from this department to visit me at my home and discuss this matter. I want justice one way or the other and if I don't get it, I will take the law into my own hands and you and Blair will be help responsible for what actions I may take. I will do something that will demand a public enquiry so everyone responsible will lose their jobs, including you.

I hope to get a positive response soon.

Yours faithfully

Mr R Steele

9. I then received a letter from the Department for Communities and Local Government on 24 April 2008 as follows:

Communities & Local Government

Dear Mr Steele

Thank you for your letter of 27 February to the Prime Minister regarding your complaint about your council. Your letter has been passed to this Department for reply and I apologise if you delay in responding. I also apologise if you did not receive replies to your previous correspondence.

I am sorry to hear of your concerns. I must explain however that local authorities act independently of central government. Ministers have no remit to intervene in their day-to-day affairs except where specific provision has been made in an Act. Local authorities are however responsible for their actions to their electorate, their Auditor and to the courts.

With respect to your request for assistance with your legal proceedings, you should consider contacting the Community Legal Advice. The service offers free and confidential legal advice on a range of issues. They can be contacted on telephone number 0845 345 4 345 or via their website at www.clsdirect.org.uk

Yours sincerely
William Tandoh

10. I once again wrote to Gordon Brown on 28 July 2008 as follows:

Clockface Road, St Helen's, Merseyside

Dear Mr Brown

This is my sixth letter to you and I have written five other letters to Tony Blair. I have been meaning to write to you since 24 April 2008 when I received a letter from the Communities and Local Government. I have sent a copy of the letter with this letter.

I wrote and told you I became shop steward in June 1996 and by July 1996 I was in dispute with management over our wages. Within 13 months I had 76 grievances with management. This made me so ill I lost my job in November 1999. I went off sick in August 1997 and never returned and have never worked since. In February 2008 the council gave my department a £4000 pay rise. This is still 50% short of what they should be on. This proves I was right all along. Jack Straw is the Justice MP and I want to speak to him personally as I want justice.

It says in the letter I have sent with this letter, the council are liable to the courts, I want this Government to pay to take the council to court and I want you to make the council pay me my loss of earnings that amounts to over £759,000 and £240,000 for damages to my health. That comes to 1 million pounds. I have to pay for prescriptions, glasses, dentist and when my mum and dad die, I will have to pay full council tax. I will also have to pay for a house cleaner as I am not well. I have paid two solicitors and a barrister nearly £10,000 and they have all told me different and I have got nowhere.

I have not lived normally for 11 years and it's how much more I want to take before I take my own life. I am an innocent person who wants to live a normal life till I get justice.

Like I say, I am an innocent person and the justice system has let me down. I just want to get a life back. Get Jack Straw to meet me and get St Helen's Council into court so I can get on with my life.

Yours faithfully

Mr R Steele

11. I received a reply from 10 Downing Street on 28 August 2008 as follows:

10 Downing Street, London

Dear Mr Steele

I am writing on behalf of the Prime Minister to thank you for your recent letter and enclosed letter.

As you can imagine, Mr Brown receives thousands of letters each week and regrets that he is unable to reply personally to them all.

I have forwarded your letter to the Ministry of Justice so that they may reply to you direct.

Yours sincerely

Mr G Edwards

12. I again wrote to Gordon Brown on 14 October 2008 as follows:

Clockface Road, St Helens, Merseyside

Dear Mr Brown

I have received a letter from the Department of Ministry of Justice. There is good news and bad news. The good news is they have helped me find two solicitors who deal with personal injury and the European Court of Human Rights. The bad news is they are privately funded. I am going to try the communities' legal services for funding and if they cannot help, it's down to you, the government to fund my case, as it was a labour council that caused my problems.

If you can bail the banks out with 500 billion, you can pay my thousands to take the council to court. Once I win my case, you will get your money back. Look on it as a personal loan.

I look forward to hearing from you as a matter of urgency.

Yours faithfully

Mr R Steele

13. I again wrote to Gordon Brown on 14 December 2008 as follows:

Clockface Road, St Helen's, Merseyside

Mr Brown

I am getting fed up with you and your Government departments. This is the seventh time I have written to you with no joy. Firstly, I want you to investigate William Tandoh who has totally ignored my last two letters to him and he works for the Communities and Local Government, copies sent with this letter. Secondly, I believe Gornall has been embezzling to this day as he is charging his clients for a service he has never had the manpower to cover the duties. He is bringing a new rota out on the 12 January 2009 and he has put a floating shift on nights. Most of the time he is only going to have two men on nights when he needs three men to cover the duties. His clients require cover and paying for. The new rota he is bringing out will not cover client's specifications.

I want your Government to meet me and investigate this matter and take them to court. It's fraud. Had the District Auditors done their job in 1998 and 1999, Gornall would have been sacked on the spot.

I want you to find the time to meet me and discuss all that has gone on. You're the Prime Minister that said you will listen to the people, then listen to what I have got to say. I want to hear from you as soon as possible and I want you or someone from the Government to come and see me and look at my files and see what you can do about my problems.

Yours faithfully

Mr R Steele

14. After complaining about Communities and Local Government not replying to my letters, I received a reply on 13 January 2009 as follows:

Communities & Local Government

Dear Mr Steele

St Helen's Council

Thank you for your letter of 14 December to the Prime Minister, about St Helen's council and its head of security, Mr Gornall. Your letter has been passed to me for response here at the Department for Communities and Local Government as the part of the department I work in has responsibility for the conduct of councils.

I am sorry to hear that you have not had responses to your earlier letters. Mr Tandoh no longer works in Conduct and Council Constitutions, but I have reviewed your correspondence and read your letters of 27 June 2007, 15 July 2007, 5 August 2007, 19 August 2007, 3 September 2007, 27 February 2008 and 16 October 2008.

I should begin by explaining the relationship between central Government and local government. Local authorities act independently of central Government. Ministers, even the Prime Minister, have no remit to intervene in the day-to-day affairs of local authorities, except where specific provision has been made in an Act of Parliament. Local authorities are accountable for their actions to their electorate and must act within their statutory powers.

This disconnect between central and local government means that public agencies exist to provide redress and investigate allegations of injustice or wrongdoing in local authorities.

If you have a complaint about the council, in the first instance you should direct your complaint towards the local authority involved. St Helen's council will have a complaints department that you can contact. If your complaint refers to corruption, fraud or misuse of public money at St Helen's, please contact the appointed auditor for that authority. To find out the identity of the auditor you may wish contact the Audit Commission on 0844 798 3131. The Audit Commission appoints auditors to local government bodies in England. Auditors are either officers of the Commission or private firms.

If you feel that you have suffered injustice as a result of the council's actions, you may well wish to contact the Local Government Ombudsman. The Ombudsman is charged by Parliament with investigating complaints by individual citizens that they have suffered injustice arising from maladministration by local authorities. The Ombudsman is independent of both central and local government to ensure impartiality in his decisions.

The service is provided free of charge. You can telephone them direct on 0845 602 1983 or 024 7682 1960. The service is available from 8.30am to 5.00pm, Monday to Friday.

I enclose information about making a complaint to the Ombudsman.

Again, let me apologise for the lapse in getting a response to you. I hope that either the authority's own complaints system, the auditor or the Ombudsman help you gain a satisfactory solution to your concerns.

Yours sincerely

Stephen McAllister

15. I wrote back to Stephen McAllister of the Communities and Local Government on 14 January 2009 as follows:

Clockface Road, St Helen's, Merseyside

Dear Mr McAllister

Thank you for your letter and contents. Firstly, I have been in contact with the Ombudsman several times and they can do nothing for me. Secondly, I have dealt with the Audit Commission since 1998 on numerous occasions and they have covered up for St Helen's Council and have covered up for their own officers, and I have the evidence to prove it. All in all, your letter and its contents were a waste of time.

Going back to your letter dated 13 January 2009, you write 'Local authorities are accountable for their actions to their electorate and must act within their statutory powers'. In other letters it states they are also responsible to the courts but you have failed to inform me of this and in my letter I asked the Government to take St Helen's Council to court and that's what I want you to do.

I am seeing a solicitor tomorrow and I will pay myself, to take them to court and claim my costs back. I am giving you one more chance to take it to court or I will do it myself. I want to hear from you as soon as possible with your decision. If I have not had a reply within 10 working days, I will instruct a solicitor to take it to court.

Yours faithfully

Mr R Steele

16. Stephen McAllister of the Communities and Local Government replied to my letter on 27 January 2009 as follows:

Communities & Local Government

Dear Mr Steele
St Helen's Council

Thank you for your letter of 14 January about St Helen's Council, enclosing previous correspondence from this Department and its predecessor.

You ask in your letter if the Government intends to take St Helens Council to court over the matter you have raised?

As I explained in my letter of 13 January, local authorities act independently of central Government. Ministers, even the Prime Minister, have no remit to intervene in the day-to-day affairs of local authorities, except where specific provision has been made in an Act of Parliament.

This disconnect between central and local government protects councils from unwarranted intrusion in their affairs by central Government and it is for this reason that independent bodies such as the Ombudsman exist; to provide redress for those with a complaint about the council.

If you have exhausted the redress available through the Ombudsman and do not consider the Audit Commission to be an effective remedy for redress then you are, of course, free to pursue legal redress yourself. Your letter mentions that you are minded to contact a solicitor about this and claim your costs back. I presume you mean claim your costs back from the authority but for the avoidance of doubt I should make it clear that the Department would consider itself in no way liable for the costs you incur should you wish to pursue a legal course of action against the authority independently.

Yours sincerely

Stephen McAllister

17. I again wrote to Gordon Brown on 20 January 2009 as follows:

Clockface Road, St Helen's, Merseyside

Brown

This is my eighth letter to you since you have become Prime Minister. You are really beginning to p**s me off. You are the organ grinder that should be looking into this matter, not your *grease monkey that keeps fobbing me off. I have been asking this s**t government for help as far back as 1998, maybe 1997 to no joy. You are also responsible for contributing for my time limits to run out. I spoke to a solicitor on Monday 12 January and he told me that not only had the limitation run out for a personal injury claim but the limitation had run out against the solicitors. And he told me that I had a potential claim,'you were looking at one million pounds plus'.*

I have had my life ruined by St Helen's Council. How would you like it if I ruined other people's lives for revenge? I have tried to get justice the legal way and as far as I am concerned, there is no legal system in this country. I want you to organise taking St Helen's Council to court so the courts can listen to my grievances against the council.

Yours faithfully

Mr R Steele

18. I again received a reply from 10 Downing Street on 19 March 2008 as follows:

10 Downing Street

Dear Mr Steele

The Prime Minister has asked me to thank you for your recent letter and enclosure.

Mr Brown has asked that your letter be forwarded to the Department for Communities and Local Government so that they may reply to you on his behalf.

Yours sincerely

S Caine

Once again my letter was passed to the Department for Communities and Local Government and once again they did not reply to my letter.

19. The letter I wrote to Gordon Brown was passed on to Ministry of Justice who once again passed it on to Communities and Local Government. I decided to write to Joanne Wells in the Ministry of Justice on 27 September 2008 as follows:

Clockface Road, St Helen's, Merseyside

Dear Joanne

I wrote to you on 21 September 2008. Now I am feeling more up to it, I will let you know the situation. I was shop steward for Security of St Helen's Council. In just over 13 months I had 76 grievances with management. It made me so ill I had to go off sick in August 1997. I will now tell you how the system and the justice system have let me down.

On 12 October 1998, Sheila Samuels, Head of Human Resources wrote to Jim Keegan, full time officer of Unison and told him, 'it is my view unless there is a frank and open debate with yourselves and management regarding these issues and all issues are put on the table, which has not been the case to date, it is likely that they will continue to fester in Robert's mind and may prejudice not only his return to full health but the ability to re-build links with the Council and facilitate a return to work'. To date this never happened.

On 27 March 1999 I telephoned work and told them I am getting a return to work note off my doctor and will be back on 30 March 1999. Peter Mavers wrote to me on 29 March 1999 and wrote, 'In respect of your statement on Saturday, I am informing you that I am not in a position at this time to allow you to return to work'. They did not want me back. I was being represented by Thomsons Solicitors from

February 1998 till around June 2000. They got me in the office and told me that because I never returned to work I have not got a case. Firstly, I tried to return to work and was refused and secondly, the solicitors should have warned me of this before the three years were up.

In 1998 Peter Moffat, Assistant Director, got me in the office and told me Gornall's in a position and staying in a position and Farrell's in a position and staying in a position, therefore I'm terminating your employment. I got sacked because of two corrupt people.

I have had four solicitors and a barrister on the case and between them have let my limitation run out and have all told me different. I don't know who's telling me the truth, if any of them. I have around 2000 pages of documentation regarding this matter and I want someone from your department to look at it. Can you let me know as soon as possible.

Yours faithfully

Mr R Steele

I eventually received a reply from Department for Business Enterprise and Regulatory Reform on 17 February 2009 as follows:

BERR

Dear Mr Steele

Thank you for your letter of 27 September 2008 about your dismissal from St Helen's Council. The matter you have raised is the responsibility of BERR. I have been asked to reply. I apologise for the delay in responding.

I was sorry to hear about your experiences. However, the Government is unable to advise on individual employment situations.

The Department produces guidance on a range of individual employment rights, which you can find at www.berr.qov.uk/emplovment/emplovment-leqislation/emplovment-quidance/.

If you have further questions, you may wish to contact the Advisory, Conciliation and Arbitration Service (Acas). Their website address is www.acas. Orq.uk. They have a national public helpline, 08457 47 47 47, which deals with questions from employers, employees and others about a wide range of employment relations matters.

Yours sincerely

Lesley Burke

BERR Ministerial Correspondence Unit

Email: Berr.correspondence@berr.gsi.gov.uk

I contacted Acas and guess what, like everyone else they could not do anything. I have been fobbed off by everyone I have turned to for justice and no one in the country has any powers to stop any councils doing what they want, even when wrongdoings are going on.

The Communities and Local Government were wrong to state they are responsible for their actions to their electorate as I was their electorate and I got told by the Council where to get off. They also stated their Auditor, I went to the District Audit and they covered up for them and they also stated the Courts and I tried taking them to court for 15 years to no joy. What a corrupt society we live in.

20. A friend of mine decided to write to Jack Straw on 17 November 2009. He sent the same letter to Her Majesty's Court Services, the Queen and Lord Judge as follows:

Redruth Avenue, Laffak, St Helen's

Dear Jack Straw

You all should know of Mr Robert Steele apart from her Majesty the Queen, as you all have received letters from him. The reason for this letter is hopefully to get Robbie justice and inform you what type of person he is.

I first met Robbie in 1992, Robbie and I eventually became good friends and he started visiting my house Robbie was a perfectionist at everything he did he gave 100%. All the security officers at St Helen's MBC did not like Mick Gornall (Head of Security). In 1994 all the security officers signed a vote of no confidence in Mick Gornall but Robbie refused to sign it. The security officers where complaining of being robbed of their wages and in 1996 Robbie agreed to become shop steward and investigate the matter. Over the coming months Robbie investigated this and had numerous meetings with the direct people involved and he was told there was no problem. Robbie also told me he had 76 grievances in total and not one was dealt with. The pressure got so bad he had to go off sick. Whilst off sick several security officers continued to pass information to Robbie, as they saw him as their best hope of getting their wages sorted.

In 1999 Robbie stopped visiting me, he showed up two to three years later and I was shocked at how much his appearance had changed. Robbie told me he had been sectioned under the Mental Health Act and that the police had threatened him. My wife then introduced him to a former work colleague Mr Peter Edwards (solicitor) and me and my wife took Robbie to several meetings involving Jackson and Canter who were recommended by Peter Edwards but Robbie found it difficult to put his case across, as at the time it was difficult for him to put a sentence together. He has shown a slight improvement each year across recent years.

A doctor O'Brien did a psychiatric report on Robbie and repeatedly said he was paranoid. I can tell you here and now he is not paranoid he is one of the most honest and truthful person you could ever meet and puts everybody else first.

By defending his members it has cost him his health,job and his home. It was not the role of shop steward that made him ill, it was the way Robbie was treated by senior management as they could not deal with his honesty.

Mick Gornall had told the lads,'I do"t know why Rob hates me so much he serviced my car a few weeks ago'. He(Mick Gornall) would continually make comments like these in order to stir up problems for Robbie). I can tell you the last thing on Robbie's mind was compensation and several psychiatric nurses can confirm this. All Robbie was ever interested in was justice for his members. I went to Robbie's first JCC meeting and Brendan Farrell (Assistant Director) stated 'a keen shop steward, I like a good scrap with the unions'. He then went on to stop Robbie from discussing his agenda by stating 'this is not the time or place' all you are doing is discriminating against Mick (Mick Gornall). Robbie's psychiatric nurses have told him over the lastfew years to put himself first and to get his compensation but Robbie wouldn't listen and continued to fight for justice for his members right up until 2008 when the council finally admitted that the pay structure was wrong and the lads all got pay entitlements. It springs to mind a conversation between Mick Gornall and Ged Philbin (current full time union official) when Ged said 'Rob Steele is like a dog with a bone, once he gets hold of something he won't let go'.

Now all the members have got what they wanted none of them will speak to him, when he calls round they don't even answer the door. Over the last few years Robbie has lent over 20 people money interest free,he has even bought me two cars and let me pay him back two years later. He is currently

*owed around £20,000.00 by six people and can't get his
money back. His bank account is now overdrawn and he is
having to pay back £22 in interest every 5 days. His Mum
has begged him not to lend money out but unfortunately he
won't listen and people just play on his good nature. Last
year alone he bought 22 Christmas presents for his friend's
children.*

*Derek Anders (current depot manager) was Robbie's supervi-
sor and another one who played on Robbie's good nature.
Robbie had repaired and serviced Derek's car for a number of
years and then in order to obtain the deputy head of security's
job,he set Robbie up and stabbed him in the back.*

*At this time there was that much pressure on Robbie he
started swapping his day shifts tor night shifts so as to avoid
management. Derek Anders stopped this whilst at the same
time allowed other officers to continue doing this. This was
not the first occasion where Robbie had shown signs of being
under stress but the management had failed to notice this.
Mick Gornall, Derek Anders and Paul Molyneux (current
deputy head of security)were the most hated people in
security and only a few weeks before Robbie went off sick he
had serviced all their cars.*

*This was similar to an earlier incident when Ged Philbin had
pulled Robbie up and said to him you were like Les Gillford,
a roaring bull. They shut him up, now they have shut you up.
Clearly there has been enough widespread incidents for a
number of people from senior management to see Robbie's
stress and illness kicking in and a duty of care plan should of
been implemented.*

*Robbie wrote to the royal courts of justice, judicial office and
has stated if he wins his case he is going to write a book
about his case from start to finish and is hoping to make
several million pounds off it and he is then going to donate*

all proceeds to Alder Hey Children's hospital in Liverpool. His friend and former neighbour who is in charge of the midwives has asked Robbie not to forget her hospital and has asked for two life-support machines for premature babies. Robbie has told me he will personally pay for this out of his compensation.

I can tell you Robbie has requested meetings with the head of the council on several occasions to confront them on his grievances and they have refused. He has also asked the head of district audit to meet with him while he challenged their report but they refused. The unions also refused Robbie's request. Robbie has also asked several government officials including two prime ministers to meet him and discuss his case and they all refused. Last of all he wanted to confront Detective Inspector Steve Lowe in front of the Chief Constable on allegations he made on Robbie and they didn't even reply to his letter. Had they have sat down with him he would have opened a can of worms on all of them. What I know I can tell you is that they have all covered up for each other and Robbie is defending himself in court and he will rip them to pieces on the witness stand.

I wrote to the law lords some time ago requesting they lift the limitation on Robbie's case as they have set a precedent by recently allowing somebody else to have their limitation lifted. Robbie recently asked the courts for the names of the people involved in this case then he can personally write to them, he has requested this several times over the last month and although having received replies to his letters they have not given him the information he has requested. In my opinion they are no better than politicians. They go all around the world but don't answer the question you have asked. I am sending copies of this letter to the following people – Her Majesty the Queen, Jack Straw Justice MP, the lord chief justice and her majesty's court services and I hope one of you will make the relevant people do something and give this lad his day in court and let him try to re-build his life.

I personally think her majesty's court service should invite Robbie to see them and put his case across to them and they can then request the law lords to lift the limitation on his case and if they are not the relevant people to discuss this, then they should find the people who lifted the limitation on this other case and let them go through Robbie's case. Lf any of you got to know him you would find him to be the most honest, kind, sincere and considerate person you could ever meet and be proud to be his friend.

Yours sincerely

Alan Bolger

Then he wrote to him again on 11 January 2010 as follows:

Redruth Avenue, Laffak, St Helen's, Merseyside

Dear Jack Straw

I wrote a letter to you on the 17 November 2009 yet my letter has not been responded too. I am again sending you a copy of the letter and maybe this time we will get a rapid response. Robbie did get a response from a letter sent to the Lord Judge after several requests and telephone calls.

The Master Eyre has sent Robbie a sample for particulars of claim. Robbie and his brother, who put the letter of claim together, don't understand the sample, therefore Robbie has spoken to solicitors about this and they told him he will have to pay to correct his letter of claim but they want to look at the whole case, this will cost over £2500. Robbie has no faith in solicitors or banisters as over the years have took money off Robbie then dropped the case at a later date. Robbie has repeatedly requested for the law lords, the courts and the

Lord Judge to give him the names of the lawlords who lifted the limitations on that case so Robbie can write to them personally to meet them and discuss his case. I feel that you personally should sit down and discuss Robbie's case with him as you are the Minister of Justice, or at least someone from your department should do as a matter of urgency.

As you will see from my letter dated November 17, it states Robbie is hoping to raise money for sick children with his story and at present you are preventing him getting justice, therefore preventing money being raised for charity.

I'm also sending you a copy of the letter of claim that needs altering and hopefully your department will amend it to the requirements for the courts as a matter of urgency so he can re-issue it to the courts. I will tell you now I am preparing a letter to the European Court of Human Rights that I don't get a response from yourself the Queen, Lord Judge or Her Majesty's Court Services by the first of February, I will be sending copies of all correspondences from all parties and will be requesting them to help Robbie get justice as this country has let him down. I have sent this letter recorded delivery so I can check on the Internet who has signed for it. I hope to hear from you shortly.

Yours faithfully

Mr A Bolger

21. Jack Straw never replied to both letters so Alan Bolger wrote to him again on 9 February 2010 as follows:

Redruth Avenue, Laffak, St Helens, Merseyside

Dear Jack Straw

I wrote to you on the 17 Nov 2009 and 11 Jan 2010 yet neither of my letters have been replied to. I am again sending you copies of both letters yet again. I am asking maybe this time we will get a rapid response.

You were also sent a letter of claim that needs altering and your department was asked to amend it for the court's requirements as a matter of urgency so he could issue it to the court's. This has not been returned as of this date. Could you please look into this and have it returned ASAP. I am also sending you a copy of the letter I received from Buckingham Palace 14 January 2010. As this letter has supposedly been dealt with by yourself and Lord Chancellor, I have put on hold sending all correspondences to the European Court of Human Rights. However, I am starting my letter to them and if Robbie does not receive a reply or receive the letter of claim by 20 February 2010 I am posting all correspondence to ECHR.

Like I told the Queen in her letter, Robbie is very disappointed that you have not replied, despite him helping raise millions for charity on a book he is hoping to write on his story and all the monies going to the Children's Alder Hey hospital in Liverpool. I have checked on the internet and the letter was delivered to South West London and signed for on the 12/1/2010. I hope this matter will be dealt with this time and he can issue proceedings without any more delay.

Yours faithfully

Mr A Bolger

22. Alan Bolger did receive a reply from the Department of Ministry of Justice on 26 March 2010 as follows:

Ministry of Justice

Dear Mr Bolger

Robert Steele

I am writing in response to your letters of 11 January and 9 February 2010 addressed to the Lord Chancellor and Secretary of State for Justice, Jack Straw. My letter also considers and responds to the letter sent by Mr Steele dated 18 March 2010. All of these letters concern Mr Steele and his claim and therefore it is sensible to deal with all the issues in this single reply.

However, before dealing with the current correspondence it is necessary for me to apologise for not sending you a copy of the earlier response dated 19 February 2010 that was sent directly to Mr Steele. I have attached this letter for your information.

In your letters you raise three issues. First, that Mr Steele would like the names of the Law Lords who handed down judgment in a limitation case. Secondly, that the Lord Chancellor or a member of his staff from the Ministry of Justice meet with Mr Steele to discuss his case and finally that the department amend his Part 7 claim form to make it suitable for use in his legal proceedings.

In respect of your first request, the names of judges who have handed down judgment in a particular case are never private. The issue is simply one of obtaining the name of the relevant case and either finding the judgment in a public reference library (such as the British Library) or using an online resource such as Bailli (http://www.bailii. Org). If you do not have access to the internet your local public library may be able to help. It is important that I make clear that the relevant judges will not be able to provide legal advice in respect of Mr Steele's particular case.

In relation to your second and third requests, these can be dealt with together. Officials from the Ministry of Justice are unable to comment on or give advice in individual cases. That being the case it would be inappropriate for officials to meet with Mr Steele to discuss his case or draft his Particulars of Claim form on his behalf. I note that Master Eyre has provided a sample Particulars of Claim form and this is the fullest extent of the assistance that we could have provided to Mr Steele.

The only advise that I am able to offer is that, if he intends to bring any proceedings or to take steps in existing proceedings, he should seek independent legal advice from his local Citizens Advice Bureau or Community Legal Advice.

In Mr Steele's most recent correspondence (18 March), he states that he has contacted Citizens Advice and Community Legal Advice and that they were both unable to assist him. I am sorry to hear this. Unfortunately, this fact does not alter our position and we are still unable to offer any legal advice.

In all the letters the point is made that Mr Steele intends to pursue this matter with the European Court of Human Rights. This, of course, is his right and is entirely a matter for him. Additionally, the point is made that Mr Steele intends on donating the proceeds of his legal action, if successful, to Alder Hey hospital. This is a worthy charitable purpose, however, it does not change the position regarding our ability to provide Mr Steele with legal advice.

I understand that this may not be the response that either yourself or Mr Steele were hoping for but the limits on our ability to help in this matter are clear. I am however happy to discuss this further should you have any questions.

I have sent a copy of this letter to Mr Steele.

Yours sincerely

Iheke Ndukwe
Policy Manager

23. Here is the letter Iheke Ndukwe sent Alan Bolger dated 19 February 2010 as follows:

Ministry of Justice

Dear Mr Steele

Limitation Periods

I am writing in response to a letter written by your friend Mr Alan Bolger dated 11 December 2009. I apologise for the delay in responding to this letter.

In the letter Mr Bolger outlines a number of facts concerning your life and some of the difficulties that you have faced. Mr Bolger concludes the letter by indicating that your cause of action is statute barred as a consequence of the limitation period having expired. He mentions that he has written to numerous people asking that the limitation on your case be lifted so that it might be heard. However, I am not clear how far your case had progressed, if indeed it has been started, or what, precisely, it is about in legal terms. I have assumed that the claim is against your former employers for the illnesses that you have suffered as a result of stress induced by events at work. Such a claim would probably be categorised for limitation purposes as a personal injury claim.

First I am very sorry to hear of your situation but I must make it clear that I am unable to comment on or give legal advice in individual cases; however I am able to provide you with general information on the law in this area. If you decide that you wish to bring any proceedings or to take any further steps in existing proceedings, I would advise you to seek independent legal advice from the local Citizens Advice Bureau or Community Legal Advice may be able to help you find one. Information regarding Community Legal Advice

can be found on its website: www.communitylegaladvice.
org.ukor by telephoning 0845 345 4345.

The principle of limitation, which requires that claims be
brought within a certain time limit, is a long-standing one in
the law of civil liability. It is found in many legal systems and
is regarded as consistent with the right to a fair trial under
the European Convention on Human Rights. Statutes of
limitation seek to hold a balance between the interests of
claimants in having maximum opportunity to pursue their
legal claims, and the interests of defendants in not having to
defend excessively old proceedings. Currently the mainstream
limitation rules for England and Wales are contained in the
Limitation Act 1980.

The Act specifies different periods for different actions,
most actions for damages in personal injury claims must be
brought within three years of either the date when the cause
of action accrued. Or within three years of the claimant's
'date of knowledge', whichever is the later. The date of
knowledge is the date on which the claimant first knew the
following facts:

– that the injury in question was significant;
– that the injury was caused in whole or in part to the act
  or omission which is alleged to constitute nuisance,
  negligence or breach of duty, and
– the identity of the defendant.

The courts have a wide discretion to disapply the limitation
period in personal injury cases when it considers it just and
equitable to do so. Section 33 of the Limitation Act 1980
contains factors to which the court should have regard to
when exercising its discretion although the discretion itself
is to all intents an unfettered one. These factors include
the length of, and the reasons for, the delay on the part of a
claimant in bringing his or her claim. Finally, because the

judges are independent of the Government, if a court decides not to exercise their discretion, politicians have no power to compel them to do so.

If a court has already decided not to exercise its discretion in your case, the way to challenge the decision is through an appeal. There are legal rules governing when an appeal can be made and I would recommend that you take legal advice if you are in this situation.

I hope that you have found the information in this letter useful. If I have misunderstood your situation, please do not hesitate to contact me again.

I have copied this letter to Mr Bolger.

Yours sincerely

Iheke Ndukwe

Policy Manager

24. I wrote back to Iheke Ndukwe on 18 March 2010 as follows:

Clockface Road, St Helen's, Merseyside

Dear Iheke Ndukwe

Thank you for finally replying to my letters of 19 February 2010. I hope you are going to reply to this letter a lot sooner (ASAP) as I would like this matter solved as soon as possible.

Firstly, from your letter I would like to point out I have contacted the Citizens Advice Bureau and they have no one qualified to deal with this matter and the Community Legal Advice number you gave me – 0845 345 4345 were a total waste of space. Stop playing games with me and give me the relevant contacts I need to sort out my letter of claim. Now where do we go from here?

I am now preparing a letter to the European Court of Human Rights for help, as this country has totally let me down and has no justice system whatsoever.

This is the last time I am writing to the Ministry of Justice as this is your last chance. I am also giving the courts one last chance and my letter will be sent to the ECHR, along with all the correspondence I have sent to all the relevant people I have asked to help me and let me down in mysearch for justice.

Yours faithfully

Mr R Steele

25. I received a reply from Iheke Ndukwe on 26 March 2010 as follows:

Ministry of Justice

Dear Mr Steele

Letter of Claim

I am writing in response to your letter dated 18 March 2010. I have also recently replied to two letters from your friend Mr A Bolger. For completeness, in addition to responding to your letter I have attached a copy of the response that I have sent to him.

First, I am sorry to hear that Citizens Advice and Community Legal Advice were unable to assist you. In the event that I was not clear in my previous letter I am unable to comment on, or give legal advice in individual cases. This includes recommending a suitable solicitor or barrister to take forward your claim. I am, however, happy to provide you with the web address and telephone number for the Law Society (http://www.lawsociety.org.uk/home.law and 020 7242 1222) The Law Society is the national professional body for Solicitors. I hope that it will be able to assist you to find a suitable solicitor to deal with your claim. I must stress here that the Law Society will not be able to provide you with any legal advice but they may be able to direct you to where such advice might be found.

I understand from your letter that you intend to contact the European Court of Human Rights. That is, of course, entirely a matter for you.

If I can be of any further assistance, please do not hesitate to contact me. I have forwarded a copy of this letter to Mr Bolger.

Yours sincerely

Iheke Ndukwe

Policy Manager

26. I never did get anywhere with any of the Government departments so I gave up with them as they did not want to see me get justice.

27. I once again wrote to Gordon Brown on 5 November 2009 as follows:

Clockface Road, St Helen's, Merseyside

Mr Brown

Since you have been Prime Minister, I have written to you eight times about St Helen's Council. I can now tell you my case is in the High Court and my claim is valued at over one million pounds, and that's no thanks to you.

I am now writing to you about an insurance company. I want you to get your finger out and do something this time. I have sent you a copy of the letter I have sent them and I want you to pass it on to the relevant department to sort it out.

In my opinion your government is a load of c**p and in my opinion the other idiot who's going to take your place next year is also going to be a c**p government. Do you know what, I'm not racist and I ended up voting the BNP in the European elections and I will be doing so in the General Election. Do you know why? Had I written to him about St Helen's Council, he would have done something about it and he would do something about this problem I have now. I bet you don't do anything about this problem I have now and I have to sort this out myself. If you don't help me, then I will contact Nick Griffin. One thing about him, he gets straight to the point and he tells you as it is. When you took over as Prime Minister you stated you would listen to the people, the last time I wrote to you, you never listened to me. Are you going to prove me wrong this time and do something about it?

Yours

Mr R Steele

The other idiot I was on about was David Cameron and I was right to call his government c**p too as I got nowhere with him either and Gordon Brown never proved me wrong and did not listen to me for the eighth time and it was his statement when he became Prime Minister – he would listen to the people.

I was banging my head against a brick wall as all I was doing was reporting corrupt people to corrupt people. Also, I got it wrong about the BNP because I approached them and they fobbed me off too.

I will never vote for anyone again because it does not matter who you vote for, none of them listen. There have been only two people that have done anything for me – that was Peter Kilfoyle MP and D Jenkins of the High Court as he helped me get my case into Court.

CHAPTER TEN

1. Alan Bolger wrote to the Law Lords on 31 January 2008 as follows:

Redruth Avenue, Laffak, St Helen's

To the Law Lords

I am writing on behalf of Robert Steele. He is unable to write to you at this moment in time due to his health. He is in severe depression and his medication has recently been increased.

Robbie has not had any form of life for the past 10½ years now and somebody somewhere must be able to assist him in his fight for justice. Until somebody listens to him and the people responsible are brought to justice, he won't ever recover and an innocent man has suffered long enough.

On 30 January 2008 you were on the national news stating that you have overruled the six-year limitation to claim against sex offenders. Robbie needs you to overrule either the three-year rule for personal injury or the 6-year rule for breach of contract so he can take his ex employer, St Helen's Council, to court.

Robbie was shop steward and in just over 12 months Robbie had 76 grievances. Robbie approached the District Audit on several occasions with some of his grievances. The District Audit took sides with the Council in their findings and when Robbie sent them copies of written evidence to back his allegations up they wrote back and told him 'it's nothing to do with the Auditors'. So why did they do a report?

A few years later Robbie went to the Police station and showed a Detective Inspector Steve Lowe six of his grievances and he told him 'there's lies, bullying and embezzlement' and Steve Lowe took it no further.

It was on national news today 31/01/08 about an MP and embezzlement and they were on about taxpayer's money and people involved in embezzlement being removed with immediate effect. This has been covered up by a number of people.

Robbie has had several solicitors on the case and a barrister and they have let the time limits run out for a personal injury claim and a breach of contract claim. Compensation is the last thing on Robbie's mind. He wants the people responsible for his illness brought to justice.

Robbie has written to Downing Street 9 times over the last 10 years and they have failed to help him. Robbie wants to come to the House of Lords and tell you everything that has gone on. If you will see him can you inform of a date when he can attend as soon as possible.

He feels discriminated against as the 6-year ruling is for certain people.

Yours sincerely

Alan Bolger

On behalf of Robert Steele

2. The Law Lords' office wrote back to me on 14 March 2008 as follows:

House of Lords

Dear Mr Steele

We have received a letter from Mr Alan Bolger who has written on your behalf as he has explained your situation and mentioned the details of your grievances against St Helen's Council. I am very sorry to hear about the negative effects this has had on your health and we are entirely sympathetic to your situation. He also quoted the ruling of the Law Lords in a recent judgment but this would have been a special case, which came here due to needing clarification of certain points of law in that particular case.

As far as your case is concerned you need to have the legal advice to guide you. Mr Bolger mentions that you have had solicitors dealing with your case and I think this is the way it has to be dealt with so they can give you the correct guidance. We cannot embark from this office in communication with members of the public no matter what their situation. There is a strict protocol across the board that judges cannot engage in correspondence with any party about their case.

I understand how strongly you feel about your grievance case and I do hope that you will receive the correct legal guidance. I also sincerely hope that your health improves and that your case will be resolved in time with the right assistance.

With kind regards

Carmen Castillo

Law Lords Office

c.c. Mr Alan Bolger

3. The Law Lords' office change their name to the Supreme Court so I wrote to the Supreme Court on 18 March 2010 as follows:

Clockface Road, St Helen's, Merseyside

Dear Sirs

I am writing to you, reference a letter from the Judicial Office, Royal Courts of Justice 15 March 2010. The reason for this letter is I would like to know the names of the Law Lords who lifted the limitation on that case in February 2008 as I strongly feel my limitation should be lifted on my case with immediate effect for my pledge to get justice I really deserve.

I have two hurdles to cross, one is limitation and the other is for someone to correct my letter of claim so the courts will accept it as it has been rejected twice. Will you please find the Law Lords who dealt with that case in February 2008 and arrange a meeting with them to discuss my case as a matter or urgency? This is the last time I'm going to request this as I have asked the courts several times for this information and they have failed to give me this. Next move is the European Court of Human Rights. The ball is now in your court.

Hope to hear from you with the names of the relevant people to contact by the end of the month.

Yours faithfully

Mr R Steele

4. I received a reply from the Supreme Court on 23 March 2010 as follows:

The Supreme Court of the United Kingdom, Parliament Square, London

Dear Mr Steele

I acknowledge receipt of your letter of 18 March 2010.

I am sorry but the Justices of this Court cannot advise on or intervene in individual cases. I can only suggest you contact a solicitor or Citizen's Advice Bureau.

Yours sincerely

Louise di Mambro
Registrar of the Supreme Court of the United Kingdom

It's funny that I was told the Justices cannot intervene in individual cases but they intervened on MRSA with the lotto rapist on the news on 30 January 2008. In my opinion it is just one cover up after another.

CHAPTER ELEVEN

1. After contacting the High Court and having nothing but problems, I decided to write to Lord Judge, the Lord Chief Justice to strengthen my case on 1 October 2009 as follows:

Clockface Road, St Helens, Merseyside

Dear Lord Judge

I have put a claim into the High Court for personal injury on 30 September 2009. Weightmans Solicitors, the Council's solicitors, are going to have my case dropped on limitation. I am going to defend my case in limitation on the grounds of new evidence and concealment. I would like to get my case into court at a first attempt. I will be going to the Court of Appeal and to the Supreme Court and if all fails, I will take my case to the European Court of Human Rights.

I have already spoken to them on the telephone and told them the situation. They have told me I will get a fair hearing there as I would not have had one in England. I don't listen to the monkeys, I go straight to the organ grinder, that is why I have come to you. This is not a normal personal injury claim. A solicitor has stated it as bizarre and a Councillor has stated it's a massive and complex case. This is a special case and needs clarification of certain points of law like that particular case the Law Lords lifted the limitation.

I have lost the last 12 years of my life through being made ill by my employer. I have had no motivation or strength in my body to do anything since September 1999. My father is 80 and my mother is 78 and they look after me. They're not going to be around forever and when they pass away I am going to have to pay people to look after me and maintain the house. My life is not much better than being a cabbage. I can tell you now, I will not have the funds to live and I have also been told by a solicitor that if I lose my case the Council will make me bankrupt.

I am going to subpoena the following people: John Vis, District Audit; Clive Portman, District Audit; Steve Lowe, Merseyside Police; Dr Fiona Page, Consultant Occupational Physician; Dr L Stephen O'Brien, Consultant Psychiatrist; Brendan Farrell, St Helen's Council, Mick Gornall, St Helen's Council, Peter Mavers, St Helen's Council and Carol Hudson, St Helen's Council. They can all defend their actions that are not true and try to lie their way out of things they have said.

If yourself and Lord Phillips came to court and listened to what has gone on you would have never come across a case like it in your lives and will never come across it in the future. If you do the right thing and give me a court hearing at the first attempt, maybe I can try to re-build my life and I hope it's not permanent damage they have done to my health.

I must warn you if I do get a court hearing, the court may need to be flexible on times as I could be available from 9am for a couple of days and then struggle to get there till afternoons. I thought my health had improved mentally. The last six weeks I have been working on this case has knocked me back. I started this letter on 1-10-09 and have finished it today, 5-10-09. I have sent with this letter a copy of letter to Weightmans dated 1-10-09, a letter to me from Weightmans and my letter of claim. This is one hell of a case and if there is a limitation problem, I seriously hope yourself and Lord Phillips will consider this as a special case.

Yours faithfully

Mr R Steele

2. I received a reply from the Royal Courts of Justice on 9 October 2009 as follows:

Judicial Office, Royal Courts of Justice, Strand, London

Dear Mr Steele

Thank you for your letter of 1 October received by the Office of the Lord Chief Justice, which has been noted.

Unfortunately the Lord Chief Justice cannot intervene in or comment upon an individual case whether before or after it is decided.

You say that your matter is a massive and complex case and therefore I can only advise that you consider seeking legal advice in order to take your case forward, but neither this office nor the Lord Chief Justice is in a position to offer such advice. You may also wish to contact your local Citizens Advice Bureau.

I am sorry that this office cannot help you more.

Yours sincerely

Susan Holleran

Judicial Office

3. I wrote back to the Royal Courts of Justice on 15 October 2009 as follows:

Clockface Road, St Helen's, Merseyside

Dear Susan

Thank you for your letter 9 October 2009. Firstly I will point out to you it was Councillor Wally Ashcroft who stated it was a massive and complex case. I have had advice from six firms of solicitors and two barristers who have all told me different. How can you tell me to seek legal advice when none of them can agree with one another and my local Citizens Advice Bureau have turned me away twice as they have no-one qualified to help me.

I would like you to look into the ruling of the Law Lords in 2008. I would like to know exactly how it was done as I am going to contact the relevant people and if need be, have the limitation lifted on my case. As I stated in my last letter, this is no ordinary personal injury case, no judge would have ever come across a case like it, this is a case that needs clarification of certain points of the law.

I may not need this limitation lifting at this point as the limitation is automatically lifted on the grounds of new evidence and concealment. The reason I am pushing for this information is to be one step ahead and if I fail on new evidence and concealment, then I can fall back on clarification of certain points of the law. Again, like I said in my last letter, I would like to get my case into court at a first attempt. If all fails and the British Courts don't help me, this case will end up in the European Court of Human Rights.

If I get my loss of earnings and enough damages to live comfortably for the rest of my life, I am going to write a book on a true story and sell it to as many countries as possible and hope to raise several million pounds and all the profits will be donated to the Children's Alder Hey Hospital in Liverpool. Don't think this is a publicity stunt as I have made it quite clear for a number of years that's where I want my money to go. My neighbour in Liverpool will tell you this is true and she asked me to buy two incubators for keeping premature babies alive, as she is a midwife. Do you know what, I will personally buy her them out of my damages.

I hope you will inform me with the relevant information asap.

Yours faithfully

Mr R Steele

4. I received a reply from the Royal Courts of Justice on 26 October 2009 as follows:

Judicial Office, Royal Courts of Justice, Strand, London

Dear Mr Steele

I am in receipt of your letter of 15 October to my colleague Susan Holleran, the contents of which have been noted.

I can only reiterate what Susan has told you in previous correspondence – that the Lord Chief Justice cannot comment on or intervene in individual cases. I note you have sought legal advice and have been to a local Citizens Advice Bureau and in these circumstances there is little further that I can suggest other than directing your queries to Her Majesty's Courts Service:

Her Majesty's Courts Service, Customer Service Unit
Post Point 1.40, 1st Floor, 102 Petty France, London SW1H 9AJ
Tel: 0845 4568770

I regret this office cannot be of any further assistance to you in this matter.

Yours sincerely

Adam Davis

Judicial Office

5. I once again wrote to Lord Judge on 24 October 2009 as follows:

Clockface Road, St Helen's, Merseyside

Dear Lord Judge

I wrote to you on 1 October 2009. I know for a fact you have not seen or read my letter. I accept you cannot intervene or comment upon an individual case. I have turned to the courts for justice. The courts should know full well I have mental health problems and it states quite clearly my employers have used a psychological approach to wear me down. This is stated in my letter of claim, page 7 2. F. I now feel the courts are using the same method.

I sent my letter of claim, along with my NI claim form with a cheque that I attached to my paperwork with a paper clip so it would not get lost in the envelope. On 6 October 2009 my paperwork was returned for the following reason – you need to provide a fee. I rang the court and asked to speak to Bailey Read. He was not in the office and another fellow spoke to me. I made it quite clear I did send a cheque and the paper clip it was attached to was still attached to my paperwork. He said they had not received my cheque and to send the paperwork back with another cheque. He also told me to put a stop on the other cheque immediately, this I did.

I again had my paperwork returned on 14 October 2009. It had been looked at by Master Eyre and was returned for the following reason: the claim does not comply with CPR 16.2 and the letter before action does not satisfy the requirements of the Particulars of Claim. I again rang the court up and asked to speak to James Lelas. I don't know who I spoke to, whether it was him or someone else, whoever it was was not very helpful and I got my brother to look on the internet to see what CPR 16.2 was. We do not know what he means by the requirement of the Particulars of Claim. I have written to the Master Eyre to explain what exactly it is he wants. I am still waiting for his reply.

I then receive a letter dated 19 October 2009 ref. stopped cheque. This is the cheque they denied receiving that they told me to cancel and I can confirm that the second cheque was cashed earlier in the week. I can tell you now this is stressing me out more than I already am. I can accept the second letter but they should have explained in more detail what it was they require. The other two letters were unnecessary and stressful.

Going back to the letter I sent you on 1-10-09, a Susan Halleran replied to your letter dated 9-10-09. I wrote back to her on 15-10-09 and I am still waiting for a reply. I have put in that letter ref. the ruling of the Law Lords in 2008 where they lifted the limitation on a claim. I require the relevant people who did this so I can contact them. As far as I am concerned you, the courts, have set a precedence for other claims and if you deny this, then it's discrimination and I will take this matter to the European Court of Human Rights.

I have sent you the four letters I have received from the courts with this letter. If you think I am going to give up or back down, then think again. I don't care how ill it makes me, I'm here to the end. Let's hope we can get things sorted and get my case into court, then I can put it to bed.

Yours faithfully

Mr R Steele

6. Alan Bolger wrote to Lord Judge on 17 November 2009. This is the same letter that was written to Jack Straw and Her Majesty's

Court Services and the Queen. I received a reply from the Royal Courts of Justice on 20 November 2009 as follows:

Judicial Office, Royal Courts of Justice, Strand, London

Dear Mr Steele

I am in receipt of a letter from Alan Bolger to Lord Judge. He asks for replies to be sent to you.

I regret I can add little further to what I said in my letter to you of 26 October. The Lord Chief Justice cannot be of assistance to you in this matter and I suggest seeking further legal advice on how to take matters forward. If you have not done so already you could also contact your local Member of Parliament. I have given his contact details below:

Rt Hon Shaun Woodward, 1st Floor, Century House Hardshaw Street, St Helens WA10 6RN Tel: 01744 24226

I am sorry this office cannot be of more help.

Yours sincerely

Adam Davis

Judicial Office

7. I again wrote to Lord Judge on 17 February 2010 as follows:

Clockface Road, St Helen's, Merseyside

Dear Lord Judge

Ref: information request

On 1-10-09 I wrote to yourself regarding my case to see if you or Lord Phillips would consider it to be a special case and lift the limitation period.

I wrote to the Judicial office, a lady called Susan on 15-10-09 requesting she sends me the names and information of the Law Lords who made a ruling in 2008 to lift the limitation on a case, in order for me to contact them to see if they can also help me.

I again wrote to yourself on 24-10-09 requesting the same information and received no reply to this issue. I again wrote to HMCS on 1-11-09 requesting the same information but nobody seems willing to provide the information requested. I appreciate you're a very busy man and to save me keep writing to you, can you please supply the information I need or help me.

Many thanks

Mr Robert Steele

8. I again received a reply from the Royal Courts of Justice on 15 March 2010 as follows:

Judicial Office, Royal Courts of Justice, Strand, London

Dear Mr Steele

I am in receipt of your letters of 17 February and 11 March to the Lord Chief Justice.

I note in your letter of 17 February you have requested information relating to the Law Lords. Their function is now undertaken by the Supreme Court and you may wish to contact them with your requests for information:

The Supreme Court, Parliament Square, London SW1P 3BD

With regards to the matters you raise in your letter of 11 March, I am sorry to hear of your health difficulties but as I believe you have been made aware in previous correspondence the Lord Chief Justice is unable to comment upon or intervene in individual cases. May I suggest contacting the St Helen's County Court directly?

St Helen's County Court, 1st Floor, Rexmore House
Cotham Street, St Helen's, Merseyside, England WA10 1SE
Tel: 01744 27544

I am sorry this office cannot be of more help.

Yours sincerely

Adam Davis
Judicial Office

9. Alan Bolger once again wrote to Lord Judge on 17 May 2011 as follows:

Redruth Avenue Laffak, St Helen's, Merseyside

Dear Lord Judge

I am writing on behalf of my good friend, Mr Robert Steele who resides at Clockface Road, St Helen's, Merseyside.

Robbie has written to you five times since 2009 seeking help and support from you. I know he needs your help more now than ever before as once again the British courts have let Robbie down.

Firstly, I attended with Robbie to the Court of Appeal when Robbie was told by the Judge he could not take his case any further in the British courts. When Robbie arrived home he contacted the Supreme Court and was again told that because his case was put in front of one Judge and not three Judges in the Court of Appeal, his case could go no further in the British courts.

Robbie asked him to put in writing for him to forward to the European Court of Human Rights and Robbie was informed to write to the courts for that answer so Robbie did. Robbie received a letter from the Master Eyre 25-10-10 – Mr Steele, your unsigned manuscript letter dated 21-10-10 has been put before me. Whether or not you have any further recourse in this jurisdiction is simply a matter of the civil procedure rules and you must make your own investigation of those.

This statement is not good enough to send someone with mental health problems. All Robbie could do is take the words of the Judge and of that person in the Supreme Court and put his case into the European Court of Human Rights.

This case was thrown out because the court found that domestic remedies had not been exhausted as required by Article 35-1 of the Convention copy sent with this letter.

You being the Lord Chief Justice, should contact Clare Ovey and inform her either your courts have given Robbie the wrong information and if that's not the case, then inform the European Court of Human Rights that they have got their decision wrong. As all remedies had been exhausted, this decision has just destroyed Robbie's life and has prevented him getting his justice he deserves.

If Robbie was entitled to go to the Supreme Court, then you should do the right thing and put his case into the Supreme Court and if that's not the case, then you should contact the European Court of Human Rights and inform them that all remedies had been exhausted in the British courts and allow Robbie to continue with his case in the European Court.

Yours sincerely

Alan Bolger

10. Alan Bolger wrote again to Lord Judge on 12 July 2011 as he did not receive a reply to his letter dated 17 May 2011 as follows:

Redruth Avenue, Laffak, St Helens, Merseyside

Dear Lord Judge

I wrote to you on behalf of Mr Robert Steele on the 17-05-11, that I never received a reply to and I am once again writing on behalf of Robert Steele.

Robbie was in the County court in St Helen's on the 8-07-11 over a Rolls Royce he had bought. The case was brought before District Judge Hassal and he made a statement to Robbie on capacity and the judge said if the case would have been for a million pounds then you would not have the capacity to deal with the matter. Even though this case is for £8,100 the judge said Robbie lacks capacity and will need a litigation friend and that Robbie's case may be a borderline case.

When I went to court in London with Robbie on 15-10-10 and the judge made it quite clear that Robbie had capacity to deal with a one million pound claim.

The statement made by District Judge Hassal confirms Robbie never had the capacity. This is once again a reason his case should be re-opened with immediate effect, as the judge in the court of appeal should not have made this statement. Robbie had capacity without medical evidence, even District

Judge Hassal has requested medical evidence on a £8,100 claim because he was not in a position to make that decision and the judge in the court of appeal was also not in a position to make the decision he made. The judge also ignored the grounds of new evidence and concealment that Robbie has set out. Copy sent.

I have also sent you a copy of Judge Hassal's notes dated 8 July 2011.

Please have the decency to use your authority and put Robbie's case back into court as this is the correct thing to do. This issue is new evidence and could you please reply to my letters.

There is also the issue that was raised with the judge in London about the victim wins right to sue Lotto rapist, like this case Robbie also received physical abuse and psychiatric injury like the victim of the Lotto Rapist.

The judge told Robbie that her limitation was lifted; because he knows what he was doing Robbie told the judge that St Helen's Council knew what they were doing and the judge never responded to Robbie's reply.

I have also sent you a copy of the Lotto Rapist report; I sincerely hope you contact Robbie with some good news so he can have his day in court that he no more deserves. Robbie has started writing a book and I have sent you a copy on a CD disc that he is half way through completion. Robbie has paid over £600 for someone to type it up for him and if you make the effort to read it you will understand why Robbie's illness will never improve till justice has been done.

That's if the damage to Robbie's health is not permanently damaged. I have also sent you paperwork on limitation, if you read concealment page 385 (11.34) and page 388

(11.37) was P under any disability while time ran and if so for how long did it last? Robbie has been under a disability since he became severely depressed in 1999 and is still under the disability today.

District judge Hassal has confirmed this by the actions he has taken on Robbie's case on the Rolls Royce.

Please stamp your authority and re open Robbie's case, as it is the right thing to do. Please have the decency to take the time to read Robbie's book and you will see how serious this case is and you will fully understand why this case must go to trial.

Please have the decency to look at all the evidence including the CD before making a decision and could you please reply to this letter.

Robbie has rung the court of appeal on Monday 11-07-11 as he misplaced two letters from the courts and Robbie is furious to find out that his case was not heard in the court of appeal, as he was led to believe but was heard on the Queens Bench. The lack of communication from the court, including the negative response and wrong information from the courts, has led to Robbie losing his case in any court including the European Court of Human Rights. This matter needs putting right with immediate effect and gives Robbie his day in court that he deserves.

Robbie has spent thousands of pounds to get his day in court and has been badly let down by lawyers and the courts. Now it's time to do the right thing and put his case into the court of appeal where it should have gone in October last year. Robbie did not know what Queens Bench was till Monday 11-07-11 when he was informed by the court that his case was heard in Queens Bench and not the court of appeal. If Robbie would have known his case was being heard in Queens Bench, then he would have known to take his case to the court of appeal. That he would have definitely done.

Robbie told me he has been to the psychiatrist today 12-07-11 and Robbie was told it's very difficult to make a judgment on capacity as things change day to day. The psychiatrist asked Robbie some questions and what Robbie had told him, he has told Robbie he has capacity today. Because of Robbie's capacity changing from day to day, it has been decided that Robbie is to take a mental health advocate to assist Robbie, as he may not have capacity on the day.

Yours sincerely

Alan Bolger

11. Alan Bolger received a reply on 31 October 2011 from Anne Coleman from the Judiciary of England and Wales as follows:

Judiciary of England And Wales

Anna Coleman

Assistant Private Secretary to The Lord Chief Justice of England and Wales

Dear Mr Bolger

Thank you for your letter of 12 July to the Lord Chief Justice, I am sorry for the delay in responding to you.

I am afraid it would not be appropriate for the Lord Chief Justice to intervene in or comment upon individual cases, unless they come before him in court. I can only suggest that you seek further legal advice from a solicitor or contact your local Citizens Advice Bureau.

I am sorry this office cannot be of further help.

Yours sincerely

Anna Coleman

12. I decided to write to Her Majesty's Court Services on 1 November 2009 as follows:

Clockface Road, St Helens, Merseyside

Dear Sirs

I have written to the Royal Courts of Justice three times. Twice to the Lord Chief Justice who I know has not read my letters and one letter to a Susan Holleran. The Judicial Office has given me your address to write to you to direct my queries to you.

On two occasions I have asked the Royal Courts of Justice to give me the names of the people who lifted the limitation on a certain case in 2008 so I can contact them to have my limitation lifted on my case. Both times they have not given me this information. I have sent you the copies I have sent to the courts for your replies.

I look forward to a rapid reply and I hope you are going to give me the answer and support I require.

Yours faithfully

Mr R Steele

13. Alan Bolger wrote the same letter he had written to Lord Judge, Jack Straw and the Queen on 17 November 2009 to Her Majesty's Courts Services and they replied on 23 November 2009 as follows:

Her Majesty's Courts Service, London

Dear Mr Bolger

Re: Your Recent Communication

It may be helpful if I explain that judges are constitutionally independent of Government and the administration. For this reason I am unable to comment on the judge's decision, nor the manner in which the judge conducted the case. Where someone is dissatisfied with a judge's decision the test of its integrity lies in an appeal to a higher level of judge, subject to prior permission being given. I can only suggest you seek legal advice as to the options now available to you.

Yours sincerely

Ms J Thompson

Customer Service Unit

14. I wrote again to Her Majesty's Court Services on 25 November 2009 as follows:

Clockface Road, St Helen's, Merseyside

Dear Sirs

I am writing to you once again. Last week I rang you to see why you have not replied to my letter and I was told they have not received it. This letter was sent recorded delivery and I will be checking up on the Internet who signed for it. Queens Bench have also denied receiving a letter and a cheque, 3 out of 3, what's going on, all recorded delivery?

I again have sent you the letters for your reply. You would have also received a letter last week from a Mr Alan Bolger who is trying to push my campaign.

Yours faithfully

Mr R Steele

15. I received a reply on 3 December 2009 as follows:

Her Majesty's Courts Service, London

Dear Mr Steele

Re: Your Recent Communication

Thank you for your letter received 1 December 2009.

I have read the contents of your letter and appreciate your frustration. However, I must explain that (HMCS) Her Majesty's Court Service is responsible for the administration of the courts in England and Wales.

Unfortunately as a court official I am unable to comment or intervene in individual cases. I can only suggest that you appeal the Judges decision if so advised or seek further advice regarding the options available to you.

I am sorry I am unable to assist you further.

Yours sincerely

Ms J Thompson

Customer Service Unit

CHAPTER TWELVE

1. In July 2009, I felt for the first time since becoming ill I could take my case on with help from my brother, on my own. I contacted the High Court and I completed an Appellants Notice form to put my case into court and they filed it on 3 August 2009. I then had to fill in a certificate of service. When I filled my claim form in for court, I had to pay a fee of £1,530.

I then receive a letter from the court sending my paperwork back on 6 October 2009. It states 'please find enclosed your claim form, it has been returned for the following reasons –

– 'you need to provide a fee'

This came from Bailey Reed, Queens Bench Division. I then rang the court as I had sent the cheque with my claim form, so I told the person on the phone I sent the cheque with my claim form. He made it quite clear to me to cancel the cheque immediately as they had not received it, so I did.

2. I then receive a letter from the court on 19 October 2009 as follows:

Her Majesty's Courts Service, London

Dear Sir

Re: Stopped Cheque 100404 Steele-v-St Helen's MBC

I am writing to inform you that I have been notified that the cheque we received from Mr R B Steele, no. 100404 in the sum of £1530 in the above matter has been returned to us Stopped Cheque.

The application has been put before Master Eyre who has required further information and we the matter will not proceed without payment.

Please send a replacement cheque for £1530 clearly marked on the back with the following reference: RD 09/10 20/10 to the above address.

If you are not going to proceed with the Claim could you inform me by letter to the Fees Office so that I can recoup the monies.

Many thanks in advance for your assistance in this matter.

Regards

Jennifer Foley

Fees Officer

As you can see quite clearly, they did receive my cheque after denying having received the cheque.

3. The court again sent my application form back letter dated 23 November 2009. With it was a copy of a letter 14 October 2009, which reads as follows:

Her Majesty's Courts Service, London

Dear Sir

Re: Issuing a Claim Form in the Queens Bench Division

Thank you for your recent claim form.

Unfortunately the claim form cannot be issued for the following reasons:

It was referred to Master Eyre who has stated: 'The claim does not comply with CPR 16.2 and, the letter before action does not satisfy the requirements of Particulars of Claim'

Please make the required amendments to your claim form and resubmit to the court for issuing clearly stating the following reference Sheet 1 Letter E for £1530.00.

If you have any queries please contact the above number.

Yours faithfully

James Lelas

My brother helped me with CPR 16.2 and a solicitor, Ruth Power from Haygarth Jones in St Helen's, helped me with my particulars of claim and I sent it back.

4. I wrote to Master Eyre of the High Court on 29 November 2009 as follows:

Clockface Road, St Helen's, Merseyside

Dear Master Eyre

I wrote to you on 15 October 2009. After a week I rang to see why you had not replied to my letter and a woman told me it is on the table waiting for you to look at it. Another week went by so I rang again and a fella answered. He put me on hold for a few minutes and told me I had not sent you a letter and they had not received one. I told him it was on the desk last week and that the letter was there, and in a split second of me telling him this, he said he had found it.

Over another week went by so I rang again and spoke to a Miss Bird. She told me you had looked at my paperwork and there was a problem 16.2. I told her that you said that in my last letter and is it the letter from October and she said 'no', the letter was dated 11 November. I said to her my brother must have got the Particulars of Claim right, I don't know how because we did not know what we were doing and I don't understand why 16.2 was wrong because we corrected that off the Internet.

I put the phone down and rang back the next day as I wanted a copy of that letter. A woman put me back on to Miss Bird and I asked for the copy of the letter. She told me there is a charge but they would send it this time. I received the letter dated 23 November and guess what, it was the letter dated 14 October. There never was a letter dated 11 November from you. This is not the first problem I have had with Queen's Bench as they denied having a cheque that they did receive.

I am now sending you another draft NI claim form and again asking you if this is now correct. Please return it and I will send you all my paperwork back if this is still wrong. Can you please tell me exactly what it is you want as I am not a lawyer and I am doing this case myself? If you can explain to me, I will correct it and get my case into court. Can you try and deal with this matter by the weekend as I want to return their papers ASAP.

Yours faithfully

Mr R Steele

5. I then receive a letter from the court on 12 May 2010 as follows:

Her Majesty's Courts Service, London

Dear Sir

Your draft claim-form and Particulars of Claim dated the 2 May 2010 have been put before Master Eyre, who instructs me to state that:

1. *This action is long out of time. As your enclosure shows, you are aware of the ruling in A. v Hoare, but Mrs A was able to show that she had a good reason for postponing bringing her action. You do not so much as mention any such reason, and moreover your allegations make clear that you knew of the relevant circumstances from the beginning. If you think that you do have a good reason, you must in your draft Particulars of Claim set out what those reasons were.*

2. *Even then, you draft falls far short of what is required, and would need the most extensive alterations. Consideration of that can await your answer to point '1' above,since,if you are unable to show that you have an action that might be within an extended limitation period, nothing will be achieved by considering alterations.*

Yours Faithfully

Mr Bailey Reed
Administrative Officer
Case Preparation

6. I wrote back to Master Eyre on 16 May 2010 as follows:

Clockface Road, St Helen's, Merseyside

Dear Sir

I am writing in response to your letter dated 12 May 2010 having received a letter from myself Mr Robert Steele date 2 May 2010.

I believe I have been misled by the courts regarding my taking an opportunity to seek justice through the courts resulting from harassment at work that led to personal injury.

On two occasions I received a rejection letter from yourself with an explanation of what I need to do before re-submitting my Particulars of Claim. After seeking costly professional advice from a Solicitor you again rejected my Particulars of Claim and issued further advice.

My letter dated 2 May included a copy of the case A. v Hoare. My particulars are similar for which I made reference to in my Particulars of Claim on Page 8 enclosed. I have been advised by my solicitor to bring this to your attention as I believe this was overlooked by you, based on the response in your letter date 12 May.

Before I invest further money, which I can ill afford, in order to start the process of a fair hearing in the courts, can you kindly review the letter before making judgment especially page 8. You will also notice that I suffered from and still suffer psychiatric injury as a direct result of my ex employer.

There has been a further development regarding my state of health. My Community Psychiatric Nurse (CPN) informs me I have been referred to see a Psychologist as part of my on-going treatment.

Yours sincerely

Robert Steele

Letter dictated by Mr Robert Steele

This letter was written on my behalf by my brother.

7. I then receive a letter from Master Eyre dated 25 May 2010:

Queen's Bench Division, Central Office

Order in Steele v St Helen's [HQ10X01949]

UPON considering the Claimant's letter of the 16 May 2010 and its enclosure AND without a hearing AND pursuant to Rule 3.3 of the Civil Procedure Rules

AND IT APPEARING to the Court that:

- *The action is on its face long out of time for purposes of the Limitation Act 1980, ss. 5 and 11.*
- *Despite having been prompted by this Court in its letter of the 12 May 2010 to set out any case for saying that the action ought nonetheless to be permitted to continue, the Claimant has wholly failed to advance any contentions to that effect.*
- *In any event, the draft Particulars of Claim show at §6, 9, 10 and 11 that as long ago as 1999 the Claimant was well aware of the possibility of bringing proceedings in respect of the wrongs that he now alleges.*
- *The action accordingly infringes Rule 3.4(2)(a) and (b) of the Civil Procedure Rules.*

IT IS ORDERED as follows:

1 *There is leave to issue the claim-form, but it must not be served.*
2 *The claim-form is hereby struck out, and the action dismissed.*
3 *Any application by the Claimant in relation to this order, whether for leave to appeal or otherwise, must be made direct to the Judge — not to any of the Masters.*

8. I wrote to the court on 7 June 2010 as follows:

Clockface Road, St Helen's, Merseyside

Dear Sir

I am writing in response to a letter I received from the Master Eyre of the High Court of Justice Queens Bench Division dated 25 May 2010.

The letter made reference to paragraphs in my Particular of Claim 6, 9, 10 and 11. I have been trying to explain to the Master Eyre through interpretation since my illness as a direct result of my treatment from my last employer in 1997. From that day onwards I have been under medication for depression, stress and anxiety. Medical evidence of my treatment can be sought from the NHS.

On the 25 of May, the Master Eyre stated that an appeal in relation to his letter must be made directly to the Judge.

From 1997 until 2009, my illness had delayed me being able to gain full reasoning and confidence. I have been receiving help in compiling letters to the courts of appeal to pursue a claim against my ex employer for justice and reconciliation for what I believe was the primary cause of my on-going illness.

In November 2009 my illness took a turn for the worst further diminishing my reasoning and confidence and ability to write and explain my intentions. I am able to explain my grievance orally rather than writing as I become irritable and confused.

With help from a family member I compiled many letters for which I have not declared I have been receiving help until I received rejections and an assortment of advice in the form of letters from the Master Eyre.

14th October 2009; 12th May 2010; 25th May 2010

Can you kindly review my Particulars of Claim and may I draw your attention to page seven Particulars of Negligence and page eight New Evidence and Concealment enclosed, in order that I can have a fair hearing in a court of law.

Yours faithfully

Robert Steele

Letter dictated by Mr Robert Steele

9. I received a reply on 23 June 2010 from Her Majesty's Court Services as follows:

Her Majesty's Courts Service, London

Dear Mr Steele

Steele v St Helen's

Your letter of 7 June 2010 has been shown to Mr Justice Maddison. He wishes you to be informed that any application for permission to appeal against Master Eyre's order of 24 May 2010 would have to be made by filing an Appellant's Notice form N161.

Though you are entitled to do all this yourself, the Judge strongly suggests that you see a solicitor before mounting an appeal. This is partly because the procedure for appealing is quite complicated, and partly because on the information available to him. Mr Justice Maddison can see no grounds for saying that Master Eyre's order was wrong.

If you want to obtain an appeal pack or want further information on lodging an appeal please contact the appeals office on 0207 947 7383.

I hope this assists.

Yours sincerely
Miss S Ali
QB Judges Listing

10. I then receive a letter from D Jenkins from the High Court on 15 July 2010 as follows:

Her Majesty's Courts Service, London

Dear Sir/Madam

Re: Steele (App) V St Helens (Res)

I confirm receipt of your appeal papers in the above matter. The appeal cannot presently be issued as you have not complied with the standard minimum requirement for submitting an appeal to the High Court Appeals Office. The following documents, indicated below, are required.

- ☑ *Appellant's Notice in triplicate (present version updated as of July 2006)*
- ☑ *Grounds of appeal (must be headed 'Grounds of Appeal')*
- ☒ *A sealed copy of the Order being appealed*
- ☒ *Any order allocating the case to track*
- ☑ *A cheque for £200.00 payable to HMCS*
- ☑ *Extension of time and reasons (made in Section 8 and 9 of the Appellant's Notice)*
- ☒ *Reasons for the Stay of execution (Section 8 of the Appellant's Notice)*
- ☑ *Other In section 2 of your Appellant's Notice you have stated that you are seeking to appeal an order of Mr Justice Maddison whereas the order you should be seeking to appeal is that of Master Eyre dated 24 May 2010. You will need to amend section 2 accordingly.*

In section 1 you should put the name of the respondent as St Helen's.

In section 4 you have ticked the box no for do you need permission to appeal, whereas you do need permission so you will need to tick the yes box. You will need to sign your name in the box seeking permission to appeal.

If you re-submit your application with the appropriate amendments/additions outlined above, you may now be out of time to appeal. If so, then you will need to request an extension of time to lodge your Appellant's Notice. Please see sections 8 and 9 of the Appellant's Notice.

We are returning your papers for the appropriate amendments.

I enclose an appeal pack to assist you.

Yours faithfully

D Jenkins
Appeals Office

I filled it in and sent it back along with Reference Grounds of Appeal, victim wins right to sue lotto rapist and my amended particulars of claim:

Clockface Road, St Helen's, Merseyside

Reference: Grounds of Appeal

1. *I feel my claim against the St Helen's Metropolitan Borough Council (SHBC) listed in My Particulars of Claim Ref: Court of Appeal Master Eyre have not been fully assed by the courts in order to allow me to lodge an appeal due to my illness and have my limitation on the grounds of ill-health lifted to allow me as the workplace Union Representative to have a fair trial against my ex employees decision to end my employment whilst I was incapacitated.*

2. *New Evidence*

   • *Inland Revenue date 27 September 2002 Ref: ECR/709/WA/WE states incorrect rates and failure to pay employees for working Bank Holidays.*
   • *An independent pay assessment (Mitchell Charlesworth) Charted Accountants paid for by the*

majority of the St Helen's Borough Council Security department employees. The review indicated discrepancies. Refer to the draft dictions from Mitchell Charlesworth date 29 Sep 2003, para 1.8 to 1.9.

- *Evidence of pay awards grade 3 inclusive to grade 2 plus allowances date February 2008.*

3. *Concealment*

Whilst on the sick, I the claimant received no communications by letter or telephone or any other means in relation to a letter dated 12 October. Reference SS/SF where Ms S Samuels (HR Manager) SHBC was arranging a meeting with Mr J Keegan a full time Unison Officer and Mr P Mavers the Assistant Director of the SHBC on the 21 October 1998. Failure to communicate with me or allowing me to seek independent representation prevented me the opportunity to provide Ms S Samuels with my personal grievances and allegations of harassment from my employer as the elected Union Representative. Letters between Ms S Samuels and Mr J Keegan suggested they had open debates regarding my grievances and my future in my absence.

Signed: Robert Steele

Victim wins right to sue Lotto rapist

(Picture removed) Lorworth Hoare in November 2007. Photograph: Owen Humphreys/Press Association

A retired teacher today won a landmark law lords ruling giving her the right to claim compensation from a serial rapist who won £7m on the national lottery.

The 78-year-old woman tried to sue Lorworth Hoare after he won the lottery in 2004, but was unsuccessful because the sex attack happened 19 years ago.

The unanimous ruling backed Mrs A and people featured in four other sexual abuses cases, some involving children. It is expected to pave the way for thousands of victims to pursue claims for damages many years after their abuse.

The five cases considered by the law lords were sent back to the high court to be reconsidered in light of today's ruling.

The law lords ruled that claims for sexual assault should be brought within three years in future – in line with other civil claims for damages – but said courts should have the discretion to extend the period to permit older claims, removing the six-year cut-off point.

In a statement read by solicitor Sandra Baker, Mrs A said she hoped her compensation claim could now be speedily settled at the high court.

'I am both delighted and relieved that my appeal to the House of Lords has been successful and that I have succeeded in changing a law which will provide others in the future with a means of achieving justice,' she said. 'It was this, rather than financial gain, which motivated me to begin this process two years ago.'

'It is to be hoped that my claim for damages against Lorwoth Hoare will now be brought to a speedy resolution without the need for me to endure further protracted litigation.'

'I hope that many others in the future will be able to benefit from the change in the law which I helped to bring about.'

The charity Victim Support welcomed the ruling but said it would help few people. Its spokesman, Paul Fawcett, said: 'It's very good news for her but the wider significance is questionable because the vast majority of offenders don't have assets to chase.'

'We have long campaigned for a public fund to allow the courts to award compensation, leaving it to the courts to recover assets from the offender and allowing the victim to walk away and put the crime behind them.'

Mrs A lost her case in the high court and court of appeal, and was ordered to pay Hoare's £100,000 legal costs. Her case was one of five appeals heard at the House of Lords on how the Limitation Act affected claims in abuse cases.

Mrs A, who received £5,000 from the Criminal Injuries Compensation Board, sought compensation from Hoare for psychiatric injury caused by the 'violent and disgusting' attempted rape in February 1988.

Hoare, 59, who had subjected six other women to serious sexual assaults, including rape, attacked her as she walked in Roundhay Park, Leeds, West Yorkshire. The retired teacher says she still suffers from nightmares and claims the brutality of the attack destroyed her self-esteem, wrecked her relationships and ruined her life.

Hoare had not been worth suing until he won £7m. He was jailed for life in 1989 and spent 16 years in prison before buying the winning Lotto Extra ticket while on day release. He was released in 2005 and is reported to live in a £700,000 house near Newcastle.

Master Eyre
Ref: Court of appeal Mr Justice Maddison

IN THE HIGH COURT OF JUSTICE   Case No:
QUEENS BENCH DIVISION
CENTRAL COURTS OF JUSTICE

ROBERT STEELE   *Claimant*
-AND-
ST HELEN'S MBC   *Defendant*

PARTICULARS OF CLAIM

1. *The claimant Robert Steele was employed as a security office by the Defendant St Helen's MBC from the 8 June 1992 until 2 August 1999.*

2. *In June 1996 the claimant was elected as the GMB Shop Steward for my local branch of the St Helen's Metropolitan Borough Council, during which time the claimant complied with the GMB rule book to enable me to carry out my duties as the Shop Steward.*

3. *In September 1996 the claimant applied for a position as a security co-ordinator. In October 1995 the claimant was handed a reference from Mr Michael Gornall (Head of Security), which stated 'the claimant shown exceptional ability and my work record was exemplary'. It also stated the claimant was honest, trustworthy and totally reliable and could be relied upon to carry out any task using my own initiative. It also stated the claimant had a pleasant courteous personality and my attendance record was excellent.*

4. *My application for the position of a security co-ordinator was unsuccessful. At the time the claimant believes my application was rejected following a conversation with Mr Brendan Farrell having brought to his attention as the Shop Steward regarding staff shortages. One of my concerns was that my department was charging Ranger Services for a contract that was not supplied due to the staff shortages controlled by Mr Gornall. This was queried in my presences, over the telephone between Mr Farrell and Mr Gornall. As a result of my complaint to Mr Farrell I believe Mr Gornall resented my openness in raising the issue regarding Ranger Services and as the manager who appointed the security co-ordinator the claimant was victimised having received a shining*

reference from Mr Gornall for another position within the council.

5. *In December 1996 the claimant started having problems with sleep deprivation and lack of concentration during my work and social activities. The claimant now believes this as being work related stress, which was the start of my illness. On the 14 of August 1997 the claimant was unfit for work, the claimant informed my employer by telephone. On the 20 August 1997, My GP, Doctor Schofield diagnosed me as suffering from a stress related illness. The doctor's note held on my file confirms the following:*

    Work Problems ++ Tension, Stress, Low mood, Poor sleep, Loss of interest, Poor appetite. Needs a break from work. Given Sick note for two weeks, Stress related illness. On the 23 of September 1997 the claimant attended an Occupational Health Physician with Doctor F Page arranged by my employer. The claimant was declared unfit for all work.

6. *In May 1998 my employer St Helen's Metropolitan Borough Council terminated my employment. The claimant appealed against this decision in St Helen's Town Hall. After the appeal my employment was reinstated. It was reinstated after the claimant provided evidence, which was backed up by Mr Peter Moffat (Assistant Director). Mr Moffat stated in front of the appeal committee that Mr Gornall and Mr Farrell were staying in their positions of employment therefore I am terminating your employment. The appeal committee having witnessed this statement reinstated my employment. At the time of my appeal I was still on the sick. After the appeal the claimant returned home still unable to return to my place of work. The claimant was now terribly affected by my treatment and attitude of my employer during my appeal.*

7. *In March 1999 the claimant contacted my employer informing them the claimant would be attending my doctor's surgery on Monday the 29 to obtain a return to work note and would be retuning to work on the 30 of March 1999. The claimant received a letter by courier delivery on the 29 March 1999 from Mr P Mavers the Assistant Director informing me that he is not in a position to allow me to return to work. The claimant found this extremely unusual and instantly felt the claimant was not welcome to return to my place of work.*

8. *On the 11 May Dr Page attended my home for approximately 15 minutes to make an assessment on my health purely based on a conversation. Dr Page insisted the claimant should finish work on ill-health. The claimant told Dr Page the claimant wanted to return to work. Dr Page admitted my health had greatly improved but stated she was not prepared to allow me to return to that environment because it would make me ill again and then informed me she is recommending my employer terminate my employment on ill-health. The claimant had no faith in Dr Page as an assessor assessing my health as Dr Page on a previous visit to her surgery; she made a comment to m,e 'I've been used' by the council.*

9. *On the 20 September 1999, the claimant received a letter informing me my employment had been terminated with seven weeks notice whilst the claimant was on the sick. My termination date was the 8 November 1999 on the grounds of incapacity to fulfil contractual duties. On the 3 of August 2000 the claimant attended an appeal to have the decision to terminate my employment reversed. The claimant handed the appeals committee a letter the claimant received from Mr P Mavers Ref: PRM/DP date 29 March 1999 to prove the claimant was ready to return to work when the claimant was in*

a fit state. The letter and following treatment which included the home visit of Dr Page caused me further anxiety and triggered stress due to the lack of communication between me and my employers until the claimant received a final letter of termination.

10. *As a result of the appeal rejection the claimant contacted Unison requesting advice on how to make a case against my employers at an industrial tribunal as a result of my state of health, which the claimant believed was caused by my employer for a failure of a duty of care during my absence from work with stress related injury. During my illness the claimant received medication for a schizo-phrenia-like illness, which was diagnosed on the 8 of December 1998 by a Dr A Dutta (Consultant Psychiatrics).*

11. *A tribunal date was arranged by Unison. The claimant was later informed by letter from Unison that I the claimant will not have representation from Unison and would have to defend myself at the tribunal. As I was not in a good state of health and under the influence of medication I was not in a position to defend myself at the tribunal. A letter was posted to the tribunal address stating the claimant could not attend the tribunal due to ill-health.*

12. *August 1998 my GP, Dr Schofield documented that the claimant was suffering from a stress related illness with anxiety, agitation and depression. My GP advised my employer that a full recovery was possible and an eventual return to work would be beneficial to my condition. Suggesting a gradual reintroduction to the work place.*

13. *In November 1998 the St Helen's Council Occupational Health Physician Dr Page again stated the claimant was unfit for work in any capacity. On the 2 of August 1999*

Dr Page stated as a result of my medical condition, the claimant fell within the Disability Discrimination Act 1995 and Dr Page could not make any adjustments which would allow my accommodation.

14. *From the start of my employment on the 8 of June 1992 and being elected as the work place GMB Shop Steward June 1996 my work was described as exceptional ability by Mr Gornall. From June 1996 until my illness the claimant was the elected workplace GMB representative, which later changed to Unison.*

15. *Since becoming the elected GMB representative and having more dealings with the senior management the claimant was subjected to bullying, harassment, threats and victimisation by the senior management, which included threats of redundancy and dismissal on several occasions. My employer took advantage during my absence from work with stress and on two occasions terminated my employment.*

Particulars of harassment:

a) *The discovery of my department pay stature was inaccurate. This was brought to the attention of Mr Gornall and Mr Farrell at a Joint Council Meeting (JCC).*

b) *Being falsely accused by Mr Farrell for misleading union members regarding a memorandum, an extract from the union handbook with reference to contract changes. This was following a complaint from a member of staff who was allegedly being threatened for not applying for the role of a Security Co-ordinator by Mr Gornall.*

c) *Prior to my applying for the position of a Security Co-ordinator. As the GMB representative, in June/July*

1996, the Head of Security Mr Gornall informed me that if no one applied for the position of Security Co-ordinator (six positions) he would replace six employees with unemployed people. This was repeated by Mr Farrell in a later meeting supporting Mr Gornall for filling the six positions, based on a first in last out policy, the claimant was one of the six employees whose employment could have been terminated. The claimant applied for the position as a Security Co-ordinator in September 1996 to secure my position with St Helens Council in order to fulfil my ambition of remaining in work and maintaining my mortgage etc. My application was later rejected by Mr Gornall. See Para 4 above.

d) *In November 1996 a meeting took place between the management, T&G, GMB members and after the claimant called for a status quo regarding the introduction of changes to contracts. The meeting was as a result of my employers introducing a change of contract without any consultation with the workplace GMB members. The claimant had a private meeting with Mr Farrell prior to the November meeting and was told the contract changes had already been passed by the Town Hall and will be introduced whether the claimant like it or not.*

e) *In 1997 the claimant in the presence of Mr Gornall and Mr Farrell, the claimant presented Mr Farrell with a list of premises that were not checked over a weekend due to staff shortages. Mr Gornall passed a comment to Mr Farrell that the claimant would not release the name of the person who supplied me with the list. This resulted in further threats by Mr Farrell stating he will return the money to the schools and threatened to sack ten men.*

f) *As a result of being the elected Shop Steward and the liaison person between management and union members in pursuit of grievances, this brought me into conflict with my employer beyond industrial exchanges. They included pressure from the senior management and constant criticism as the then Unison Representative, which contributed to increased pressure and stress.*

g) *Mr Farrell, off his own back and without written notification from the work force on any inclination that the claimant had resigned as the Shop Steward, wrote a letter to Mr Eddie Tickle the Unison Branch Secretary stating the claimant was no longer recognised as the work place elected Shop Steward and refused to provide me with trade union facilities. However the claimant was still being requested by the senior management and recognised as the elected Shop steward. This is evident in the letter Ref: BMF/DP 31 July 1997.*

h) *Whilst on a rest day, the claimant received a telephone call from Mr Gornall to attend a meeting at 1600hr at the council depot. The claimant was not informed what the meeting was about but volunteered to attend during my rest day. At the meeting were senior management, personnel and the Unison Branch Secretary. The Branch Secretary earlier informed me the claimant did not need to attend the meeting. As the claimant had already agreed to attend with my line manager Mr Gornall, the claimant contacted Mr Gornall who confirmed the claimant was to attend the meeting.*

i) *Upon my arrival and as the claimant sat down Mr Farrell who also attended the meeting launched a verbal attack against me claiming the claimant was militant, a trouble maker and the claimant caused more trouble than all the shop stewards altogether. As the claimant was not informed of what the meeting was about the claimant was shocked following the sudden verbal attack. My response was one of disbelief and a heated defence followed. The Unison Branch Secretary and the claimant left the meeting for a short period for me to calm down and get my head around why the claimant was asked on my rest day to attend the meeting.*

j)   *The final straw was on the 14 of August 1997 during a JJC meeting when the claimant was accused of being a liar by Mr Gornall. The claimant was enraged and as the claimant got up to leave the JJC meeting the claimant grabbed my table to release my frustration after being called a liar. The claimant reported to my place of work that evening. This was the last shift the claimant completed as a security officer with St Helen's Council as the pressure of the treatment the claimant was receiving made me unable to attend work the following day. This was the start of my illness.*

k)   *Whilst on the sick the claimant went to work. In the rest room the claimant was having a chat with lads when the co-ordinator came into the room and said Mr Gornall said the claimant was not welcome here any more.*

l)   *Part of the harassment included requests for me to attend a meeting with the management whilst on the sick after the management were instructed not to call me into work as the claimant was very poorly.*

m)   *Whilst visiting St Helen's market, a market officer employed by the council invited me for a cup of tea in the market security room. As the claimant was leaving and passing through the market, a council security officer and the liaison officer on passing stopped for a chat. The clamant spoke to the security officer. The claimant was later informed that the liaison officer made an allegation that the claimant had grabbed the security officer around the neck and made threats to him. This allegation is totally false. The claimant was also informed that Mr Gornall wanted the security officer to agree that he had been grabbed as this was a sackable offence and they could sack the claimant.*

n)   *On the 1 of October 1997 at Dr Page's surgery I was advised to give up the Union Shop Steward's role as this was causing me with stress related issues. As the claimant was on the sick and not getting involved with Union matters my contact with my employers was to seek justice and the truth from my senior managers relating to the treatment the claimant received from my employer from when I became the elected GMB Work Place Shop Steward in 1996.*

o)   *A meeting was held in October 1998 (letter Ref: SS/YG) for which the claimant did not attend nor was the claimant notified of the outcome of the meeting from either my employer or UNISON representatives.*

p)   *The actions of St Helen's Council went far beyond acceptable standards of behaviour and the negotiations in the workplace context and amounted to a culture of bullying.*

Particulars of Negligence:

a)   *My employer knew of my stress related illness based on my doctor's notes from August 1997. My employer did not recognise any changes in my behaviour as stress related or offer counselling or help on a confidential basis.*

b)   *Knowing of my condition, my employer continued to bully and harass me as the workplace Shop Steward. One example is both the claimant and another colleague were sick at the same time. The claimant was sick for two weeks my colleague for five weeks. The claimant was selected to attend the Works Occupations Doctor; my colleague was not requested to attend.*

c) *My psychiatrist informed me during a home visit that in his opinion my senior management team were carrying out a psychological approach to wear me down.*

d) *The claimant was not approached to provide further evidence or given the opportunity to clarify my allegations against grievances the claimant had raised, 76 in total. In November 1998 the claimant raised Grievances and allegations of harassment to Mr P Mavers unaware that the claimant had an opportunity to do this at the meeting with Ms Sheila Samuels and Mr J Keegan in October 1998.*

e) *The claimant was not aware of any assistance or recommendations from my employer regarding improvements to my health and framework to return to work.*

f) *My employment was reinstated following a successful appeal. The clamant did not return to work as the conditions that caused my health deterioration were not addressed by my employer, nor did the clamant receive any payment from the employer.*

Particulars if Injury:

The claimant suffered from psychological illness, with schizophrenia like symptoms, stress and depression that required on-going support from the Community Psychiatric Nurse, Psychiatrist and local Doctor with on-going medication which is or a severity that rendered me as unfit for work.

Particulars of Financial Losses

Legal cost to date £8,745.13
Loss of home due to unable to pay the mortgage
Loss of earning for continuation employment as a security officer
Payments into my Private Pension Scheme

The claimant was to have attended an employment tribunal in 2000. Unfortunately and due to my being incoherent, my Father acting on my behalf, wrote a letter to the employment tribunal explaining why the claimant could not attend the hearing.

The claimant should have been made aware that there is a limitation issue in relation to proceeding.

Due to my state of health the claimant was also unaware of letters Ref: SS/SF and SS/YG dated 10 November until the claimant started to collate information to pursue a claim for compensation for the treatment the claimant received from my employer which contributed to my being ill when the claimant was the elected Workplace Shop Steward.

New Evidence

- *Inland Revenue letter date 27 September 2002 Ref: ECR/709/WA/WE states incorrect rates and failure to pay staff for working Bank Holidays.*
- *Independent pay assessment (Mitchell Charlesworth, Chartered Accountants) paid for by the majority of the security department employees indicated discrepancies. Refer to a Draft Discussions letter date 29 September 2003 para 1.8 to 1.9.*
- *Evidence of pay award grade 3 inclusive to grade 2 plus allowances (Feb 2008)*

Concealment

Whilst on the sick – the claimant received no communications by letter or telephone in relation to a letter dated 12 October (Ref: SS/SF) where Ms S Samuels was arranging a meeting with Mr J Keegan and Mr Peter Mavers on the 21 October.

Failure to communicate with me prevented me the opportunity to provide Ms S Samuels with my grievances and allegations of harassment. The letters between Ms S Samuels and Mr J Keegan were discovered by a barrister acting on my behalf in 2006.

AND the Claimant Claims:-

1.   *Damages exceeding £300,000.00.*
2.   *Interest thereon pursuant of Section 35A of the Supreme Court Act 1981.*
3.   *Costs.*

STATEMENT OF TRUTH

I believe that the facts stated in these Particulars of Claim are true.

Signed :   *Claimant*

Dated :

11. I then receive a letter dated 3 August 2010 as follows:

Her Majesty's Courts Service, London

Dear Sir/Madam

Re: Robert Steele (App) v St Helen's MBC (Res)

Thank you for your Appellant's Notice received on 3 August 2010.

This appeal has been allocated the reference number QB/2010/0442. Please use this reference number in all further correspondence. This appeal will be handled in the High Court Queen's Bench Appeals Office.

We return a copy of your Appellant's Notice for your own record, together with sealed copy (or copies) for service on the Respondent(s). It is your responsibility to effect service on the Respondent(s). Service by first class post is deemed to have taken place two working days after posting.

If your Appellant's Notice includes an application for permission to appeal, no other documents should be served on the Respondent(s) at this stage. The Respondent(s) need not take any action until such time as notification is given that permission to appeal has been given.

Please send to this office, the certificate of service required by CPR 52 PD 5.21 (1) and (2) as soon as possible.

I am sending your appeal papers to a judge at this stage. I will send you a copy of his / her Order in due course together with any other directions which may be made. Apart from service on the Respondent(s) (see above) you need take no further steps until you have heard further from this office. If your Appellant's Notice includes an application for a transcript at public expense or a stay, I will notify you of the judge's decision in due course.

Yours faithfully

Queen's Bench Appeals Office

12. I received an Order on 28 September 2010 from the Honourable Mr Justice Edwards-Stuart as follows:

*In the High Court of Justice Queen's Bench Division
High Court Appeal Centre Royal Courts of Justice
Order of Master Eyre dated 24 May 2010 Case number:
HQ10X01949 Appeal ref: QB/2010/0442*

BETWEEN
ROBERT STEELE
Claimant and Appellant
and

ST HELEN'S METROPOLITAN BOROUGH COUNCIL
Defendant and Respondent
ORDER

*Before the Honourable Mr Justice Edwards-Stuart sitting in
the Royal Courts of Justice Strand London WC2A 2LL on
the 27th day of September 2010.*

WITHOUT NOTICE

IT IS ORDERED THAT:

1.   *The Order of Master Eyre dated 24 May 2010 striking
     out the claim form is to be stayed pending the determina-
     tion of this application for permission to bring this
     appeal and, if permission is given, the appeal itself.*

2.   *Appellant's application for permission to bring this
     appeal out of time, and, subject to such permission
     being granted, for permission to appeal with a total
     time estimate of 1 hour, will be heard before a High
     Court Judge at the Royal Courts of Justice, Strand,
     London WC2A 2LL at 10:30am on a date to be fixed.*

3.   *If the Appellant wishes to seek permission at the same
     time to amend his claim in order to rely on section 33
     of the Limitation Act 1980, he must serve an amended*

Particulars of Claim on the Respondent and the court by no later than 4 pm on 13 October 2010, together with a witness statement in support of that application which must deal with the matters mentioned at section 33(3) of the Act (insofar as relevant).

4. *The appellant must file, within 35 days of service of this order, a full appeal bundle, which must contain the documents specified in PD 52 paras 5.6 and 5.6A (but noting that there is no judgment and therefore no transcript). The appeal bundle must be paginated and indexed, and must contain all relevant documents to enable the appeal court to understand the full circumstances giving rise to the appeal.*

5. *NOTE: This is not the hearing of the appeal. It is an application only for permission to appeal. If permission to appeal is granted, directions may be given for the hearing of the appeal.*

27 September 2010

I also received a letter dated 28 September 2010 with the Order as follows:

Her Majesty's Courts Service, London
Dear Sir/Madam

Re: Steele v St Helen's MBC

The hearing in accordance with paragraph 1 of the order of Mr Justice Edwards-Stuart dated 27 September 2010 has been listed for 15 October 2010.

Enquiries should be made, the day before after 2.30pm, via the Queen's Bench Office on telephone 020 7947 6010 to confirm the time and location of the hearing.

The attendance of the Appellant is required.

The Respondent(s) may attend or submit written representations before the hearing but will not usually be awarded the costs of doing so.

If a Respondent submits written representations or other written material it must be served on the Applicant (or his/her solicitor if any) at least two clear days before the hearing.

Special arrangements can be made to provide access to the Royal Courts of Justice for those with a disability. If you anticipate any difficulty in attending any hearing please let the Listing Office know as soon as possible.

Please acknowledge receipt of this letter by either fax or post to the above.
Yours faithfully

Appeals Office

I rang the court the day before as in the letter and I was told that the hearing had been cancelled. I told them I was in London and that I had not cancelled the hearing so I got a hearing the next day at 2pm.

13. I attended the hearing with Mr Justice Nicol and I took Mr Alan Bolger with me to get me to the hearing. The judge said to me that I'm not well and should he cancel the hearing? I told him I'm here now and I want to go ahead with the hearing.

Mr Justice Nicol listened to the Council's barrister with their defence. The barrister told the judge that I may not have had capacity till 2006. What I cannot understand is the Council got a Dr L Stephen O'Brien, Consultant Psychiatrist to do a report on me and he made it quite clear I had capacity throughout 1997 to 2006. He did say that there was a gap between 2001 and 2002. One could postulate that at the time he was too unwell to act.

In my opinion this does not prove incapacity. This d******d had never met me or discussed my illness with me and made an assertion on my state of capacity.

On another case in the County court in St Helen's on 8 July 2011, District Judge Hassall made a statement that if my case would have been for 1 million pounds, I would not have capacity to deal with it. He also stated even though my case is for £8,100, I lack capacity and will need to bring someone with me to act as a litigation friend and that my capacity may be a borderline case.

Again in the County court in St Helen's on 16 April 2012, District Judge Foden made a statement that he was concerned that I did not have capacity to deal with the same case District Judge Hassall was dealing with and District Judge Foden put the case back to 31 May 2012 where I took a litigation friend with me.

Between 8 July 2011 and 16 April 2012 on the same case I saw a District Judge Fitzgerald in the County court in St Helen's and he too showed concerns about my capacity and told me to bring someone with me, i.e. a litigation friend.

This is now three separate judges at different times have seen me and have all shown their concerns about my capacity status, yet on 15 October 2010, Mr Justice Nicol told me I had capacity since 2006, yet when we first went into the court room he was on about postponing the hearing because I was unwell, in my opinion another p***k. When I saw my psychiatrist, Dr Whally in 2011, he told me that capacity changes on a day-to-day basis and that other psychiatrists have their own opinions on capacity. I'm not a stupid person, I know my state of mind and since 1999 I have had capacity for around 5% of the time. I could have put this book together in one month, two months max and because of my capacity status, it's taken me two years to get to here.

Going back to Justice Nicol, when I was in the court room he mentioned the case against the lotto rapist and told me that the reason the limitation was lifted on Mrs A was because he knew what he was doing to cause Mrs A a psychiatric injury and I told him that St Helen's Council knew what they were doing to cause my psychiatric injury and the judge never commented whatsoever. Mr Justice Nicol threw my case out on capacity. If I would have had capacity on the day, I would have challenged him on the issues he had raised and also on the new evidence I presented to the courts in July 2010.

I told Mr Justice Nicol that I am taking my case to the Supreme Court and then to the European Court of Human Rights. I told him I had a letter from the European Court and he asked to see it, so I showed it to him. Again, he never commented on it.

Here is a copy of the letter from Clare Ovey dated 9 September 2010 as follows:

European Court of Human Rights
Application no. 21381/10 Steele v the United Kingdom

Dear Sir

I acknowledge receipt of your letter of 3 September 2010 and accompanying document. They have been included in the file concerning the above application.

The answers to all the questions in your recent letters are addressed in the enclosed 'Note for Guidare'. As you have not exhausted all your domestic remedies your case file has been opened prematurely at this Court. If you wish to pursue a case before the Court at a later stage you may do so.

Please note that no acknowledgment will be made as to the receipt of subsequent correspondence. No telephone enquiries either please. If you wish to be assured that your letter is actually received by the Court then you should send it by recorded delivery with a prepaid acknowledgment of receipt form.

Yours faithfully
For the Registrar

Clare Ovey
Head of Division

14. A few days later after the 15 October 2010, I received a letter from the High Court as follows:

IN THE HIGH COURT OF JUSTICE,
QUEEN'S BENCH DIVISION
Claim No. HQ10X01949, Appeal No. QB/2010/0442
Before The Honourable Mr Justice Nicol

Applicant   Mr Robert Steele

Respondent   St Helen's Metropolitan Borough Council

An Application was made by Appellant's Notice dated the 3 August 2010 by the Applicant in person for permission to appeal the Order of Master Eyre dated the 24 May 2010.

And Upon Hearing the Applicant in person and Counsel for the Respondent

And the Judge having read the written evidence filed

IT IS ORDERED that this oral application for permission to appeal is refused.

Dated: Friday, 15 October 2010

By the Court

15. When I got back from London, I rang the Supreme Court up to put my case into court as I thought when I was in court in London, I was in the Court of Appeal. I spoke to a fella on the

phone in the Supreme Court and I told him I had my case struck out of the Court of Appeal and he asked me 'were there three judges or one judge?' I said, 'one judge'. He said I cannot take my case any further in the British courts. Had there been three judges, then I could have appealed. I asked him could he put it in writing so I could send it to the European Court of Human Rights and he said I will have to write to the courts, so I did.

I received a reply from Master Eyre on 25 October 2010 as follows:

Date:	*25 October, 2010*
To:	*Mr Steele*
Re:	*Yourself v St Helen's HQ 10X01949*

Mr Steele – Your unsigned manuscript letter dated 21/101/0 has been put before me.

Whether or not you have any further recourse in this jurisdiction is simply a matter of the Civil Procedure Rules, and you must make your own investigation of those.

Yours sincerely

Telling someone with mental health problems and who lacks capacity to make your own investigations is one big joke so I took the word of the fella in the Supreme Court and I approached the European Court of Human Rights as I had exhausted all avenues in the British Courts.

CHAPTER THIRTEEN

1. I decided to write to the European Court of Human Rights to let them know what was going on. My brother wrote the letter on my behalf on 2 April 2010 as follows:

Clockface Road, St Helen's, Merseyside

Sirs

I am writing to you to seek help advice and justice in relation to my current state of health, which started in August 1997 whilst employed as a security officer for the St Helen's Borough Council in Merseyside, England.

My health started to deteriorate as a result of treatment from my employer whilst representing the workforce as a union representative for which at the time I was being victimised after discovering bad practices and the mis-management of payment to employees over a period of years. In 1998 whilst absent from work with severe stress I received a letter to attend a meeting with the Assistant Director and the HR Manager and was informed my employment had been terminated.

After talks between my Union, Unison and my local MP, my employment was reinstated following a successful appeal. I did not return to work as the conditions that caused my health deterioration were not addressed by my employer, nor did I receive any payments from my employer.

On 27 March 1999 I informed my employer that I was ready to return to work. On the 29 March I received a letter from the Assistant Director informing me he was not in a position to allow my return to work. I had no further contact with my employer until May 1999.

In May 1999 I had a home visit from Dr Fiona Page, the council's works doctor who recommended I should finish work under the Disability Discrimination Act 1995.

In September 1999 and without any further consultation, I received a letter informing me my employment had been terminated. In November I received a final payment from my employer of approximately £4,000. I assumed this was back pay, holiday pay etc. as I did not receive any pay between September and November 1999. My mental health worsened to such a state I was being cared for by my elderly and retired parents in their home at the above address in which I still reside, and am still being cared for, as I have not fully recovered.

Another appeals committee was arranged by Unison in 2000. At the time I was suffering from deep depression. I attended the appeal without any representation from Unison. The appeals committee told me I would not be reinstated.

An Industrial tribunal was arranged between Unison and my ex employer. I received a letter from the Industrial Tribunal stating the date and time of the tribunal. Unfortunately due to my state of health I could not attend the tribunal. From the date of receiving the letter to attend the tribunal, I have not had or received any correspondence relating to attending another tribunal.

During my recovery to my current state of health for which I am still under medication, I have spent thousands of pounds trying to pursue justice for the treatment and pressures I was put under by my employer from June 1996 to 2000.

I have been failed by solicitors and barristers, for whom, two solicitors and one barrister received payment.

I have exhausted all channels to have a fair and proper trial to state my case against the St Helen's Borough Council.

The advice I receive by letter or through telephone conversations revert me to the start point that is, I should either speak to Citizens Advice Bureau or seek advice from a Solicitor.

As a last resort I am appealing to the European Court of Human Rights to provide me with help and assistance in order to have a fair trial, relating to the conduct of my ex employer who I believe could have identified and assessed my health deterioration between 1996 and 2000 and continued treatment.

I hold a correspondence file containing letters since 1996.

Yours faithfully

Mr Robert Steele

2. I again wrote to the European Court of Human Rights on 3 April 2010 as follows:

Clockface Road, St Helen's, Merseyside

Dear Sirs

The letter dated 2 April 2010 was prepared by my brother on my behalf. I have also sent you a copy of my letter of claim that was rejected by the High Court before 15 October 2009. I have tried everything possible to amend the letter of claim dated 20 September 2009 and not one person will help me with this.

I contacted the Supreme Court on 18 March 2010 and I received a reply on 23 March 2010 from a Louise Mambro. I am sorry but the justice of this court cannot advise on or intervene in individual cases. I rang her to confront her on this statement on 26 March 2010. She tried to tell me this was the case then I confronted her on a case where the Law Lords lifted the limitation on a case in February 2008. She tried to wangle her way out of it. I told her I had seen this case on the Internet and I'm getting a copy of it. She told me I can complain to certain people and when I asked her for their contacts she told me she was in the middle of a meeting and had to go and put the phone down. I don't believe this for one minute.

I have sent you a copy of this case that was put on the Internet. I too have suffered psychiatric injury. Mine was caused by physical and mental abuse. The actions of St Helen's Council went far beyond acceptable standards of behaviour and the negotiations in the workplace context amounted to a culture of bullying. If I have any hope of getting my case into the High Court I have to get my letter of claim sorted and the other issue is the limitation problem sorted. The courts and the Government have been hostile to me in every way possible. The only way forward is for the European Court of Human Rights to intervene and give me my day in court. That, I fully deserve.

Yours faithfully

Mr R Steele

Ps I would like to come to Strasbourg and meet someone from the European Court of Human Rights and discuss my case with them. To discuss everything that's gone on over the last 14 years will take a good three days so a meeting would have to be arranged for three days. I need a meeting as a matter or urgency. Please read all correspondence thoroughly. Thank you.

3. I received a reply from the European Court of Human Rights on 19 April 2012 as follows:

European Court of Human Rights

Our Ref 21381/10

The Registry of the European Court of Human Rights has received your communication of 2 April 2010, from which it appears that you intend to lodge an application with the Court. Your file has been given the above number. You must refer to it in any further correspondence relating to this case.

In order to process your application more efficiently, please find enclosed a set of 10 barcode labels for your use exclusively in this case. If you send the Registry a letter or any other correspondence, please stick one of the barcode labels on the top right-hand corner of the first page of the correspondence.

You will also find enclosed a document containing a copy of the Convention and its Protocols and the official application form with an explanatory note for prospective applicants.

If, after a careful study of the foregoing documents you are satisfied that your case meets all the appropriate criteria, you should fill in the application form carefully, legibly and completely. It should be accompanied by copies of all relevant documents (unstapled and numbered pages), in particular any decisions of national courts or authorities which you wish to challenge before the Court. Please note that if you send original documents, they will not be returned to you by the Court.

You should return the completed application form not later than eight weeks from the date of the present letter. In other words, the date on which you send back the completed application form must not be later than 14 June 2010. Failure to comply with this time-limit will mean that it is the date of the submission of the completed application form rather than that of your first communication, which will be taken as the date of the introduction of the application. Your attention is drawn to the fact that it is the date of introduction that is decisive for compliance with the time-limit set out in Article 35 § 1 of the Convention (see para 18 in enclosed notes to applicants).

For safety reasons, any object sent to the Court without having being expressly requested by the Registry will be destroyed immediately together with the cover letter. If you consider sending documents other than on paper, you should first get in touch with the Registry.

The file opened in respect of your communication will be destroyed without being submitted for judicial decision, six months from the date of the present letter, unless the duly completed application form has been received in the meantime.

Enc: Application package

4. I again wrote to the European Court of Human Rights on 8 May 2010 as follows:

Clockface Road, St Helen's Merseyside

Dear Sirs

I wrote to you to help me get justice and I needed your help to put my letter of claim right. I have now managed to do this and my case is back in the High Court in England. If I lose my case, then I will be going to the court of appeal and then to the Supreme Court and if all fails, I will be coming back to you in the European Court of Human Rights.

I am sorry there has been a misunderstanding. I am not ready to apply to you yet but if all fails in the British courts, then

I will contact you again. Let's hope the British courts do the right thing and I get the justice I deserve.

Yours faithfully

Mr R Steele

5. I received a letter from the European Court of Human Rights on 21 May 2010 as follows:

European Court of Human Rights

Application no 21381/10
Steele v the United Kingdom

Dear Sir

I acknowledge receipt of your letter of 8 May 2010.

The above case fill will now be destroyed.

Yours faithfully
For the Registrar

Clave Ovey
Legal Secretary

6. I wrote again to the European Court of Human Rights on 25 June 2010 as follows:

Clockface Road, St Helen's, Merseyside

Dear Sirs

I am writing to you to see where I stand with the European Court of Human Rights. If I don't get a fair hearing in Britain and the reason for this is based on limitation. I was told by a lady in the European Court of Human Rights on the telephone I would get a fair hearing in your courts as I did not get a fair hearing in Britain. Can you please confirm this is the case?

I have also sent you a copy of a letter where the Law Lords lifted the limitation on a case 19 years old. I have put this to the courts that my case is a similar situation where I too have suffered a psychiatric injury. As at this moment in time, the courts have ignored my request to lift the limitation. I still have the court of appeal and the Supreme Court to go before coming to you for a hearing.

The reason for this letter is for you to confirm to me I will get a fair hearing in the ECHR even though I have a limitation issue in Britain. Hope to hear from you soon with a positive answer.

Yours faithfully

Mr R Steele

7. As I got no reply to my letter dated 25 June I wrote to the European Court of Human Rights again on 27 July 2010 as follows:

Clockface Road, St Helens, Merseyside

Dear Sirs

I wrote to you on 25 June 2010 and I have not had a reply to this letter. I have sent you a copy of the letter with this letter for you to reply if you did not receive the letter.

The reason I am now writing is to find out how much it costs to put my case into the European Court of Human Rights. At this moment in time, my case is in the court of appeal and if it's struck out on limitation, I am going to the Supreme Court, then I am coming to you for a hearing.

Can you please send me the cost of the court so I will have the money ready?

Yours faithfully

Mr R Steele

8. I received a reply to my two letters from a Clare Ovey on 20 August 2010 as follows:

European Court of Human Rights

Application no 21381/10
Steele v the United Kingdom

Dear Sir

I acknowledge receipt of your letters of 25 June 2010 and 27 July 2010, the contents of which have been noted.

I refer again to my letter of 21 May 2010.

Yours faithfully
For the Registrar

Clave Ovey
Legal Secretary

9. I again wrote to Clare Ovey of the European Court of Human Rights on 31 August 2010 as follows:

Clockface Road, St Helens, Merseyside

Dear Clare

I am writing to respond to your letter 20 August 2010. Firstly, you did not give me answers to my questions, this I would like answers to, the way you have replied to my letter.

The above file will now be destroyed. So what you are saying is I cannot have a hearing in the European Court of Human Rights. I have never asked for this file to be opened in the first place. I wrote to you for help and advice and at the end of the day I could end up coming to the ECHR to have my case hear in the ECHR.

I again have sent you copies of the letters dated 25-6-10 and 27-7-10. Could you please give me the answers to my questions? I will be writing to Jean Paul Costa and asking him why I am getting a negative response from the ECHR for me receiving justice for the wrong doings from my former employer.

I hope this time I will get a positive response to my questions.

Yours faithfully

Mr R Steele

10. I wrote to the European Court of Human Rights on 3 September 2010 telling them they have put my case into court too early. I received a reply from Clare Ovey on 9 September 2010 as follows:

European Court of Human Rights

Application no 21381/10
Steele v the United Kingdom

Dear Sir

I acknowledge receipt of your letter of 3 September 2010 and accompanying document. They have been included in the file concerning the above application.

The answers to all the questions in your recent letters are addressed in the enclosed 'Note for Guidare'. As you have not exhausted all your domestic remedies your case file has been opened prematurely at this Court. If you wish to pursue a case before the Court at a later stage you may do so.

Please note that no acknowledgment will be made as to the receipt of subsequent correspondence. No telephone enquiries either please. If you wish to be assured that your letter is actually received by the Court then you should send it by recorded delivery with a prepaid acknowledgment of receipt form.

Yours faithfully
For the Registrar

Clare Ovey
Head of Division

11. I again wrote to Clare Ovey on 8 November 2010 as follows:

Clockface Road, St Helen's, Merseyside

Dear Clare Ovey

I wrote to you on 28 October 2010. I am again requesting for the application form to put my case into the European Court of Human Rights. As of the 15 of October, my case had finished in the British courts. I have also written to Jean Paul Costa and I have sent you a copy of the letter I sent to him.

When you send me the application form, can you let me know how much it's going to cost for the court fees?

Yours faithfully

Mr R Steele

12. I again received a reply from the European Court of Human Rights on 16 November 2010 as follows:

European Court of Human Rights

Our Ref 66263/10

The Registry of the European Court of Human Rights has received your communication of 2 November 2010, from which it appears that you intend to lodge an application with the Court. Your file has been given the above number. You must refer to it in any further correspondence relating to this case.

In order to process your application more efficiently, please find enclosed a set of 10 barcode labels for your use exclusively in this case. If you send the Registry a letter or any other correspondence, please stick one of the barcode labels on the top right-hand corner of the first page of the correspondence.

You will also find enclosed a document containing a copy of the Convention and its Protocols and the official application form with an explanatory note for prospective applicants.

If, after a careful study of the foregoing documents you are satisfied that your case meets all the appropriate criteria, you should fill in the application form carefully, legibly and completely. It should be accompanied by copies of all relevant documents (unstapled and numbered pages), in particular any decisions of national courts or authorities which you wish to challenge before the Court. Please note that if you send original documents, they will not be returned to you by the Court.

You should return the completed application form by post not later than eight weeks from the date of the present letter.

*In other words, the date on which you send back the com-
pleted application form must not be later than 11 January
2011. Failure to comply with this time-limit will mean that it
is the date of the submission of the completed application
form rather than that of your first communication which will
be taken as the date of the introduction of the application.
Your attention is drawn to the fact that it is the date of introduction that is decisive for compliance with the time-limit
set out in Article 35 § 1 of the Convention (see para 18 in
enclosed notes to applicants).*

*For safety reasons, any object sent to the Court without
having being expressly requested by the Registry will be
destroyed immediately together with the cover letter. If you
consider sending documents other than on paper, you should
first get in touch with the Registry.*

*The file opened in respect of your communication will be
destroyed without being submitted for judicial decision, six
months from the date of the present letter, unless the duly
completed application form has been received in the meantime.*

Enc: Application package

13. I once again wrote to Clare Ovey on 6 December 2010 as
follows:

Clockface Road, St Helen's, Merseyside

Dear Clare Ovey

*I have now received my application form for the European
Court of Human Rights but I have not had a reply from you
telling me how much the legal costs are.*

*I am getting help filling in the application form from the
British Legion next Monday. I have addressed the envelope*

to you and there should be three files arrive at the same time. When you receive them could you please let me know you have received my three files and my application form? At the same time, can you let me know how much I need to send a cheque for and who to address it to, ie. pay ECHR one thousand pounds.

My friend Alan Bolger is going to write to Jean Paul Costa. He will be sending you a copy of that letter.

Yours faithfully
Mr R Steele

I would also like to know how I go about issuing a subpoena to 8 people to court as I want to put them on the witness stand and cross examine them.

14. I wrote to Clare Ovey again on 30 December 2010 as follows:

Clockface Road, St Helens, Merseyside

Dear Clare Ovey

As you are the Head of the Division for the European Court of Human Rights, I have sent you all my correspondence to Jean Paul Costa, the head person of the European Court of Human Rights. As you are aware, I have sent the 8 people I am subpoenaing to court letters out to them and I have sent you their names and contact addresses to contact them personally when a date has been arranged. As you were made aware, I had to be the first person to contact them as I have waited 13 years for that day.

All I am now waiting for is the date of the hearing as I will be staying at Holtel Aux Trois Roses, 7 Ruede, Zurich, Strasbourg and I will be flying from Liverpool to Amsterdam and changing at Amsterdam to Strasbourg. All I am waiting for is the dates to book my hotel and flights. I will be bringing Mr Alan Bolger with me to act as my chaperone as he took me to London to court as I am not well enough to get there on my own and he would also like to have a say on this matter.

It is going to take me more than a day to cross-examine Mr Michael Gornall and Mr Brendan Farrell and the other six will take no longer than several hours. I will need three days to cross-examine them and for me to give evidence. I am booking 8 days in Strasbourg as I will be celebrating my victory of justice as I know 100% my case is condemning against the 8 people I am subpoenaing to court. Thank God we have the European Court to allow me to have my Human Rights.

Can you please push my case forward as I would like a hearing by October 2011? I would like to thank yourself and Jean Paul Costa for listening to me.

Yours faithfully

Mr R Steele

Ps The book I told you I am writing is going to be headed 'My 14 Year Battle for Justice' and you know exactly where the proceeds are going.

I also sent the names of the eight people I was subpoenaing to court with this letter as follows:

Here are the names and contact addresses I will be subpoenaing to the European Court of Human Rights:

Clive Portman, Audit Commission, 2ⁿᵈ Floor, Aspinall House, Aspinall Close, Middlebrook, Bolton BL6 6QQ; John Vis, Audit Commission, First Floor, Block 4, The Heath Business & Technical Park, Runcorn WA7 4QF;

Dr L Stephen O'Brien, MB CHB FRC PSYCH, Consultant Psychiatrist, Ferndale Unit, University Hospital, Aintree Hospital, Lower Lane, Liverpool L9 7AL;
Inspector Stephen Lowe 8403, Merseyside Police, PO Box 59, Liverpool L69 1JD;
Mr Peter Mavers, Assistant Director, Hardshaw Brook Depot, Parr Street, St Helen's, Merseyside WA9 1JR;
Mr Michael Gornall, Head of Security, Hardshaw Brook Depot, Parr Street, St Helen's, Merseyside WA9 1JR;
Carole Hudson, Chief Executive, Town Hall, Corporation Street, St Helen's WA10 1HP;
Mr Brendan Farrell, Head of Human Resources, Town Hall, Corporation Street, St Helen's WA10 1HP

15. I again received a letter from Clare Ovey on 3 January 2011 as follows:

European Court of Human Rights

Application no 66263/10
Steele v the United Kingdom

Dear Sir

I acknowledge receipt of your documents, received at the Court on 20 December 2010, the contents of which have been noted.

Please note that to date you have not completed and returned your application form. In order for the Court to process your case you must return the application form before 31 January 2011.

Yours faithfully
For the Registrar

Clare Ovey
Legal Secretary

16. I again wrote to Clare Ovey on 6 January 2011 as follows:

Clockface Road, St Helen's, Merseyside

Dear Clare Ovey

I know I have been bombarding you and Jean Paul Costa with letters. The reason for this is I am determined to get justice in the European Court of Human Rights. If you have not already looked at my three files, would you please look at them and you will see how massive and complex case it is. I don't tell lies, nor do I exaggerate the truth.

I first felt unwell in December 1996. With the behaviour of my employer things got so bad I had to go off sick in August 1997 with stress. My employer refused my plea to sort out the problems for me to return to a healthy environment and decided to terminate my employment in 1998 because the two people I was complaining about were staying in their employment. I was reinstated because of this. I stayed on the sick as my employer still refused to sort out the problems that made me ill in the first place. I tried to return to work in March 1999 and my employer refused to let me back into my workplace and again terminated my employment in November 1999.

Around this time I became seriously ill where I was sleeping for 23 hours a day and I stopped talking. This went on for three years. My health did gradually improve slightly over the years and in November 2009 I started to deteriorate again and in September 2010 I had an assessment and I'm suffering with a severe depression. I am very worried how I am going to cope physically, mentally and financially when my parents are no longer here to care for me. My body is physically and mentally drained. I have no motivation in my body whatsoever and I have been like this for the last 11½ years.

I am not being greedy but I'm being realistic and I will be claiming for my loss of earnings, loss of life and care and I will also be claiming for my personal losses because of my illness. I have done everything possible to convince you to give me justice, it's now in yours and Jean Paul Costa's hands to let me have my day in court.

After the way I have been treated by my ex employer, no-one deserves justice more than me. They have totally destroyed my life and they need to be brought to justice. You are my last chance.

Yours faithfully
Mr R Steele

17. I wrote to Clare Ovey again on 12 January 2011 as follows:

Clockface Road, St Helen's, Merseyside

Dear Clare Ovey

Thank you for your letter dated 3 January 2011. I am very concerned that you have not received my application form as it was sent on the 13 December 2010 with my files you say you have received. I sent the three files and the application form in separate envelopes and all four had to be signed for.

I rang the European Court up yesterday and she told me they had received a letter on 6 January 2011 and I asked her was it my application form and she said 'possibly'. I told her I need to know if it's my application form as I have only got till the 31 January 2011 to get it into court. She said 'have a good day' and said 'goodbye' and put the phone down. Could you please let me know if it was my application form you received?

I want to win my case more than ever as my great nephew has been admitted to the Childrens Alder Hey Hospital in

Liverpool with Leukaemia. This is the hospital I am trying to raise several million pounds for. As you can understand, I am now more determined than ever.

Yours faithfully

Mr R Steele

18. I received a reply from Clare Ovey on 17 January 2011 as follows:

European Court of Human Rights

Application no 66263/10
Steele v the United Kingdom

Dear Sir

I acknowledge receipt of your letter of 13 December 2010, with enclosures, including a completed application form.

The Court will deal with the case as soon as practicable on the basis of the information and documents submitted by you. The proceedings are primarily in writing and you will only be required to appear in person if the Court invites you to do so. You will be informed of any decision taken by the Court.

You should inform me of any change in your address. Furthermore, you should, of your own motion, inform the Court about any major developments regarding the above case, and submit any further relevant decisions of the domestic authorities.

Please note that no acknowledgment will be made as to the receipt of subsequent correspondence. No telephone enquiries either please. If you wish to be assured that your letter is actually received by the Court then you should send it by recorded delivery with a prepaid acknowledgment of receipt form.

Yours faithfully
For the Registrar

Clave Ovey
Legal Secretary

19. I again wrote to Clare Ovey on 2 April 2011 as follows:

Clockface Road, St Helen's, Merseyside

Dear Clare Ovey

I sent you the first seventy-three pages of my book. I have also sent them to Jean Paul Costa to read. There have been several alterations to those pages. I have sent you a memory stick with one hundred and sixty-six pages on it. Will you please copy them twice and send a copy to Jean Paul Costa and both of you read my part of the book very carefully and you will see exactly what has been going on in St Helen's Council. There is still some way to finishing my book and I still have another 29 personal grievances to add to it.

I am taking some time out on the book as my anxiety is running high re-living my problems and is causing me sleep deprivation. When things settle down, I will send yourself and Jean Paul Costa the next stage of my book. I do hope you understand my efforts for getting justice. Once you read my book you will see I fully deserve it.

Once you have copied my memory stick, can you please return it to me at the above address?

Thank you for your time.

Yours faithfully

Mr R Steele

20. I again wrote to Clare Ovey on 17 April 2011 as follows:

Clockface Road, St Helen's, Merseyside

Dear Clare Ovey

I sent you a memory stick two weeks ago. If you have finished with it could you please return it to me? I hope yourself and Jean Paul Costa read what's on the memory stick. The personal grievances I have put on it are only half of them, there are another 29 to add to the memory stick.

Getting a hearing in the ECHR will change my life and the book I am writing. I am hoping to sell one million copies of £10 profit on each book giving a total of ten million pounds. To build a wider market to sell the book, I am donating two million pounds to 5 charities as follows – Royal Society for the Prevention of Cruelty to Animals, National Society for the Prevention of Cruelty to Children, Cancer Research (Clatterbridge Hospital), Help the Heroes (for the armed forces) and the Childrens Alder Hey Hospital in Liverpool.

Winning my case in the ECHR will greatly improve my book sales as people will want to read how I managed to seek justice after 15 years. At the end of the day, it would have been my sheer determination in getting justice that made it happen. I am relying on yours and Jean Paul Costa's support in making my dreams happen.

Yours faithfully

Mr R Steele

21. I again wrote to Clare Ovey on 25 April 2011 as follows:

Clockface Road, St Helen's, Merseyside

Dear Clare Ovey

I have sent you a copy of a leaflet from a Mr David Lawrenson who is hoping to be elected as a local councillor for St Helen's. As you can see he has suffered similar problems with St Helen's Council and if you look in my blue folder at grievance number 41, pages one and two, you will see I also received a harassment order to shut me up.

I sent yourself and the Sun newspaper, a memory stick. The Sun newspaper never received it so I am sending you a CD with my book on it. Once again, could you please read it all and give a copy to Jean Paul Costa as I find this relevant to yourselves making a decision in my favour for my case in the ECHR.

There is a total of 166 pages on the CD and like I have already stated, I have another 29 personal grievances to add to my book and total of around 150 pages to completing my book.

I do hope you find David Lawrenson's leaflet of interest as I am not the only person who has been in conflict with St Helen's Council.

Yours faithfully

Mr R Steele

22. Clare Ovey wrote to me on 26 April 2011 as follows:

European Court of Human Rights

Application no 66263/10

Steele v the United Kingdom

I write to inform you that on 19 April 2011 the European Court of Human Rights, sitting in a single-judge formation (VA de Gaetano), decided to declare inadmissible your application lodged on 2 November 2010 and registered under the above-mentioned number. The Court found that the requirements of the Convention had not been met.

The Court found that domestic remedies had not been exhausted as required by Article 35 § 1 of the Convention, since you had failed to raise in time – either in form or in substance – in an appeal to domestic courts, lodged in accordance with the applicable procedural requirements, the complaints made to the Court.

This decision is final and not subject to any appeal to either the Court, including its Grand Chamber, or any other body. You will therefore appreciate that the Registry will be unable to provide any further details about the single judge's deliberations or to conduct further correspondence relating to its decision in this case. You will receive no further documents from the Court concerning this case and, in accordance with the Court's instructions, the file will be destroyed one year after the date of the decision.

The present communication is made pursuant to Rule 52A of the Rules of Court.

Yours faithfully
For the Court

Clare Ovey
Head of Division

23. Alan Bolger wrote to Clare Ovey on 6 May 2011 on my behalf as follows:

Redruth Avenue, Laffak, St Helens

Dear Clare Ovey (Head of Division)

I am writing to you on behalf of Mr Robert Steele residing at Clockface Road, St Helen's, Merseyside.

I have been a good friend of Robbie's since I met him when he commenced work on 8 June 1992 as a work colleague.

I knew how he was when he was well and I know how much damage St Helen's MBC have done to his health over the last 15 years. I can tell you now Robbie would not take sides or have a bad word said about anyone and is the most honest person I have ever known.

All Robbie has done is stand up for his members to get them justice against the bullies in St Helen's Council. I have seen today 6-5-11, your letter dated 26-4-11. I can tell you that Robbie has been knocked for six and his health has deteriorated dramatically since I saw him a few days ago.

It's just like when he appeared at my home in 2002 after disappearing for three years. I am finding it very difficult to have a conversation with him again, it's like you have knocked back his recovery by nine years.

I am now going to stand up for Robbie. As you have stated, the court found that domestic remedies had not been exhausted as required by Article 35 of the Convention. I can tell you, you and the single judge VAde Gaetano are wrong. I attended with Robbie to the court of appeal when Robbie was told by the judge he could not take his case any further in the British courts.

Robbie told the judge he had a letter from the European Court of Human Rights, the letter being from yourself dated

9-9-10. The judge asked to see it and read it. The judge knew Robbie's next move was the European Court of Human Rights. Copy sent for your attention.

Robbie also contacted the court on 21-10-10 and was told by them his case could go no further in the British courts. Either the British courts have lied to Robbie or you have got it wrong.

I personally think you should look at his case again as it states European Court of Human Rights and you have denied him his human rights for all the wrong reasons.

If the British courts have told him his case can go no further in Britain, then Robbie has to accept that and his next step is the European Court of Human Rights and as far as Robbie was aware, all domestic remedies had been exhausted. Everyone in Britain and yourselves in the European courts who have dealt with Robbie have destroyed an innocent man's life. All he ever wanted was for someone to listen to him and put right all the misdemeanours that were occurring in St Helen's MBC. Had this been the case, Robbie would still have his home, his job and his health.

Because of all the corruption he has got nothing. He has told me he doesn't know what he's going to do when his parents are no longer here to look after him. Please look at this case again and do the right thing and give Robbie his day in court. You know as well as I do you've got it wrong. Remember his human rights too.

He has also told me he has sent you a CD disc with a copy of his book on it. Try and find time to read it and you will see for yourself why he's like he is. Please re-consider your decision for his sake.

Not only has he experienced problems with the High Court and the court of appeal, he has also had a bad experience with the County court. Seven people have taken advantage of Robbie's illness and have received money from him. He has taken two people to the County court and they have no powers to recover his money. Between the seven mentioned people, they owe him over £18,000 that he will never see again. I find these people despicable taking advantage of someone with severe mental health problems.

Robbie has never been in it for the money but for justice. Had he wonhis case he was trying to raise ten million pounds for five charities giving them two million each. This is typical of the person Robbie is. Your wrong decision is not only denying Robbie his justice but also denying him the chance to raise for the five charities. Like I have already stated, Robbie's health has deteriorated rapidly because – (1) you have totally got the decision totally wrong or (2) the British courts have lied to Robbie which has led to this problem.

The evidence is there for you to do the right thing and change the decision that will be the right thing to do under the circumstances. A letter was also sent from myself to Jean Paul Costa on 6 December 2010, copy sent.

Yours sincerely

Alan Bolger

Cc Jean Paul Costa

24. I received a reply from Clare Ovey on 28 July 2011 as follows:

European Court of Human Rights

Application no. 66263/10 (inadmissible)

Steele v the United Kingdom

Dear Sir

I acknowledge receipt of your letter of 6 May 2011.

I should remind you that the European Convention on Human Rights does not contain any provision for appeal against a decision by which the European Court of Human Rights has declared an application inadmissible. The Court's decision declaring your application inadmissible is therefore final.

I should also point out that, by virtue of Article 35 § 2 (b) of the Convention, the Court could not deal with any further application by you which was substantially the same as the above application and which contained no relevant new information.

Yours faithfully
For the Registrar

Clare Ovey
Head of Division

The British courts cost me my day in the European Court of Human Rights. If they had been reasonable with me this would never have happened.

25. I wrote to the following people on 13 December 2010 telling them I was subpoenaing them to the European Court of Human Rights as follows:

Clockface Road, St Helen's, Merseyside

Dear Mr Gornall / Dear Mr Farrell

I am writing to you to let you know I am subpoenaing eight people to court in the European Court of Human Rights and guess what, you're one of the eight people.

I will be putting you on the witness stand and it will be me personally cross-examining you and if you continue to tell lies, I am going to ask the judge to do you for contempt of court and perverting the course of justice and that is a prison sentence. You have had plenty of warning to get your passport ready. Not turning up to a subpoena is also a prison sentence.

Merry Christmas, see you in Strasbourg in the New Year. Happy New Year from Rob Steele.

Yours faithfully

Mr R Steele

Clockface Road, St Helen's, Merseyside

Dear Mr Mavers

I am writing to you to let you know I am subpoenaing eight people to court in the European Court of Human Rights and guess what, you're one of the eight people.

I will be putting you on the witness stand and it will be me personally cross-examining you and if you wish to tell lies to protect your colleagues, then I will ask the judge to do you for contempt of court and perverting the course of justice. As you being a magistrate, you will know this is a prison sentence. You have had plenty of warning to get your passport ready. Again, you will know not turning up to a subpoena is a prison sentence.

Merry Christmas, see you in Strasbourg in the New Year. Happy New Year from Rob Steele.

Yours faithfully

Mr R Steele

Clockface Road, St Helen's, Merseyside

Dear Mrs Hudson

I am writing to you to let you know I am subpoenaing eight people to court in the European Court of Human Rights and guess what, you're one of the eight people.

I will be putting you on the witness stand and it will be me personally cross examining you and if you wish to continue to tell lies then I will ask the judge to do you for contempt of court and perverting the course of justice and that is a prison sentence. You have had plenty of warning to get your passport ready. Not turning up is also a prison sentence. There is no point going to lover boy about this letter because Steve Lowe would have received his the same time as you.

Merry Christmas, see you in Strasbourg in the New Year. Happy New Year from Rob Steele.

Clockface Road, St Helen's, Merseyside

Dear Steve Lowe

I am writing to you to let you know I am subpoenaing eight people to court in the European Court of Human Rights. Guess what, you're one of the eight people.

I will be putting you on the witness stand and it will be me personally cros- examining you. I 100% remember everything you and that DC said to me and if you don't tell the truth, I am going to ask the judge to do you for contempt of court and perverting the course of justice. You being an ex DI will know that is a prison sentence. You have had plenty of warning to get your passport ready. Not turning up to a subpoena is also a prison sentence.

Merry Christmas, see you in Strasbourg in the New Year. Happy New Year from Rob Steele.

Yours faithfully

Mr R Steele

Clockface Road, St Helen's, Merseyside

Dear Clive Portman / Dear John Vis

I am writing to you to let you know I am subpoenaing eight people to court in the European Court of Human Rights. Guess what, you're one of the eight people.

I will be putting you on the witness stand and it will be me personally cross-examining you and if you continue to protect St Helen's Council with lies, then I am going to ask the judge to do you for contempt of court and perverting the course of justice and that is a prison sentence. You have had plenty of warning to get your passport ready. Not turning up to a subpoena is also a prison sentence.

Merry Christmas, see you in Strasbourg in the New Year.
Happy New Year from Rob Steele.
Clockface Road, St Helen's, Merseyside

Dear Dr Stephen O'Brien

I am writing to you to let you know I am subpoenaing eight people to court in the European Court of Human Rights. Guess what, you're one of the eight people.

I will be putting you on the witness stand and it will be me personally cross examining you and if you don't tell the truth and lie, I am going to ask the judge to do you for contempt of court and perverting the course of justice and that is a prison sentence. You have had plenty of warning to get your passport ready. Not turning up to a subpoena is also a prison sentence.

Merry Christmas, see you in Strasbourg in the New Year. Happy New Year from Rob Steele.

I really thought I was going to have my day in court in the European Courts of Human Rights but Clare Ovey, Head of Division, made sure I did not with the help of the British courts. I felt I had been set up by the British courts.

26. In January I was talking to my Community Psychiatric nurse, Suzanne Hall and in conversation she mentioned I had seen a private psychiatrist before Christmas. I said 'no, why should I have then?'

Suzanne told me Dr Raj, in-patient consultant received a phone call from an unknown consultant psychiatrist. He felt Robert was mentally unwell. Dr Raj conveyed this to Dr Whalley who then spoke with Suzanne who confirmed no noted concerns with Robert's mental health. Here is the EOL activity record report from Suzanne Hall:

Eol Activity Record Report

Team:	*CMHT South*
Service user name:	*Robert Steele*
NHS number:	*PAS Code:*
SU ID:	*D.O.B:*

Activity ID:	*Appointment ID:*
Date added: 24 Dec 2010 13:49	*Booking event ID:*
Added by: Suzanne Hall	
Practitioner name: Suzanne Hall	
Intervention: Other	
Activity date: 24 December 2010	

Activity type: Telephone contact with other proxy
Borough: St Helen's   *Location seen: Other*
Outcome: Took place
Service user status: Domiciliary / home visit
App'tment scheduled time: 0:00
Time service user arrived: 0:00
Time activity started: 0:00   *Time activity ended: 0:00*
Individual or group: Individual
Summary of clinical notes:
T/c from Dr Whalley. Informing me that he'd received a phone call concerning concerns raised by a private psychiatrist that Robert has recently seen regarding his court case.
I confirmed with Dr Whalley that I had no new concerns and see Robert every 2 weeks for his depot and that he is due to attend clinic on 29/12/10.
The team are aware Robert is an angry man with long-term fixed beliefs and he will subjectively report issues for secondary gain to add weight to his long term feud with his ex-employer.

I told Suzanne that I wrote to a consultant psychiatrist, Stephen O'Brien just before Christmas telling him I was subpoenaing him to court. This is the psychiatrist that wrote a report for Weightmans Solicitors on behalf of St Helen's Council stating I had capacity and when he thinks he is to give evidence in the European Court of Human Rights he told my psychiatrist that I am mentally unwell. This fella wants his cake and eat it.

CHAPTER FOURTEEN

1. I decided to write to the head person of the European Court of Human Rights, Jean Paul Costa on 28 October 2010 as follows:

Clockface Road, St Helen's, Merseyside

Dear Jean Paul Costa

I am writing to you to see if you will answer my questions. I have taken my case to the top as I cannot take it any further in Britain. My case was struck out on limitation of time. Will this affect my case being heard in the European Court of Human Rights?

As I suffer from mental illness caused by my employer 13 years ago and I need to seek justice I rang the European Court of Human Rights up a few years ago and a lady told me I would get a fair hearing in the ECHR as I have not been given one in Britain. I also need to know how much it costs to put my case into the ECHR. I have tried a number of organisations to help me fill the form in to the ECHR and many people told me they cannot help me. I am going to need help filling it in. I'm going to have to fill it in myself and you will have to be patient with me as I don't know what I'm doing.

I do need my case being heard, as I should be working and earning £500 a week. Because my employer made me ill and I'm claiming sick pay, I only get £78 a week. Because I lost my job I also had to sell my house because I could no longer afford it.

The people I reported for bullying, harassing, threatening and victimising are still in the job earning £30,000 plus and

£50,000 plus. I also reported them for embezzling their clients and there was a cover up and it was me who lost their job. Now it's time for the ECHR to give me justice. My case was struck out for the last time on 15 October 2010 and I was told I cannot take it any further in the British courts. I have sent you a copy of the conclusion I have written out laying out the reasons why you should give me a hearing in your court. I will be sending a file with the summary of facts and chronology of events to the ECHR with my application form.

Hope to hear from you soon.

Yours faithfully

Mr R Steele

2. Because I never received a reply from Jean Paul Costa, I decided to write to him again on 22 November 2010 as follows:

Clockface Road, St Helen's, Merseyside

Dear Jean Paul Costa

I wrote to you on 28 October 2010 and I also wrote to Clare Ovey the same day and I also wrote to her on 8 November 2010 and I have not had a reply from either of you.

I can tell you I have over 57 issues concerning myself with St Helen's Council and I have over 60 grievances as my time as Shop Steward. All these issues need to be addressed in the ECHR as none were dealt with in the British courts. I also challenged the British courts on limitation where they lifted the limitation after 19 years. The Supreme Court told me it was lifted because it was a special case so I wrote back and told them mine was a special case. Then I was told at the Court of Appeal that the limitation was lifted because he knew what he was doing and I told the judge St Helen's Council knew what they were doing and both times I was ignored.

A Councillor, Wallace Ashcroft, wrote to the District Audit and told them it's a massive and complex case and is too big for him to handle. The District Audit allied with St Helen's Council and did nothing. Not one person in Britain has sat down with me and discussed the problems I was trying to seek justice for. This is no ordinary case; this is a special case that needs a court hearing.

I am being cared for by my elderly parents and if anything happens to them I have serious problems. I have been singled out as a number of people would lose their jobs had this gone to court or been dealt with by St Helen's Council. I had a lovely home and spent thousands of pounds doing it up and I left it fully furnished when I walked away from it. I have sent you photocopies of it.

Once I get to the ECHR and win my case I will have enough damages to live comfortably for the rest of my life and to have the money for my care for the rest of my life. I will be writing a book about my ordeal and hope to make several million pounds and I am giving it to the childrens Alder Hey Hospital in Liverpool as I don't like seeing children ill and hopefully the money will save many lives.

I hope you will send me the forms to fill in for my day in the ECHR very soon.

Yours faithfully

Mr R Steele

3. Alan Bolger wrote to Jean Paul Costa on my behalf on 6 December 2010 as follows:

Redruth Avenue, Laffak, St Helen's, Merseyside

Dear Jean Paul Costa

I know Robbie has written to you on several occasions and you have not replied to his letters. Robbie will have sent Clare Ovey his application form, plus three files regarding his case.

I am asking you personally to please look at these files and see for yourself that the justice system in Britain has let him down badly. I personally have written to the law lords asking for Robbie's limitation to be lifted as of Mrs 'A' in the lotto rapist was lifted after 19 years. They replied saying that was a special case. Robbie has suffered in the same way as her and therefore, his case is a special case.

I went to the Court of Appeal with Robbie in London. The judge told Robbie the reason the limitation was lifted was because he knew what he was doing. Robbie told the judge that St Helen's Council knew what they were doing. The two reasons for lifting the limitation fell in the same category as Robbie's case but they ignored the situation.

I have known Robbie 18 years and I can vouch for him, he would absolutely help anyone out. When Robbie first became ill, he had to sell his house as he could no longer live or many to live on his own. He also had several thousands in the bank. In 2006 people began taking advantage of his illness and kindness. They borrowed sums of money from him and promised to pay him back; unfortunately once they got the money they never paid him back. I know he is owed the sum of £18,000 at this moment in time and only one person is paying it back out of six people. Until his illness took hold, Robbie never loaned money to anyone. Had Robbie not become ill and was still living in his own house in Liverpool, he would never have loaned out any monies at all.

St Helen's Council have to be held responsible for all this and when Robbie goes to court, any outstanding debt St Helen's Council should be responsible for paying. As if they had not caused his illness, he would never have done this.

I enclose two references, one from the Army and one from Mr Mike Gornall, his line manager. I hope these will show you what type of person he is. I have also enclosed copies of a letter from myself and my wife, in fact my wife has written this letter on my behalf as my handwriting is unreadable. She has also re-written a letter dated 17 October 2006. These letters will show you just how much damage St Helen's Council have done to Robbie's life.

Robbie needs his day in court because until he gets that, he is never going to get better. I believe there is a possibility that the psychological damage done, he will suffer from for the rest of his life. He is definitely not the Robbie I first met back in 1992.

I am asking you sincerely to lead Robbie's campaign and get him his day in court and finally the justice he so deserves.

Yours sincerely

Alan Bolger

4. My father decided to write to Jean Paul Costs on 15 December 2010 as follows:

Clockface Road, St Helen's, Merseyside

Dear Sirs

I am most concerned about my son Robert currently seeking support from the Court of Human Rights.

He has for some years, been trying to get members of St Helen's Council and the District Auditor to investigate certain aspect of the corruption which he observed whilst he was employed by St Helen's Council which came to no avail.

Robert did however, on several occasions, secure a meeting with the Leader of St Helen's Council, Councillor Mike Doyle. On one occasion, which I also attended, Councillor Doyle listened attentively to Robert's allegation of embezzlement re. Pets Corner not having the service it was paying for, which Councillor Doyle admitted he had heard about from another source, unknown to Robert.

Councillor Doyle went further and admitted that much of Robert had told him would appear to have involved some senior members of the Council. He also promised that he could have a panel of six Councillors to have an open debate with the management and Robert.

A Detective Inspector Steve Lowe, the District Auditors and Robert's Trade Union appear to have allied themselves with the Council against Robert, together with the Chief Executive, Carole Hudson and three Council leaders; Mike Doyle, Marie Rimmer and Brian Spencer and two Assistant Directors; Peter Moffat and Peter Mavers.

All failed to sit down with Robert and Management and thrash out Robert's allegations.

All the above led Robert to suffer a severe health breakdown and severe depression, changing him from a very active, healthy individual to someone with lack of motivation, chronic fatigue and tiredness, disordered sleep pattern and chronic anxiety.

Since late 1999, we his parents, now in our late seventies and early eighties, have been his registered carers and our main concern is what happens to our son when we are no longer here to care for him.

For the first time since 1999, in August 2009, Robert felt confident he could put his case together, with help from his brother, but within weeks he had burned himself out again.

His brother continued to put his files together until December 2010 when they were completed.

Robert had help to fill his application form in for the European Court of Human Rights by Royal British Legion Care Workers but found some sections too complicated to complete. I fervently hope that this will have no effect on Robert seeking justice.

I remain,
Yours sincerely

JP Steele

Note: *This letter's gone to Clare Ovey of the European Court of Human Rights and to Jean Paul Costs, Head Person of European Court of Human Rights*

5. I wrote once again to Jean Paul Costa on 25 December 2010 as follows:

Clockface Road, St Helen's, Merseyside

Dear Jean Paul Costa

You would have received letters from Mr Alan Bolger and my father, Mr John Steele who have written on my behalf. I am desperate to get justice and put my case to bed once and for all so I can try and re-build some sort of life. The damage St Helen's Council have done to my health is quite possibly permanent.

I have written to 8 people prematurely and told them I am subpoenaing them to the European Court of Human Rights. I did this as I wanted to be the first person to inform them as I have waited 13 years for this day and I 100% believe you will give me my day in court.

The British courts are a joke and have not been honest with me, nor have they listened to what I have told them. Clare Ovey would have received my files on my case and if you read them you will see for yourself how big my case is and the evidence is there to back it up. I want to get the eight people on the witness stand and cross examine them to prove they have all set me up and destroyed my life. I have been used as a scapegoat to protect officers of the council for corruption and alleged embezzlement. All the issues I have reported and have on file have been dealt with and introduced illegally.

Since I have become ill, I have spent thousands of pounds on cars and have lent thousands of pounds to people. This is something I have never done till I became ill. I have lost in the region of £90,000 and I fully blame St Helen's Council for the change in my behaviour. I have also lost £50,000 in the sale of my house. I have sent you photographs in an earlier letter showing you the high quality of life I once lived. Since September 1999 I have had no quality of life whatsoever. I pray to God that you give me my day in court and I get the justice I deserve.

As a reward for my justice I am going to write a book on my time with St Helen's Council and all my problems on the road to justice and all the proceeds are to go to the childrens Alder Hey Hospital for sick children in Liverpool.

Will you please reply to this letter and I am also sending a copy to Clare Ovey and I hope she will write to me to confirm she has received my three files. The eight people

I want to cross-examine need to be brought to justice. This is how I spent my Christmas day grovelling for help.

Hope to hear from you soon.

Yours faithfully

Mr R Steele

6. I wrote again to Jean Paul Costs and Clare Ovey on 13 February 2011 as follows:

Clockface Road, St Helen's, Merseyside

Dear Jean Paul Costa / Clare Ovey

Before you decide on the outcome of my case, I have sent you the first 43 pages of my book and when the next lot are typed up I will send them on to you. Please take it home and read it in your own time as it is a true story. There are about eight swear words in it. I cannot change them as it's a true story and they are facts.

I hope you both realise why I deserve a hearing in your court.

Yours faithfully

Mr R Steele

7. I wrote again to Jean Paul Costs and Clare Ovey on 14 March 2011 as follows:

Clockface Road, St Helen's, Merseyside

Dear Jean Paul Costa / Clare Ovey

I am sorry for taking so long to send the next part of my book, unfortunately my depression got worse and I had to rest. I should have part three and four done by April so I will send them as soon as possible. I do hope you find it interesting and you can see my employer went far beyond normal exchanges. When you read parts three and four you will see for yourself how badly I was treated, not only by the Council but also my Trade Union turning on me to protect the Council.

Everything I have written in my book is 100% true and not been exaggerated in any way whatsoever.

Once again, I hope you both realise why I deserve a hearing in your court.

Yours faithfully

Mr R Steele

8. Out of all seven letters sent to Jean Paul Costa, he never had the decency to reply to any one of them and I gave up sending him any more letters and gave up with the European Court of Human Rights when Clare Ovey replied to Alan Bolger's letter dated 28 July 2011. I thought the name the European Court of Human Rights meant they are there to given human rights to individuals who have not received human rights in their own country. How wrong I was. The British courts didn't help fobbing me off when I turned to them when I wanted to know if I could take my case any further in the British courts and a fella from the Supreme court said I cannot and when I wrote to the court to put it in writing the Master Eyre told me it's up to me to find out myself. All I could do is take the advice from the fella from the Supreme Court and apply to the European Court of Human Rights. What a corrupt society we live in.

CHAPTER FIFTEEN

1. I decided to contact Shaun Woodward MP again as the corruption was still going on in Security 20 years later at the clients' expense and to bring to justice Mick Gornall for his wrongdoings, i.e. charging his clients for a service he cannot provide. I wrote to him on 17 October 2011 as follows:

Clockface Road, St Helen's, Merseyside

Dear Shaun Woodward MP

I spoke to John Fullam today and he has told me to put it in writing to you that the Security Section of St Helen's Council have been charging its customer for their services that they cannot provide to contract. This has been going on since 1991 when Mick Gornall took over as Head of Security. Because of a constant lack of Security Officers, he has to take men away from one duty to help out elsewhere at the clients' expense. If a client is paying for the service, then they should receive it.

If I go into Security with you and we get the RLS sheet, the duty sheet and the rota out and colour the duties in, you will see that the rota is short staffed and has been for the last 20 years.

I have sent you a CD disk with half of my story on it. Will you please have the decency to read it to the end and you will see just how bad I have been treated for trying to have the department run properly. Once you have read my CD, I hope to meet up with you and discuss the matter.

Yours faithfully

Mr R Steele

2. I received a reply from Shaun Woodward MP on 24 October 2011 as follows:

Rt Hon Shaun Wooodward MP, House of Commons, London

Dear Mr Steele

Thank you for approaching me with your concerns.

I have sent a copy of your letter and your DVD to Mrs Hudson CBE at St Helen's MBC and asked her to respond. I will let you know as soon as I receive a response although I can usually expect a full reply within three weeks.

Once I receive that reply I will, of course, get back to you but in the meantime please do not hesitate to contact me.

With all good wishes,

The Rt Hon Shaun Woodward MP

3. I again received a letter from Shaun Woodward MP on 7 November 2011 as follows:

Rt Hon Shaun Wooodward MP, House of Commons, London

Dear Mr Steele

You will recall that I wrote to St Helen's MBC on your behalf and I can now enclose their reply regarding the concerns you raised with me. Although I know you will not be happy with this response it is important to note that your concerns have been reviewed on several occasions and unfortunately they do not warrant additional review.

If you think that I can be of further assistance in this or any matter please do not hesitate to contact me.

With all good wishes,

The Rt Hon Shaun Woodward MP

Here is a copy of the reply St Helens Council sent:

St Helen's Council, Legal & Administrative Services, St Helen's

Dear Mr Woodward

Thank you for your letter dated 24 October 2011, addressed to the Chief Executive, regarding your constituent, Mr Steele.

I have briefly examined the information, which you provided, as requested. The issues which Mr Steele raises are not new and have been raised previously. The Council has provided its response to those issues previously. It is acknowledged that Mr Steele has never been satisfied with the Council's response, but there is nothing further which we wish to add.

Thank you for raising this matter with the Council. I return the information provided.

Yours sincerely

Angela Sanderson
Assistant Chief Executive
(Legal and Administrative Services)

4. I wrote again to Shaun Woodward MP on 8 November 2011 as follows:

Clockface Road, St Helen's, Merseyside

Dear Shaun Woodward MP

I am disgusted with the Council's response. I want to go into Security with yourself and the Police as the Council has admitted to you in their letter of 2 November 2011 that issues have been raised previously and the Council has provided its response to those issues.

I can tell you now that the Council has only seen nine of the issues out of the 83 in total and would not give a direct answer to those issues. Like I said to you in my last letter dated 17-10-11, the charges to the client have been going on for the last 20 years when they cannot provide the service to the customer because of a shortage of manning levels and the people of St Helen's have a right to know what's going on their council.

When you are in St Helen's, I would like you to arrange for us to go to Security Monday to Friday with the Police and I will show you what's going on and that it has been going on for the last 20 years.

Briefly examining the information is a cover up as there should have been a thorough investigation but the Chief Executive is not going to allow that as she is in it up to her neck. I strongly advise you to read my CD or get John Fullam to read it as it's in great detail and get him to report back to you on his findings.

My next move is to send these letters and a copy of my CD to ITN news desk and Granada Reports as I am not going to let this matter drop.

I look forward to receiving a date for us to go into Security and I will prove what I am saying is 100% true.

Yours faithfully

Mr R Steele

5. I once again wrote to Shaun Woodward MP on 24 November 2011 after having a meeting with him that day as follows:

Clockface Road, St Helen's, Merseyside

Dear Shaun Woodward MP

As stated in our meeting today, Thursday 24 November 2011, I have sent you two copies of the letters from Unison dated 6 March 2000 and 23 June 2000 stating Unison is no longer able to act for me in my case. Like I stated in my book, every member who has left the Council has become a honourable member of Unison apart from myself. Once again I have been singled out.

Also agreed, I have sent you Peter Kilfoyle's last letter to me dated 31 March 2010. I noticed you have printed off my book that is only halfway to completion. Please take it with you and read it as it is in great detail and you will see how everyone has ganged up on me to protect the Council. I have only exposed John Vis and Clive Portman from the District Audit. I have not yet got to the other three auditors who have closed ranks and covered up for the Council like John Vis and Clive Portman. You also stated to me today, that I have already been through enough, now it's time to put wrongs right as until justice has been done, I cannot let go as it's eating at me every day of my life.

Yours faithfully

Mr R Steele

6. Shaun Woodward MP wrote to me on 29 November 2011 as follows:

Rt Hon Shaun Wooodward MP, House of Commons, London

Dear Mr Steele

Thank you for taking the time to attend my surgery.

I have reviewed the copies of correspondence you have forwarded and reflected on the your case file and our conversation last week and I remain of the opinion that you the issues you remain focused on have been reviewed on several occasions by several authorities, independent from one another, and unfortunately they do not warrant additional review.

As you know your employment concerns are now time-barred and if current employees have concerns they have access to their trade unions or can seek legal advice in order to address their own concerns.

I appreciate that you are unhappy with the situation but opportunities for redress have been explored and exhausted and I am afraid that I cannot assist you further on these matters.

With all good wishes,
The Rt Hon Shaun Wooodward MP

As you can see, Shaun Woodward covered up for the Council as he was made well aware that Mick Gornall had been charging his clients for the last 20 years and not giving them the service they are paying for. I wanted to go into Security with him and the Police and prove it to them. If anyone knows where to look it's me. It's now December 2012 and it's still going on. Once again, it shows just what a corrupt society we live in.

7. I decided to write to Shaun Woodward MP and let him know exactly what I think of him on the 8 November 2012 as follows:

Clockface Road, St Helen's, Merseyside

Woodward

I am writing to you to tell you I have no respect for you and to let you know exactly what I think of you. Firstly, I believe you have allowed St Helen's Council to get away with a number of misdemeanours including alleged embezzlement. You even printed off 300 or so pages of my book when I sent it you on CD so you know exactly that has gone on and the last time I contacted you on 24-11-11, you were made well aware of my concerns and you sat back and did nothing. It is now the 8 November 2012 and Mick Gornall can still not fulfil his contracts to his client's as he has not got the correct amount of staff to carry out the service the client is paying for.

The last time I spoke to you about this was in 2011 and you should have got the Police to investigate Mick Gornall and you sat back and did nothing. In my opinion you are gutless and have not got the balls to put the wrongdoings right. I feel you should stand down as an MP and let someone who has got the balls to stand up to St Helen's Council have the job. You have a commitment to your constituents to see that things in St Helen's Council are run properly and you have not.

One disillusioned constituent

Yours

Mr R Steele

Ps You will never get my vote.

I have sent this letter recorded delivery as I may not receive a reply to it.

8. I received a reply from Shaun Woodward on 13 November 2012 as follows:

Rt Hon Shaun Wooodward MP, House of Commons, London

Dear Mr Steele

Thank you for your letter dated 8 November 2012.

You will recall that I addressed the issues you raise in my letter dated 29 November 2011 following our meeting at my surgery and I do not propose to revisit them again.

With all good wishes,

The Rt Hon Shaun Woodward MP

As you can see, he still will not involve the Police as Mick Gornall cannot provide the staff to fulfil his clients' requirements. In my opinion he is defrauding them out of money. They think they are getting the required service they are paying for and they're not whatsoever.

9. *St Helen's Star* did an article on St Helen's Council on Thursday 15 November 2012 as follows:

Local authority will appeal judgement affecting more than 1,000 workers

St Helen's Council could be forced to settle a £70 million equal pay compensation bill after an employment judge ruled in favour of unions representing more than 1,000 workers.

Many of the claimants are in line to receive considerable compensation following a reserved judgement delivered after a pre-hearing review in Liverpool.

They include local authority employees ranging from cooks and cleaners to clerical staff, classroom assistants, caretakers and technicians.

According to a senior council source the cash-strapped local authority – which is already dealing with £50m budget cuts – will mount an appeal in an effort to overturn the judgement.

However, if it is unsuccessful it may have to apply to central government for loans or sell off land or property assets to raise revenue.

Steve Fay, from the St Helen's branch of Unison, said: 'This is a great result for our members. The council failed to establish a defence against (accusations of) discriminatory action'.

'There is also a long way to go to determine what may actually be paid to each individual (and) we understand that the council may exercise a right of appeal.'

A written judgment seen by the Star, states Unison and GMB brought the equal pay claim after Town Hall managers 'protected' higher earnings of employees, such as bin men and street cleaners, between 2000 and 2008.

Workers in other roles, in jobs that were classed as being of equivalent value, were on the same salary grades but were getting paid less money.

The 'payment protection' effectively kept in place a bonus or additional payment that workers, such as bin men, had been receiving historically.

Documents from the tribunal stated that in 2004, the council decided to protect the earnings of the bin men rather than reduce them to the rate at which they had been assessed during a wide-ranging review of pay grades.

According to the ruling, it was intended that, in the course of the 'pay protection period' the bin men would not receive cost of living allowance, to erode the pay difference.

However, this did not happen and the basic pay increased in line with cost of living increases, though the 'consolidated bonus' did not rise.

The council conceded that pay arrangements in place were tainted by gender but argued there was justification for its decision.

The council claimed that levelling up (increasing the claimants' wages) would have cost £70m, arguing an 'unaffordable' move would have left it unable to deliver satisfactory services.

There, were other routes available, however, one of which included finding a middle ground of earnings by increasing the wages of the lower earners and dropping pay of higher earners.

An employment judge ruled that the council, which had known about the discriminatory pay in 2000, could not justify the entire overpayment for such a lengthy period.

The judge concluded the council had not 'adopted proportionate means of achieving their legitimate aim'.

Asked about the judgment and the potential liabilities it faces, St Helen's Council issued a statement which read: 'The council is considering its legal position in response to the judgement – and it would be inappropriate to comment in any detail at this stage.

'However we can confirm that the council received an adverse judgement in a pre-hearing review. This process however, does not award financial settlements.'

10. As this exposed Unison for not doing their job in 1997, I decided to write to the General Secretary, Dave Prentis on 19 November 2012 as follows:

Clockface Road, St Helen's, Merseyside

Dear Dave Prentis

I am writing to you about an article in the St Helen's Star ref. Equal Pay. It states in the paper Unison and GMB brought in the equal pay claim after Town Hall managers protected higher earnings of bin men and street cleaners between 2000 and 2008. I was the GMB shop steward in 1996 and I reported the low wages in our department (Security) to the GMB and I was told I had opened a can of worms that should have been left alone so I came to your union around January 1997 as Eddie Tickle and Kevan Nelson both said they would sort out all the problems in our department including the wages and your union stabbed me in the back.

That led to me being seriously ill which led to me losing my job, my home and my health because of yours and the GMB's ignorance. That has come 16 years too late for me. Had you done your job properly in the first place, all these people would have got their money many years ago and would have been backdated to 1990. One of the General Secretary's, Rodney Bickerstaffe and Mike Fitzsimmons, Head of Local Government, were both well aware of the issues I had with St Helen's Council and the main priority was the wages and in my opinion Mike Fitzsimmons filled me full of b*******t why we were not entitled to a pay rise.

I will now be seeking advice whether I have a possible claim against you for ruining my life and doing something about the wages issue 16 years later. Had you and GMB done your job in the first place, I would still have my job, my home and my health and would have been on a good wage.

One disillusioned ex shop steward of Unison.

Yours

Mr R Steele

If the unions had done their job in 1996 and 1997, St Helen's Council would have had to pay out at least £240 million to date and not £70 million. They are going to have to pay out for the last six years. The unions let them get away with it by not doing their job in the first place. This would have been backdated to 1991 and this would have given the opportunity for all the other departments to claim as far back as 1991 and not 2012.

11. I received a reply from Unison on 26 November 2012 as follows:

Unison, London

Dear Mr Steele

I acknowledge receipt of your letter dated 19 November 2012, received on 21 November 2012, addressed to the general secretary.

In line with the union's complaints procedure, your complaint will be investigated by your UNISON region. Your letter has therefore been passed to the following:

UNISON North West, Arena Point, 1 Hunts Bank, Manchester M3 1UN
Tel: 016 1661 6701

If you have any further questions about how the investigation will be carried out please contact the region.

Please let me know if you need a full copy of the complaints procedure. It is also on the union's web site: www.unison. org.uk

Yours sincerely

Glen Turner
Member Liaison Coordinator
Member Liaison Unit

As you can see, they say my complaint will be investigated. It is now 11th March 2013 and I still have not received a reply to their investigations and I doubt I ever will.

CHAPTER SIXTEEN

1. We lived at Quarry Road, Bootle, Liverpool 20 and when I was three years old, I fell off a kiddies scooter in the back entry and a fella picked me up and carried me into the back yard and my dad carried me into the house and phoned for an ambulance. I was taken to the Children's Alder Hey Hospital in Liverpool and I was kept in as I had broken my leg. In the next bed to me was a young lad about the same age called Freddy with no legs or arms. When I got older I always wanted to raise money for Alder Hey Hospital and when I thought I was going to get a claim against my employer, St Helen's Council, I thought I would write a book and I was a bit optimistic and thought I would sell one million copies and make ten million pounds for the hospital.

I became more determined to raise the money for Alder Hey Hospital when my great nephew got leukaemia in January 2011 and was treated at Alder Hey Hospital. Then I thought I would give to five charities to increase my book sales, as people supporting those charities would buy my book.

The charities are – Royal Society for the Prevention of Cruelty to Animals (RSPCA), National Society for the Prevention of Cruelty to Children (NSPCC), Cancer Research, Help for Heroes and Alder Hey Children's Hospital.

I now have to put myself first as I want to replace the home I lost. If I can sell one hundred and sixty thousand copies of my book it will raise £960 thousand pounds profit. My great nephew took a turn for the worst in December 2011 and sadly passed away in January 2012 aged 11. They took him to Clair House Hospice in Clatterbridge. What I want to do is add Clair House to the other five charities and if I can make my goal of £960,000, give the six charities £80,000 each that will leave me with £480,000 and after tax, will leave me £240,000 to buy a new home and fully furnish it. I also told my friend, Liz Lloyd who is a midwife that I would buy out of my damages, two life support machines for premature babies and if I get more money than stated and covers the cost of the incubators, then I will honour my promise to her.

2. In an attempt to get legal help, I wrote to Mr Al Fayed, Harrods owner to sponsor my case. I got no joy so I wrote to Simon Cowell, as he does charitable work and I sent the letter to Louis Walsh's management team, 24 Courtney House, Appian Way, Dublin 6, Ireland to pass it on to Simon. As got no reply from Simon, I wrote to Cheryl Cole at her record company, Polydor Records, 364-366 Kensington High Street, London W14 8NS and asked her to pass a letter on to Simon. I still got nowhere so I then wrote to Frank Bruno as he had suffered depression and knows what it's like. Again I got no joy.

I was watching a programme on television and either Piers Morgan or Alan Titchmarsh was on about Rupert Murdoch being the most powerful person on the planet so I decided to write to him to support my case. I wrote to both his English and American addresses and again came to no joy. I don't believe that any of the above people actually received the letters I sent them as their personal assistants would have made sure of that.

3. As already read, I had three small claims in the County court against St Helen's Council, 2 for damage to my wheels and tracking caused by potholes and the other for flood damage to my car. I attended court in September 2010 to deal with the pothole damage and when I got to court they had put all three claims on the same day. It was before Deputy District Judge Goodwin and the Council sent five members of staff and a barrister to give evidence against me. Judge Goodwin said I would have to go back to court, as there was not enough time to deal with the three claims. As I felt intimidated with how many people were there, I told Judge Goodwin I was not going back to court and to drop my two pothole claims and to deal with the flood damage to my car.

Two members from Highways Department gave evidence that my car did not get flooded as the water does not get deep enough to flood my car and the barrister said my car did not flood because the car had door seals and that the engine would have flooded. Judge Goodwin said two people stated my car did not flood and I lost my case. Basically, she call me a liar and that's one thing I am not. My car did flood and I asked the Council for £30 to valet my car and they refused so I took them to court for a new carpet and mats as they were soiled with sewage from the grid. This was recommended by Howard Nulty of St Helen's law.

CHAPTER SEVENTEEN

1. I will now tell you how St Helen's Council causing my illness affected my life.

Because of my illness, I had to go on the sick and I had my benefit forms filled in by the benefit people and around April 2004, I got a letter from the benefit office to go and see them. I went and saw them and they told me it's serious and I need a solicitor. I went back and I was accused of benefit fraud and they wanted to look at my bank accounts. They asked me about a certain bank account and I knew nothing about it and gave them permission to contact my bank. They called me back and said the bank doesn't know anything about this account and asked me what it was. I said I didn't know, if the bank did not know about any account how was I supposed to know.

They also asked me why I did not tell them about my pension. I said I was never asked. They said it was their error and I was taken off benefits and had to pay back £17,228.05. A fella came out from the benefit office and asked me what income I was getting and told me that I was entitled to the money I was on.

2. I don't get any help with prescriptions, glasses or dentists. If ever I have to move into rented accommodation I will have to pay full rent and Council Tax as I cannot claim benefits. Because I could not claim any benefit I had to sell my house in Liverpool and move in with my parents as my outgoings were a lot more than what I had coming in. I can thank St Helen's Council for this.

3. When my depression hit me in 1999, I was sleeping 23 hours a day most days and I went from 14 stone to 21 stone with the medication they had me on. Years later, I still sleep up to 16 hours a day and I have spells where I have sleep deprivation where I can go 80 hours without sleep. I have been given several types of

sleeping tablets to get me to sleep that don't work. My doctor gave me diazepam that people on drugs take. I was reluctant to take it but I got so desperate for sleep I took two in one night and I still never got any sleep. I have managed to lose weight over the last two years and I am now 17 stone and to keep my weight off, I can only have one to two cooked meals a week.

4. Since my depression started in 1999, I find it difficult to live any sort of life. In 2012 I had one bath, washed my hair twice and I don't cook, iron, wash my clothes or anything else. I really struggle from day to day. My parents, who are in their eighties, care for me and when they are no longer with me I am going to have to pay someone to care for my needs. There are days where I wake up uncomfortable and have not got the strength to turn myself over in bed and have to lie there till I fall asleep again and when I do get up, it takes me ages to get dressed. I shave every three to four days in the evening when I am a bit more alert. Before I became ill, I used to wash my hair and shave every day and have a bath once or twice a week and also have showers. I don't know what's happened but my body has totally shut down.

5. I had £90,000 in the bank to pay my legal costs against St Helen's Council and when Robert Spicer dropped my case for the second time I sunk very low and to cheer myself up I went to Car Craft and bought two cars. It picked my mood up a bit and after a couple of weeks the novelty wore off. This happened several times. I ended up buying five Jaguars, three Ford Focus and a Rolls Royce and kept selling my cars cheap to Brian Wright. He had two Ford Focus and two Jaguars off me. Trying to cheer myself up, I squandered a big chunk of my money I had put aside for my court case. I put this down to my illness.

6. When St Helen's Council terminated my employment the first time, I contacted the people of my private pension. A fella came out to my house and he told me I would get £10 a year if I want my pension now. I told him that the fella who sold me the pension told me I would get a £44,000 lump sum and a pension of £200

a week when I retired. He told me I would have to increase my monthly payments to £200 a month to get that sort of money.

I decided when the problems at work were sorted, I was going to cancel my private pension and join the work's pension when I returned to work. That would have been March 1999 but St Helen's Council refused me a return to work and sacked me again in September 1999. The fella that sold me my private pension, Ken Page from Cheltenham, totally misled me on my pension and if I had known sooner that my pension was not worth a bean, I would have joined St Helen's Council pension scheme when I started in 1992.

When I retire at 65, my private pension will be around £10 a week. Had the Council let me return to work in 1999 when I was ready to return, I would have now been in the pension scheme for the last 14 years. Once again I have been left to struggle and let down by the system.

7. I always said I would never take on other people's kids and when I became ill and over a twelve-year period, I took on three kids and I was going to adopt two of them. I thought if I looked after them when they were young, they would care for me when my parents are no longer here to look after me. How wrong I was. After the way they treated me, I have no time for John and Cuz and just say hello to Josh when I see him at his nan's. John and Cuz were hard-faced and asked for everything they got. Josh asked for very little but got the most as I had been a dad to him from the age of two years old. Between the three of them they had over £20,000 out of me.

Would I do it again? If someone caring and understanding came along and things got serious I would adopt their kids. I would like to meet someone around 40 and have a child with them. The girlfriend I was living with in 1988 got pregnant and could not settle in England and went back to Germany. I have tried finding her with a private detective from Germany and my friend contacted long lost family but they never replied. I would like to leave my kids my inheritance when I am no longer here and if I did adopt any kids, they would also be included in any inheritance.

If this is not to be, then I will leave my inheritance to children's charities – Clair House, Alder Hey Hospital and the NSPCC.

8. On Saturday 19 December 2009, I had family problems and walked out of the house. At about 11pm I went to Peasley Cross crisis team to talk to them. There was no one there so I stayed outside all night. About 8.30am this fella turned up and he told me he had come in early to sort paperwork out and no one will be in till 9am. I asked him if I could use the toilet as I had been there all night. He put his face close to mine and said, 'I don't know you, do you know where I'm coming from?'

I said, 'I don't know where you're coming from' and he told me to go home. I told him I would wait in my car and he went inside.

About 5 to 10 minutes later he came out and told me to go home and ring up later. I told him I didn't have a home. He told me if I was homeless to go to the Millennium Centre. He finished by telling me to go away so I said to him I would jump off the f*****g bridge over there and I pointed to it. He just walked off and went inside so I went to the bridge and stood at the edge and a Police car came past. He stopped and stayed for several minutes and drove off. I climbed onto a concrete ridge and stood there thinking. It hailstoned and I was stood there shaking with the cold. A tanker driver came down the hill blasting his horn as he had seen me on the bridge. I still stood there thinking and I thought if I jump that b*****d is going to get away with it, meaning the person that turned me away. After a couple of minutes I got off the bridge and went to a friend's house and on 30 March 2010 I reported this person to Simon Barber, Chief Executive, 5 Boroughs Partnership, NHS Foundation Trust, Hollins Park, Hollins Lane, Winwick, Warrington.

An investigation did take place but I was told he gave a different version of what happened and never got disciplined and I was told the matter would be noted in case it happened again in the future. This incident nearly cost me my life.

9. Until well into my illness, I never lent people money. I have been friends with one family for 36 years now and about seven years ago I got Gary Brennan a car and he was paying me back £50 a week. I got him another car, still paying me £50 a week. In February 2007 he lost his job through his own fault and since then he keeps telling me he wants to pay me back but has been out of work for the last five years and he has owed me £3,555 since 14 January 2011. I think if he ever decides to get a job he will pay me back.

I got his sister, Paula Brennan three cars over the last five years and she kept telling me she would never do what Gary has done to me and in November 2010 she stopped paying me. When I went round to her house she would not answer the door so I fell out with her. She still owes me £2,390.

Not only did I get Paula three cars but I also paid the insurance on them that I never got back. Also, her kids did not go to school as her washing machine had broken and they had no clean clothes to go to school in so I got her a brand new washing machine and a tumble drier so she could get the kids back to school. Once again I never got paid back for that either.

She buys over fourteen twenty packets of Lambert & Butler cigarettes a week for herself and her boyfriend and son, that she has been giving cigs to from the age of twelve, out of her benefits and on a Friday she was broke with no food in to feed the kids so I used to take Sarah, her twelve-year-old daughter to Iceland and Tesco for food for them and pay it on my Visa. The food was to last till Tuesday when she got paid.

I remember her borrowing £10 on a Monday and sending me to the shop for twenty Lambert & Butler and five packets of giant parmaviolets for herself and when I got back to her house the kids were asking to be fed. She had no money for food for them. I went home for my tea and I felt sick eating it as four kids were going hungry. I borrowed some money off my dad and went to the chippy and fed the four kids and her.

Over weekends and Mondays I used to buy her kids a McDonalds or a chippy meal or go to Pizza Perfect on a regular basis because there was never any food in the house or money to buy any. In my opinion well over £100 a week is spent on cigarettes out of the kids' benefit. I believe she puts her cigarettes and giant parmaviolets for herself before food for her kids.

She also asked me to get her boyfriend, Dave Smith, a car for him to get back into work. He wanted to drive the car around with no insurance so I paid for his insurance so he would not get the car taken off him by the Police, to make sure he could pay me back. They were both living at 16 Richmond Avenue, Haydock, St Helen's and he was working since 2001 and she was claiming benefits for a single parent.

The benefit people investigated her three times and in believe she lied her way out of it. They split up in November 2009 and got back together in December 2010 and are both living at 77 Central Drive, Haydock, St Helen's and to this day, she is still claiming single parent benefit.

I have never reported anyone but the way she treated me I reported her to the benefit office and they did not want to know. I know for a fact they have had over £120,000 in benefits. Dave Smith still owes me £260 since April 2010.

Paula had no money to buy the kids Christmas presents in 2009 so I ended up lending her the money for a laptop and a phone for herself on contract and she kept running big bills up on them and never paid me back. By this time she had fallen out with me and I had to pay the contracts of 14 months. I also lent her the money for the kid's Christmas presents that I never got back. So much for knowing her 36 years.

I sold Brian Wright of 102 Taunton Avenue, Sutton Leach, St Helen's, Merseyside two Focus and two Jaguars. I had known Brian since 1992. On the second Focus he did a deal with me where his mate Stuart paid me £60 a week for 52 weeks and he paid me £100 for 20 weeks and for doing it I would make an extra £120. Stuart stopped paying me when he paid £2,800 and I told Brian he still owed me £320. Brian had told Stuart he could have the car for £2,800 and told me Stuart had bought for car for £3,120. Brian spoke to Stuart and I got my £320. Stuart overpaid me by £60 and I told Brian to tell him to come and collect it. His wife came and I gave it them back.

Brian then struck a deal on the second Jaguar between myself, him and his mate Phil Hewitt of 3 Warwick Street, St Helen's, Merseyside WA10 4BE, where he paid me £100 a week for 50 weeks and his mate Phil Hewitt paid £100 a week for 78 weeks. The car Brian sold Phil kept breaking down and as there was £5,820 outstanding and to save falling out with Brian as he had stood guarantor, I paid for the repairs on the car as Phil Hewitt was using the car as a taxi and with the car off the road, Phil could not pay his payments.

I eventually fell out with Brian as Phil was not making the payments on the car. As there was over £7,000 outstanding I took Brian to court on 7 November 2012 and the case has been adjourned till 5 March 2013 because Howard Nulty, Brian Wright's solicitor, stated myself and Phil Hewitt had entered into a new agreement behind Brian's back. What Brian has failed to tell his solicitor and the judge is he was also sent paperwork to sign for that agreement and he refused to sign it so I never started the new agreement with Phil Hewitt. For this reason, as far as I was concerned, the new agreement was void as there were three signatures on the original agreement and to change it you would need three signatures to do so.

I contacted Ruth Powell of Haygarth Jones solicitors who I went to to recover my money and she wrote new contracts for the three of us to sign. I rang her and told her that the judge stated because new contracts had been made up, Brian Wright is no longer guarantor and I asked her if this was true. She said she didn't know. She mentioned me paying money and to go and see her. I have not got the money to pay solicitors.

I attended court on the 5th March 2013 and I lost my case because the Jaguar Brian Wright sold Phil Hewitt kept breaking down so I paid for the repairs to Phil Hewitt vehicle in an attempt to recover my money back without falling out with Brian and because I wanted the money back for the car repairs before paying off the debt that Brian Wright had stood guarantor for because Mr Hewitt could not pay me any money without his car being on the road as this was his means of income taxi driving. If I had not put the car back on the road Brian Wright would have had to pay me £5,820 had I taken him to court instead of me paying for the car repairs, doing Brian Wright and Phil Hewitt a favour and paying out another £4,132.50 to Phil Hewitt on top of the £5,280 owed by Brian Wright. I now have to pay Brian Wright's solicitor's costs for being kind enough to pay for Phil Hewitt's car repairs and not taking Brian Wright to court at that time. In my opinion Brian Wright and Phil Hewitt both swore on oath and told blatant lies to the judge and judge Fitzgerald knew they were telling him lies and at the end of the hearing Judge Fitzgerald thanked me for being an excellent witness. As far as I am concerned they both should be charged with perjury, for lying on oath in a court of law and I will be writing to judge Fitzgerald about this matter. Howard Nutty and his firm of solicitors have not complied with certain parts of orders by judge Mc Cullach on the 21st March 2012 and judge Fitzgerald on the 2nd August 2012 and again to judge Fitzgerald on the 14th November 2012 and got away with it.

You can see why the British courts are considered to some be an ass. Later that afternoon I could not settle as I wanted my money back off Phil Hewitt so I went round to his house and as I got their he drove off in his taxi so I followed him and kept signalling him to pull over and he drove to the police station so I followed him there. Hewitt pulled over a police car and told a police officer I had lost my case in court and I have followed him and he does not know why I was aggressive and the police officer made Phil Hewitt sit in his car and I discussed with him the problem. I was really annoyed and I told him I want to put a gun to my head and shoot myself and take them with me meaning Phil Hewitt, Brian Wright and Howard Nulty. The police officer got hold of me and told me he was going to lock me up as I was a danger to myself he then asked me, was I a gangster and I said no. He then asked me was I a bailiff and I said no. He said I can see you are upset and to go home, I did say to him I want to speak to Phil Hewitt about the £7,000 plus he owes me and he would not let me discuss it with him I then asked him would he like it if someone owes you £7,000 and won't pay you back he said no then I left.

I then decided to write to Judge Fitzgerald on the 9-3-2013 as follows.

09-03-2013
Clock Face Road
St Helen's
Merseyside
WA9 4LD

Dear judge Fitzgerald

On the 14 November 2012 you told Howard Nutly of St Helen's Law that lies are being told and you let him amend his clients statement (Brian Wright) On the 5 March 2013 you got myself Brian Wright and Phil Hewitt to swear an oath on the bible and I believe you knew they both told blatant lies and that most of their evidence was lies I now insist you change them with perjury for telling lies on oath in a court of law. I am also not happy with your decision in favour of Brian Wright. I know you read out terms of another case that I believe they had no bearing on my case. Firstly there was three signatures on the original agreement for guarantor as it does not matter whether I state verbally or in writing to Phil Hewitt that want the money back for the car repairs. First as it was not put in writing and signed for by all three parties and all three parties would have to agree to it also the payments for the car repairs and guarantor were on one bill. Secondly I went to Haygarth Jones Solicitors and Ruth Powell wrote out new agreements for myself Brian Wright and Phil Hewitt to sign and on the 13 May 2012. Myself and Phil Hewitt signed ours and Brian Wright refused to sign his. These proposals were put in front of you and they show quite clearly that the further payments made by Phil Hewitt were taken off Brian Wright debt and not taken off the car repairs as I wanted. I am also dissatisfied that District Judge Mc Cullach ordered on the 21 March 2012,the claimant and the defendant will file and serve the witness statements of all witnesses to give evidence by 11 April 2012, the claimant and the defendant will each give standard disclosure by 28 march 2012 and Brain Wright solicitors did neither and once they received my disclosure they did their defence and put it into court months later putting me at a disadvantage and you accepted it. You yourself on the 2ndAugust 2012 ordered the defendant shall have permission to serve on the claimant and the court by 4pm on the 2ndAugust 2012 an amended defence which shall not include any matters not already referred to in the defendants original defence and you personally let Howard Nulty, Brian Wrights solicitor put new evidence into court that went against me. Again you yourself ordered that permission to the defendant to amend his defence in order to (A) clearly set out how the written agreement between the parties should be interpreted. (B) particularise what payments have been made by either the defendant or Mr Hewitt to the claimant (C) clearly set out (as the defendant now contends) how and why the agreement between the parties has been discharged or otherwise negated my belief as none of these were complied with and were not dealt with by yourself on the 5th March 2013. I believe you let them get away with murder I don't know the law but I am going to challenge your decision and if I have to take this matter to the Court of Appeal in London I will I am sending a copy of this letter to Lord Judge the Lord Justice as I am well dissatisfied. I can inform you now I can only afford to pay Howard Nulty £1 per week and the courts and Howard Nulty can do nothing about it as long as I am making an effort to pay. I've been there and wore the T-shirt with Phil Hewitt, Gary Brennan, Paula Brennan and Dave Smith I am informing you I have written a book and if you want a copy it's called *Rough Justice,* A True Story by R Steele and part of this case is already in it and I am adding what happened on the 5th March 2013 in court and the contents of this letter. The book is at the publishers at the proof reading stage. The book should be on sale by the end of May 2013 if not before.

Yours Faithfully

Mr R Steele

cc Lord Judge (Lord Chief Justice)
Brian Wright
Howard Nulty

I wrote to the Lord Chief Justice Lord Judge on the 11-03-2013 as follows

Clock Face Road
St Helen's
Merseyside
WA9 4LD

Dear Lord Judge

I want to make a complaint about a hearing I had in St Helen's County Court on the 5th March 2013 with Judge

Fitzgerald. Firstly I would like Brian Wright and Phil Hewitt charged with perjury for telling blatant lies on oath in a court of law and I also want to know why Judge Fitzgerald let Howard Nulty, Brian Wright's solicitor get away with orders by the judge. Get away with it three times. I have sent you a copy of the letter I sent Judge Fitzgerald dated 09-03-2013 I was also not happy when I was leaving the courtroom Judge Fitzgerald telling Howard Nulty,'you did put it in late.' I believe this to be the defence that lost me my case this is the new defence that Judge Fitzgerald stated, which shall not include any matters not already referred to in the defendants original defence I would like answers why Judge Fitzgerald allowed this as this decision cost me thousands of pounds that I can ill afford to lose. I look forward to a positive response.

Yours Faithfully

Mr R Steele

Once again this case will end up a case of *rough justice* like my other cases I will most probably get fobbed of by the Lord Chief Justices office like before like I have previously stated the law is an ass.

10. I visited Dr O'Donnell at her surgery and I told her what I told Dr Dutta, Consultant Psychiatrist, for him to say I had a schizophrenia type illness. She said it's not necessarily schizophrenia, it could be frustration. I said to Dr O'Donnell, 'that's exactly what it is'. I have always stated I have not got schizophrenia.

At my next visit to the surgery I was telling Dr Kurzeja what Dr O'Donnell had said and he said to me 'come on Robert, you're paranoid and a schizophrenic'. I went and saw Dr O'Donnell and told her I wanted her to be my doctor from now on. I told her I had no time for Dr Kurzeja and I will never go to him again.

I did get a report from Dr Kurzeja on 19 June 2006 as follows:

Four Acre Health Centre, St Helens

TO WHOM IT MAY CONCERN

Dear Sir or Madam

Re: Robert Steele, Clock Face Road St Helen's

Mr Steele suffers from Schizophrenia and is currently under the care of the local Mental Health Team.

His current ill health sees him with the following mental health issues:
- *Lack of motivation*
- *Chronic fatigue/tiredness*
- *Disordered sleep pattern*
- *Chronic anxiety*

Naturally these have an on-going effect on his ability to pursue and perform normal day-to-day activities. He is clearly unable to live a normal lifestyle.

Yours faithfully

Dr J A Kurzeja

As you can see, it states I suffer from schizophrenia when in fact it should be severe depression. The rest of his report is 100% accurate. I visited Dr Whalley, Psychiatrist in 2010 and I told him I had never had schizophrenia and he sent me to a Dr John Traverse to find out one way or the other.

I was supposed to have had six visits with him and after two visits he told me I didn't have a personality disorder. Here is John Traverse's report dated 13 September 2010:

5 Boroughs Partnership, Personality Disorder Hub Service

Dear Suzanne

Re: Robert Steele

Clock Face Road, Clock Face, St Helen's, Merseyside WA9 4LD

I have completed my assessment with Mr Steele and I do not believe that he has a Personality Disorder.

However, he does appear to be suffering with severe depression, which includes some very fixed beliefs and obsessive thoughts.

He has agreed to try a brief course of CBT to work on his fixed belief that he cannot stop until he has seen justice done and that he must have his day in court.

I recommend that he might have six meetings of CBT to see whether it may help. However, if there is no progress I do not think that prolonged CBT would be likely to be beneficial. I have discussed this as a possible approach with Mr Steele and he would like to try it.

I have discharged him from the Personality Disorder Hub Service.

Yours sincerely

Dr John Traverse
Lead Consultant Clinical Psychologist

As you can see, I have not got and never have had schizophrenia.

11. On my visit to Dr Whalley, Psychiatrist in 2011, I told him I was having dizzy spells from the anti-depressant tablets I was

taking. He told me it was low blood pressure and changed my anti-depressant and I was still having dizzy spells. They changed my anti-depressant five times to no joy. I went for a medical to my doctor's and my blood pressure was very low and she got me to stand up and it was still low so I was taken off the anti-depressant for good. This leaves me in a depressed state but I'd rather be like that than keep falling all over the place.

I have had numerous health problems over the years. I have had chest pains several times, numbness in my head and feeling really ill and every time I go to the hospital or the doctors they tell me it's anxiety. Considering all the stress I've been put through, I am lucky I have not had a massive heart attack or stroke. The last two times I have had my blood pressure taken it has been normal since coming off the anti-depressant tablets.

12. I visited Dr Whalley, Psychiatrist on 17 July 2012 and in conversation, Dr Whalley asked me could I ever see myself getting better? He told me it's been too long and he can see me never getting better. I asked him about schizophrenia and depression and he told me there is a positive side and a negative side to schizophrenia. The positive side is you hear voices and the negative side are the symptoms I am showing and you never get better. The depression is the symptom I am showing and you do get better.

I still think I have severe depression and the reason I have not get better is because I cannot let go. It is now January 2013 and I still have severe depression, lack of motivation, chronic fatigue, tiredness, disordered sleep pattern, chronic anxiety and stress.

I worked from the age of sixteen for nineteen years without any problems and lived a normal life. I had a double garage workshop at the back of my house and it was fully equipped to do all car repairs, paint spraying and welding and I carried out work for people who could not afford garage prices. I was very hyperactive and always on the go seven days a week. Since September 1999 when my depression kicked in, I have not done anything whatsoever and I am clearly unable to live a normal lifestyle. Like my Community Psychiatric nurse, Suzanne Hall said to me, no one would want to live my life as I just exist. I have had no life whatsoever since September 1999.

13. I had a lovely home and here are some pictures I have taken when doing it up to the finished article. I lost it because of all the issues in this book with St Helen's Council.

14. Here is the cartoon picture Damian Finnan drew of Mick Gornall and Keith Hackett put Hitler's head on it. It just shows what the workforce thought of Mick Gornall.

Chapter Eighteen

FINAL CONCLUSION

1. Mick Gornall had three men on nights and if an alarm went off in Rainford he would send two men and if another alarm went off he would send the third man to get a good response time and in fact, he would have to wait in his vehicle for either another security officer or the Police if available, that was hardly ever, to attend before entering the building, so the response time was a sham as it could be an hour or longer before the building was actually checked and between 5am and 7am the third man was on a static duty and opening the parks and that meant the third man had to be taken off Pets Corner in Sherdley Park or taken off opening the parks that the client has paid for.

A few years ago Mick Gornall changed the rota and put one of the three night turns on a floating shift so if he has sickness or holidays he will take one man off nights. There is no doubt this will happen on a regular basis where there are two men on nights and he still has to cover for three men making it impossible to get good response times.

Mick Gornall will tell you they call the Police to assist but nine times out of ten they are too busy to send someone. It is totally impossible for two men to cover the night shift; even three men cannot cover client's needs on the night shift. This matter has been raised numerous times to the relevant people and they have all given Mick Gornall the green light to rip off his clients.

2. Mick Gornall gave his officers Scale 2 and 3 plus allowances in 2008 giving them a £4,000 pay rise. If those officers contact Chris Benson, Lawyer, who was on *ITV News* on 24 October 2012

reference equal pay and gave him a copy of my book, they would definitely get Scale 4 and 5 plus allowances and back pay of six years. That would get them another £4,000 plus and back pay of at least £24,000. They can contact him on 0207 650 1200.

If I still worked for the Council I would definitely contact him and Security have been robbed of their wages since 1991 when Mick Gornall took over Security. He made sure himself and his close buddies in Security got the correct Council rates of pay and ripped the majority of his staff off.

Security officers, Supervisors and Co-ordinators, again the relevant people were informed of this matter and again they gave Mick Gornall the green light to rip his staff off.

3. Mick Gornall has in my opinion cut corners in every way shape and form, especially with the safety of his officers. This has been stated quite clearly in this story and he has got away with it for the last twenty-two years. Once again the relevant people have been informed of these issues and Mick Gornall has been given the green light to put their lives in danger.

4. St Helen's Council did everything in their power to prevent the eighty-three grievances I had issues with them coming out and also the fifty-seven personal grievances I had with them. All these issues should have been put on the table and sorted.

The reason I was threatened with the sack eight times and sacked twice was because they could not buy me like they did everyone else and, for that reason, all they wanted was me out of the Council and out of my job at whatever cost and were protected by everyone involved.

5. St Helen's Council and all the other councils in the country have got the power to do whatever they like and know they won't be challenged. They will tell you they are responsible to the Audit, the electorate and to the courts. I was their electorate and they did not have to answer to me. I went to the Audit and they covered

up for them and I also tried taking it to court with no joy. Why we have courts, Prime Ministers and senior governing bodies in this country God only knows as none of them have any powers to do anything, especially where St Helen's Council is concerned.

In my opinion here is a list of people's lives destroyed by Gornall and Farrell who worked in Security:

1. Keith Jones	2. Eric Clarke
3. Alec Grant	4. Gary Wainwright
5. Peter Waine	6. Alan Proctor
7. Jimmy Johnson	8. Keith Hackett
9. Cath	10. Phil Kearns
11. Terry Cunliffe	12. Mick Rimmer
13. Graham Davis	14. Bernard Day
15. John Swift	16. Rob Steele
17. Alan Bolger	18. Damian Finnan
19. Peter Woodcock	20. Chris Gearing
21. Phil Deighton	22. John Sexton

The word embezzlement in this book has been misinterpreted, in my opinion the word could be fraud, theft or stolen as money was taken from peoples wages and from clients that didn't get the service that they were paying for.

Lynn Davidson, director of the Memoir Club Ltd, publishers, took £4,500 off me to publish this book. She refused to pay me back the £4,500 that I requested on the 30th January 2013, 8th February 2013, 22nd February 2013, 12th March 2013 and 22nd March 2013 because she changed the terms that was agreed and in my opinion is telling me lies.

I would like to finish off by saying what a lovely corrupt Britain we live in.

Lightning Source UK Ltd.
Milton Keynes UK
UKOW041331240513

211168UK00002B/40/P